Praise for the Novels of Carol Berg

The Spirit Lens

"In this superbly realized leadoff to Berg's quasi-Renaissance fantasy trilogy . . . Berg shapes the well-worn elements of epic fantasy into a lush, absorbing narrative."   —*Publishers Weekly* (starred review)

"Rich with vivid characters and unforgettable places. . . . [Berg] spins an infectiously enjoyable series opener that fans of thought-provoking fantasy and intriguing mystery should appreciate."   —*Library Journal*

"A super opening to what looks like a great alternate Renaissance fantasy. . . . Fans will appreciate this strong beginning as science and sorcery collide when three undercover agents investigate the divine and unholy collision of murder, magic, and physics."   —Genre Go Round Reviews

"Berg is entirely adept at creating a detailed and nuanced fantasy world, made all the more impressive by noting that other books she has written seem to be about other worlds with other rules."   —I Don't Write Summaries

"A genuine page-turner that should please both mystery and fantasy fans."
                                                                       —*Booklist*

"A nonstop ride to a superb ending that left my appetite whetted for the next installment."   —Fantasy Book Critic

"Berg is a master world builder that novice fantasy authors would do well to study. This first installment in a new trilogy, Collegia Magica, is a winner."
                                                                       —*Romantic Times*

"*The Spirit Lens* is an incredibly enjoyable fantasy adventure for those who love unexpected heroes, web-worked plots, magic versus technology, and librarians with a skill for investigative spying."   —The Reader Eclectic

continued . . .

Breath and Bone

"The narrative crackles with intensity against a vivid backdrop of real depth and conviction, with characters to match. Altogether superior."
—*Kirkus Reviews* (starred review)

"Berg's lush, evocative storytelling and fully developed characters add up to a first-rate purchase for most fantasy collections."　　　—*Library Journal*

"Replete with magic-powered machinations, secret societies, and doomsday divinations, the emotionally intense second volume of Berg's intrigue-laden Lighthouse Duet concludes the story of Valen. . . . Fans of Marion Zimmer Bradley's Avalon sequence and Sharon Shinn will be rewarded."
—*Publishers Weekly*

"Berg combines druid and Christian influences against a backdrop of sorcerers, priestesses, priests, deep evil, and a dying land to create an engrossing tale to get lost in . . . enjoyable."　　　—Monsters and Critics

"An excellent read . . . a satisfying sequel."　　　—Fresh Fiction

Flesh and Spirit

"The vividly rendered details . . . give this book such power. Berg brings to life every stone in a peaceful monastery and every nuance in a stratified society, describing the difficult dirty work of ordinary life as beautifully as she conveys the heart-stopping mysticism of holiness just beyond human perception."
—Sharon Shinn, national bestselling author of *Quatrain*

"Valen is unquestionably memorable—in what is definitely a dark fantasy as much concerned with Valen's internal struggle as with his conflicts with others."
—*Booklist*

"Chilling fantasy."　　　—*Publishers Weekly*

"Fast-paced. . . . Berg creates a troubled world full of politics, anarchy, and dark magic. . . . The magic is fascinating."　　　—SFRevu

"Carol Berg has done a masterful job of creating characters, places, religions, and political trials that grab and hold your attention. . . . Don't miss one of 2007's best fantasy books!"
—Romance Reviews Today

"[Berg] excels at creating worlds. . . . I'm eagerly awaiting the duology's concluding volume, *Breath and Bone*. . . . An engrossing and lively tale, with enough action to keep you hungry for more."   —*The Davis Enterprise*

The Bridge of D'Arnath Novels

"A very promising start to a new series."   —*The Denver Post*

"Berg has mastered the balance between mystery and storytelling [and] pacing; she weaves past and present together, setting a solid foundation. . . . It's obvious [she] has put incredible thought into who and what makes her characters tick."
                                        —*The Davis Enterprise*

"Berg exhibits her skill with language, world building, and the intelligent development of the magic that affects and is affected by the characters. . . . A promising new multivolume work that should provide much intelligent entertainment."
                                        —*Booklist*

"Imagination harnessed to talent produces a fantasy masterpiece, a work so original and believable that it will be very hard to wait for the next book in this series to be published."   —*Midwest Book Review*

"[Seri] is an excellent main heroine; her voice, from the first person, is real and practical. . . . I'm truly looking forward to seeing what happens next." —SF Site

"Gut-wrenching, serious fantasy fiction."   —Science Fiction Romance

Song of the Beast
Winner of the Colorado Book Award
for Science Fiction/Fantasy

"The plot keeps twisting right until the end . . . entertaining characters."
                                        —*Locus*

"Berg's fascinating fantasy is a puzzle story, with a Celtic-flavored setting and a plot as intricate and absorbing as fine Celtic lacework. . . . The characters are memorable, and Berg's intelligence and narrative skill make this stand-alone fantasy most commendable."   —*Booklist*

"It would be easy to categorize it as another dragon fantasy book. Instead, it is a well-crafted mystery. . . . Definitely recommended for libraries looking for high-quality fantasy and mystery additions."   —*KLIATT*

THE
SOUL MIRROR

A NOVEL OF THE
COLLEGIA MAGICA

CAROL BERG

A ROC BOOK

ROC
Published by New American Library, a division of
Penguin Group (USA) Inc., 375 Hudson Street,
New York, New York 10014, USA
Penguin Group (Canada), 90 Eglinton Avenue East, Suite 700, Toronto,
Ontario M4P 2Y3, Canada (a division of Pearson Penguin Canada Inc.)
Penguin Books Ltd., 80 Strand, London WC2R 0RL, England
Penguin Ireland, 25 St. Stephen's Green, Dublin 2,
Ireland (a division of Penguin Books Ltd.)
Penguin Group (Australia), 250 Camberwell Road, Camberwell, Victoria 3124,
Australia (a division of Pearson Australia Group Pty. Ltd.)
Penguin Books India Pvt. Ltd., 11 Community Centre, Panchsheel Park,
New Delhi - 110 017, India
Penguin Group (NZ), 67 Apollo Drive, Rosedale, North Shore 0632,
New Zealand (a division of Pearson New Zealand Ltd.)
Penguin Books (South Africa) (Pty.) Ltd., 24 Sturdee Avenue,
Rosebank, Johannesburg 2196, South Africa

Penguin Books Ltd., Registered Offices:
80 Strand, London WC2R 0RL, England

First published by Roc, an imprint of New American Library,
a division of Penguin Group (USA) Inc.

First Printing, January 2011
10 9 8 7 6 5 4 3 2 1

RoC REGISTERED TRADEMARK—MARCA REGISTRADA

LIBRARY OF CONGRESS CATALOGING-IN-PUBLICATION DATA:
Berg, Carol.
   The soul mirror: a novel of the Collegia Magica/Carol Berg.
     p. cm.
   ISBN 978-0-451-46374-6
   I. Title.
   PS3602.E7523S68 2011
   813'.6—dc22   2010034844

Set in Bembo
Designed by Ginger Legato

Printed in the United States of America

PUBLISHER'S NOTE
This is a work of fiction. Names, characters, places, and incidents either are the product of the author's imagination or are used fictitiously, and any resemblance to actual persons, living or dead, business establishments, events, or locales is entirely coincidental.
   The publisher does not have any control over and does not assume any responsibility for author or third-party Web sites or their content.

For those who are shy, reserved, or introverted, who lack self-confidence, or who just can't ever come up with a punch line until a day late . . .

ACKNOWLEDGMENTS

Thanks, as always, to Linda the Muse, aka the spirit of Lianelle, for literary lunching and launching. To Susan, Laurey, Brian, Catherine, Curt, and Courtney for their support and tough, careful reading, and especially to Glenn, fine man, fine friend, fine writer. To Markus for sharing his combative expertise. To my dear readers for their constant encouragement. And most especially to the Exceptional Spouse for love and support above and beyond.

CHAPTER 1

"Here we are, Damoselle de Vernase." My escort drew aside the overhanging pine branches so I could better view the disturbed ground. A raven flapped away, screeching, scraping my already stripped nerves. The shallow ravine was heavily wooded, preventing any glimpse of the severe gray walls or the round, slate-roofed towers my younger sister had called home for the past seven years.

Lianelle had once told me that forests were the perfect representation of magic: roots that delved deep into the rich, layered loam of all that had come before, shadow and light, growth and decay, mystery and life. All of it connected and balanced, ever changing, yet old beyond history. My sister had lived for magic. And now she had died for it—all her merry teasing, her laughter, her brilliance wasted on lies, dead dreams, and superstition.

The wiry little man shuddered and licked his pale lips with an overlong tongue. "Mage Bourrier says that for the last tenday Acolyte Lianelle has scarce been seen about the collegia. Whatever she was working on, it was certainly *not* her assigned duties or lessons. The alchemical stores were dreadfully out of order and the aviary unswept, and she had not yet submitted her essay on theoretical formulae for shape transformations. One of the tutors found her out here. Evidence bespoke a magical explosion . . . as I told you. Horrid."

And then they had dug a hole and thrown her in without a song or a prayer or a kinsman's touch to bid her farewell. A girl of seventeen. *Horrid* could not even begin to describe it. What of *despicable, vile, unconscionable?*

Yet another spasm of pain shivered my heart. Anger and resentment burned in my chest like fiery ingots, and I wanted to yell and weep and curse every stone of this place and every bastion of Heaven. But I swallowed the knot in my throat and clamped my jaw tight. Anne de Vernase did not crumble before strangers.

The patch of raw earth scraped out of the scorched bracken had been outlined with salt and sprinkled with herbs, likely some magical foolery intended to keep evil away—or contain it. Unbelievable that anyone could countenance such nonsense, when academicians could view the structure of a salt crystal through magnifying lenses and write treatises cataloging its properties. Every day scholars and academicians unmasked another enchantment as a fraud.

Only Lianelle had ever been able to fool me into thinking there was any substance to sorcery. "Certainly not in the common practices," she would say with a mixture of excitement and worldly wisdom laughable in a girl who had spent almost half her life within these walls. "Most large magical workings are illusion, and anything for sale in the marketplace is a waste of good coin. But the fundamentals—spellwork, binding power, elemental linkages between natural objects—those are real. That's what I study at Collegia Seravain." And then an oriole would settle on top of her head or the hearth fire would flare into stringy flames the deep blue of iris, and Lianelle would swear she had not thrown lamp oil in the hearth to make it burn so strangely or sprinkled seeds in her hair to attract the bird, but had done it all with magic. Laughing.

I folded my arms in front of me as if by force of will I might not lose the last bits of her. My sister. My dearest friend in the world. How could she be dead?

Their salt barrier had not lasted even a sevenday. Rain or animals had already blurred and broken the white lines.

"You've not marked her burial place with so much as a stick," I said, the magnitude of the hurt leaving privacy and dignity in ruins. "Did no one recall she had family to mourn her, to give her honor to ease her Veil journey? Why was she not taken to a proper deadhouse?"

My companion's fluttering hands dismissed my concerns, his bony wrists protruding from his sleeves as if he had put on a younger apprentice's gown. "The chancellor determined we could afford no delay in such untidy circumstances. A master mage came from Merona and laid heavy enchantments about her body to ensure nothing of her mistakes lingered to harm others. Being ungifted, you perhaps would not understand."

Ungifted. Paeans to the Pantokrator and his saints that I was ungifted in the ways of magic! Better to be plain, plodding Anne than dead like my gifted sister or locked away, unable to tell day from night, like my gifted mother. With my brother four years hostage to an angry king's vengeance, I seemed to be the only functioning member left of a family my father had once proclaimed "as perfectly balanced as the elegant ellipses of the planets." My father, who had explained the world to me, only to prove his every word a lie. My father, the royal diplomat, the man of science, the traitor.

I squeezed my arms tighter, fingers pressing to the bone. "This land belongs to the collegia?" I scanned the rugged landscape for some fence or marker.

"Yes. Though much of our lower, flatter land has had to be sold off—a disgraceful result of the king's new tax levies—the forest reaches and cliffside lands remain under our hold."

"Then certainly the mages will not object to my placing a stone marker scribed with my sister's name here. A small thing. Out of the way." Too little, too cold, too hard to remember a bright spirit. "She died while in the school's care."

"Um . . . I will have to inquire, of course. I was told only to show you." The balding man, not a day younger than fifty years, chewed his nails like a schoolchild. The masters of the collegia had sent an aging apprentice—a nobody—to guide me here. Someone who could answer not one of my thousand questions. No adept, no mage, and certainly no master could spare the time to explain why a sixth-year student at Collegia Magica de Seravain had been found half buried in last year's leaves, her flesh scorched and her fingers missing. I supposed I should be grateful they had notified me at all.

My guide scuttered up the slope of the ravine on his way back to the forest path.

FOR TWO HOURS I SAT outside the collegia gates, awaiting word that the mages would allow Lianelle's grave to be marked. The autumn day waxed warm and hazy. Fibrous streaks of cloud left the sky brownish gray rather than blue, promising rain by nightfall, a welcome change. Even the leafy wood that crowded the narrow lawn appeared dry, its greens grayish, the undergrowth already dying. I crushed the surging emotions of the previous hour until they had subsided to a familiar fevered dullness. Until I felt dead, too.

"Damoselle de Vernase!" The balding apprentice called out from behind a wicket gate in the gatehouse wall. "Chancellor Kajetan agrees to the marker. The stone must be cut small and designed to lie flat on the ground. When it is ready, the stonemason should apply to the grounds-keeper, and he'll be taken to the site. Now, will there be anything else?"

Anything else? Everything else! My skin flushed hot, then cold, then hot again. Choked by events I could not allow myself to feel, I could spit out only the mundane. "My sister's things," I said. "I should take them with me."

The jittery apprentice glanced over his shoulder. Well behind him, in the rectangle of sunlight at the far end of the dark gate tunnel, a broad-shouldered man leaned on a white stick and stared back at me. His features were indistinct, save for dark brows and thick black hair that threatened escape from a bound or braided queue. A silver band glinted from his neck—a mage collar.

"If anything of a personal nature is discovered, it will be forwarded to you along with the girl's death warrant," said the apprentice. "This concludes our business. Divine grace, damoselle." The wiry man slammed the wicket and retreated into the shady tunnel. Once he exited the tunnel, the arched rectangle of light was empty.

So, that was that. The sorcerers of Collegia Seravain had not allowed me even to step inside their door. Suffering such disrepute as they were already, they likely feared my unsavory family connections would taint them irreparably.

Five years previous my father had enlisted three sorcerers of the Camarilla Magica in his scheme to overthrow his oldest friend, the King of Sabria. The three had been caught using grotesque, murderous means to "enhance their power for magic" and paid the price on the headsman's block. My father yet eluded capture. The penalties for *his* infamy had been paid only by his victims and his family.

I hiked the long, dusty road down the hill to the whitewashed village of Seravain. As constant practice taught me, a rapid walk helped loose the knots in one's belly.

In the village I endured another two-hour wait, this time for the stonemason to return from mending a customer's springhouse. A contract with the stonemason to engrave a small plain marker with Lianelle's name and embed it in the ravine took two silver kentae and no time at all.

The stonemason gave me the name of the village baker's half-wit son, who might be spared long enough to drive me down to Tigano. From there I could take the evening coach back to Vernase. I'd be lucky to get home before middle-night.

"Damoselle Anne! Anne de Vernase!" I'd not yet rounded the village well to the baker's house when the shout halted me. A fair-haired man came pelting down the road from the collegia, the long sleeves of his gray gown flapping behind him like pennons in a Feste Vietre parade.

I waited for him in the middle of the deserted road.

"You're Lianelle's sister?" He skidded to a stop not a handsbreadth from my nose. Sweat dribbled through the fine layer of dust coating his boyish face and plastered tendrils of pale hair to his high forehead.

I stepped back to leave a more comfortable space between us. "Sonjeur?"

"I'm Guerin—Adept Guerin—Lianelle's instructor in semantics: lexicography, cryptonymics, and all that. And her friend, I think."

My sister had written about her semantics instructor a number of times. *Wizardly talented*, she had called him, *and wickedly handsome*. Lianelle had never been temperate in either speech or living.

"She mentioned you."

"We were just beginning—" The adept's voice faltered. Puffing out his cheeks, he released a long, shaking exhale, then held out a small roll of red leather tied with string. "The day before she died, she asked me to post this to you. But I'd not gotten around to it, and, in the upset, forgot I had it. When I heard you were here today . . . Oh, saints and angels, damoselle. I am so sorry."

His sorrow enveloped me like a fire-warmed blanket on a winter night, more welcome than any word or artifact. But I dared not accept such seductive gifts. Grief had broken my mother.

I nodded and said nothing.

His fingers were slow to release the leather packet. The bundle was heavy for its small size, the smooth leather warm and damp from his hand. A folded paper protruded from the flap.

"They've had me into her dormitory cubicle to decode some papers. Said she was plotting with her father. But they were only notes she took in my tutorials." His frowning gaze lingered on his hands, as if the troublesome bundle remained there. "I had no idea her father—your father—was—"

A woman banged open her door and yelled at her daughter to come in for supper.

Guerin glanced about uneasily. "I must get back, before— I've duties."

His imminent departure raised a fluttering panic, questions crowding and bumping to get through my constricted throat. "They'll not tell me what happened," I blurted. "Only that she was trying to work some enchantment that was too advanced. What was she doing? I swear on my hope of Heaven, she had no dealings with our father. And why would they bury her so quickly? Why in secret? Why in that ravine?"

"I know little more than you." His wide brow knotted. "She was upset that morning. Begged off my tutorial, swearing me not to report her absence. Said she had something dreadfully important to do. She asked if I still had this, and when I said I did, she pulled out that paper and scribbled your name on it—so I would be sure to get it right, she said. She could have been going anywhere. Students often cut through the ravine to avoid the door warden. But I had this awful, sick feeling about her all day. When she didn't attend her afternoon tutorial, I went looking for her the first moment I was free."

He tightened his jaw and closed his eyes for a moment.

"A small, focused explosion killed her," he went on, "damaging her chest and her hands. But whether the fire or the impact or the magic itself did the mortal damage, I couldn't tell. There were no particles lying around—no objects used in the spellwork—that might tell me what she was attempting. The magical residue was of a kind wholly unfamiliar to me, and once I'd summoned my superiors, I wasn't allowed to examine her again. But my mind refuses to let it go, as it just doesn't make— You see, your sister was a very good student, damoselle. Talented. Eager, but not rash. She should have been a first-rank adept long ago."

A frigid hand squeezed my heart. "Are you saying that someone else did this to her?"

"No. The magical signature was hers alone. There was not so much as a boot print near her." He rubbed his arms and stepped backward. "I am so sorry. So very sorry."

This could not be everything. Though it scalded my tongue to speak of it, I had to know. "Adept, surely you know the kind of vile sorcerers my father was involved with, and what they did to Ophelie de Marangel, to others. Lianelle wasn't—"

"Certainly not!" He hushed me with the words, his eyes darting at the windows and doors opened to the cooling evening. "No one was bleeding her, damoselle. Nothing I saw . . . nothing I knew of her . . . suggested she was being used for power transference. Divine grace, lady."

Before I could ask more, he was trotting back up the road.

Certainly Lianelle could have made a deadly mistake. She was forever

7

rash and always headstrong. I'd spent half my life cleaning up her messes. And a determination to prove she was more than just a traitor's daughter could easily have led her to overreach. But someone had failed her. Failed in protecting, failed in teaching, failed in caring.

Inexpressible fury set my whole body trembling, so that every step down the road required an act of will. My sister was dead and no one would tell me why. But she was the daughter of Michel de Vernase, and slander already tainted her memory in a place that should have been her shelter. Had her tutors murdered her before fifty witnesses here in Seravain village square, no one in the world would care, and I could do not a blasted, bloody, wretched thing about it.

"LET ME ROUST REMY, DAMOSELLE. He'll parse you up to the house. It's past middle-night." Mistress Constanza, the proprietress of the Cask, watched the Tigano coach rattle out of her rutted innyard. Her ample figure filled the bright-lit doorway of the sole inn in Vernase. Wavering yellow light spilled around her robust silhouette, along with the sounds of hearty laughter, boisterous conversation, and well-lubricated singing. "If you'll pardon my saying, dearie, you've got the look of a rug's been beat too many times."

"I think I'd rather walk home tonight. Thank you, Constanza. The rain has left the air so pleasant after the hot day."

"Sure you won't come in and ease your bonesprits with a cup?"

"Not tonight, mistress." I could not bear the thought of company, the sidewise glances, knowing nods, and incessant murmurings: *Treason . . . unholy sorcery . . . wife near burnt the place down . . . the wild boy prisoned . . . the youngest so odd . . . that plain'uns the eldest, no feelings, corked tight as a swollen bung, damned her own father . . .* Gossip helped fill the friendly Constanza's ale mugs, but my family had provided enough of that for a lifetime of swilling.

"As you will, dearie." As I picked my steps carefully across the innyard, she called after me. "Is your brother hale, then, damoselle? Such a direful confinement in the river damp. I suspected perhaps this journey . . . so sudden . . . Or was it the contessa, sweet angeli comfort the poor dear lady? Still helt in the mountains with her kin, is she? Her brothers tend her, I think."

"My brother endures, mistress." Though when I wrote Ambrose this day's news, he would surely batter his head to pulp against his prison walls. "And my mother's condition is unchanged. Thank you for your concern."

My aching back would have appreciated transport, even in Constanza's rickety donkey cart, but I had used up the last of my ready money for the stonemason and the coach fare. I'd not so much as a kivre to tip Remy. On another day, the petty humiliation of such impoverishment might have bothered me more. But all such nagging worries had long coalesced into a single overriding truth: My family was broken, and nothing in the wide, starry universe was ever going to repair it.

THE STEEP HIKE UP TO Montclaire stretched very long and very dark. The only sentient being I encountered along the path was the soldier assigned to that particular portion of the estate's encircling watch posts. Four years they'd kept up this stranglehold, lest the traitor *conte* abrogate his celebrated intelligence and attempt to visit the family he had abandoned.

The insolent guardsman near singed my hair with his torch as he examined my face and questioned my late excursion. With well-practiced hauteur, I rebuffed his attempts to pry out gossip. By the time I let myself through our outer gate, climbed the last swell of the hill, and used the faint light from the stable lamp to step carefully through the churned muck of the yard, the moon had set.

A sturdy man, more grizzle on his chin than on his round head, awaited me on the flagstone terrace, lamp in hand. "Mistress Anne, we have a—"

"It'll have to wait until morning, Bernard. I can't think another moment."

Underneath the spreading walnut tree, that dearest of men traded his lamp for my cloak. He wore the faded purple jacket and breeches, meticu-

lously white linen shirt, and threadbare hose that he donned in the evenings when he became footman, chamberlain, and porter after a day spent
as gardener, vintner, carpenter, and steward. "My lady, I must tell you—"

"Please, not now."

Even his urgency could not penetrate my leaden spirit. Almost everything Bernard had to tell me was urgent: The grapevines were dying; the
roof needed patching; the chimney in the reception room was clogged
with starlings' nests. Always and ever.

But, of course, he did not deserve to be chastised for it. I summoned
one more breath of control. "Thank you for waiting up. Angels' peace be
with you this night. And to Melusina the same."

Bernard's wife, Melusina, also played multiple roles: cook, housekeeper, laundress, and maid. In truth, we three did everything around
Montclaire, and it was never enough. The most beautiful house in Sabria
was slowly falling to ruin, yet today and tonight I could not care.

"Is it true, then, about the little one?" he called after me softly, as I
started toward an open door into the house.

I looked back. "Yes, it's true."

The soft circle of lamplight illuminated his round, ruddy face as it
crumpled in grief. His sorrow tore at me like hot pincers. If I stayed to
comfort him, I would be undone.

But when I stepped into the small parlor beyond the open doorway I
at last grasped what Bernard had been trying to tell me, what a burning
stable lamp and fresh muck should have told me, considering I had sold the
last of our horses two years past. An unfamiliar cloak lay over a small
traveling case, and a tray bearing the bony remains of boiled fish sat on a
small table beside a half-empty decanter of wine.

We'd had no visitors at Montclaire since a few months after the trial,
when my mother's irrational behavior had grown severe enough that we
could no longer mask it. Only creditors, or wanderers in search of work
or custom, neither of which we could provide, had wandered by. And, of
course, yesterday's messenger from Seravain. Saints shield me from worse
news.

Leaving the lamp behind, I peered through the inner doorway into the foyer. A slim, stiff-backed gentleman with close-trimmed brown hair and hands clasped behind his back was examining my father's telescope, on display between the curving arms of the grand staircase. Though richly made, the visitor's garments were unadorned and conservative in cut. Black and gray. No puffs, no ruffs, no trailing lace or colored ribbons. His modest height topped me by little more than a handspan. Familiar . . .

I eased past the arched doorway, hoping to glean his identity before choosing to engage or escape his attention. But he must have heard my footsteps. He pivoted sharply.

"Damoselle Anne," he said, bowing slightly and exposing the back of his left hand on his right shoulder as Sabrian law required of those born to a family of magical inheritance.

The law required the same of me, no matter that my father was not born to the blood and that I took no supernatural gift from my mother's family. But anger erased every other concern at recognizing the slight, soft-spoken man. This was the questioner. The wheedler. The Royal Accuser. The king's odious secretary or investigator or *agente confide*— whatever he was—who, with relentless pursuit and irrefutable logic, had destroyed my family.

"Sonjeur de Savin-Duplais," I said, wrestling to find words contemptuous enough to drive him away. "How dare you come here?"

CHAPTER 2

36 NIEBA, MIDDLE-NIGHT

"My apologies for intruding, damoselle, especially in this difficult time. I'd not planned to impose upon your hospitality, but your man said you would be late. It was necessary I speak with you as soon as possible." Four years had not altered his chilly demeanor. Always assessing. Always judging.

Many would discount Portier de Savin-Duplais, neither young nor old—middle thirties, perhaps—and so physically unexceptional. Before he took on the task of investigating the conspiracy that surrounded my father, he had served as librarian at Collegia Seravain. I would have preferred the company of an adder.

"*Necessary*, sonjeur? What could possibly be so important?" My bravado stemmed solely from Bernard, who had taken up a protective stance in the doorway of the dark dining room.

My father, the diplomat, had avowed that not even the most profound shyness or the most determined reserve could prevent an honest man from meeting a steady gaze. My visitor's eyes flicked from one of the twelve arched doorways to another, then swept the stair and upper gallery, as if my father's corruption might be visible as creeping mold or cracked mortar.

It pleased me that Bernard, Melusina, and I had managed to keep this part of the house respectable, at least. Our finest tapestries hung on the cherrywood panels. The lamps were bright. The blue slate floor was clean. As a fond duty to my mother, Melusina had set pots of fresh snapdragons about in nooks and crannies, and alongside the priceless Lefage mirror Mama had brought from her home in Nivanne. In front of the mirror, the telescope's brass gleamed, its ornate mounting free of dust, its mirror spotless, the engraved signature of the renowned astronomer Germond de Vouger—my father's longtime correspondent—prominently displayed. Yellow, blue, and green marbles representing the sun and the planets perched firmly atop the polished spindles that fixed them in the planetary. My father's prized possessions remained in the house because they were rare and valuable, not in any relapse of sentiment.

Returning his attention to the vicinity of my head, Duplais drew a folded paper from his doublet. "I've brought a summons."

My fists released their hard clench. He'd not brought ill news of my hostage brother or notice that my father's ashes had been *scattered in an unknown location, according to the law of Sabria,* as the king's judgment prescribed. Yet a summons could mean anything.

The paper was heavy and rich, my name in bold, sweeping script. I turned it over and my spirit petrified. The red wax was imprinted with the royal seal of Sabria.

A glance revealed only Duplais' back as he examined the gleaming brass ellipses of the planetary. I broke the seal.

> *By order of His Royal Majesty Philippe de Savin-Journia y Sabria, Anne de Vernase is hereby summoned to attend His Majesty's Court at Merona no later than the fifth day of Ocet, making all prudent preparations to fulfill her duties as king's ward and gooddaughter, such duties to include investiture as a maid of honor of the queen's household and all such proper engagements and alliances as His Majesty may specify.*

Engagements . . . alliances . . . I read the message four times before I comprehended its full meaning. And when I did so, the reek of betrayal sickened me.

The King of Sabria—my goodfather by my parents' wish, my guardian by law, which said that an unmarried woman of property who lacked competent parents became the king's ward, no matter her age—desired to use me as a diplomatic pawn, like an estate or a forest range or ten paces on a disputed border. Handsome, noble, knightly Philippe de Savin-Journia, whom I had adored from the day I could walk until the day he sent his soldiers to arrest my father, wanted to sell me for whatever pitiful return a traitor's daughter could fetch.

Duplais had now abandoned his studious pretense, his eyes narrowed and posture stiff, as if he expected a torrent of hysteria, or that I, the daughter of a condemned felon, might somehow produce a weapon and attack him. My own mind fixed itself upon absurdity. I had lived in the country my entire two-and-twenty years, and had maintained no contact with noble society since I was sixteen. For my life, I could not remember how to curtsy.

"By departing Montclaire at third hour of the afternoon watch tomorrow, I determine we can make it as far as Tigano by nightfall," said Duplais, "which should bring us to Merona four days after, in concert with His Majesty's orders. Naturally, I shall provide you female accompaniment. Your own attendant can follow with your luggage."

"Tomorrow?" Impossible. But then, five months or five years would not be enough. The estate was my responsibility. Bernard and Melusina and I, working all day every day, could scarce keep it up. I mustered what calm I could scrape together. "I cannot possibly leave Montclaire so abruptly. You must inform His Majesty. The house, the accounts . . . We begin the grape harvest in less than a tenday. You *do* understand my mother does not reside here anymore."

He ought. For the first year we had lived under the shadow of my father's disappearance, my mother had been our mainstay, her strength inspiring, uncompromising. But then the king had ringed Montclaire with soldiers hunting Papa, and this Duplais had come here with his dreadful mage. They had poked about the house, pried, questioned, brutalized my mother with insinuations and threats until her spirit had fractured. By the time of Papa's trial and condemnation, her distress had deepened into mania.

Duplais' slender face remained cold. Long dark lashes shielded his eyes.

"You needn't concern yourself with Montclaire any longer, damoselle. The Ruggiere titles and lands have been granted elsewhere."

As a fox empties a meadow of birdsong, so did this announcement silence my heart. Papa's crimes had already exiled Mama, Ambrose, and Lianelle. Now it was my turn. And to my shame, though the terms of my departure were trivial beside madness, prison, or death, I was not sure I could bear it.

Montclaire's expansive vistas, the abundant richness of its soil, the warmth and unpretentious comforts of the rambling house had created a nest for my life's nurturing. Though the echoes of laughter and playacting, sword fights, my mother's whimsical singing, and debates over everything from politics to mathematical proofs to shoes were fast fading, I felt safe here, embraced by the warm stone and sweet airs and the robust quiet that I could not seem to find in any city or village.

The reprieve that had kept us in our home had always been temporary. I'd known better than to credit the king with some lingering belief in Papa's innocence that I myself did not hold. My father was a betrayer and a murderer; he was never coming back.

Like an automaton, I gestured toward the doorway where Bernard waited, his expression bloodless with shock. "Our steward will show you to a room. It's very late, and it appears we've a great deal to do tomorrow."

"Indeed. As I informed your man, a clerk will arrive in the morning to begin an inventory. You may set aside your family's personal belongings. Everything else remains with the house."

"Yes. Naturally. I understand." My lips spoke the proper words, the only words possible.

Duplais did not move immediately to join Bernard. His sharply inquisitive gaze fixed on me, as if he could sight straight through my bones. "Have you——? You understand I must ask, damoselle. Why is your sister dead?"

"They told me she overreached in her magical studies. I don't know what that means. Perhaps you could tell me."

"Have you any further information on your father's whereabouts or activities?"

"I have not." Despite his burrowing stare, I refused to drop my eyes. I was guilty of nothing.

"You understand, surely, an intelligent young woman, a daughter so close in mind to her father, that this death signifies some change in his situation, some rising conflict with allies or rivals. I urge you to share whatever you know." When Duplais came to Montclaire that first time, he had lured us into exposure with this same reasoned urgency. Only at my father's trial had I observed his steel blades fully bared.

"You know nothing of my relationship with my father, sonjeur. Nor do you know anything of my mind."

"Very true. I do not." He bowed, stiff as an oaken door. "Angels' peace, damoselle."

Foolish to bait him. Silly, angry bravado, the kind of response for which I had always berated my brother. But I could not grasp his purpose, and the long day and its grinding emotion had deprived me of any more reasoned response. My father had called me the child of his mind. Then he had set about torturing and murdering a girl younger than me. How could I ever come to terms with that?

I stumbled up the stair to my own bedchamber. Once behind a closed door, I sat on my bed and screamed into a lapful of pillows, indulging anger and outrage and a shameful dose of self-pity. I would grieve forever for my beloved sister and my mad mother, for my wretched hostage brother, and for the false memory of a father I had worshiped. But for that one hour I mourned the end of one life and the dismal prospects of the next, raging and weeping and cursing my treacherous parent and his cruel king and their damnable conspiracy to steal away the home that was as much a part of me as heart and bones.

SELFISH EMOTIONAL INDULGENCE AIDS NOTHING, of course. Certainly not sleep. When my crusted eyes blinked open in the dark hours before dawn, the harsh facts remained unchanged. Even after stripping off shoes and travel-stained skirt and climbing under the sheets, I could not banish them with dreams. My thoughts were already snarled in packing, choosing, leaving.

But I refused to yield these last quiet hours alone to Portier de Savin-Duplais and his summons. Some things were more important. Traveling in the dark, lost in the storm of grieving, I had not yet read my sister's letter.

The candle Melusina had left burning on my table was naught but a puddle of wax, but I found another, coaxed a spark from the ashes of my bedchamber hearth to light it, and set it on my family altar beside the stone figurines representing my Cazar grandmother and a young cousin who had died ten years previous. Until I received Lianelle's death warrant from the Seravain deadhouse, our local verger would not sanctify a tessila for her.

Although I had long abandoned my childhood beliefs in the trials of Ixtador Beyond the Veil and the Ten Gates to Heaven in favor of reasoned ethics in this life and speculative ignorance about what might follow, I found comfort in the rituals of remembrance. I invited the memories of my sister to fill my heart as I extracted her packet from my discarded skirt, untied the string, and pulled out the paper bearing my name.

The crumpled letter was spotted with candle wax and varicolored blots of ink and tea. Not unexpected from the perennially messy Lianelle. Wiping my eyes with the back of my hand, I smiled and broke her seal. The letter was initially dated ten days past, but the two pages appeared to have been written in fits and starts. I wrapped a shawl about my shift and settled down to read.

Dear Ani,

I believe I've discovered some things to make you believe in sorcery at last. I'm posting them secretly, as the mages are so very strict about students working on enchantments that are "beyond one's level." Certainly they must consider almost everything of interest to be beyond my level as yet, and seem determined to keep it so. They forever find reasons to refuse me the examinations for adept's rank, though I've mastered work well beyond most third- and second-rank adepts already.

But their pigheadedness shall not prevail. A few days ago, I was researching an essay, and the library hound, Adept Nidallo, refused as always to admit me to the vault where they keep all the oldest books. So I returned after hours and let myself in.

Hush your scolding, elder sister! Were it not for picklock magic, I'd have learned nothing these six years! Everything of interest is kept in the vault.

Someone had been there before me and left a book open on the work-table. It was one of an odd collection usually stuffed in a corner because no one has been able to read them since the Blood Wars—not even Dullfish Duplais when he was librarian. Though the bindings are worn and the books are spellbound, they bear no titles, and all their pages are blank. Seeing one left open pricked my curiosity. If someone else at Seravain had learned to make something of them, I could too. So I absconded with one from the stack.

Over the next few days, I dabbled with some encryption spells Adept Guerin and I had been working on—and there it was, <u>A Discourse on Gautieri Personal Protections.</u> After a few days, I traded that book for another and then another. Ani, these books are a revelation!

The Gautieri methods seem to rely more upon innate power than exact balancing of the divine elements, and on reasoning and desired results instead of the specific formulas and endless memorizing that pass for learning here. One book called <u>The Gautieri Invariants of Dimensional Mind and Spirit</u> describes enchantments I've never heard of anywhere.

I've used these books to make three marvels especially for you, because I <u>do</u> want you to understand why I stay here instead of coming home to be with you. If I learn enough, I might be able to help Mama or set Ambrose free of the blighted Spindle. I know the power is in me.

So. Your gifts. The silver bead in the ring is a <u>courret</u>, a wardstone. It will glow blue if you're in danger from spellwork, red if you're threatened by fire, and black if poison is within arm's reach. The book lists many more variations of the ward, but they are devilish complicated, and I just didn't have time. It's unlikely a volcano is going to pop up at Montclaire anytime soon! You're not likely to be poisoned, either, but the poison ward was the easiest to work and the easiest to test.

I am not going to tell you exactly what the powder in the case will do, but only say that you could run naked through Vernase, snatch a chocolate comfit from the little box beside Mistress Constanza's couch, and no one would ever know! Shocking, yes? Mix a pinch of the powder in two spoonfuls of wine. Make sure you're alone, and taste it only in the smallest amounts. Each drop prolongs the effects for about a quarter hour. The keyword is <u>aventura</u>.

The pendants are the most amazing. They're called nireals, or soul mirrors. One is mine, a gift to you, and one is for you to bind and send back. Hold mine tight in your hand, speak the keyword, <u>soror deliria,</u> and you'll see what it does. To complete your own for me, you must focus all your mind and spirit on it, then think of all the things you love best in the world—and only those. Once you feel the magic open to you, and you certainly will, say the word you wish to key the spell—in Aljyssian, remember! Send me your pendant along with the keyword you've chosen.

You've always been the strongest of us, Ani, and the cleverest, and the wisest—the rock that will hold while the rest of us wander. But you mustn't hide yourself away at Montclaire forever. Perhaps my little gifts will make you bold enough to venture out.

All my love,
Lianelle

She had stuffed the red leather packet with scraps of old linen. Nestled in the soft folds was a gold ring, fashioned in the likeness of a falcon's head. A silver bead had been fitted as the bird's eye. The packet's weight derived from a palm-sized round case made of ivory, filled with a coarse gray powder. The nireals must be the two thumb-sized oval pendants of untarnished silver. Pretty trinkets. It was only the thought of magic working that left me queasy. Smoke and mirrors and lies.

The letter revealed no hint of the anxiety her wizardly instructor had described. I read on into the second page, a jumble of snippets scrawled in different inks.

I've had no occasion to post this, as Mage Bourrier has stuck me on the restriction list again—for demonstrating that his "talking door" could be made wholly inarticulate by applying a rasp to the hinges, and silenced altogether with a healthy dollop of grease. As usual, I am named insolent and self-aggrandizing. Ah, but not stupid at least!

Last night, I sneaked into the vault to exchange the <u>Invariants</u> book and, to my horror, charged straight into Chancellor Kajetan, who had chosen that particular night to wholly rearrange the vault collection. Of course he threatened to dismiss me from Seravain for lock-picking and being where I wasn't supposed to be in the middle of the night. But I convinced him that Librarian Nidallo detests me and has spitefully refused to allow me into the vault to research my essay. I took the occasion to explain how frustrated I am with my tutors' excuses, and how I am determined to sit for my adept's examinations this season. I knocked over a stack of books, and in all the distraction, managed to return the Gautieri volume without him noticing.

The old crock is very kind, and whenever he speaks on the subjects of sorcery and history and destiny, I go all gooseflesh. He touches a kindred part of my soul, the same that drives me to all this trouble. I do so wish you could speak with him. Perhaps then you would understand my determination.

Anyway, Kajetan promised to instruct Nidallo to supervise my work in the vault, which, of course, is not at all what I want. To spite them both, I pilfered another book from the "Gautieri stack," the last one I've not read, and smuggled it out in my shift. This one has visible script. Unfortunately its wickedly complicated encryption has resisted my best efforts. I'm thinking it isn't from the same collection after all.

Today Chancellor Kajetan stopped me in the yard. He has banished Bourrier the Toad! Master Charlot, the new vice chancellor, whose head

*is perfectly round, by the way, is to be my principal tutor, and he is
ordered to schedule my third-level examinations. Huzzah! Now I'm
off for one more joust with this useless book, then return it before Charlot the Prig finds an excuse to hold me back. A wizardly kind friend has
agreed to post this letter for me.*

*Do not breathe a word about these books! For your life, Ani! Do not
trust ANYONE. I've set events in motion. Heed both mind and heart to
understand.*

This last scrap was scrawled with the same pen and ink that scribed my
name on the outside of the letter. So she had written it the morning she
died. Whatever had happened before or after she returned her magic book
to the Seravain library, whatever events she had set in motion must have
driven her to the mistake that killed her. How could I *ever* understand?

Hurt settled like lead weights in my bones. Its barbed edges gouged a
raw and ragged wound in my heart. I had once believed no pain could be
worse than testifying at my father's trial, hearing my own words expose
his treason and murder and seal his condemnation. But then I had watched
my terrified brother clapped in irons and dragged to prison when he was
but fifteen. And then I had watched my mother's fractured spirit decline
into madness, and I had been forced to beg her family to confine her in
their mountain fortress, lest she harm herself or others. And now this . . .
How could a girl of such life and spirit be lost to this world? What had
frightened her to her death?

"I'll try to be bold, little sister. Somehow, I'll find out what happened
to you. I swear it." Though I had no idea how to go about it.

I poked at her charmed trinkets with a hairpin, as if they might yield
me answers. The back of one silver nireal had been engraved with a frog—
Lianelle's, surely. She had once filled my bedchamber with no less than
fifty frogs that she claimed to have called to her service with sorcery. The
back of the second pendant was engraved with a single olive tree on a
hill—a symbol of strength and home. My chest ached as if it might crack.

As I rewrapped the trinkets in the linen and leather, a small triangular scrap of paper fell loose. A single word, *andragossa*, was written on it. An Aljyssian word, no doubt the keyword for the ring spell. Stomach churning in rebellion, I stuffed the scrap in the packet with the rest.

Though I treasured my sister's sentiments, not even her wizardly talented Guerin nor her revered Mage Kajetan could persuade me to touch her unnatural gifts. Had poison killed Lianelle, I would not swallow it to learn how. Had she fallen from a cliff, I would not jump after her to discover why.

Perhaps some magic was honest and worthy. Perhaps there existed some true enchantments that could not be exposed as duplicity or explained by natural laws of alchemistry, biology, or physics. I doubted it. But from my earliest memory, the very notion of spellwork—some kind of unnatural energies fermenting inside one's veins, perverting the natural order of creation—had repelled me. As I grew older, the revulsion had become a physical thing, the merest suspicion of nearby magic unsettling my stomach. Now its pursuit had brought ruin to everyone I loved. I wanted nothing to do with it. My own mundane gifts must carry me on this wretched journey.

CHAPTER 3

1 Ocet, afternoon

"Damoselle, we really must be on our way." Savin-Duplais hovered in the doorway of the library, poised at the edge of my leaving, as he had been all day, like a gray sparrow ready to take flight at the flick of my hand.

"My parents have lived here for twenty years, sonjeur. I cannot sort out our belongings in a few hours."

I dropped a magnifying lens into the satchel at my feet, laid my mother's sketch of Ambrose, Lianelle, and me in the box of her drawings, and riffled through the packet of my father's years of correspondence with Germond de Vouger. Some collegia would surely treasure these papers, the evolving outline of an entirely new theory of objects in motion from the preeminent natural philosopher in the world.

"The driver is waiting."

I threw the priceless letters into the empty drawer of my father's desk and slammed it shut. As I rose from the chair, I surveyed the ranks of books, denying tears for the hundredth time since dawn. These volumes were my childhood, my education, my refuge and delight.

"The books remain with the house, damoselle," snapped Duplais, as if he could read my thoughts. "If some particular volume has sentimental value, you may write to Sonjeur de Sejain to request it."

Sejain would be highly unlikely to yield anything. The squinting inventory clerk had attached himself to my shoulder upon his arrival as if he were the new owner of Montclaire and I a thief. He had come near apoplexy when I made to retrieve my mother's jewel case. Duplais, to his credit, had sent the creeping weasel off to inventory the plate and porcelain.

"One more day, sonjeur," I said, desperation breaking my resolve not to ask Duplais for so much as a spoon. "I sit a horse well and have no need to be bundled off in a coach. If we ride to Merona instead of driving, we cut off two days, allowing me to arrive well within His Majesty's deadline." A stupid deadline. What urgency could be attached to a waiting woman? I doubted Queen Eugenie, deprived of my attendance, would flounder in filth and loneliness, unbrushed or undressed.

"Within the hour, damoselle." Daylight had not thawed the frozen stick.

I would not beg a clerk for my books. Gritting my teeth, I snatched four or five volumes from the shelves of story collections and histories and slammed them down beside the stack of personal belongings to be stored in Mistress Constanza's attic at the Cask. Among the salvaged items were the box of Mama's drawings and the pages of Ambrose's poetry I had transcribed through the years. Though possessed of an unlikely gift for verse, my brother had refused to write down his creations. Running, riding, and swordwork were his life's breath. Angels protect his mind, confined for so long.

Turning back to the shelves, I pulled out Papa's favorite manual of swordwork, a star atlas, and a book on river birds. I stuffed them into the satchel I would take with me to Merona. Perhaps I could celebrate with Ambrose on his birthday, a month hence.

Of a sudden, my despite for the King of Sabria swelled to choking. Had Ambrose's approaching majority triggered this sudden rush to revert the Ruggiere demesne? With a father five years missing, Ambrose would, by statute, inherit the Ruggiere titles on his twentieth birthday, thus making it more complicated to strip away the demesne. Unless it was already granted elsewhere.

"Damoselle . . . the time." Duplais' tapping boot must surely dent the floor. His right hand, pocked with ugly red scars, pointed at the door.

"Very well." I stacked a few more books beside the boxes of drawings and letters, and stuffed one more into my bursting satchel. Hefting the bag, I brushed past Duplais, mumbling, "Creator forbid that Sabria topple because we're late for my brother's disinheritance."

Duplais' naturally deep complexion took on a decidedly scarlet cast. The Royal Accuser knew exactly what I meant.

Mistress Constanza's donkey cart had been waiting since third hour of the afternoon watch, and it was already half past the fourth. As I entrusted my list of the family's personal belongings to Bernard, and spoke to Melusina about packing the garments laid out on my bed, Duplais twitched like a cat's tail. I had scarce begun exchanging farewells with these two, a part of my family since before I was born, when his slender patience cracked. "Enough of this!" He grabbed my arm. "You may write your friends once you are settled in Merona."

He propelled me through the front doors and up to the splintered seat beside the slouching Remy. Bernard had not even brought Duplais' own mount from the stable as yet. Evidently that did not matter, as Duplais tossed my book satchel in the cart and slapped the donkey's rump. I groped for a suitably scathing comment to yell back at him. As ever, it eluded me. No doubt a memorable gibe would occur to me on the morrow.

We'd not even rolled through the gates when a violent jolt jounced me out of the emotional backwash of my departure and almost out of the cart. Remy had headed off the road onto the rutted track that led through the vineyards and around the backside of Montclaire's hilly terrain, a much longer and rougher route to the village.

"Whatever are you doing?" I said, clinging to the seat lest I be bounced out altogether. "Duplais will have apoplexy!"

"No'm. He paid me to take you down by Jaugert's and meet him at Vradeu's Crossing."

"In the name of sense, why?"

Remy shrugged and bawled insults at the mule, while the wind caught our plume of yellow dust and rolled it back over us.

Goodman Jaugert owned a ramshackle stable just north of Vernase. Unfortunately, anyone desiring to avail themselves of his tender hands with horseflesh or the healthy grazing of his pasture had to travel five kilometres upstream to Vradeu's Crossing and back again, or risk fording Pelicaine Rill, which was more kin to a rapids than a rill alongside his property. Only Montclaire's food baskets kept his seven children from starving.

Such a circuitous route made no sense at all.

"ANI! ANI! ANI!" A FULL hour after leaving Montclaire, five dirty-faced urchins with near-white hair chased the donkey cart into Jaugert's yard, swarming onto the step and the box before we had rolled to a stop. A gangly girl held back and dipped her knee, while at the same time snatching the collar of a freckle-nosed boy trying to climb my skirt. "Divine grace, damoselle."

"Divine grace, Kati. I'm so sorry I've brought nothing today." I patted several warm white heads and told myself guilt was irrational, which did nothing at all to cure it.

As Remy went off in search of Jaugert and the noisy swarm dispersed, I motioned Jaugert's eldest up close. "Kati, you must get up to the house tomorrow early and tell Melusina I said to fill you as many baskets as she can. I'm called to the city, and there will be a new lord at Montclaire. A new family. Do you understand?"

"Aye, damoselle." Though her shy flush died away, her proud manners held.

A child of eleven should not have to understand what I'd just told her. But her mother had died birthing the baby that clung to Kati's hand, and her father was waiting for a charm singer to cleanse his house before considering a new wife to care for his brood. Unfortunately, the Camarilla, the council of master mages who supposedly protected Sabrians from magical charlatans, had the habit of branding charm singers on the forehead and hanging them up in the public markets until they confessed their false practices—or starved.

I never knew who to despise the more: the lackwit grannies and hedge wizards who perpetuated these superstitions, the brutal mages who insisted people hold faith in—and pay for—only their particular variety of charms and spells, or the believers like Jaugert who allowed magic to impoverish their lives.

"Damoselle Anne, divine grace be with thee this sweet even'," said Jaugert from the barn door. "Guess me fair who I've got fer ye." The wiry little man led out a bright-eyed little silver-bay mare, who nickered and bobbed her head in greeting.

"Ladyslipper!" The happy surprise almost destroyed my hard-won composure. Holy saints, how I detested such sentimental weakness.

"The laird what sent you here paid me sum enow to fetch one of yer own beasties from the hostelry in Tigano. Shall ye ride her down to the crossing, or would ye rather stick with Remy and his balkish ass?"

So Duplais had intended me to ride all along. Why hadn't he told me? I doubted he'd done it from generosity.

Ladyslipper nuzzled my shoulder. I stroked her neck and apologized for my empty pockets. Though she looked a little thinner, her brown coat was glossy, her pale mane combed, and her hooves well trimmed.

"I'll ride," I said, throwing my arms around the bony hostler—which was entirely unlike me. "Thank you, Jaugert. Such a kindness you've done me." He could have used Duplais' coin to hire me a bone-racking hack and pocketed the difference.

Jaugert fastened my book satchel to the saddle, but I couldn't bear to wait longer and had him give me a hand up. Yelling to Remy that we'd transfer the rest of my bags when we joined Duplais at Vradeu's Crossing, I took out across Jaugert's meadow. Allowing Ladyslipper her head in the soft evening was almost enough to outrun grief. We certainly outran Remy and his ass.

As THE TRACK ANGLED BACK toward the fretting ribbon of Pelicaine Rill and the crossing, I slowed the mare to a walk. An evening haze had settled over the gray-green stubble of Barone Vradeu's lavender fields, half obscuring the vertical white rocks that bounded the valley. Remy and his cart were the merest dust cloud behind me. The wind and pounding rhythm of Ladyslipper's exuberant run had cleared my head.

Yet my contentment was short-lived. Duplais awaited me at the top of a short incline. Behind him the track leveled and plunged through a sea of rippling wheat before vanishing into a thick stand of oaks and beeches.

"Well-done, damoselle," he said, pulling his little chestnut around before I could halt. "We've time enough to get through the wood and across the ford before dark. We'll have moonlight the rest of the way to Tigano, and the road's easy enough. Quickly, if you please."

If he was in such a dreadful hurry, why had he brought me the long way around?

All at once, the harsh realities of my situation stung like a slap on tender skin. We had encountered no sentry on the back road, and Vradeu's Crossing would deposit us well outside Vernase. No one in the village and none of the encircling guard would have seen me leave Montclaire with Duplais. Deception. Duplicity. Lianelle had said to trust no one.

"Wait! Sonjeur!"

He brought his horse around again. "What is it?"

"I must wait for Remy and the cart," I said.

"Impossible."

"But I've left bags on the cart. My clothes. Valuables." I wasn't going anywhere without the leather case I'd tucked under the seat of Remy's cart. It held my mother's jewelry and my own few pieces, my grandmother's and cousin's tessilae, a few coins I'd taken from Montclaire's iron box, before consigning it to Bernard's custody . . . and Lianelle's packet.

"The cart will proceed to Vernase, where the innkeeper will send on your belongings. I've left her funds for just such necessity. We must go *now*, damoselle."

A few times on his first visit to Montclaire, and for a certain moment after my father's trial, I'd imagined Duplais possessed of some small portion of compassion. In the years since, I had marveled at my naïveté.

Everything he'd said and done had been aimed at convicting my father and his confederates.

My newly wakened mistrust emboldened me. "Why *must* we?"

Had I been an artist like my mother, I would have sketched Portier de Duplais' smooth, narrow face as chiseled ice, seamed with cracks spewing steam. At my question, the cracks split.

"Because, damoselle, my king has charged me to deliver you to Castelle Escalon intact. As you so recently discovered to your distress—and my own—your father's rank in the brotherhood of traitors no longer ensures his children's safety. I was followed to Montclaire and have no reason to believe those followers friendly. Now, will you please ride?"

The horrors I'd dismissed at Seravain came rushing back. "You believe my sister was *murdered*. For what?"

"Vengeance," said Duplais, his gaze roaming the path and the shadowed boundary of the wood. "Your sister revealed secrets that brought down three powerful sorcerers and stalled your father's plot to upend Sabria. Those who dabble in murder and unholy sorcery invite retribution in like coin. Or perhaps someone believed she knew more than she told and wished to silence her . . . or tried to pry out her secrets for their own use." He cast his keen-edged scrutiny on me. "Something's changed in the world. Now they're coming after you."

"But I know nothing of use to such people!" The assertion, repeated a thousand times before the trial, sounded false even to me. Because now, of course, I *did* know something. Yet Lianelle had warned me not to speak of her magic books. *For your life, Ani . . .* I'd thought her exaggerating.

Without waiting for more argument, he goaded his mount to a trot. Ladyslipper took out after the chestnut, though every morsel of my own spirit yearned to hie back to Montclaire and barricade myself in the study.

Fear welled up like a black, sour flood. Ambrose could not run. "What of my brother?"

"A well-guarded hostage is not so easy a mark as a lone woman in the country," said Duplais. "But I've warned the Spindle warder to bolster his guard."

No matter how I detested Duplais, I could fault neither his logic nor his thoroughness. *Naive* was too bold a word for me, who had wasted these four years pretending I could stay hidden and safe at home forever. *Dunderheaded* described me better. No matter that Duplais had tried to tell me, I had not considered what Lianelle's death might mean about my father.

One of Lianelle's fellow students, a young girl named Ophelie, had become involved in the illicit practice of blood transference in an attempt to grow her power for magic. Lianelle had known her friend's secret and tried to help her. But my father and his confederates had abducted Ophelie and imprisoned her, and the three sorcerers had used her blood for themselves. For one brief hour, the dying Ophelie had gotten free of them, providing the first evidence that led to my father's conviction. At the trial, Duplais had used Lianelle's continued life as evidence of Papa's supremacy in this magical conspiracy. Now she was dead, and with only this flimsy explanation.

The lowering sun slipped through scattered clots of purple and gray cloud. Hawks and kites circled, dodging angled sunbeams as they surveyed Vradeu's wheat field. The drying wheat rustled like a showering rain. But as we passed under the canopy of oak and beech, the noise of the Rill, the wheat, and the birds fell silent. The spongy woodland turf muffled hoofbeats and muted the light.

"Damn and blast." Duplais' soft epithet sliced through the breathless damp like a saber. "Stay close, damoselle. Follow my direction, whatever comes."

No amount of peering into the gloom revealed what concerned him. I nudged Ladyslipper to Duplais' side as he slowed, though every part of me wanted to kick her to a gallop. I had no other defender.

"Hey up, steward . . . wimman's *heinend* . . . whateer th'art called at present day." The flat, contemptuous hail snapped through the woodland like a whipcrack. "And tha, too, lahddee fair."

CHAPTER 4

1 OCET, EVENING

The variegated gloom disgorged three bulky men in hammered leather. Heart thumping, I hauled on Ladyslipper's reins. She came around sweetly, but two riders blocked our retreat. Duplais sat petrified on his chestnut.

"There's noort ta go, lahddee fair." The cloaked swordsman who stepped forward wore a full leather mask, shaped so like a human face, one expected the narrow lips to issue a blessing. Deepening shadows hid the gaze behind the eyeholes and the human lips behind the mouth slot. A heavy brown hood, tied to the mask, hid his hair. "We've a small bizn with tha; thence can be on yer way. Doon, now. Ta ground tha go."

The big man's bizarre costume transfixed me. Not a squared centimetre of his skin was exposed. Horrors could lie beneath so perfectly sculpted a mask.

"Do as he says, damoselle," said Duplais, taut as wind-stretched canvas. "Resistance gains nothing."

The secretary, so imperious this day past, had shriveled, appearing diminished and subservient before the masked giant. Wholly a coward. Face pale and rigid as a limestone cliff, he dismounted hurriedly and offered me his hand.

I ignored his stiff courtesy and slid to the ground. He'd be no protection against these five. He did not appear to carry so much as a knife. Not that I was better prepared. My zahkri, a Fassid bandit knife given me by my Cazar grandfather, remained in Remy's cart. When my uncles had tried to teach me its nastier uses, I'd practiced only long enough to make them happy before escaping to less barbaric enjoyments.

The leader's thick accent spoke of Norgand, the ever-hostile tribal lands of rock and ice and fire that constricted Sabria's northern sea routes. But these were neither marauders come downriver nor other common highwaymen. He had called Duplais *steward* and a woman's *heinend*, or bond slave. They knew him. But their *bizn*—business—was with me.

I was not so frightened as I would have expected. Though the cruel nature of my father's crimes implied the like from any rivals, facing danger seemed easier than anticipating. But if I was to survive, I'd best pay attention.

The masked man motioned to his companions. One held our horses' bridles, while the other threw my satchel to the ground. Duplais' shabby leather case soon joined it. These two and the two riders who'd come up from behind wore simpler masks and no hoods, which left their hair and necks exposed. I judged them no cadre of Norgandi mercenaries, either. Ebony skin and black, tight-curled hair named one man a Fassid. Norgandi believed the Fassid to be Fallen and would never work side by side with them.

The two behind dismounted and joined their fellows, weapons bristling.

"We've naught of value, *wegheind*," said Duplais, naming the leader an ox's rear, as the Fassid cut his purse and a velvet spall pouch from his belt and dropped them beside our bags. "The coins in my purse won't cover the first bribe for your jailer. And surely you were taught that those who dare touch sanctified spalls are doomed to wander Ixtador Beyond the Veil for a thousand years."

Kneeling beside our belongings, the masked Norgandi emptied Duplais' spall pouch into his hand and examined the three stone chips—struck from tessilae to be constant reminders of honored dead. "We're nae worrt by yer god's punishings o'er splits of stone. Die with honor, and the Mariner sails un direct ta Skyhallow. Nae cruelish wanderwalks out of time. As tae valuing, oor bizn is oor own."

Duplais' glare roved from one of the masked men to the next as if committing them to memory. One of the four was missing a finger on his left hand. One wore gold hoop earrings, and a zahkri at his belt, yet he was not Fassid, but rather brown-haired and thick boned.

Discarding pouch and spalls over his shoulder, the leader dug into my book satchel. Spiderwebs brushed my face and hair.

"Ah! Look-see . . ." He pulled out the books I'd packed for Ambrose. One by one, he examined the titles, riffled the pages, and carefully traced his fingers over random text.

I drew back, a creeping, wriggling certainty churning my gut. As sure as my name, the masked man was using spellwork to examine the books. His mask covered his neck, so I could not see if he wore a mage's collar, and his gloves hid any blood family's handmark.

One by one he discarded my books. With a muffled curse, he upended my bag and pawed through the papers and silly oddments I had snatched up to bring with me. Family birth warrants and the Camarilla validations of our handmarks. My parents' marriage contract. Montclaire's planting book, which I would need to return to Bernard, merited a brief look. A thumb-sized portrait of my mother. The journal I'd not written in since I was an overimaginative twelve-year-old. The magnifying glass from the study. The engraved silver scissors Mama had given me on my sixteenth birthday. Bits and pieces of a life in splinters.

The Norgandi seized on the journal at once and set it aside. Had I not been increasingly sick at the thought of his magic working, I would have laughed at the consideration of desperate criminals reading my lurid speculations on male anatomy, "women's mysteries," and what went on in my parents' bedchamber.

The planting book went with the journal. The papers he reviewed and tossed aside.

The scissors and the glass also merited study. The masked sorcerer laid the magnifying lens on a silver plate from his cloak, encircled them with the length of yarn, and mumbled a word that sounded something like *fya-cor* or *fillator,* words that meant *starfish* or *evil brother* or something like. My Aljyssian vocabulary had evaporated for the moment.

Though he blew a note of disappointment, the Norgandi tossed the magnifier atop the journal. His examination of my scissors resulted in the same.

"Baggage seems a mite scant for a lahddee traverling." Though its molded expression remained serene, his displeasure battered me like hailstones. He jerked his head at his men. "Outen their pockies 'n see what's else hid. Soft wi' the lahddee. Nae want 'er mussed till we scoff 'er *spiniks.*"

What were *spiniks*? My head was spinning. Not jewels. Treasures? No. Something to be *scoffed*—stolen. Thank the stars that the cart carrying Lianelle's letter and charms had lagged so far behind us.

As he dumped clothes and sundries from Duplais' case, two of the others sheathed their weapons. While the fellow with the hoop earrings stood behind Duplais, the Fassid searched the secretary from neck to boots. Duplais stood rigid, as the brigand tossed a slim leather-bound book, an overlarge silver coin, and a small, tarnished brass case to the ground.

Then it was my turn. The man with the hoop earrings laid his thick-knuckled fingers on my shoulders and slid them down my arms all the way to the wrists.

My flesh shrank away from my skin.

When he returned his creeping hands to my shoulders, his thumbs strayed above my bodice to my bare throat, and stroked the skin with a slow, discomforting pressure. Then his fingers splayed wide and his thumbs circled downward. The fire in my gut blossomed.

"Don't touch me!" I said hoarsely, bringing my forearms up sharply between his and slapping them outward, knocking his hands away. At the same time I lurched backward, right into the arms of the Fassid. I flailed at him and dodged to the side before he could grab me. "I've no pockets and nothing you would—"

A guttural screech split the gloom. Something huge and dark swept out of the trees. A rider.

Pandemonium erupted as someone's grunting curse turned to a bub-

bling shriek. Duplais' chestnut reared. Ladyslipper whinnied. With frightened snorts, our horses vanished into the wood.

As I strained and twisted, Duplais enveloped me in his arms and
slammed me to the ground. A second horse and rider charged into the
fray, so close the wind of their passing fluttered Duplais' collar into my
eyes. They must have crossed the very spot we'd been standing.

Duplais' heart drummed through his coat as I tried to wriggle out
from under him. Two steps away, the Fassid lay unmoving, an arrow protruding from his eye.

"Into the trees," Duplais growled into my ear, before rolling off me.
Gripping my hand and pressing my head low, he half led, half dragged me
deep into the twiggy underbrush.

"Fitch the lahddee! Fitch 'er!" The breathless Norgandi sounded as if
he were too busy to *fitch* me himself. Savage grunts accompanied the
clank and scrape of steel.

Duplais gave me no chance to heed my footing. When I tripped on a
mass of roots, he had me up again before I could spit out the dirt and dead
leaves. We'd gone perhaps twenty metres from the road when he backed
me against a tree. Stronger than he appeared, he forced me still and pressed
a finger to my lips. I shoved his finger from my mouth, but bit my lip and
stayed quiet.

The weapons fell silent. Hoofbeats retreated toward the crossing. But
Duplais did not move until a nighthawk, which did not sound exactly like
a proper Aubine nighthawk, trilled plaintively.

"I believe we can go back now." Duplais stepped away and straightened his doublet.

The Fassid and two others lay dead. My eyes dwelt on the blood-
slathered bodies only long enough to see that neither the leader with the
shaped mask nor the man with the earrings was among them. I hoped
they were collapsed around the next bend.

A broad-chested, mustachioed man, his sweating skin the rich golden
tan of long-brewed tea, moved from one body to the next, kicking them
to elicit signs of life. He carried himself soldierly, and his leather armor
was spangled with steel plates, which spoke of true battle experience, so

my father had taught me. But his hair fell all the way to his jaw—most unsoldierly. I knew why when his head whipped around at our approach. Slow and purposeful, he drew his black locks behind his ears—horribly mutilated ears.

I quickly dropped my gaze, my skin flooded with shame. Only a determination to decency forced words out of me. "Captain de Santo, it appears you and your"—I glanced about in vain for the rider in black—"friend saved our lives. Thank you."

"I was asked," he said, jerking his head at Duplais, "else I might have thought different."

My father had done this. To hide his own duplicity, Papa had made a distraction of de Santo, once captain of the king's guard, by accusing him of jeopardizing the king's life. He had badgered and bullied and rushed the captain to judgment, cropping his ears with an ax, thus condemning him to everlasting humiliation and disgrace far worse than the pain of the mutilation. It had cost a good soldier his honor, his livelihood, and his family.

De Santo had testified at Papa's trial, as I had. I hoped bearing witness against his tormentor had restored his honor in his own mind, even if no one in the world would ever see past the testimony of his cropped ears.

"The others got away?" Duplais was examining the bodies, yanking off the masks, searching for anything to identify them.

"The shadow man took after them," said de Santo. "The henchman's skewered already. I doubt he'll tell us aught when he stumbles. I stayed back, lest they've friends about."

Indeed, moments later, the black horse dragged a fourth body—that of the man with the earrings—into the trampled glen.

"No luck with the leader?" said Duplais.

The "shadow man," dressed and cloaked in the color of midnight, shook his head. A black silk scarf wound around his face and neck hid all features save his eyes, and a flat, wide-brimmed hat shielded those from view. As soon as de Santo untied the rope, the rider moved off into the trees, denying me any chance of identifying him in the future, except that he was more graceful in the saddle than any horseman I'd ever observed.

More even than Ambrose, whom my father had forever sworn to house in the stable.

Duplais yanked the mask off the newly arrived body.

"Welther!" The name popped out of my mouth the moment the scarred cheek and bristling jaw came into view.

"Who?" Duplais' question rang sharp as a bell strike.

"Welther de Ruz. One of my father's aides, years ago." The burly soldier's stares and insinuating smiles had blighted a year of my girlhood, until Papa noticed my increasing reluctance to leave my bedchamber. "My father dismissed him for impropriety. Not . . . kindly."

"So these might be your father's rivals, and yet . . . tell me, damoselle, did you recognize the leader?"

Glad he didn't force me to dredge up more, I answered readily. "The Norgandi? No."

"What if the accent was false?"

False? I tried to think back to the Norgandi's diction. The dialect had been pervasive and perfectly accurate. And without seeing the man's face— Heaven's lights, the mask! At the trial Duplais had described a mask worn by the villain he called the Aspirant, the man he judged to be the ringleader of the conspiracy—my father. Duplais' unwavering gaze scrutinized me as he might a treasure map.

"That man was not my father. I would know."

But would I? Frightened, confused, and grieving as I was? After five years' absence? With his being cloaked and masked, voice disguised by the thick patois? As I reviewed the scraps and snippets of his Norgandi phrases, I could detect a false perfection. No one, especially a man of common background as the masked man's words bespoke, enunciated his own language without some local or regional variation. So he had learned the Norgandi language later and was better educated than he seemed. But Papa? I called it up again and listened.

"He was not my father. His voice's timbre was all wrong. But neither was he a native speaker."

"Good enough." Duplais seemed surprised at my offering so much. "What was he after? If he'd a mind to abduct you, he would have clobbered me, dragged you off, and searched your baggage later. If he had wanted blood to leech, they would have taken both of us and to perdition with baggage. He was hunting *something*."

The three of them waited. De Santo glaring. Duplais calculating. The black-cloaked man in the shadows listening.

"I've no idea." I knelt on the soft earth and began to collect my belongings, brushing off the dirt and flattening what had been trampled before placing each item back into the satchel. The Norgandi had gotten off with my journal, Montclaire's planting book, and my magnifying lens, but he had dropped the scissors and the other books. "Perhaps they were like you, sonjeur, digging where there is nothing."

My lies glared like a temple dancer's spangles. Duplais expelled a disbelieving epithet, and stomped into the wood to consult his shy friend.

Self-discipline rid me of the shakes and set my mind to work again. The marauders had been after a book. Lianelle's own journal, perhaps? Or had she never returned the doubly encrypted Gautieri book? Considering their interest in the scissors and magnifier, I surmised they were also interested in anything Lianelle had made *using* the books. For certain they hunted the same thing as Duplais: *spiniks* . . . secrets.

CHAPTER 5

As Duplais, my chaperone Margriet—an old friend of Captain de Santo—and I crested yet another scrubby hillock, journey's end spread out before us. Beyond yellow-gold grass dotted with rust-colored poppies lay the broad bronze loops of the river Ley and the royal city of Merona, glowing this afternoon in a golden haze. Sketchy shapes of sails and barges clustered at the crescent harbor, whence Sabrian ships sailed into the unknown reaches of the world. Atop a modest bluff overlooking city and river sprawled shapely walls and towers of pale yellow stone—Castelle Escalon, where the kings of Sabria had held court for more than four hundred years.

I dreaded the place. Tens of thousands of people lived inside Merona's walls.

My parents had assured me that my aversion to crowds was merely excessive shyness certain to be outgrown, like my belly-churning reaction to magic and my spring sneezing fits. So far I'd seen no relief from any of them. The few towns and villages on this journey had already left my ears itching and buzzing, as if a swarm of insects had been trapped inside my skull.

In contrast, Duplais' spine visibly uncoiled as our path hairpinned down the hill toward the Caurean highroad. For three days the tight-wound librarian had pursued a convoluted route of game tracks, bridle paths, and roads little more than faint wagon ruts. We had spent our nights at deserted loggers' cabins and a meager hostelry that had likely not hosted a customer since the Blood Wars. Captain de Santo and the black-cloaked man had never left us, lurking among the trees or behind hillocks. Indeed, we had traveled from Montclaire to the royal city without being abducted, slain, or even noticed—whichever the danger Duplais feared most.

None of this odd behavior ruffled Margriet. Truly, I doubted an outbreak of man-eating wasps could have made the formidable woman blanch. She ate her own provisions, slept like a fallen tree trunk, and jogged along on her mule, exhibiting not the least trace of curiosity.

As we rounded a curve on the lower slope, the view expanded to include the dark thumb of rock protruding from the river's deepest channel. *Ah, saints have mercy, little brother.* Bleak, harsh, isolated, the Spindle Prison had been Ambrose's entire world since he was fifteen. The sight choked my heart beyond bearing and roused a guilty urgency that distant imagining could not.

"Sonjeur, will I be permitted to visit my brother?" I said, nudging my mount up beside his. My ingrained hostility to Duplais suddenly seemed childish. "He is a hostage, not a convict. Yet he's been allowed no visitors. I've petitioned, written letters . . ." Everything I could think of. Few had even bothered to reject my petitions.

"I've no influence with the Spindle warder, damoselle. You'll need to take it up with him if your duties permit. Move along faster, if you please. Prod that balky ass, Mistress Margriet." He spurred his mount well ahead of me.

If eyes could truly launch daggers, mine would have pierced his straight, slim back.

The highroad stretched like a braid of dust toward Merona. "The city gates are closed at sunset," said Duplais, as our course merged with the city-bound traffic, "and the only hostelries outside the gates are wholly unfit—especially for women. Worse than we've seen."

I doubted they were so dreadful. Duplais clearly detested traveling. His mouth had hardened at the rough accommodations, and he did naught but pick at the food we carried with us: dried meat, sweating cheese, and fruit sorely bruised by heat and saddle packs. At each juncture, he had offered terse apologies, as if I were a discommoded queen.

Unwilling to ease his discomfort, I had chosen not to mention that my father had often taken Lianelle, Ambrose, and me into the wild to sleep on the ground, snare our supper, and live "rough" when we were children. We had called ourselves the Gardia Ruggiere, and considered ourselves well prepared to take on King Philippe's worst enemies. Who would have imagined a day would come when our goodfather would regard us as those very villains?

An hour of Duplais' prodding, and we arrived at the clogged approaches to the city gates. Market carts laden with potatoes and beets, and wagons hauling wine casks, coal, tin pots, or anonymous crates of merchants' wares were strung out fifty deep at a customs station bristling with soldiers. We three were halted in a queue of horse and foot traffic almost as long.

"Soul charm, damoselle? 'Tis Camarilla approved." A pock-faced woman draped in dusty scarves dangled a glittering bracelet of glass and silver beads where the sunlight could catch it. "Protect thy sight and soul from haunts and daemons, spectres and ghoulies. Twenty kivrae only . . ." Her left hand rested on her right shoulder, exhibiting a blood family mark. Its smudged lines testified it to have been drawn with ink, however, and not the indelible birth-marking of the Camarilla.

I refused, and the woman moved on, deftly avoiding the scrutiny of a collared mage in the striped robe of a Camarilla inspector.

A sultry breeze off the river swirled the dust rolled up from cart wheels, boots, and hooves. As the orange-hazed sun slipped toward the horizon, the crowd of travelers grew fractious. Our line lurched toward the massive gate tunnel from time to time in the mode of a caterpillar. The thrumming in my ears worsened with every centimetre, making my cheekbones throb and my teeth ache.

"Will they truly shut the gates with all these people outside?" I asked, to take my mind off the unpleasant sensations. "We're not at war."

"It's disturbances inside cause the gate closings." Duplais did not shift his roving gaze from the crowd, examining the multihued sea of faces as if a magistrate might arrive to explain further. "Officious fools believe they can lock out the wind."

Before I could ask what he meant, Duplais rose in the stirrups and waved to a sober, soft-cheeked gentleman who had just emerged from behind the customs station. "Henri! Over here."

The man squeezed his way through and handed over a rolled page, tied with a ribbon. "You're a fortunate man, Portier," he said, blotting his forehead and bearded chin with a linen kerchief. "Chevalier de Sylvae provided this just before he left for the country. You're right that the imbecile can expedite tricky matters, though I'll throw myself in the river if I must listen to one more crocodile story."

"Many thanks. I had to leave in such a rush, I'd no time to arrange for a gate pass."

"She's still not bound for the Spindle?" The man lowered his voice, eyeing me without staring.

My cheeks scorched. This Henri, his close-barbered beard and mustache encircling an ill-defined mouth, had been one of Duplais' witnesses at Papa's trial.

"She's the king's gooddaughter," said Duplais, "and deemed little threat should she be in custody of a forceful ally. The dowry His Majesty settled on her in infancy will attract notice from a number of useful quarters."

I wanted to vomit. For these long three days in the saddle, I had relived the bizarre attack in the wood, wrestled with the heartache of leaving Montclaire, the impossibility of Lianelle's death, and Duplais' implication of murder. I'd given my own future no thought at all. Now here it was, laid out before me like the view from the hilltop.

My father had been a king's First Counselor, ensuring that I would take substantial property, connection, and influence into a union. Since my first inkling of what marriage meant, my father had assured me that any husband would be my own choice, a choice of the heart, as my parents' had been. Yet observing my mother's heartache every time Papa rode out, often absent for months at a time, I had decided that love and inti-macy created a bondage every bit as confining as arranged marriage. Friends, family, study, and travel were everything I wanted. But in this, as in all, Papa's crimes had changed everything.

"Best not let word get out who she is," said this Henri. "A mob demol-ished a cult shrine last night, screaming they were sheltering the Traitor. Night begets rumors of hauntings like a corpse begets maggots. And pick your route up the hill carefully."

We never heard his reasons. The crowd shifted, quickly engulfing Duplais' friend, as a rider in dusty scarlet livery charged through the press. "Make way! Step aside! Royal dispatches for Castelle Escalon!"

Duplais pushed his mount into the wake of the royal messenger, shout-ing at Margriet and me to keep close. The deft maneuver slid us to the head of the queue, where he presented his scroll. To the disgruntled mur-murings of other travelers, the gate guards passed us through after only a glimpse.

"Why would anyone believe a shrine would shelter my father?" I said as we rode through the gate tunnel.

"It was a cult shrine—the Cult of the Reborn," said Duplais. "Since your father's conviction, Merona has suffered a plague of . . . unnatural . . . happenings. These *hauntings* or *incidents* spawn rumors that the Great Trai-tor seeks to raise an army of revenants to overthrow the king. The fright-ened and ignorant lash out at any group who speaks of souls returning from the dead."

The Cult was a small, devout branch of Temple worshipers. They be-lieved that our saints were actually heroic souls who had turned their backs on Heaven, reborn repeatedly to succor humankind in times of our direst need. Yet I'd never heard that Cult beliefs encompassed *necromancy*, an aberrant—and wholly unsubstantiated—practice anathema to the Temple and renounced by the Camarilla. And an *army of revenants*? What nonsense! People must be truly frightened.

We emerged from the gate tunnel onto the ring road between the thick outer bastion and a less imposing inner wall, draped with straggling vines grown right out of the mortar. What struck me first was the quiet.

Not only was the ring road almost deserted, as if the passage of the gate tunnel had transported us much farther than thirty metres from the noisy throng outside, but the quality of the sounds themselves seemed muted. A gaggle of street urchins pelted past us, making no more noise than if they tiptoed. Our own mounts' hooves made more of a dull *thwup* than the ringing *clop* one would expect.

The dimness was less surprising. Sunlight might yet stream across river and vineyards, but the orb itself hung low enough that shadows collected in the gorge between the walls. Even so I would swear that someone had draped a gray veil between the city and the silvered sky.

The wind tore green leaves and full-hued blossoms from the rattling vines, whipping them into odd whirlpools that rose high like dust devils in fallow fields. Odder yet, the wind was not the usual sultry breeze off the Ley, stinking of river wrack, but dry and cold enough to sting my cheeks and mock my light clothing. Had I not noted Margriet's shivering as Duplais counted out her pay, I might have assumed I'd caught a chill along the way.

"We must move quickly," said Duplais, heading up the road as Margriet and her mule vanished down the steep way toward Riverside. The odd light grayed his complexion, as he scanned the road, the walls, and the towers.

The rapidly deteriorating light had evidently sent many people home to supper early. Streets and markets were deserted, booths and stalls locked up. A number of streets were blocked off by barrels of sand or piled stones. At every barricade stood a quartiere—an iron pole with three crosspieces, hung with animal bones, bells, or strips of tin and copper, and topped with a snarl of laurel—a magical artifact supposed to ward off malevolent spirits. One spied quartieres in the countryside from time to time, but never in cosmopolitan Merona.

Indeed almost every house we passed sported runes painted on its lintel or inverted lamps hung in the windows or some other charm or witch sign near its threshold. The king's city bled superstition and fear—enough to shiver my skeptic's blood and loosen my tongue.

"What is everyone so afraid of?" I said as we took yet another detour into a street entirely deserted. My skin prickled in the gloom.

Duplais pointed a finger at a shabby tenement, painted all over with witch signs. A burning torch had been mounted in a bracket beside the door, yet the stoop, the door itself, and the lintel, carved with the open hand sign of a moneylender, remained indistinguishable in the gloom. In fact . . .

"The light seems bent," I said. The fire glow curled around the left side of the house and illumined naught but an alley choked with smoke. The smoke itself streamed round the corner in a direction directly opposite the wind.

"Moneylenders throughout the city are particularly beset with such strangeness. Pawners, too. Did your father have difficulty with his debts?"

"I've told you repeatedly, I know nothing of my father."

In the next street, he pointed out a cracked signboard painted with three gold balls, dangling by one corner over the door of another house. The windows and door gaped black like empty eye sockets. Air rushed into them as if they were sucking every breath out of the world.

"You're going to tell me this is sorcery." Worms riddled my stomach.

"Give me a scientific explanation for such unnatural spectacles. They've spread throughout Merona like plague. There are streets in Riverside where fire does not heat food or melt iron. Others where wild pigs have taken up residence. Sorcerers have repaired some, only to see other disturbances break out. Just this past tenday, I've heard report of an incident in Sessaline—a village fifteen kilometres north. Here, this is interesting, too . . ."

He led me past a small district that had been leveled by fire—recently, from the rising trails of smoke and the heavy stink of char and refuse. The area was an exact square, the bordering houses lacking even a trace of soot. "This was a street of solicitors and small banking houses. It burnt three years ago."

No response came to mind. I was, after all, plain, plodding Anne de Vernase, who could speak seven languages but could not come up with a witty retort until a day late, who preferred a book to any adventure, who believed that everything in the world had a rational explanation, save my father's great betrayal.

Duplais urged his skittish mare closer to Ladyslipper. "Keep moving, damoselle. Sunset is the riskiest time."

"Wouldn't it be better to make straight for the palace if we're in such a hurry?" I said as Duplais detoured through yet another narrow lane, behind Merona's Temple Major.

"There is no *straight* in Merona just now. Damnation . . ."

Duplais' mount shied, dodging sideways and forward all at once, near unseating the man. Only my most insistent persuasion kept Ladyslipper from doing the same. A soft hissing, as of spewing steam, swelled into a pulsing, whining, scratchy rush of sound from every side. Rats flooded the alley before and behind us. Pouring from the shadowed verges as if birthed by the brick walls, they surged toward the temple's back steps and its servitors' entry as if summoned to the god's service.

A bolt of violet light shot from Duplais' raised palm, halting the squirming, screeching vermin before they started climbing our horses' legs. A second bolt parted the flood in front of us. We kicked the horses onward, bursting from the alley in disarray. Sweat dripped down my back and from my brow, the air suddenly a furnace. Appalled, disgusted, it was all I could do to maintain any sort of calm instruction for the quivering Ladyslipper. Duplais mumbled epithets and wrestled his mount into nervous compliance. "Saints and spirits, should have known he'd not exempt the Temple . . ."

Which comment I understood not at all. But I needed no urging to stay close and move faster. We turned onto a wide, paved boulevard, divided by a row of spreading plane trees—the Plas Royale. Duplais glanced up at the deepening sky, now the hue of charcoal, then released an unhappy exhale. "Watch your step, damoselle."

Duplais reined in to a slow walk, picking the way up the broad street as carefully as he'd done on the narrowest hillside track. Grand stone buildings with sculpted facades and fluted columns lined the Plas Royale: the Academie Musica and the Collegia Medica, and merchant halls such as the Vintners' Consortium and the Wool Guildhall. Farther ahead of us stood a striking edifice of deep green granite, the Bastionne Camarilla. I could just make out the sculpted figures that stood atop its facade—a pair of robed male and female mages, each with one hand upraised to Heaven and one opened in generous provision to the onlookers below.

Despite the benevolent images and the elegance of its carvings and polished granite, the headquarters of the Camarilla Magica had always made my skin creep. Its lack of windows brought to mind an eyeless face. And that was before I had learned that inside those impenetrable walls, magical practitioners who violated Camarilla strictures were routinely whipped or branded in the name of preserving magical purity, even if they were naught but ignorant countryfolk. In its deepest bowels, so it was said, the prefects executed the most serious violators, as they had my father's magical accomplices.

"Great Heavens!" I said. As we closed on the Bastionne, it became clear disaster had struck. Two of the fortress's walls and a third of its slate roof had collapsed, exposing the blackened skeleton of its interior. Floors hung at rakish angles, and massive columns leaned like felled trees, supported by the piled rubble that shifted . . .

I blinked.

A few faint lights—pale green and yellow—flickered through the dark interior. Their pulsing movement must have fooled my eyes into seeing the rubble expand and contract as if it were a wounded man's chest instead of crumbled stone.

"A moment." I halted Ladyslipper and squinted into the deepening gloom. Shadows had pooled just at the spot where the two collapsed walls would have joined. And like a pond, the blackness had swelled and shifted when a carved capital tumbled much too slowly from an upper floor and penetrated its boundary. I squinted, my eyes refusing to accept what they encompassed. The scene was entirely *wrong*.

"Sonjeur de Duplais, what's happened here?" I whispered. My heart, still racing from the encounter with the rats, rattled my ribs. "That hole . . ."

"An unfortunate shifting of the earth," he said. "The collapse occurred a year ago. The Camarilla announced that some natural cavern in the rock beneath the fortress gave way—perhaps an instability caused by excessive rain. The prefects are weaving spells to ensure the integrity of the remaining foundation before they rebuild."

"Who would risk going in there to work with the structure in such a precarious state?" I said, watching the colored lights multiply like gleaming fireflies in the deepest corners of the ruin.

Without shifting his gaze from the pavement in front of us, Duplais urged his mount forward. "No one goes *inside* the collapsed wing. It is forbidden."

"But . . ." Green sparks drifted across an open span where the great rib of a vaulted ceiling lay below. The livid glow reflected on a bulbous metal object—a lamp or an urn or a cooking pot—that chose that moment to slide off the edge of a raked floor and drop . . . no, settle slowly, like an autumn leaf, and vanish into the pooled night.

My head, already aching, rattled like a tin drum full of squirrels.

Impossible. I didn't believe in sorcery, certainly not sorcery that could collapse walls or cause . . . whatever I had seen. Yet as I followed Duplais up the road to Castelle Escalon, I kept my eyes on the pavement lest nature open an abyss under our feet, and all my strident intellectual protests produced not a single principle to explain why metal pots and blocks of granite might fall so much more slowly than physical laws predicted, or why their landings might cause ripples in the dark. When Duplais nodded to the palace guards and ushered me into my new home, I blessed my priggish escort and welcomed the closing gates behind me as I never imagined I could.

CHAPTER 6

4 Ocet, evening

"I'm to provide chamber service for you, damoselle, as I do for the queen's other young ladies. As you've brought no personal maid, I've been told to attend to your dressing and hair, as well. I'll bring your supper here when you've no other engagements."

The queen, dressing, hair. The topics were so at odds with my current preoccupations, they might have been foreign words. The venture through the city had left my head like porridge.

"I'll come back tonight once I've finished my other ladies, and see to the unpacking. Here's your bedchamber." The round-cheeked girl, lugging my heavy book satchel, opened the door at the end of the wide passage and allowed me to enter first.

The small, tiredly elegant room was possessed of a single casement, no hearth, and a clutter of furnishings. It was also occupied.

The woman inspecting my piled luggage whirled about. "Well, here you are!"

Did I not know Eugenie de Sylvae nearer five-and-thirty than five-and-sixty, I might have assumed that the woman extending her arms in welcome was the Queen of Sabria. A trim woman of mature age, she had gowned herself in purple velvet heavily embroidered in gold. A stiff ruffled collar rose to the crown of her pyramid of black and gray curls—an ancient style seen on ruined Fassid temples or potsherds.

Many women of little taste and enormous wealth might have adorned themselves so, but one glance at her face warned that this particular lady must be approached with certain caution. Her eyes were very like olive pits, small and hard-edged. And in the style of Fassid empresses, she had completely plucked her eyebrows, an artifice that gave her an expression of either permanent surprise or permanent disdain.

"Dear, dear Anne, I do hope the wretched journey has not pummeled you into dust! Knowing how difficult this time must be for you, I simply had to welcome you right away."

The serving girl gave me no clue as to the woman's identity, save confirming her rank. She dropped instantly into a low curtsy, pasting her gaze to the floor. Her "Your Grace" was so faint as to approach a sigh. The lady tapped her elegant toe on the floor thrice, and the girl dropped my satchel and scuttered away, closing my door without so much as a click. I hadn't thanked her, nor so much as asked her name. Had I forgotten every trace of civilized behavior?

I followed the girl's lead and dipped my knee, laying my left hand on my right shoulder to expose the Cazar family blood mark as the law required. The woman clucked and patted my cheek, reminiscent of Mistress Constanza at the Cask. Then her jeweled fingers encircled my wrist and drew me up and around my heaped baggage to sit beside her on the bed.

"When I heard Duplais had brought you on horseback—astride, for love of Heaven, like some wild, immodest Kadr girl—when you have such obstacles before you already, I told my daughter we should string him up for the whipsman. We shall convict him of criminal obtuseness . . . obtusity . . . obtusativity. . . ."

Her words flowed like honey, embracing, enveloping, mind clogging. It likely wasn't useful to protest that my mother had insisted that no true horsewoman would ride sidesaddle. But, of course, my mother was mad.

"You will have to correct me, *caeri*, as I understand you have a stellar intelligence. Such a blessing"—she swept me with such a comprehensive gaze, I'd no doubt she could recite the number of my hairs out of place—

"in a—now, let us be honest, as I prize honesty above all things—a plain girl. Really, the three of us must see to the dullard's punishment. I've never quite understood what quality Eugenie sees in Duplais—a *failed* sorcerer, so dull and craven even Philippe cannot tolerate him."

Despite her prattle, her eyes had not softened so much. But I could now guess who she was. Queen, indeed. Wife of a king, now dead, and mother of a king, also dead—the dowager Queen of Sabria.

My mother had long maintained that Antonia de Foucal was the most powerful person in Sabria. She had actually ruled as Queen Regent in the first few months after her husband died, leaving only their son, Soren, a boy of thirteen. At one-and-twenty, Soren had married Eugenie de Sylvae, a child of eight years, and Lady Antonia had adopted her son's child wife.

Soren had fallen in battle before Eugenie was old enough to consummate the marriage, and his heir, my goodfather Philippe de Savin-Journia, had ended up marrying the widowed Eugenie to consolidate his claim to the throne. Mama had always said that Philippe and Eugenie had grown into love in spite of their marriage, and in spite of Lady Antonia.

"Sonjeur de Duplais got me here safely, Your Grace. Now I'm eager to learn my duties."

She tutted and creased her browless forehead. "Of course you are, *caeri*. And we must give that some careful thought. Interesting that Philippe's brought you here. Clever. Of course, he leaves such women's matters as noble marriages to Eugenie, but I do my best to relieve her of tiresome burdens. Well, we shall do what we can. You *must* improve your dress and hair." She pinched my cheeks. "And so pale. You're not ill?"

"No, my lady."

My cheeks surely took on a more fashionable blush as she inspected me. My mother and brother were dark-haired, physically strong, and graceful, with rich-hued skin and luminous eyes. Lianelle had taken the best of my father's fairer coloring and gold-flecked brown hair, and had surpassed me in height by the age of fourteen. Yet despite my dull complexion and plain features, I despised face painting, rejecting the world's consuming passion to look like something one was not. I certainly didn't care what these people thought of me. Humiliating, nonetheless, to hear my lacks laid out so baldly.

Lady Antonia squeezed my shoulder. "Good health is assuredly a blessing. But, of course, the family connection is the great difficulty here. How are we ever to match a woman whose father's name is so reviled, the king will not have it spoken in his presence? Or convince a suitor that lunacy will not taint his children? I shall have to apply my best wiles! A modest presence in the palace will enhance your prospects."

As if I wished to be here! I crushed a rising heat. "Certainly, Your Grace. As you say."

She fixed her great surprised eyes on my face, as if she could read my heart. "And one more thing. As your devoted well-wisher, I must advise you: You must not practice even a tat of sorcery. With your father's history—his collusion with such disgusting, unholy practices—everyone will be watching. Do you understand me, *caeri*?"

I bit my tongue yet again. "Such would be impossible, my lady. I possess no power for sorcery."

"But, Anne, your sister studied at Seravain! And your mother's family . . ."

"It is long proven that neither my brother nor I carry the Cazar factor in the blood. Only my late sister."

She took up my left hand and with a dry finger ringed in emeralds, traced the Cazar zahkri imprinted there when I was born. "Even those ungifted *use* magical artifacts, spells purchased at the market or given them by others. Her Majesty's mage advises you refrain from that, as well—even the seeming. You understand."

"Certainly, my lady." Though I didn't, really. Happily, my inclinations favored her advice.

"Now, *caeri*, you'd best get settled in. Tomorrow you must work with all diligence. You're far behind the other girls."

In flurry of kisses and pats, she was gone. Angry, humiliated, and entirely flustered, I could not think what to do next.

A sneezing fit broke my paralysis. A combination of the lady's abrasive perfume and the scent of the dried rosemary and lavender sprinkled over bedclothes and floor set my nose dripping and eyes itching.

Squeezing past the luggage and the table, I wrestled with the heavy iron window latch and shoved open the casement. The heavy air scarce moved, the night swollen and inflamed like a septic wound. Floating lights, bent shadows, pits and pools of blackness, impregnable fortresses in ruins . . . Perhaps it was not *so* surprising to find people installing quartieres near their homes.

The formidable Lady Antonia had left me feeling as if I'd been trampled by horses. Instead of unpacking, I unbuckled my little traveling case and installed my two tessilae on a small stone altar table set beside the bed, calling up fond remembrances of my grandmother and my cousin Raynald. Little Raynald's death of summer fever had fed my doubts about Ixtador Beyond the Veil. What god worthy of honoring would be so cruel as to set children wandering alone in a barren wasteland? My mother's belief, unsanctioned by the Temple, insisted that children could find their friends and family in Ixtador. At least that way Lianelle might have Grandmama and Raynald to companion her.

Settling on my bed, I pulled out Lianelle's letter. Her exuberant voice was so clear in those pages, as if she sat in her room at Seravain, awaiting my answer.

As I completed a third rereading, someone tapped on the door. "Come," I said, stuffing the packet back in my case, blotting away tears so as not to make a spectacle of myself.

"A bit of supper, damoselle." The chambermaid carried in a lighted candle and a tray draped with white linen serviettes. She looked about in dismay, first at the luggage blocking her way, and then at me, stumbling to my feet, red-eyed and sniffling. Lianelle was entirely wrong about me being strong.

"Here," I said, "let me move this." I shoved my clothes bag into the corner beside a blanket chest and threw the book satchel onto the bed. As the girl squeezed through and set the tray on the table, I rescued the wobbling candle. "Tell me, what's your name?"

Eyes averted, she dipped her knee. "Ella, if you please."

Though a handspan taller than I, she could be no more than fifteen. Freckles sprinkled her face, and the wisps of hair that peeked out from under her ruffled white cap were orange-red. In the past hour she had inked a green witchknot below one ear. Perhaps she thought it might protect her from the Great Traitor's daughter.

On our way up from the steward's office, I'd noted several other people wearing witchknots or chevrons on temples or cheeks—warding sigils one saw among country people from time to time. The practice was akin to burying a lock of a rival's hair under a thorn tree to afflict her with pustules, or kissing your altar stone whenever you had a wicked thought about a dead relative, lest the kinsman's shade send a daemon to make you soil the bed. To see servants in a royal residence displaying such open superstition was astonishing.

No matter trepidation, Ella whisked the candle from my hand and returned it to my supper tray. With brisk competence, she checked the untouched water pitcher, then unlatched an old-fashioned painted armoire and pulled open every drawer, leaving them ready to receive my things.

"If that's all, then . . ." She dipped a knee and headed for the door.

"No! Wait. Please!" Perhaps the fear so palpable in city and palace had infected me, or perhaps it was only that my emotions had been so thoroughly wrung out, but this efficient child suddenly seemed like an anchor of reason.

"No one's told me what I'm to do here." An entirely inappropriate comment to address to a palace chambermaid, who would be taught to display no evidence whatsoever of possessing a mind. "I've no idea where I'll be expected tomorrow."

The girl glanced up briefly. "If you like, t'morning, after I've seen to the other young ladies, I'll fetch you where you're to be."

"That would be very kind. Thank you, Ella."

"Will you be needing aught else, damoselle? Help with your unpacking?"

"No, I've not so much." The leather case with its precious contents glared at me from the bed. "Not unless you could tell me where I might keep a few valuables out of the common eye." Duplais would come hunting Lianelle's trinkets. And Antonia . . . was it ridiculous to imagine she'd been snooping about my belongings?

The girl cocked her head, as if considering whether I was trying to trick her. "Might could," she said at last. "I've cleaned a few of these older closets." She poked around the ancient armoire, tapping on splintered moldings and fumbling under drawers and behind shelves.

"Hah!" She slid a scalloped corner piece aside to reveal a small drawer and even produced a tarnished key from inside it. "None but a chamber girl like me's going to figure where that is. I'm sure I'll forget it myself."

She dropped the key back in the drawer. Her white cap bobbed, and she was out the door, so quiet and quick in her movements that once she was gone, I wasn't sure she'd even been there. For the first time in days, I was smiling.

My mother's jewelry went into the hidden drawer. Lianelle's packet would go in as well, once I'd read the letter one more time. I sat down on the bed . . .

. . . AND NEXT thing I knew, a hammering on my door brought Ella, a pitcher of hot water, and a morning of brilliant sunshine.

"It's just gone half past eight of the morning watch, damoselle. I'll be back to take you along soon's I've seen to the others."

The solid sleep had done me good, and I decided not to allow Antonia de Foucal to intimidate me. As quickly and thoroughly as possible, I scrubbed away the sludge of sleep and three days' travel, then set to buttons, skirts, and lacings. I tied my tangled, unruly mane of bark-hued curls—the bane of my life until I had learned what the words *traitor* and *madhouse* meant—into a knot at the back of my head, ran my fingers through the remaining twists that framed my face, and called my toilet good enough. By that time, Ella was back.

"All right, show me where to go."

Ella's heels clicked on the marble floor as she led me through the queen's household—the east wing of Castelle Escalon. My childhood visits had been confined to my father's haunts in the west wing and the palace's public rooms and gardens. I didn't know this place at all.

A long gallery, its arcade windows bright with a rain-scrubbed sky, and then a few steps and a quick turn to the right led us into a wide passage. Painted huntsmen, half-dressed dancing girls, knights, satyrs, and an interminable variety of sheep peered down from the vaulted ceiling.

"That would be Lady Antonia's apartments, damoselle." Ella gestured toward a pair of paneled doors flanked by man-high portraits of courtiers portrayed in sentimental versions of pastoral myth. "That one"—she gestured to a more modest doorway—"is where the queen's young ladies, the maids of honor like yourself, meet for their instructions. Very like you'll go there every morning until . . ."

"Until when?"

She blinked. "Until you're sent somewhere else."

Though she remained properly expressionless, I detected a sharpness in her gray eyes before she lowered them. I ventured a smile. "That makes good sense. Divine grace, Ella."

The girl dipped her knee and vanished. Somewhere in the vast reaches of Castelle Escalon, a bell struck nine.

I CLOSED THE DOOR BEHIND me and tiptoed across the chamber.

". . . protocols, placings, and appropriate dress for an intimate hunt dinner. We shall discuss guest selection and suitable entertainments. . . ." The elegantly long-necked woman of middling age nodded to acknowledge my arrival, but did not interrupt her commentary.

Ten scarcely distinguishable young women sat in a half circle, facing the lady. All were expensively dressed in ruffles and silks; all were rosy of cheek, smooth-haired, and still in their teens. Every one of them wore painted witchknots, chevrons, or calligrams on a perfect cheek, forehead, or temple. Perhaps the practice was not fear and belief but fashion. Had I ever worn a witchknot in my girlhood, whether at Montclaire or in Merona, I would have been laughed out of the room.

I took the only empty seat, feeling quite old and dowdy at two-and-twenty.

Maids of honor were the third tier of aristocratic women engaged to serve the queen. At the highest level were the few like Lady Antonia, women who had a strong personal connection to the queen, such as kinship or girlhood friendship. Given titles such as Mistress of Gowns, First Lady of the Bedchamber, or Overmistress of the Queen's Gardens, they set the queen's schedule, arranged the seating at dinner, and the like. At the second level were ten ladies-in-waiting, women linked to the throne by politics, history, or strategic interests. They stood at the queen's side at every public appearance.

The young women busily assessing my turnout were the unmarried daughters of important families, brought to court to affirm their families' alliance with the throne. Every summer a new group was summoned to Merona to serve as the queen's companions, as decorations to her court, and as attendants to the ladies-in-waiting. My father had promised he would never allow my talents to be wasted on such frivolity. A small betrayal beside the rest.

I folded my hands in my lap as the others did and listened carefully. ". . . preferred application of scented linens to offset unpalatable odors . . . provision for weaponry and game bags . . . extra gloves . . . would never permit flushed complexions . . . immodest activities . . ."

My mother, the kind of hostess who could seat a beggar and a king at table together and make both feel valued and at ease, had made sure that I was knowledgeable in the graces of hospitality, but never would I have imagined that the details of a properly constituted hunt dinner for the royal family and two hundred intimate acquaintances could fill two hours in the telling.

Despite the trivial subject, our mentor's voice was pleasant and her approach intelligent. My companions addressed her as Lady Cecile. The lavender band embroidered on her left sleeve declared her a widow. The lack of any painted ward against evil marked her as independent minded, a skeptic, or perhaps inordinately devout. While accepting magic as an element of divine Creation, the Temple stood stalwartly opposed to luck charms, daemon wards, and other superstitious practices, calling them the muddy boundary between earthly magic and divine mystery.

For the next hour, my mind wandered off in circular patterns. At least I was not required to contribute to the discussion.

". . . white gowns for your court introduction." Lady Cecile had risen. The rest of the women followed and dipped their knees before dissolving into chattering twos and threes as they left the room.

Startled out of my meanderings, I jumped up and offered the same genuflection. A slight twitch of the lady's two fingers instructed me quite explicitly to sit down again.

As I sank back into my chair, one of the young ladies, a willowy young woman with pale hair like spun silk and eyes so large and so blue they could cause a border war, raced forward and flung her arms about our mentor. "Dear Lady Cecile!"

The tall, cool woman kissed the girl's cheek, at the same time maneuvering herself free of the untidy exuberance. "Sweet Belinda, such a pleasure to see you returned to health."

"Whatever am I to do about the Hematian letters?" Though the two women stood at the far side of the chamber, Belinda's piping tones were piercingly clear. "It's less than a month until Prince Dessin arrives. Hematian customs are so dreadfully peculiar."

The lady herded the girl toward the passage door. "Come to me this evening at the usual time and we'll see to it. Prince Dessin shall not find you lacking in appreciation of his culture."

The door snicked shut behind the young woman, creating an instant and welcome quiet, as if I'd been sitting in the midst of a gaggle of geese, now dispersed. With a quick survey of the courtyard, Lady Cecile pulled the paned doors securely shut. Then, to my pure astonishment, she engulfed me like the incoming tide, drawing me from my chair and kissing me on each cheek in the robust fashion of Nivanne. "Dearest Anne."

"My lady . . ." I tried to draw away, but she wrapped an arm about my shoulders.

"Horrible, horrible," she said, her voice barely above a whisper. "This awful thing about your sister . . . and your poor, dear mother. You are very like her. You may have your father's coloring, but you certainly have those incomparably deep Cazar eyes. My father always said Madeleine epitomized the beauty of another age—the fey, wild spirit of ancient Sabria. But, then, he adored her inordinately, ruing the long days of winter when the bandit kin dragged her home."

Understanding dawned. "You're Cecile de Blasencourt! Mama's school friend."

In my mother's day, few collegia had admitted women, and my grandfather Cazar had adamantly opposed formal education for his daughter. But Lady Cecile's father, fascinated with modern learning, had invited a number of young women into his home for *extended visits*, secretly hiring the finest tutors to mentor them. Cecile's marriage into a demesne on Sabria's frontiers had kept the friends apart since I was small.

"Indeed." Lady Cecile released my shoulders with a firm little shake, as if to imprint her affection on me before stepping away. "Delighted as I am to see you, Anne, I've grave misgivings about your presence. For anyone to bring you here behind Philippe's back, to risk his wrath . . ."

"The king himself summoned me, my lady."

"Unlikely. He cannot abide Castelle Escalon. The past years he visits here only to pursue his duties to his bloodline. And this border uprising in Aroth will take him off to war again after the new year, so I doubt that issuing invitations to prospective maids of honor has been a concern." Folding her arms, she drifted back to the courtyard doors and peered through the glass. "No, someone else has brought you here—someone who can issue a summons in Philippe's name."

My thoughts reverted instantly to the Royal Accuser. "Savin-Duplais fetched me."

Her long fingers dismissed the notion. "Duplais is a nothing, an ambitious little toad who follows someone else's orders if it gives him some advantage. I don't know why Eugenie keeps him on. He's clever enough for a household administrator, I suppose, but he's not a schemer."

Her opinion surprised me. The king had repeatedly deferred to Duplais' opinion at Papa's trial. The man was anything but stupid. Lianelle had once told me she would feel sorry for Duplais, had he not been so

ruthless in his prosecution. She said he knew more about magic than anyone in Sabria, despite failing the most rudimentary tests of spellworking
in his student days. And queen's administrator—in essence, a housekeeper?
How odd.

"Perhaps it was the new Conte Ruggiere," I suggested. "Duplais says
the Ruggiere titles have been granted elsewhere."

"Well, that was bound to happen, though I've not heard who might be
in line for it. Ah, Michel de Vernase, crush your granite heart, what were
you thinking?" Her hands clenched as if she could scarce restrain herself
from hitting something. "He once told me that magic sapped our will to
learn of nature."

The palace bells pealed the hour's change. Lady Cecile gathered me up
and urged me toward the door. "I'll advise you to avoid any involvement
with sorcery. Any! You've enough reason to fear Philippe's displeasure. I
can't begin to imagine the uproar should he hear your name in the same
breath as *magic*."

Why did everyone feel it necessary to warn me off? I was not an idiot.
I knew my father's crimes. "I've no talent for magic, my lady."

"Talent has little bearing. Ghost charms, witchknots, spellworked per-
fumes . . . there was a time you'd not see such things in Philippe de Savin-
Journia's house." Lady Cecile's voice and manner were consuming in their
intensity. "But now these mysteries . . . disturbances . . . drive fools to try
anything. It's all happened since the Exposition, since that dreadful
mage—"

Voices carried from the passageway.

"Stay alert, Anne. Someone has a blade destined for your back . . . or,
more truly, for your father's back, but you can be sure it will go through
his women first. Only a cretin would imagine Madeleine de Cazar could
lose her mind from grief. And now your sister."

Shock had me stammering. "So you believe they *purposely*—?"

The latch clicked and a party of gentlemen peered in at us. Cecile
stepped back and raised her voice. "Report to my apartments this evening
at half past seventh hour so that we may begin to review the discussions
you've missed."

"As you—" But she was already out of the room, and a haughty young man in pale blue livery was holding the door for me. His left cheek bore a blue-painted witchknot.

As I retreated to my bedchamber, I could not leave off thinking of Cecile de Blasencourt's accusation. Duplais had brought a sorcerer to Montclaire on the day my mother's mind collapsed. A fearsome sight he had been, cloaked, hooded, and gloved so one could not see a bit of the human person. Yet Duplais had done all the questioning. The mage had but touched Mama's hand. How could a single touch drive a person mad?

Later, when I'd heard our guards whispering of the queen's devilish mage and his exhibition of sorcery that had frightened the wits out of half the court on the night of the Grand Exposition of Science and Magic, I assumed it was the same sorcerer.

My breath caught. What had the apprentice guide at Seravain said? *A master mage came from Merona and laid heavy enchantments about her body.* And I'd seen a mage watching me through the gate tunnel—broad-shouldered, dark-haired, leaning on a white staff, as had the mage at Montclaire . . .

The same mage, certainly. Duplais' comrade. They had called him Dante.

I slammed my bedchamber door as if Portier de Savin-Duplais stood in its path. How weak and stupid I had been to believe civilized men incapable of horrors. The Royal Accuser had brought me here, but as sure as I lived, his reasons had nothing to do with marriage portions. He believed I could help him capture my father. Certainly he knew what had happened to my mother—he and his mage. Had they murdered Lianelle as well?

It was as if I had leapt suddenly from childhood to adulthood. Why had I accepted the Collegia Seravain's account of Lianelle's *accident* so meekly? I should have rattled the collegia gates and demanded to see the mages.

Why hadn't I bartered with Duplais? Not one step from Montclaire until he told me everything he knew. His every word, every move these past days had been veneered with lies and withholding. Why had he not made a show of our leaving from Montclaire, trusting public view to protect us? Why had he not insisted the Guard Royale escort a maid of honor and royal messenger as far as Merona? We could have slapped our mounts and galloped easily past the three thugs on the forest road. Duplais had seen I could ride well and had even provided me a familiar mount. He had brought de Santo and the other man to defend us. . . .

With only this modicum of reasoning a new and startling truth—stark, vile—lay exposed.

In these recent days, as ever in my life, crises had ensnared me in girlish emotion, self-debate, and hesitation. Words of useful eloquence or forceful wit had died in my throat because I could not formulate them fast enough. Only now, after the events, did my thoughts shed their cobwebby confusion and display answers like a swordmaker's wares, bright and keen-edged. Duplais had *allowed* us to be caught by our masked pursuers. He wanted to see if I would run to my father or bargain my safety to be taken to him. He had entrusted our lives to his confederates, so that he could judge what our assailants were after and how I would respond.

As if by an alchemist's hand, anger fused festered guilt and grieving into molten iron. Spirit and flesh pulsed with its heat, and its weight settled into my belly. I had to grow up. Trust no one. If I were to find justice for Lianelle, Ambrose, and Mama, I'd no more leeway for sentiment or timidity. I had to become as bold as Lianelle imagined me.

Lianelle's lockets and ring went into the hidden drawer in the armoire, mixed up with my mother's jewelry. The key to the drawer went around my neck on a silver chain. The ivory case would sit on the dressing table with my toiletries until I could decide what to do with the powder inside it. As an afternoon storm yielded to a mournful drizzle, I read Lianelle's letter one more time, committing every word to memory. Then I lit the papers with my candle, dropped them on my emptied plate, and watched them reduced to ash. No one would learn my secrets until I was ready to share them.

CHAPTER 7

I stood at my bedchamber window, watching the storm clouds roll in from the south, in a race with the night deepening in the east.

"It's best you take the inside way round to the ducessa's apartments, damoselle," said Ella from behind me. "Cutting through the ballrooms makes it quick enough."

"I don't understand. I can walk straight through the inner courtyards to the west wing. If it rains, I can detour through the Rotunda. It will take me half the time."

"Please, you'll not want to do that, damoselle." Ella's freckles pulsed on her pale cheeks. Green chevrons gleamed from beside her eyes. "It's already raining, and"—the words gushed from her in a torrent—"the Rotunda's a dreadful place. Haunted."

The palace tower bells had just rung seventh hour in the evening watch, and I was more than ready to set out for my evening tutorial. Surely in the privacy of her own chambers, Lady Cecile would speak more freely. I had a thousand questions, but before all, I wanted to hear what she knew of my mother's illness. And surely the ducessa could advise how I might get permission to visit Ambrose.

I latched my writing case and took the mantle Ella held waiting. "I'm sure that if a ghost wished to haunt Castelle Escalon, it would prefer the dungeons in the old keep to the drafty Rotunda. My sister and brother and I played ball or echo games there when we would visit Merona. Not a single phantasm ever showed up to frighten us away."

People who could slaughter a seventeen-year-old girl with impunity or break a woman's mind, hiding their misdeeds behind a cloak of magical mystery, terrified me more than spectral gossip. The afternoon's mundane tutorials had given me time to consider the disconcerting sights in the city. Likely everything I'd seen could be reasonably explained: the floating lights by some gaseous emissions, the oddly falling objects by optical illusion. And every waterfront city had problems with rats. Duplais might think it useful to frighten me.

Ella stacked my supper cups and plates and wiped the table. "The haunting's only been since the Grand Exposition," she said, not at all mollified. "A gentleman fell ill that night and died in the Rotunda. Some say his ghost lingers, as he left unfinished business behind. Others say it's the dark mage who cursed the place that night—and mayhap the whole city as well." The girl's voice and spirit shrank. "He raises the dead, you know, for the queen, so she might comfort her poor mites as they travel Ixtador. But the Temple folk are too scared of him to look into it. None goes into the Rotunda twice and never, never at sunset. Don't do it, miss."

My heart seized. Not from the fancies of ghosts or hauntings. Nor from the vile chicanery of deadraising, though it was despicable that anyone should exploit Queen Eugenie's tragic history—four children dead in infancy. Rather it was the memory of an act of indisputable human evil. Edmond de Roble, a gentle-spoken young lord, the fairest gentleman I had ever seen, had not fallen ill on the night of the Grand Exposition of Science and Magic. He had been cruelly murdered.

"I don't believe in ghosts or deadraising," I said, breathless with the hurt. "The Pantokrator has created the Veil to divide the demesnes of death and life."

I dismissed Ella and hurried off in search of answers, though some questions could never in the world be resolved.

I had met Edmond de Roble only once, a few months before Papa's disappearance. But I had noticed a singular, pleasurable . . . *warmth* . . . deep in my stomach whenever I thought of him, and decided that if Papa would not allow me to remain an independent woman as I wished, Edmond would be a fair compromise. Papa had held the young lord in great regard, or so I had believed.

I could scarce recall Edmond's true visage anymore. It was Duplais' description of the young man's mortal torment, recounted at Papa's trial, that would be forever etched on my spirit. Evidence said that my father, whom I had believed the strongest, wisest, most honorable man in the world, had systematically lacerated Edmond's flesh, drained his blood, and ordered his body deposited like offal on the floor of the Rotunda. What daemon had come ravening from Dimios's frozen demesne and eaten my father's soul?

I emerged from the ground floor of the palace into an expansive puzzle of open plazas and gardens. My path to the middle section of the west wing, where Lady Cecile resided, must cross the vast open space, now awash with autumn rain. Or I could detour slightly to my right through a vaulted arcade and into the ancient gray-domed structure that intruded on the newer palace like a troll's barrow pushed from under the earth.

The bells rang the quarter hour. Rain sluiced down the walls and drainpipes. Dreadful memories were not ghosts, nor were shame or grief or an anger that scalded my blood. I set out for the Rotunda.

I remembered the dim, cavernous Rotunda as a refuge in summer heat, its thick walls retaining the night's coolness until late afternoon. Indeed, when I tugged open the heavy door, a chilly flood set me shivering. Foolish, Ella's talk of ghosts and deadraising. *The dark mage* . . . this Dante again, Duplais' comrade—the only one of the queen's consilium not executed as my father's conspirator.

My slippers echoed lightly as I hurried through the deserted foyer, between the circled ranks of columns supporting the crowning dome, and into the vast open space. A feathery touch brushed my cheek. I blinked, just as a thread of purple light caught my eye high in the dome.

My heart, ignoring reason, rattled in my breast. *Silly girl.*

I peered into the gloom. King Philippe had suspended a great pendulum from the peak of the dome for the Grand Exposition. And though my brother's remarks were sauced with spite, Ambrose had confessed it a wonder, its path scribing the very circle the theories of the earth's rotation predicted. Perhaps the purple light was some part of the pendulum structure.

I moved on more slowly, eyes drawn upward. Another soft brush on my forehead. Another on my hand. No sooner did I give in and blink than rose and green threads floated beside three purple ones. I stopped again. The soft rhythm of my slippers seemed to continue, a tap embedded in a sigh of moving air.

Near the center of the Rotunda, a vertical gray wire stretched into the dark heights, a ball of dulled gold suspended from it. The unmoving pendulum.

The muted taps soon sounded more like the chink of metal on firm-seated metal, hammer on chisel. A tide of cold air flowed from across the chamber. I blinked a'purpose, and the threads of light—hundreds of them now—drifted downward from the dome like falling leaves, coalescing in the air near the stilled pendulum. Soon I could see them even without blinking, settling themselves into some pattern. The sight reminded me of a game played with a beam of light in a dark room . . . where a reverse image was formed by light thrown through the design cut into a paper.

But neither will nor diversion could obscure my horror at the crime that had happened here.

The threads shaped an upraised hand. The shadings of pale flesh streaked with scarlet must surely be the odd light, illuminating one of the mosaic figures in the dome. Yet the hand seemed too large, too close, too real. Not far from the hand, mottled gray threads wove themselves into wide diagonal swaths, shaded folds, and then glimmers of scarlet joined and pooled across the gray. And even as I named the red stains blood on fabric, more flesh took shape above the gray garment . . . a chin . . . a cheek. . . .

Father Creator, send thy angels!

A well-proportioned mouth, the straight nose, wide-set eyes, closed in repose, bruised and abraded flesh, blood everywhere. *Edmond*. The very image that had occupied my mind since leaving my bedchamber.

As if fed by my grief and outrage, the image rapidly reached its completion. No sacred mosaic, the figure took on bulk as well as dimension—a young man bound, hands over head, as if he dangled from the king's pendulum. Yet still the atrocity was not done, for the light-sculpted figure began to writhe, and soon the lacerated face was ridged and seamed with agony. The pale lips stretched, and a whisper in my ear resolved into a faint keening as of a wounded animal. The eyes flicked open, black and wholly empty.

Pain crushed my heart and ribs, near blinding me with heated colors that smeared and melted into blazing scarlet.

"Stop this!" I could not have named the target of my outrage.

The image shattered. In a frenzied explosion, the thready lights sprayed across the vastness of the dark before collecting like fireflies around a human-sized silhouette not five metres away from me. The cloaked figure twisted in my direction so fast, the face was but a pale blur streaked with black. But I could not miss the white staff in his grip.

Get away. Get away. Get away. Throttling a whimper, I raced across the chamber toward the golden pool of lamplight that marked the far doors. Under the colonnade. Through the vestibule.

I stretched my hand toward the door, only to have the bronze slab fly open before I'd touched it. Gray evening outlined a figure in the doorway. I yelped like a dog who'd been stepped on.

"Hold! Hold, damoselle!" He grabbed my flailing hands.

"Let me go!" I thrashed and struggled to get loose, straining to see through watering eyes.

"What's happened here?" He held firm. His hands were warm and solid, his form slender and of modest height. Not monstrous. "Damoselle Anne?"

Only as I forced myself still did I recognize him.

"Duplais!" I craned my neck, looking back into the depths of the Rotunda. Retreating footsteps echoed through the emptiness.

"Have you seen something here? Tell me." Insistent. Concerned.

I stumbled over words, unable to explain, not sure I should report such mad visions. "Nothing," I blurted at last. "A servant . . . someone . . . startled me. That's all."

"Naturally." His manner reverted to his usual brittle chill. "What brings you to the Rotunda on your first evening at court, damoselle? The queen's household does not encompass this place."

"Let me go. I'm late." That was all I could say without my voice quavering. Stupid to be so wrecked by a few lights, a lurker, and a vivid, morbid imagination.

I wrenched my hands free and fled. Duplais' gaze burned my back until I was inside the west wing, traversing a portrait gallery under the watchful eyes of Sabria's last twenty monarchs. *Answer me this, householder,* I thought. *If the queen's household does not include the Rotunda, then what business do you have there?* Meeting the mage with the white staff, I'd wager.

The bells struck the half hour as I turned into a modest passage painted the color of claret and halted before the second door. As I raised my hand to knock, the door opened.

A gentleman reared backward in surprise at seeing me so near with a raised fist—and surely a grim and violent aspect.

"Oh!" I said stupidly, straining to see that the birds carved on the lintel were indeed peacocks. "These are the Ducessa de Blasencourt's rooms?"

"I d–doubt I should speak truly, d–damoselle. You've no intent t–to harm her?" His square-jawed face wore a severe expression, blunted by the trace of a stutter and belied by a spark in his eyes. Close-trimmed, white-threaded dark curls framed a strong, symmetrical visage, adorned by a meticulously groomed mustache. A pleasant, intelligent face. Mature, nearer fifty than thirty.

"No. Certainly not. I was summoned." My heart's thuttering slowed. He was a large man, both tall and broad. Trim, fit, but substantial.

"Then b–be of good cheer. You have arrived," he said quietly, dropping his eyes. He bowed modestly and stepped aside to allow me through. "Ah, here is noble Slanie to c–carry you onward. Angels' peace, damoselle."

Cheeks afire, I dipped a knee, already marshaling my questions. A serving girl in a frilled bonnet showed me into a cluttered sitting room. Books and teacups sat atop tables and shelves, alongside fans, beadwork, painted clay pots, and other artifacts from the ducessa's travels.

Lady Cecile rose in welcome, not for me, it appeared, but for a large woman wielding a cane, who marched in behind me like an invading legion. "Make yourself comfortable, Eleanor," she said. "Anne, don't hang back. Come in and join us."

The serving girl vanished. Ensconced on the couches were the fair-haired Belinda and a tiny red-haired marquesa, who had lectured us for an hour that afternoon about petticoats.

I could have chewed the carpet.

"Eleanor, Patrice, this is Anne de Vernase," said Lady Cecile. "And you know dear Belinda."

"Divine grace, my ladies," I croaked. My curtsy would have been better made by a bricklayer.

The ladies vouched me voiceless nods, while Belinda offered a smile that could have outshone a lighthouse. As if I could not feel her shrink away.

The four of them settled into a discussion of Hematian marriage protocols, including the necessity for a prospective bride to pen elaborate descriptions of her family, her childhood, and her education for each member of her betrothed's family in the Hematian language. Belinda near fainted at the prospect. "I'll never manage it!" she said.

"Perhaps I could be of some help," I said, having spent the tedious hour reclaiming my equanimity.

The ladies stared, a bit shocked, as if they'd forgotten I had a voice and weren't sure I should have one.

"I've studied Hematian and, though my pronunciation is merely passable, I'm quite proficient with the written language." No sympathy or interest in Belinda's betrothal prompted my offer. I merely craved some halfway intelligent occupation. All the better if it quieted their endless nattering.

"I understood you grew up in the country, damoselle." The red-haired

marquesa, Lady Patrice, was sharp-tongued and trim of figure at an age
no less than seventy. From her sour expression, one might have thought
the country a sewer or a mine shaft, where such things as lessons were
unknown.

"My family traveled widely when I was twelve and thirteen," I said.
"And my father believed women had quite as fine intelligence as men,
thus the same need for education."

At least two of the four women hissed when I mentioned Papa. Belinda's great eyes rounded.

"And as Lady Cecile knows, my moth—"

"A most useful refinement, languages." Lady Cecile snatched away the
conversation with practiced larceny. "It would be most kind of you to help
Belinda with her letters, Anne. You can set her to work in these evening
sessions as we review your own deficiencies. Now, we've done for tonight.
Divine grace, dear ladies."

Lady Cecile rose, and though I watched carefully, her fingers did not
signal me to stay behind. Yet as she swept me to the door with the others,
she held my arm for one moment, her eye on Lady Patrice's back. When
the brisk little marquesa disappeared around a corner, Cecile whispered in
my ear, almost spitting. "Do *not* mention my connection with your mother.
Not to anyone. Do you understand?"

"Certainly, Your Grace," I said, my cheeks heating. "I understand
completely."

So she was no better than the rest.

I departed, seething, having extracted only two scraps of information
in the hour's session. First, that Belinda de Mercier, a young woman who
lit a room like a streak of sunlight and possessed an excruciatingly rich
father, had an intellect the size of a pea. And second, that my expectation
that I would detest this place was entirely correct.

The storm had passed. Mist hung thick in the courtyards and lightning
danced in the starless heavens. Unwilling to visit the gloomy Rotunda, I
set out through the dark, wet gardens.

As the damp air bathed my overheated face, I brought reason to the
experience of the night. What I had seen in the Rotunda was no mani-

fested spirit. Despite its movements and sounds, the body had projected no quality of humanity. Those fathomless eyes could project no personhood, no soul.

More likely I had witnessed a terrible trickery—a manipulation of lenses and prisms by the cloaked mage hiding near the pendulum. A camera obscura, perhaps. And it made sense they would project an image of the man who'd died there. But why would anyone do such a thing? To frighten serving girls and palace guards? Neither the mage nor Duplais could have imagined *I* would enter the Rotunda this night.

A touch on my sleeve and a glimpse of pale flesh near startled me out of my shoes—until my scrabbling fist caught a clump of wet leaves. The little grotto was choked with oleander. A pale marble statue of a naked javelin thrower hid behind the leathery leaves as if to protect his modesty.

Unfortunately, reason could not repair a good fit of the shakes. I bolted for the nearest door and took the long way through the palace to my bedchamber.

To FIND MY ROOM DARK surprised me, as Ella had promised to leave a light. I groped for the bellpull and sat on the bed to wait. The room felt odd and uncomfortable, the inky blackness squirming like the heat shimmer of summer afternoons. By the time Ella tapped on the door, I was trembling, as if thready lights might flood through the doorway and shape another agonized visage.

Ella's candle illuminated only her round cheeks. "Damoselle?"

I felt ridiculous as Ella lit the lamp on the dressing table with her candle. "I asked to have a lamp burning when I'm out after dark."

"But I—" She shut her mouth firmly and dipped her knee.

"Tell me what's wrong, Ella. I don't want to be unreasonable."

"Sorry, damoselle. It's just I came to light the lamp not an hour ago. But I saw the light under the door. As you didn't say come when I knocked, I figured you'd no need."

"But that's imposs— Wait." I spun around. The emptied letter packet lay on the dressing table exactly where I'd dropped it, but the string . . .

One fold gaped, though I had tied the roll of red leather tight, ready to discard. And had I left the ivory case, filled with Lianelle's mysterious powder, beside or behind my brush? I couldn't recall. I glanced up quickly, but Ella's wide-eyed confusion seemed innocent enough.

"That's all right, then. I'm sure it was only another maidservant come to the wrong room."

"Aye, damoselle." Her gray eyes were wide as she dipped her knee and left.

When she had gone, I unlocked the hidden drawer in the armoire. My mother's jewelry appeared undisturbed and Lianelle's ring and lockets intact, exactly where I had put them. I debated whether to hide the packet and case in the drawer. But the damage was done. Better to leave them out and pretend I didn't know someone had been here.

As the night waxed I lay abed, practicing the strict mental disciplines my mother's family had taught me. If Duplais and his mage could bend my mother's mind to breaking, I needed every tool I could muster to fight them.

CHAPTER 8

S unbeams arrowed through the tall, narrow windows of the Royal Presence Chamber, striking the gold-crusted coats and jeweled turbans of the Arothi delegation. The resulting spits of light rivaled the sparkling showers of red and green fire launched from the balconies flanking the hall. Jugglers' balls of faceted silver flew through the shimmering air, while leaves and rose petals drifted into carpets on the floor.

The Arothi fireworks were not magic, as they claimed; my father had shown us the explosive power of powdered sulfur, nitre powder, and charcoal packed in paper cylinders. The display was breathtaking nonetheless.

On my seventh morning at Castelle Escalon, Eugenie de Sylvae sat on a cushioned velvet throne beneath the glittering dome at one end of the Presence Chamber. With the king away, it fell to his wife to receive the annual tribute delegation from the kingdom of Aroth.

As the maids of honor had not yet been officially presented at court, we stood near the back of the hall. From so far away, the queen's elaborate court gown, robes, and jewels masked any semblance of a real woman. I'd grown up thinking of Eugenie as an angel—tall, lovely, and soft-spoken. But those were an impressionable girl's fantasies. At best she was a weak-minded woman who had allowed herself to be deceived by conspiratorial advisors plotting her husband's overthrow. Even now she sponsored this mage Dante, encouraging his wickedness in some unhealthy hope of clinging to her dead.

The mage would be the sapphire-robed man at Eugenie's right hand. The white staff and the silver collar were unmistakable. I could see no more than that.

A spray of green fireworks announced a parade of half-naked bearers. To the bone-thudding rhythm of tree drums, they paraded a fascinating array of exotic gifts through the hall: painted casks of Arothi brandy, porcelain masks as tall as a man, gold cages occupied by multihued birds and small furred creatures, nasty-looking things with intelligent eyes, sharp teeth, and jeweled collars. The Arothi ambassador, a slender man with a stiff mustache, described the trials and prosperity of his homeland for the past year, while the bearers laid the symbolic gifts at the queen's feet. No doubt the bulk of the tribute payment was already safe in the Sabrian treasury.

The event was a welcome change from the household routine. Every morning began in the sitting room with lessons on precedence and the peerage, Her Majesty's preferences in dress, and every sort of trivia. Afternoons I spent in the queen's salons with some fifty household ladies, who played cards, embroidered, recited turgid poetry, and gossiped. Infinitely tedious afternoons. The queen had not joined us even once.

A few steps away from me a gentleman bent down to retrieve a few of the rose petals magically "transformed" from the fireworks. The close-trimmed curls named him the mature, fine-featured gentleman I'd met leaving Lady Cecile's apartments. Twice since then I'd passed him in the east-wing corridors. Twice he had stood aside and bowed with a sober gallantry. Upon a third encounter, in the Kings' Portrait Gallery, he'd seemed on the verge of addressing me, but had withdrawn with a wry smile when the doughty Lady Eleanor had hobbled around the corner.

"Dianne"—I edged closer to the most unrepentant gossip among the maids of honor—"who is the gentleman standing on the other side of Marie-Claire?"

She squinted, crinkling her nose and exposing dreadful teeth that left her status, if not her actual rank, as low as my own. "That's Roussel, the queen's new physician. A commoner, I've heard, a cobbler's son or some such. Of course, even if he'd a fine demesne and was rid of his speech affliction, who'd care to be touched by a man who puts his fingers in wet noses and bloody pustules? Not even a royal appointment's going to make him a decent match."

Eligible marriage must ever be a maid of honor's highest priority. Considering what kind of nobleman might find my modest dowry advantageous enough to overcome the stigma of my name, a cobbler's son with a courteous manner might be a fine catch, even if his fingers traveled unfortunate places. A smile teased at my lips as I watched him sniff the rose petal, ply it with his fingers, and scrutinize its shape and coloring. He was a scientific man.

Despite aching feet and lingering frustrations, I enjoyed the two-hour exhibition, pleased that I could understand most of what the Arothi said, though I'd not studied their language as intensively as others. As the crowd dispersed, I hung back, trying to summon the courage to address a native speaker for the first time. Before I could decide, a commotion broke out not ten metres from me.

A skinny young man in gray robes had tripped over an Arothi birdcage, fracturing the fragile wood and releasing a flock of screeching redplumed birds and a shower of feathers. The man's stumbling propelled him into the back of Mage Dante, knocking the sorcerer face-first into a column of spiraled marble. A horrified gasp rippled through the departing courtiers.

The staggered mage whirled about, his unshaven jaw hammered iron, black brows lowered over deep-set eyes. Above the shoulders of a field laborer, the wide silver collar bound a sinewed neck. Body quivering, cheeks darkened with rage, he pointed his staff at the man sprawled on the floor. "Never touch me."

Bloodred light streamed from the staff, but it was the mage's thundering voice that projected truer menace. The poor adept backed away crabwise, attempting to distance himself. The mage followed, at each step jerking the staff in a circular motion that resulted in a burst of scarlet flame and a shower of sparks. "One would think an aspiring practitioner of sorcery with the mind of a pigeon and the talents of a stump would not wish to draw attention to himself."

Another step. Another burst. Spits of fire rained upon the fallen man, who slapped clumsily at his exposed skin. "You *will* clean up this mess. Lick it up, if you must."

With every burst, my intestines twisted, raveling and unraveling themselves like knots of string. Disgusting to think the mage had once touched my mother's hands. Surely he was vile enough to break an innocent woman's mind or to bury a young girl without grace. Murder? That, too.

As abruptly as it had begun, the assault ended. The mage turned his back and strode out of the Presence Chamber.

Staggering to his feet, the unfortunate adept flapped his hands and brushed his face, arms, and garments, as if the drifting sparks from the flaming staff yet stung him. Indeed the hall reeked of burning. The stench of scorched flesh and feathers set me coughing.

Piles of leaves and rose petals smoldered or flamed. The young man hurried from one to the next, stomping them out, his face stormy. A sharp-boned face . . . dark wedge of a beard . . .

The adept, too, had been at Montclaire on the day my mother was stricken! Perhaps he knew what this Dante had done to her. Surely he could be no ally of the man who had just shamed him before the entire court of Castelle Escalon. Somehow, at a better time, I'd find out what he knew.

As I hurried toward the doors, I could not shake the image of the mage's flaming staff. The wood itself had not charred, nor had it splintered from the explosive energies. Yet the sparks had ignited true fire, hot enough to roast two birds. What was the mechanism?

"Damoselle Anne! Anne de Vernase!" Duplais stepped away from a group of chattering householders, hand raised to stay my steps.

Heads turned. Conversations died. I was tempted to pretend I had not heard and keep on walking. But a certain severity in the administrator's tone promised more conspicuous consequences if I snubbed him. Better to give the gawkers nothing to titter at. "Sonjeur?"

He clasped his hands behind his back, like a nursery tutor. "Damoselle, perhaps I did not clarify the conditions of your presence here when I fetched you from the country."

Molten heat flooded my cheeks. "Excuse me?"

"Surely you recall His Majesty's three small requirements: to report to my office twice in each tenday, to submit your letters for inspection, and to offer your parole before witnesses that you will not leave Castelle Escalon without my permission."

"But you never—" I tightened my lips. Nothing but gossip would be served by naming him a liar in such a public venue. "I am ever grateful for the clarification, sonjeur." I moved to go.

"Damoselle?" He motioned to the onlookers—twenty or thirty secretaries, aides, and gentlewomen. "We have witnesses *now*."

I hated him then, the officious little twit, aggrandizing himself before his minions. Pretending to seek truth and justice while playing with other people's pain.

"You have my parole, Administrator," I snapped. "As you say. But I can see no reason to seek you out. *Fetch* me when you wish me to grovel."

Shocked titters followed me out of the Presence Chamber. In the foyer Lady Cecile was engaged in serious conversation with Mage Dante's red-faced assistant. An interesting sight after her warnings for me to avoid anything to do with sorcery or sorcerers, but then, I would guess that hypocrisy ranked close to vanity in the palace hierarchy of virtues.

12 OCET, EVENING

IT REQUIRED ONLY ONE CLEAR moment to realize that my rebellious intent to avoid Duplais was doomed. Unless Queen Eugenie herself overruled his strictures—and I had yet to have a personal exchange with her—I must seek Duplais' permission to visit Ambrose.

Distance from the event did nothing to explain Duplais' lie. Though anger named his display churlish, reason judged it more complicated. Portier de Duplais was a man of mature and relentless logic. His every move was well considered—such as allowing the ambush at Vradeu's Crossing to test me. So why would he wish to demonstrate my humiliation so publicly, even as he took such care to convince everyone at court he was insignificant? He must believe someone was paying attention, which set me forever looking over my shoulder.

Thus it was with an entirely sour disposition that I attended Lady Cecile's review session two evenings later. The evening promised naught to revive my spirits. I had now attended four sessions with Belinda, Lady Cecile, and one or both of our overbearing instructors. At no time had the ducessa offered the least sign of interest or familiarity. I'd begun to doubt my memory of her welcome.

"Eleanor and Patrice are at cards with Her Majesty this evening," she said when I arrived at the evening's venue—the Rose Room, a writing room set aside for the queen's ladies. "We shall have to proceed without them, which is why I've brought us here. Belinda, you must continue copying your letters, now Anne has so kindly written them out for you. It is critical that they be sent in your own hand. Hematians are very sensitive to such personal touches. As for you, Anne, Her Majesty has expressed particular wishes that all her young ladies be trained to serve in her bedchamber."

At least I might advance this ridiculous course toward its completion tonight. I had often wondered what "review" I was supposed to accomplish when the entirety of our evening sessions had been devoted to Belinda's impending betrothal.

"This entry is not for common use." Lady Cecile pressed the latch of a plain door in the corner of the Rose Room and motioned me through.

We entered the royal apartments through an octagonal waiting room of scarlet silk and velvet. Two blue-liveried guards snapped to attention as we entered, and a bald gentleman in blue brocade bowed. "Divine grace, *bellassi* Cecile," he said in heavily accented Sabrian. "Time be for serving lessons tonight?"

"Yes, Doorward. Damoselle Anne is new to Castelle Escalon this season. Her Majesty is at cards, I understand."

"Indeed so. Damoselle, welcome. I am Rulf de Viggio, Doorward

Hereditary of the Queen's Household." The gentleman briskly opened an elaborately carved door three times my height.

Lady Cecile ushered me through an extensive series of luxurious apartments, done up in shades of blue and lavender. I'd no time for any impression beyond high ceilings, refined comfort, and gracious simplicity, at least not until we arrived at a large sitting room.

None could miss the evidence of pervasive superstition: a bundle of dried herbs in every doorway, a grapevine wreath over every window, a bunch of small brass bells and colored feathers on the marble mantelpiece. Charms, I knew, but whether intended to ward off sickness or poison, to freshen the air, to prevent mold, or to keep ink from drying too fast, I had no idea.

An altar stone held a place of honor along one wall. Hung with pimpernel, toadflax, and deep green, wax-leafed ivy, it held far too many tessilae for a woman not yet forty.

Above a white marble hearth, a grand watercolor depicted creatures from faerie tales, dancing in a forest clearing bathed in moonlight. Male and female dancers, some wearing stag horns or goat's legs, some humanlike and draped in spidersilk, were depicted in such lifelike rendering, I could almost feel the wind of their spinning. The artist had created them almost transparent, fading into the flowers and grass and mighty oaks. Transcendent beauty, imbued with overwhelming sorrow . . .

"Sit over here." Lady Cecile's command startled me. I rubbed my prickling arms and took a place on a settee next the cold hearth. She sat across from me. A few locks of graying hair fell loose from their precise pinning and dangled across her cheek. She didn't seem to notice.

"I regret it's taken so long to have a private word," she said, keeping her voice low, "but I feel it critical to belie any suspicion of familiarity between us. You must keep a tighter rein on your feelings, Anne. One is always under observation at court."

"Of course, my lady. I can see that."

"Here, at least, we'll not be overheard." She gathered her shawl tighter, as if she'd taken a chill, and she glanced about the open doorways uneasily. "Perhaps I should not have spoken."

Her pause was so long, I feared my questions would go begging yet again. "My lady, you hinted my mother's condition was no accident. You implied I could be in danger."

"Yes, yes, but I've only bits and pieces and no idea how they fit together." She heaved a deep sigh and leaned forward. "Tell me about your father, Anne."

Of all questions. "Lady, my father is a coward, a murderer, and a traitor."

There, I'd said it. Was this a test of loyalty? Must I swear upon my mother's muddled head to prove I spoke my true belief? Perhaps I should mark my face with blood, as mountain folk did to call their gods to witness.

Cecile rapped her finger rings on the arm of her chair in agitation. "What I need to hear are details of his birth and family, and what reasons might lead him to betray the author of his fortune. Trust me, Anne, for your mother's sake."

In no way did I trust her. Perhaps that would come; servants and ladies uniformly adored her. Yet my father's history was no secret.

"What would you hear? My father was raised at the regimental headquarters in Delourre by an elderly chevalier and his dame. The dame, at least, was not his blood kin. Her kitchen maid had run away, leaving him in a basket by the stove. Papa assumed he was the chevalier's . . . byblow."

Lady Cecile's expression registered no shock. Papa had certainly found no shame in his questionable birth. He had snorted at Mama's kinswomen who clucked and scowled about it, and he had laughed at courtiers who tried to insult him with it, proclaiming it a badge of good fortune that he was the fruit of "youthful passion." His laughter had rumbled Montclaire's floors and filled its rooms like spring windstorms.

I squeezed my mind shut. The man of those memories did not exist. Had never existed.

"Chevalier de Menil moved from one border posting to another, perpetually short of money. He used every kivre he had to see Papa knighted, falling so far in debt he held my father's investiture feast in a tavern. He died in the same battle in which my father saved Philippe de Savin-Journia's life." The old man had never known that his beloved protégé had become the Conte Ruggiere on Philippe's coronation day, given all the wealth, honor, and influence a decent man could want.

Of course, my father had demonstrated that he was a particularly *inde*cent man. "Should I continue?"

"I want to hear everything, even things you might not consider important."

So I told her of Papa's service to King Philippe, of how in our childhood it was most often riding at the king's side in battle, but that as time went on diplomatic missions—negotiating alliances, inspecting outposts, raising levies of men and money—replaced martial ones. She seemed interested in the smallest detail: that he stayed home teaching the three of us when he was not on campaign, that he preferred books of natural philosophy to any other, that he engaged in lengthy correspondence with a few old friends, soldiers like Basil de Reyne, governor of Kadr, and men of science like the astronomer Germond de Vouger.

". . . No, none of those friends or acquaintances dabbled in sorcery, my lady. Why would they?"

I could have told her a great deal more. When Papa came home from his travels, my mother would hear nothing of dangers or intrigues that might haunt her the next time he had to leave. Ambrose would not sit still for any stories beyond war and combat, and Lianelle was preoccupied with magic. But my father delighted in history and politics, cities, temples, and strange cultures, just as he delighted in languages, astronomy, and mathematics, and I was the only one in the family who shared his fascination with all of it. Until those last few journeys, he had told me everything. Or so I had imagined.

What I would give to erase treacherous memory! I would *not* grieve for a man so depraved as to leech the blood from a young girl to feed some sorcerer's odious magic.

"Why would your father become enamored of sorcery after proclaiming skepticism for twenty years?" Cecile said, her pale knuckle rubbing her upper lip. "It doesn't make sense."

The ducessa's unrelenting intensity reminded me of Duplais. Increasingly uncomfortable, I averted my eyes. "This is all so long ago, my lady. I was only sixteen when he vanished."

The strands of pearls dangling from her ears clicked softly as she shook her head. "I wish I could tell you more. Your father's background is of immense interest to several most influential people. Which leads me to think— Well, it just doesn't make sense. But I refuse to believe your mother has succumbed to nervous collapse. I've heard insinuations that her condition was precipitated. And now your sister is dead."

"What was done to my mother?" I blurted. "Who says it? For mercy's sake, if we knew what was wrong with her, we might find a remedy."

She shot to her feet, uncertainty dismissed. "I'll not betray my informant's trust, any more than I would betray yours. Not yet. Just . . . tread carefully. Now, we must move on before the queen returns."

"My lady, please!"

"While Her Majesty is unendingly gracious and lenient in matters of protocol, she does have a few very particular requirements. One window on the east and one on the south must be opened each night, no matter the weather, and each must have . . ." Lecturing serenely, as if she had never imagined purposeful madness or murder, Lady Cecile led me into Queen Eugenie's bedchamber.

After a quarter hour of fruitless fury, I became caught up in my bizarre schooling. The queen must indeed be the *most* superstitious of women. Nighttime rituals involved more of placing charms and burning enspelled herb bundles than of tooth cleaning or hair brushing, and of lighting particular fragrant candles to burn through the night than of smoothing sheets.

". . . and always to close the bed curtains before the lamps are lowered." Lady Cecile demonstrated how to refasten the silver clips once the heavy silk curtains were released about the wide bed. "Except for this one."

She led me around to the side of the bed nearest the windows, the side one might assume the first to be curtained off against the chill and the last to be opened. The curtain at the head of the bed had been sewn in two panels, and she showed me how to release the wide panel nearer the center of the bed. The narrow panel nearest the bedpost and pillows was always to be tied open unless the queen herself closed it.

"Now bring a lamp and we'll examine her medicine box."

As I made to follow, the strangest thing caught my eye. Half hidden behind a painted screen, a metallic ring perhaps a metre and a half in diameter had been embedded in the wood floor between the bed and the open window. The ring seemed to suck the golden beams right out of the lamp, stretching them impossibly thin and bending them around its perfect circumference.

"What *is* this?" Fascinated, I sank to my knees and brushed a finger along the ring. To my surprise, it was not metallic at all, but more akin to amber glass. And the stretched light beams were not some trick of sputtering flame and startled vision, but actually streaked around the circle of amber, regardless of my viewing angle. Likewise the shadows were not just the inverse of the light beams, but shooting splinters of blackness independent of the light.

"Ouch!" I snatched my hand away. A snap of heat had shot straight up my arm to the center of my forehead, like a charge of the *virtu elektrik*.

The air in the sitting room stirred, as if an open door had let in a winter draft. The lamp guttered and almost went out.

"Anne?" Lady Cecile peered around the bedpost. "Grace of angels, girl. Never touch that."

"Whatever is it?"

"That sorcerer's filth." She spat her answer in such a way as to close off further probing.

That sorcerer. Dante.

We spent a half hour with Eugenie's extensive collection of potions and tonics. I would never remember it all, especially as a ferocious ache in the center of my brow grew worse every moment. The lamplight glancing from the faceted glass vials and bottles sliced through the air like sabers.

When the west tower clock struck ninth hour, Cecile began reordering the medicine box, which required pulling out a few remaining items lying loose in the bottom—a flat tin that rattled as if filled with buttons, a drawstring pouch of gray silk, a bundle of cinnamon sticks tied with string—and installing everything again. "Always leave things tidy, and be aware: Antonia's word is law in this room."

"Our mistress might dispute that, dame."

My spirit froze. No mistaking the resonant baritone from the doorway behind us, though it was bereft of madness on this night. Not the least sound or movement had warned of his presence.

Lady Cecile jostled the cabinet as she twisted around, clinking and rattling the bottles and vials. "Master Dante," she said, "why are you here?" Her challenge was undermined by a slight quaver.

"Our lady queen bade me survey her chamber before her return. To make sure there be no . . . unwanted intruders."

He entered the pooled lamplight, a dark-haired man of modest height and simple, sober garb—black breeches and hose, and a full-sleeved shirt the hue of overripe plums. His silver collar glinted in the lamplight, bright against the shadowed hollows of his face.

Close to, the mage appeared far younger than I would have guessed—no more than thirty—though his eyes . . . My skin shivered. Set in a fine spiderwork of sun creases, his eyes were not black, but the deep, intense green of a sunlit wildwood. They hinted at experiences more remote than those of my great-grandsire Cazar, who had witnessed the ending of the Fassid Empire and the last, lingering scourges of the Blood Wars.

"I ween I should bespeak an introduction, dame." The cool interest, voiced with the slight patois of the northern mountains, might suggest him a more disciplined sort than the man who had beaten his adept in the Presence Chamber, save that one of his black-gloved hands gripped the infamous white staff.

"Certainly, Master. May I acquaint you with Her Majesty's new maid of honor, Anne de Vernase?" Familiar forms seemed to restore Cecile's more customary calm. She took my hand and drew me forward. "I am training the young lady to the queen's service. Anne, Master Mage Dante, Queen Eugenie's First Counselor."

Grudging, I inclined my head. My forehead ached and burned, as if a carpenter had attacked it with an auger, but I summoned anger and resentment to reinforce Cazar discipline. This man would not see me quail at his mere presence. No matter this mannered arrogance, no matter his true allegiance, he was a brute. If the ducessa was right, he had slaughtered my mother as truly as any knife-wielding barbarian.

"You expose a braver soul than mine, Dame Cecile, to bring the Great Traitor's daughter to this chamber. Mayhap I should banish her, as I do haunts and spectres." He drifted across the room toward the windows, passing between us and the bedstead, inspecting the various charms and wards tucked here and there along the way, touching this one, adjusting that, breathing a whispered word on another. He touched every bottle and jar in the medicine box. "What danger do you represent, damoselle?"

"None, sonjeur," I said to his back, purposely failing to acknowledge his rank, as he had with the ducessa. "What grievance could I have with Queen Eugenie, who demonstrates such tolerance as to welcome me here?"

He reversed sharply, his back to the tall windows. His eyes were narrowed, his black brow raised skeptically. "You carry many a grievance, I think. Your traitor parent searches for sorcerous power he cannot wield himself. Who better to benefit from his findings than his nurtured childer, who carry the mark of blood inheritance? Have you nae wish to take your share of his discoveries and right the wrongs of the world? Your mother's nerves remain fractured, I hear."

Hatred exploded in my breast, shooting fire to every limb. I felt as if I could have lit a bonfire with a touch. How dare he speak of my mother? "You know nothing of me, mage. But be sure of this: Were I gifted in the practices you call magic, I would not share in my father's work, or your work, or any such vileness, even were it the sole means to heal my mother's injury, so *cowardly* inflicted, or return my innocent brother's freedom, or turn back time itself to prevent my sister's diabolic murder!"

The clang of tuned bronze sliced through air turbulent with lamplight and shadow, as the palace bells pealed the half hour. Lady Cecile, pale as stone dust, used the interruption as an excuse to drag me toward the door. Her heart's pulse rattled like a rabbit's. "Time runs. We must abandon you to your duties, Master, and return to our own. Come, Anne."

He may have answered. He may have laughed. I couldn't hear, for the world blurred as she bustled me through the dim-lit rooms and past the bowing guardians in the scarlet waiting room. By the time we stood in the deserted outer salon, I was shaking. Dizziness threatened to drop me on the gray carpet.

"Are you an entire fool, girl?" she spat through clenched teeth. "To speak like that to *him*?"

"Angels defend us, my lady. What is he?" I said, clamping my trembling arms around my stomach. Not even Duplais' razored questioning had left me feeling so raw.

"The queen's current favorite is what he is. Dangerous beyond dreaming is what he is. Some say it was no earthshaking but this mage caused the destruction of the Bastionne Camarilla—yet the prefects do not, cannot, touch him. There are more reasons than border uprisings or disaffection that keep the king away from Merona." She smoothed her hair and mustered her more accustomed dignity. "Now, are you quite well? I must get back to Belinda."

She must have interpreted my tremors as affirmation, as she hurried back to the Rose Room without allowing me to speak. "Not at all well," I whispered to her back.

My childhood memories of Eugenie de Sylvae were like the sweetened versions of old tales told in the nursery, all starlight, elvish singing, and happy endings. Present truth seemed more like true folk tales: monsters, dark deeds, and unexplained evils—all personified in this one man. Why did she keep him here? What had possessed me, whom my family named unflappable, to insult him? I felt as if I'd been ravished by a horde of stinging ants.

Returned to the Rose Room, Lady Cecile finished inspecting Belinda's work and bade the two of us a peaceful night. As Belinda stacked her letters, I broached the subject of my brother.

"I've no influence with the king, Anne," said the ducessa, cool as a spring night, "and know naught of prison protocols. I'll see you tomorrow morning, as usual."

I could have gnawed my way out of an iron cage.

———

SLEEP ELUDED ME THAT NIGHT. Telling my father's story had brought the best of him to life for me again. Yet the letter that had sent Edmond de Roble to torture and death was scribed by Papa's hand, as was another asserting he would never again be subservient to a king. My father had vowed to see Sabria overturned, and I, the daughter he had once called the child of his mind, could not deny his guilt. My testimony had affirmed my father a traitor and left my brother hostage to a king's wrath. Paralyzed by guilt and fear, I had retreated to Montclaire and for four years had never looked beyond its walls again. What kind of traitor did that make me?

CHAPTER 9

Over the next few days I was steeped in the lore of Sabrian nobility and the outfitting of a queen's household, learning more than any person could ever wish to know about demesnes major and minor, property settlements, the advantages of silk made in Tallemant over silk imported from Hematia, and the particular linen sheets the queen preferred. The voyages of exploration King Philippe sponsored had brought enormous wealth to Sabria, as well as new fabrics, foods, artworks, and ideas. On one morning we were taken to an importer's warehouse down at the docks and shown a grand variety of things I'd never seen before.

In years past, I would have reveled in such an outing. But the restless anger grown in my viscera would have been better satisfied by smashing porcelain than by admiring it. What was wrong with me?

More than tenday gone and I'd learned nothing to explain my sister's death. I had applied to every undersecretary in the steward's office and the chancellor's, as well as to the Temple Minor and the king's First Secretary, for permission to visit Ambrose, but no one had been able or willing to help. Though I scoured the royal library, hoping to discover what poisons might destroy a woman's mind or how else such a thing might be accomplished in the matter of a day, I had found no answers. Neither sleep, study, exercise, nor conversation had provided relief for the agitation that afflicted me when thrust among strangers. Bees might have been nesting in my ears.

On the long afternoons I roamed the edges of the queen's salon or sat by a window, trying to stay inconspicuous and avoid screaming with boredom. I knew I should speak to people, try to make acquaintances, or at least convince someone I was not leprous. This was my life now, and I needed to make something of it. I listened to gossip and collected rumors of more strange incidents in the city—including a violent whirlwind that had destroyed the Plas de Gierete, the Punishment Square where criminals were publicly whipped or executed.

Every day I swore to find someone among the women who might enlighten me about Lady Cecile or Duplais or exactly what services the mage Dante provided for the queen. But whenever one of the less-intimidating ladies in the room was between conversations, my mouth went dry and my head seemed entirely abandoned by any idea worth expressing.

I needed to see Ambrose. Perhaps if I could pour out the tale of these events, the two of us together might make some sense of them.

A FEW DAYS AFTER MY unsettling encounter with the mage, I dawdled too long in my bedchamber, writing a letter to Bernard and Melusina. As I hurried down the window gallery, late for the first of a flurry of evening engagements, none of which I anticipated with pleasure, a light touch on my shoulder spun me around so fast I near burst my skin.

"Damoselle de Vernase. Would ye come with me, damoselle?" A trim young serving man whipped his hands behind his back, only to pull one out again to dash a lock of yellow hair from his eyes. "My master would have a word with you."

"Who are you? Who is your master?" My address was much too abrupt, but if he answered Dante, I was sure to heave up my lunch.

The young man grinned cheerfully. "I'm Heurot, damoselle, saints please ye for asking, gentleman's attendant and aide to Sonjeur Portier de Savin-Duplais, Administrative of Her Majesty's household. My master bids you report to his chambers as you are required."

Every day since the humiliating spectacle at the Arothi tribute ceremony, I had expected Duplais' summons. Hoped for it, once I'd accepted him as my only route to Ambrose. I'd have damned pride and sought him out, but my time had been occupied at every hour he was available. And again tonight . . .

"I'm expected by the Ducessa de Blasencourt just now, Heurot. Tell Sonjeur de Duplais that I'll attend him after the presentation tonight."

Heurot looked distressed. "But, damoselle . . ."

"Later, I promise."

The gloomy afternoon had grown chilly and threatening as I hurried through the inner courts toward the west wing. I was to sit an early supper with the other maids of honor and meet with Lady Cecile for another hour of frustrating nothing. The evening's culmination was to be our formal presentation to Queen Eugenie. The prospect was unbearable. With an ache as sore as any wounding, I longed to be home.

Halfway down the portrait gallery leading to Cecile's apartment, a youthful figure hovered beneath a greater-than-life-sized image of Philippe de Savin-Journia, my king and goodfather. The youth popped to attention as I passed. "Damoselle, please wait."

"Heurot! How did you—? I told you I've engagements for the next few hours."

"My master does sincerely wish a word with you, damoselle. He is most insistent."

Resolution faltered, then hardened into a different shape. "All right. Give me a few moments."

The women were picking at poached pears and lettuce when I was shown in and promptly begged leave to withdraw with a headache. Though I believed the lie must be written on my face for all to see, none of our three mentors seemed particularly surprised. Lady Patrice flared her nostrils in disapproval, but she could hardly object. The other maids of honor, including her especial favorites, fostered headaches enough for a regiment of unhealthy young women.

"We'll see you at the presentation, then," said Lady Cecile. "Angels' peace, Anne."

I was surprised when she rose from the table and escorted me to the door. As I lowered my guilty gaze and bade her a peaceful evening, she pressed a small leather-bound book into my hand. "Read this for our next meeting," she said quietly. "Be prepared to discuss it. I believe it relevant to our discussion of several days ago."

My eyes shot up. Her smooth, elegant forehead was seamed with worry, and her usually rosy complexion had a dreadful gray cast to it. A damp sheen coated her upper lip. "My lady—"

"Be off now." In a swirl of plum satin, she returned to the others, beckoning her maidservant, Slanie, to close the door behind me.

Alone outside the door, I examined the worn little book. The title, scribed on red leather in faded gold lettering: *A Brief History of the Demesne Gautier.*

Heaven's gates! *Gautier* was the name on Lianelle's books of sorcery!

I was instantly torn. Heurot waited in the gallery, ready to take me to Duplais. My yearning to hold my brother in my arms, to comfort him in his lonely prison and share the dreadful events of the past month had swelled to bursting, and the only way I could see to ease that ache led through the queen's administrator. But this book . . . Dates and names and lists, sketched maps, and genealogical charts tantalized me as I thumbed through it. An entire section was titled "Collegia Magica de Gautier." Surely this book was enlightenment.

But the needs of the living must trump the concerns of the dead, no matter how dreadfully, hurtfully, they had passed beyond the Veil. I stuffed the little volume deep into the pocket of my underskirt. First I must persuade Duplais to get me into Spindle Prison. Then be "presented." Then I would delve into Lady Cecile's book.

"My master says he's chosen a venue less likely for interrupting," said Heurot cheerfully, as we bypassed the turning to Duplais' office chamber.

I was skeptical. Even more so when the young manservant led me down and down into a gloomy bricked passage that must penetrate Merona's bedrock. Certainly it was a season removed from the autumnal warmth upstairs. I wished I'd brought a shawl.

"Here, damoselle." Heurot indicated an open doorway, snapped an inexpert bow, and hurried back the way we'd come.

I had the impression of a spacious room, but in truth I could make out nothing but two chairs drawn close to a well-grimed hearth. A small fire snapped in the grate, creating a modest circle of light and warmth. The room's most noticeable feature was an enveloping quiet. For the first time since riding into Merona, I could hear myself think.

"Divine grace, damoselle." Duplais stepped out of the shadows behind the high-backed chair. Exposing his marked left hand, he sketched a bow. "Please sit," he said, indicating the chair opposite his.

I exposed my Cazar mark and sat.

Duplais remained standing. "Are you well, damoselle? Settling in? Our journey was not too taxing?"

Had he lost his mind? "I'm well recovered, sonjeur, and becoming familiar with my duties."

That seemed to satisfy his scheduled allotment of banter. He picked up a few folded papers from a shelf above the hearth, passed them to me, and retreated behind his own tall chair, where the firelight could not reach his face. Only his slender hands remained visible, resting on the back of the chair, left hand marked, the right pitted with small angry scars.

I glanced at the papers. Letters, addressed to me. Seals broken.

Heat, nothing to do with the fire, suffused my cheeks.

"The king insists," he said, before I could speak. "I take no pleasure from it. Take the time to read, if you like."

To wait and read the brief missives later would demonstrate more self-command, but I could not bear the thought that this man knew more of my business than I did. So I read.

A letter from the temple minor in Seravain stated simply that the verger of the Seravain deadhouse had issued a death warrant for *Lianelle de Vernase ney Cazar, age seventeen years, dead by calamitous incident.* The warrant would be forwarded to the temple major at Tigano, at which time the family of the deceased could apply to Tigano's verger for a sanctified tessila.

"I have taken the liberty of notifying the verger at Seravain to forward your sister's warrant to Verger Rinaldo at our temple minor here instead," said Duplais.

I did not thank him.

The second letter, somewhat longer, was from Bernard, scribed with his usual careful lettering and direct prose.

> *Damoselle Anne,*
>
> *May the blessed saints find you well in your new state.*
>
> *No new master has yet arrived at Montclaire. Melusina and I bide. We shall do our duty until told not. The grapes swell.*
>
> *Three nights after your departure, the very night the Guard Royale took down their watch, unknown ragpockets invaded the house. To my shame, my crotchit skills did not suffice to hold them off. Neither Melusina nor I can descript the fiends, as they wore masks. They pried into every barrel, bin, and box, as well as rifling the desks and inspecting every volume from the library.*
>
> *Truth be told, these were no common filchers. The only items taken were a few oddments you had tossed in the dustbin: a looking glass, a leash, a knot of ribbons, and the like. Also a stack of letters rummaged from the library desk. They also took a packet come by post messenger that very day, a handspan square, more or less. It was sent from Seravain. We'd set it by to send on to you.*
>
> *We've neatened the house as we can and sore regret that we lost the packet what must sure have been a value to you, as it appeared to be sent from the little one now dead. We hold her dear in our thoughts and deeds.*
>
> *Angels grace thy soul, dear lady, and the good young lord's, and the sweet mistress's broken spirit.*
>
> > *Thy servant always,*
> >
> > *Bernard*

As a curiosity, I heard later that the cellar at the Cask was tumbled ear-lier that same night by men in masks.

HORRID TO IMAGINE BERNARD AND Melusina beset by men like those who'd accosted Duplais and me in the wood. The stolen oddments were all from Lianelle's room—trinkets from her childhood, things she had tried to work spells on before she went to Seravain. Nothing of value. Nothing I wanted to keep. She had given me the shell-backed looking glass years ago, but I had returned it, as the glass was poor quality. Using it left me dizzy. The packet, however . . .

"So they found what our masked bandits were seeking in your luggage." Duplais echoed my thoughts so clearly, it was startling. "I suppose you've no idea what these *oddments* might be, or the letters or the packet from your sister. A book, possibly?"

Though I would rather yield nothing to the hateful man, I would cooperate. I was determined to learn what he knew of Lianelle's death, and I needed his approval to visit Ambrose.

"The only letters left in the drawer were my father's correspondence with Germond de Vouger, a gifted man of science. They're valuable to those who treasure the power of intellect and scientific advancement. Perhaps they think to sell them."

"I know of de Vouger. A physicist and astronomer. He was a friend of your father's?"

"Not a friend, not in the personal sense. I don't know that they ever met. But they corresponded for many years about the role of science in society and the imperative to stretch the boundaries of exploration, both in the world and in the mind. And about de Vouger's own discoveries, naturally. Nothing treasonous, you can be sure."

Duplais tucked that away without expression. "And the packet?"

"My sister hoped to sit for her adept's examinations this winter and feared she wouldn't be allowed to study what she needed. The librarian despised her. So from time to time she sent books home to read on holidays. How could I know which one? What could be so important about her books?"

"Books are valuable and fragile. They can be damaged by shuffling around the countryside. Or lost. Or passed on to a villain who should not have them—a soul-eating villain who recruits his own daughters into his dangerous games."

Duplais' distaste for despicable parents might recommend him if I didn't suspect him and his mage of harming my mother for *their* own purposes. Had his dogged pursuit of the king's enemies become a campaign for his own private gain? A failed sorcerer, a king's cousin of incisive logic and intelligence reduced to assigning apartments for ladies-in-waiting, might be willing to use anything, even this rogue Dante, to gain access to my father's secrets.

"What information might be of such desperate interest to my father?" I said, acutely aware of Lady Cecile's book in my pocket. "Or to his rivals, if your theories about those highwaymen at Vradeu's Crossing are correct?"

"That's certainly the question, is it not?" he said. "What were these other articles the brigands took from Montclaire?"

"I discarded many items of little or no value before we left. As you well know, I refused to leave any of my family's personal belongings for the new Conte Ruggiere."

I was as curious as Duplais. Was it the specific artifacts Lianelle had made from the books that they hunted . . . or was it *anything* she had touched?

Duplais' scrutiny did not waver. "Damoselle, that night we met outside the Rotunda, you seemed frightened. Have you been threatened in some way? Accosted here in the palace?"

"Certainly not. I was merely late for an appointment. It was my first day here." I would share facts, not foolish megrims.

"Did you meet anyone in the Rotunda?"

"I glimpsed a man adjusting the lamps near the pendulum. I assumed him a watchman or servant."

"*Lamps?* Do you think me an idiot who has no idea what goes on inside the Rotunda?" His fingers gripped the chair back as if ready to throw it at me. "What are you *doing* here, damoselle? Are you waiting for someone to contact you?"

"I am in Merona by His Majesty's command. You yourself brought the summons."

"We know there's more!" he snapped. "Are you dealing with someone inside the palace? Are you a player or a pawn?"

We? The room was suddenly sweltering. Sweat beaded my neck. Was his mage partner here?

"I've no idea what you're talking about. I neither expected nor wished to come to Merona. Did my jailer give me leave, I'd walk home this very night."

Surely some revelation lay just beyond his words, if I could but nudge his fraying patience a bit further.

"Perhaps you could be more specific," I said. "Or is this a determination to punish my father's kin because you're too incompetent to catch him? You've destroyed my mother. You've imprisoned my young brother in a place reserved for murderers and traitors. And for *what*?"

"For *sorcery*!" he blurted. "Don't play the ingenue with me! You devoured every word spoken at your father's trial. This is all about sorcery."

"What could I know of sorcery, Sonjeur de Duplais? I've no schooling in it. It's likely some few magical workings are natural phenomena that scientific academicians do not yet grasp. But the bulk of them are no more than hypocrisy and lies—illusions of light or mechanics portrayed as the supernatural by deceivers like you to enthrall the gullible."

"Confound it, damoselle. Your father is not a stupid man, so his favored child could not be so. Your father's associates pursue magic of a kind we've not seen in ages of the world, sorcery that corrupts the laws of nature. Do you think you can play with it? Tease with it? Sell it to the highest bidder?"

"I cannot help you, sonjeur," I said, holding tight reins on my rising excitement. "I've neither seen my father nor communicated with him in five years. Perhaps if you told me—"

"Be very careful with these games, damoselle." He bit off each word, fury quenched so thoroughly, one would think he'd donned plate armor. "You do not behave as the innocent you claim to be. Others see this as well as I do. I've a powerful friend who can protect you, do you but ask."

Against all intent, the septic anger festering in my belly erupted. "You can be sure this is no game to me, Sonjeur de Duplais. Yet *your* powerful friend would be the last I'd choose to aid me. I'm not sure who to fear more—those who perpetrate these crimes or those who prosecute them. Somewhere the differences between the two parties have blurred. My mother is mad and my sister dead, and neither you nor your vile mage has told me why, though I believe you know very well."

"My vile— You speak of Dante." Wariness clipped his tongue.

"I came here willing tonight, because your public posturing ensured I cannot leave the palace without your permission. So, perhaps your *powerful friend* can help me with this: I have not been allowed to see my brother in four years. I have appealed to every authority I know, from my good-father to his lowliest secretary, but have received naught but vague referrals to other faceless names. I doubt half my letters reach my brother's hand. Even if they did, I cannot tell him of our sister's death on paper. I must speak to him. You serve no justice to forbid it."

He considered this for a moment. "Perhaps we could exchange favors."

This despicable offer left me speechless. Before I could recover my wits, the cheerful manservant popped through the door. "Sonjeur, it's time."

"We'll continue this another day, damoselle," said Duplais with a curt bow. "Meanwhile, I'd advise you to have a care with accusations. Court politics will ever overtake justice. As for Master Dante . . . he is no ally of mine. As I tell Heurot, here, and anyone else who might listen: Keep as far from him as your duties allow. Divine grace."

I neither reflected the blessing nor gave him any more words to twist.

CHAPTER 10

"Your master is a cold man," I snapped to Heurot as we ascended the endless stair. "I wonder he allows you to smile."

"He's ever been kind and considerate to me, damoselle. Still does mostly for himself, though he raised my pay when he hired me on to work for him alone. And I've never known another gentleman to help his man with an education. He's determined I'll be a fit secretary for him someday."

"He intends us all to be useful to his schemes." Of course he would want me to stay away from Dante, so I could not learn what wickedness they planned.

"Respectfully, damoselle, I believe you've misunderstood him." Heurot frowned and shook his head as if I'd slandered his mother. "I only dare speak out so bold because a certain person tells me you're a kind mistress who appreciates honest talk, and I'm certain my master would never wish to offend a gentle lady."

"I doubt he notices whether I am a woman or not."

"Likely that's your misunderstanding of him, damoselle. Confidentially, he's not at all easy with ladies, being dreadful . . . inexperienced . . . in that line. And then it haps the first lady he came sweet on turned out to be the traitor's handmaid what was condemned to die and then escaped the Spindle Prison. *That* set him back, it did."

Duplais had *loved* Maura ney Billard? I could scarce believe it! Lovely, good-hearted Maura. My father had once saved her life, then callously manipulated her into complicity in treason. Duplais, as the Principal Accuser, had laid out the case against her and signed the king's judgment condemning her to death. Never once had he wavered or shown any hint of withholding. True, the lady had miraculously escaped from prison. But Duplais remained here, pursuing my father. Either he was the coldest lover ever to walk the earth or the most deceitful or . . . I wasn't sure what. The man confounded me.

As Heurot and I slogged up the long stair, reason cooled my fury. Duplais believed the mysterious bandits had found what they searched for at Montclaire. A book, certainly, and perhaps some of my sister's things. Every one of the items mentioned had been Lianelle's, save de Vouger's letters. Why the thieves would take those letters was a mystery.

My sister claimed she had been working sorcery entirely different from what the Camarilla taught, Gautieri magic she called it, derived from the Seravain books. I squeezed Lady Cecile's book, weighing like an anvil in my pocket. *Collegia Magica de Gautieri.* Was magical authority the problem? Lianelle had told me how protective the Camarilla felt about their rites and formulas. Yet why would the Royal Accuser in the matter of Michel de Vernase care about Camarilla infighting? Unless even a failed sorcerer could be a partisan in such a battle. Unless the conflict was not *petty* infighting.

The Blood Wars, begun in clan warfare among sorcerers, had brought Sabria to the brink of ruin: half our people dead, cities and villages burned to ash, scholars and teachers executed, entire families—many of them blood families, but also other noble families who had founded and built Sabria—entirely wiped out. Now Duplais' Mage Dante, who had made himself indispensable to the Queen of Sabria, had reportedly destroyed the Bastionne Camarilla. . . .

Images of objects falling from the ruin much more slowly than physics prescribed slowed my steps. *Sorcery that corrupts the laws of nature.*

Somehow Lianelle's encrypted books were linked to my father and blood transference and the plot to bring down King Philippe. The marauders' Norgand ringleader had used a mask like that described at Papa's trial. It was all part of the same mystery.

"I do appreciate your honesty, Heurot," I said. "I'll not betray your confidence. And I'm glad to hear Sonjeur de Duplais treats you better than his friend the mage treats *his* poor servant."

"Oh, damoselle, if you thought . . ." Pausing at the last bend of the narrow stair, Heurot shook his head and lowered his voice. "My master is no friend with *that* one. Sonjeur de Duplais was employed by Master Dante when they both first come here, but the mage near burnt him to ash in displeasure at his work, and near broke my master's neck on that barge what burned. That's the day my master's hand got burnt by the devil's firework. Some say the dark mage was trying to cripple my master or kill him by leaving him to burn. And everyone knows there's more ill feeling between them than that."

His witnessing shook me a bit. Those ugly pocked scars on Duplais' right hand were visible evidence. But with only the good-hearted Heurot to support it, I was not yet ready to yield Duplais' benevolence.

When we reached the east-wing stair, the youth halted and bowed. "Heed his warning, damoselle. My master is the wisest man in Merona, and sure there's naught he fears in the world more than the dark mage."

THE MEETING WITH DUPLAIS LEFT me no time to read Cecile's book before the court presentation. Though it was easy to say which activity I'd prefer, I knew better than to risk Lady Antonia's wrath by skipping the formalities.

The queen sat amid her ladies and gentlemen. Bless all bright spirits, the mage was not present. But Duplais was there in a discreet corner, sober and proper, journal in hand. And the physician Roussel, his aspect pleasant as always, stood to one side, observing the fanfare. Hundreds of people lined the Presence Chamber, despite the lack of fireworks or exotic splendors. Tonight was an exhibition, not of science or magic but of politics, influence, and rank.

"Belinda de Mercier, daughter of Gerard de Mercier Conte Fermin and Beatrice de Marquay y Mercier-Fermin . . ."

One by one they announced our names. Each young woman strolled the length of the Presence Chamber, escorted by a gentleman of the household, and made formal obeisance to Eugenie. Each was applauded and cheered as the queen handed her a white rose, and the young lady took her place at the queen's side. My lack of rank placed me last.

"Anne ney Cazar, daughter of Madeleine de Cazar." At court, I was the child only of my mother. Perhaps I should adopt the Cazar name as Lianelle had.

A moment's resounding silence greeted the announcement. An immensely tall, slim man in a slashed doublet and tight breeches of peach-colored satin stepped to my side. Resplendent, perhaps a bit overresplendent, in pearl-studded gold embroidery and trailing lace, he swept a bow and took my hand, holding it raised in front of us as if my fingers were fragile and precious.

A tide of whispers swelled behind us. The carpet seemed to stretch a thousand kilometres. Skin blazing, I clenched my jaw and fixed my eyes on the gilt-edged painting of the Pantokrator looming over the queen's head. After the turmoil of the past hour, a meaningless ceremony before people I detested should not faze me, yet my hand shook like a coward's knees.

"You mustn't mind them." My escort's gaze remained forward, his expression the vague and meaningless hauteur of an experienced courtier. But his eyebrows flicked upward several times, and his head tilted ever so slightly my way. "Think of them as a flock of geese. I always do. Just attend your steps as you leave the hall, lest you foul your most charming slippers."

The fiery bands constricting my chest loosed just a bit. "Thank you," I murmured, without moving my lips. Never in my life had I been so grateful for a word.

His hand, encased in ridiculously long-fingered peach satin gloves, squeezed my fingers.

When we reached the end of the carpet before the throne, I dropped my eyes and curtsied deeply. My escort raised me. Without releasing my hand, he swiveled on his heeled boots and swept an elegant bow. "A pleasure, Damoselle de Vernase."

His use of my proper name popped my glance upward. I blinked. His pale hair was cut in an eccentric style, left long on one side and cut short on the other, where it could reveal an ornate dangling earring set with tourmalines. He rolled his merry blue eyes and retreated.

"Welcome, Anne." When I stepped forward at her soft greeting, the queen, exquisitely regal in midnight blue and diamonds, handed me a rose from the alabaster vase at her side. Her gaze remained lowered, as if she were the demure maiden. Her flawless cheeks bore a faint flush.

"Your Majesty."

I took my place with the other maids of honor, marveling at the power of good humor. My escort stood behind the other gentlemen of the court, a head taller than any of them. He made no effort at sobriety, winking, making faces, and twiddling his peach-gloved fingers at this person and that. Emboldened by his kindness, I swore to speak to him as soon as the ceremonies were over, rather than escaping at the first instant, as was my wont.

The queen dismissed the assembly and swept out of the hall, dragging a train of courtiers behind her like a comet's tail. My escort remained behind, speaking with a portly older man. He did most of the talking, waving his hands and making comical faces all the while, only occasionally bending his head low enough to hear the other man's words. He touched one satin finger to his lips whenever he laughed.

Slowing my steps, I practiced what I might say. *Good morning . . . sonjeur . . .* or *my lord. . . .* Guess too low, and I would insult him; too high, and I'd look the fool. They'd not have paired anyone too well regarded with me. *Thank you . . .* For what? His pity? *Why are you so accustomed to tittering gossip at court?* That would certainly recommend me! *Have you a felon in your family, too? Dementia, perhaps?*

He exchanged elaborate bows with the portly gentleman, then strolled toward the doors opposite my own destination, waving and throwing kisses. He seemed to know everyone.

My feet tried to retreat, but I reminded myself that *he* had made the overture of kindness. Simple politeness permitted a response. Demanded it. *Say something. Quickly, before he leaves the chamber.*

No sooner had I sped around the crowd and between two slender columns, ready to intercept him, than he pivoted abruptly and headed back into the hall, quickly subsumed in the mob on the far side. Sorely disappointed, I joined the swarm bumping and pushing to exit the doors.

"Damoselle Anne de Vernase!" The loud pronouncement of my name made me flinch. A yellow-gowned stick of a woman wearing a topknot of the most unnaturally red hair stood midstream in the flow of courtiers, pointing at me. "Her Grace commands your attendance."

I didn't have to ask which *Her Grace*. Everyone in the palace knew the red-haired Morgansa, Lady Antonia's universally reviled waiting woman.

"This moment, please."

The crowd parted for the red-haired waiting woman. I raced after, lest she disappear before I knew where to go. We returned to the Presence Chamber, where Lady Antonia was engaged in animated conversation with a small group of courtiers. I could have located her with my eyes shut; her abrasive scent filled the air for a hundred metres in any direction. I hoped not to attract more ill favor with a sneezing fit.

After a suitably awkward interval, Antonia waved a jeweled hand. "Ah, dear Anne, come here."

Most of her little cadre melted into the departing crowd. A favored few adjourned at a short distance, whispering behind fluttering fans and gloved hands. Only one remained at her side—the tall young gentleman in peach-colored satin.

"This is the young woman I spoke of, Ilario. His Majesty's good-daughter . . ."

My spirit congealed. She was displaying me, putting me up for bids to one of the few people in this warren I cared to know.

He was not unattractive—a narrow, refined face, unscarred by disease or warfare, of the boyish kind that would leave his age unguessable well into his dotage. If a bit vacuous, the light eyes were certainly nicely proportioned. And if his mouth was a bit too wide, and his nose a bit too prominent to match an artist's ideal, who could care? A generous humor could make up for far worse blemishes.

He dabbed at his long, straight nose with a lace handkerchief. "Dearest goddess of maternal feeling, as I've said before, I do most enthrallingly value His Majesty's regard. And as you well know, your own desires are as the angels' wishes to my hand, but these matters are not—"

"You have lost yourself in frivolity for too many years, Ilario. It is time you settled."

Ilario . . . maternal feeling . . . Was it possible the kind, handsome, loquacious gentleman was Queen Eugenie's half brother? I knew him only by reputation. If Castelle Escalon had a court fool, it was Ilario de Sylvae.

The poor man was squirming. "Your Grace, you need not trouble your ever-lovely head. While exhilarated to make Damoselle Anne de Vernase's acquaintance"—he bowed gracefully in my direction—"and superiorly delighted at the prospect of a deeper friendship, which would allow speaking with her at length on the topic of foreign travel, which I understand is her singular specialty"—he slapped his hand on his lace-ruffled breast and tilted his body in my direction—"because, Damoselle Anne, you must understand that the idea of foreign travel simply petrifies me. Giant reptiles . . . ferocious birds . . . secret languages . . . Saints Awaiting, such a multiplicity of dangers!" He swiveled toward Lady Antonia yet again. "Yet, dearest, most honored goodmater, your excessive wisdom must tell you I could not possibly enter into any manner of serious negotiation that could wrench me from Geni's side. Whoever would see to her ladies' comforts and entertainment? I've neglected them terribly this tenday I've spent in the country—so tedious to deal with roof repairs and vine pests and mural painters, who are, perhaps, the god's most sensitive creatures—"

"Fires of Heaven, boy, quench your babbling!"

Cheeks scorching, unable to look at the man, I scoured my head for something to say that might alleviate the excruciating moment. Lianelle had always teased me for rehearsing conversations in my head. *Speak up, Ani! You never realize how very little you say, and when you do actually engage in a conversation, it comes out as stiff as a bone corset.*

"I—I am presently mentoring a young lady in Hematian customs, my lord . . . and would . . . be pleased to address your travel . . . concerns . . . at any time."

"*Sancte angeli*, damoselle, I shall anticipate such prospect of enlightenment with supreme elevation! Perhaps one day in my sister's inestimably hospitable afternoon salons." His fair complexion glowed as scarlet as a stormy sunrise. "Now, if you will please excuse me, *sacre mater*"—he bowed deeply—"and Damoselle Anne."

As he hurried away, the dowager queen threw her hands up in exasperation. Her elegant lady and gentleman followers snorted or rolled their eyes and drew in close around her.

This most extraordinary encounter had left me as worn-out as if I'd just played a game of chase and hide with my brother and sister. Only as I recovered could I parse the single important bit of information from the verbosity: The gossip naming Lord Ilario as the most ridiculous, empty-headed dandy in the court must certainly fall short of the truth.

The ducessa patted my arm. "Well, it was only a whim, *caeri*. Ilario does have some decent property and a fine income, thanks to an overindulgent and entirely inappropriate father. But perhaps even a bastard imbecile knows to beware a misalliance. Never fear, dear Anne, we shall find a man to provide you a comfortable establishment. A man . . . perhaps that's the problem here."

With a limp wave of dismissal at me, she gathered her friends, who burst into laughter as they drifted out of the hall.

I ground my teeth. To be publicly portrayed as a grasping conniver rankled sorely enough. But for the gentleman . . . Lady Antonia was his foster mother. No matter his vanity or less than stellar wit, I had felt the pulse of a generous heart. He deserved better of his own parent, even an adoptive one.

As I escaped in the opposite direction, I passed the physician Roussel in the shadow of a column. He inclined his back with a sober familiarity, as in our frequent encounters in the east-wing corridors. My cheeks blazed hotter than ever as I dipped my head to acknowledge his courtesy. From his position he would have heard everything. Stupid to care what a stranger thought of me. But in the case of this gentleman, a polite man new to court and uninvolved in my family's history, I did care.

I could not return to my own chamber fast enough. Churning with all the direction of beans in a boiling pot, I passed through the galleries into the queen's household. The other maids of honor were gathered at the top of the queen's stair, all talking at once. Though curious at their choice of meeting place, I'd no desire to join them. I'd had enough of court society for one day.

"Dearest Anne, did you hear the awful news?" Belinda de Mercier's flutelike voice, half choked with sobs, called down to me. "Lady Cecile is dead."

CHAPTER 11

17 OCET, NIGHT

Her heart had given out. The tale flew about the east wing like a trapped bird. By the time I'd changed out of my court gown, Lady Patrice summoned the household to the outer salon to await news of funeral arrangements and our related duties. Once we were gathered, she bustled off to the queen's apartments, bidding us remain close though the hour was late.

The ladies were quieter than usual. Frivolous occupations like cards and games were eschewed in favor of needlework and whispered gossip.

"Who would have dreamed Cecile was so ill?" murmured one after another.

Ill? I didn't believe it. Cecile de Blasencourt had been a healthy woman of middle age. She had walked energetically on our excursions, eaten well, and tried to reform those younger women who constantly complained of faintness or vapors, insisting that modern men no longer found cultivated frailty attractive.

Gravely worried? Certainly. Our last conversation nagged at me like an insect bite: the puzzle she was trying to put together that had something to do with my father, her warnings of danger, her concern that I not expose her connection to my mother.

The more thinking I did, the more difficult it was to sit still. I needed to learn what she had discovered. The book, back in my pocket, might have been ablaze.

Scarce three hours since, Duplais, a man who was a great deal more than the ambitious dullwit he projected in the household, had claimed that these events—which I took to mean this five-year chain of vanishings, murder, and betrayal, plus my sister's death and the attack in the wood—were all about sorcery. At Papa's trial, he had called their aim chaos, implying something more than the upheaval of a royal assassination or a traitorous queen. But corrupting the laws of nature? If the laws of nature had been set in place by a divine creator, then challenging them was a matter far beyond political upheaval. *Magic of a kind not seen in ages of the world.* Was such knowledge enough to seduce a man of science like my father? It was certainly enough to frighten a man of reason like Duplais.

"Damoselle Anne, your attention!"

The sharp remonstrance right over my head yanked me back to the present. Marquesa Patrice stood tapping her foot.

"Forgive me, my lady."

"Her Majesty wishes to send personal notices of Cecile's funeral to a number of her acquaintances in Hematia and Thanitar. She requires someone with language skills and a sensitivity to protocol to accomplish this task." Her lips pruned, as if acknowledging my competence might cause her own heart to fail.

"I'll be pleased to do whatever I can."

"Come to the Rose Room tomorrow afternoon at first hour."

I used the settled meeting as an excuse to leave, taking one of the candle lamps set out on a table beside the door. When sent on an errand a few days before, a wrong turn had taken me into a dusty little corridor that paralleled the outer wall. Evidently someone had miscalculated when the east wing's interior walls were rearranged for such amenities as stool closets and ventilation. The sole doorway off the corridor opened onto a small balcony cluttered with scraps of stone and broken plaster. I had sought out the balcony several times to get a private breath and allow birdsong or raindrops to muffle the incessant buzzing in my ears.

Unwilling to be interrupted as I read Cecile's book, I sped down a servant's passage that appeared to end in a blank wall, around the corner into the odd little stub of a corridor, and through the door onto the balcony. The night was sultry, the stars obscured by haze as I settled down to read.

The book purported to be a history of Delourre and Grenville, two northern demesnes major. The *Grande Demesne Gautier* the book called the two together, named for a blood family that had once claimed huge swaths of the mountains and heaths for its own.

Dated some twenty years previous, the book contained facts about the geography of the region, the ancient peoples who had settled it, the villages, towns, and holy sites. It detailed myths that had their origins in the area. The Gautieri had built their collegia magica in Delourre in the year 356—more than five hundred years ago. It had been the largest school of any kind in Sabria for more than three centuries.

The author proposed that rivalry between the Gautieri and another blood family, named Mondragon, was the root of the Blood Wars. Neither family nor the collegia bearing the Gautier name had survived the savagery. Papa had always said that whatever truth and nobility might once have existed in magic had surely been squandered in the Blood Wars. My mother's family, the Cazars, had foresworn magic entirely in repentance for their deeds during the wars.

I flipped through the pages, hunting a notation, a marker, anything that would explain why Cecile had given me the book. She couldn't know about Lianelle and the Gautieri books, unless someone from Seravain had told her. *Some relevance to our discussion of a few days ago*, she had said. Yes, my father had been born in the demesne of Delourre, but had never lived there since going off to war at eighteen. He had never mentioned the Gautieri or their collegia magica or the rival Mondragons.

Half an hour's pondering left me no closer to the answer. Convinced I had seen what was to be seen in the book, I headed for my bedchamber. Restless feet drove me past my proper turning. My head felt like an overstuffed partridge.

The storm had broken at last, and a warm, steady rain confined my walk to interior rooms and sheltered promenades. It had been raining the last time I had visited my mother in Nivanne. She had huddled in the corner of her locked room as a steady drizzle splattered on her brother's courtyards. Her dark hair, once as glossy as silk, straggled dull and limp. The eyes my father had compared to midnight oceans lit by stars stared wild and senseless from the smudged hollows of her face. For three days my once-beautiful mother had wheedled and begged me to take her away. But she could not remember my name or the violence she had done that caused me to beg her brothers to confine her. Three times she had come near leaving Montclaire in ash by setting fire to my father's bed, his clothes, or his study.

From the palace towers, from the temple, and from the town clock tower in Merona, bells pealed the middle-night shift from evening to the night watch—twelve strikes—their varied timbres making a somber conversation tonight instead of their usual peaceful changes. Even so late, the palace hummed with activity. An army of footmen flitted through corridors and stairs, tending the lamps. Chambermaids, messengers, seamstresses, hairdressers, and visitors crowded the passageways and galleries leading to the ladies' chambers. The passersby carried ewers, trays, or shoes, and information to be delivered with their services. *Lady Eleanor had breakfast with Dame Catrin. . . . Someone sent flowers to Lady Patrice. . . . They were arguing when I took Lady Collumet her tea. . . . The Baroness of Winternitz had three new gowns delivered. . . .*

As of their own mind, my feet took me past the Presence Chamber and ballroom, and around one of the giant mechanical clocks the king had placed in the heart of every wing, its shining cogs and gear wheels a reminder of the rational world. Soon I strolled the Kings' Portrait Gallery, spending a good while in front of my goodfather's likeness, trying to read the familiar features for some clue that would explain my father's long-buried resentments.

Before I knew it, I stood in the quiet passage that led to Lady Cecile's apartments. A footman wearing the ducessa's yellow badge stood at honors outside her door. He glanced my way. Curious.

My skin broke into a sweat. What was I doing here? I fled.

Back in my own room, I threw the red leather book on my bed. To solve a mystery, one needed clues. Cecile de Blasencourt had hinted she possessed more than just the book. But now she was dead, and I'd never know what she might have told me.

As distant thunder rumbled outside my window and a nearby drainpipe gurgled, conviction settled about me like a net about a fish: I needed to examine the ducessa's room before it was stripped of her belongings. Yet I dared not be seen where I didn't belong. What would I say to the guard, or to the lamplighters or servants or deadhouse attendants who might discover me there?

Anne the Upright, my sister and brother had called me—the elder sister who couldn't tell a lie without instantly confessing it, who chastised them for picking locks or pilfering sweets or keys or wine. Lianelle or Ambrose, either one, could have managed this better than Anne the Recluse. Anne the Coward, who refused to sneak out after bedtime on Midsummer's Eve, because she was terrified she might actually *see* faeries. That was in the days before science and reason had relieved me of my nighttime fears.

Perhaps my little gifts will make you bold enough to venture out . . .

I fingered the key hung round my neck and envisioned my mother in her filthy shift, chewing her fingernails to the quick, staring into nothing. *Your mother's condition precipitated . . . your sister dead . . .*

Lianelle's ivory case glared at me from the dressing table. I didn't need to run naked through Vernase, but I did need to walk unseen through the unsleeping west wing of Castelle Escalon. Was it possible?

I dipped a fingertip into the gray powder. Was it merely my distaste for hypocritical practitioners that caused this horrid wriggling sensation in body and spirit? Or was it the "sorcery" itself—the unexplained forces of nature some few mages were able to harness, pretending them the outgrowths of their singular power?

If the world was built upon the rules of physics and mathematics as I believed, a pinch of this would do nothing except perhaps intoxicate me into dreaming whatever I wished. Yet Lianelle had known I was a skeptic, and yearned for me to believe as she did. Something about her trinkets' making—whether one called the principles she had used magic or natural science—had gotten my sister murdered. No longer could I hide childish terrors behind science and reason.

I rang for Ella and asked her to fetch me wine. As I waited, I stowed the red book in the hidden drawer alongside Lianelle's ring and pendants. Once Ella had left me a pitcher of wine and a pewter cup, I emptied a green glass vial of nettle tincture Melusina made for my autumn sneezing and rinsed it clean. A pinch of the gray powder went into the vial, followed by two spoons of wine as near as I could estimate. As I shook it, the opaque mixture cleared to amber.

I pulled out the glass stopper and sniffed the contents. Odorless—no trace of the wine's bouquet. I let a drop fall from the slender glass rod back into the vial. Thin and watery. The next drop I let fall on my tongue. Tasteless.

Nothing happened.

Ridiculous. Did I truly expect my body to vanish?

I plugged the stopper back into the vial and slammed it onto the dressing table beside the key to the hidden drawer, and remembered . . . *The keyword is* aventura, my sister had written.

If the world was as I believed, speaking a random Aljyssian word should not make a speck of difference in the effects of a potion. But I whispered, *"Aventura,"* and dispensed another droplet on my tongue.

A frosty finger traced my spine. The outlines of the furnishings and walls smeared like watercolors. Then, as if I'd jumped from Sante Paolo's Pillar, the bottom dropped out of my stomach.

I gripped the bedstead, and in the moment's stillness objects re-aligned themselves. But at the same time the ever-present hissing and buzzing in my ears shaped itself into whispered words. Voices. From the passage. From outside the window. Through the walls. Louder and louder . . . from above, from below, inside, outside . . . quiet, angry, tearful, droning . . . and behind them all, like the reinforcing wall of troops behind a charging brigade, an onslaught of grief and terror, excitement, exaltation . . .

I slapped hands over ears to quiet the growing pandemonium.

It made no difference. Louder yet, innumerable streams of jumbled words and feelings flowed, boiled together until they became a mighty river of sound. Meanwhile tables and chairs stretched themselves and rebounded into proper shapes. Madness!

I stumbled to the door. No daemon throngs waited in the passage. Nauseated, I shoved open the casement. No unholy mob had gathered beneath my window. Clinging to the sill, I gulped the damp night air. Stupid to take secret potions, no matter who had made them. Trembling, terrified, I held out my hand. It was visible, of course.

How could I imagine such a thing could work? Sorcerers would tell me I had mixed it wrong or spoken the keyword too loud or too softly or that the stars were not properly aligned. Was this what had caused Lianelle's death? Rampaging voices in her head? A physical world that refused to steady, that somehow forced her into a mistake in her magic working?

It was lunacy to call the individual strands in the snarl *voices*. I closed my eyes and tried to shut out the noise. Mental discipline, my mother's family taught, was a matter of metred will. One step to suppress desire, another step to address each sense, controlling perceptions that might trigger desire. One step for each passion of the body, so that hunger, thirst, fear, or need might not drive one to yield. Summoning every practiced skill, I created an island of quiet in the torrent, a rock, a small fragment of reason. I clung to it, concentrated . . . until the babble receded to the edges of my mind.

Moving slowly, so that beds and chairs stayed in their shapes, I returned to the dressing table and the mirror that hung above it. *Stars and sky!* I blinked and squinted. I waved my hand before my face. My hand was visible . . . but only one. The actual hand. The mirror displayed no reflection. Even when I pressed cold fingers to the glass, only my bedchamber was visible.

A knuckle pressed to my mouth, I throttled panic. *The world is rational. Men and women who study the properties of light and lenses and optical instruments could explain what I see or do not see. First principles . . .*

I looked again, closer, straining my eyes until they hurt. I glanced behind me and then back at the mirror. All right. It was not that I was invisible. What I saw in the mirror was not what existed directly behind me. Lianelle's potion must have skewed my eyesight, just as it had afflicted my hearing. This was not magic but optics and alchemistry.

I rang for Ella.

The door opened. "Damoselle, did you need more—? Oh! S'pose not."

I held motionless and silent as she straightened the bedclothes, blotted a spill of water beside the basin, then pulled the door open again.

"Ella," I whispered.

She swung around and looked in my direction. But her glance passed through and over me, flicking away and darting about the room. "Damoselle?"

When I did not answer, she shivered and slammed the door. Ella had not tasted the potion.

Frost fingers traced my every bone.

Think, Anne. Perhaps the mixing had caused light itself to bend. Without analyzing the absurdity of this reasoning, I stepped into the passage. A liveried footman stood outside Belinda's door, a few metres down the corridor. A youngish man sporting a narrow mustache, he slouched against the wall, yawning and idly twisting one of the blue silk ribbons that dangled from his pouffed sleeves.

I tiptoed down the passage, halting directly in his line of vision. He did not move or acknowledge me. I waved my hand. His eyes shifted up and down the corridor, but did not rest on me.

Halfway back toward my room, I turned and spoke quietly. "Footman."

He immediately stood up straight and squinted up and down the corridor. At a loss, he spun and tapped on Belinda's door.

I fled to my bedchamber and slammed the door. Madness yet hovered at the verge of my thoughts. But whatever this chance, I had to take it.

Each drop a quarter of an hour. I retrieved the vial, removed the glass stopper, and dripped eight more drops on my tongue. *"Aventura."*

I would have two hours.

―――――――

LADY CECILE'S DOOR WAS NOT locked. The footman wearing the yellow badge was nowhere in sight. Exulting in my luck, I waited until a pair of chambermaids carrying clay pots of heated herbs passed by, then slipped through the door.

The ducessa's chambers were dark, the hearths and lamps cold, and the draperies drawn. I'd not thought to bring a lamp, but had no difficulty seeing my way. A wash of pale blue light limned the familiar furnishings as with winter moonlight.

During our tutorial sessions, the sitting room had always been comfortably cluttered, with writing materials near to hand, extra shawls or light blankets left on the chairs, teacups, playing cards, books and papers, and spools of embroidery silk scattered here and there. Now it was perfectly tidy. Books were returned to the cupboard by the hearth, leaving no evidence of the ducessa's choice of reading materials in her last days. Only blank sheets of paper lay on her writing table. No item of clothing or jewelry; no bit of needlework lay ready to hand. Even Belinda's stack of Hematian letters was gone.

The bedchamber was the same. Silver brushes were lined up like armored soldiers on her dressing table. The bed was smooth. Clothes hung straight and still in her wardrobe. Nothing was left to indicate that anyone had actually lived in these rooms. Someone had been here before me.

Disappointment weighed my spirit and feet with lead. The strain of keeping the rampant voices at bay threatened to blind me.

I didn't even know what to look for. I picked through the wide drawer in her writing desk and found no correspondence, no lists, no sketchbooks, no notations of any kind. Her bookshelves revealed a preference for romances and travel memoirs, none of which exhibited any quality of interest beyond any other, and a somewhat surprising interest in physics. She owned every one of Germond de Vouger's works.

I was searching her armoire, thinking I might find clues tucked among her scarves or undergarments, when a door shut softly. My heart near stopped.

"It must be here somewhere." The woman's voice, sharp as struck brass, came from the sitting room. "Orviene babbled to her incessantly. She's the only one who could have taken it, the meddlesome thing. What interest could she have had? Why is it *you're* the first to tell me? They should have come to me four years ago."

A lower voice, a man's voice, mumbled a response I could not decipher. Orviene had been one of my father's sorcerers, executed for treason. Silently, I closed the armoire and ducked behind a folding fabric screen in the corner beside the doorway, the best of bad alternatives.

"You can't be seen here," said the woman. "It would be remarked. I don't know why you insisted on coming."

Fabric rustled—satin skirts and softer fabrics. Hinges squeaked. Cabinet doors slammed, followed by a series of muted thuds.

As the litany of noises continued, I peered cautiously past the edge of the screen and through the sitting room doorway. Though her back was to me, the piled curls were unmistakable. Lady Antonia. She was pulling books from the shelves, flipping through the pages, and tossing them onto the floor alongside cushions, pillows, and shawls.

Her male companion was no more than a darker mass in the shadows by the outer door. Yellow light streamed from his extended hand. I could see no lamp. My eyes must be playing tricks. My stomach heaved, and the noise in my head threatened to swamp my barricades and engulf reason.

When Antonia had tossed aside the last volume, she spun around. The yellow light danced across her face, her painted lips thin and angry. "Stupid cow. Where could she have hidden it?"

She charged straight toward me, the screen quivering as she swept into the bedchamber. The yellow light followed, gleaming from the doorway.

Holding my breath, I pressed myself into the corner. Through the stretched, painted gauze of the screen, I watched her poke and prod the pillows and bedding, shaking out the hangings, and even kneeling to peer underneath. She pulled every drawer out of the armoire and dumped out its contents. Discarded cases and enameled boxes spilled jewelry, pens, buckles, and keys onto the floor. She pawed through the debris, mumbling curses. Clothing followed, gowns, shifts, undergarments, hose, skirts and sleeves. She examined every fold and pocket.

Unlike me, she seemed to know what she was looking for. The little red book, perhaps?

Angry and frustrated, the dowager and her companion soon retreated to the sitting room, and I breathed again.

"All right, so it's not here. I'd best get someone to straighten these chambers, or we'll have another scandal."

"So she didn't have it. You've been too hasty . . . endangered your plan . . ." I could only hear a few of the man's whispered words, but his tone of reproach rang clear.

Lady Antonia joined him at the door. "Easy for you to quibble. We intercepted a letter she wrote to her scholar friend in Tallemant. She claimed to have *the key to unravel the conspiracy and root it in the Blood Wars.* Perhaps she knew. Perhaps she lied. Either way, she was getting too close. The damnable woman was talking of going to Seravain to get the truth of the girl's death! No one would be able to silence the rumors once word got out. It *had* to be done."

Revelation rocked me on my heels. This woman, once Queen of Sabria, Queen Eugenie's own foster mother, spoke of murder.

The two stood by the door, arguing in whispers, not even half of their words audible. ". . . not afraid of taking action," said Lady Antonia. "We'll settle this tomorrow night . . . after cards . . . examine the codices. . . ."

"I'll go first," said the man.

As soon as Lady Antonia had followed her companion out the door, I scuttled across the room and peered into the passage, hoping to identify the man. But the corridor was deserted.

The certainty that I'd been right to come, right to suspect that this death was linked to Lianelle's, that all these terrible events were connected, cleared my head for the moment. An idea had struck as Lady Antonia emptied the wardrobe. The *key*, she had said. I thought I might know where to look.

I first picked out every key from the litter on the floor. She'd paid no attention to them, so clearly she had known these weren't the type of key she sought. Clutching the slips of brass, bronze, and silver, I poked around the decorative corners and scallops of the painted armoire—quite an old piece. Sure enough, behind a piece of green-painted scrollwork, similar to that in my own wardrobe, I found a keyhole. Many false starts later, I pulled open a long, narrow drawer. With a fierce joy, I snatched up the sole article in the drawer—a small pouch. I relocked the drawer and tossed the keys in the scattered debris.

As I slipped into the passage, Morgansa, Lady Antonia's red-haired waiting woman, rounded the corner with a pale, scrawny serving girl in tow. I flattened myself to the wall, skin awash with sweat, floundering for excuses. I'd no idea how much time had passed. The potion would wear off at any moment.

The woman bustled past, murmuring sharply to the child. ". . . tell no one or we'll have your mam thrown into the deepest dungeon in Sabria." Neither of them looked my way.

I sped through the corridors. To my dismay, a guard had taken up a post, blocking the passage to my bedchamber, and, of all people in the world, Portier de Savin-Duplais stood talking with him. There was no alternate route. My head throbbed so viciously, I was near screaming.

I slipped around the guardsman, and edged carefully past Duplais.

The Royal Accuser whirled in my direction. No more than three paces from him, I dared not move or breathe.

"Who's there?" he called, his glance attending the crossing passage, the silent doorways.

"N-none's here, sonjeur," said the guardsman. "Who could be here?"

I crept a step backward. Duplais shook his head. "Someone . . ."

Eventually he moved into the main passage. The guardsman pulled some kind of amulet from underneath his armor and kissed it. I ran.

By the time I reached my bedchamber my entire body shook with exhaustion. I threw myself on the bed, pulled a pillow over my head, and fought to hold on to my defenses. But fabric and feathers could not hold off chaos.

Confusion, terror . . . those were my own. But the voices themselves encompassed every possible expression: a child crying with a nightmare, a mother's comfort, a lover's whispers—oh, sweet heaven, I had never imagined such tender eloquence—a husband's grief, a woman's hunger, an argument over money, a drunken tavern tale . . .

Wonder and amazement nibbled away at my terror, and I began to truly listen, thinking of each voice as a distinct mind that existed somewhere in the encompassing night beyond my window. Madness! Yet as the clamor began to fade, I found myself straining to hear more, opening my ears, my mind, my soul—wherever this strange phenomenon was occurring. Two distinct presences lingered long after the rest.

One was little more than a cool stillness, quiet and wary. Surely it was my own mind that shaped unspoken curiosity into a word. *Who?*

And the second, so faint, yet clear as honed steel, embedded a dagger in my soul. A voice that testified to pain beyond bearing. A voice—great Creator of Heaven and Earth—a voice I knew, though I had never heard it so bereft of hope or joy: *Impossible. Impossible. Yet you feel so near tonight. Hear me, child of my mind, daughter of my heart. I am not what they name me. Help me. By the bones of Heaven's Gates, Ani, help me. . . .* It was my father.

CHAPTER 12

18 Ocet, midmorning

"Papa!" The cry burst from my lips as I shot up from my pillows, my heart galloping. Sunlight glared through my window, accusing me of loitering while lives hung in the balance.

Doubt, skepticism, all those things I expected to overwhelm me as I roused to the new day were nowhere in evidence. Scarce more than a dozen words sorted from chaos had shattered Reason—the truest god of my two-and-twenty years. The sense of my father's presence had been immense, so vivid, so *real*, as if for that moment I had lived inside his flesh. Somewhere he existed in torment, captive, innocent of the crimes the world laid at his feet . . . that *I* had laid at his feet. Neither wish nor dream, that moment had borne the undeniable, sharp-edged clarity of truth.

Beyond the horror at his state, beyond the guilt of my own betrayal, the certainty of his life limned every moment with a joy I had not felt in five years. I had to find him. I *would* find him.

The green glass vial stood innocent on my dressing table, tempting me to taste its contents once again and open my mind to mystery. Was the potion magic? Did it spur some intervention of the saints and angels I'd scorned since I was fourteen? I had to consider, for what science could explain my walking about unseen, or hearing the prayer of a man I believed more vile than any daemon?

I had succumbed to the temptation repeatedly on the previous night—twelve more drops, three more hours of racked senses. The unceasing battery of human joy and grief, anger, longing, hatred, and ecstasy near shredded my mind, yet I had held together, listening, tasting, examining every word and emotion until exhaustion hammered me to sleep. Not another whisper of my father had I sensed. Yet still, on this bright morning, I believed. Magic. In the result, if not the act.

Though shallow sunlight insisted that half the day was gone, I was not late for my duties. All was changed this day. Lady Cecile was dead—murdered.

Amid the turbulence of my spirit, I could scarce grieve for a woman I hardly knew. Yet she had not deserved to die in the vigor of her middle age. Justice demanded that I report what I knew, but who would believe it on my word alone? The dowager queen, once the Queen Regent of Sabria, a murderer. And for what?

I patted the empty pockets of my skirt, searching for the prize I'd snatched from the ducessa's wardrobe. I surveyed my floor and the dressing table, yanked open the armoire and the night cupboard. Anxiety rising, I rummaged among the bedclothes I'd rumpled in my restless night. And there it was.

A palm-sized pouch of gray silk. Familiar, though I couldn't recall where I'd seen one like it. But inside . . . I unclipped the brass ring at its neck, tore at the laces that held it closed, and upended it over my palm. A tight roll of thin paper slipped out.

I smoothed it on my table. Three diagrams appeared on the flimsy page, not printed but precisely scribed in ink, and not recently, from the faintness of the marks. Each was a triangle, embedded in a circle. Words and symbols annotated the circled triangles, but in a language and symbology wholly unknown to me. Beneath the diagrams was a single line scribed in Lady Cecile's florid hand, this in common Sabrian.

"M vitet" or *"G vitet"—the essential question is which?*

Perhaps it was only because I'd read Lady Cecile's book that I immediately associated the *G* with the Gautieri and the *M* with the rival Mondragon family. *Vitet* was the Aljyssian word for *life*, which illuminated
nothing.

Disappointed, I replaced the little roll in the silk bag. No word leapt
out as a spellkey, and the drawings made no sense, especially as a cause for
murder. Yet I could not discount them.

These events were all about sorcery and, even as a skeptic, I had learned
enough throughout the years to comprehend the enormity of what Lianelle had stumbled into. My sister's spellwork had profoundly altered
nature, the test of true magic, so she'd always said. I had merely mixed the
powder and spoken the keyword she'd given.

Spirits of night! In moments I had unlocked my own hidden drawer
and pulled out the scrap of paper fallen from Lianelle's leather packet,
along with her lockets and wardstone ring. On it she had scribed a single
Aljyssian word: *andragossa*. I had assumed it the spellkey for Lianelle's
wardstone ring. But she had written the keywords for the vanishing
powder and the lockets in her letter. Why would she not mention the
ring's keyword in the letter, too, if it needed one? This was for something else.

As a story depicted on Syan screen paintings, the tale of my sister's
murder began to unfold. On a morning twenty-five days ago, Lianelle,
frightened and agitated about something she had discovered in an encrypted book of magic, had reclaimed her red leather packet from Adept
Guerin, scribbled a warning note to me, and inserted this scrap—perhaps
the keyword to open that very book. After returning the packet to her
friend, she had raced through the ravine behind Collegia Seravain to the
village and posted the book to me at Montclaire. On her return journey
through the ravine . . . Perhaps the murderer had laid an explosive trap, or
perhaps he drove her to mistakes that destroyed her. But sure as sunrise,
Lianelle's death was no simple accident.

Since that day, the murderer had been hunting the book, its key, and
any artifact my sister had created that might relate to them. Though the

villain had now retrieved the book from Montclaire, he couldn't use it. Cecile's paper was linked to the mystery, too, but I believed the key Antonia and her allies sought lay in my hand.

So what to do about it? For certain, my life was not worth a snip of tin, should they suspect I had it. And the danger was not mine alone. How long before someone pried into Lianelle's especial friends at the collegia and focused their attentions on Adept Guerin?

Over the next half hour, I dashed off a warning to my sister's friendly tutor. New evidence had convinced me that my sister's death was not accidental, I wrote, but had been deliberately caused by my father's rivals, who were likely residents of Collegia Seravain. Knowing the horrors befallen the conspiracy's victims, he must take every precaution not to meet the same fate. In addition, I begged him to forward any of my sister's personal belongings to me at Castelle Escalon. Surely the man was intelligent enough to infer that the packet Lianelle had been so anxious to annotate on the morning she was murdered left him in mortal peril.

The next letter had to be short and careful. Antonia had spoken of Lady Cecile's scholar friend in Tallemant, and the ducessa had owned every work by Germond de Vouger. Indeed, my father's longtime correspondent taught at the Collegia Astronomica in Tallemant. Using the book collection as an excuse, I delivered the sad news of Cecile's sudden demise and asked him to pass on the news to anyone in academic circles who knew her. As an aside, I mentioned her kindness and determination to help me sort out the dreadful entanglements of my father's treason. I hoped he would choose to take up the lady's cause or at least share what he knew.

I had just sealed the letter when a tap on my door propelled me to my feet. I whipped the silk bag and the letters behind my back. "Come."

"You're up, damoselle." Ella lugged in a steaming jug and filled my basin. "I peeped in earlier, but you were sleeping so hard." Setting down her burden, she assessed me frankly. "You'll be wanting a fresh gown, then. A sober one, in respect for the poor lady."

"Yes, certainly. And Ella"—as she selected skirt and jacket from the armoire, I smoothed the rumpled bedclothes, stuffing the gray silk bag under my pillow—"I've letters need posting, one to Seravain and one all the way to Eldoris in Tallemant. Sonjeur de Duplais insists on reading anything I send, but these are private matters, family matters, not at all anyone's business. Can you suggest someone who might do me the favor?"

She rubbed her lips with a plump finger, hesitating . . . considering.

"I swear to you, Ella, on my poor sister's Veil journey, these letters are wholly innocent. My sole purpose is to see justice done."

She squared her shoulders. "I'd be pleased to pass them to my brother. He mucks stables for the man who runs the coach route to Tigano and is friendly with the coachman. The coachman could post the Tallemant letter and take the Seravain one himself. Will that do?"

"Perfectly." I offered her a few coins from my slim purse. "For their trouble and yours."

"I'll pass it on. I don't need none of it. I'm happy to serve you, damoselle. Truly."

"I've another question, then. Who in the queen's household is considered reliable and . . . helpful . . . in private matters? Someone of influence, if you know what I mean."

Ella might be only fifteen, but every day as we became more comfortable, she'd become freer with her opinions. I'd found her observant and insightful. She pondered my request as seriously as if I'd asked what prayers to say at temple.

"The Ducessa de Blasencourt was one to help young and old, that's sure—angels guide her through Ixtador's trials. Some say Adept Jacard, Mage Dante's assistant, is ever ready with a kindness to a young lady, but he promises more than he keeps." She peered carefully at my face, then rubbed her ear with a thoughtful finger. "Perhaps he's not the one you want."

Though I'd felt a sympathy for the beleaguered adept, he could well be Antonia's partner.

"Well, you've had a say about Administrator Duplais from time to time, but I've heard from . . . reliable persons . . . that he's a generous man." The sudden glow of Ella's complexion affirmed my suspicions about the girl and young Heurot.

"No, not Duplais . . . and, please Ella, I trust you'll never mention my *private* business to anyone, even the most handsome, charming, and reliable young men."

"I never would, damoselle!" Her profound shock at the suggestion testified to honesty.

"So, what of the physician, Roussel?" The man's courteous demeanor and engaging humor, not to mention his comely aspect, had kept him in my thoughts. Without conscious direction, my eyes sought him in every crowd.

"I've not heard so much of that gentleman, damoselle. He's new just this summer, and stays quiet and apart from the householders. A bit shy, it's said. But then, I've heard no ill, neither. But if it's Her Majesty's favor you need, there's only one certain, though it's not the kind of one I'd think of, with you being the— Pardon, damoselle." The pale skin beneath her freckles glowed crimson as her hair. Her hands helped me into slightly less wrinkled skirts of black and indigo.

"Speak freely with me always, Ella. I'll never take it ill. I promise."

"It's just you're serious-minded, so quiet and always reading, thinking so much and of everything at once, while my other ladies— Well, you're just different is all, and this person is not a bit like you. But if you want Her Majesty to heed a request of yours, the one to ask is Chevalier de Sylvae. Though, god's truth, you must swear him to silence on his father's tomb, else he'll blab about it from here till Desen's month."

"Chevalier—you mean Lord Ilario?" Kind, yes, but I could not imagine the foolish gentleman in lace carrying weight with anyone. He'd been assigned to escort *me*, for goodness' sake.

Ella slipped the tight black velvet jacket over my arms and applied herself to the buttons. "Aye. The queen quite dotes on him, though lots, including *very* important personages, scoff and say— Well, they're not respectful. I'm sorry I couldn't come up with better."

"No, you've helped immensely. I thank you, as ever, for your truthfulness and discretion." The girl took my letters, dipped her knee, and departed.

Lord Ilario. So Eugenie de Sylvae doted on her foolish brother. I instantly thought better of her.

Tonight I must be watching when Lady Antonia left her card game to meet her partner in murder. Solve Lady Cecile's murder—the nearer one—and I would be closer to solving Lianelle's. Learn about the magic—*magic not seen in ages of the world*—and perhaps that would lead me to my father. Yet before all, I needed to see Ambrose. I needed to share all this with him. If murder stalked the conspiracy's victims again, then neither of us was safe.

My first official duty of the day was writing funeral notices in the Rose Room in the afternoon watch. But the household would already be gathered to gossip and mourn. Evidently when he was in residence, Lord Ilario was a fixture in the queen's salon.

I pulled the gray silk bag from under the pillows and tucked it into my jacket for safekeeping. Then I combed my hair carefully, hung my mother's gryphon pendant about my neck, and for once set out for the royal salon with anticipation and purpose. Somehow I would persuade Lord Ilario to get me into the Spindle.

NEVER HAS ANTICIPATION BEEN SO quickly frustrated. Lord Ilario did not attend the salon that morning. No one did, save Lady Patrice. "I'm sending everyone to see to their mourning clothes," she said, fluffing the black lace at her sleeves. "Her Majesty keeps to her bed today. After such news, a troubled night is only to be expected. Here's the message she wishes conveyed to Cecile's friends in Hematia and Thanitar. . . ."

I RETIRED TO THE ROSE Room and for five hours wrote and rewrote the same message. By the end I could not have said what language was my own or whether my script was at all readable. The marquesa herself had abandoned me hours before.

I wriggled and unkinked my stained fingers, stacked the letters to await the queen's seal, and left them as the marquesa had directed me. As I turned to go, the door from the inner room burst open.

"Maman! Maman!" The Queen of Sabria stumbled through the doorway, clad in a rumpled white shift. Her unseeing gaze darted about the empty room. "Don't go home, Maman! I smell smoke. I hear the dogs . . . the horses . . . Old Tomas screaming. . . ."

"Soft, my lady," I said, taking her arm as gently as I could, remembering how my own mother had soothed nightmares. "These are but imaginings. Let's call the angels to bring you sweeter ones."

I led her through the doorward's chamber—surprisingly devoid of guards or Doorward Viggio this afternoon—and through her apartments, into her bedchamber. None of the queen's ladies occupied the nearby retiring room. The chamber itself was dark as pitch, the heavy drapes drawn, the bed curtains down.

Eugenie swayed and stumbled. I wrapped my arm about her slender waist, hoping we would make it to the bed before she crumpled. My head only reached her chin.

"Here," I said, drawing the curtain into its silver clip. But as I helped the queen into the bed and smoothed the silk sheet over her bare legs, I could not help but notice that the inside of the bed enclosure reeked of smoke and charred grass and—disgusting—burnt meat. The half curtain on the far side—the one that was never to be closed—hung heavy with the rest.

Once Eugenie slipped into an unsettled sleep, I opened the narrow panel. Then I examined the bedclothes, the frame, the tester, not at all sure what I was searching for. On my knees I peered into the narrow gap between the rope sling and the floor, stretching out my arm to reach what the gloom hid.

I knew it when I found it. My fingers touched a strand of barbed metal, and the world burst into searing, choking flame. I yanked my hand back. It wasn't flayed, nor was the chamber burning. Using a shoe, I fished out the barbed bracelet and wrapped it in a linen towel from the bedside table.

A few days before, I would have called the thing a mechanical mystery. On this day, I was not so sure. Anyone with access to the bedchamber could have put it there.

"Sleep well, sad lady," I said, and left the way I'd come.

On the way back to my room, I detoured by my little balcony and tucked the wrapped bracelet under a pile of debris. My caution felt entirely justified when I noted that Duplais had moved a bench to the junction of the main passage and the corridor where the maids of honor were housed. He stood and bowed, then replaced his spectacles and resumed jotting notes in his journal. But his scrutiny scorched my back as I passed him by.

IT REQUIRED ONLY A BRIEF, discreet questioning of a drowsy sweeping woman to discover where Lady Antonia was to play cards that evening—a small suite of rooms perched on the highest level of the east wing, where they could catch the morning sun and the fairest breezes from the south. According to the servant, the queen had used the out-of-the-way suite for childhood lessons in music, dancing, and painting. Currently, she used them for games and other quiet activities she wished to pursue away from the unending bustle of the household. Nervous excitement put me on watch early.

The suite's atrium, open to the night air, could be accessed from above or below. A short steep stair led down from the sheltering bulk of the northeast tower. And shallow flagstone steps spiraled upward from the east-wing galleries.

It was a lush night. A profusion of stars glittered through the arches, and the mild, heavy airs promised lingering summer instead of early autumn. Perhaps it was the unsettled season that ran my blood so cold. The breeze smelled of dead leaves and rot, when it ought to smell of ripe apples and meadow saffron.

I couldn't blame my megrims on the potion. Not wishing to waste it, I'd not taken it yet. I remained well hidden, tucked behind giant clay pots of scarlet hibiscus and whimsical bronzes of giant beetles, moths, and dragonflies. The position gave me an excellent view of the entry door and a liveried boy, who sat on a bench beside it, tending four lamps.

As I suspected it might, the evening had stretched well past the bells of eleventh hour. My back ached from sitting so long on stone. Just as I considered changing position, the door opened and the lamp boy leapt to attention.

"Divine grace, sweet Geni, *sacre mater*, and lovely young lady whose name I've most atrociously forgotten." Unmistakably Lord Ilario. "I must to my bed, as tomorrow I must notify my stewards to cancel my plans for Feste Morde. Dreadful as it is to utter, I do wish poor Cecile had found a more convenient time to pass the Veil. I was so hoping to sponsor a masque for this year's feste. Such a display of beauty and cleverness, music and camaraderie must surely honor those who journey Ixtador, and why not allow them the extra benefit of displaying it during the holy days? But then, a mourning term must not be violated in such times as we live in. Saints Awaiting, the terrible things I've heard . . . and, no, *mater amore*, I shall not repeat them. But now I'm wondering if the Temple might approve a *mourning* masque, all of us in black and dancing to seriously sober music—"

Muted voices interrupted Lord Ilario, and a long, fair arm shoved him out the door.

"There, you see, sister mine, you *are* capable of laughter even in a grievous time. Though I don't see why it must be at my expense, when I've worked so diligently all evening to cheer you. I'll expect proper gratitude tomorrow!"

This last he pronounced as the door closed in his face. He accepted a lamp from the boy. "Always do your best to bolster grieving ladies, young pup," he said to the snickering lad, flipping him a coin. "Bolster!"

I shook my head at his inanity, while quite understanding why the queen kept him near. How could she ever be cross with one so singularly dedicated to the purpose of lightening her heart?

For a fleeting moment I considered following him down the stair to present my petition. But the opportunity to identify Lady Antonia's confederate might not come again. So I let him go.

Next out was the "lovely young lady" whose name the chevalier could not recall. To my surprise she was one of the maids of honor, a tall, plain girl named Marie-Claire, daughter of the Duc de Tallemant, the wealthiest lord in all of Sabria. Gangle-legged and haughty, she'd never once spoken in our morning sessions. The door closed behind her and she soon vanished down the flagstone steps, carrying her lamp.

Antonia would likely be leaving soon. "*Aventura,*" I whispered as eight drops of the tasteless potion slid down my throat.

The voices came first this time. Or perhaps I just was listening so intently for them. Whispers quickly swelled into a clamor of excitement, anger, and nightmare. I swallowed hard and allowed them to grow unchecked, though my skull felt like to crack and surely my eyes bulged from their sockets. Searching, listening, I whispered silently: *Papa, can you hear me?*

I'd no illusion that it could be so. I wasn't even sure if the words I heard were voiced in actuality or in thought, or if somehow they were shaped solely from the very stuff of life.

The game room door swung open again. The lamp boy jumped to his feet. I forced the dizzying cacophony aside, blinked until the smearing colors of the scene settled into shapes, and stepped out from behind the hibiscus. Better to test my state of visibility with the boy.

I stomped my foot. Alerted, he squinted straight through me into the dark. Picked up a lamp and turned it brighter. And vouched no sign of noticing a woman standing five metres from his nose. I breathed again.

Lady Antonia soon emerged. "Her Majesty wishes to linger for a while," she said to the boy, as she took the proffered lamp. "Fetch a flask of oil from the guard post and return here to await her pleasure. I'll snip your ears tomorrow if I hear her lamp was dry when she was ready to go down."

"Aye, Your Grace." The boy snapped a bow, hung the sole remaining lamp on a hook beside the door, and raced up the steep stair toward the tower.

Antonia raised her lamp high and examined the atrium. "Where are you?"

I froze. Her inspection passed over me three times. Holding my breath, I peered over my shoulders to make sure I wasn't jostling a branch or otherwise signaling my presence.

But she paid me no mind. After a moment, she lowered her lamp and threw back her head. With a low, throaty laugh that unnerved me soundly, she spun in place until her silk skirts billowed and the lamplight scribed a circle of fire around her. "So near! So near! I *do* feel you close, dearest, as if you breathed on my cheek. I cannot wait for you tonight. But soon, love."

Still chuckling, she headed down the stair, her steps as light as a girl in her teens.

I'd never have picked Lady Antonia as a woman for romantic passion. But then, I'd never have picked her as a murderess, either. Who was she expecting?

My slippers scarce whispered as I slipped down the stair after her. Movement blurred the silver-blue wash of light before my eyes, forcing me to follow more slowly than I liked. But that was the only thing saved me from careening headlong into the man who rounded the corner on his way up.

I hugged the wall.

Ruddy-skinned and compactly muscled, he was the kind of man who, while not exceptionally large or exceptionally beautiful of feature, exudes a confidence that demands admiration. His thick brown beard, longer and fuller than most courtiers wore, imparted a strength to his jawline that might or might not be accurate. Though he seemed familiar, I could not place him in my recollection of the king's household lords, nor in the once-rich stream of Montclaire visitors. He was not a man one would fail to notice.

Dressed in fur-lined cloak, puffed satin breeches long out of fashion, and a rakish, feathered bonnet that shadowed his face, he sped past me, his long stride devouring the stair. Perhaps it was my gasp of surprise or my heart's pounding that alerted him, but he peered over his shoulder straight in my direction. But he said nothing and did not slow. He could as easily have been examining the rustling bougainvillea that draped the wall behind me. So I told myself, as the mellow breeze sent shivers chasing up and down my back.

Antonia's footsteps clattered on the lower stair. She had not challenged the man, so *she* must know him. Yet I could not but think of the queen left alone, without even a lamp boy within hail.

Damn and blast. I reversed direction, reaching the atrium just in time to see Eugenie de Sylvae standing in the open doorway, hand pressed to her mouth as if to suppress a cry. The wind swirled through the open arches, rattling the hibiscus leaves, lifting the queen's loosened hair into a dark tangle around her flushed, lovely face, painted tonight with butterfly wings beside her eyes.

The man had dropped to one knee in front of her and spread his arms wide, the perfect image of a lovesick chevalier, his cloak draped gracefully behind him, revealing the hilt of his sword—a coiled dragon studded with rubies. He reached for her hand and leaned forward to kiss it.

Another gust rattled the lamp and set it swaying on its hook. The gold flame flared inside the glass chimney and winked out.

In a rustle of silk the man rose, and the two shadowed forms retired together. The door closed softly. Eugenie knew her visitor and was not afraid of him. No help was needed.

I knew how things worked in courtly circles. Certainly no one in the household pretended the royal marriage thrived. Yet I felt disgust as I retraced my steps in pursuit of Lady Antonia. For certain *she* knew the visitor. She had facilitated the assignation, getting rid of the boy long enough for the man to arrive unobserved. That alone was enough to set my back up.

THE DOWAGER QUEEN WAS HURRYING past the royal apartments when I caught up to her. She did not acknowledge the bobbed knees or inclined backs of servants, nor even the greetings of what few courtiers passed so late of an evening. Her pace changed noticeably as she descended the stair into the window gallery. She might have been out for a leisurely, late-evening stroll. Pausing in one window niche after another, she gazed on the middle-night view of the city.

I loitered a few metres away, the certainty of my invisibility assured when a footman ducked into the window niche beside me and relieved himself. If the blood rushing to my cheeks did not expose me, naught was going to do it.

Only when the gallery was entirely deserted did Antonia resume her determined path, reversing course and scooting into a wide passage that ended in a tall window bay. I slipped along behind her as she hurried past two doors, chained shut, to the far end of the passage. Just outside the last door sat a writing table covered with untidy stacks of books, grimy canvas bags, and innumerable ink bottles. A large ledger book sat atop all.

Antonia rapped sharply on this door, retracting her hand just as quickly. When no one answered, she used a book from the desk to depress the latch and nudge the door open. She poked her head in. "Are you here?"

Recognizing that I had only moments to act, I slipped off my shoes, stuck them in my belt, and pelted down the passage, slipping through the doorway just behind her. It was all I could do to keep from bumping into her. Only after I was inside did I have time to call myself an idiot. Sorcerers claimed they could detect spellwork, and this was assuredly a sorcerer's den.

To my left the apartment nearly sagged under the clutter—two tall cupboards, doors open to expose haphazard stacks of papers, books, and instruments I could not identify in the dark. Bottles, jars, and tins burdened shelves mounted on the walls. Three long tables and the floor were piled with everything from baskets of sticks to rolls of linen to entire plants uprooted.

Lady Antonia betook herself to my right, a neat and pleasant space, where a single long divan fronted by a low table faced an entire wall of windows, unmasked by any shred of drapery. Were it daytime, the room would be flooded with sunlight.

The lady set her lamp next an unlit one sitting atop a tall stool. The stool was a type tutors favored. Its lid, raised, would reveal a boxlike cavity where the tutor could tuck away papers or maps—or the mechanical toys sneaked into lessons by annoying little brothers. The wall where I stood, adjacent to the door, supported the only other furnishing, a set of whitewashed bookshelves crammed with books.

Antonia flopped on the couch for a time, then bounced up again and paced in circles. Agitated. Waiting.

I remained beside the door, lest I need a quick escape. A marble hearth gaped dark and cold on the wall opposite me. A great ring of amber or glass was embedded in the bare wood floor just in front of the hearth. A subtle gleam, as if the great ring had captured stray beams of Antonia's lamplight, sketched out its dimension—perhaps twice the diameter of the one in Eugenie's bedchamber.

Uneasy, I shoved the muted voices deeper behind a wall of silence. A withering quiet engulfed me, a weight upon my spirit as ominous as the fiercest thunderstorm of summer in the hour before its breaking, a wrongness that crept through my soul like settling frost.

I blinked and shuddered, welcoming the starry expanse visible beyond the wall of windows.

Blowing sighs of exasperation, the lady snatched up her lamp and strolled past the cluttered tables and shelves. She touched nothing. All her actions shouted *caution*. Before very long, she picked up her lamp, moved past me to the bookshelf, and began reading the titles. On the stretch of bare wall beside the bookshelves, just next my shoulder, hung the room's sole decorative item: a small, exquisite painting of a lighthouse standing sentinel on a rocky headland, sending its beams into a stormy sky.

The tower bells tolled first hour of the night watch. I fingered the vial in my pocket. By half past second hour, I'd need to drink more of the potion.

"Where are you, fool?" Antonia muttered, slamming her lamp on the schoolmaster's stool. "Who knows how long we have?" Her fingers tapped rapidly on the table, diamonds and sapphires sparkling in the light beams. Of a sudden she leapt up and charged straight toward me, wrenching the door open to peer into the passageway. Did she raise her elbow, she would plant it in my chest. Her abrasive scent tickled my throat. I shrank to the wall and tried not to breathe.

She moved away, only to circle back before I dared shift my position. A low bench, cluttered with empty cups and pitchers, prevented me sliding farther from the door.

I swallowed a cough and pressed my hand to my nose. Ludicrous. By the miracle of Lianelle's potion, I lurked unseen, poised on the verge of uncovering a murderous conspiracy. Yet at any moment I could be exposed because of this woman's proclivity for foul perfume!

My eyes watered. Throat clogged with phlegm, I buried my mouth in my sleeve, but soon felt the onslaught of an uncontrollable spasm. I had to get out or be discovered.

On the lady's next approach I gathered my skirt and sleeves into the slimmest possible profile. In the moment she yanked open the door, I squeezed through, nudging it only slightly as I passed. Before reaching the end of the passage, I sneezed three times over and began coughing as if my lungs would burst.

Any hope of returning to the mage's chamber or lurking in the passage to see who arrived was quickly overthrown. The vile scent lingered in my very pores, and the coughing spasm simply would not stop. The door opened and Antonia stepped out. . . .

Furious and frustrated, I fled, speeding through the windings of galleries and stairs in search of a remedy, moving fast enough the lonely footmen or light boys could not remark a disembodied sneeze. Common sense took me to a buttery that served the deserted reception rooms on the ground floor. Not only did I find stiff, bitter brandy amid the wine and ale casks, but also honey and spices.

I threw together a pale imitation of Melusina's favorite nostrum, sipped my crude concoction, coughed, sputtered, and sipped again. By the time the syrupy elixir had done its work, I sagged, on the verge of tears, against an ale barrel. My head throbbed, chaos battering at my feeble control, my morning's fierce optimism blighted by the knowledge that my father's agony had stretched one more sun's turning, and I'd come not one step closer to easing it.

The tower bells struck a quarter past second hour. I'd be visible soon, and I had no wish to prolong this exhausting state. I dragged myself to my feet.

A blinding concussion staggered me. Back to the stone wall, I raised my arms in feeble defense. No assailant stood within the silver-washed shadows, yet the hammer blows continued. A brutal, merciless barrage. Anger. Malevolent fury. Murderous indignation. Inside me. Filling me like a poisonous flood. Drowning me in feelings that were not mine.

I crumpled, hands clutching my head. *Stop!* I screamed it. In voiced word or in mind only, I could not have said. *Please, stop! Have mercy!*

Abruptly as it had begun, the noise stopped. Or so it seemed for one brief, blessed instant. But perhaps the source was only drowned in turn, for my discipline collapsed, unleashing the flood.

For some incomprehensible time, I huddled in the corner, arms thrown over my head as my mind ached with unknown joys, raged with unknown anger, sobbed with unknown anguish. Burying my own cries in my arms, I wept for the sorrows and fears of thousands.

Only as the voices faded and silence crept across the dusty flagstones did I hear an echo of the previous night. Not my father's voice, but the other. The quiet, curious one.

Who? As a silken sheet it floated over my knotted limbs. As a pallet of eiderdown it cradled my hurts. *Are you injured? In danger? Is this new to you?*

Naught had been so terrifying as this. These words were not random passions, not a collection of scraps, but the communication of a single mind purposefully directed at me. Impossible. Madness. As if one could hold a conversation wholly without speech.

Have you any idea what you've done? Just speak clearly, focused on my voice, and I'll hear. Gods, there has been no one . . . ever. . . . Not even my father's pain had spoken such loneliness. *Trust me.*

Even were the speaker real, how could I trust? No face to read. No background, no reputation, no identity, no consequence for falsity. This overwhelming mystery that he—for of all things, I understood the speaker was a man—seemed to comprehend, but I did not. Madness, waiting to ensnare me.

One word . . .

But I did not, could not, answer. And when true silence enveloped me, thick and safe as a winter cloak, I crept back to my bed and let sleep hush my weeping.

CHAPTER 13

SOLA PASSIERT, MORNING

On the morning after my frustrated spying adventure, the queen's salon was crowded. An array of delicacies had been spread on a sideboard: peeled oranges with cinnamon, breads, sliced cheeses, sugared pastries, and baked apples sprinkled with nuts. A towering crystal sculpture was draped with fat, firm grapes. Unable to remember when I'd last eaten, I filled a plate and perched in a window seat that gave me a good view of the comings and goings.

The ladies of the queen's household shifted about the room, murmuring and fretting in soft, quick movements, like doves in a dovecote. A few gentlemen stood here and there, sober anchors in the fluid landscape, ready to offer soft grunts of sympathy or affirmation as the ladies required.

The gentleman the queen had welcomed so late was not among them. I'd yet to recall where I'd seen him before. To my disappointment, Lord Ilario was not among the gentlemen, either.

Duplais stood diagonally across the room from me, jotting notes in his ever-present journal, as householders brought him requests or questions. As the queen's household administrator, he dealt with accommodations and servants for her ladies and gentlemen, arrangements for entertainments, and every trivial matter from supplies of hairpins to arranging a

nursemaid for Baroness Agnecy's mother. A man of his acuity and determination could not be satisfied in such a position, something between a
steward and a nursemaid for seventy women and their requisite servants,
one mage, one adept, and a physician. Portier de Savin-Duplais was more
than that.

Lady Antonia flitted back and forth from the inner rooms, snapping at
ladies and servants equally. She dispatched messengers to fetch the royal
seamstress and a ribbon merchant, as we of the household must wear black
badges on our sleeves throughout the mourning period for Cecile. She
organized a party of ladies to sit with Eugenie when Verger Rinaldo came
from the deadhouse to discuss funeral rites, as the Ducessa de Blasencourt
had no children to see to such details.

Antonia looked stretched, as if her skin could barely contain her hostility, not at all the woman who had danced like a maiden in the night air.
Her meeting with her partner in murder must not have gone well, even
after I'd run away.

The difficult thing on this morning was pursuing the necessities of the
day rather than the experience of the night before. *Who?* I could ask that
myself. Someone in this very room? Though the immediacy of the experience tempted me to imagine the speaker as someone nearby, it was clear
that the other voices I heard came from every level of society and every
possible kind of person. Some would assume the voice daemonic, but the
memory bore no taint of evil. Its owner had responded to my cry of
pain—heard me, just as I heard all the others.

Reason insisted it was but dream or madness. Yet the bits and pieces—
the quality of that voice, the restrained emotion, the caution and care,
curiosity and longing—felt genuine, fragments of a single whole. A person. Real. Which implied that *all* the voices I heard were real. Angels'
mercy, my father lived.

The sun bathed my back with warm, soothing fingers. A farewell of
sorts, for this was the day out of time, Sola Passiert, the Day of the Sun's
Passing. From today until spring, night would be longer than daylight.

Oddly, on a morning of such dire certainties and pressing anxiety, the
food tasted extraordinary, and not simply because I was famished. Rich,

sweet, crisp, and tart, every bite exuded flavor. When a red-haired serving girl offered a tray of warm couchines, I could not resist. The sweet's thin layers were bathed deliciously in butter, honey, and ground almonds, and I relished the first sticky bite as if I had never tasted food at all. Such pleasures seemed obscene in light of my family's disaster, in light of Queen Eugenie's dead children and tormented dreams.

"D-damoselle Anne de Vernase, I believe." Physician Roussel bowed gravely as I came near choking on a flake of pastry. I'd not even noticed his approach.

I could no more than bob my head in answer as I fumbled for a serviette.

"Her M-majesty requests your attendance within."

"Now?" I croaked, between futile attempts to clear my throat.

His gray eyes sparked, and he relieved me of the plate, which threatened to dump its sticky remnants in my lap at any moment. "Unless you lose c-c-consciousness from an overdose of c-couchine, I believe you will be summoned when she is finished with her c-current guest." The hard *c* sounds creased his brow only fleetingly. Though he worked diligently to minimize his afflicted speech, he seemed at ease with it.

"With Lord Ilario, perhaps?" I said as he set the plate aside, whipped out a kerchief, and presented the spotless square of linen to me.

"None so amiable." The humor fled his square face, and his forefinger touched his gray-tinged mustache as if to hush his own opinion. "She c-consults her mage at present."

"Ah. I'll wait, then." I dropped my eyes and dabbed at my fingers, trying to force my own expression into proper neutrality. "Divine grace, sonjeur."

A moment passed. I glanced up, surprised to find him still there.

He cleared his throat. Clasped his hands behind his back. "It's never foolish to be w-wary of sorcerers."

Better not to acknowledge the softly voiced sentiment, no matter how fiercely I wished to agree. Instead, I returned the now-sullied kerchief. "Thank you . . . uh . . ."

I could not decide whether to reveal that I knew his name.

He must have taken my hesitation for maidenly encouragement. "Roussel," he said. "Ganet de Roussel. Though we lack formal introduction, D-dame Fortune seems intent on our meeting. I doubt I've c-c-crossed paths with any of dear Cecile's young ladies with such frequency." A smile softened his well-proportioned lips, once he'd gotten the difficult sounds out of the way.

A knot of pride and anxiety had forever choked me in the presence of "eligible men." Taking resolution in hand, I swallowed hard, met his gaze, and returned the smile. "Would you care to share the window seat as I await my summons, Physician Roussel?"

His turn to hesitate. His eyes darted about the chamber.

Embarrassment scorched a path from my toes to my cheeks. "I'm too forward."

"Alas, damoselle, a physician without title is c-c-considered distasteful, unfit company for the q-queen's salon. And he is often"—his pale gray eyes returned to mine, introducing a certain deliberate quality to his sentiments—"*c-counseled* as to whom he may address and whom he may not. Perhaps on another day, in a d-different window seat, I might be allowed such a p-pleasure."

He bowed and left the room, a finer figure than any man present.

Stupid, this business of rank. I could not fault the shadings of bitterness in his manner. I supposed a physician of unremarkable background might not be considered a useful enough match for a king's gooddaughter, even the Great Traitor's child.

A flush of ferocity supplanted all other considerations as I reclaimed the knowledge of these past nights. Papa was *not* a traitor. I wrenched my gaze from the doorway, only to find Duplais watching me from his corner.

With irreproachable sobriety, I nodded to him. No more childish rebellion. No more slips of control. Not until I understood his purposes and what use I might make of him in order to locate my father.

"Damoselle Anne de Vernase." One of the household ladies held open the inner door. I rose, cursing sticky pastries as I dusted my lap for flakes. Duplais' eyes, and a number of others, followed me as I left the room.

———

As the queen's gentlewoman and I traipsed through the octagonal waiting room, down the passage, and into the royal apartments, it crossed my mind that I might have an opportunity to beg the favor I needed from the queen herself, bypassing her foolish half brother. Yet how great could be the influence of a queen involved with traitor sorcerers in the past and so blind to her own foster mother's wickedness?

My first glimpse of the company in the queen's sitting room deepened my doubts.

Eugenie herself might have been one of the moonlit dancers depicted on the canvas behind her. Cocooned in layers of blue silk, her slender form seemed fragile, her softly flushed cheeks as transparent as watercolor, and her eyes larger than a human woman's ought to be.

Lady Antonia had planted herself on the couch beside the queen, Eugenie's hand firmly in her jeweled grasp. Her stiff curls brushed the queen's smooth black tresses, as she murmured to her adopted daughter in such low tones, none else could possibly distinguish the words.

Lord Ilario, resplendent in vermillion brocade, sprawled on a divan much too small for his long limbs. As I made obeisance to his royal sister, he twitched and snorted as happens with those who've dropped off to sleep from boredom.

To my dismay, Mage Dante hovered behind the queen, near the hearth, where an entirely unnecessary fire burned. The mage looked ill on this morning, gray-skinned and drawn, leaning heavily on his staff as if he were a much older man. His hard-edged eyes had sunk yet deeper beneath his dark brow. He served as the *mortuis memore* in this tableau—the death's head crafted into every painting, every sculpture, and every building created since the Blood Wars as a reminder of our trials to come in the realm of Ixtador Beyond the Veil.

The crimes of both civil authorities and the rival sorcerous families during that conflict were so grievous, so the Temple taught, that the Pantokrator had altered his creation, requiring the dead to traverse a bleak and barren wilderness, assaying ten barred gates to find their way to Heaven.

The consideration of Ixtador's trials roused the steel in me, just as the *mortuis memore* was intended to do. The souls of the dead could not progress through the gates without our honorable deeds on this side of the Veil; so we were taught. Did we fail them, they would wander until the last day of the world, when the Souleater would carry them off to the frozen netherworld.

More doubter than believer, I nonetheless appreciated the principle. What better could I do for Lianelle's memory than to succor Ambrose and rescue Papa? Justice—identifying her own murderer—would surely follow.

"Anne! Welcome!" Queen Eugenie's open hand brought me to my feet, but it was her face and voice that startled me. A soft smile transformed her entirely, as if the artist had laid a wash of diamond dust over her person. And a solid vigor imbued her speech, as a deceptive autumn breeze can ripple hair and skirts so gently while at the same time tumbling stripped leaves across the countryside. "I insisted on hearing who had penned these many letters, as I know Escalon's scribes have a shameful incapacity when it comes to foreign tongues."

My box of pages, now folded and sealed, sat on the floor beside her.

"It must have taken you a day, at least, and all in so lovely a hand and perfectly worded, as far as my own poor skills can attest. You have my deepest gratitude. My dear Cecile must certainly be well begun on her Veil journey, thanks to those like you who have offered such care in her memory." Her language reflected a pleasant animation of spirit, embracing and welcoming.

"I was pleased to be of service, Majesty." I floundered, hunting more words. This opportunity to request access to Ambrose must not be missed. "The ducessa was ever kind to me. Sadly, she was unable to—"

"Anne is such a talented girl," Antonia broke in. "Cecile was working to refine her manners in hopes we might secure the best match suitable to her unfortunate circumstances. We must do all we can for her."

Resentment heated my cheeks and sparked a cold ember in my depths.

"I'm sure Anne's manners are of the most excellent kind, Dama—natural grace without artifice, schooled with love by a gracious lady." Eugenie patted Antonia's hand as if to gentle the reproach, while maintaining her focus on me. "In truth, Anne, I have ever admired your mother, her devotion to her family, and her strength . . . to make her own life. And so lovely. Tell me"—in the span of two words, pain etched Eugenie's glowing skin—"how does she endure?"

The queen's kindness but fed the cold fire inside me. Dared I say what I believed about her two companions? I could not but feel the mage stirring across the room. Yet what safety did I gain by withholding my theories?

"The events of four years ago broke my mother, lady, though not of her own weakness. When I have solid evidence, I'll tell you and my good-father exactly the evil cause of her illness."

"Evidence is wicked limiting. Is it not, damoselle?" Mage Dante moved swiftly away from the hearth, taking up a protective stance beside the queen's couch. "It can prod belief in one theory over another. But alas, belief cannot prove the theorist's position. In fact, truth often eludes both evidence and belief. Is that not so?"

"Conceded," I said, the sap of debate rising in my blood. His argument could have come from my father's lips. "I should have said, When I have solid *proof*, the history of my mother's madness shall make a tale worthy of note."

Antonia tapped her bony fingers on the queen's hands. "*Caeri*, it's time for a rest. . . ."

But Eugenie's attention did not swerve. Shock etched her features. "Madness? Truly?"

Now, Anne, I told myself. *Say it now.* "Four years ago, when my mother was questioned about my father's disappearance, she suffered a sudden and catastrophic nervous collapse. Her condition deteriorated to such a dangerous state, we were forced to have her confined. She cannot remember her children, lady, nor how to clean herself, nor where she is, nor even her own name."

The shocked queen turned sharply to her mage. "But, Dante, you must visit poor Madeleine! You once treated diseases of the mind. Healed them, so I heard. You've been so generous with me. . . ."

Healed! Generous! Hatred and contempt swelled to monstrous proportion, propelling me past caution. "I'd not think of luring Master Dante from Castelle Escalon, Your Grace. Surely he must remain on call to see to your needs. Tell me, lady: You appear so much more rested since your daytime sleep yesterday afternoon. Was it this mage who soothed your troubled dreams?"

Lady Antonia's browless gaze snapped to Dante, as if a wire stretched between them.

The same man who had brutalized his adept in a public venue now armored himself in stillness. Was anyone in this love-forsaken palace so controlled as he?

Not the reckless idiot Anne de Vernase, who had to clasp her hands at her back to prevent him spying their tremors, whose jellied knees scarce held her up.

Not Eugenie de Sylvae, who sat back, surprised, and cocked her head. "Indeed, as you say it, that must be why I'm thinking so clearly today, despite a late night . . . at cards." Her cheeks took on the hue of her snoring brother's garments. "In the afternoon the dreams came, as always. But they never reached conclusion. And then last night, I thought other events had overshadowed. But I'll vow I did not dream at all! Master, is this blessing your doing?"

"Nay," said Dante. "Though 'tis a boon, to be sure. Someone other must take the credit."

For the first time, I glimpsed a true emotion from the mage. As the abandoned hearth fire took that moment to die in a spurt of yellow smoke, an oddity which none but I could have seen, his left hand, sheathed in a glove of black leather, caressed his white staff. One corner of his mouth twitched into a mirthless smile. My challenge had amused him.

No words sufficed to describe my fear.

———

ANTONIA SAW ME DISMISSED BEFORE I could broach the subject of Ambrose. Shaken, berating myself for allowing anger to trump wiles yet again, I returned to the salon.

The hour was too early to retire. I couldn't even walk or seek refuge in the library, as the ladies-in-waiting insisted we remain available for Her Majesty's needs until third hour of the afternoon watch. Unable to bear the stares and whispers, I wandered into the courtyard garden.

An elderly gentleman sat on a shady bench, playing mournful dances on the flute. Unfortunately, half his notes came sour. Every few bars, he would halt and examine his instrument, twist or shake it, and try again.

The morning had turned sour, too, a suffocating, anxious mantle I could not shed. I believed Lady Antonia a murderess who was embroiling the Queen of Sabria in her plots. What had possessed me to reveal so much or, saints' mercy, to spar with the mage? Master Dante frightened me beyond anyone in Castelle Escalon, yet I had so much as told him I'd removed his vile artifact from the queen's bedchamber.

"Excuse me, damoselle." A serving girl dipped her knee. "A gentleman said I was to bring you this, and ask if you would prefer wine or a bracing tisane." Her flowered dish held a hot couchine.

"Neither, I think," I said. "Nor the pastry." I could not have ingested a morsel, yet I relished the offering. "Return it to the physician with my thanks," I whispered, smiling at the red-haired girl. "Or have it yourself. You have my permission."

No sooner had the serving girl departed than a small commotion broke out inside. I gleaned only bits and pieces. "But surely she's not gone! You ladies are ever devoted to your duties, all your clever needling and witty discourse . . . especially wished to speak to her . . . no one woke me . . . considering an expedition to the Isle of Naasica . . . giant turtles that expire when brought . . . Good Portier, have you seen . . . ? In the courtyard, you say?"

I was not so astonished when the lanky lord in vermillion brocade poked his fair head out the courtyard door and begged the indulgence of my time to advise him on Naasican expeditions.

"Perhaps we could remain out here, as the weather is quite blissful," he said, when I offered to follow him inside. "I *do* so delight in the outdoors, but perhaps I could send for your maidservant to bring you a hat, as I was thinking I should have John Deune bring me one, but truly I don't believe the sun warrants it, autumnal as it is, and John, my manservant, gets testy when I bid him hither and yon unnecessarily."

"No need, but my thanks for your consideration." Truly one could not dwell on frights when this man got to babbling. And the opportunity . . . Hope blossomed anew.

Hands behind his back, Lord Ilario chattered on about his proposed expedition as we strolled across the garden. Carefully and properly remaining within sight of the broad doors, we appropriated the shady bench the flute player had abandoned.

As we sat down, the chevalier's cheeks took on the scorching hue of his garments. "Damoselle de Vernase, I must beg your pardon and indulgence. I do most assuredly wish to probe your experience with regard to the excitements and dangers of viewing giant sea turtles, but I must first give up a confessional that such is not the entire subject of my address this morning. And I will beg, on my knees if required, that what I say be held in the most direst privacy."

I blinked, confounded. "Certainly, my lord. I'm happy to discuss whatever you wish in confidence."

Taking a deep breath, he leaned his head close. "I was not asleep."

He might have been Ambrose at seven, confessing the sin of raiding the kitchen for raisins.

"In my lady's chamber just now?"

He half covered his mouth as if to prevent anyone reading his lips. "I often pretend to doze during tedious discussions."

Despite the dark threads of that earlier conversation, I barely suppressed a smile. "I don't think you're alone in that, my lord."

"Our papa—Geni's and mine were the same, you know, though our mothers were not—used to feign sleep from time to time, especially when *women's matters* were being discussed. He said true sleep was better, if one could manage it, but as long as the ladies didn't *know* you weren't sleeping, you could avoid being held responsible for the information."

Solemnly, I acknowledged the point. "Indeed, very wise."

His long pale hands, so like his half sister's, gripped his knees. "Thus I heard you and Geni speak of terrible things . . . your mother's state . . ."

Naught to do but nod and let him get it out.

"I am most profoundly sorry to hear such news, as I've met your mother several times on her visits to Merona. As Geni said, she was—is—a beautiful and gracious lady." He crinkled his smooth forehead and raked fingers through his flaxen hair. "My sister, you must understand, has experienced great sadness in her life, as you have. And since the . . . incidents . . . of four years ago, she's come deeply under the influence of this dreadful mage." He huffed in resolution. "The man frightens me, damoselle. Though I am a Knight of Sabria, I can say it no plainer. And I am not the only one in the palace to feel disturbance."

He surely read agreement in my face.

"In this recent conversation, where I was not asleep, you referred to Geni's dreams—which delicacy instructs me not to mention, save that I must in this instance. You see, our parents—our papa and Geni's blessed mama—died in a rapacious fire only a few months after Geni was brought to Castelle Escalon as King Soren's bride, and only a few days after I was brought to Castelle Escalon to companion her. She was but eight years old, and I eleven. This is a sorrow that torments her most awfully of late, by way of these wicked dreams." He leaned even closer. None but I could have heard him. "Yet you spoke of an ending to the dreams, as if you knew of them. As if you knew why she was indeed able to sleep yesterday afternoon and last night, as she has not in months. How, damoselle? And how did you stop them, for even a weak-wit such as I heard you *challenge* this terrible mage with the knowing. And he yielded the point!"

Great Heaven, I had guessed right!

Lord Ilario's exposed love and worry for his sister compelled me to answer truthfully, without endless self-argument. If ever a man were honest in his testimony, it was surely this one. Indeed, the ugliness of what had been worked on Eugenie enlisted me instantly in her cause.

"Yesterday, as I sat in the Rose Room writing out those letters, the queen appeared in the doorway, distraught with nightmare . . . sleep-walking, it seemed. None of her ladies were nearby, which struck me as exceeding strange, and no guards or footmen, either. It was but happenstance that I was near. So I guided her back to bed. . . ."

I told him of the closed curtains, the reek of burning, and the barbed bracelet.

". . . and, suspecting such an ugly artifact might be the cause of her distress, I removed it."

Lord Ilario gaped at me, speechless. Which silence lasted all of an eyeblink. "But why would the mage torment her dreams? She's done nothing but indulge him."

Though I longed to ask in what ways Dante was indulged, it was more important to focus Lord Ilario's flighty attentions on warning Eugenie. "Chevalier, as I am so new at court, I've spent a great deal of time observing and listening. More courtiers than just this mage frighten me. I've solid reason to believe Lady Cecile's death was no accident, and the evidence points to someone in the household, someone *very* close to the queen, who can dismiss servants and ladies from her bedchamber without question, and who could be working in concert with this mage, who does such awful things. Lord, your sister must not trust *anyone*, save you. Not friend, nor even kin, no matter how devoted that person might appear . . ."

Lord Ilario had bowed his head, and his fingertips pressed the center of his forehead, hiding his face. A gold ring fashioned in the shape of a phoenix flashed in the sunlight. He did not unmask when next he spoke. "You've proof of all this?"

"I've hidden the bracelet. As to who left it, I've no proof a Royal Accuser would account, especially coming from me."

"You've shared this information with Duplais?" His head popped up, and the question rang short and sharp as a pistol shot.

"Certainly not!" My response returned equally sharp. "Duplais brought Mage Dante to my home. My mother began her decline that very day. I don't trust him."

"Ever-righteous *Duplais* in league with malfeasors? That I simply cannot *grasp*. He was my secretary, you know. A stiff little pup of a man, but he's got the intellect of an encyclopaedia and the perceptions of a Saint Reborn, which I once thought— Well, never mind that. And he has the patience of a rock with anyone but a lackwit chevalier whose inane babbling drives him to head pounding. He'd never do something so dastardly wicked. Why, he alone uncovered the transference plot and prosecuted the trait—" His complexion bloomed scarlet yet again.

"It's all right, my lord." I hadn't meant to involve my mother's plight, but if it drove him to protect his sister and find someone trustworthy to help her, it would be worth the risk. "I know it's difficult to reconcile Sonjeur de Duplais' behavior. I've wrestled with that myself. But a person so ruthless in the pursuit of answers might be led to compromise his integrity for what he considers righteous. I cannot, will not, trust him."

"None could blame you, damoselle. Certainly not. But what shall we do with this dreadful artifact? Someone should look at it. Parse it for clues."

"I think it had best be taken far from the queen."

"Ah, most delightfully sensible. What if I had my valet fetch it from some location you specify and dispatch it to my house in the country? I'll tell him it's a token from a young lady. We would have it out of the way, while yet keeping it under our eyes, so to speak. I could locate a reliable person to examine it."

That sounded as good as anything. I'd send it somewhere myself, save for the surety that Duplais inspected my outgoing packets as well as those incoming. I told Lord Ilario where his valet could find the wrapped bracelet. "Please keep in mind, lord, that the threat is more than just this one thing. Those responsible are still here."

"I'll take your caution most sincerely to mind. If I could but persuade Geni to listen to you . . . But she tolerates my meddling only so far. In some matters, her stubbornness rivals even Portier's."

He bent his head and rubbed his neck, such an image of humble dejection, I wanted to pat his head. Such an odd person. Far more thoughtful than anyone would guess. And the phoenix ring . . . no wonder he incessantly invoked the saints awaiting. He must adhere to the Cult of the

Reborn. I certainly wished I could garner assistance from the Cult's hero saints.

"My lord, I must confess something of my own."

His head popped up again, all frowning attention. "How so?"

"I came in this morning apurpose to speak with you." Though he did not change positions on the bench, I felt the distance between us stretch. The subtle movement bade me continue quickly. "Please, do not imagine this a tit for tat. Can you do nothing for my personal situation, I would not change my testimony or my warning or my sincere concern for Her Majesty's health and safety. Your devotion to your sister gives me hope that you might heed a sister's plight."

"Go on."

"My brother has been the king's hostage since he was fifteen. . . ."

The chevalier listened gravely, and when I was done, leapt to his feet, slapped one hand on his sword hilt, and the other on his heart. "Damoselle de Vernase, no Knight of Sabria could fail to apply his talents to such a tragic lapse of mercy. King Philippe, while just and sober in his necessity to confine a traitor's son, could not have meant to punish his goodchildren in so severe a fashion. Alas, his noble person is preparing to defend Sabria from these wildman uprisings out of Aroth, else I'd present this petition to him directly. But I swear to you on my honored father's head that before the sun sets on this day, you shall clasp your brother to your heart."

CHAPTER 14

SOLA PASSIERT, LATE AFTERNOON

L ord Ilario was as good as his word. Lady Antonia dismissed the
queen's household at third hour. By the time I reached my bedchamber, a footman awaited me in the passage.

"With Chevalier de Sylvae's compliments," he said, extending a rolled
parchment tied in blue ribbon.

To the Warder of Spindle Prison, Greetings:

*By order of Eugenie de Sylvae y Savin-Journia, Queen Regent of Sa-
bria in the absence of Philippe King, the visitation restrictions imposed on
Ambrose de Vernase, detainee of Spindle Prison, are hereby abrogated to
the sole benefit of Anne de Vernase ney Cazar for the period of four hours,
to begin at fifth hour of the afternoon watch. Such temporary abrogation
shall be construed as neither a reversal of judgment nor mitigation of the
detainee's designation as a Danger and Risk of Collusion with a Known
Traitor to the Crown of Sabria, and shall in no manner affect any other restriction, privilege, or regulation imposed by the Warder in the fulfillment
of his charge.*

"The chevalier says that a mount and an escort will await you at the stables at fourth hour. Will there be anything else, damoselle?"

"Tell the chevalier—" My heart had swollen to the size of Mont Siris. "Convey to him my most profound gratitude and humble appreciation."

"As you say, damoselle. Divine grace."

Joy and excitement winged my feet. Trepidation sped my hands. I could not move fast enough. I changed into riding clothes. Pulled out the few shirts of Papa's I'd brought, thinking they might fit a young man of nineteen. Saints' mercy, he would have grown so much. Of course, they might have provided him new clothes. He was a hostage, not a prisoner.

He'd written so rarely—a few times the first year when he was so angry, twice in the second, once in each of the last two, each scarce more than a scribble, and nothing of his circumstances. He was alive. He tried to keep fit. He heard no news. He valued my frequent letters.

Stars and planets, I should take him paper and ink, sticks of plummet for drawing or if he should run out of ink, and I mustn't forget the books I'd brought for him.

Your spirit is a maelstrom.

Startled, I glanced up from the cloth bag I'd stuffed with clothes and books to see who had come in. Not Ella. Her voice was . . .

Until you learn—and are ready—to initiate and respond, it is your upheaval that allows me to forge this link that binds us.

Father Creator!

You have an immense gift. Do you understand that? You are not mad. Not cursed. Not evil. Quiet. Careful, as if tiptoeing through glass. *Do not fear your gift. Do not fear me.*

And then he was gone. I knew it as certainly as if someone had stepped out of my bedchamber and closed the door behind.

I hadn't taken any of the potion. This was not a lonely girl's longing for her family, nor some hysteria induced by a magical concoction. A man, a stranger to me, yet most assuredly the one I'd heard before, had been as close to me as my own thoughts. A genie, trapped inside me instead of a lamp. The image raised a smile. Not mad. Not cursed. A *gift*, he said. Though . . . had my mother heard voices?

The bells pealed the third quarter of the hour. No time to consider mystery or madness.

I spun wildly. What else should I take? Stupid not to have given it more thought.

The vial of Lianelle's potion sat on the corner of the dressing table, glaring, obvious. To provide a Spindle detainee magic of any kind was surely forbidden. I could pass it off as a family tonic, and yet what if the warder had some way to detect spelled artifacts? Perhaps the powder unmixed . . . a small amount . . .

I cut a scrap of cloth from a clean shift, wrapped up a pinch of the powder, and stuffed it in my shoe. Then I rang for Ella. The blessed girl was quick.

"I need a small flask of wine," I said. "Sealed properly, as from the vineyard. Bring it to me at the stables by the fourth-hour bells, and I'll provide for your children's children until world's end."

"Won't pass on that." A grin set her freckles glowing. As she ran, I heard her laughing. "Must've got the favor you wanted."

"MAY I SEE THE QUEEN's warrant, damoselle?"

No alchemist could have transformed my heart to lead so efficiently as did the sight of Savin–Duplais awaiting me in the stableyard. The requirement to notify him had never crossed my mind.

"I've scarce met the chevalier," I said, "so I never expected this favor. And then the time was so short." How had Duplais learned of my journey so quickly?

"I'll speak to Her Majesty to clarify the situation," he said, stiff as granite. "Naturally, I cannot contravene her will as written."

As my heart and fists unclenched, he pocketed the warrant and waved to a man in Chevalier de Sylvae's spring green livery. The footman led two horses forward. To my delight, one was Ladyslipper. To my chagrin, the other was Duplais' favored gelding.

Duplais took the reins. "Assist the lady up, if you would. You may inform the chevalier that I've relieved you of escort duty."

I should have expected this. Had propriety allowed, the man would surely have moved into my bedchamber. It was not going to be easy to shake him off once I set out to find Papa. That was exactly what he waited for.

As I settled into the saddle, Ella pelted across the stableyard. "My children's children, damoselle." Duplais looked on, puzzled, as she pressed the wine flask into my hand.

"I'll not forget."

Only fourteen days had passed since Duplais and I had entered the royal city, yet it seemed a lifetime. The flag-draped Plas Royale teemed with citizens and soldiers, as it was Transfer Day, when a fresh complement of the Guard Royale relieved that posted at Castelle Escalon. Two full gardias, more than a thousand men, were parading up and down the boulevard.

"I'll be able to get transport at the docks, yes?" I said, feeling precious time slide past as we pressed through the mob. "Is it a particular boat that serves the Spindle?"

"A Spindle shallop will be waiting, as long as we're there before sunset. Come, let's get out of this." Duplais shouted and bullied his way to the edge of the crowd, taking us into a side lane.

"Did it not cross your mind that leaving the palace grounds could be dangerous?" he said, directing me into a quieter lane.

"I would risk a great deal to see my brother, sonjeur." Bathed in full afternoon sunlight, the city did not oppress me as before. But as we descended toward Riverside, I did keep a wary eye out for rats and sinkholes.

"You're carrying no contraband?"

"I'm carrying only the same items you put at risk at Vradeu's Crossing—no valuables at all."

That reaped a sharp glance and thinned lips. "Be sure of that."

Something in the day had him worried. His eyes never stopped scanning the shop fronts, the passersby, the road before and behind us. Yet it struck me that if he feared some assault, he might have insisted Lord Ilario's burly servant accompany us. Were Captain de Santo and his black-cloaked friend lurking along our route?

Once we crossed into the lower city, it was not soldiers but snarls of wagons and pack mules hauling goods from the harbor to upper city that drove us off the main road and into the heart of Riverside. It was as if the sun had set three hours early, the tangle of steep, muddy lanes so narrow that the upper stories of the houses came near touching. Quartieres blocked almost every side lane. Many tenement rows were interrupted by blackened gaps where rills of yellow and purple flames burned untended. In some cases the houses on either side were half charred, the raw edges still smoking as if being eaten away by invisible flame. Unnatural flame.

"What's happened here?" I said.

"Your father happened," said Duplais. "Dante happened. Ride faster. Come sunset, we could be equally beset. Come sunset of Sola Passiert, the possibilities are worse." Sola Passiert—when night overbalances day.

It was a relief to emerge from Riverside's gloom into the afternoon bustle at the harbor. The river sparkled like diamond-dusted satin. A swarm of small boats threaded their way through anchored barges and fishing vessels to a newly anchored caravel like ants to a discarded bun, each hoping to be the first to glean news or scoop up rare finds, to sell spirits, limes, or luck charms to returning seamen, to deliver letters and collect harbor fees.

But as soon as I spied the forbidding finger of black stone rising from a rock in the deepest channel of the river, all other concerns dropped away. Ambrose . . . my exuberant, never-still-a-moment brother. *Saints have mercy.*

Duplais paid a tallyman's lad to watch our horses, and we trudged down to the waterfront on planks laid across the muddy banks. Gulls swooped and screeched or marched around the mud flats, pecking at mussels and crabs. Black posts flanked one of the docks, where a dark-skinned man with a pistol at his belt lounged in a small boat, picking his teeth. His eyes sat atop his face as if the Pantokrator had near forgotten to put them there. "Summat thinks to visit the Spindle?"

"I am escorting the lady to visit a prisoner," said Duplais. "We carry the queen's warrant."

"Warrant don't mean fishbones to me," said the rower, stretching his shoulders. "I'm just Scago the ferryman. Come aboard."

As he goaded the little boat through the slopping current, Scago grumbled of unstable tide flows, tricky rocks, and unnatural fogs that had tormented river men of late. I did not heed his chatter. The Spindle demanded my full attention, huge and dismal, a blight on the day.

The black granite had been smoothed and glazed, and barred slot windows had been inserted into the featureless stone. Elsewise, one might have thought the tower sprouted naturally from its rugged base. The gray-green water of the Ley chopped and frothed against the ugly lump of black rock. Barely enough mass extended from the base of the tower to allow the waterbirds a gathering place.

The sole entry to the Spindle lay beyond an iron gate anchored in giant rock pillars that protruded from the water. The gate, the first of three, so I'd read, clanked upward when Scago blew a whistle in a stuttering pattern. The pattern changed by the day, he told us.

With a few heaves of the ferryman's powerful shoulders, we lurched beneath the weedy, dripping gate only to face a second at least six stories high, its bars wrought with outlines of monstrous beasts bound with chains. The first gate groaned, scraped, and plunged into the water behind us. Ambrose had been brought here at night. In chains. Hearing that dreadful sound must have felt like the end of the world.

As our boat bobbed in the slurping channel between the gates, growing dread gnawed my spirit. The murky water stank of sewage. And my ears itched and buzzed, as if I stood in the heart of a great city—as if the effects of Lianelle's potion were just wearing off. "Magic . . ."

Duplais' head jerked around. I'd not meant to speak it aloud.

"Aye," said Scago, feathering his oars to maintain our position. "Spindle were enchanted before the Blood Wars, when sorcerers ruled. You'll see nae spit of rust on gates, locks, or bars. And none's been able to escape the wards, save the Treacher's whore four year ago. None knows how that was done. Magic, likely. Magic's comin' back, you know. World's changing. All can see it. Maybe the Spindle won't hold no more. Or maybe it'll be locked forever and none'll ever go free."

World's changing. I drew my thin cloak tighter. The "Treacher's whore" was Maura ney Billard, my father's dupe. I glanced over my shoulder at Duplais. For once his stony face was staring at something . . . or someone . . . a long way from me.

"I'll see your warrant." A short, smiling, round-cheeked man greeted us from the far side of the second gate. "I am Pognole, Warder of Spindle Prison."

Warder Pognole appeared sturdy as a rock fortress himself; almost as broad as he was tall, his head bald and leathery, his garments of padded canvas and leather sewn with steel plates. His thighs might have been more of the granite pillars. He could likely bend the iron bars of his gates without losing his smile. I prayed my face revealed no smuggler's guilt.

Scago eased the boat to the gate so Duplais could pass the royal warrant through the bars.

Pognole glanced up sharply from the document. "Damoselle de Vernase! Indeed! And come to the Spindle of your own will. Bravely done. And who might you be, sonjeur?"

"Portier de Savin-Duplais, administrator of Her Majesty's household, sent to supervise Damoselle de Vernase."

The warder's glance scanned the warrant again. "Alas, you needs must remain out here."

"But I am required—"

"You're not *Named.*" The warder rolled the page and stuck it in a pouch slung from his belt, opposite a plain, battered sword. "Don't matter who you are. I've a method here. Those not Named in the warrant don't enter. Out the boat and onto the bench, or I'll have Scago tip you out."

The bench was a slimy wooden platform bolted to the gatehouse wall some ten centimetres above the wavelets. The only way to get anywhere from the bench was to climb a sheer stone wall or swim through the palm-width gaps between the bars of the gates.

Duplais, red-faced, seethed as he clambered from boat to bench. But he didn't bother to launch into bombast or otherwise assert privilege. No one with a mind would believe that useful. Warder Pognole could crack his spine like a dry stick.

Once the administrator was perched on the bench, knees drawn up to keep his boots out of the river, the second gate clanked and groaned, rising slowly from the water. Not a speck of rust marred the thick bars.

"Maintain your dignity, damoselle," Duplais called, as Scago rowed under the second gate. "You are Her Majesty's gentlewoman. And consider: False hopes are worse than any bars or gates."

Unlike his usual pronouncements, these did not sound like warnings from a Royal Accuser to a suspect. His head sank to his knees, and I wondered if he thought of sweet Maura, condemned by his own relentless pursuit of treachery.

The second gate clanged shut. Across the stretch of churning water, a wooden dock stretched out from the mouth of a narrow cavern that penetrated the Spindle's rocky base. No evidence of the third of the Spindle Prison's notorious water gates was visible. Scago shipped his oars, and the boat bumped gently against the bollards.

While the oarsman tied up his boat, the warder offered me a hand up to the dock. A few metres' walk took us onto the apron of rock that fronted the cavern.

"I'll see the bag now, damoselle," said the warder, grinning cheerfully. An ugly, pale scar creased one ruddy cheek from brow to chin. "Can't have any naughtiness brought into my prison."

He laid out books, clothes, paper, ink, and wine flask on the ledge of a barred window hacked from the stone to provide light in the cavelike gatehouse. He sniffed the ink, shook out the bag and the shirts, and quickly thumbed through the books and papers.

Clicking his tongue in disapproval, he held up the bulbous green flask. "Don't like books or wine for prisoners," he said. "Don't like 'em forgetting what they are or where. It's discipline gets 'em through the days. Not coddling."

"Perfectly understandable," I said, trying not to bristle. "But of course my brother is hostage, not prisoner. I assumed you would permit a few small reminders of home."

"Maybe. Don't imagine he'll care. He's not a friendly sort. Nor studious."

Mumbling, he passed a pewter charm over the wax plug sealing the wine flask. He frowned and rubbed the charm with his thumb. Mumbled again. This was no Gautieri brilliance, but the kind of magic I'd seen growing up—unreliable and inefficient at best. Pognole tried his charm three more times until satisfaction replaced the frown. "Spell seal seems to be intact. So you've not put something ill inside the flask."

"The wine was brought straight from Castelle Escalon's cellar."

He chuckled. "That's no recommendation. But I'll bring it along once I've put it in a skin. Not allowing the young rapscallion to have a bit of glass, now, am I? Might break. Might cut."

He set the flask aside, his smile crinkling the leathery skin around his eyes. He breathed through his mouth, nasal, liquid breaths, as if his nose was clogged by the river damp. "Have you weapons on you, damoselle? Or magics? Pretty little daggers or pox charms or unlocking spells? 'Twould be a foolish deed for a girl by rights should be living here alongside her kin."

"Certainly not." I mustered innocent indignation. But I dared not add more words. Stammering would make him suspicious.

His thick fingers curled, rubbing idly together as his gaze roamed over me. "We've no females here to inspect you, and I don't trust these charms to detect all. 'Twould be sufficient grounds to turn you away. You see, I've just got the boy tamed. Don't like the thought of him getting riled up again."

Of a sudden the barrel-necked warder's round cheeks, thick fingers, and crinkle-eyed smile sickened me. How had he *tamed* and *disciplined* my brother, who would have been wild with terror when they brought him to this horrid place?

Maintain your dignity, Duplais had warned. I summoned the hauteur of Eugenie's highest-ranked ladies. "Warder Pognole, the Queen of Sabria has expressed her especial trust in me by that document you hold. She can hold no fond memories of this place, having herself been unjustly imprisoned here. And as Sonjeur de Duplais will tell you, and as you yourself noted by so rightly forbidding him entry, she will allow no whim to contravene her warrant."

Pognole's smile became chipped flint. For a moment I thought he might topple me into the gray-green water. But I did not flinch, and with a motion deceptively quick, he shoved the two shirts and one of the books into my arms. The rest of the materials he returned to my bag, which he slung over his thick shoulder. "I'll provide the wineskin. But I'll pass the detainee the rest of your bounty only as he deserves. Hostages, just as prisoners, must be taught proper behavior. Come."

The warder snatched a torch from a bracket. Leaving Scago snoring in his boat, we climbed the slanted walkway into a natural rock cavern. Walls and ceiling were slimed with moldy seeps. Every step required attention, as the flat floor was riddled with cracks and channels, some no more than a finger's width, some spanning almost a metre. Water slurped and gurgled in the inky depths.

As we left the afternoon behind I felt, more than heard, the warder mumble a word. Iron bars shot up from the water, from the lip of the cavern ceiling, and from either side of the opening, slamming, screeching, clanging into an impenetrable grate behind us.

The metallic dissonance faded into a profound quiet.

Pognole parked his torch and pointed up a narrow, twisting stair lit by gloomy daylight. Every twenty or thirty steps, a barred window open to the weather illuminated a landing and two or three iron doors.

The wind gusted through the barred portals, skirling up and down the stair. Together with the distant, lonely cries of river birds, it composed a song of misery that only compounded the silence from behind the doors.

"How many are prisoned here?" I asked as we climbed.

"Only three just now." He was sorry for it.

The warder did not stop until we had reached a single iron door at the topmost step of the Spindle stair. As the damp wind whipped my hair, Pognole unbolted a hinged steel plate and peered through a square grate in the door. "Seems he's at home. No surprise, eh?"

From inside came the sound of soft, quick breaths.

Pognole pushed a key from his belt ring into the lock. The door swung open and the warder stepped through, motioning me, in no questionable terms, to wait. But around his sturdy bulk I glimpsed a blur of long limbs, whirling, lunging, one brief pause to balance, then another spin-and-slash executed with grim, mute precision. Martial exercises.

My heart raced from the climb, from anticipation, and now from the fear that the tall, hard man I'd glimpsed—dark hair trimmed close to his head and jaw, gaunt limbs rippling with corded sinews—could not possibly be my brother. Ambrose had adored both fighting and dancing, and practiced them with equal devotion, but always laughing, a handsome, rangy youth whose flowing hair glinted with copper, whose easy grace and careless beauty had roused both pride and jealousy in his elder sister.

"Display before your warder, prisoner. 'Tis not a day to play your games. You'll rue the choice."

The prisoner had moved out of sight. After an overstretched moment, Warder Pognole motioned me into a semicircular room of rough stone, the barred, slotlike gaps in the wall open to the weather. A thin mat leaking straw, a single blanket, a battered tin pot—nothing more occupied the room, save its resident.

He stood, back to the door, arms spread and hands flat against the curved wall, legs splayed wide, bowed head pressed to the stone. A mortifying posture. Indecent. Slops of common canvas scarce reached his knees. A filthy shirt stretched thin and tight across his shoulders, sleeves ragged. No hose. No shoes. Angry red scars glared on his wrists. Impossible . . . yet the back of his left hand bore the imprint of an angled knife— the zahkri, the mark of our Cazar blood.

"Ambrose," I whispered.

He did not move, and for a moment, my fear returned.

But then Pognole widened his vile grin. He sidled up to the man leaning on the wall and brushed his hand slowly across the quivering shoulders and down the rigid spine to his buttocks, where it lingered just long enough to claim possession. "Is the boy not well disciplined, damoselle?"

Even yet, Ambrose held still. I prayed he was responsible for the scar on Pognole's cheek.

The warder almost danced back across the stone floor to the door. "At ease, prisoner. Enjoy this happy hour." He slammed the iron door behind me and locked it.

"Forgive me," I whispered to that rigid back. "Saints forgive me, I didn't know."

CHAPTER 15

SOLA PASSIERT, EVENING

The prisoner's splayed hands curled into fists. Then he drew in his arms, folded them around his chest, and swung around to settle his back against the wall. Ankles crossed casually, as if he were waiting for Melusina to set his place at supper, he nodded in emotionless greeting. "Good afternoon, Ani. You look well."

I ached to embrace my brother, to comfort, to soothe, to erase the loathsome history so callously exposed, to convince him it changed nothing about his worth. But naught in this man's manner invited intimacy. I could not comment on his knuckle-length hair, his bristling chin, or his impressive height—grown almost half a metre since I'd seen him last—any more than I could have tweaked Duplais about his scrawny body or teased Chevalier Ilario about his long straight nose. We were strangers. Even the common greeting wish of the Creator's grace seemed presumptive, and most assuredly a mockery in a place so utterly alien to grace.

"My first visitor in four years and she does not speak. Is this *Pignole's* idea?" His voice had settled into a timbre deeper than my father's. Arms, legs, and spirit displayed a web of scars. A few inconspicuous iron loops and hooks fixed high on the stained walls glared at me in accusation. Ambrose would not have been tamed easily.

My arms clutched the materials I carried as if they were the keystone that held the world in place. Ambrose was a *hostage*, not a prisoner. How could I have known what he lived with? And even if I had, what could I have done differently? Yet excuses were dross.

"I've so much to tell you," I whispered, choking. "I don't know where to begin."

"Sit if you wish." He jerked his head to the thin pallet. "Do not assume privacy."

Indeed the metal plate over the door grate remained open, and I could almost hear Pognole's sibilant breathing outside it. Vile. Disgusting. Imagining his eavesdropping began to transmute loathing into anger and resolution.

"I doubt the good warder would be listening in," I said, stringing a warp of lies and hoping my brother could interpret my truer belief. "He has no wish for me to report a gift of Castelle Escalon's finest vintage stolen. Her Majesty has sent a flask of wine, and the gentleman has promised to decant it into a skin and bring it here. He seems to think a glass container might incite you to misbehavior. Could that be true?"

Ambrose snorted. "Did you not witness, damoselle? I am well disciplined."

He existed beyond bitterness. Had anyone cut him, he would have bled sand.

In the hard silence that ensued, my senses, so heightened in these past days, noted soft steps descending the stair. Clutching the paltry comforts the warder had allowed me to bring, I surveyed the barren chamber that would be a sultry furnace in summer, and a cold, wet, windy agony all winter. I could not believe our goodfather intended this deprivation. Not for a youth who had committed no crime.

"They would not allow me to come before now," I said softly. "I tried. I wrote everyone who might have influence. Every plea was returned. I paid a lawyer"—who had taken the fee and done nothing, claiming that no one would hear a petition from Michel de Vernase's kin—"as I wrote you . . ."

His expression remained blank.

My brother's few letters had never mentioned his situation. Nor had he responded to my questions or complaints, to the news of our mother's illness, to anything specific.

"Ambrose, did you get *any* of my letters?"

"The pig said I could read them when I stopped trying to tear his eyes out," he said, quiet and harsh. "And then he said it could be when I stopped trying to rip a hole in these walls with my fingernails. And then it was to be when I chose to eat again, as he hated the mess of forcing me. And then it was to be when I licked his boots. And then it was to be when I would lick . . . whatever he wished to be licked. Always another condition. So no. But I always appreciated the intrinsic heat of paper and ink. You see, he would burn them a centimetre or two from my hands or my eyes or whatever he chose that day. But always"—one small, shaking breath—"I recognized your hand, Ani. I knew you had—"

He slammed the back of his head to the wall, jaw clenched, nostrils flaring. He might have been formed of that very granite.

So he knew nothing of Mama or our struggles at Montclaire or how sorely he was missed. Pognole had likely told him every kind of lie. Ambrose wouldn't have believed him, but in the absence of any alternative, the lies would have eaten at him. So long not knowing.

"You have been in my thoughts every day, brother. Every single day." I propelled each word across the chamber with the force of a mangonel slinging stones. "Only fourteen days ago was I brought to Castelle Escalon, where I at last found an advocate. I've so *much* to tell you. We've only a few hours."

A heavy breath slipped his tight lips. "He's not found, then."

Of course Papa would be foremost in his mind. Ambrose could not be free until Papa was arrested, if even then. And angels' mercy, that was not the hardest thing I had to tell. "No."

"But you're not held? Nor Mama nor Lianelle?"

"No. But I have to tell you what's happened to them. . . ."

Perhaps it would have been more merciful to keep the news from him. Yet he deserved honesty, and whatever lie I told gave Pognole another weapon for torment. Perhaps anger might give him something to hold on to, something to live for, even if it was hollow vengeance.

But his hands did not so much as twitch. His face did not sag or twist or reflect the slightest pain. His silence frightened me. It felt as if I'd murdered what splinters of him remained.

It did not ease matters that the warder's boots rang on the stair just then, and a mocking command accompanied the rattle of keys. "Discipline, prisoner!"

Ambrose flushed, closing his eyes.

As he spun face to the wall, I moved to one of the window slots. At least sixty metres of polished granite lay between the barred opening and the cruel rocks below. The city sprawled along the riverbank and bluffs, barely visible through the afternoon haze. The caravel in the harbor might have been a toy ship.

A groan of iron hinges, and the warder sauntered in, swinging a wineskin. "Here you are, damoselle. As promised. Are you two getting on? Remember, I don't reward misbehavior."

"My brother was always ill behaved, Warder. Wild. Stubborn. Your results are impressive." I snatched the wineskin from his fingers. "Now you may leave us. I've estate business to discuss . . . vineyards, tenants, my marriage portion. In a few days I'll be sending a lawyer with documents for him to sign. It's why the queen agreed to send me. I'd not waste your time with such tedium."

I doubted Pognole was fooled, but at least he didn't argue. And when I called after him to request a lamp, as the days were getting shorter, and it would be unseemly for a queen's maid of honor to be closeted in the dark with an unmarried man, even a kinsman, he grumbled but set a blazing torch in the bracket outside the door.

Having no illusion that we were left unsupervised, I moved to the pallet and smoothed the filthy, rumpled blanket as if it were Eugenie's silk sheets. I sat back to the wall, skirts spread modestly over my knees, which I'd drawn up in front of me. "Come sit beside me. I've brought you a book."

"He won't allow them, Ani. As soon as you've gone—"

"You could study it *now*. It would give you something new to think on." I propped the rare folio of river birds on my knees and leafed through the wide, expensive pages. Expanses of unmarked space set off the short descriptions and delicate sketches. Shielded from the open door grate, where only Ambrose could see, I produced a stick of plummet from my pocket. "It's important to make good use of time."

The man's eyes met mine for the first time. Nowhere in those deep, cold layers of despair could I find the bright youth I had known. He joined me on the pallet, though maintaining a solid distance between us. I could understand his need to keep his armor intact. I would have enslaved my soul to Dimios himself to have some hope to offer.

"I thought you might have an opportunity to observe these birds while you were here and record the sightings to keep the family records complete. I've left a fresh supply of ink and paper with the warder, and I'm sure he'll allow you to have them. Now I'm resident in Merona, a member of the queen's household, I'll be checking up on you more often."

Or so I hope and pray, I wrote above a hoopoe's beak, angling the book where he could see.

Thus I continued for two hours, speaking of birds, Montclaire's grape harvest, and court life, while filling the pages with what I knew of Lianelle's murder, Mama's illness, the Gautieri books, and the strangeness in the city that everyone linked to Papa's sorcerers. I regaled Ambrose with details of my "honored" position as the king's goddaughter and queen's maid of honor, but at the same time sketched out the cipher that was Duplais, and the circumstances of Lady Cecile's murder and Antonia's complicity, and I affirmed his suspicions of the hooded mage who had visited Montclaire.

Dante, I wrote. *All of these events are connected, and they all come back to this Dante. At the trial they said the conspirators' purpose is chaos severe enough to topple the king. But there must be more. Why else manipulate the queen? She has little actual power.*

When I came to the tale of Lianelle's magic trinkets and my certainty of Papa's innocence and captivity, I would have sworn my brother stopped breathing.

"Examine this heron's configuration," I said, while sketching the odd diagrams I'd seen on Lianelle's bit of paper. "Have you seen this one here on the river? Or any of these species?"

"Spirits and daemons, Ani," he muttered, "when could I have seen anything?"

"Time is what you have, Ambrose. Eyes and ears. And a mind to focus outward . . . or *inward*. Have you seen *anything* like? A purple heron? A Louvel tern?" I brushed my hand over the filled pages detailing magic and conspiracy. "Any marvels like these? *I* never cared for rare birds before. I didn't believe they were real, because I hadn't seen them for myself. But that sole glimpse . . . I believe it now."

"Let me see the cursed book."

I shifted the book to Ambrose's knees and the stick of plummet, more than half worn away, to his cold hand. Torchlight streamed through the door grate, the pattern of the bars growing ever more distinct as evening faded into night. He flipped pages until he came to an inked sketch, labeled PIED AVOCET.

"This one. I might have seen this one. . . ."

He tapped on the page but quickly sketched a hand, then overlaid it with an *X*. I touched the blood family mark on my left hand, and Ambrose dipped his head. *A sorcerer* . . .

"It settled on one of these ledges one night. Stupid bird, to visit here, as I had nothing to give it. Kept coming back, always at night. Not sure of its markings or . . . decorations. I was . . . sick . . . in those days. Wasn't seeing so well. But I'm sure it was one of them."

"To know the markings would be essential," I said. "The decorations, too." As in whether the visitor wore a mage collar.

As Ambrose rambled on about birds supposedly spied through the slotlike gaps, he scribbled notes on the page, desperately fast. Stark, bleak notes that curdled my blood.

Wanted to die. Tried starving. Almost worked, but then he came . . .

He tapped a finger on the marked hand.

Never saw his face. He taught the pig how to force food down me. Came another time and cut my thigh. Used a . . .

His hand paused. I could feel him searching for the word.

. . . bladder to squeeze something into the cut. Thought my leg would fall off. Wished for it. Sick for months. Dizzy. Puking. Pissing blood. Lunatic dreams. Saw things couldn't be real. He came again and again. Always in the night. Sneaking. Always asking what I saw. But I wouldn't tell him. Wouldn't give him the satisfaction. Drove him loony. One night, a different one came—a mage with a white staff, just like the one who came to Montclaire. Said he'd been told to get some use out of me. He tried. Felt as if he boiled the inside of my skull. At the end, he said I was worthless. Broken. He was right. Haven't dreamt since. Haven't seen anything, anyone. Can't think straight anymore.

He paused for a moment, then wrote the last and circled it, pressing so hard he bent the stub of plummet.

I don't believe Papa's innocent. You're just wishing. But all the wishing's been torn out of me. I want to deliver him to the Souleater myself. I can't stay here. Can't.

". . . damnable birds never came back. Should've strangled them. You can keep your fool book." He stuffed it back into my hands.

Night had closed in. The flickering torch provided too little light to read or write, especially with tears blurring my eyes. I had been planning to give Ambrose the powder in my shoe and tell him how to use it, should I fail at proving Papa's innocence. But desperate as my brother was, he would surely try it right away, without thinking it through. He'd be caught and punished, named a lawbreaker in his own right, which would justify everything that had been and would be done to him. And sure as sunrise, he would force them to kill him before they could drag him back here. I could not allow that.

"Oh, one more," I said and opened the book to a new page. Duplais was right. I could not give him false hopes. *ENDURE*, I wrote in large capitals. *FOR MAMA. FOR LIANELLE.*

"Ani . . . ," he whispered.

"Watch for birds," I said. My fingers touched the words I had written. "Remember their markings. You're the only person who understands the importance of these things. The only person in the world I trust. I *need* to know you're watching . . . until the day you walk free."

The roar emerged from the depths of his being, erupting in an agony that shook the Spindle's rocky foundation. He leapt to his feet and ripped the book from my hands. Raging, cursing, he tore out its pages one by one, shredding the delicate drawings, the glowing colors, all the harmony of science and art that had gone into its making. "Birds . . . courts . . . walls . . . magic . . . family. I. Hate. All! Don't patronize me! Don't come here again!"

As if in echo of his rage, wind thundered through the portals, cold and pitiless, and the faint bells of the city pealed ninth hour. The warder shouted for him to be silent or be chained. As Pognole burst the door open, Ambrose stuffed the gathered scraps of the book through a barred portal. The wind scattered them like ghosts through the night.

"To the wall, traitor spawn!" A whipcrack split the blustering air. "Do you see the fruits of indulgence, girl? One lapse and we've lost all discipline."

Pognole circled toward the portal, snapping his leather strap yet again. Sparks! Holy saints, blue and yellow sparks flew from it. Ambrose backed away, the sparks reflected in his eyes. No matter how he tried to mask it, he was terribly afraid. It was not just main strength and cruelty the warder used to control him.

"To the wall, boy, or the next falls on your back! What have you been up to?"

As the warder squinted through the barred opening, Ambrose, shaking, threw back his head and inhaled deeply. His arms tightened about his ribs. "Get out of here, Ani. For love, for mercy, get out and don't come back."

"Ambrose . . ."

"*Now*, Ani."

The warder, seething, marched back to the door. "Come, damoselle. Your warrant is expired. Time for you to go, as this rude lout has said."

"You've no right to harm him," I said as Pognole hooked the coiled whip to his belt and herded me out of the door. "He is the king's goodson and is convicted of no crime."

"Our king saw fit to confine the boy to a prison, damoselle. Good order in a prison is the warder's province. Who could expect a delicate lady to understand that?" He slammed the door. "Did he accuse me of harming him?" Menace barbed the question like iron thorns.

"Naturally, my warning was only hypothetical," I said, reining in my hatred. "But I've observed his condition now, and as he promises good behavior, I will expect to see no deterioration when I come back. And I *will* come back. He has promised to watch for birds!" I made sure to speak clearly through the open grate.

My brother made no answer as he spread arms and legs and turned face to the wall.

DESPAIRING SCREAMS FOLLOWED US AS Scago rowed us downriver. Were they in my ears, in my head, or solely in my imagining? No matter which, I believed them to be my brother's. I did not block them out. Even as they heated the cold darkness in my belly, I honed the blade of logic. To determine how to get Ambrose out of the Spindle, I had to know who wanted him there, who wanted him *tamed*.

The administrator did not attempt to question me. That, at least, was a mercy. He did eye the few scraps of soggy parchment caught by the current. He snagged one pale, limp fragment and peered at it through the spectacles he wore from time to time. "A hoopoe?" he murmured, puzzled; then he threw the disintegrating scrap back into the river. Ambrose had saved our secrets.

"Tell me one thing, Duplais," I said as Scago began his return journey to the Spindle and the two of us set out across the mudflats. "Who hired Warder Pognole?"

Duplais shook his head. "Merona's First Magistrate, I suppose, or perhaps the commandant of the Guard Royale or . . . I've no idea. Why?"

It had occurred to me that Pognole served two masters. No matter what royal official had jurisdiction over the Spindle, and no matter what rules the king had laid down for Ambrose's confinement, the warder held the keys to the water gates. Pognole had allowed the man with the handmark and Dante to torment an innocent man, but he had sneaked them in at night, outside of public view. It had been necessary to keep their presence secret from his legitimate overseer.

"You told me you had notified the warder to double Ambrose's protection. But, then, twice nothing is nothing. If you mean what you say about protecting my brother and me, you'd best not trust the warder to do it. Else tell me why Mage Dante and some other mage were allowed to see him."

"Dante! When?" Genuine surprise. An unusual slip. Duplais was a bottomless well, taking in everything and yielding nothing.

"I don't know. He sneaked in during the night to finish the work his friend began."

Duplais could not be either of Pognole's masters. He had been genuinely furious when Pognole forbade him to accompany me into the prison. And Ambrose would have recognized the Savin mark on Duplais' hand as the same device marked our goodfather's hand. But someone had installed the devilish warder apurpose. I'd vow it was the same person who held my father.

Duplais did not question me further. His attention seemed wholly preoccupied with our surroundings.

Perhaps it was overwrought nerves, perhaps it was the poisonous atmosphere of the Spindle, lingering to addle my head, but the world seemed fundamentally altered now dark had fallen. The harbor was deserted. On a mild autumn night, gleaners should be scouring the mudflats and the docks. Fishermen should be unloading a late catch. But scarce a light could be seen anywhere, and the only sounds were the faint clangs of buoys and the slop of the river about the docks. *World's changing*, Scago had said. *Magic's comin' back.* As if magic were a personality of itself—or a defeated legion come to reconquer what it had lost.

Ladyslipper was already skittish when we reclaimed our mounts from the tallyman's lad. The boy snatched his fee from Duplais' hand, and without a word grabbed his lantern and sped up a dark dockside lane. Duplais tried four taverns before finding torchmen to light our way back to Castelle Escalon, and had to pay ten times the usual fee.

We'd gone no more than half a kilometre up the Market Way when a flock of birds erupted from a warehouse to our left—thousands of them flooded into the night, screeching, fluttering, blocking out half the sky as they spiraled upward. The storm wind of their wings snuffed one of the torches, and our bearers threw down Duplais' coins and streaked back down the hill.

"Ride!" Duplais shouted, as the tip of the spiral reached its apex and arced downward again, on a course to intercept us at the boulevard that divided Riverside from the upper city.

The horses scarce needed a nudge to break into a gallop. The wind stung eyes and nostrils like summer wildfires in the maquis. Fluttering wings mimed the wavering thunder of the flames. As Ladyslipper's breath chugged beneath me, we approached the deserted boulevard.

At the moment we crossed, Duplais flung one hand backward and shouted, *"Carriamente!"* The air rippled as if a transparent curtain had been drawn. A few birds plummeted to earth, and the bulk of the wild flock arced away. A glance behind and I saw the birds spiral downward into the dark masses of tenements. Faint cries fractured the silence. An infant's wail threaded the settling quiet.

In tandem Duplais and I reined in and coaxed our mounts to a walk. My head throbbed with pent chaos. Yet I could not take time to inquire how it was possible that a failed student of Seravain had worked this seeming . . . magic . . . to turn aside the maddened birds, as he had the rats the first time we rode these streets. A patch of thicker night, very like a fog collected in a hollow or river gorge, drifted in front of us. Unwilling to retreat, we rode through it. I could not see Ladyslipper's ears. Thinking of rats and sinkholes, I bent low over her neck. "Careful, careful of your steps, sweetings. Take us home. To the stable. To the warmth. To the light."

When we emerged from the thick dark, Duplais nudged his mount closer. "Do we encounter another such, halt. I'll dismount and lead them both."

Such patches hung everywhere in the streets. When we could not avoid another, I stopped as he'd said. But the dark reached out to enfold me, and I could neither hear my companion nor feel his presence. "Duplais?"

He didn't answer. Panic rose in curdling waves. But for Ladyslipper's sake I whispered soothing nonsense. When we emerged from the blackness, Duplais was waiting.

"I halted," I said, accusing. "I waited, called, but you didn't answer."

"I called you, as well. I don't know." I did not need to articulate the question he had answered. And so we rode on into the Plas Royale.

The drifting purple and green lights had multiplied in the ruin of the Bastionne Camarilla. And some few drifted into the roadway, like bladderfish floating on an incoming tide. Duplais halted to let them pass or detoured to avoid them. I followed his lead, sickened when one came too near, a pocket of cold that stank of char and soot.

"What are they?" I whispered when we had navigated and arrived at the palace gates.

He shook his head and breathed deep, as the guards approved his identity and opened the gate. "Honestly, damoselle, I have no idea." It struck me as his first entirely unguarded opinion since his appearance at Montclaire.

We dismounted and gave our horses to a waiting lad. "Sonjeur . . ."

Duplais had tried to help Ambrose in the days before Papa's trial. The "officious prick," so Ambrose said, had prevented him pronouncing some salacious opinions of King Philippe within hearing of the Guard Royale, warning repeatedly that reckless speech from a youth on the verge of manhood was no game. And at the trial, I had listened as the Accuser had recounted Ambrose's behavior honestly before the king, yet left out the full extent of my brother's foolishness.

". . . my brother has been obscenely, horrifically abused in the Spindle. They've used sorcery to torture him."

"Damoselle, your brother's status is entirely out of my purview. Please present your findings to someone who might have an interest." Torchlight glinting on his stony face, he bade the waiting soldiers divine grace and walked away.

"Damn your grace and your honor and your king," I spat, but under my breath, like the coward I was. And then I cursed my own foolish notion that Portier de Savin-Duplais might actually possess a heart.

CHAPTER 16

I slept little after my visit to the Spindle. Black fogs infested my dreams, deadening sight and sound and every sense. Suffocating, I flailed at the patchy night until it shattered into birds, thousand upon thousand of starlings fluttering, screeching, spiraling into a leaden sky, only to reveal Ambrose chained to the Spindle wall, screaming, his body limned in colored fire. Duplais stood between Ambrose and me, silver light streaming from his hands, creating a barrier I could not cross. Magic. *Real* magic. *His* magic. But before I could decide whether his power caused Ambrose's torment or shielded me from it, another black fog engulfed me, and it all began again.

Well before sunrise, I lay listening to the mournful drizzle outside my window, cursing my choice to keep the potion from Ambrose. I should have allowed him to decide his own future.

Inevitably the palace day began. Ella greeted me with dreadful news. Physician Roussel had fallen prey to a virulent flux in the night. No one knew as yet if he would live or die.

Stunned, I raced into my clothes and joined the household in the queen's salon. Eugenie and the ladies-in-waiting were attending Lady Cecile's rites at the deadhouse. Without the senior ladies to manufacture errands or instigate activities, the maids of honor and other householders were at a loss for occupation. Exchanging fearful rumor must suffice until late afternoon, when the combined households and the local nobility would sit down at a feast in the ducessa's honor.

Not long after my arrival, word arrived of a servant who had succumbed in the night to a virulent flux. Tales had already linked the red-haired girl's death with the physician's illness. The kitchen servants were in terror of an epidemic, examining one another's tongues and dosing themselves with saffron and teas made from pomegranate, sage, and white oak bark. The world seemed mantled in dread.

I could not force myself to conversation. Could not settle. Not even reading could tempt me on such a day. Though I grieved for the dead girl and hoped the best for the kind physician, it was fear for my brother had me pacing.

My goodfather was no tyrant, but a strong, pragmatic, and enlightened king. Thus, like a fool, I had believed my brother safe in the Spindle. Agitated by confinement and restriction, yes, but never deprived of the most basic comforts. Never in physical danger. For certain, never so ignominiously, so vilely, abused. What in the name of all saints was I to do?

I considered another appeal to Lord Ilario, or perhaps directly to Eugenie herself, who had been willing to dispatch her servant to succor my mother. But Eugenie and Philippe were estranged, and no one but the king himself could set Ambrose free or, at the least, commit him to less odious confinement. Logic insisted I must appeal to the king yet again.

An ornate writing table sat in a remote corner of the room, set with jade inkpots cleverly carved in the shapes of elephants, and an ivory monkey embracing a brass pot of quills. But a quick investigation determined the desk and its charming accoutrements entirely decorative. What I would have given for a hammer to smash the useless thing!

". . . claimed it was a couchine!" The word snatched at my attention, as two women strolling the perimeters of the salon arm in arm passed within range of my hearing. "So like a doctor to share food with a servant. Do you know the disgusting things physicians do?"

A shared *couchine* . . . a red-haired serving girl . . . Physician Roussel . . .

My skin broke into a fevered sweat. As if it hovered in the air before me, I could see the steaming couchine on its flowered plate. Intended for me. But I had sent it back: *Return it to Physician Roussel or have it yourself.* And so the girl must have done. And they had shared it. And she had died. Truth glared at me like a skull and bones. Poison.

Roussel, sick himself, could not have been the poisoner. Yet he had sent me the pastry . . . or had he? A gentleman had sent it, the red-haired girl had said, and I had assumed that person to be the amiable physician. But others could have witnessed our exchange about the pastries. And now the girl was dead, unable to say if I had returned the plate to the same gentleman who intended it for me.

Hand pressed to my lips, I fled the room, caring naught for protocol, for duty, or for Duplais, perched on a stool next to the door, absorbed in his journal. Any man or woman in that chamber could have dispensed poison in the couchine. *Here, child. Leave that plate for a moment and fetch me a cup of tea.* Or, *Trade me that little pastry for this larger one, girl. I've not touched it; none will mind. Tell her a gentleman sent it.* The child would have obeyed the villain, just as she had me. And now she was dead. Like my sister. Like Cecile. Like Ophelie de Marangel and all those other victims four years ago and who knew how many since.

"Ah, Damoselle Anne!" Chevalier Ilario's chirruping greeting as I entered the passage struck my clamorous spirit as the scrape of steel on glass. His mustard-striped taffeta scorched my eyes. "Your felicitous family reunion, was it satisfactory?"

"I must beg your indulgence, lord chevalier. Please excuse me."

"Certainly. I only wondered—"

Rudely, I left him gaping. I owed him every courtesy. Of everyone in this horrid place, he had shown a willingness to aid me. But to thread the needles of conversation was beyond me just now. Someone wanted me dead.

Grieving for the red-haired child and praying the Pantokrator's angels to succor the kind physician, I sped through the east wing, unable to still my shaking no matter how tight I wrapped my arms.

So distraught. So afraid . . .

It's nothing.

Clearly not. Is it the voices in your head?

Only then did I realize what was happening. The intruder had joined me again, nudged me gently, and without thought I had responded.

"No, no, no, no!" My hands gripped my temples. "Go away!"

The door inside me closed, and he was gone. But it was not silent inside my skull. Saints' mercy, the voices were still there, potion or no.

Choking down a cry, I broke into a run, passing the turn to my own room. I needed to escape these poisonous walls and this growing strangeness in my head. I sped down the broad stair and into the window gallery.

A movement just ahead of me. A startled face whipped round—a pale and dark smear. "Hold up—ungh!"

The collision was unavoidable. A hard, solid point struck just beneath my breastbone.

Objects went flying. The world blurred. The pain in my middle bent me in two. I could not cry out. Could not breathe. Could. Not. Breathe.

The face swam before my own. Words. A laugh aborted. Hands fumbled at me as I crumpled. Awkward . . . slipping . . . dying . . . The solid collision of head and the hard ground scarce registered.

"Damoselle Anne . . . hold on . . . easy . . . easy." As if from the bottom of a well.

Cold marble held my back. *Dead . . . dead . . . dead . . . stupid girl . . .*

With a painful whoop, my lungs sucked in air; then I was coughing and curling up to soothe my bruised middle.

Cold fingers tapped nervously at my cheek, and an arm slipped tentatively around my shoulders. "Damoselle, forgive me. I just stepped out. Wasn't watching. Do tell me you're all right."

He helped me sit up. Crossing my arms tight across my breast, I blinked away the blur and looked up. Mage Dante's mournful assistant knelt before me, aghast.

"Saints Awaiting! What's happened?" a second man called from behind me.

"Only a small collision, lord chevalier. Knocked the wind out of her. I'll see to her."

The sorcerer helped me to standing. Too busy inflating my burning chest to speak, too shaken to repudiate his attentions, I allowed him to lead me down a passage and sit me on a stool behind a writing table littered with books and papers. "Stay here. I'll fetch something. Only a moment. You're not going to topple off?"

I managed a positive finger wag, confident of remaining upright only because he'd propped my hands on the table. He wrenched at the latch on a lower pane of a tall window. Damp air bathed my face as he scurried off in the direction we'd come. Concentrating on moving air in and out, I dared not turn my aching head to see where he'd gone.

He was back in moments with a cold wet cloth that he dabbed at my forehead.

"Does this help? I've always heard *damp cloths*, but I'm thinking perhaps you should be lying down."

"One. Moment," I whispered. Gradually the world was coming back into focus and the cramping behind my ribs was easing. I straightened my back a little and kneaded my midsection. He wore a gray academic gown, not spiked armor, and he carried no pike or bludgeon. "Don't know what hit me so hard."

He blanched and stuffed the wet towel into my hand. "Oh, daemon spawn! I'll be back!" And he raced off again.

Holding the towel to my somewhat clearer head, I glanced around at where he'd brought me. The writing table sat along the wall of a passage, lit and cooled by the great window bay in its end wall. Odd, a desk in a passage.

A rush of realization tinged with fear spurred me off the stool. I knew exactly where I was. This was the same corridor I'd visited two nights previous to spy on the murderous Lady Antonia.

The panting young man reappeared and dumped eight or ten books onto the desk atop the rest. "Ah, you're up. Most excellent. It was these injured you, I'm afraid," he said, stacking his volumes more carefully.

"You slammed into— Well, my studies take up a great deal of time I'd rather spend with ladies, but I've never had books come between a lady and me in so dire a fashion. I was on my way to the palace library to return this hodge-podge."

"My fault entirely." I passed him the towel and began a retreat. "You've been very kind, Adept—"

"Jacard," he said, grinning and sweeping a bow, exposing a handmark in the shape of a winged lion. "Jacard de Viole. And you, of course, are Anne de Vernase, the queen's racing maid of honor. Are you always in such a hurry?"

"It must seem like it." I glanced at the door behind him. A murderer's door. Dante's door, I believed. Could I make some advantage of this? Learn something? "Tell me, is your master truly so terrifying as he appears? When he looks at me, I feel . . . sullied."

"Everyone does." Jacard bobbed his head, keeping his voice low. "But truth is, he's mostly bluster and bald arrogance."

"But I've heard he's responsible for inexplicable horrors—bird storms, fires, ruin." Artifice could mask strength as well as weakness. It would take the Pantokrator himself to convince me Dante was not the most dangerous man I'd ever met.

"Oh, he's talented, no doubt. But he's like a racing horse that shows all he's got in the first half kilometre, then keels over."

"He's despicable"—the memory of Eugenie's dreams and my brother's despair set fire racing through my veins, scalding limbs, cheeks, tongue— "cruel and vicious, abusing his servants, tormenting our queen, torturing helpless prisoners—" I clamped my mouth shut, cursing my incautious tongue.

But Jacard heard exactly what I never should have spoken. He edged closer, his back to the mage's door. "I heard you visited the Spindle yesterday." Quiet. Eager. "Has my master done something awful there?"

I near choked on my idiocy. Never could I allow anyone to believe Ambrose had identified his middle-night visitors. "I've certainly no evidence. My brother seems very confused. Cowed. But it's clear that he has been . . . disciplined . . . with magic. Indeed, he is covered with scars and bruises, and I recalled that terrible incident at the Arothi reception where Master Dante beat— Well, it sounded something the same."

Jacard's scarlet brow could have lit a cellar.

I babbled on as if I hadn't noticed. "I asked my brother if Master Dante had done it, and the stubborn boy said he didn't know, that he'd been told to keep his face to the wall. But the mage is the most frightening person I know and I attribute everything despicable to him. Why would a kind gentleman like you stay on? I understand Collegia Seravain has fine tutors and a library filled with magical texts. Surely you'd be welcome there." Let Jacard think me a dimwit maiden.

"Tedious schoolbooks and mediocre masters don't suit me," he said, purring like a barn cat at a saucer of milk. "But Dante . . ." He leaned close and dropped his voice. "I've a theory he possesses some source or device that makes his work more potent than other magic. There are tales of daemon-wrought jewels that can give a man power beyond imagining. Dante does his best to obscure it with this show he puts on."

"You don't think— He's not involved in this despicable practice my wretched father perpetrated?" Let feigned horror mask my own hunger for information.

"Blood transference? He could be, though none will ever prove it. He's wickedly clever at covering his tracks." Jacard lifted a thin little volume from the desk, smoothing its crackled cover absently with his thumb. "You see, the puzzle is not just the power he uses to bind spellwork, but the nature of the work itself. His magic demonstrates complexities unknown in current practice. *Someone* needs to pay attention."

"So that's why you stay?"

"More than four years I've put up with him, despite the insults, the petty errands, the demeaning gossip. But every moment, I edge a little closer to uncovering his secrets. Soon, now, I'll show them all that he's not what he claims."

He forced a sheepish grin, seeming to realize he'd displayed more than he intended. He'd twisted the slender book so hard a binding stitch snapped.

"I get a bit hot about the man, of course," he said, tossing the volume back onto the heap of books. "Takes a bit of convincing not to take the next ship bound for Syanar. Instead, I'd best be off and get these back to the library. The mage has been on a rampage about history and symbols and blood-family genealogy of late. He devours more books than food, and with the same ferocity that he devours his servants. I'd like to throw the man and his precious books into a mine shaft. That would unnerve him right enough."

"My position here seems entirely to be sent on errands," I said, ideas bumping and crowding one another. *History . . . symbols . . . blood-family genealogy.* The very things I needed to understand the scraps of evidence I held from Lianelle and Cecile. "Indeed, my duties take me to the library this morning. Could I express apologies for my heedlessness by delivering these for you?"

"Honestly, I'd welcome the relief," he said, astonished and pleased. "I've a tenday's work he's expecting done by this evening. But are you sure you're feeling up to it?"

I breathed deep and felt only a slight bruising. "Now my lungs recall their duties, I seem quite well. I'm happy to help. Please indulge me." I held out my arms.

With mumbled doubts and repeated solicitations, he transferred an armload of books and bundled scrolls to me. The collection was more awkward than heavy.

I didn't swallow the purity of Jacard's motives—his willingness to risk proximity to a such a dangerous man because someone needed to "keep watch" on him. Jacard wanted Dante's knowledge to elevate his own position. But that was a very human aim, ordinary and understandable. One thing certain: He despised Dante as much as I did. The adept could be a most useful acquaintance.

"Do take care, Adept. You're a braver soul than I."

He bowed, momentarily sobered. "And you, damoselle. I'd be pleased to encounter you under circumstances involving no violence. Slow your steps, perhaps?"

Vowing to do just that, I returned to the window gallery at a more deliberate pace, and with one suspicion confirmed. The laboratorium with the grand windows, the apartment where Lady Antonia had gone to meet her partner in murder, belonged to Master Dante.

I reversed my earlier course and headed for my bedchamber. Running away would accomplish nothing for the dead girl or the physician or any of those who awaited justice.

Jacard's estimate of Dante's work intrigued me. *Complexities of magic unknown in current practice . . .* There it was again, the hint of some internal dispute fueling these events. Had Lianelle and Lady Cecile stumbled on something deeper—a war *already* being waged between factions of the Camarilla? Dante might have been summoned to Seravain to uncover why a rival had killed Lianelle or to mask the circumstances of her death. His destruction of the Bastionne could be a remnant of such an internecine battle.

Duplais could be a participant in the war, too, proclaiming himself a failure at magic to deceive some rival faction. For I had seen his empty fingers create a barrier to turn away the attacking birds . . . and the brilliant light he'd shot at swarming rats. What could I call it but magic?

Magic. Like a mighty fortress wall undercut by sappers with picks and knives, my long-held denial was on the verge of collapse. Twisting the possibilities of mechanisms or alchemistry to explain Duplais' deeds or how Ella and Antonia had looked straight through me had become more difficult than the admission: Some spells worked. And if so, then, like any objects of value, they could cause a war.

Magical rivalries did not explain *Antonia's* interest in the matter or the vile manipulation of Eugenie's dreams. Perhaps these were but distractions from the villains' real purposes. And none of this explained why my father remained alive. He had been convicted as the daemonic Aspirant, the perpetrator of the grand conspiracy to overturn my goodfather's reign. What further use had his captors for him? Or for my brother?

The answer must be found in Lady Cecile's scribbled diagrams, and in the books Lianelle had read, the magic she had worked from them, and the magical key she had sent me. The key to what?

A serving lad halted in midstride, gawking as I topped the stair. Oddly, he didn't offer to take my armload of books. Two kitchen girls sped past, but not without a glare.

The encounter with Jacard had set me on course again. Once returned to my bedchamber, I took up my pen to compose the letter to my good-father. While acknowledging a sovereign's historic right to constrain the grown son of his avowed enemy, I protested the particular restrictions imposed in the name of prison discipline. I did not mention Pognole by name, nor detail the most shameful abuses I only suspected. But mentions of hooks and scars and the particular deprivations and degradations I had witnessed could not but lead any intelligent man to certain conclusions.

The letter signed and sealed, I rang for Ella. As I waited for her, I examined Dante's books. They might give me some insight regarding his areas of interest. The collection included an herbal, a genealogy of the kings of Sabria, and several general histories of Sabria, including a basic treatise on the Blood Wars that I had read years ago in my own studies. I was surprised to discover one of the books to be a brand-new scientific text on the eye, based on the most modern theories of the transmission of light through the air, glass, and water. Another, more appropriate to my ideas of a mage's studies, was titled *The Proven Magicks of Gemstones.* Though the crudely stitched codex had innumerable colored sketches of gems and settings, the text was little more than an agglomeration of folklore and outlandish superstitions. I doubted even a sorcerer would find it useful.

The last volume puzzled me the most. *Divine Harmonies and Discords of the Air* seemed to record a dry, philosophical dispute on whether music was a specific gift of the Creator to humankind, provided whole and entire as a means to guide us through Ixtador's gates, or whether it was entirely man-made, a bold insolence that created a breach in the wall of Heaven. I could not envision Mage Dante caring for such pedantry.

A tap at the door announced Ella. "Damoselle?"

"I've a letter to post," I said, jumping up from my chair. "I was hoping you might prevail upon your brother again, as I'd like it sent outside the common way."

"Don't know," she said. "It's a risk for him." The girl's freckled face was composed as always. But her back was stiff, her eyes averted. Something was wrong.

"Is there bad news?" I said. "Is it the physician? Have more fallen ill?"

"No more've sickened, damoselle. And I've heard the physician recovers, which is a relief to all but poor Naina and her mam. Is there any other service you need of me?"

After a whispered thanksgiving, I raised Ella's dropped chin. Suspicion had turned her gray eyes to stone and plump lips to a hard line.

"This Naina brought me a couchine," I said. "She told me a gentleman sent it. I believed that gentleman to be the physician, and the thought . . . gladdened . . . me, as he has treated me kindly, and I've not had a gentleman friend for a very long time. But I'd had a fright that morning and couldn't eat, so I told her she could take it back to the physician and taste it herself, if he didn't want it. She was obedient, and I never imagined that the sweet might have come from a person who might wish me harm. You must believe me, Ella. Never, ever would I do something to harm an innocent girl. Never."

"Didn't think it," she said softly. "Didn't want to think it. But Eune the footman said he saw you give her the plate, and she carried it straight to the physician. And she was such a good girl. She'd never have took it to eat on her own." Ella swallowed a sob, the first chink I'd ever seen in her servant's armor.

I threw my arms around her, drawing her sturdy warmth to my breast. I had relied on her so much, and she was so young. "Her death is vile and unjust," I said. "Creation's balance seems wholly askew, and you just want to scream at Heaven."

Ella's stiffness melted away in my arms. When her sobs quieted, I nudged her to arm's length. "Tell me, is someone collecting a handsel for Naina's family? I'd like to offer something for it."

"Aye. Her mam's sickly and there's none else to earn for her. We've hopes summat will take her in if we can give a bit to help out."

"I'm going to find out who's responsible for this crime, Ella. I promise. But for now, I really need this letter sent—in hopes of saving another innocent."

"Alonso'll see to it. He's my brother's coachman friend, and he'll—" Her eyes widened as she recognized the name of the addressee. "He'll do it most careful, damoselle."

After another embrace, I sent her off with a silver piece for the coachman and another for Naina's handsel. The donation could not soothe my conscience. Only discovering the perpetrator could do that, for sure as I was born, the girl had died instead of me. Murdered for what?

I pulled out Lady Cecile's history book. *Gautier.* That name linked all of this: my father, my sister, and her encrypted books, the sorcery Duplais had called a kind *not seen in ages of the world.*

Clearly the writer was an admirer of the Gautier. Gautieri architecture had been *elegant and innovative.* Gautieri students were *the most diligent at any collegia magica.* The family's pursuit of knowledge had probed the farthest reaches of mysticism and magical practice, and the library at Collegia Gautier—twenty thousand scrolls and codices, an extraordinary number even by modern standards—had been the most complete literature ever recorded of any academic discipline.

One footnote caught my particular interest because of its mention of encryption and blood transference:

Historian Georg de Veon-Failleu posits that jealousy of the Collegia Gautier library and its restrictions on access, implemented by extensive encryption, lay at the root of the Mondragon-Gautier rivalry. The Mondragons were historically weak in their practice of the mystic arts and regularly enhanced their skills through the extensive use of blood transference. Their scholarship and investigative skills were substantially weaker even than their practical skills. Few Mondragon practitioners were literate.

The theory struck me as illogical. Why would anyone start a war over access to books they could not read? But then, history was often distorted. Papa had always said the first task of victors in any war was to rewrite its history in their own favor. But both families were exterminated by the end. No one had won the Blood Wars.

Duplais could likely explain more. Of all things, I had granted him the virtues of intelligence and intellectual honesty. Yet now that I believed my father innocent, even that was suspect. Had Duplais even a notion that his conclusions were wrong? The man was a cipher, and his hateful disregard for my family stung bitterly. Yet if I could learn what I needed no other way, I must learn from him, even if I had to take Lianelle's potion and follow him around.

I opened the treatise on the Blood Wars. Names leapt out from the page.

> *Germond de Gautier, lamed by a Mondragon potion in retaliation for his sending a spy into the Mondragons' desert fortress, labored for thirty years to develop a magical defense wall that could shield innocents from Mondragon spellwork. The Ring Wall was under constant siege by Mondragon raiders who called up daemonic spirits to burn every hovel and household in the district. The daemons ravished maidens and boys, bringing evil magics to bear upon the Gautieri works until they crumbled.*
>
> *In 693, Reviell, the last Conte Mondragon, wearing a horned helm, left a path of spectres, ravaged souls, and charred villages in his wake as he pursued the weakened Gautieri to their doom.*
>
> *Abandoning the broken Ring Wall, the Gautieri retreated into the Voilline Rift at the base of the holy mount. Backed deep against the foot of the crags where Ianne, the first of the Reborn, brought human-kind the gift of fire, the valiant Gautieri mage line unleashed the fires of Creation against the Mondragon legion. Whereupon the Mondragons called upon the Souleater and his earth-bound daemons, wrenching the sun from the sky and thrusting it into a pit to swallow their sworn enemies.*
>
> *It was said that the dead walked on that foul day, and trees curled back into the earth, and arrows reversed upon the archers. Frost blighted the vineyards though it was the midst of summer, and throughout Sabria, infants crawled back into their mothers' wombs. For ten days and nights the battle raged, until both sides lay bloodied and exhausted.*

The remnants of the two families had fled, but the Sabrian king and his subjects had declared them pariah and exterminated the lot of them.

The other histories sounded the same notes. The collegia and its library had been wonders of the world. Yet scholarly achievements had not saved the Gautieri. Whatever the level of their magical or academic skills, the Mondragons were acknowledged as capable strategists who pushed their hated rivals to the brink of destruction. A length of string marked a page in one of the volumes.

> *Reviell de Mondragon's incineration of Collegia Gautier and its library in 693 threatened to send all of the known world back to the age of pictographs and stone tools. For this depredation, even more than the blood-leeching wreaked on hapless victims, even more than the systematic extermination of the noble Gautieri line, did the Camarilla Magica break its long tradition and execute the savage conte in public. On the day the Concord de Praesta was ratified by King Pascal and Camarilla, Reviell, the last Mondragon, was bound on the Plas Royale and flayed by Fassid knives. Scyllid scorpions, gathered from the deserts of Kadr, were unleashed upon his skinless flesh before his entrails were drawn and burnt. Defiant to the end, the devil conte warned the watchers that their beloved dead would "pay the price of Gautieri greed." From that day forward, the family mark of the Mondragons was altered to dueling scorpions, reflecting the stinging poison of depraved sorcery. . . .*

The lurid descriptions nauseated me. And I marveled at yet more skewed logic. If the Mondragons were jealous of Gautieri spellwork, why would they destroy the very library where they might have learned how to imitate it? If my young sister could decrypt the Gautieri books, then surely the Mondragons could have found someone to do so. Fools, then. Perhaps the Creator's saints did protect the world from its worst evils, ensuring our worst villains were either too stupid or too clumsy to carry their plans to completion. That did little to ease the pain they caused along the way. Pain and chaos . . . the Aspirant's aim, so Duplais had said at Papa's trial.

A disharmonious clamor of bells from city, palace, and temple announced both the fourth hour of the afternoon watch and Cecile de Blasencourt's journey feast. Saints and daemons, I'd used the entire afternoon. Dante's books would have to be returned to the library later.

As I returned Cecile's history book to the drawer, I fingered Lianelle's magical trinkets. The fortress wall of my convictions sagged. If her powder left me unseeable, then what of these other things? True magic. Gautieri magic, right out of these history texts. I doubted the pendants would have meaning without a sister to share them, but the ring . . . She'd said the falcon's head ring could warn me of poison. Why hadn't I been wearing it the previous day?

Something had changed. The conspirators had wanted Lianelle's book—which they'd gotten. They also wanted these things she had made, but they'd never shown any interest in me. Now someone was trying to kill me. Perhaps I was getting close to the truth.

The fire smoldered in my gut. "Show me your worst," I snapped. "I am Michel de Vernase's daughter, and you'll not take me down so easily."

I slipped the gold circle onto my finger, locked the hidden drawer, and set out for Cecile de Blasencourt's journey feast. Everyone would be there.

CHAPTER 17

The Minor Hall of Castelle Escalon housed a glittering assemblage. At least forty long guest tables had been ranked across the hall and laid with fine linens and painted porcelain. The raised head table sat crosswise to the others in front of a newly completed mural that depicted *The Creation of All That Walks* in vivid colors and astonishingly lifelike detail.

Every lady and gentleman of the court seemed to be present at the journey feast—we maids of honor sprinkled amid the others like sugared plums on a cake. Tucked away in the corner behind the high table stood Duplais, his hands at his back, primly overseeing guests and servants alike. Chevalier Ilario, pensive in froths of black lace and taffeta, topped by a gray-plumed hat, sat at Queen Eugenie's left hand. On her right Mage Dante slouched in his chair. Bored and disdainful, his gaze roved the crowded tables below the dais. When one person shuddered and turned away, his shadowed attention moved on to the next.

A permanent position as the object of Mage Dante's scrutiny seemed more attractive than my own seating arrangement. My assigned dinner companion had inflamed my complexion to a heat that could roast the duck on my plate.

"The lady says ye ride astride like a man. Is't true? As skill it's fine, for Gurmedd paths are too steep for dainty saddling. And truth, the considering of a right lady spreading her legs rousts my rod. But then, I've a wonder about yer maidswatch." The Honorable Derwin de Scero, Barone Gurmeddion, wiped his mouth on his grease-spotted sleeve and lubricated his most astonishingly vulgar conversation with yet another mug of ale. "Bad enough to take on traitor's spawn, but I'll have no bride broke without I do it myself."

"I am a skilled rider," I mumbled, solely because failure to respond would cause him to repeat his vile speculations louder. The scandalized ladies and gentlemen seated across the table and to either side of Derwin had already averted their faces and retreated as far as the close seating permitted, but they would not ignore such ripe fodder for a long winter's gossip.

Only the barone's avowal that he relished women who battled his will, "begging to be tamed" had quashed my fervent desire to smash a plate into his ugly face. Instead I had restrained my temper, spoken as little as possible, and distracted myself by searching the faces for Queen Eugenie's late-night liaison. Such a strikingly confident man would stand out even in such a crowd, especially if he made a habit of out-of-fashion apparel. No luck at finding him. No luck at persuading Derwin to shift his attentions elsewhere.

"Ye must speak up when addressing a lord, girl," declaimed Derwin. "Women are best silent—and I teach 'em that right off—but when I ask, I expect a firm and truthful answer. No squirreling. No dainty-mouthing. Whispering bespeaks liars and sneaks. Won't have it in my house."

Lady Antonia had snagged me as I hurried into the hall. Called me *caeri* and dithered over "this new and exciting prospect" like a child unwrapping a birthday gift, then whisked me off and introduced me to the most singularly unattractive man I had ever met. Leathery brown skin appeared to have shrunk to fit his hard, bony frame. Sparse gray-brown hair bristled on his knobby skull and jutting chin. His expensive camlet was splattered with remnants of a month's meals, and the reek of sour flesh near had me gagging as he circled me, appraising as if I were a horse for hire.

"I've not bedded a blood-kin woman before. Don't you imagine to use your witching on me, though. There's iron enough in Gurmedd's crags; magic don't work there. But please me with your *female* tricks"—his tongue darted out from wide-stretched lips—"and I'll treat ye fair."

Antonia had lavished the lord—a very minor lord—with flattery, insisting that his warriors' unmatched prowess, his staunch alliance with the king, and his determined stewardship of the most remote mountain passes between Sabria and Norgand kept our northern borders impregnable.

The Honorable Derwin could be a duc or King Philippe's sworn brother for all I cared. This particular alliance would *not* happen. I'd use Lianelle's potion and walk to Syanar first.

Derwin raised a grease-slicked hand. "Here, boy," he shouted to a passing servitor. "More of that meat, and plenty of skin with it."

The musicians in an upper gallery began a new tune—a somber, driving pulse of tambours overlaid by shawm and pipes, sinuous melodies in the mode of ancient Sabria. A troupe of veiled dancers whirled and leapt down the wide aisles between the guest tables, the bells and links about wrists and ankles chinking in rhythm.

The barone shifted his chair around to get a better view, dripping fat on his soiled garments while chewing the slab of duck breast impaled on his knife. He paused from time to time to lean toward the nearest gentleman and blurt lewd comments on the female dancers' physical attributes and their movements or positions.

The Temple taught that only family or dedicated mystics could, by their deeds of honor and righteous living, speed a soul's journey through the trials of Ixtador Beyond the Veil. But most people of my acquaintance presumed the Pantokrator would not discount the offerings of close friends and liege lords in the weighing of a soul's worthiness for Heaven. Queen Eugenie seemed to share that view. She had hired the city's finest players and musicians to send Lady Cecile off on her Veil journey with dignity. Even assuming the Pantokrator cared at all for humankind, I doubted Derwin's presence accorded the dead ducessa much benefit.

With the barone's attention diverted, I sought to clear my own thoughts of their murderous bent and focus my meditations on Cecile's welfare. I trained my eyes on my hands, folded in my lap. The falcon's head on Lianelle's ring stared back at me with its silver eye.

The exercise merely roused the inner voices I'd fought so hard to mute since slipping the gold circle on my finger. They forever lurked in the nooks and niches of my mind, waiting to be heard . . . as they had since childhood. Since I discovered that being around cities and crowds caused hissing and buzzing in my ears. The thought mystified and terrified me. Proximity to my sister's magic seemed to swell them to a volume and intensity that threatened sanity. All my determination could quiet the din only to this muffled rumble. I would yield five years of my life to go back to Montclaire and the quiet countryside.

There you are.

I glanced up at Derwin's back as he strained to see the performers, and then at my equally absorbed neighbors, before grasping the source of the quiet words. Inside me. The clarity of his voice left the others but a murmur.

I've no wish to terrorize you. I glimpse you now and then, but I've stayed back to give you time.

Glimpse? All gooseflesh, I peered around the hall, examining every man within line of sight without moving my head.

Not with eyes. Don't you understand? We could be ten kilometres apart or a thousand. I glimpse you in the mindstorm . . . in the aether, where the unseen energies of life are expended. I hear you despite the damnable noise, though what we do is no more connected to ears than these words I send you are connected to a tongue. It's easiest to find you when strong emotion carries you into the aether, as on that first night. But with this gift you can open yourself to the storm at quieter times. Any time. Your voice is so clear, so distinct, I could pick it out were a whirlwind battering bricks round my head.

His presence surged, as if he felt the need to expend his thoughts before I dismissed him again. The feasting company receded to a blur.

If you'd rather I not intrude, I'll honor your wish. But I've grasped this is new to you, and I'd like to reassure you. Selfishly, because it is so . . . fine . . . to hear another, to know I'm not the only one . . .

Rushing now, like a stream broken loose of its channel. Because I did not stop him. Because I'd no desire to be trapped again in the vile present with Derwin of Gurmeddion. This voice reflected so much the barone was not.

You needn't fear it exposes you in any way. The very nature of the gift protects you . . . protects us both. I can only know what you reveal in words or by the tenor in which you speak them. Clearly you are a woman of strong passions who has experienced some upheaval of late—maybe only the unveiling of this gift. Yet were I standing at your side, I could not recognize you. I cannot know your face. I cannot know the place where you stand . . . or sit . . . or sleep. Try it. Tell me where I am just now. You cannot. I doubt you'd believe it anyway. Think of all you've divined of my history . . . my circumstances . . .

Which was nothing, of course. He was a man, not a child. He seemed thoughtful and well-spoken. Educated, his vocabulary and articulate grammar attested. Alone. Longing laced his every word. I told myself to be rational. He could be skilled at masking.

It's only natural you're skeptical. But there is no lying in the aether. Withholding, yes, but untruth galls the inner ear. Let me demonstrate. I'll tell you three things, and you must judge their truth. I live in Merona. Jolly pipe music will always lift my spirits. I spent one year of my life without speaking.

Two statements flowed past me, clean and sure. One scraped my spirit, discordant, like a vielle played with a stick instead of a bow. Closing my eyes, I shaped words in that private darkness behind my eyelids: *You detest jolly pipe music.* Then I nudged them into the chaos.

Pleasure . . . relief . . . a deep and resonant joy swept through me like a spring zephyr . . . feelings not my own, yet vigorous enough to crease my cheeks with a smile. *Exactly so,* he said. *Now you. Come, test me.*

Silk embroidery is my favorite pastime. I have delivered a foal with my own hands. I was born in a tent. The game came easy, so like those played at Montclaire. And I was well practiced at masking any feeling that might register in face or voice. Perhaps the skill might hold me impassive for this odd communication, as well.

So you are a woman of strong passions, born in a tent, who has helped a horse give birth and dislikes . . . detests? . . . embroidery. To despise mindless triviality makes perfect sense, but that you feel so strongly about the horse intrigues me. The birthing in a tent even more. Somehow I don't imagine you a shepherdess. Those who labor in the rough world are rarely the gentle spirits noble ladies imagine—yet you could be. Such gifts flourish most often in those close to the natural world. Perhaps you are a warrior woman riding across the steppes of Syanar. I cannot say how far this bond might stretch. Almost all I know of it has come from study—a mention here, a whisper there, a great deal of listening and experimenting.

I did not respond to this probing. Caution had not completely deserted me. But now I had engaged him, I desperately wanted to know more. That first time, I'd heard my father, too.

And so I ventured a step. *You say only we two can do this, but I hear many, some very clearly.*

Yes, the mindstorm. You hear the strong emotions of thousands. I do, as well. And yes, sometimes they are shaped in words—spoken or unspoken—and sometimes in feeling only. But none is directed at us. They just exist. The aether is the medium of souls. The mindstorm itself fluctuates like the weather—sometimes violent, sometimes serene, surging, fading. We cannot control who we hear any more than we can control the clouds and rain.

But if I picked out one voice from all these thousands, someone sorrowing or in pain, I could speak to him like this. . . .

Alas, no. We witness. We speak. But unless the other shares the gift, we cannot be heard. That's why it's named a curse.

Not even someone familiar . . . family . . . friends?

The negative response came before he spoke it. *Only the gift makes it possible to hear the voices of the mindstorm. Familiarity . . . acquaintance . . . plays no part. Nor have I discovered anything to suggest the gift runs in families, as magical talent does.*

He didn't know everything about it. I had heard my father's voice. That could not be coincidence. *So it's a form of magic?*

No. Everything I've read and heard insists they occur together, feeding and enriching each other, but the tangle curse is a separate—and extremely rare—gift. Or curse, as you may see it; I've questioned that often enough since my own gift's waking.

But I've no— I cut off my protest. This was getting much too intimate.

You don't have to tell me anything. And you shouldn't. You've no reason to trust me.

Questions whirred like a plague of gnats.

"Damoselle Anne . . ."

Alarmed, I blurted, *I thought you couldn't know!*

Yet even as his puzzlement reflected through me, I recognized the one who'd spoken my name was not the one inside—the speaker who existed in the medium of souls.

A terrible imagining swelled then, obscuring all else, as if one gnat from the swarm had grown to the monstrous proportions shown by an opticum lens. *Great Heaven, are you dead?*

Reflected shock . . . and then a wry amusement. *No, not dead. Just buried in a place I'd rather not be.*

"Damoselle Anne!"

The snapped address wrenched my eyes open. Senses registered the noisy clatter of knives and plates, the babble of five hundred tongues, the sawing cadence of a string consort. I felt as might a fish leaving the cool, peaceful depths of the ocean to breach the surface of a bustling harbor.

Directly in my line of sight was an oval of fine, crosshatched wrinkles caked with powder and rouge, and framed by tight curls of hennaed hair. Yellow eyes peered down at me as if I were a blotch on the floor.

"Dame Morgansa! So sorry. I was . . . meditating." I sat up straighter and tucked my hands under my crossed arms, shaking off the encounter that already seemed as remote as dream stories.

"You're bidden to attend. Come now."

Derwin glared at me from one side of the waiting woman, his beard glistening with duck fat. He licked his lips. "Snooty little trollop, ben't she? 'Twould be pleasureful, I'm thinking, to bend her. Tell your mistress."

Other faces turned our way as I left the disgusting lord behind. But their attention quickly reverted to the end of the hall. Afternoon sunlight beamed through the clerestory, transmuted to arrows of jeweled fire that fell upon the guests. A troupe of male singers behind the head table spun a transcendent elegy, so lovely that it surely traveled those jeweled beams straight to the Pantokrator's Heaven.

As I followed Morgansa through a side door, empty seats glared from the head table. Eugenie's. Antonia's. From his corner Duplais stared at me, eyes narrowed in speculation.

"What does your mistress need of me?" I asked Morgansa, as we threaded a swarm of hurrying servants carrying trays of meat, salads, and cheeses.

"'Tis Her Majesty bids you. She wishes a lady to attend her. The ladies-in-waiting are required to maintain the feast, and the other maids are encumbered with family duties. That leaves you." One would have thought Morgansa herself an empress, forced to treat with a barbarian.

Fraught with misgivings, I followed Morgansa down a short passage bristling with guards. Without waiting for an answer to her tap, we entered a small chamber, luxuriously appointed with damask couches, ebony tables and chairs, and even a narrow bed. From the music lapping at an inner door, I assumed this a retiring room behind the dais.

Flushed and breathing rapidly, Queen Eugenie sat stiffly upright on a padded chair so large it would have swallowed my father. Lady Antonia dabbed at the queen's forehead with a towel. Chevalier Ilario stood a few steps away, fidgeting with his hat.

"Here's the girl as you requested, Majesty," said Morgansa, sinking into a curtsy so obsequious, she could scarce untangle herself from it. "May I supply anything else for your comfort? A cushion? A soothing ice? A comfit?" Her weedy whining set my teeth on edge.

"No, thank you," said Eugenie softly. She caught her foster mother's arm in mid-dab and pressed it away. "Dearest dama, now Anne is here, you must return to my guests. I'm only a touch dizzy. After so long a rite at the deadhouse, I'm sure I drank my wine too quickly. But I'll not have Cecile's feast founder because of my weak head. Only *your* hand is firm enough to keep the ship righted and on course."

Antonia could have filled a ship's sails with her pained sigh. "But, *caeri* . . ."

"Please, dama. A royal presence is needed to supply proper honor."

"All right. Certainly. But you must sleep for a while. If anything should happen . . . as with the physician last night . . . this choice will haunt us both." The lady dithered, arranging Eugenie's garments, smoothing her hair, pressing the towel into her hand.

"My fair knight will protect me," said Eugenie, reaching out her hand to Lord Ilario. "All will be well."

My cheeks blazed.

Antonia curtsied in a sinuous motion, then turned to go, casting such a damning glare my way that my hand flew to my heart as if to make certain it remained in place. She commanded Morgansa to "supervise the chamber service," and slipped through the door, onto the dais.

The door snicked shut, silencing the singing. Eugenie immediately dispatched Morgansa to fetch a vial of smelling salts from her bedside table. Curiosity superseded apprehension. What was going on?

The answer came as soon as the scowling waiting woman had gone. The queen sagged in her chair. Lord Ilario had his arms around her before she could topple onto the floor. "Damoselle, if you would assist . . ."

Together we assisted Eugenie to the bed. Her skin burned through her clothing. I arranged the pillows under her head and fetched a shawl from one of the chairs to cover her when she began to shiver. "I'll be all right," she whispered, all strength departed from her voice. "I just feel so strange. I could not bear anyone to see . . . to start up the rumors yet again."

"Geni . . ." The chevalier was truly distressed.

"Fetch me some of Roussel's shellblade tisane, sweet brother. You know how it invigorates me. Honestly, I'll be well if I can but rest a little. Anne will sit with me, and we'll talk until you're back. I'm so happy you suggested her."

With a helpless glance, the chevalier hurried off.

"Surely you are more than just dizzy with wine, my lady. Someone with medical knowledge should see to you." Though who that might be, I didn't know. "Let me raise your feet a bit." I knelt at her bedside and tucked another cushion under her feet.

"There, you see, this is exactly why I've summoned you. Intelligent, perceptive, and kind." Her hot hand stilled my own. "Your mother's grace lives in you, Anne, and you need no further training in trivialities. I've a favor to ask."

"Whatever you need, my lady."

"For a little over two months"—her cheeks took on an even deeper scarlet—"since the king's last visit to Castelle Escalon, I've been subject to certain fevers and weaknesses. Though the sensations are . . . different . . . from the past, and my physician doubts, I believe I may be with child again. A blessing unexpected. But, you see, I cannot allow anyone to know. Not until we're sure. Perhaps not until the saints have blessed us fully with a healthy—" She breathed deep and steadied herself.

"Divine grace succor you, lady." Eugenie had suffered one child dead in infancy, one stillborn, and two more lost before carried to term.

"I need a female companion, someone quiet and trustworthy, who understands the difficulties of my position. The other maids of honor are sweet and devoted and so very dedicated to doing their best for their families. But they are quite . . . inexperienced." It seemed almost painful for her to cast such slight aspersion. "As for my dear ladies-in-waiting, truly, with my goodmother as she is, who needs more mothering? If you'll pardon my callousness, it helps that you are not in comfortable communication with my husband. He, in particular, must not know of this until I tell him myself. Another failure and he'll— Well, I cannot bear thought of the consequence."

But I already knew. The king's counselors, including my father, had long pressured Philippe to set Eugenie aside so that he might ensure an heir of his blood. At least in part it must explain the wedge that divided them. "I understand the need for discretion, lady."

"Ilario suggested you. Though few take his opinions seriously, my brother is an exceptional judge of character."

I bowed my head that she might not read my curiosity. If she worried over my goodfather's loyalty, then why in the name of the Creator did she dally with another man? Political marriages naturally spawned more fractured vows and adulterous intrigues than pairings founded in mutual desire and affection. That was one reason Papa had promised I'd never be subject to such an alliance. Yet both he and my mother had believed Philippe and Eugenie to have discovered such affection despite their entirely unpromising circumstances.

"Would you accept this charge, Anne? I know my favor will subject you to more gossip, and of all people, I'm aware of the harm gossip can do. To bring Sabria a healthy heir, I need a companion I can trust. But the choice is yours. I'll think no ill if you refuse."

"Certainly I will, my lady. I am deeply honored." Astounded, to be exact. Yet the more I was around her, the more I came to think that Eugenie de Sylvae's difficulty was not so much a weak mind or a careless attitude toward evil, as I had once believed, but a heart that imbued every person's behavior with the fairest possible motives.

"I'll need you to—"

A sharp rap on the door halted her thought. "Come."

I jumped up and retreated.

"Majesty, I could not wallow abed when I heard rumor of your illness." Sallow complected, hair askew, and clothes rumpled, Physician Roussel dropped to his knees at Eugenie's bedside.

"Ganet! How is it you're out of your sickbed?" said Eugenie, sitting bolt upright.

"I'm of robust constitution, Your Grace, and my illness denotes no element of contagion. How could I stay away when I hear you've collapsed in front of your court?"

"It was only a moment's weakness—this same devouring fever. Distressful, but nothing different from the other occasions."

"I should judge that, lady. Please . . ."

Sighing, she allowed him to take her hand in his broad one. Tracing the lines, he examined her palm, then curled his steady fingers around her wrist. After a moment's quiet, listening with his eyes closed, he brushed back her dark hair and pressed fingers to her temples, and then to her slender neck and her ankles. A twirl of his hand, and she stuck out her tongue for him to inspect. His steady thumbs lifted her eyelids. The brisk examination done, he withdrew his hands, sat back on his heels, and rubbed his head tiredly, causing his hair to stand even more on end.

"I see no change. We'll do a more thorough examination tomorrow, Majesty. Drink the shellblade tisane and sleep."

Eugenie laid a hand on his shoulder. "Thank you, Ganet. Now, before you scurry back to your lonely chambers to recover *fully* from this illness, I would like to introduce you to my dear handmaid, Anne de Vernase. Anne, this is my tireless, faithful—and wretchedly shy—physician, Ganet de Roussel."

He leapt to his feet and bowed. Whether his color or mine more nearly reflected the crimson velvet of the chamber's furnishing, I could not judge without a mirror glass.

"Physician, I cannot tell you how glad I am—"

"Damoselle! I am so gratified to see that—"

Our words tangled in the air, yet somehow communicated enough of our sentiments that guilt and apology were unneeded. My relief felt unbounded; he blamed me no more than I did him.

"Madame, I have made the lady's acquaintance briefly. I feared— Last I saw, she was enjoying a couchine. Needless to explain, I am immensely gratified she did not choose the spoiled one that felled me and the poor kitchen girl."

Perhaps it was only that I was watching exceptionally closely, but when Roussel caught my eye, he gave the slightest shake to his head. Warning me off the topic? If anyone, a scientific man should be able to distinguish the different effects of spoilage and true poisons.

Eugenie demanded a thorough explanation. And no matter the physician's dismissal of the incident as lamentable happenstance, she picked up at once on the sinister implications. "Rumor ever natters of dread conspiracies in Merona, and it is impossible to sort any crumb of truth from it. But a young woman dead? And the two of you at such risk? Ganet, report this to Lord Baldwin at once. His duty as my husband's First Counselor is to ensure the safety of this house. And both of you promise me you'll take more care. Anne, consider well the added risks of serving me so intimately."

"I am honored and pleased to serve you, Your Grace. No further consideration is necessary."

I *WAS* PLEASED, I THOUGHT, late that night as I closed Eugenie's bed curtains. Not merely for the selfish reason that I might learn more of Dante and Duplais and the murderous Antonia by orbiting the perilous sun that was Eugenie de Sylvae, but because the lady herself, open-hearted, loyal, and kind, deserved to have some ally beyond her foolish brother. Though Lord Ilario was not, perhaps, as inept as he appeared. The chevalier had gotten me into the Spindle within hours. And a single day after expressing his wish that Eugenie might listen to my warnings, I was her new maid of the bedchamber.

I finished tidying the room and tiptoed into the passage.

Lady Antonia had near split her skin when Eugenie informed her that I was to assume her bedchamber service. Antonia herself would take up Lady Cecile's duties, training the maids of honor. A good thing I was already wary of the woman.

I paused at the door to Doorward Viggio's chamber. Soft footsteps padded through the quiet apartments behind me. Thinking it might be Eugenie needing something, I retraced my steps.

Indeed she was up again and wearing the deep blue bedgown that flowed around her in elegant simplicity and set off her fair skin and dark hair. But she was not alone. The glow of the watch candle I'd left on her dressing table illuminated a romantic tableau, as a bearded man in voluminous scarlet sleeves kissed her hand. His out-of-fashion blue velvet chamarre fell to his knees, its lappets and hem banded richly with pearls. The elegant gentleman, the same I'd seen before, must have slipped up the servants' stair.

Embarrassed, I retreated quickly. Her friends were her business.

FOUR CHAMBERMAIDS AND A FOOTMAN stood in a whispering huddle at the corner of the passage where my bedchamber lay. Furtive glances my way seemed to intensify their murmuring. I almost reversed course rather than pass them by. But I was done with cowering. "Divine grace," I said, exposing my hand as I passed.

Some choked the proper response. Two girls bobbed their knees. None looked at me.

Gratefully, I pulled the bedchamber door closed behind me and sank to the bed. Heart and mind whirled with the strange and terrible day just past: poisoning and death, the wonders of this tangle curse and the strange intimacy with a person I had never seen, the vile prospects of alliance with Derwin of Gurmeddion, the intrigue of my new position, the pleasant prospect of getting to know Ganet de Roussel, and my deep and abiding fear for my brother.

I pulled off the falcon's head ring and tucked it away for the night with the potion vial. As the voices I'd held at bay—the *mindstorm*, my mysterious correspondent had called it—faded into the more familiar, subtle disturbance beyond my senses, I found myself sorely tempted to seek out the one who lived in the aether, *where the unseen energies of life are expended.* It was not so much that I could lay out the puzzle of poisons and pregnant queens, magical heresy, and ancient rivalries, but to hear a voice without suspicions, without connection to the tangled mysteries of Castelle Escalon, a person who could speak only truth and took such joy in sharing his strange gift.

Common sense scolded. Why would I believe his insistence that he could not lie?

No reason any sensible person would admit. But I did.

A booming staccato on my door propelled me to my feet. Before I could do more, the door burst open to a sour-mouthed, gray-haired fellow wearing a gray academic gown. Beside him stood a tall figure draped in flowing black robes. An enveloping green hood left only a raptor's nose and pair of seedlike eyes exposed to view. A mage's silver collar encircled his neck.

The gray-haired man waved a rolled parchment and shoved a heavy garment of dark wool into my arms. "Anne de Vernase ney Cazar, the Camarilla Magica summons thee to Witness in a matter of Treason and Sorcery."

CHAPTER 18

19 Ocet, night

Suffocation had never been one of my terrors. Not until the Camarilla inquisitor dropped the hood of wool and iron over my face. My shoulders already bore the weight of a voluminous gown, designed to mask a Witness's identity, and sewn with iron rings, designed to confound spellwork. So the gray-haired man had explained to me.

The inquisitor himself or herself—there was no way to know—had not spoken and would not. His silence signaled to all that the Camarilla would hear no plea, no testimony, no bargaining or command until the Witness had been taken to the Bastionne Camarilla and properly questioned.

"You've no right to question me. I've done nothing." I stumbled backward, wrenching the thick wool away from my mouth. "I am King Philippe's gooddaughter, the queen's maid of honor. This is the *king's* house."

I struggled to keep from babbling. Did they believe I had poisoned the serving girl? How did one prove innocence?

A body behind me halted my retreat.

"The Concord de Praesta prescribes that the Camarilla needs no authority but this warrant to enter any house, even a palace, or to summon or detain any Witness, even a king's goddaughter, pursuant to investigation of criminal matters involving sorcery." The gray-haired man's voice quivered with excitement.

"Then name my crime." I scrabbled at straws. Poisoning was not equivalent to sorcery.

"All will be revealed in time. Unless you are accused, you shall be returned here without prejudice. If you cooperate, we'll have no need for shackles."

Saints defend, shackles . . . the Bastionne . . .

They tugged the hood downward, deadening sound and cutting off the light, leaving me in the dark, accompanied by images of the gaping ruin and its floating lights. My stomach lurched as if I were plummeting from the splintered floors into the pooled darkness. My spirit boiled with fear.

We moved briskly, the adept holding one arm, the inquisitor the other, supporting me firmly enough I would not stumble. Heat and fear made my head swim, and I quickly became confused at the turns. No one spoke to me. I was alone with my jerky breaths and thudding heart.

Camarilla inquisitors had led Adept Fedrigo and Mage Orviene to their execution in shackles, shrouded in these same awful garments. Orviene had wailed from beneath his hood, *Do you know what they do to you in the Bastionne?*

No one did. Rumor spoke of terrible magics. My father had said that, whether or not the flesh displayed scars or bruises when a Witness emerged from the Bastionne, the spirit certainly did.

I considered calling on my friend in the aether. If he was close, he could get a message to the queen . . . someone. Or what if the inquisitors could detect such things? Hearing voices . . . speaking to them . . . they'd accuse me of practicing sorcery without Camarilla sanction, which would put my fate solely within their purview. He might even be one of them.

My father had railed against the Camarilla's prerogatives to adjudicate all matters of sorcery. He felt it an unwarranted infringement of civil authority. The Camarilla insisted that no civil authority was fit to judge the particular demands, requirements, and possibilities of magical practice.

But Papa had argued we might as well give the Temple sole authority over believers, or fishmongers sole authority over fishermen. No, the Camarilla would bear no good feeling for Michel de Vernase's daughter.

But as my captors rushed me down steep stairs and through short turns, alternating sudden halts with bursts of haste, I came to the most unsettling impression that they were sneaking me out of the palace. If no one saw them take me, who might guess my whereabouts when I turned up missing? Panic won out. "Wait!"

Another short descent—stone steps without enclosing walls—and we trod on gravel and dirt. I flailed within my shroud. Screamed. Dragged my feet. Surely someone would see. But as iron fists crushed my arms, a hand thrust under my hood and forced a bitter draught into my mouth. Muffled in the heavy wool, unable to get a breath, I had no choice but to swallow.

"Wildcat witch . . ." The two words were all I heard before slipping into a terrifying blackness.

AWARENESS RETURNED WITH HELLISH NOISE. Saints save me, my cranium rattled with a din worthy of Dimios the Souleater's return at world's end—the mindstorm in full bluster.

". . . supposed to be a last resort, you toadwit! Why dose her when you've already got her in hand?" The woman stood close by.

My face lay on a firm surface of scratchy linen. Cool air bathed my cheek. My upper arms throbbed but were under my command, causing me immense relief, until I recalled where and why they had been trapped. Saint's mercy, I was in the Bastionne Camarilla. I blinked my gritty eyes but did not move.

"Adept Vronsard said—"

"Adept Vronsard is not a *prefect*, fool! Tell me what prefect wrote the warrant, and I'll—" She stopped abruptly. "Natti, you blighted, ignorant dunderhead. When I find out what lackwit summoned a Witness—*this* Witness—at middle-night without notice or preparation . . ."

"A high-level sanction was called. The plan says, in that case, we pick her up." The man's spindly silhouette manifested itself from the blur. "Can't help it no one's ready."

Grinding the heels of my hands into my eyes, I wrestled the internal clamor into submission. Then I sat up. A searing white brilliance did naught to soothe the pain in my head. But I held my eyes open and mustered every shred of my wits. My life could depend on it.

"Awake, are you?" said the belligerent woman, little more than a shadowed shape within the fracturing light beams. "Give trouble and we'll dose you again. Probably ought to anyway."

I knew better than to imagine this was all a mistake, but perhaps these two weren't so sure. "You've no cause to hold me," I said, managing to sound calm and reasonably sure of myself despite a frog in my throat. "I am no sorcerer, nor do I pretend to be. I wish the queen notified of my whereabouts."

"You are a Witness in a crime of sorcery, here to answer what's asked of you." The stout woman, shapeless in a gray gown and clearly unhappy over her assignment, passed her hand across the source of the blinding light, which began immediately to fade. "None cares what you wish."

My eyes squeezed shut briefly, grateful for the reduced glare, and opened again to a windowless box of a room. A single door centered the whitewashed wall in front of me. I sat on a padded bench fixed to a similarly bare wall. Naught else occupied the space but the three of us.

The woman pressed the bronze door latch. "I'll advise that truth is your best ally. You'll not want us to extract it. We can and will. And don't imagine we won't know the truth when we hear it, no matter your family *brilliance* that mocks and destroys whatever stands in your way."

Oh yes, she hated my father. And, indeed, the matronly woman, blessed with eyebrows thicker than a shoe brush and hands worthy of a blacksmith, appeared quite qualified to wrest truth from anyone—woman, man, sheep, or bear.

"Natti," she said after a moment of contemplative scowling, "we'd best put Damoselle de Vernase in a resident cell. Put her in a day cell and we'll have every accountant and registry clerk gaping at her by morning, especially once people guess who she is. We must proceed carefully. And get out of that gown. If a prefect sees you . . . by my mother's womb, *you'll* be resident here."

"*You* take her! Prefect Angloria said we shouldn't go down there."

"Prefect Angloria has naught to say about this one. And don't you be prattling to her about it."

The ill-favored young man she'd called toadwit voiced his objection in a high-pitched squeak. He busily stripped off the black gown that flapped about his gawky frame, then unhooked the dull green cap that dangled around his neck and stuffed it into the gown's sleeve.

That odd green cap . . . *He* was the formidable Camarilla inquisitor! Yet I'd have sworn he'd worn a mage's collar when he arrested me.

"Then send Vronsard to transfer her." Natti afforded me only the briefest of glances, as if I might not hear his whispering if he weren't actually looking at me. "She's a wolverine. Felt her claws straight through the Witness gown when I searched her pockets."

I breathed in relief that I'd put away the potion and the ring before the inquisitor arrived.

Sputtering in disgust, the woman yanked open the door. "I'll send your rival in idiocy, Natti, and pray for the day we've acolytes who can follow procedures and control a slip of an untrained girl. If it's the master from the palace who's called this sanction, I suppose we must proceed. If it's one of the others, I'll have that one skinned and roasted."

My brief surge of assurance withered. The *master from the palace* could only be Dante. *The others* . . . Other masters? Others from the palace? Who?

The woman slammed the door behind her.

"This is all a mistake, isn't it?" I said to the bony Natti. "I'm not supposed to be here."

"Sanction was called," he mumbled.

I gambled. "Best take me back. Master Dante will flay you for deviating from his plan."

"Wasn't his plan! He's not got the authority for—" His complexion faded to the color of whey. "You be quiet."

Whose plan had been triggered too early, if not Dante's? To *call sanction* to the Camarilla must mean to accuse a person of illicit sorcery in a way more serious than rumor or suspicion. And the Camarilla would likely investigate a serious accusation from any person, sorcerer or not.

I considered threatening or bribing the awkward young man to get a message to Eugenie, but this whole thing might be a trap aimed at her—her attendant, the traitor's daughter, arrested. Better to stay calm and learn more. Never had I felt closer to the heart of this conspiracy.

Natti's help arrived. Adept Vronsard was the gray-haired man who had stood in my bedchamber and issued the summons.

"You've no metal on your person, damoselle?" said Vronsard, examining my neck and wrists. "It's not allowed here."

"None. Why?"

"Can't have prisoners working magic, now, can we?"

I'd not considered the particular problems of imprisoning sorcerers. Metal was involved in most spellwork. I knew that much. But, of course, previously devised spells could be attached to artifacts of wood or stoneware, shell, liquid, or powder, creating charms and potions that anyone could use, as Lianelle had done for me. Mages attached their favorite worked spells to their ancilles—wands, rings, or staffs, like Dante's. Lianelle had once shown me a drawing of the ancille she planned to create—five silver rings, each attached to a bronze bracelet with a delicate silver chain—a *gauntlet of magic*, she'd called it.

One man on each side of me, we paraded through a huge, windowless, whitewashed room, stuffed with a hodgepodge of tables and chairs piled in teetering towers, rolled carpets and tapestries, cobbled-together racks hung with robes, crates stacked upon crates and every other kind of container. It appeared like nothing so much as an attic or undercroft where unwanted household furnishings were stored.

Yet desks and worktables were tucked into every possible niche amid the jumble. Between two overloaded book cupboards, two women stirred the contents of a copper pan over a small burner that belched green flames. A gowned man sat writing at a desk tucked into a nook of half-charred casks. These things must have been rescued from the ruined wing of the Bastionne.

Once past the far door, a long passage stretched before us, evidencing the Bastionne's more somber purposes. Cells, barred with stone latticework, lined the left side of the passage. Most were empty. A young woman with painted eyes and long greased curls hissed at us as we passed. Two old men in adjacent cells played cards by laying out their game outside the bars, though neither could see the other's face. The inmates would likely be offenders dragged in from the marketplace and kept for a few hours for questioning.

"These are what you name day cells," I said.

Natti jumped when I spoke, glancing at me suspiciously, as if I were using some magic to steal his knowledge.

"It's so," he said as we started down a flight of black granite steps.

Resident cells were likely for longer-term prisoners of the Camarilla. My throat knotted.

The downward stair led us into a tangle of dim lower passages. And surely I recognized the moment our path took us into the lower reaches of the ruin on the Plas Royale. Natti opened an iron door that groaned and complained as it scraped the well-worn floor. Misery, horror, and despair whispered through the corridor, tickling my ears as if the voices inside me had escaped through my skin. Though torches had been mounted on the passage walls, the gloom sapped their luminance. And when I blinked, faint threads of purple light floated into view, hovering on the periphery of sight. Just as in the Rotunda.

The wide passage reeked of camphor. It was notched on one side by square nooks, empty and of a size matching that of the day cells. Wood latticework had been embedded in the stone walls, floors, and ceilings. Oddly, no bars closed them off. Odd, too, the nooks were spaced irregularly, as if the builder had forgotten to open the passage wall for some few . . . or as if those had been walled shut. Sealed.

"Don't leave me down here," I said. "For love of the holy saints, please don't. . . ."

"Resident cell five," said Adept Vronsard, halting at the corner of one empty niche. "You'll work no illicit magic here. Step in, damoselle."

"I've done nothing. I can't work magic. I've been tested. I'm not responsible for my father's opinions . . . my father's crimes. . . ." I babbled shamelessly, all notions of truth or pride, honesty or loyalty vanquished by fear of being walled up down here with the purple lights and the burgeoning mindstorm.

Vronsard crammed a folded blanket and a stoppered clay flask into my arms.

"The Prefect Inquisitor will determine your innocence," said Natti, as the two of them shoved me into the empty niche. "We'll retrieve you when he's ready."

"A prefect?" I yelled, spinning in place, "or the Aspirant?" A fourth wall stood in place.

Throwing down the blanket and flask, I hammered my fists on the wood-latticed wall, and then all the way around the cell in a panicked hunt for a way out. Half a minute, and I could not have said which wall fronted the passage.

An ash gray gleam emanated from the stone, enough to reveal a thinly padded stone shelf fixed to one wall and a lidded commode in one corner. But no sooner had I lavished thanks on the Creator's messengers than the gloom faded to black. The sole illumination emanated from the drifting threads of purple, green, and rose. The only sounds were the faint whispers, just this side of hearing. Even the mindstorm had fallen silent.

Wholly unnerved, I retreated into a barren corner and wrapped the scratchy wool blanket around my shoulders. I didn't want to see what might take shape from the floating lights. This time it might be Lianelle, her chest caved in by explosive magic, or Lady Cecile, lips stained black with poison, her elegantly long neck twisted as she gazed on me with dead eyes.

Talk to me, I said. *Friend, please.* With all the strength I could muster, recalling every nuance of his presence . . . the sound of him . . . the sense of his pleasure at our exchanges, the muted longing, I reached into the night. I dared not tell him where I was, but I was desperate to hear a friendly voice.

The aether felt dull and impenetrable. No voices. No friendly, curious intruder. No mindstorm. Nothing.

Shifting air riffled the enveloping blanket and my skirts. Warm, dry, the gusts bore a pungent, resinous scent—juniper or cedar—that mingled with the unpleasant camphor and musty stone. The colored threads floated past, their movements unaffected by the eerie breeze. Their touch tickled my skin, giving off bursts redolent of sickness and decay.

I waved them off. Blew on them. Whispered, yelled, clapped my hands. But no action affected their random wanderings. They passed straight through my hand, and through the walls and ceiling.

As the time ticked away, they gathered about me, their sighs and whispers a swelling canon of failure and loss, anger, avarice, and . . . hunger. . . .

I searched out the flask Adept Vronsard had given me, uncorked it, and sniffed. Water. After a welcome swallow, I poured some onto the floor. The threads flocked to the puddle until it glowed . . . and the whispered pain surged as if I dangled a crust of bread just beyond the reach of a starving prisoner.

I'm sorry. Sorry. Hastily I splattered and smeared the water into smaller puddles and droplets, overcome with the feeling that I had committed some incalculable cruelty, though exactly what or against whom I could not guess. When the shifting air had dried the last of it, the whispers receded again. My trembling did not.

Bathed in cold sweat, I huddled in my corner, closed my eyes, and practiced the exercises Papa had used to banish my nightmares. I calculated the time it would take to ride a horse from Merona to Abidaijar. I reconstructed Ludaccio's proof of the invariant ratios of squared triangles. . . .

A clatter and scrape of steel and stone shattered my concentration and sent me scrabbling to my feet. A narrow door stood open in the wall opposite the bench. Backlit by the torches in the outer passageway, Mage Dante stood watching me.

CHAPTER 19

19 OCET, MIDDLE-NIGHT

"An ugly place to find an aristo lady." Save for the band of silver about his sinewed neck, the mage might have been any ruffian out of Riverside. Worn canvas breeches, russet shirt, and buff jerkin could more likely suit a pikeman newly returned from campaign than the Queen of Sabria's First Counselor.

But I was not fooled. Every nerve, every sense quivered with danger. I chose my words precisely. "I've been brought here in error, Master. I am no sorceress, thus I do not fall under the authority—"

"Hold your arguments. I know naught of Camarilla rules." He leaned against the doorframe, half in, half out of the cell, as one of Montclaire's neighbors might when stopping in for a taste of the new vintage. "I was waked from a sound sleep and told a Witness had been brought to the Bastionne to be questioned. As this was a very special Witness, and the designated inquisitor was not available to record a preliminary interrogation, I was to do it. Yet no one bothered to inform me as to what this person was witness to, so I'm at a loss to know what to ask. Perhaps you could tell me. Have you been misbehaving? Following in your wicked father's footsteps?"

I refused to let his barbs prick me to anger or his easy posture lull me to carelessness. "No one's informed me of my offenses. Take me to this designated inquisitor, and we can inquire together."

"None's going to tell *you* anything. And I'd have to spook it out of him. I've no yen to play games so late of an evening."

Yet he was so clearly playing games. The beams from his staff glinted in eyes of green adamant. I drew the blanket around me, hoping he would not notice my shaking.

"Then perhaps you could educate me as to your own designs," I said. "Every despicable place I find myself, you seem to have left your vile handprint already."

"Brave talk. Especially for one who's lagged her first stay in a sorcerer's hole." He cocked his head. "Does the lady ween the like of a sorcerer's hole?"

The unfamiliar term was not so hard to interpret. "Detention impervious to magic working, I'd think. Iron locks? Magical barriers?"

"More than that." He stepped inside, poking his staff idly at the strips of wood in the wall and the floor. "Whitebud laurel—the camphor laurel. If you chipped your way through the stone facing, you'd find a layer of cypress wood, banded with iron. An enclosure comprised of these materials and kept entirely free of the divine element of spark inhibits a true sorcerer's use of magic."

I poked my finger at one of the green light threads, refusing to shudder at the stink. "Then surely the prefects realize these cells are already breached."

"Ah, this little problem. But you see"—he jarred the heel of his staff lightly on the floor and white flames blossomed from its tip, highlighting his prominent cheekbones and brow ridge, now stretched in a moment's ferocity—"all is not as we might assume." Over his shoulder, he snapped, "Now!"

The door's outline merged instantly with the solid wall. The flames of his staff blinked out in that same moment, leaving the fading gray gleam from the stone as our sole illumination. "There. Magic quenched. Speaking as a sorcerer of some capability and a man of ungenteel origins, I can tell you that felt as if someone yanked my entrails out through my nose."

I cared naught for his discomfort, only for the implication. "So these threads are not of magical origin."

"Not as *I* know magic. But you . . . likely you know more than you claim about the matter."

"That's preposterous."

Was he saying natural philosophy—science—could explain the light threads? An alchemical reaction? An optical device? The idea of an explanation based in reason gave me some comfort.

Dante rapped three quick bursts and two slow on the wall behind him. The door slid open again.

"Come, Witness. I've a notion to pursue your questioning in a more interesting locale." The mage was out the door faster than an arrow from a longbow. I darted after him, breathing much harder than ten quick steps should warrant.

"Betake your knocking knees back to the south wing," he said to the whey-faced Natti. "You've served your use, and this woman's less like than you to puke up supper."

"But I was commanded—"

Scarlet fire leapt from the mage's staff to Natti's arms. "I said depart, worm-prick."

Slapping his arms and moaning, the bony "inquisitor" bolted.

Dante waved me deeper into the bowels of the ruined Bastionne. "Best keep a good pace. You'd not like me to aim my stick at you."

I'd no wish to linger. The floating lights swarmed in the passage. Now we had left the cell, the mindstorm built like thunderheads behind the walls I held against it. So a sorcerer's hole broke the connection with the tangle curse, as well.

I dismissed the whim of calling on my friend. I'd not dare use the gift with Dante's eyes on me and, saints protect the feebleminded, I was wretchedly curious as to what the mage wanted with me.

"To the right . . . and again . . . now left . . ."

Three turns, four. Torches set in wall brackets provided less and less light the deeper into the ruin we went, until the flames appeared to be little more than gray sputters.

At the base of a stone stair, the mage jarred the heel of his staff on the floor. White sparks spat and died. Another whack and the staff remained dark. At the fourth solid hit, a rill of livid flame oozed from the head and spilled down the shaft and across his gloved hand.

Something was dreadfully, horribly wrong in the ruins. Dante's every attempt at spellworking laced my nerves with fire. Every step forward tainted my spirit as if we slogged through sewage.

Two flights of cracked steps took us up to some kind of intermediate level that overlooked a cavernous darkness. We picked our way over fallen balusters to the next level, a gallery of toppled statuary. There I first glimpsed the jagged outlines of broken walls against the stars. A whining wind roved freely through deserted hallways. We circumnavigated buckled flooring and angled roof beams by threading a warren of ruined apartments.

"Here we are." The mage held his staff high. Only two and a half walls and half the ceiling remained of the long chamber. Beyond the broken walls gaped the inky night, hills and ridges and pits of blackness scattered with glimmering stars or lamps. The pricks of light were indistinguishable, as if the Pantokrator had drawn the mantle of the night sky across the body of the sleeping city.

The floor, tilted outward toward the yawning drop, creaked and groaned alarmingly as we entered. Dante's livid light exposed the remnants of a sorcerer's laboratorium, identifiable as such only because I had visited his own apartment in the palace. The explosion—or earthshaking or destructive hand of the Souleater or whatever it was—had smashed glassware, crates, and boxes, and scattered metal pans, brass instruments, and bits of unidentifiable materials about the chamber, along with the remains of toppled cabinets and shelves. The wind riffled papers and clothing spilled from an armoire. Amazingly, one table next to the interior wall remained untouched, glass canisters, boxes, and books stacked neatly and sorted by size.

"Do you recognize anything here?"

Mesmerized by the strangeness of the place, it took a moment for his question to make sense.

"How could I?" I whispered, unable to convince myself that too loud a word would not send us sliding down the wooden slope and plummeting into the pooled darkness below.

"I thought perhaps he had a place like this tucked away at Montclaire, as well. Well hidden, if so. I certainly didn't detect it on my visit." He stepped gingerly to the armoire and picked up an empty boot that he dangled in the light of his staff. Even as I stared at the boot—a horseman's knee-high boot, well worn, well cared for—he dropped it back into the heap and drew out a cloak of dark wool banded with gold braid and bearing a red-and-gold badge: Sabria's golden tree on a scarlet field.

My breath caught.

"Perhaps you've seen this." From his leather-clad fingers the mage dangled a pendant, a great topaz set in a triangle of oddly cut bronze, each side fashioned in the shape of a key. "Or this?" He pulled out an old-fashioned dagger with a cruciform hilt and a broken blade.

"Papa . . ."

The pendant was unfamiliar. But my father had carried that broken stub of a weapon with him everywhere, a relic of the soldier who had raised him. The cloak, worn from one end of Sabria to the other, had marked him as King Philippe's First Counselor. And I could not mistake his favorite boots, meticulously waxed and oiled and mended because he'd never found another pair to match their comfort.

I yanked my eyes from my father's belongings and reassessed every article in the apartment. Maps and charts—astronomical charts, anatomical charts, and alchemical tables—were fixed to the walls. A mangled opticum lay on the floor. Shattered bell jars. A small pump. This was a scientist's laboratorium, as well.

"Whose place is this?" I demanded, grief and hurt swollen to anger. Why were my father's prized possessions here?

Dante raised his staff to illuminate a nest of brass rings behind an up-ended chair. As if the gleaming rings formed a great lodestone, I was drawn to drag the chair aside and kneel by the warped and bent planetary, touching the dusty marbles that represented the known moons and planets. Beside it lay a thick leather mask, one side of it crushed, and the other a sculpted male face, inhumanly beautiful. Beneath it lay a sheaf of papers, scribed in a bold hand so agonizingly familiar that when Dante spoke, I already knew what he would claim.

"Your father's, of course."

"That is not *possible*." There were no chains here. No scourges. No barred iron doors. My father was not the daemon who wore that mask.

"And how are you so sure of that?"

It was a question I could not answer without speaking of aethereal voices that could not lie, a mystery of the mind that properly belonged to saints and angels. But, of course, all that could be deceit and illusion, as well.

"No answer?" said the mage. "Like you, my master relishes his secrets, including his name. So I thank you for affirming my notion of his identity. 'Tis useful to know one's friends as well as one's enemies. One never knows when roles will . . . switch." Arrogance and despite sheathed the mage's every word.

His master . . . the Aspirant . . . the architect of murder and treason. Did I have the smallest faith anyone would believe me, I would have run to the chamber's verge and screamed Dante's sideways admission to the sleeping world. Yet none of this made sense.

"Even if my father is what you imply, why would he keep an apartment in the Bastionne Camarilla? And why would the mages here risk charges of conspiracy to hide him? Someone's been living here." The dust of its destruction could not disguise the feel of recent habitation. "And why would he require a sorcerer's paraphernalia?"

"Matters of interest, to be sure. The Aspirant enjoys confounding observers. Come now. Before we're interrupted, I've a mind to try a small exercise that might explain more."

His black glove encircled my wrist like a shackle and drew me to a stool beside the door. "Sit."

The mage drew a small book from inside his jerkin and pressed it into my hands. Bound in darkened leather, crudely stitched, the book sat more solid than such a slender volume warranted. Traces of gold gleamed from the worn edges of the pages.

"You've a talent for tongues, I hear. Can you read this? It might be of interest to us both."

I paged through the flimsy leaves, hand-scribed in a language entirely unfamiliar. "No."

As I peered at the odd script, the weak and shifting light caused the characters to blur and squirm. Was it encrypted? *A handspan square, more or less*, Bernard had written. Heaven's gates, was this *Lianelle's* book?

I dared not speak the word she had sent me on the torn scrap: *Andragossa*. Not in front of Dante. My hunger to know was so great, I could scarce keep my shaking fingers from scrabbling through the book, seeking the page with its corner torn off. Sure as my soul, I would find one.

Blinking and squinting, forcing myself to breathe normally, I riffled lightly through the pages. The book fell open to the title page. In its center, someone had inked a pair of dueling scorpions.

"The Mondragon mark!"

"Indeed so." Surprise and satisfaction oozed from the mage like cooling tar. "But how does a young lady entirely unfamiliar with magic know anything of such evildoers? Since the Mondragons were exterminated two centuries ago, it has been forbidden to teach of them."

"I read history," I whispered, choking.

"Let's see how well." And before I could blink, he snatched the book away and gripped my right hand with his left. He yanked me to my feet, twisting until I faced his back, my right arm wrapped about his waist.

"Stop! What are you doing?" I hammered his back with my free hand, but he clamped my forearm between his ribs and his bicep like a plank in a vise. My thumb blazed with steel-cut fire.

"Curse you forever!" I yelled, the images of forced bleeding risen into present horror.

Relentless, he squeezed my pierced thumb and dragged a cold, smooth implement across the wound.

My heart thundered like stampeding horses. My head buzzed and spun. It was all I could do to keep rein on the mindstorm waiting to break loose. I grabbed Dante's thick tail of dark hair and wrenched hard.

His implement clattered to the floor as he reached back and grabbed my hand, squeezing and twisting in a bone-crushing grip until I yelled and let go.

"Release her immediately!" Savin-Duplais snapped the command from the direction of the door. "Are you entirely mad?"

Never had I been so happy to hear another's voice.

"Librarian!" The mage's cool baritone resonated through his broad back. "I should have expected insects to scuttle out of the corners as the storm approaches. Do your hairdressers and seamstresses not keep you busy enough?" The mage dragged me, stumbling, to his side. "Or have you gone sleuthing again? Is the girl your quarry or your partner?"

Duplais, out of breath, doublet unbuttoned, cloak askew, looked as if he'd crawled from his bed and into a hurricane. Yet he did not flinch under the mage's eye. "The queen has filed a grievance with Prefect Angloria. This woman is her servant and her husband's gooddaughter, and has performed no act that subjects her to Camarilla jurisdiction."

"Yet *I* am the queen's First Counselor," said Dante.

"Civil rank matters nothing in the Bastionne," snapped Duplais. "Here you serve the Camarilla, and the Camarilla has no authority to place Damoselle Anne in the hands of a rogue mage they do not and cannot control. Or have you chosen to swear false allegiance to those you despise? Have the prefects learned your true opinions of their magics?"

"Do you *threaten* me? Do you imagine anyone in this city would heed a talentless clerk whose sole accomplishment in life is to link a chain of flimsy conclusions to convict a man he has never met and cannot find of a crime he cannot fathom? Damoselle Anne, view your brave defender who hides his inadequate intellect and dreams of talent behind aristo ladies' hairpins, one who dares not examine his own mind for fear of what he might find there."

Dante shoved me back to the stool and retrieved his staff, propped in the nearby corner. The Mondragon book lay facedown at my feet.

"It is not I who have become the performing monkey in an aristo menagerie, mage," said Duplais.

Dante did not bite. His demeanor could hardly be icier. "If I have found enticing opportunities in the palace and the Bastionne, the responsibility lies with you, does it not? Who was it arranged my introduction here?"

"You extracted the price for that misjudgment long ago." Heated bitterness welled from Duplais' depths. "Corruption requires an act of will. Do not lay yours at *my* feet."

Dante tutted, as if to a child. "Still so righteous. Consider well the value you place on your righteous wits, librarian. I've learned a great deal since we played our wicked games—"

All my imagining of a secret confederacy between these two was erased by their exchange, not only in the insults spoken, but in those left unvoiced—the vitriol of broken trust and festered grievance. As they spat and hissed like feral cats, I draped my skirt over the dropped book. When convinced both men had forgotten me, I slid the little volume into my pocket. That book was my sister's death price. It was everything. Even an hour's examination might reveal some truth.

"Master Dante!" An iron gray woman in a scarlet mantle swooped in from the corridor, edging Duplais aside. "Explain yourself. Why ever have you chosen such a dangerously unstable chamber for an interrogation? And why in the name of the Everlasting Fire were you summoned to this task?"

"Prefect Angloria." Unfazed, as if he had been expecting her all along, Dante executed a curt bow. "I maintain good reasons for all. But first I might ask you how it is a failed acolyte is allowed to wander the inner chambers of the Bastionne Camarilla."

"Sonjeur de Duplais claims the Witness was brought here in error. Queen Eugenie supports his view."

"Then accept my apologies," said the mage, entirely unapologetic. "I believed the Camarilla Magica empowered to act as it saw fit in matters of sorcery. I had no idea that whining from a witless aristo and her sweeping boy were sufficient to interrupt an interrogation."

He did not cow Prefect Angloria, whose steady presence brought a brick wall to mind. "Be sure I yield no jurisdiction to the crown. But we deem it intelligent to *consider* royal opinion before flouting it. And *I* shall judge the strength of Sonjeur de Duplais' allegations, not you."

"As you wish. Then perhaps someone should attend to the Witness. She acquired a splinter from the wreckage—bound with a nasty little enchantment that could not be allowed to fester for an instant. I'm afraid I quite shocked her with my abrupt attentions."

"There was no splinter," I snapped. "The mage manhandled me and pierced my thumb."

"Let me see it." The scarlet-robed prefect extended a hand.

"It was no splinter!" I said again. "Is a mage permitted to *cut* a Witness? Three of your own were executed for that, were they not?"

"I would caution you to consider well before making accusations, damoselle," said the prefect, her manner cooling dramatically. "Several of our people have suffered septic woundings while working in this wreckage. If such is its origin, you're fortunate that Master Dante took quick action. If it's something more sinister, we shall detect it."

I wasn't at all sure of that.

Dante's staff provided light as she examined my throbbing hand. The tiny puncture on the pad of my thumb welled a single drop of blood. Indeed a splinter might have made it. Duplais, his narrow face fierce, near shoved the prefect aside to get a look.

"I sense no mortification," said the woman after a moment. "And, to answer your concerns, I sense no enchantment, either. Let us leave this dreadful place. We'll look again in better light, and meanwhile sort out the matter of your summoning." Clearly Prefect Angloria was not accustomed to arguments. "Walk with me, Master. You may enlighten me as to this awkward business along our way. Sonjeur de Duplais, see to the Witness. You will recall the penalties for interfering with a Camarilla investigation, I'm sure."

Angloria and Dante led the way back, heads together and far enough ahead we could not hear their conversation. Two robed adepts closed in behind Duplais and me. I was somewhat surprised when Duplais took my arm as if to support me over the rubble. "Where did you leave the Camarilla warrant?" he murmured, keeping his face pointed straight ahead. "I couldn't find it in your bedchamber. I need to know what this is about."

"I saw no warrant. He waved a scroll at me . . . Vronsard . . . Adept

Vronsard was his name," I said, spewing pent fear and anger before some-one silenced me again. "But he never showed me. He threatened shackles, put that horrid hood on me, and forced some potion down my throat. Sneaked me out of the palace. I was afraid no one would know."

"They didn't let you *read* the warrant?" he said, fiercely quiet. "Who else had a hand in this? Was Dante there?"

"Just Vronsard and an inquisitor. A woman met us here, but I never heard her name. She was unprepared, upset with the two of them, said things were irregular. She called the inquisitor Natti, and I believed he was a mage, but I'm not sure he's even an adept. He said the summoning was a high-level sanction. What does that mean?"

"It means someone has serious reason to believe you are a danger to the Camarilla. What were you and Dante doing in the ruin?"

"They put me in a cell at first, a sorcerer's hole, the mage called it. Then he took me to that chamber. He tried to make me believe it was my *father's* chamber, and said he wanted to identify his master. Then he showed me—"

I hesitated. To mention the book, an anchor weight in my skirt, was to admit that I attached some significance to encrypted books, opening the door to all those things I had tried to keep from Duplais.

My fist closed over my burning thumb. The hateful words Duplais had spoken in the past yet confused me. But his actions spoke clearly. He had tried to protect me—in the wood at Vradeu's Crossing, in our excursions through the city, even at the Spindle. He had raced here, setting himself squarely in Dante's path, to get me out. Such a debt required payment.

"The mage showed me a book that bore the mark of the Mondragon family. He asked if I could read it."

Duplais' head came around sharply before reverting to its determined forward-facing posture. "And could you?"

"No. That's when he cut my thumb."

"Ixtador's Gates!" His exclamation was little more than a sigh, but its tenor left no doubt that I had thrown him a wholly unexpected prize. I just wished I knew what it was.

CHAPTER 20

Before we could say more, Angloria led us into a cramped study in the unruined part of the Bastionne. Dante and Duplais remained standing as she examined my punctured thumb in the steady brilliance of a painted lamp. Blotting it with a bit of linen from a drawer in a desk, she concluded, "A splinter, perhaps. A cut, perhaps. But neither septic nor in any fashion reminiscent of transference."

Solely by virtue of Duplais' timely arrival, I guessed.

Taking a seat behind the desk, Prefect Angloria stared at the two men for a moment. "Master Dante has presented a compelling argument for the young woman's retention until the confusion of her summoning can be clarified. He refuses further information. I don't like that. But given the history of the Witness's family, I am inclined to agree that we should await the issuer of the inquisitorial warrant. Sonjeur de Duplais, tell me why I should not heed the master's advice."

"Because, honored Prefect Angloria, you have a terrible mess on your hands. The Witness claims she was not allowed to read the warrant—a clear violation of the Concord. She could be lying, yet she has no reason to be familiar with Camarilla protocols. As no warrant remains anywhere in Castelle Escalon and no one else has seen it, we've no way to determine if it was properly presented . . . or properly issued. Perhaps Mage Dante could tell you which prefect signed the warrant, and you could obtain a copy to verify the basis for the summons."

No matter his mussed hair or half-buttoned doublet, I recognized *this* Duplais—the Royal Accuser who had so skillfully laid out the case against my father.

"Unfortunately, there seems to be no copy of the warrant," said Dante, mellow as cream.

"An administrative error, certainly." Duplais acted as if he did not take note of the color risen in Angloria's cheeks. But I knew how unlikely that was. "More troubling is the status of the two who fetched the Witness. I understand that the inquisitor who visited this warrant upon Damoselle de Vernase—the man who emerged from the inquisitor's gown upon their arrival back here in the Bastionne—answers to the name of Natti, not at all a common name. My employment at Seravain familiarized me with most young people who study the magical art. The sole bearer of that name is a young man who could scarce qualify for the post of laboratorium sweeper, much less mage inquisitor. I doubt the Concord de Praesta has been amended to permit a raw acolyte to parade about in a mage's collar."

The gray-haired woman's flush deepened to a scarlet that matched her prefect's gown.

Duplais drew himself up, as if he had himself taken on the stature of a prefect. "Prefect Angloria, Camarilla representatives—Adept Vronsard and Acolyte Natti—have invaded the king's house illegally and *abducted* his gooddaughter. Whatever chain of events led to this violation is yours to investigate, but I respectfully submit that the young lady must be released and returned to Her Majesty's household. I believe it most fortunate that I, a man who values and honors the traditions of the Camarilla, was called in to investigate this incident."

"If these allegations are proven, then I would agree with you, sonjeur. You will excuse me briefly." Angloria spun like a scarlet typhoon. "Mage Dante, with me!"

The woman departed the room in such haste her silver collar left glimmering streaks in the air. Someone would feel her wrath.

Dante paused at the door, bowing to Duplais, a mirthless smile twisting his face. "Well-done, librarian . . . and damoselle. A fine pair you make. I'll see you again, of course. Especially if anything important should turn up missing."

When the door clicked shut behind Dante, I closed my eyes, trying to pretend that icy green stare had not seen straight into my pocket. Foolish to imagine he would have forgotten the book.

"What did he mean?" Duplais' quiet question slapped me in the face.

When I pulled out the book, I thought he might vomit on my shoes.

"Creator's grace, no!" His hands flew up when I offered him the little volume. "Dante could detect my handling it. But show me."

I opened to the title page where the pair of scorpions fought their endless duel. In the matter of a moment's scrutiny, he could have reproduced every ink droplet on the page.

"Why did he want my blood?"

Shaking his head, Duplais dragged his gaze from the book. "He must believe your blood has some efficacy when it comes to decryption spells. Is this the book they retrieved from Montclaire? Your sister's book?"

"I don't know. *Honestly*, I don't," I said, adding the confirmation when his wiry body stiffened at my first denial. "She mentioned reading encrypted books of magic. *Gautieri* books."

Duplais raked slim fingers through his short dark hair. "She broke Gautieri encryption? A girl of seventeen? I'd vow to Sante Ianne himself that was impossible, yet Dante must believe it. A *vitet* might explain it." He bit off his mumbling.

"A *vitet*?" I said, pouncing on the word. *M vitet* and *G vitet* had been written on the scrap of paper I had retrieved from Lady Cecile's hidden drawer.

"A spell created using blood as a particle—as a physical piece of the working, rather than as a source of power, as is the case with transference. He must think the encryption spell was built using blood. Hers, and thus yours."

"I might know someone who could help," I said, thinking of Lianelle's cryptonymics instructor. "If we took this to him, we might understand her capabilities." The book held the answer to Lianelle's murder . . . to so many things. I was sure of it.

"Dante knows you have it. Walk out with it, and the Camarilla will have you again before you can sneeze, this time with every backing of royal authority. Mondragon books are forbidden to any without permission of a Camarilla prefect. Hsst!" He held up a hand. Footsteps approached the door.

Duplais moved away, holding me to silence with a gesture to his ear and the door. No one came in. But no footsteps moved away.

When the latch rattled at last, Duplais held stiffly across the room from me, hands behind his back, annoyance written in every muscle. But his posture changed when a tall, silver-haired mage in prefect's red burst into the room and enveloped him in a hearty embrace.

"Portier!" boomed the newcomer. "Bless my heart, lad, it's good to see you! Angloria told me you were here trying to sort out this debacle. I told her I must pop in before you got away."

"Master! I believed you still hunting books in the desert. When did you get back?" Duplais expressed genuine pleasure.

"Mid Nieba. How is your mother getting on?"

"She speaks no more of sense than she has in thirteen years. I apply a little more patience than I have in the past, so she does not shriek quite so loud when I arrive, nor weep quite so voluminously when I leave. Our visits are rare. My duties tie me to Merona."

The mage's abundant silver brows slanted downward from the center of his forehead, giving a pleasing crinkle to the corners of his eyes. The loosening folds of his aging skin hung over supremely elegant bones. As a younger man, he must have been the idol of every woman he met.

He laid a long, beautifully formed hand on Duplais' shoulder. "Ah, Portier, why must you—?"

"I beg you not renew this argument, Master. My position at court is not negotiable. Though not my vision of my future, it brings great honor to my family. Now, sir, we've business here . . ." He extended a hand in my direction. "The queen's handmaiden."

"Spirits, yes!" The man whirled about, as if he had wholly forgotten my presence. As if he had not examined me with astonishing thoroughness at his entrance. "Damoselle de Vernase, excuse my rudeness. Portier here is as near a son as I can claim in this world. We so rarely cross paths, restraint is difficult."

"Mage Kajetan," I said, recognizing a person who could describe magic's history and destiny in a way that made students go all gooseflesh. "My sister had only good words to say of you."

"Ah, Creator's Hand," he said, the brilliant smile bending into perfect sorrow. "The little girl. Such a talent, just revealing itself. She would have made a fine mage. I am so very sorry for your loss. For *all* your losses." Every word Kajetan spoke was infused with a fervency that must attract the sympathies of everyone who listened. Except me, perhaps.

Duplais pulled aside a drapery, revealing a walled courtyard and an ash-hued sky. "Dawn is near, Master. Both the lady and I have duties to our mistress." Duplais' dismissal of sympathy was a marked contrast to his mentor's exuberant offering. "Have you brought us word of Prefect Angloria's decision?"

"Yes, yes," said the prefect, scowling at Duplais. "And an explanation. Evidently this unfortunate mistake was made by the ever-diligent inquisitorial staff. A crime committed in the evening hours was attributed to Damoselle de Vernase and judged to be within Camarilla purview. But the jackanapes who raised the alarm did not do the least work to verify his assumptions. The lady is incapable of the magic used. And a few simple inquiries have shown her to be in public view in the entire time frame of the event."

"What event?" Duplais and I voiced it together.

"The ancient wards of Spindle Prison were shattered tonight, and its warder murdered with a spelled knife. For good or evil, as you may see it, lady, your brother is nowhere to be found."

The news sent my spirits soaring, but only for a moment. That the vile Pognole lay dead did not trouble me a whit. But Ambrose was sure to be accused of murder and named a fugitive. Those were the best of possibilities.

"How is that possible?" said Duplais. "If the boy had magic enough to murder the warder and escape the Spindle, he would never have waited four years."

Yes. That exactly.

"It was assumed he had help from his sister," said Kajetan. "Evidently there was a recent visit where plans could have been made."

"I did no such thing!" I said. "My brother was a hostage, dreadfully, wrongfully abused, but innocent of any crime. Even if I could work magic, the last thing I'd do is make him a fugitive." Or a murderer. Or a conspirator in treason. Exactly why I'd not left him Lianelle's potion.

"I believe you, damoselle," said Kajetan, overflowing with sympathy.

The Aspirant had taken him. I was sure of it. He had tormented Ambrose into months of sickness, thinking no one would notice, but my visit had threatened exposure. "My brother has been abducted, sonjeur. The king must be notified."

"That's as may be. But Angloria, that woman of clear head and good sense, has ascertained that *you* were incapable of this crime. You're free to go with the sincere apologies of the prefecture."

He *sounded* quite sincere. Yet I could not shake the sense that I was watching a play unfold. If Chancellor Kajetan was so grieved by Lianelle's death, why had he not written to me? If he valued Duplais so highly, why did he speak to him as if he were a twelve-year-old child? I would detest anyone who patronized me so. Natti and his confederates had been expecting a prefect.

"Master Kajetan, upon my arrival repeated references were made to a plan to spirit me into the Bastionne," I said, exaggerating only a little. "Is it presumptuous to ask why?"

"Not at all. And for this I make no apology." He propped his backside on Prefect Angloria's writing table. "For years, your father worked to convince the people of Sabria that sorcery had failed them. He claimed the Camarilla had nothing to offer in a new world shaped by natural philosophy. I believe that Michel's sponsorship of heinous magical practice, and the public association of depraved sorcery with royal assassination, are but a continuation of that assault."

"You believe my father sponsored blood transference and murder in order to discredit sorcerers?"

Kajetan inclined his head. "The ultimate aims of his strategy, I cannot fathom. But we of the Camarilla are engaged in a war for our survival, damoselle. Sadly, the children of principals in that war are themselves players who must be accounted for."

"As my sister and brother have been?" I could not withhold bitterness.

"Who could blame you for assuming the magical community responsible? For my part, I believe your sister's death was the tragic result of a girl overreaching her talent in order to prove that she was *not* her father's child. Believe me, the last thing the *Camarilla* would do is destroy a determined, legitimate talent who might, if we were fortunate, stand with us in this war. Your brother? I find it far more likely that your father found it expedient to retrieve his son than that a young lady with no inclination to power unlocked the old magics of Spindle Prison. We of the Camarilla cannot begin to unravel such spellwork as exists in the Spindle."

His arguments sounded entirely rational. Except that I knew Lianelle had uncovered some unexpected danger that left her terribly afraid. Except that the Aspirant and his servant, Dante, had been given access to the Spindle. Except that my father was a captive, not a player.

"Ambrose would have strangled Papa rather than go anywhere with him."

Mage Kajetan shrugged. "Others might see profit in holding Michel's heir."

Duplais had turned his back to the discussion, favoring the view of the dawn-lit garden beyond the window. It was left to me to push further. "And who might that be? Our goodfather would welcome that information, I'm sure. When he hears of this, his wrath will shake this kingdom."

"Ah, yes . . . well . . . let us say that there are factions even within our community who disagree about the best way to fight the threat Michel de Vernase represents."

I could read the warning signs as clearly as I had read Sabria's woeful history. Rivalry parading as reason. The siren trumpet summoning sorcerers of the blood to defend their lives and passions. Skirmishes were already being fought in the haunted streets of Riverside, in the halls of Collegia Seravain, and the palace of Sabria's king. When would it break into open combat? When would cities and collegiae and libraries begin to burn?

"Is *discretion* how you account for this mage, Dante, who threatened and assaulted me here under your own roof?"

The mage's long finger rubbed his lips, crunched in a rueful grimace. "Mmm . . . not quite. Dante is the enigma. He bears no intrinsic loyalty to any faction, yet each hopes to lure him to its service. You could call him a mercenary, an extremely talented and well-protected mercenary. I would advise you to be wary of him, as we all are."

"Dante is no cipher, Master," said Duplais, still perusing the sky beyond the window. "He is rogue. Dangerous. He entirely lacks moral grounding."

"I need no lecturing, Portier." Even gently spoken, Kajetan's reproach must have stung. "You know my thoughts. Knowledge must not be forbidden. Study must not be forbidden. Proven acts of illicit sorcery are already subject to our law, so bring me proof if you would stop him."

Duplais pivoted, acknowledging his mentor's admonition with a shallow bow. "Pride of intellect and prejudgment remain my worst failings. For my sins, I must now revert to tedious duty and return this lady to her mistress. Perhaps you and I could dine together before you return to Seravain."

Pride of intellect and prejudgment. I almost laughed. How often had Mama warned me of the same? Had Duplais addressed that confession to me? Did he suspect that his meticulous case against my father was flawed?

"I would like that very much, lad."

"And I must ask"—Duplais dropped his eyes—"might you provide us escorts for our return to the palace? These quiet hours are often the most dangerous. I was sent down in such a hurry I failed to arrange proper protection for the lady."

"Certainly. Give me a moment. Damoselle"—Mage Kajetan inclined his head politely—"if I learn anything of your brother's fate, I'll do what I can for him. We'll hope he merely took advantage of some unrelated assault on Warder Pognole and will soon be returned to his goodfather's safekeeping."

The vibrant prefect's departure left a void in the room. Did no one else in the world feel his contempt for us all?

Duplais patted his pocket, nodding to me and to Angloria's desk, his unspoken message clear.

To leave Lianelle's book behind, knowing it the key to these mysteries, was wretchedly difficult. Yet the trap was obvious, now I had sense to see it. I had no wish ever to return to the Bastionne Camarilla.

"You'll have another chance," Duplais said softly. "Keep pushing. You've thrown them off balance. Tonight they made a series of terrible mistakes, and mistakes will undo them. Have you guessed who recommended Pognole to the Overseer of Prisons?"

Only one name made sense. Someone of devious purpose and high influence. "Antonia?"

His head jerked assent. "Be very careful. But do *not* count on me to help you again. I've exposed far more than I wish tonight. Someone trustworthy will contact you in the coming days, offer help, advise you."

A trustworthy contact! The idea sparked an excitement . . . and relief . . . I could not hide. "Who?"

He shook his head. "You'll recognize him, as you've already spoken. If you believe yourself in imminent danger or discover something truly significant—something that changes everything—tie a love knot to your window at sunset. Just understand, when you take that step, forcing a contact, you'll put lives at risk."

"Why haven't you said something before? I've floundered . . . so stupidly. I've needed help."

"I'd no way to judge your intents or true loyalties."

Simple. Obvious to a person who had not allowed prejudice to cloud her judgment. "This storm that's coming . . . magic . . . the king . . . the queen, too . . . it's the Blood Wars all over again, isn't it? Just as you said at the trial. And now they've got my brother. What must I do?"

"Hold your secrets close," he said. "Pretend—*live*—as if we had never spoken. Right now you are poison, a traitor's daughter of unknown talents who could be anyone's tool or anyone's spy. Every eye in Merona is trained on you, which is not a bad thing at all for the rest of us. We all have our own parts to play in the search for truth. Unfortunately, most must be played alone."

A suspicion nipped at me then, a distracting idea that I could ill afford to consider until I was alone and safe. I wished he would look at me, allowing me to learn more by what I could read in his face. Perhaps revealing even so much as he had put his "part" at risk. On this night a righteous strength and conviction lay behind his words, leaving me satisfied. Only for the present, however, as his every answer opened up a thousand other questions.

Reluctantly I placed the little volume on the desk, brushing my fingers over the cover. My punctured finger left a thin film of blood on the faded gilt of the title. "*Andragossa*," I whispered, little more than a breath, more a determined wish than an intentional act.

Falling . . . falling . . . My head spun, stomach surging into my throat, as if I had jumped from the tower. The faded gilt characters writhed and twisted beneath my fingers.

I blinked, then snatched my hand from the book, thumb scrubbing the blood smear away.

Duplais whirled about. "What have you—?"

His demand was cut short, as two Bastionne adepts, neither of them familiar, appeared in the doorway. "We're here to escort you out, sonjeur. There's mounts waiting."

"You said you wished to pen a message of appreciation to Prefect Angloria," said Duplais, peering over my shoulder, his body rigid as a steel post.

The cool leather displayed naught but gibberish.

"I . . . yes," I said, trying not to allow tremors to show. A message to leave with the book.

I borrowed paper and ink and scribbled my thanks for the prefect's even-handed investigation of my situation, adding a note that I had inadvertently carried away a book Master Dante had asked me to translate. As the book was wholly illegible, I chose to leave it behind on her desk.

Making use of the lamp, I dripped a blot of wax on the folded paper, and handed the sealed missive to a door guard as we followed the adepts out of the Bastionne. Let Dante answer Angloria's questions about an encrypted Mondragon book.

AS THE LIGHT GRAYED AND the city began to stir, Duplais and I rode up the Plas Royale in silence. The Camarilla aides held much too close behind for us to speak freely.

We dismounted inside the palace gates and Duplais dismissed the two adepts. Only when we walked under the gate tunnel on our way into the busy inner bailey did we have a moment out of sight and hearing of the world. "Thank you, Duplais. I see now what I should have recognized much earlier."

"I've not been able to trust my instincts for a while," he said there in the dark. "I'm happy to see they were correct in your case."

"One question." I could not leave it unspoken, because if I heard the wrong answer, I must reclaim what grace I had yielded Duplais this night. "Your mentor . . ."

"Thirteen years ago, Kajetan saved my life, my sanity," he said with urgency and conviction, as if he had guessed what I wanted to ask. "He is my true father, a man who fights with words, not bloody lancets, who seeks to inspire by the power of ideas, not fear and chaos."

"But do you trust him?"

Our footsteps rang on the cobbles. "Saints forgive . . . no."

Honesty won him the night's prize. "Dante's book is titled *Diel Schemata Magna*," I said. The words unmasked by my blood were seared into my mind with fiery script. "*The Book of Greater Rites*."

CHAPTER 21

"**S**ante Ianne," said Duplais, scarce breathing. "Tell no one of this . . . of the words . . . or that you recognized them . . . or how. For your life, lady." He began to move away.

"That book holds their plan, doesn't it?" I said, blocking his path before he could run away again. I wanted answers in return for my revelation.

"Possibly. Now—"

"Saint's mercy, Duplais, my sister *died* for that book!" I moved to block him again, feeling his rigid frame centimetres away from me. He would have to strike me to move past. "Tell me why. What do they plan?"

"Four years I've devoted to discovering that answer, and, saints forgive, I do not yet know." His muted anger was directed inward, not at me. "We need to go. This isn't safe. . . ."

The night beyond the portals of the gate tunnel spoke of the ordinary: a gate guard's laugh, a sharp siege of barking followed by a cat's yowl, the snap of torch flames and watch fires. Our escorts' retreating hoofbeats were fading.

"Let the watchers think I fainted from fright," I said. "Say whatever you like to whomever questions, but I must know why Lianelle died and what they want with my brother. I can help you. I will. I'll do as you say: forget you, ignore you, learn what I can, be the worm wriggling on your fishhook. But these things I *must* know."

"It's rooted in history," he said. "You have to understand the history first."

"Then *tell* me."

He retreated a few steps and pressed his back to the damp wall. The air thudded with his life's pulse. Or perhaps it was my own heart galloping, for his story came quiet and reasoned. "In all the centuries of their existence, the blood family named Mondragon produced very few written works. But among them were four codices, intended to testify to the supremacy of Mondragon magic over that of their greatest rivals."

"The Gautier family."

"Yes. One of the volumes, *Diel Voile Aeterna*, was an index to the other three, a listing of experiments and results gathered over generations. *Diel Mechanika* described how to make various enchanted devices—amulets, talismans, lenses, and the like. *Diel Revienne* recorded their learnings about necromancy, forever the most compelling perversion of the Mondragons. The fourth, *Diel Schemata Magna,* recorded certain rites developed in these investigations. Rites, in the magical sense, are complex constructions of multiple spells designed to accomplish a single purpose." He paused on a questioning note.

"All right."

"Together, these volumes detail the Mondragons' investigation of death, life, and the *voile aeterna*, the eternal Veil that divides those divine demesnes. I've no idea what these particular rites were designed to do, but I believe it is—and has ever been—the Aspirant's goal, the goal of this conspiracy, to break that book's encryption and use the Mondragons' great rite. *That's* what's coming."

"To what end? A new king? Civil war? Anarchy?"

"I don't know. At the least, they will cause some profound disturbance in the natural order—like these disturbing sights we see in Merona. But are those the goal or merely side effects? I've pieced together a story from Temple records and civil writs, from legends in Delourre and Arabasca, from every source I could tap without announcing my true interests to the world. Evidently, at the height of the Blood Wars, a Gautieri spy stole these four codices from the Mondragon fortress in Arabasca and took them to Collegia Magica de Gautier. The Gautieri had a habit of encrypting the books in their library to protect them from ill use. The stories I've unearthed—and these are not the matter of any official history, but tales passed down in Delourre, where Collegia Gautieri and its library once stood—say that the spy eventually turned traitor, and returned three of the four volumes to the Mondragons. Evidently he was caught and executed—buried alive—by the Gautieri before he could return the fourth. Here and there in the tale of these books and the Veil, enough to know it is no error, I've found reference to Ixtador."

"But the Temple only proclaimed the teaching of Ixtador *after* the Blood Wars," I said, "when the Mondragons and Gautieri were all dead." The Pantokrator had imposed the realm of trial and journey between the Veil and Heaven as punishment for human savagery.

"So we've always been told. But the first mention is associated with the Mondragons, and only later crops up among the Gautieri."

Smoke wafted through the tunnel, mingling with the odors of must and urine. So ordinary beside my companion's dreadful tale. "Where are the other books?"

"Mage Gaetana gave *Diel Revienne* to Dante right before her arrest."

My bones shivered. *The Book of Return.* Necromancy. Phrases from the histories I'd just read leapt into mind: *The Mondragons wrenched the sun from the sky . . . trees curled back into the earth . . . arrows reversed upon the archers . . . the dead walked.* History told a story, exaggerated, skewed by the politics of the writer or the prospective reader, but rooted in fact. And now rumor claimed Dante raised the dead.

"*Diel Revienne, Diel Mechanika,* and your sister's book were likely part of a collection I retrieved from a chest discovered in a Mondragon ruin in Arabasca."

"Stolen from the Collegia Seravain vault by Mage Gaetana," I said. "You used the theft as evidence against her at the trial."

"Yes. But the devices she created, like the spyglass named in evidence at your father's trial, were flawed, inexpert, as if created from hearsay and not the true source. Dante has done better."

"So he has *Diel Mechanika—The Book of Devices—*as well, and can *read* them."

"Yes. Somehow, using sheer, stubborn magic he can unravel the layers of Gautieri and Mondragon encryption, which his partners cannot. Yet when I saw him working at it four years ago, the translation required debilitating expenditures of power. Your sister, it seems, found an easier way. If I'd had any idea . . . saints' mercy. And now you." He drew a breath of resolve, as if venturing an exceedingly difficult task. "So, you can work this kind of magic, too?"

"No! She sent me a spellkey. That and the blood from my thumb unscrambled the title."

"Which explains what Dante wanted with you." The cogs and gear wheels of Duplais' mind spun and meshed. I waited for him to explain.

"Once she broke the layers of encryption, your sister must have worked a new encryption spell of her own, keying it to you by using her own blood. We must pray her encryption talents were as robust as those she used to decipher the Gautieri locks."

"What of the fourth book?" The index that put it all together.

"*Diel Voile Aeterna,* the index, must be the volume the traitor spy did not reclaim for the Mondragons. It's logical that he would leave the summary volume until last. I've a mind that the list of experiments and results in the index gave the instigator of this conspiracy the very notions that sparked it: lenses and mirrors that show us things we're not meant to see, deadraising, magic powerful enough to create pits that swallow light, to drive birds and beasts mad. These things you've seen and others you've not."

Which brought us back to Lianelle and her discovery. My turn to yield information. He had to know the truth. "My sister took the *Book of Greater Rites* from the vault at Seravain. From what she explained, I believe they were laid out precisely for her to find. Your mentor, this Kajetan, *caught* her in the vault on one of her visits to exchange books. She believed she had distracted him from her pilfering. But he killed her, didn't he? Hand of the Creator, she trusted and honored and believed in him, and he killed her."

Duplais did not respond, though I might have heard a mumbled curse.

I pushed harder. I believed history had erred in one respect. "Duplais, what mark does Mage Kajetan wear upon his hand?"

Duplais' answer came so readily, it was clear he had anticipated my question. "A peregrine falcon, the symbol of excellence . . . of perfection in knowledge . . . of devotion to learning. Exactly as he has lived every day that I've known him. The Saldemerre mark is a very old one and strictly controlled. And it cannot be confused with either the dueling scorpions of Mondragon or the three keys of Gautier."

"And what mark does the Aspirant wear?"

"At my first encounter, he wore gloves. When he bled me, I noted no mark, as your father wears none . . ."—he paused for a very long time—"but, in truth, I was in no state to be certain of anything."

I came near crumbling at this simple, difficult admission, the first crack in Duplais' case against my father. But I summoned an image of my brave sister and remained upright, controlling all but the gravel in my voice. "The Aspirant came to my brother's prison in the night and infused Ambrose's veins with some potion that drove him half mad. Though he, too, was too sick to recognize any mark on his hand, Ambrose indicated the man worked magic. Duplais, my father is *not* the Aspirant."

Duplais' face was but a pale blur in the dark as he moved me firmly . . . carefully . . . aside. "Do not blind yourself with false hopes. Even if another wears the Aspirant's mask, which I am not yet ready to concede, the evidence against your father—evidence scribed in his own hand, evidence of his own acts and his orders to others—remains intact." A brief, kind touch on my shoulder gentled the sting of his words. "Now you must go. Nudge. Push. Knock them off balance. Put me out of your head and wait for my messenger to contact you. I'll do what I can to discover what's become of your brother. With your help, we *will* sort this out."

One more thing I had to be sure of. "Dante is not your man?"

"He was. Once." Profound weariness accompanied this admission, as if Duplais had long fought and lost the battle to arrive at it. "I hired him to spy on Orviene and Gaetana. He warned me from the first that he had no use for any of us. Yet I liked him. Believed we'd come to be friends. Then I betrayed his trust—a stupid, terrible, unredeemable mistake. Though I knew he walked a moral precipice, I did not believe a man of such brilliance, of such extraordinary insight into nature's working, could be so brittle of soul as to let a friend's error topple him from it. His crimes are my responsibility, and this sorcery he pursues drives him even deeper into the dark. Believe me when I say: However dangerous you imagine him to be, the truth is far worse. Do not engage him. Do not challenge him. Do not make yourself of more interest to him than you must inevitably be as your father's daughter. Be dust at his feet. Now we go."

The air stirred. Boots scuffed. When I stumbled from the tunnel's mouth into the glaring torchlight of the inner courts, Duplais had already vanished.

A SHORT TWO HOURS' OBLIVION separated the dread adventure in the Bastionne from my first morning as Eugenie's maid of the bedchamber. Despite Ambrose's disappearance, my father's belongings in the Bastionne Camarilla, this mesmerizing Kajetan, so coolly explaining how my family had become pawns in a war, I had to keep my focus on gowns and hairbrushes. To retain my new position, my most promising avenue to learn what I needed, I had not only to satisfy the queen herself, but to convince her murdering harpy of a mother I was no threat.

The queen's bed curtains were yet closed when I arrived at the royal bedchamber. A clinking noise drew me to the wardrobe room, where Lady Antonia was rearranging a shelf of scent bottles.

"Divine grace, my lady."

She snapped her head around at my greeting. "Anne! I didn't expect . . . Well, here you are."

Though her eyes remained flinty, the dowager queen's lips curled into a smile. She set me immediately to work, arranging the painted silk screen that shielded the royal commode from the open doorways.

"Divine grace be with thee, Your Majesty, and with thy ancestors, and all thy lost and beloved," said Antonia, drawing the bed curtain open as I scurried off to retrieve the refreshment tray servants had left in an outer room.

I laid the morning rose correctly on the tray, warmed a cup with hot water, then poured fragrant tea over the dollop of honey said to promote clear eyesight. By the time I returned, Eugenie was emerging from behind the commode screen, wearing a sky blue morning gown. Her hair was a cloud of midnight framing a feverish complexion.

Despite the early hour, she managed a welcoming smile. "Dear Anne, such a kindness to relieve my sweet dama of this burdensome bedchamber service."

"Surely serving you is no burden, Majesty," I said, setting the tray on the ebony table nearest the eastern windows. Gold shafts of sunlight poured the promise of a perfect autumn day through the open draperies.

"Others would disagree," said Eugenie, sighing and curling up on the small couch next the table. "You'll need to be a brave girl to serve me, Anne." She drew the gown around her as if the sunbeams were frost laden.

Her grim warning imbued my natural curiosity with urgency . . . and a bit of a shiver, as well. "What *courage* would anyone need to serve so gentle a mistress?"

"I maintain this appointment is a mistake, daughter." Antonia did not allow her to answer, barging in between us like a Norgandi longship bristling with paint-streaked warriors. "Your husband rules the mightiest demesne in the Middle Kingdoms, and your state—and respectability—must reflect his position at all times, not for your own comfort, but to instill awe in his allies, his subordinates, and his enemies. Already we've had queries from the Camarilla about this girl, and now some common Riverside magistrate needles Philippe's bailiff about Spindle Prison and—angels guard you—murder. To afford personal intimacy to a girl of such appalling notoriety is idiocy."

Eugenie's smile melted away. "Dama Antonia, I choose to believe it is your vigorous care for me that so taints your words with insult."

Quicker than a hummingbird's flight, Antonia was sitting next the queen, kissing her hand. "Oh, dear child, forgive," she said, raw and tremulous. "Injustice and treacherous circumstance ever raise my ire. Naturally, Anne bears no personal fault in these matters. We women are forever at the mercy of the men we love." For that single instant, Antonia might have been a player entirely stripped of wig, rouge, and mask.

Astonishing that a quietly spoken reproof could induce so desperate a retreat. Gracious, Antonia had spoken slightingly to Dante. What could frighten her more than the vile mage? Surely she had numerous resources of influence and wealth to weather a minor pique from her daughter—who seemed the least likely person to hold grudges of anyone I'd ever met.

"Philippe's bailiff told Ilario it was all a mistake. Anne was not in the least implicated in the unfortunate events at the prison," said Eugenie, laying a hot hand on mine. Firm, far stronger than one would ever expect, that touch communicated a harmony of trust and sympathy. "What honor would I gain for Sabria were I to bend to innuendo and rapacious gossip aimed at me through my handmaids?"

Eugenie kissed her foster mother's hand and picked up her tea, thus dismissing the matter of Ambrose and my detention. The queen had far more of kindness in her than I. Had Lord Ilario caught my hint about Antonia? Had he warned Eugenie?

Antonia snapped her fingers at me and pointed to Eugenie's dressing table. Anger and spite sparked behind the dowager's tight smile, a reaction that cheered me ferociously. Antonia's stranglehold on Eugenie seemed exactly the correct place to keep pushing, as Duplais had advised. Her handprints were everywhere in the conspiracy. What did she gain from it?

I prepared the dressing table as I had been taught, selecting hairbrushes, combs, pins, and adornments to suit Lady Patrice's wardrobe selection for the queen's first engagement of the day. Eugenie's engagement calendar, a stiff page of meticulously inked times and places, lay on the writing table where Lady Eleanor left it before dawn each day.

At midday Eugenie would dine in the Peony Courtyard with the wives of the knights and officers preparing to accompany the king on the spring campaign to quell a border uprising. Immediately following she would make a round of ten calls, one to the merchant headquarters of each demesne major in celebration of another successful voyage returned from Syanar. Journian nobles would escort her on her rounds, as a reminder that the king's own house would claim first shares of the voyage's profits. The round would end with supper at the Journian merchant guild. Just reading the plan exhausted me.

Antonia dosed Eugenie's tisane with a red tincture, insisted she swallow two spoons of a peppermint elixir, and passed her a little box containing pastilles of pressed herbs to suck on, should she become nauseated during the afternoon's activities.

As I brushed Eugenie's luxuriant hair, I noted a few strands of gray, the clear signal of her constricting future. Her age must be near five-and-thirty. If she failed to bear her king a healthy child soon, she would be declared *cerrate vide*—an empty cask—and my goodfather's counselors would force him to set her aside. The words must beat an unceasing tempo in her heart. Indeed, as I clasped a delicate carcanet of diamonds about the queen's long white throat, her racing heartbeat pulsed beneath her heated skin.

Once Eugenie was dressed and awaiting her escorts, Lady Antonia ran me through my paces. She seized every opportunity to confuse me, listing fifty-six separate steps for drawing Eugenie's bath, declaring that Her Majesty never wore green on Third Days, as it was bad luck, and insisting that her cup of chocolate before bed must be exactly warm enough to wilt a rose leaf, but no warmer. While never contradicting her foster mother aloud, Eugenie made sure to arch her brows in such gently humorous fashion as to reassure me that this was all a bit of exaggeration.

By the time the two women had departed, my head was bulging with minutiae. I retired to the salon with a journal I'd brought to record just such information.

My eyes wandered to Duplais as I wrote. As ever, he sat apart from the ebb and flow of ladies' emotive conversation, giving serious attention to the mundane queries of all who approached him, jotting notes in his journal as if Lady Alice's cracked teacup was on par with necromancy. So intense a mind. Such a singular focus.

"Good morrow, dear ladies, gallant gentlemen! Divine grace be with all of you on this delectable morn!" Chevalier Ilario bustled into the salon with his usual exuberant disruption. "Such news I have for you! But hold, I must prepare our shepherd."

He moved straight for Duplais and settled into a long conversation, illustrating his exchanges with gesticulation appropriate to a marketplace orator. The chevalier's overexpressive manner and ruffled finery—today expressed in vermillion satin and yellow lace—left the administrator almost invisible. Duplais might have been a door facing. How did he hold patience with people such as Lord Ilario?

Duplais had done his best to put distance and public hostility between us over these past two tendays since he'd fetched me here. By leaving me exposed and isolated, he had deflected attention from his own pursuits, as well as giving me an opportunity to prove my loyalties. Fair enough. Racing to the Bastionne to rescue me had compromised that carefully crafted position. Thus I had to live as if nothing had changed between us, push forward on my own to find answers to the mysteries that plagued me—and Sabria, too. For if I had learned anything from the trip to the Bastionne, it was that Lianelle had exposed no simple magical rivalry.

The Book of Greater Rites. That was the incendiary agent, a match awaiting only my blood and Lianelle's key to strike fire. And Mage Dante, the mercenary, was the touchhole, the meeting place of fire and nitre powder at the center of it all. I just could not comprehend the shape of the conflagration to come. I needed to know more about magic.

With Duplais unavailable, I was left with few choices. An unreliable link of ink, paper, and distance lay between me and Lianelle's friend, Adept Guerin. Jacard lived in much too close proximity to Mage Dante. Perhaps the trustworthy ally Duplais had promised could provide answers. All in all, it was reassuring to feel that I had *two* allies here—even if we could not communicate freely as yet.

Of course, I had one other acquaintance who knew of magic. Dared I trust a man I had never met in person? He could be a Camarilla prefect, for all I knew. I'd heard not a whisper from my mysterious friend all morning. Unless . . .

A frisson of wonder washed through me, and I glanced over at Duplais yet again, only to find his eyes peering over his spectacles, straight at me. He ducked his head even before I did. A man of quiet intensity, of intelligence and education. A man of secrets, who made himself invisible, who could work magic yet buried his talents in mediocrity, allowing even his beloved mentor to believe him incapable. Who could be lonelier than one who lived so? Was it possible . . . ?

"Hear, hear, sweet ladies, generous gentlemen!" Lord Ilario climbed onto a couch to address the assembly—entirely unnecessarily, as he topped anyone in the room by a head. "I bear grand tidings! As these abbreviated days inform us, the year wanes, drawing down on our heads all the tedious business of harvesting and tidying up and fluffing pillows and blankets and such that entirely fill one's head with dust and smoke and make one's housekeeper and steward entirely grumbly. And with the change of season arrive the duties of demesne lords, which are also tedious, certainly, but do give one the chance to see a variety of people and connive a celebration or two or at least a festive dinner party along the way. But, then again—"

He halted abruptly, clapping one lace-draped hand to his forehead. "Now, where was I? Oh yes, the news! His Majesty, being a most diligent and gracious lord of his demesnes, has decided to make his quadrennial progress through the demesnes major of Sabria an entire year early—and we shall certainly not discuss the bellicose circumstances on the northeastern borders that might preclude such an extended journey next year, as they are quite too depressing to express before such a gentle assembly. Rather we shall rejoice at news that must surely dispatch this gloom that so blackens our fair kingdom. For King Philippe has notified Lord Baldwin that he shall begin his tour *here* at Castelle Escalon in a tenday's time!"

Lord Ilario leapt off the couch, jostling the elderly dame who sat at the opposite end, and promptly began relating the same information in much elaboration to each person in the salon in turn. His ringing tenor was instantly drowned out by an explosion of conversation. The most reliable gossip had indicated the king was not expected at Castelle Escalon until the new year. And now this . . .

Duplais' expressionless attention was again focused on his journal. I imagined I heard his pen scratching on the pages. Was my goodfather's change of plans his doing?

I stifled an impulse to call out for my quiet friend. Satisfying curiosity—even so intimate a curiosity—must wait. If Duplais and I were to keep our secrets hidden from those who might use them for harm, I must tuck that particular speculation deep inside.

Restless, uneasy, I abandoned my trivial occupation and wandered into the courtyard garden. The day had changed. It was as if the ocher haze that colored the daylight had thickened and grayed, settling into a bastion of cloud on Sabria's horizon. The storm was rising.

CHAPTER 22

20 OCET, EVENING

The queen returned to her chambers in late evening. As soon as her waiting ladies departed, she sagged, limp and exhausted, into a chair. Her head drooped onto her fist, the wisps of hair at her neck and temples damp with sweat. Her complexion was flushed, her lips rosy and swollen.

"Sleep . . . dreams . . . are all I can think of." She drained a goblet of wine in two swallows, licking her lips as if to savor the taste. "The officers' wives are such brave women to send their men off to war. I near drown myself in sleeping potions and silly amusements when Philippe is on campaign, and he is the king, who sits at the back, well protected. They must think me horrible and proud, as I could not stand and receive them individually. My knees would not hold me so long."

"Is such exhaustion usual, Your Grace?" I knew very little about pregnancy and didn't want to raise an alarm unnecessarily.

She waved me off. "Everyone assures me it *is* quite usual in these early days—as normal as anything in such an awkward time. But such vivid sensations run wild in my body . . . such heat . . . this craving for a man's—" Her flush deepened. "I've not experienced the like. Four times, it's been. Perhaps *different* signals a better outcome."

I wondered if she had managed to eat anything during the grueling day. I guessed not, but refrained from inquiring. Better to not annoy her with an excess of mothering right at the beginning. "Let me help you with your gown, and then I'll bring tea and salt biscuits."

"That would be lovely. Dare I say this bodice squeezes the breath out of me? Such would be a certain sign." A wistful sigh blossomed into a smile. "There, you see, I am much too intent on interpreting my every hiccough! It is a dreadful, selfish way to live—and unhealthy, too, so Roussel informs me."

"The physician seems a sensible man . . . and caring."

"Very much so. I've held no faith in ordinary medical practice since my son's death. Mages might have saved Desmond had Philippe allowed me to call them in early enough. And despite my blind idiocy in trusting Gaetana, Orviene, and Fedrigo, I've not relinquished my beliefs. But I felt I owed it to Philippe to try again with a scientific man. Duplais found Ganet for me."

In the light of my newfound belief in Duplais, I found this information quite reassuring.

"So Master Dante does not prescribe for your health?" Dante had paid particular attention to the queen's medicine box when he'd barged in on Lady Cecile and me.

"No. The mage serves . . . other needs. I know he quite terrifies everyone in the household, but we have an understanding." Sadness settled about her shoulders even as I unclasped the diamond-studded carcanet. "He does not coddle me or make promises he cannot keep. That's refreshing."

"You're braver than I, lady," I said, removing the diamond comb from her hair. "I cannot bear him even to look at me."

"Foolish and stubborn, not brave. But the Creator gave us magic for a purpose, and if I am to endure a life I did not choose, then I shall have my way in the matters of my heart's need. Even if it means I shelter one of the Fallen for a while. Put Dante out of your head, Anne. I'll see he doesn't trouble you." She shook out her hair vigorously, as if to rid herself of unpleasant thoughts.

Would that was so easy! I brushed out the looped strands of hair, and she sighed in pleasure.

"Have you made friends in the household, Anne?"

"I'll confess I am not . . . sociable . . . in the way of your other maids of honor, so I'm not familiar with anyone save Sonjeur de Duplais."

"Whose presence must cause you great distress." She reached up and patted my hand. "I'm sorry for that. He is very good at his tasks. You must speak to my brother. Ilario knows everyone. He can certainly make introductions for you."

"Lady Antonia introduced me to the chevalier at my court debut." My cheeks heated as I recalled the occasion. "I do believe she had ideas of matchmaking."

Eugenie turned around so fast I thought she might topple from her chair, her hand flown to her face, masking uncontrollable laughter. "Oh, my dear girl!" she said, when the smothered fit had passed. "You must have been wholly shocked!"

I could not deny it. "I've since learned how kind he is."

"Indeed he owns the kindest, most loving and loyal heart in this world, and the Creator has endowed him with an innocence that reminds me every day of the world's goodness. He is dearer to me than I could express in a thousand years of trying, but I'll not deny that he can appear so . . . outrageously . . . foolish. And marriage? All these years, he has never once expressed an interest. I've sometimes thought his urgencies leaned in other direct— Well, I cannot imagine what Dama Antonia was thinking. No girl could ask for a better person, but for an educated woman like you, who must yearn for wit to match her own . . ."

I laid aside her jewels and sleeves to put away later. "Yearnings cannot matter. And yet—"

"No. They cannot." Eugenie turned away before I could broach the subject of her foster mother's latest attempt at matchmaking. "Tell me, Anne, had you a gentleman friend in the country, before you came here?"

"No, my lady. My responsibilities have kept me much too busy these past few years."

"I'm sorry to hear that."

"No need to be sorry. If I am to marry according to the king's desire, as is only right and has ever been my expectation"—a small lie—"it seems better I have no ties of affection to leave behind." I slipped the wine-colored gown from her shoulders and set to work on the numerous buttons of her bodice.

"Not better. No. I think an affection—a friendship—nurtured away from marriage, away from political considerations, away from court and counselors, goodfathers and parents, must be something pure and lovely, like clear glass, blown into the simplest, thinnest shape. It would ring with perfect clarity and catch only the truest colors of the light."

She pulled away and sought out the angled sunbeams so quickly retreating from her south window. The light caressed the bared arms she crossed over her breast.

"Love is so very deep a thing, Anne, so complex, so sweet and yet so engulfing, that when it rises amid these other considerations, wrapped and punctured and bound, the heart's yearnings become too complex, its shape twisted beyond sorting out. It saddens me you've had no chance to experience that rarity."

Nor had she, of course, wed to King Soren as a child of eight years, and widowed and wed again at twelve. I couldn't think of anything to say that wasn't maudlin. Perhaps such pure affection was what she sought with her gentleman friend. But what did *he* seek? His face was so familiar, yet I'd never glimpsed him in the corridor or salons. Was he one of the conspirators as well?

Gentle, kind, damaged Eugenie was surely a pawn in this great struggle, only I could not see where she fit. Was this estrangement with my goodfather a true rupture, or did he stay away in some attempt to protect her from arrows aimed at him? Someone had certainly fed her falsehoods to soothe her fears for his safety. My father had told me that not even the royal herald rode into battle ahead of Philippe de Savin-Journia.

Dismissing her pain with a smile, Eugenie enfolded me with a warm embrace. "So, tell me, now, Anne, what games did you play at Montclaire? I'll confess to enjoying quiet distractions, silly things like cards and charades and sonnets whispered in moonlight. . . ."

As I laid a sheet and the featherlight coverlet over her, I told of guessing games, word squares, and card stacking, of mock debates and blind chase and mute plays. Memories of Montclaire would ever be fraught with sorrow, yet the pain of loss had already dulled. That life was gone, so remote in the face of my current preoccupations as to seem like a myth.

Once Eugenie had slipped into a peaceful slumber, I arranged the bed curtains, keeping a wary eye on the sorcerer's ring in the floor. Could it be a device like the barbed bracelet, set to channel wickedness here? Yet it was so brazenly displayed. The bracelet had been hidden, though not *well* hidden, come to that. Perhaps that was part of the scheme. Who would expect a nasty charm in the bedchamber when a sorcerer's ring was fixed in place so openly?

It was tenth hour of the evening watch by the time I had put everything away and bade a peaceful night to Arabella de Froux, the lady-in-waiting who sat in the retiring room through the night hours. Though I relished the thought of my own bed, once shed of gown and hairpins, I found myself too tight wound to sleep. The chamber in the Bastionne—spirits of night; Papa's boots and dagger—and the encounters with Dante and Kajetan and Duplais churned in my head.

What a pleasure it would be to leave Castelle Escalon for a while, to spend an hour wholly engrossed in matters other than murder, grieving, and conspiracy. I'd last experienced such removal at Cecile's journey feast, while talking with the quiet intruder. Astonishing to think that had been only yesterday.

The more I relived that strange interlude, the more I longed to revisit it. Quickly resolved, I shut down the lamp, reached into the dark, and invited the mindstorm. *Friend . . . are you there?* I formed the words, careful to speak only truth. *I can't sleep and need . . . company.*

Chaotic noise filled my head. With swelling disappointment, I began to shove the unruly emotions and clamoring voices behind my inner walls again. But a sharp jolt of confusion stayed my closing, as if I had collided with someone in a dark tunnel. A surge of astonishment was followed by a profound stillness in the heart of chaos. He was there. So much communicated without a word.

I'd like to get to know you better, I said. *Is this all right?*

When he did not respond immediately, I felt an idiot. The sun had long set over Merona. He might be asleep . . . or with friends . . . or a wife. . . . Or, if my suspicion was correct, he might be sitting in his east-wing office, laboring over the royal household accounts or trying to unravel Dante's latest move. I quickly shut that image out of mind, lest it color my speech. Better we remain anonymous. *Never mind. You're likely busy. I am so sorry. I didn't think—*

No, no, it's well-done. Truth. Every word. He *was* pleased. Quiet joy washed through my body like warmed wine on a cold night. *His* joy, so much deeper and more powerful than words, more a surging ocean than a rushing river. *You're not afraid of me.*

Shivering, I drew my shawl around me and gazed out at the lights of the city, winking beyond the dark palace gardens. This was so immense. *There are so many things in the world to be afraid of,* I said. *I thought, perhaps, we could talk of something wholly ordinary, as if our true lives did not exist. You weren't asleep?*

Ought to be. But I don't sleep easily. I'd as soon work. Or read.

What kind of books? My question followed so naturally it startled me. And it frightened me a little, too. Every word between us needed consideration. If I had asked what kind of work or why he did not sleep well, he might well ask the same of me. And if he were not Duplais, then he could be anyone . . . a gossip, a thief, an enemy. I didn't want to know.

Tonight, a treatise on the heavens. His answer felt constrained somehow, though it carried no hint of untruth.

A vast topic, I said, *whether astronomically speaking, or religiously speaking . . .*

. . . or addressing the weather or the possibility of astral divination or a more philosophical tack—the nature of pleasure. Interest and amusement surged as he completed my thought.

Divine Creator, how could I know that?

All fine aspects of the topic and worthy of exploration, I offered. All of them the interests of an educated man. All far removed from Castelle Escalon and its sordid secrets. A certain hunger drove me onward, making me bold as I had never been with men. *Should we address them alphabetically or in order of importance?*

Any. Certainly. I've never— I'd surprised him again. *I suppose . . . I'd a thought to take a walk to study some night-blooming plants. I could be persuaded to look up instead.*

It was a glorious night my friend walked—balmy, star-filled, scented with woodsmoke and autumn apples. That same night flowed through the open casement into me, around me, shared as we spoke of Gossorein, who had sketched the movements of the planets around the sun, using the language of mathematics as charcoal and paint. And I leaned on the sill and watched the same star-sprinkled sky he observed as we discussed Fleure's impossible project, a catalog of the stars. In a rapid-fire exchange, we proposed schemes of naming, measuring, and distinguishing between them. Our repartee infected me with the fevered delight of a new-healed paralytic stretching long-dead muscles. With a finishing flourish I proposed hiring a sorcerer to snuff out the stars and relight them in more regular patterns.

Abruptly he fell silent, closed as absolutely as a book between its covers.

No sorcerer could do that, he said after a moment, *not if the stars are truly suns like our own.*

It was only a jest. Silliness. It had been Lianelle's idea when she was five.

Ah. Spoken as if I had referred to some odd custom he had heard of, but didn't quite comprehend. Which told me much of him.

I fumbled at what to say next. I yearned to probe his knowledge of magic and its limits, but this was far too early for a topic fraught with risk. He assumed I was a practitioner. The idea did not repulse me as it once would have done—a surprise in itself—but my mother's family had tested me as a child and found no predictors of magical talent. He must himself be one, though, an adept or mage or student . . . perhaps a member of the Camarilla . . . perhaps an illicit practitioner, which would explain his shyness at discussing himself. Or he could be a once-failed student who had come to his talent late and in secret. Dangerous ground.

Thus I diverted our talk to the constellations, and he marveled when I told how Hematians saw quite different things in the same arrangements of stars—sea creatures, ships, or anchors, where Sabrians might see plows or warriors or cups overflowing with grapes. He knew only the commonest Sabrian names.

You must have made a special study of constellations, he said. *Are there so many books about them? My own studies have not explored folk tales.*

My family would often sit outside at night, I said. More treacherous ground. But yielding or withholding came easier with every word. *My parents would point out the Archer or the Dragonfly or the Creator's Hammer and require one of us children to tell the story. When we traveled, they insisted we learn the local stories and tell those, too.*

Another long pause. *It is not our talk of star patterns that leaves you melancholy.*

He did not couch this as a question. Yet a sense of his puzzlement prompted a response. *I'm fostered*, I said. Truth. And many noble families sent their daughters to live near collegiae or mentors or marriageable suitors. *My guardian is generous, but I miss my family very much.*

Ah, he said again.

This time he diverted the conversation. We were both somewhat skeptical of astrologers who claimed to read the future in the stars, but he mentioned, with excitement, how a philosopher in Eldoris had recently proposed that planets obeyed the same physical principles as a stone dropped from a watchtower.

Germond de Vouger, I said. *An astonishing thinker.* When I expressed my uncertainty that this new theory could ever be proved, my friend provided such a clear explanation, I felt as if I could draw de Vouger's diagrams myself. Papa had given me de Vouger's letters outlining his grand theory, and I had studied them for half a year, yet still I had floundered.

How can one person come up with such a grand idea? My friend's wonder was as clear as the stars. *Are insights born in our bodies like the language we speak or the ability to walk, ready to display themselves when we've reached a proper turning point? Or must one find a teacher who sculpts and hones the growing mind?*

I told what I knew of my father's correspondent. De Vouger's father had been a sailor who lived by the stars and taught him young to watch the sky. His mother had been an acrobat who spent her life being tossed into the air until she broke her back in a fall and died of it, not a month after his father drowned in a storm. Another of the acrobats had taught the youth to juggle, and his juggling took him to Eldoris, where he entertained the students and scholars of the Collegia Astronomica . . . and met Gossorein himself, the astronomer and teacher who changed his life.

My friend contemplated this story for a moment. *You know the names*, he said, *whereas I know only the ideas. I never considered that names and histories could connect ideas, like markings on a map. And yet my own story—* For a moment, scarce any sense of him remained, as if all I could hear was his breathing.

But I babbled on, unwilling to relinquish the best pleasure I'd had in months. *De Vouger still teaches at the Collegia Astronomica de Eldoris*, I said. *You could travel there and hear him lecture. You have such an astonishing grasp of the subject. Great Heaven, did you study with him there?*

Alas, I am not free to travel so far as Eldoris. His voice had turned cool. Distant. *Perhaps* you *could go and ask your questions.*

And then did the magnitude of my discourtesy overwhelm and shame me. When he had backed away from a mention of his own life, I had selfishly pressed him with a direct question, a question I would not wish asked of me. If he answered, he could not lie. Yet the matter was more complex than that. If he said *anything*, while leaving himself so open as he had been on this night, I could perceive emotions that he might rather keep private. As he had perceived my melancholy about my family. His comment had given me fair warning.

Forgive me, he said, before I could choose how to remedy the problem. *To speak of myself . . . Please understand—it's awkward. I am a teacher of sorts. Were word of this curse to get out . . .*

The fault is mine, I said, hurrying to make it up to him. *You don't know me. And you've been everything of patience since the beginning. I promise I didn't mean to push or pry. Indeed, I, too, live in awkward circumstances . . . unmarried.*

Ah . . .

We should swear on our mutual gift to leave sordid mundanity out of our con-versation, I said, whimsy giving my words flight, *and pretend we are wholly normal people in a pleasant sitting room, which, as it happens, we can reshape according to our imagination. Do you so swear?*

I imagined him smiling . . . though puzzled, too. He was clearly unaccustomed to whimsy.

I swear, he said.

And I do, as well.

The tower bells struck the third quarter of the hour. Eyelids heavy with sleep, I wasn't even sure *which* hour. He said he had come to the end of his walk, and so we bade a hasty farewell. Embarrassed at my missteps, I did not press for assurance that we would talk again. That he had taken pleasure in the exchange, as I had, led me to hope such urging was not necessary.

CHAPTER 23

A s I put away Eugenie's jewels and garments from her morning activities and readied what she might want for her evening supper party with the Duc de Aubine, brisk footsteps in an outer room brought Lady Antonia into the bedchamber. She surveyed the room, her plucked eyebrows, as ever, giving her an appearance of surprise. I gestured toward the closed bed curtains. Eugenie, exhausted from receiving a delegation of Journian vintners, was napping.

With a jerk of her head, Antonia beckoned me into one of the adjoining rooms.

"Dear Anne, I must apologize," she said as soon as we were out of the bedchamber. "My objections to your service must seem quite harsh."

"Your care for Her Majesty's reputation reflects credit on you, my lady," I said, swallowing my true feelings in the way of all servants. "None would dispute your concerns about my reputation. Believe me, I am humbled by Her Majesty's trust and will do everything in my power to deserve it."

She beamed at me and reached for my hands. "Of course you will, *caeri*. I was sure you'd understand. Eugenie is of such sweet and ingenuous disposition, she is easily taken advantage of. With the continued elusive-

ness of your despicable father—I know you share this view of him, else I'd
not state it so frankly—and the brazen unpleasantness of this Mage Dante,
the scandal of my daughter's unfortunate choice in magical counselors has
not died down over these four years, as it should have. Every spiteful word
lacerates my spirit on her behalf. But as ever with her wishes, I am quickly
reconciled. I beg you consider me your mentor, not your overseer."

This effusive declaration radiated such motherly concern as I might
welcome did I believe one eyelash's worth of it.

"So, have you any concerns or questions for me?"

I demurred. Taking my arm, she strolled through the rambling apartments, as if we were old friends exchanging girlish gossip. "Such tedious
events we endure these days! Today these groveling vintners who cannot
trim their fingernails without Philippe's approval and cannot bother to
clean them before seeking it. And yesterday that roomful of maudlin
women, bemoaning their men going to war with their king. The whining
cows should be clapped into the Spindle for treason."

"Her Majesty tires so easily," I said. "And seems constantly fevered.
Whom should I call if she falls ill—saints protect and defend—and you are
not available to advise me?"

She halted in midstep, giving the question genuinely serious consideration. "Both," she said at last, "Dante and Roussel. Though *she* may instruct you otherwise, I'll not have my daughter left at the mercy of any
man without proper supervision. Despite her unfortunate experiences,
Eugenie views the magical arts with the most profound respect and admiration. Those of us privileged to live in her household must, perforce, do
the same, even when the purveyor is himself somewhat common . . . and
entirely disagreeable."

"Of course." Interesting that Antonia was so reluctant to engage her
partner in mayhem.

"Which reminds me that you'll not be needed after Eugenie returns
from supper tonight. The maids of honor have no activities on their schedule, and my own entertainments for the evening have fallen through. I do
so enjoy performing this little nighttime service for her comfort. After all,
I've put Eugenie to bed since she was eight."

"Certainly, my lady. I understand." All that remained on Eugenie's schedule was supper with her cousin and Prayers at eleventh hour. "Naturally, I'll stay alert until the hour passes." Especially now I knew Antonia didn't want me there.

Antonia began walking again, this time more purposeful. "Your family maintains a man of business here in Merona, yes?"

"We did. But he's no longer on retainer." I'd had to drop Simon's contract two years previous, when roof repairs devoured the last of our ready money. "May I ask why?"

"Philippe's resident secretary must review the existing Ruggiere grant before any papers are signed. We understand there were codicils appended after the original was placed in the archives. So we need your man's name."

Ah yes, that other grief—my lost home. "Simon de Bois of Laurent Square. So, is it announced who is granted Montclaire?"

"Oh, *caeri*, this is not about the demesne grant!" She wrapped her long arm about my shoulders in an affectionate squeeze. "This is about *you*. Eugenie and Philippe will be so pleased. The Barone Gurmeddion has made an offer this very morning. We'll sign the betrothal contracts tomorrow. You'll be married before the new year dawns."

"No! I can't! I won't!" Horror banished all caution.

"Certainly you can, *caeri*." Antonia, smiling, squeezed a little tighter and gave me a shake. "And you shall. The king's secretary in residence has already given his approval."

My life dissolved into a puddle of spit at my feet.

She abandoned me with a cold, triumphant kiss on each cheek. How could I have thought to match wits with a woman of her experience?

No, no, no, no, no. Denial hammered with my life's blood, with my footsteps, with the fury pounding in my head. Had I held an ax, I could have razed a forest. I would *not* be bound to that crude and mindless grotesque for the rest of my days. Her colleagues of the Camarilla might have plans for me, but Antonia just wished me dead. Poison was a woman's weapon, my mother had always said, and failing poison, who better than a woman would understand the particular death of forced marriage?

I returned to the queen's wardrobe rooms, forcing myself to ready Eugenie's toilette for the evening. Eugenie would sympathize, but she bore no influence with the king's advisors. Neither could I use Lianelle's potion to run away, not with Papa's life and Ambrose's life and other important matters resting on my investigations.

As I set Eugenie's shoes on the lavender-scented shelf, I spied a tangle of ribbons heaped in a basket. I snatched out a silken strip of scarlet. Love knots were tied of red ribbons.

Immediately, I threw it back. If using the signal put lives at risk, I'd best assess the threat first. Eugenie would sleep for two hours, time enough for me to find Simon de Bois' office in Laurent Square and glean my prospects.

I notified Doorward Viggio to fetch Lady Eleanor if the queen rang for attendance before fifth hour, and stepped into the outer passage.

"Excuse me, please."

Warmth flooded my skin when I heard the friendly greeting. My steps halted, and I responded with a vigor that must surely explode in his skull. *My friend! I'm glad of a distraction.* Head bowed, eyes closed, I listened . . . released my barriers a bit . . . but could not detect the familiar presence. Likely I was too agitated. *Friend?*

"Might I speak to you for a m-moment?" The inquiry came from behind me, not inside.

I spun in my tracks, heart thumping, head noisy with the unleashed voices inside it. "Physician Roussel!"

He loomed large in the shadowed doorway across the passage. His head tilted, concern creasing his square face. "Are you quite well, damoselle?"

"Just startled," I said, half sick, half pleased, entirely fuddled. "You appear immensely improved, sonjeur."

Indeed, fresh garments, a well-applied comb, and a more natural ruddy color in his complexion had restored his ever-meticulous appearance. His thick, perfectly trimmed mustache sheltered the beginnings of a smile. "While you look the same as always, d-damoselle, entirely without need for improvement."

His eyes dropped quickly after this quiet compliment. Eugenie had spoken of him as wretchedly shy. My own cheeks could have heated a snow cave. He had been waiting for me.

"I thought . . . hearing of your new p-post . . ." He glanced to either end of the passage, quiet in this resting hour. "I mustn't— I'm not allowed to c-come into the queen's apartments without specific summoning. Her Majesty's condition concerns me, and I hoped I might prevail upon you to encourage her to attend her health more c-carefully."

"Lady Antonia encourages the various tonics in Her Majesty's medicine box. I assumed those originated with you. She's quite insistent. I doubt I can do more."

Roussel stepped closer, stooping to whisper. "In truth, I've p-prescribed little but the shellblade root tisane. Most of the rest originate with the lady mother. *The mage* sends things along from time to time."

The physician might as well have told me arsenic or adder's venom filled the queen's vials.

"What would you have me do?"

"Her Majesty eats far too little, and not enough of liver and other b-blood meats that might sustain her. And she should drink more ale, take more exercise, and retire earlier. Such good habits would help her sleep more soundly. She is so restless, p-plagued with nightmares."

"That, at least, seems improved," I said. "I understand some kind of a spelled device was found under her bed and removed."

"If one b-believed in magic . . ." His glance darted up and down the corridor. "Even if such a thing were possible, who would afflict the queen, so gracious to everyone?"

Sensing a fellow skeptic, I felt more freedom to speak. "I've thought perhaps the thing harnessed some natural energies—like sounds that set one's nerves on edge. As to who, there are deadly conspiracies afoot in the household. Your own illness tells you. The couchine . . ."

"Aye. I g-guessed it was intended for you. D-damoselle, you must take care."

The quarter hour rang from the bell tower. "I'll do what I can in both matters," I said. "But you must excuse me now. I've an urgent errand in the city."

"My duties take me to the academie this morning. P-perhaps I could escort you. Assist in whatever way you might need."

My heart stuttered, then blossomed like a lily at sunrise. Was *Roussel* Duplais' trustworthy advisor? An outsider, self-effacing. Duplais himself had recommended him for his post. "An escort would be most—"

Men's voices blasted from the outer doorway of the queen's salon, halfway down the passage. Roussel and I hurried to see what transpired.

Mage Dante had his left arm wrapped about Adept Jacard's neck and was dragging him across the threshold from the courtyard, as if the young man were a sheep being hauled to slaughter. "Out of my way, peacock," he bellowed at Lord Ilario, who scurried in retreat to cower beside the stalwart Doorward Viggio. Everyone else in the room shrank toward the walls.

Jacard's feet scrabbled furiously to keep himself from being strangled in Dante's grasp. "I've done nothing!" he croaked. "Madman! Someone, please . . ."

As the ladies of the household gasped and moaned, the few gentlemen shouted at Dante to release the poor fellow. From a sizable distance, to be sure.

"Master, please, if you've a grievance, let us speak in private." Duplais, at his most officious, advanced from his corner.

"Step aside, librarian. I'll have no schoolboy interpret my saying to the royal. This belch in the world's hind gut is a sneak and a thief."

But Dante had slowed, giving Jacard a chance to draw his legs under him. The adept's head still poked from under the mage's arm like a market pig's. "Was only studying," he croaked. "You ordered me—"

A jerk of the mage's encircling arm strangled whatever the adept might have said. And a small, purposeful gesture from the black-gloved hand elicited a guttural moan that rose from Jacard's viscera into a wailing terror that chilled my soul. Spittle poured from his mouth. His hands pawed weakly at the mage's shirt, as his tongue swelled and blackened and his hair bristled like porcupine quills.

"Master Dante! Stop this!" Duplais' shouts drowned out even the adept's mewling. "The queen is not here! Tell him, damoselle!" He waved helplessly at me.

My stomach churned and my skin itched, as if scorpions swarmed me head to feet. Yet I could not fail to recall Dante's calculating demeanor in the Bastionne, only a few hours since, and his cool responses to my challenge in the queen's chambers. This brawl could be naught but show.

"Queen Eugenie is engaged with the Duc de Aubine for supper and cards," I said. The half-truth spilled from my lips easily. But every discipline of mind and body was required to hold my ground when the quivering mage rounded on me.

Unreason blazed in the green eyes. The skin stretched tight over his gaunt cheeks had darkened to an unhealthy flush, and the muscles of his mouth and jaw twisted and twitched. The air thrummed with murder. This was no game.

"My lady will not return until late." As with a rabid dog, I took care not to show my fear. "Shall I add an appointment to her engagement sheet for tomorrow?"

The world held its breath . . . as did I.

As if a guillotine had severed his fury at its root, Dante shoved Jacard aside. The adept crumpled into a shapeless, choking heap. The mage's color cooled; his leather-clad hands steadied.

"As you will, damoselle-of-the-mysteries." None but Duplais and I could have heard Dante's clipped menace. "But you should beware. Friends are ever faithless."

The mage's smoldering gaze affixed to mine. The emerald heat of it pressed on my skull, my bones, my viscera until the room spun. Colored silk, alarmed faces, and sunlight smeared in a blossoming of agony.

But I clenched my will and did not crumble. And before I could blink in relief, the mage grabbed his staff from where it was tucked under his right arm and spun slowly, pointing it at each quailing observer in turn. "Tell the royal lady . . . each of you, so that none might distort my saying: This spying shitheel has violated the privacy of the queen's First Counselor, attempting to steal the very work the lady's hired from me. He is banished from this house by tenth hour of this evening's watch, else I betake myself to fairer climes, leaving her to failed schoolboys and peacock soldiers who tremble at their own shadows."

He poked the quivering Jacard with his stick. "Your womanish tongue may serve you again once you're quit of these walls. Or it might not. Best behave yourself."

Dante swept out of the salon.

A whimpering Jacard scuttled on all fours until he collided with a blue couch, then wrapped his arms about his head and vomited up a tenday's meals. For a long moment, no one in the room twitched an eyebrow. I, too, stood numb.

Two men approached Jacard but, after some awkward shuffling, retreated and summoned cowering servants to clean up the mess. Wine was ordered all around.

"Spirits of Heaven and Earth. My chest is pounding like the Creator's mighty hammer!" Lord Ilario sagged against the doorframe and slapped his hand to his ruffled chest—the same hand that, moments before, had been resting on the hilt of the sword he forever carried about like a child with a favorite toy. I had no doubt he would sincerely place himself in danger to succor his sister, but I wondered numbly if he had the least idea how to use the thing, especially against a man of Dante's physical strength and magical prowess.

Duplais was left to offer Jacard a hand up . . . and to fetch a serviette from the sideboard to wipe the foulness from his hand when the adept stumbled out of the salon with no thanks, no glance, no word for anyone. All Jacard's cocky assurance was left in that mess on the floor. All his eagerness to learn Dante's magic and his determination to expose Dante's "false power." I felt sorry for the adept . . . and afraid for myself and Duplais and anyone else opposed to the mage's works.

My neck yet tingled. What of this experience had been magic and what sheer lunacy?

"Are you q-quite well, damoselle?" Roussel's breath riffled my hair. Close enough he could surely sense my trembling. "Such courage to face him down so c-calmly."

Even had I not known his stammer was a natural affliction, I would not have gleaned anything but calm from him. A physician must see every variety of behavior in the course of his profession.

I turned and choked out a laugh. "In a year or so, I'll be well," I said. "Why in the name of Heaven does she keep him on? How can the king allow it?"

"Our lady is strong-willed. You've not been p-privy to the master's daemonish works as yet?"

I shook my head. "Have you?"

"They do not invite me to the d-deadraising. I like to think he fears a man of science might point out the improbabilities in his mirror play. But I am required to attend other p-proceedings, as we are partnered to—" Scarlet bathed his deep-hued cheeks. "I should not speak. I'm sworn."

The mention of deadraising and "other proceedings" did nothing to quell my shivers. Nor did the shivers dampen my curiosity. "The mage does not harm the queen? It would be wrong to keep confidence if so."

Roussel's wide brow knotted. He retreated into the passage, farther from the babbling denizens of the salon. "His mystical nonsense? Likely not. Raising her hopes that she might bear a healthy child? I know too little of noblewomen to say. Do you believe in sorcery, damoselle?"

So solemn was his question that I could not pass it off with nonsense as I ought. "For many years I would have said no. Nowadays, I'm not so certain as I once was."

"I'd like—if you would grant me the privilege—to speak with you a little more about these matters. But it must not be here."

"Yes. Certainly." Even if he was not Duplais' promised help, he might tell me a great deal. His manner lent me confidence that I could rely on his discretion.

"Stone and steel! What's happened here?" Lady Antonia's intonations, so like a clanging fire bell, resounded from the salon. "Where is Anne de Vernase?"

One might think me responsible for the ruined carpet and the frightened, unhappy household.

I had not retreated far enough to escape curious eyes, thus I could not ignore the lady's queries. "But it seems our talk must be another day. Soon, though."

LADY ANTONIA REQUIRED A PRIVATE recounting of the dreadful event. Once she had wrung me out, she summoned Duplais and forced him through it all again, as if I must have omitted some detail that would clarify the whole matter.

As we gave our accounts, she paced from one end of the small sitting room to the other, crossways and back again. Her small hands, glittering with rings, knotted and unknotted in front of her. Her stiff curls bobbed with her rapid gait.

His telling complete, Duplais added that he had already sent a report of the incident to Lord Baldwin, Philippe's First Counselor.

"You what?" She halted in front of us, her complexion already the hue of fuchsias.

Duplais remained unruffled. "With the incident of the kitchen maid and Physician Roussel so closely following upon Lady Cecile's untimely death in the prime of healthy womanhood, Lord Baldwin asked to be kept informed of any further unusual incidents in the queen's household. It is an unfortunate result of the events four years ago."

"You incompetent, simpering, cowardly ass!" Antonia's lashing tongue could have drawn blood. "Did you happen to consider how this reflects on your mistress? Does Baldwin insinuate that there is some connection between a ducessa's weak heart, a disease-riddled imp, and a petty argument between two high-strung courtiers? These matters are the fodder of kitchen gossip, not serious attention. Philippe is just waiting for an excuse to take over this household."

I had always supposed the genius of revelation must present itself in grandeur—the astronomer with his arms stretched to the heavens, or the alchemist shouting, "Gloriosa!" with colored fire spewing from his steaming potion. But mine came while standing on tired feet, with the stink of vomit exuding from poor Duplais' hands, and the dowager Queen of Sabria shaking with fury and . . . terror.

The woman was near apoplectic. Not that her mad mage might have killed his assistant in the full light of day, or that her own villainy might be brought to light—I doubted there was any evidence left to convict her of either Cecile's murder or Naina's. It was the mention of Lord Baldwin had overturned her, the fear that another scandal might curtail Eugenie's autonomy, thus her own autonomy.

For six months after her husband died, Antonia had ruled Sabria, only to be set aside in favor of men. And then she had seen her son—her remaining link to power—cut down early. But she still had Eugenie. Now Dante was charged with seeing that Eugenie produced a healthy child. Antonia herself smothered Eugenie, isolated her, lost no opportunity to belittle her husband and all men, encouraged her unhealthy yearnings for her dead children. What Antonia wanted was the sovereign power she had tasted and lost.

And this was the link between the Camarilla war and Antonia de Foucal and Eugenie de Sylvae. Antonia provided the Aspirant and his servants with a nursery for their magics: unlimited funds, access to materials and people of all kinds, a shield behind which they could experiment with illicit practices, spellwork that the tetrarchs of the Temple or others of their own kind would otherwise condemn as unholy. In return, the conspirators were going to provide Antonia a grandson to be King of Sabria . . . her own king to raise and nurture.

"Her Majesty herself insisted Lord Baldwin be notified of such incidents." I heard myself speaking in the same even temper as Duplais. "Physician Roussel can attest to it."

"Roussel!" Antonia's astonishment quickly curled into a sneer. "Roussel is a cobbler's son. His presence in this household is an offense."

Of course, her favored mage was likely some coal miner's son. Dante's peculiar patois was heard nowhere but the grimy mountain villages of Coverge, Sabria's poorest demesne major. That a son of illiterate Coverge had come to be a master mage was a mystery in itself.

"Neither of you shall speak more of this to anyone. I'll present the case to Eugenie myself. She'll send word of her decision to the mage and the adept, assuming the imbecile's not crawled into a hole by now. Thieving from a man like Dante . . . Jacard hasn't the sense of a pigeon."

It was easy to see how matters would sort out. Poor Jacard would be discharged with no references. Dante's work would continue without any assistant to threaten exposure.

Antonia dismissed Duplais and dispatched me to make sure Eugenie's water pitchers were filled afresh. But I backtracked through a gardener's room and caught up to Duplais just as he opened the door to the doorward's chamber.

"*You* hired Physician Roussel, did you not, sonjeur? He came well recommended?"

"Yes. His references were impeccable."

"So it was someone outside the queen's household . . . and unattached to the magical community . . . who vouched for him?"

Duplais studied my face carefully. "I requested a reference from the man who sponsored Roussel's studies at the Collegia Medica—Germond de Vouger, a man of science well-known to His Majesty. To you, too, perhaps?"

"Impeccable, indeed. Yes. He's been my fath—our family's—longtime correspondent." The most famous thinker in Sabria. It was all I could do to keep from embracing Duplais in relief and satisfaction. "Thank you, sonjeur. I wished only to understand how the good doctor came to the household. He is most concerned about Her Majesty's health. Divine grace, sonjeur."

His gaze heated my back as I followed the passage into Eugenie's rooms.

THE BELLS RANG A QUARTER past fourth hour as I opened a window in the ladies' retiring room off the queen's bedchamber. The garden maze was awash in autumn colors, the sunlight golden, the shadows stretched long. No time remained to consult with Simon de Bois about guardianship agreements just yet. Eugenie would be waking soon, preparing to dine with Antonia's nephew, the corpulent, bird-loving Dumont, Duc de Aubine. And when she returned, she would make her prayers, which Antonia did not wish me to attend.

I'd vow the event was more than praying. Eugenie did not pray with fanfare. She offered devotions at her private altar every time she walked past it, with a touch, a kiss passed from finger to tessila, or just a pause with her eyes closed. Her beloved dead never left her mind.

The vial of Lianelle's potion waited in my pocket, as always nowadays. I would be watching whatever occurred tonight, Antonia's will or no.

As for any scientific investigator, my moment of insight had woven threads and mysteries into a comprehensible pattern. In friendship for my mother, Cecile had started up her own investigation of my father's disappearance. Somehow she'd obtained the page of diagrams from the conspirator Orviene, perhaps linking the plotters to Gautier and Mondragon magic. But she didn't know what she had. Lianelle's death had spurred her to action again, and she had written to her "scholar friend" that she might pursue the mystery at Seravain—a risk of exposure that threatened Antonia's connivance with the Aspirant. Cecile had knocked the conspirators off balance, and Antonia had reacted with murder. The Aspirant must be furious with Antonia.

The pattern of Eugenie's seduction into the infamous plot came clear as well. The queen, in the throes of grief and helpless anger at her infant son's mortal illness, had turned to sorcery for answers, a first wedge between her and her husband. Had Antonia purposely made the child ill? Murdered him? Certainly plausible. After two more miscarriages, Eugenie would have been in despair, dependent on her foster mother, and entangled in depraved sorcery. When the time was right, she had delivered a child, only the infant was a girl, Catalin Jolie. And the babe had died that same hour—murdered, perhaps, because in Sabria a female heir must make a strong marriage to hold her rights, which was not at all Antonia's plan.

Thus was Eugenie left yearning to comfort her children as they traveled the desolation beyond the Veil. I was not yet ready to admit the possibility of raising souls from the dead. But the skills that had created the image of Edmond de Roble might be bent to any number of purposes.

Whatever the actual course of events, whatever the bargains made, the chain that bound Eugenie and Dante had been well forged. The queen's fragile shell housed a fierce will, and as long as that bond remained intact, the conspirators' plot could proceed. No wonder Antonia would be furious at the thought of me, of all people, slipping in between her and Eugenie in a most intimate way.

Which left me with the remaining mystery, as yet unsolved from four years previous. What end did these sorcerers pursue in the shelter of Antonia's obsession? What was the Mondragon rite supposed to accomplish? Duplais did not yet know.

But the Royal Accuser, relentless and ever patient, was still searching, and he wished me to do the same. Throw them off balance. Force them into mistakes. This was a siege, not a single battle. Once a healthy boy child was brought to birth, Philippe and Eugenie would surely die. And though Antonia intended to be her grandson's regent, I doubted such was the *Aspirant's* plan. His object was all to do with magic . . . magic not seen in ages of the world. Mondragon magic.

CHAPTER 24

Queen Eugenie's mind was elsewhere as she dressed for her supper party. I would help her with one garment, only to find her off in another room when I returned with the next. No sooner did I finish linking her bracelets than she was off in the wardrobe room, peering into a lacquered basket. I had to fetch her back to her dressing table so that I could tidy her hair. Her spirit trembled like that of a child on birthday eve.

She said little and made no mention at all of my goodfather's coming visit. The afternoon's events, too, were quickly dismissed. When Jacard could not be found to defend himself against Dante's charges, she had no choice but to render the verdict her First Counselor demanded.

Even if I'd had some idea of appealing Antonia's choice for my future, the dowager bounced in and out of the room as if afraid Eugenie might disappear. It was a relief when they left.

Before leaving the bedchamber, I addressed a lingering worry, grown more urgent since my talk with Roussel. Over the next hour I opened each bottle, jar, and packet in Eugenie's medicine box while wearing Lianelle's wardstone ring. *Black if poison is within arm's reach*, she had written, and *blue if you're in danger from spellwork*.

The wardstone remained silver. Either the ring did not work or the medicine box contained nothing untoward. Reason suggested the former; faith insisted the latter.

I removed the bottom tray from the wooden box. Nothing in the shallow space underneath had moved in the tenday since my last view. Nonetheless, I tested each of these items as well.

The bundle of cinnamon sticks passed muster, as did a flat tin of pastilles, so hard they must have been compounded before the Blood Wars. Several empty paper packets crumbled to scraps in my hand. All that remained was a gray silk pouch, fastened by a bronze clip.

Stars of Heaven . . . since my first tour of the medicine box, I'd seen another identical to it. Pulled from the hidden drawer in Lady Cecile's armoire, now tucked into my own, the other pouch held the torn paper containing the *vitet* diagrams.

With fumbling haste, I unfastened the clip and emptied the bag. A small circlet of copper dropped into my hand. Too large for a ring, too small for a bracelet, the circlet was intricately worked in the shape of a long-jawed beast and a wing-swept bird, clashing snout to beak. Garnets had been inlaid for eyes. It prompted no nerve-grating disturbance, as the barbed bracelet had done. The wardstone testified that any enchantment connected with the circlet was benign, as it remained a cool silver.

The idea teased at me that Cecile had shown me its hiding place apurpose, as if she had known I might one day hold her other evidence and make the connection. As if she had known she might not be here to show me. That last night when she gave me the book, her complexion had been gray and drawn—ill. Or frightened.

I returned circlet and bag and everything else to the box, just as it had been. I would get Eugenie to tell me what it was.

By the time I returned to my own room, it was far too late to visit Simon de Bois. He would already have left his office for his wife's house in a village outside Merona—much too far to go in three hours. At eleventh hour I needed to be in place in Eugenie's bedchamber to spy on her prayers. I wrote a quick message, begging Simon to find some way to stop the impending betrothal, or at least delay it until the king returned to Merona. Ella promised to see the message delivered right away.

I dared not lie on the bed, lest my restless nights take their toll. Without urgent occupation, waking brought nothing but vile imaginings. In the secret hours of girlhood I had dreamt of my virgin night . . . of handsome Edmond de Roble's hands gently unlacing my chemise. To think it might be Derwin of Gurmeddion instead, licking his crusted lips . . .

To keep from vomiting, I yanked open my window and curled up in the seat, trying to let my mind go fallow, but the mindstorm broke upon me like a storm sea on the Caurean shore. Like great rivers that emptied in a common sea, anger, disappointment, irritation, and envy, wordless and violent, mingled in the storm surge. Were a god to judge the world this hour, surely he would see it colored in blood.

A stormy night in the aether. As a slow eddy in a sheltered cove, so did my friend's voice break the torrent of emotions.

Indeed so, I said, allowing his quiet to draw me from chaos like a proffered hand. *I'm afraid it's my own voice disturbs your studies tonight.*

I'm likely a contributor as well. My work does not go well of late. Answers elude me. I don't like that.

And I'm to be betrothed to a man not of my choosing. I had to restrain myself from telling him everything. I, who had never been able to initiate a conversation unless I had known someone five years, who could not ask a question of a stranger without analyzing it ten ways.

Nonconsensual marriage is barbarism.

Certainly this one would be. In ancient times Cazar women wore their zahkris to bed. I might have to adopt such a custom.

I hope the man is civil, at the least.

Not civil, I said. *Nor civilized.* Grotesque *and* vile *are the best that can be said of him. You've rescued me from heaving up my dinner at the imagining.*

Then you must not cooperate. Women know how to manage these things, do they not?

I fear nothing can be done.

There is always something to be done. He is noble born?

A very minor lord.

He paused for a moment. *Can you go out on your own . . . into the city at night . . . without being followed?*

Did we meet in the flesh, I would never answer such a question. *Yes. My guardian's house is not so secure as he might think.*

Good. If you like . . . I know a woman in the temple district, a broker of sorts. Not a nice woman, but knowledgeable about people—scandals, illegal dealings, loyalties—and absolutely true to her word. She owes me a favor. I could arrange for you to meet her, swearing her to keep your business secret, even from me. Impressions filled me: an odd mingling of trust, wariness, and warmth, and a certain ruthless edginess with regard to the scandal broker. *If there was naught to be done—and perhaps there's not—but if so, she could tell you. I swear on this gift, I would not use the opportunity to pry into your business.*

His promise blazed sincerity and truth. Yet I hesitated. We had agreed this friendship would remain beyond our separate lives. The nature of this unique connection, its possibilities unknown and unexplored, left me reluctant to move too quickly. Once we knew more of each other, we could never go back to this. There might be no one else in the world.

Forget I spoke of it, he said quietly, not waiting for me to voice my rejection. *I'm not so forthcoming, either, as you've noticed.*

I thank you more than I can say, and if I can come up with no other resource . . . perhaps. I'm hoping some solution will present itself.

But my appreciation renewed his urgency. *I study intricate and disagreeable problems. Perhaps I am just dim-witted, but you can be sure no solutions ever present themselves to me. Think on my offer. Tonight and the next tenday, I'll have the broker send a runner to the temple major at middle-night. Wear a white ribbon in your hair. When the runner asks who sent you, say "the son of Salvator." To prison such a gift as yours with an unworthy partner . . . it would be abomination.*

Though not one whit of my situation had changed for the better, his vehemence improved my mood. *I appreciate your good favor. Even before coming of age I decided to remain unattached. Certainly no one of substance would have me now. I am plain, dull, poor, prefer books to ladylike amusements. And I've certainly no family connection likely to lure a desirable suitor. For now I am happy to have a friend with whom I can talk.*

Good. This is a pleasure . . . a great pleasure . . . for me, as well.

We spoke for a while of mathematics, finding neither of us enjoyed mathematical rigors for themselves, but only for the language they provided for nature's wonders. But in books we found a wealth of common ground. He had treasured them from early on, as I had.

My family did not value learning, he said, when I made reference to books on my shelf at home. This statement settled in our ramblings as might a thick gray wall in the garden maze. Family was a topic we would not touch. But there were many, many more that we could . . . and did.

Divine grace, I said, when the bells reminded me of spying yet to be done. *May your studies progress well and let you sleep tonight.*

The temple major steps at middle-night, he said. *A white ribbon. Do not squander your gifts.*

Some half an hour after we bade good night, a persistent hammering called me to my door. I pulled it open to find a relieved footman massaging his sore knuckle. "Sorry," I said, gathering my shawl about my gown. "I was dozing."

"You're wanted in the queen's bedchamber, damoselle."

"Certainly." Perhaps Eugenie's prayers weren't so secret after all.

An hour serving tea and brushing Eugenie's hair, and I was back to my room again. The queen had been quiet and unreceptive to conversation, offering no explanation for Antonia's desertion or my summoning. Her air of disappointment might simply have been a reflection of my suspicions; I had thought *prayers* might be a code word for some magic working. Indeed Eugenie made no prayers save those I had noted before—a kiss of her fingers and a lingering touch on the many tessilae on her altar.

Wide-awake now, I watched the scattered lights of Merona winking in the night. Which lamp or candle was his? He was out there somewhere, my friend of the mind. A teacher, he'd said. Duplais might name himself a teacher after all his years in Seravain's library. I imagined my friend to be a serious, scholarly man like Duplais, though my sensibilities placed him closer to my own years. Certainly he was not some balding elder, but a fair and fine-looking fellow with frayed cuffs and ink-stained fingers, studying by candlelight at the Collegia Physica, perhaps, or more likely the Collegia Biologica. He had been going out to study night-blooming plants, after all, an area of interest that seemed unlikely for Duplais. Of course he valued my friendship, alone with this gift that no one in the world shared, that no one would believe and many would call madness or daemon-touched. How fortunate I was that he'd been there to guide me through the terrors of beginning. Unless it was all a lie.

No, I could as soon believe this court life a lie. Our friendship had skipped the fripperies and formalities of society, the layers of family and manners and rank that conspired to hide the true person. This had not begun in artifice, but deep in our centers . . . my fear . . . his solitude . . .

The dome of the temple major swept a dark arc from the star-filled sky. Scarce a kilometre distant. If my instincts were true, in less than an hour, a runner would be waiting there for the teacher's friend with a white ribbon in her hair. And if I did nothing, I might spend the rest of my days not with a quiet scholar who loved books, or even a warrior/diplomat who relished learning, but with an obscene and mindless grotesque. His food-flecked beard would brush my face, his leathery head lie on the pillow next to me. . . . Heaven's gates, I could still smell the stale wine and sour body.

Banishing doubt, I downed two drops of Lianelle's potion—enough to get me out of the palace gates and through the city. A white lace pulled from my spare chemise would suffice for a ribbon. As the smeared colors of the world took on their blue-limned mystery, I threw on a dark cloak and hurried through Castelle Escalon and into the night.

LITTLE TIME WAS REQUIRED TO have me questioning the wisdom of the excursion. Only a few passersby peopled the streets of Merona—a guardsman here, a hard-breathing laborer hauling a coal barrow there, a gentleman on horseback who, from his wandering path and mumbled singing, had indulged excessively in the pleasures of a Riverside tavern. But I might have been pushing my way through thousands of souls, with their stinks and spittle, their resentments and anxieties. Hungers. Spite. And fear everywhere. Lianelle's magic left me naked. I could not get this done fast enough.

The mindstorm receded as I passed the gates of the temple precincts and entered the desolate gardens. The air stank of dust and urine and sour vegetation.

Visible now, I tied the white lace on my braid and ran up the wide steps. After scouring the portico from one end to the other, I stood next the bronze doors in the wavering torchlight, caution thrown aside. Not a soul moved on the porch or plaza. Weeds torn from the deadness skittered past, joining a thorny pile at the far end of the porch.

Common sense demanded I retreat. But this opportunity might not come again.

"Fine lady, has you a kivre for a girl's not et a bite this day? Or a charm or trinket a body might sell to quiet the gnawish?"

Though prepared for a sudden appearance, the brassy greeting sent a cold shock across my nerves. She sat in the shadow of a column not twenty steps from me.

My one hand slipped the zahkri from its sheath. The other clutched a potion vial. Invisibility would serve me better than my fighting skills. "I've naught to give," I said. "I've come to meet a friend."

Far across the temple plaza, a hobbling, lumpish figure dragged a small wheeled cart. The wheel squeaked in a slow rhythm.

When I glanced back at the girl, she stood at the edge of a different column's shadow. Tall as Ambrose, whip slim, her gleaming skin the hue of walnuts, she must move quickly as a hummingbird. A crimson shawl sagged in large, graceful folds about her arms and shoulders and down one side, caught up at her waist with a silver link belt on the other. The asymmetric garment revealed long, slim legs sheathed in well-worn boots reaching to her thighs. Fassid, surely. Cazars were said to have a trace of Fassid blood, an exotic beauty visible in my mother and Ambrose and entirely lacking in me.

"Mayhap your *friend* would have a coin," she said. "If the friend be a live one. A lady-born wandering the city at night might pretend a friend or seek out ghosts."

"*You* travel alone in the city."

She had circled around so the torchlight glared in my face. "Indeed so. But I be customed to it. And not defenseless."

"Nor am I defenseless." I shifted my position as well, backing up to the very column she had deserted, stretching my ears and eyeing the rest of the pooled shadows for any hint of movement. I raised the zahkri.

Her sidling steps halted. "Mayhap . . ."

"*Feste kistaro ju!*" I said, which meant "Leave me alone unless we have business." It was my only Fassid phrase. My grandmother had used it to scatter annoying children.

The girl, perhaps my same age, burst into full-throated laughter. "What a fierce little creature! So, tell, who sends tha?"

I inhaled deeply. "The son of Salvator."

"Very interesting, serious friends have tha," she said, the torchlight glinting on silver earrings. "One, certain, who thinks of tha highly. Raissina Nialle's services do not come light. Fortunately for a lady-born having a tight fist and no silver, such a friend has covered thy fee. Though I do not think he comprehends thy full state."

In a seeming eyeblink, she had bridged the gap between us and was fingering the emerald silk of my court gown. "Perhaps the fee should be larger."

"Your mistress decides that, I'm sure," I said, yanking the skirt from her fingers and berating myself for not taking the time to change clothes. "Take me to her, if you please. I've little time."

"Testing for a fight, ben't tha? Tha'rt quite the little scrag-dog. Come."

She led me across the wide portico, down the steps past the tangle of dry weeds snagged by a short fence, and into a small fountain court. Water trickled from the moss-slicked statue of a sinewed woman locked in an endless struggle with a sea monster. My skin prickled.

My guide sat on a bench facing the font, spread her arms along the back, and stretched her long, booted legs in front of her. "Welcome to my abode of business, girl wearing the white ribbon. None shall overhear us in this place. Speak your need."

For a moment, I was fooled, hunting the source of the deeper, richer voice. But only the runner and I occupied the fountain court, as solitary inside the dribble of the water as we might be in the cave behind a waterfall.

Then I understood. I sheathed the zahkri and extended my open—and empty—palms in her direction. "Raissina Nialle, may the winds of war and commerce fill thy sails and coffers. May our exchange be of honor and to our mutual benefit."

"Better! A start more friendly than fierce." Here where the torchlight scarce reached, I could not read her face. But the air seemed less taut between us.

"I am to be betrothed to a man I despise. I wish to stop it."

Her arms swept a gesture large enough to signify me and my situation. "Marriage is difficult to counter if law permits and those who rule the family decide. Yet, occasionally, obstacles can be found. The son of Salvator specifics I cannot ask the lady's name. But I must know the man's."

"Derwin de Scero, Barone Gurmeddion."

Her hand clapped over her mouth. The odd noises squeezing past her fingers told me variously that she was in the throes of a fit or choking on her dinner in compatible revulsion. But before very long her shaking shoulders clarified her reaction. She was convulsed with laughter.

I located a nearby bench, sat down, and waited for her to regain composure. "Ah, poor dearie, dearie, dearie. Be tha a devil spirit? Whoever pawns this loathsome mate on tha must think it. Weren't I a businesswoman, I'd do this for naught but air and glory!"

She dealt with a fit of the hiccoughs and wiped her eyes. I waited, hopes rising, relishing what she might tell.

"Be tha easy, lady-born. The ways this marrying can be obstructed are numbered more than Riverside rats. No need to consultate my sources. To begin, this Gurmedd lord has a wife living. Not pleasured about it is she, but breathing, nonetheless . . ."

The Fassid woman reeled off a history of murder and larceny enough to fill Spindle Prison were each offense committed by a separate man. Surely Derwin's wife chained in his cellar must be sufficient to halt any marriage contract.

". . . yet tha knowst a scurrit lord so large as this one is crafty, else he'd not have so long a tally for the Fallen to punish. So I'll advise ta move with caution, else ye'll join poor Elliana in his cellar. He'd lick his lips at that." She shuddered, all laughter spent. "And now you've what I can give. To diddle the law on your behalf would be a new tally on your own account."

Her warnings were well given. I'd need to use this information with care, else I could end up in Derwin's custody with vengeance to be served on top of lust—a prospect to make a future with the Souleater a pleasurable idea.

I rose and opened my palms to her again. "My need is served, Raissina Nialle. Our commerce ended. No diddling required just now."

"Ah, but 'tis wise to deposit a bit on account with me. Naught but a name . . . a demesne . . . for a fierce little lady-born pledged to the Gurmedd snake . . . who comes fearless through the middle-night, knowing a smat of the Fassid tongue and politenesses of my kind. The prospect of your tale curls my toes. Be certain 'twill be held in trust until you've need again."

"Or until someone pays you for it."

"With no deposit made, the cost for service in the future grows higher. A kinsman's name, perhaps, or a bit of gossip gleaned in your . . . very high . . . circles. Tell me a name friendly; then I've no need to go hunting for who might be talking of Gurmedd links."

"I admire an honest broker, Raissina, but you are a broker nonetheless. I've no wish to make a deposit just now. I shall report our satisfactory dealings to the one who sent me. He swore you'd hold these 'smats' of knowledge about me to yourself as part of his payment, yes?"

She drew in legs and arms, as if closing her shop. Slow and sinuous, she rose to her full height and bowed deep. "It is so. Tell him we are square, all bargains held."

I'VE DONE IT, I SAID, my shaking hand covering my eyes. *I've arrows now, but no idea how to loft them.*

Good. That's very good. You'll find a way. You didn't . . . give . . . her anything? I should have warned you she'd try to wheedle. . . .

She tried. I refused. Nor did I ask for more information than your bargain with her specified. You can *rest easy about that.*

I wasn't— He bit off the blurted denial, the lie so easily recognizable. *Sometimes it's difficult to trust.* And that was truth.

CHAPTER 25

On the morning after my venture into Raissina Nialle's shop of bargains, *Prayers* appeared on Queen Eugenie's schedule yet again. Again Antonia informed me I would not be needed after supper. She did so as she held my arm and guided me into the reception room off the east foyer for our meeting with Simon de Bois and the king's secretary in residence. I'd not even had time to decide how to use the information my friend of the mind had bought for me. Accusations must be supported by proof—records, witnesses. I could get them, but not quickly.

It is intolerably easy to sign away a woman's life. Indenture for debt requires an appearance before three magistrates on three days running. A tenancy agreement with a lord requires five witnesses from the community, only two of whom may be the estate's current tenants. But a marriage contract requires only a representative of the woman's guardian and a representative of the prospective husband. My presence was no more required than my consent. Antonia's presence was to ensure the event took place. Simon's presence was, as Antonia indicated, to raise any assurances that the king might have given my father when the Ruggiere grant was made—a formality at best.

My goodfather's representative was his secretary in residence, Gerard de Physto, a scarred former soldier who could not bear walking outdoors for fear of a conflict erupting in the vicinity. His post had likely been Philippe's kindness, as he claimed never to have signed anything beyond requisitions for provisioning the palace garrison. Though scarce older than Duplais, his hair was thinned to infantile wisps, and every footstep or pen scratch made him flinch. Antonia's presence could be naught but a living torment to such a man.

"I'm sure my goodfather would wish to review this contract for himself," I said.

"Nonsense," said Antonia, grabbing de Physto's collar before he could escape. "He retains secretaries to relieve him of petty annoyances such as women's matters. A good soldier knows how to keep the road clear for his commander."

The road this man wanted clear was his path out of the room. Which required his signature on the contract.

The avuncular Simon de Bois had kissed my cheeks on his arrival, whispering an apology at the same time. "I've little of help, Ani. I'm sorry." He held me away, appraising. "Despite all, you've bloomed, girl. Getting away from the past has put color in your cheeks and a spark in your eye. You've a touch of your mother after all. And he"—he lowered his voice and jerked his head at the man sitting at the head of the table— "he doesn't look so bad."

"That's not Derwin."

The man he noted was Derwin's eldest son. Dagobert de Gurmedd, sleek and wiry as a viper and just as sly, maintained a less rancid outward appearance than his father. But he never stopped grinning and never took his eyes from me. Whenever Simon and the secretary conferred or examined documents, he opened his mouth and fingered his wriggling tongue. I'd never seen a habit so disgusting.

"The contract is in order," said Simon, easing back in his chair. "As the Ruggiere demesne grant is void, due to the Writ of Judgment that renders Michel de Vernase a felon, the provision of the grant giving Damoselle Anne the privilege of consent to a marriage partner is also void. In essence, there are no restrictions at all on betrothal as long as the signer is a legal representative of the lady's guardian."

My soul froze. "The partner could be a Norgandi, then, or a commoner? He could be an embezzler or wife murderer or tax cheat?"

"Any of those," said Simon, "however—"

Dagobert snatched up the pen, waggling his tongue openly now. His age must be somewhere about sixteen.

"Hold, sonjeur!" Nostrils flared in disgust, Simon held up his hand. "I have shown Secretary de Physto a writ of guardianship, signed by Philippe de Savin-Journia on the occasion of Damoselle Anne's birth, which occurred six months *prior* to the Ruggiere demesne grant. In this writ, the king has included a codicil that the girl may not be wed without his presence and consent. Though the language does not preclude betrothal, it does impose restriction on the wedding itself. And as it precedes the deleted grant, it takes precedence."

Fear wiped away Dagobert's grin. "My sire would plug the wench before leaving Merona. How can I go back and tell him he's got to wait?"

"By the saints, sonjeur!" boomed Simon, as nausea sent my world spinning. "Where is your dignity . . . and the lady's?"

"Wedding is but formality, Dagobert," said Antonia. "The girl is Derwin's as of this hour."

"Not to contradict, Your Grace," said Simon, gathering every gram of authority his bulk allowed, "and custom notwithstanding, I would not advise any man to . . . claim . . . the king's gooddaughter without his required consent. His Majesty arrives a mere eight days hence. Meanwhile, the lady has full freedom to contest the contract."

Simon's bluster seemed to confuse Dagobert and wound the cringing secretary.

"I most definitely wish to contest the contract," I said, handing Simon the charges I'd written out from Raissina's information. "My goodfather will stop this."

"Sign the papers," snapped Antonia, looking as if she might yank de Physto's remaining hair out. "We'll allow the king to decide if a traitor's brat is worth insulting the commander who holds his northern border.

And we shall leave it to Barone Derwin to decide how vigorously to pursue his marital happiness."

The papers were signed. All I could do was return to the queen's bedchamber to work, praying I could exonerate my father before testing my goodfather's forbearance.

22 Ocet, ELEVENTH HOUR OF THE EVENING WATCH

EIGHT DROPS FROM THE VIAL, I decided. Two hours. *"Aventura."* I dripped the tasteless liquid on my tongue. Come the day when I became Derwin's bride, I might drain the entire vial and walk out Merona's gates. But for now, my focus must be on the sad lady of Sabria, and what the villains thought to do with her this night.

I didn't think I would ever become accustomed to invisibility. To walk brazenly into Doorward Viggio's velvet demesne in full view of the bald functionary and two guards was not so difficult. But then I had to decide how to get through the inner door without them noticing. Returning to the salon, I heaved a porcelain vase through the garden door, then waited as the three of them stepped out to investigate the clatter. The last overtones of the eleventh-hour bells faded as I tiptoed into Eugenie's bedchamber . . .

. . . only to find it deserted as well. No Dante. No Antonia. No Eugenie. Only air the color of ash, despite burning candles set in every sconce and on every horizontal surface.

The engagement sheet testified I had not erred about the time. Pots of willow branches had been placed around Eugenie's bed. The cold, dry air, the drifts of incense smoke, and an underlying stench of burnt grass bespoke the extraordinary, yet where were the participants? Was it already ended?

I pressed hand to nose and mouth to prevent an untimely sneeze. As my eyes grew accustomed to the dimness, a soft amber glow drew me around the bed to the sorcerer's circle. The ring pulsed softly. At evenly spaced points on the broad ring sat a clay dish heaped with earth, a bone cup filled with water, and a pierced bronze canister that exuded the smoke of smoldering incense. In the exact center of the ring, bathed in the golden shimmer, sat a silver sphere large enough to fill my cupped hands. Beside the sphere, atop a fringed purple sash, lay a folded square of silk-embroidered cambric, a carved wooden horse, a ball, a stuffed doll dressed in white silk, and a boat the length of my hand. Children's things.

I tried to set my suspicions aside lest they paralyze me. Whatever this was, it could not be finished, else Eugenie would be abed. Where would they be? *Think, Anne.* Not the mage's own rooms. The sorcerer's circle there seemed little different from this one. Not the queen's girlhood refuge. Unthinkable that she would take Dante to the place she met her lover. Only one place in the palace spoke vividly of unholy enchantments. . . .

LIGHT BOYS, NIGHT GUARDS, THE sleepy serving girl . . . what must they have thought when I ran past them? Heads turned, a blur in my enchanted sight. One guard called out, startled when I almost ran into him as I burst through the ground-level doors into the courtyard gardens. I had no mind to hush my footsteps. Let them imagine a ghost racing the palace halls.

The ungraceful bulk of the Rotunda rose from the sprawling shrubs, sculpted by lamplight strayed from a window, by watch lanterns hung here and there along the graveled paths, by the star shimmer my friend and I had joyfully reduced to first principles, angles, and formulas. Through the Rotunda's rose-petal windows, the delicate flickerings of purple, green, and crimson swarmed like fireflies over a rain pool.

Once inside the east doors, caution slowed and hushed my steps. I crept through the colonnade to the periphery of the cavernous chamber. But my will to move forward wholly failed as I viewed what lay in the center of the Rotunda.

Amid the swarming scraps of color, a sea green luminescence billowed from Master Dante's white staff like steam from a boiling cauldron and spilled groundward in a gauzy cascade. The mage gripped the staff as if the raging light might suck him into its wash and fling him into the glittering vault above his head.

But it was the scene unfolding within the veils of light that thrilled and terrified me. Eugenie de Sylvae knelt on the marble floor, playing ball with four young children. A ginger-haired boy in a nursery smock clutched the cloth ball to his chest with pudgy fists, as if to keep it away from everyone else, then released it with a gleeful crow to bounce across the floor toward a tiny girl with raven curls. She giggled and pounced on it, only to roll it toward two infants sitting next to each other. Their plump, rose-gold cheeks, pale wisps of hair, and sturdy legs hammering with excitement on the floor could have belonged to any healthy infant in the world.

The vision struck me as a lovely, homely portrait . . . until the little girl, jumping exuberantly in a circle, turned square into my view. White and unreflective, her eyes might have been shaped of ivory or a well of sheerest moonshine. They reminded me of nouri, statues of the dead purposely made with solid black eyes so that we might not mistake the artifice for a living being.

My aching heart near cracked at the sight. What cruel daemon would give Eugenie this and claim it to be her lost children?

Were these four entirely creatures of Dante's sorcery—illusion—or could they be some true manifestation of wandering souls? Certainly they were no phantasm of memory, for even Prince Desmond, the only one of Eugenie's babes to live past birth, had been but a year old when he died.

The ginger-haired boy squealed and scooped the ball from one of the infants and ran to Eugenie, dropping it in her lap. And when she rolled it toward the girl child again, he threw his arms around the queen's neck for one brief moment. She reached out for him, but he slipped her grasp and trotted off toward the others.

I must have gasped or sighed then, or shifted my feet unintentionally, for the boy snapped his head around and focused those blank white sockets exactly on my face. No mistaking. His cheery smile widened and he laughed aloud, clapping his hands in my direction, as if I might be yet another playmate come to entertain him.

My skin flushed hot and dry, then cold and damp at that empty gaze. But a babbling "Ba-ba-ba" from the little girl diverted the boy back to his game.

Soon the four began to lose substance. My gaze passed straight through the little bodies so that I could glimpse the golden bob of the king's great pendulum stilled behind them. The boy's hands fell limp to his sides. His head drooped. The infants quieted. The girl child began to wail softly. Fading . . . fading . . . the four soon became no more than misty outlines in the light. And then they were gone.

Eugenie's empty arms wrapped about her breast, and she curled forward slowly until her head rested on the floor. Dante's veils of sea green light dispersed in a sparkling spray. The mage shifted position only when the last wisp vanished, and then but to rest his head on his gloved hands. The ball rolled slowly to a stop.

As if the weight of the Rotunda's dome had anchored my feet and was now removed, I was able to move freely again. Yet I did not leave. I needed to hear what Eugenie or the mage might say when recovered from the apparition or whatever it was.

"Your skills are unmatched, Master. As ever, awe steals my breath."

Body and mind froze. The harsh, muffled voice, a male voice bristling with superiority, had originated behind a column not three metres to my left.

"Where is the witch?" said Dante, lifting his head, not in the least surprised. Despite the vastness of the Rotunda, his brittle baritone carried so far without visible effort on his part. " 'Tis enough to service an aristo's maudlin whims. I'll not play nursemaid, too. It's all she's good for."

"She waits in the garden. Fair Antonia is seized of a mighty craving for power, but wilts from its full exercise. She cannot fathom designs more sophisticated than brute murder—her answer to every obstacle. I've warned her about her stupidity, but alas . . . Can this lady royal truly not hear us?"

Mustering all I knew of stealth, I slid backward and sideways just enough to see a crouched form rise to his full height. Voice low and harsh, hooded and cloaked in floor-length black, he was scarce distinguishable from the shadows under the colonnade. He could be almost anyone.

"The witch doses her with something that leaves her drowsy. It takes no excess skill to nudge her into sleep when we've done here." Dante stretched his shoulders, then strolled across the few metres to the motion-less Eugenie. He stared down at her for a moment.

"Ah, you charm me still, Master. *No excess skill*—to accomplish spell-work your fellows starve to touch. Tonight's exhibition was superlative, the breach more distinct, longer lasting, the manifestations more substan-tial. Better already than anything *Diel Voile Aeterna* suggests. Our time approaches."

The *Book of the Eternal Veil* . . . a *breach* . . . *manifestations* . . . Did these two truly imagine Dante had breached the Veil between life and death? Weak faith wrestled with the ghostly evidence of my eyes and an oppres-sion that blighted the spirit.

"If your self-proclaimed prophet cannot stop grooming his beard and learn to work a proper spell, we'll never be ready," said Dante, moving out of the fading green light to retrieve something from the shadows. He held up a silver sphere, like the one centering the sorcerer's circle in the queen's chamber, and examined it in the pale light of his staff before stuffing it in his robe. "The nireal working yet eludes me. Naught pro-ceeds until I've deciphered its proper making . . . and the rite itself. You promised me the key. You promised me the missing guide. I've seen neither."

"I've every confidence in your abilities at translation and interpreta-tion, as well as sorcery. You've done well enough so far without the key."

Dante whirled about and pointed his flaming staff at the other man. "Then tell me the rest," he roared. "I do all the work: dandle mincing aristos, suckle your incompetent protégés and cover their mistakes, squeeze words from these daemon-ciphered books, and devise spellwork that your feeble talents cannot seem to reproduce, and *still* you refuse me!"

The sorcerer's rage rent the air between them, crackling like the sparks of the *virtu elektrik*. Bonds of conspiracy might hold these two in partner-ship, but no ties of friendship or brotherhood.

"Not yet, Master. Soon, but not yet," said the throaty whisper, smooth as oil on water. "Be assured, your talents have made you indispensable. You've earned the vengeance you crave . . ."

The white flames vanished as quickly as they had burst forth. Sputtering in disgust, Dante strode through a shower of floating lights and vanished into the gloom.

". . . And nothing in this wide universe shall ever again be as it was." The observer's conclusion could not have been heard beyond the two of us. He did not speak in metaphor.

How could this man's detachment be so much more frightening than Dante's rage?

The cloaked man turned to go. Framed by the drooping hood was a face of leather, a mask shaped and smoothed into a serene beauty that struck my soul with morbid terror.

The Aspirant poked a finger through a purple wisp, and, chuckling softly, melted into the night.

CHAPTER 26

Clutching my skirts that he might not hear my own movements, I pursued the sinister intruder through the Rotunda's colonnade. Every few steps I paused to listen for creaking leather, rustling garments—anything that might tell me his course. But echoes confused the soft sweep of fabric on marble and the hushed pad of a big man's hurried footsteps. And before long I stood at the west doors of the Rotunda, staring into the thick plantings of the courtyard gardens. Not a twig or leaf moved. Not even a birdcall enlivened the dull night.

Quivering with disappointment, I abandoned the pursuit and returned to the Rotunda. Eugenie was gone. The stink of Antonia's perfume lingered in the vast chamber amid the floating wisps of color. Taking a lamp from its bracket, I hunted evidence of Dante's work.

Near the place where the mage had produced his fountain of light stood a waist-high bronze candle stand of sufficient breadth to have supported the silver sphere. The nireal, he'd called it. Lianelle had named the two pendants she'd sent me nireals. What were they? Curiosity and excitement almost sent me straight to my room. But I needed to finish this.

Dirt littered the floor where the children had played, along with scant puddles of water collected in shallow depressions in the stone. I'd not noticed the mess while watching the ball game. Surely I'd have noticed the children's hands or their cloth ball getting wet or soiled.

Ranging farther afield, I discovered two open barrels and a water butt upended next the stilled pendulum. Spilled earth and water littered the floor around them.

As I stared at the mess, willing it to make some sense, the floating lights collected around the puddles as they had in the Bastionne. As before, greedy, angry whispers swelled inside me.

What were they? Daemonish fancy named them dead souls. But reason—even modified by my newfound acceptance of unnatural mystery—insisted they were too incomplete to be the essence of a human life. Unlike the voices of the mindstorm, they expressed no individuality, no variety, impressing me more as dust particles in a sandstorm than singular minds. Yet they thirsted mightily.

The lights did not so much frighten me as suffocate me. Believing I'd found what was to be seen in the Rotunda, I hurried away from the pendulum. I must find some way to tell Duplais what I had witnessed. Perhaps this night did not change everything, but he might make some sense of it.

The shadows lay thick under the colonnade, swollen into blackness in the vestibule beyond. I'd left the lamp beside the pendulum and the barrels. A glance over my shoulder left me unwilling to go back to fetch it or to cross to another door. An army of lights swarmed in a jewel-hued spiral—amethyst, emerald, sapphire, and ruby—down from the mosaic dome toward the pitiful splotches of water.

Annoyed at my cowardice, I plunged into the dark vestibule. No one lurked there. The Aspirant was long escaped.

It appalled me to know the arch-villain was here in Castelle Escalon— and excited me, as well. He must be instantly recognizable to the other players, else why his persistent use of an all-enveloping disguise? Dante himself was unsure of his master's identity. So who was he?

My suspicions of Prefect Kajetan had overflowed in the Bastionne. His passion in defense of his art was not feigned, nor was his concern for Duplais' welfare. Yet he had easily relegated Lianelle's fate—and Ambrose's—to the necessities of an internecine struggle. Such a man could have seen Ophelie de Marangel's self-mutilation in pursuit of magical prowess as a god-provided opportunity. He would have had no compunction about handing her over to Gaetana to use as a weapon in their war.

Yet I could not afford to blind myself to other possibilities. Kajetan would be uncomfortable spying on Eugenie de Sylvae's despair. He seemed the sort who would avoid witnessing the sordid results of his grand ideals. So who else might it be? A big man who could come and go at will in the palace precincts.

My thoughts flitted to Lord Ilario, the tallest man at court and the most recognizable, overlooked as a fool, yet cleverer than he seemed. Yet he wore no sorcerer's mark on his hand, and he was anything but broad, though padded cloaks could easily disguise that.

I paused at the steps down to the garden, recalling the tall, graceful swordsman who had swept down from the woodland at Vradeu's Crossing. Cloaked in flowing black, he had rescued Duplais and me from the brigands hunting Lianelle's book. He had hidden his face behind a black silk scarf and a simple hat . . . exactly the sort of disguise Ilario de Sylvae would require. Just a few hours earlier, I had scoffed at the thought of Lord Ilario challenging Dante, yet his hand had rested quite naturally on his sword hilt and moved away only when the threat was moot. Could the chevalier be another of Duplais' allies?

The tower bells pealed middle-night. With unexpected warmth at my imagining, I sped down the steps and plunged into the overgrown gardens.

Fog had rolled up from the river, leaving the air close, heavy with moisture and thick with the scent of damp earth and fading lavender. I headed for the east wing, thinking to look in on the queen before collapsing in my bed.

My mind raced faster than my feet, dispersing my moment's buoyant cheer. Speculation did nothing to solve the matter of Mage Dante's purposes or the intended results of their dalliance with necromancy.

Necromancy was true deadraising, so I had always understood—the act of returning a passed soul to a physical presence in the living world: a revenant. The Temple pronounced such interference with the Creator's intent as blasphemy and punished suspected practitioners severely. But was such an act even possible? The spectre of Edmond de Roble had been horrifyingly real, but hardly a true physical presence. But those children . . . imperfect, but so lifelike . . . no mere image in the mind's eye, but laughing, giggling, reaching, reacting to one another and to Eugenie. I'd never heard any claim that the dead *aged* while traveling Ixtador.

The most startling revelation of the encounter had been that necromancy was not solely a payment to Eugenie for her protection. The Aspirant had spoken of the manifestations as more distinct on this night, and of a longer-lasting breach, as if they were practicing the enchantments. As if necromancy itself was a part of their ultimate scheme.

Tendrils of fog brushed my face. Petticoat and sleeves grew sodden from constant brushing of the untrimmed plantings. The soft movement of the air set me shivering. I'd best pay attention to my path, else I'd be wandering until sunrise.

The peaceful dribble of water to my left elicited relief. The Grotto of the Warrior Angels marked the exact center of the Rotunda gardens and an easy marker for the path to the east doors. But my feet slowed as I rounded the corner. A low, cheerful hum announced that I was not the only person passing this way.

Clutching soul, spirit, and garments, I tiptoed forward and flattened myself to the brick arch that led into the little nook. I listened for any hesitation, any change in the slightly off-key melody. Hearing none, I peered ever so carefully around the brick pillar.

Through the fog I could make out the back of a man garbed in voluminous sleeves of white and black stripes, and a soft, slouching bonnet sporting a white plume. Too unfashionable to be Lord Ilario. No sign of cloak, hood, or mask. The man crouched . . . or sat . . . beside the font, idly swirling one hand in the water as he hummed a roundelay my mother had favored. He appeared to be waiting for someone.

I wanted to see his face. Circling left to keep my distance, I crept into the grotto. The humming ceased and he looked around. Easy. No guilty start.

I halted, heart leaping to my throat.

"Is it not late for court maidens to be wandering the gardens in the damp?" A wholly attentive posture, his deep-timbred, mellifluous voice, and a charming, lopsided smile welcomed me. He did not rise, did not expose a hand, but he most definitely *saw* me.

Yet I cared naught for his manners or personal attractions, nor did I heed my rapid calculations of the time elapsed since my dose of Lianelle's potion. The sorely out-of-fashion gentleman sitting cross-legged on the rim of the font was Queen Eugenie's late-night visitor.

Exposing my left hand properly, I curtsied deep, as if he'd pointed a finger to the ground. Such effortless mastery of the moment rarely manifested itself outside the nobility. "I was unable to sleep, my lord."

"Oh, dear. Don't say you've weighty matters preying on your mind. High-born young ladies ought never have serious thoughts. Or perhaps"—his voice dropped and his body leaned my way, as if to confide a titillating secret—"it's these strange times keep you wakeful."

The mist and the bonnet's white plumes conspired to obscure most of his face. Even so, recognition hovered just on the verge of memory.

Determined to get a closer view, I clasped my hands behind my back and strolled toward the fountain as if my sole interest lay in the three wounded angels whose sculpted bodies were bathed so gracefully by the streaming water. Even if he was the Aspirant, which his immaculate, exuberant attire made unlikely, his posture could hardly have been less threatening.

"Indeed these are strange and dreadful times," I said, wondering if he'd any idea of what had so recently transpired inside the Rotunda. "I'm new to court and have trouble sorting truth from rumor."

"Best believe the worst you hear," he said dryly.

He swiveled to face me directly, planting his elegant, knee-high boots on the damp paving. The plumed hat revealed full lips encircled by a meticulously trimmed brown beard and mustache. His broad hand, jeweled with rings, patted the benchlike rim of the font. "Sit beside me, lovely maiden of the mist, and converse a while. Company would please me. Tell me of your activities here. Your viewpoint on the news of the day. Whatever gossip you've gleaned about the denizens of this mighty seat of power. Where have you come from that you are new to court?"

I did not sit. The situation was too odd, the language of his smiles and posture too intimate for a stranger, and he had neither asked my name nor offered his own. Instead, I cast my line into the stream, hoping to learn more of him. "I grew up in a country house, my lord. Less than a month ago, I was summoned to serve Queen Eugenie as maid of honor. Though I was reluctant to leave home, her generosity and kindness have astounded me."

"Hmm. You've not the air of a household lady, no matter how elevated. Perhaps it is these weighty concerns, which rarely occur in a mind bent solely on profitable marriage. Or perhaps it is this accursed fog. What house?"

I blinked. No coyness about Eugenie. No reaction at all to her name or my compliment to her. "Montclaire, lord. At Vernase."

"The Ruggiere demesne? Life's breath, I adore that house! A prospect to rival the view from yon castelle tower, as well as superb grapes, and the finest hunting in Aubine."

"Indeed, lord. True on all those counts." No mention of Papa? Of treason or conspiracy? "So you've visited Montclaire?" Perhaps that was where I'd seen him before. He could not be so much as a decade older than me.

He cocked his head sharply, setting his plumes aquiver. "Not for a goodly while."

The bells pealed the quarter hour, bringing him abruptly to his feet. "Alas, I must depart," he said, buckling the sword belt about his waist. Rubies gleamed from the weapon's hilt as if they released their own light. "Dreams await."

Smiling broadly, he stepped forward and reached for my hand. His touch was featherlight. His kiss the merest brush of his soft beard. Only as he straightened and turned to go did I at last get a peek under his plumes. His eyes were nicely spaced alongside a stalwart nose. Sun-creased at their corners. And entirely black, deeper than the midnight around us.

Frozen in place, hand outstretched, I watched him go. He cast a last ravishing smile over his shoulder as the mist enfolded him. I could not say whether he dissolved or walked away.

When I could move again, I raced after him across the gardens and into the east wing, no doubt leaving a tale of haunting behind me. Three mirrors along the way testified to the continued efficacy of the invisibility potion.

The man . . . ghost . . . revenant . . . moved swiftly, too. When I topped the stair to the queen's private gaming rooms, black-and-white-striped sleeves were just visible through the closing door. I could approach no closer. Lady Antonia had pulled a chair in front of the door and sat herself there like Doorward Viggio's apprentice. Even unseen, I could find no way past her.

I did not return to my own room. Rather I sped back through the palace halls, fevered to confirm the suspicion rising in me. Past Castelle Escalon's public rooms, through the west-wing doors, up steps, down passages until I reached the gallery I had traversed so often to reach Lady Cecile's apartments—the Kings' Gallery.

And there he was, taller than life, one hand on a ruby-studded sword hilt fashioned in the shape of a dragon, one on the hip of his out-of-fashion trunk hose, a short purple cape thrown artfully across one shoulder. Brown beard and narrow mustache shaped carefully around full lips, quirked to give the merest hint of a disarming, lopsided smile. A gallant, commanding, captivating presence, even rendered in oils. Soren de Maslin-Nivanne, sixty-first King of Sabria, a man more than twenty years dead.

Antonia's adored son had fallen in battle with the Kadr witchlords when he was but six-and-twenty, before his child wife, Eugenie de Sylvae, was old enough that their marriage could be consummated. And now he visited her in the night.

Back to the wall, hands to my temples, I slid to the floor of the gallery in front of the portrait, reason, emotion, and body entirely exhausted. I could not move.

You're awake late. Another curse we share. Would you talk? But neither practiced self-discipline nor the clear voice of my friend of the mind could hold back the mindstorm.

23 OCET, DAWN

"TIME TO BE UP, DAMOSELLE. Sixth hour every morning, you told me."

I jerked upright to see Ella's freckled face bathed in candlelight. No earthshaking, but her hand on my shoulder, had startled me into waking. "Yes. Certainly. I need to be awake."

My mouth felt stuffed with wool; my head with rock. At some dark hour of the night a footman had found me sleeping in the Kings' Portrait Gallery, and somehow I had staggered back here to bed. The Aspirant's leather face and guttural voice had haunted me through hours of fitful slumber, along with a girl child's moonglow eyes and a dead king's air-touched kiss.

I kneaded my right hand where I could yet sense the brush of his beard. An apparition . . . a phantom . . . conversing, gesturing, thinking, reacting like a human person. Impossible.

Duplais had to know what I had seen. I'd tie a love knot to my window. But what was I to do between now and sunset? Idleness would drive me mad.

Ella brought cheese and baked apples. As I dressed and ate—checking my ring, holy saints, always checking my ring—I tried to devise some strategy for the day. I had an hour until I would be expected in the queen's bedchamber. If I could get my hands on the Mondragon *Book of Greater Rites* and find out what magical working required raising the dead, perhaps we'd know what Dante and the Aspirant planned. I could use the potion, steal the book from Dante's room. But I'd need Duplais to help decipher its meaning.

Perhaps I had time to learn something of nireals. Shoving the remains of breakfast aside, I pulled the two pendants from the armoire. Though the same highly polished silver as Dante's palm-sized spheres, they were but solid, flat ovals the size of my thumb. They bore no markings save the frog on Lianelle's and the olive tree on the unbound one she had made for me. *Soul mirrors*, she'd called them. There was only one way to learn more.

Barricading the rising mindstorm, I grasped the pendant my sister had named hers and invoked its key. *"Soror deliria."* Silly sister.

And she was there. As if she had run past me only a moment before. As if I might glimpse her through the sun glare did I turn my head quickly enough. So close . . .

Heat and blazing Aubine sunlight, blinding swaths of gold and green and rich brown, scorching hair and blistering skin. She'd been traipsing through the maquis . . . the fragrant oils of juniper and madder, smilax and sagewort hung sticky on her clothes . . . and the smell of dog. She never went anywhere without the dogs . . . wrestled with them in the grass . . . napped with them in the heat of the day. The dry ground crunched beneath her boots as she ran. . . .

Saints, Nel, do you never walk *anywhere?*

Whistling at woodchats. Yelling at the shrike to scare it off the particular lizard she was hunting. Forever hunting, for herbs or insects, for leaves or roots or arrow grass, for pebbles or eggs or carob buds on the verge of bursting, for bits of glass or bark, for a cloud shape, for a raindrop, a scent, a nut, for sand or clay or green stones . . . Insatiable. All to feed her magic.

For a moment, I felt as if I were falling . . .

. . . and then did the immensity of my sister's desire rattle my bones, like the substance of the earth rising through my feet . . . and then her talent, forked fire touching every piece of the life she loved—the natural world, learning, adventure, Ambrose, Mama, me—and binding it with laughter and rebellion and teasing and the vow never, ever to stop, to hide, to be quiet, to stay in one place, to serve, to forgive, to be satisfied, to hold back, to fail, to be ordinary . . .

. . . and then I felt words, not spoken in the present moment, as my mysterious friend did, but waiting for me in this magic to be graven in my spirit for now and forever. . . .

Don't be scared of this, Ani. I want you to understand. We're not the same and that's good. Magic is my calling. War and poetry and prison will drive and shape Ambrose. But you are our true warrior, our defender. Your mind and heart are our bright center . . . our fortress . . . our home.

I dropped the pendant. Bent double, I clutched my breast, racked by dry, barren sobs. How could talent and life so large fit in one single heart? And how could it all be snuffed out? For all these years, even before Papa rode away, before Mama went mad, I had chided and scolded Lianelle because she was not some imitation of me. Someone polite and tidy and reserved. Someone ordinary. "I never knew, Nel. Never understood. And I'm not what you thought. I've lost you and lost Ambrose and failed. . . ."

A sharp rap on my bedchamber door wrenched me from grief and regret and deposited me alone in my bedchamber.

I blinked, fist clutching at the hurt in my breast, stunned by the incomparable wonder and undeniable terror of the pendant's magic. Lianelle had been present in a manner far more deep and true than memory, more substantial than the person just beyond that door. And Dante had created something similar that he used to summon the dead. Was that why they seemed so *real*?

The visitor rapped again.

"Yes, all right. Coming." I pinched my cheeks and pressed my temples. The turgid gray beyond my window had taken on a rosy cast.

"Heurot!"

Duplais' yellow-haired secretary, lacking his usual grin, bowed and passed me a folded paper, sealed without any device. "This was left at the main gates day before yesterday, damoselle. The gate warders sent it to Sonjeur de Duplais, as that had been their standing orders. But my master was out most of yesterday, and now he says you've been raised up in the household and his mandate did not allow what was the rule before. He begs your pardon for the delay."

"Yes, all right. Thank you." I hurried him out and wasted no time breaking the unadorned seal. No signature. An unfamiliar hand.

Damoselle, I've business with you in reference to our last meeting. As a result of your timely message, I'm off to foreign parts, thus my visit to Merona will be brief. I'll watch for you outside the postern at sunrise three days running. I sincerely hope this finds you, as this time I've no assistance to get your name correct.

A riddle. But from whom? I dared not bite without knowing. Ambrose would not dare come here, even using someone else to write the message. The grammar was not Bernard's, and Melusina did not write. The writer referred to a *timely message* . . .

Adept Guerin! I'd sent Lianelle's instructor a warning about the dark deeds at Collegia Seravain. He was here in Merona, and the third sunrise was not a quarter of an hour away.

"Heurot, wait!"

Saints be thanked, the youth had dawdled outside my door. He leaned on the passage wall, laughing with Ella and another serving girl. But he popped to immediate attention, while the girls melted into adjoining bedchambers.

"Take a message to your master. His interruption of my post and messages has been despicable. He must notify the stewards and the castellan immediately that I must be accorded the respect and privacy due Her Majesty's ladies. But first he must inform Lady Eleanor that my chambermaid has spilled ink on my day gown, thus I shall be two hours late to the queen this morning. While I see to Ella and her laundering, I'll *respond* to this horribly delayed message."

"As you say, my . . . uh . . . damoselle." Heurot's good manners handled shock and a bit of confusion well. He bowed and retreated, while stealing glances at my unsullied skirts.

I disliked blaming Ella for an untruth, but Lady Eleanor, on duty in the bedchamber before dawn, would approve such an excuse for my lateness. The dull, excessively proper ducessa viewed the need to discipline servants as a divine mandate.

I darted back to my room just long enough to return the nireals to the drawer and dig out my zahkri. Blessed Melusina insisted on sewing a fitchet into my every skirt and petticoat. Strapping the Cazar knife to my thigh behind the hidden knife slit, I set out for my dawn assignation.

CHAPTER 27

The postern was far busier in the dawn hour than were Castelle Escalon's main gates. Coal wagons, farm carts, boys wheeling barrows, and girls herding pigs passed in and out of the narrow gatehouse in a steady stream. Scullery maids and sweeping girls pinned on caps as they ran or yelled at the guards to let them by before milady or the chamberlain sacked them. A broad-chested understeward haggled acrimoniously with a fishmonger over the night's catch. A tinker had set up a booth and was banging on a dented cauldron, while acrid smoke bellied up from his stove, further graying the murky morning.

Frustrated, I scanned the crowd from the shelter of the wicket gate, seeing no sign of the boyish adept. With the pain of Lianelle's death so fresh in mind, I was in a frenzy to know what Guerin had come to tell me. If he was truly leaving Sabria as a result of my warning, I might never hear.

A fellow ambling alongside a coal wagon broke off when the wagon rolled to a stop at the guard post. He strolled around behind the tinker's booth and vanished. Curiously, he emerged back down the road and tagged on to another party. His dark green jerkin, leather breeches, and

304

worn rucksack were wholly ordinary. But surely this was the third time he'd done the same.

I drew a gray shawl over my hair and strolled out of the wicket, setting a course to intercept the man as he approached the tinker's booth again. Fair hair peeked out from his broad-brimmed felt hat.

"Divine grace, sonjeur," I said, matching my pace to his. "We've business, I think."

The young man puffed a relieved breath. "Blessed angels, damoselle. I was about to give up."

"Palace confusion delayed your message. You've abandoned Collegia Seravain?"

"Can we get out of the way?" he said, his eyes darting hither and yon. "For sure someone'll notice if I go round again. Skin's been crawling since Tigano."

"Follow me up the path behind the sheep sheds," I said. "I know a place."

I kept a businesslike pace, skirting the animal pens and coal stores that sprawled along the road, then angling across the rocky slope toward the ridge top. Guerin strolled along behind like a shop clerk taking the morning air.

Ambrose and Lianelle and I had often played adventurers or chase-and-hide on the ridge behind Castelle Escalon. I knew every crevice in the rocks, most particularly the steep stair someone had hacked out of a fissure. Almost obliterated from centuries of rain and rockfalls, the narrow steps led to the highest point on Merona's toothy spine.

Long before the Sabrian kings built Castelle Escalon, a watchtower had stood atop these crags of slate and granite. Little remained of it. A weedy clearing tucked amid great slabs and boulders. An arc of its west-facing foundation that jutted from the height like a scrap of jawbone. A few rough-dressed blocks scattered in the apron of slabs and boulders that spilled all the way from the foundation arc to the flatter shoulder of the ridge where the palace stood. It was as if a god had sent a bolt of lightning purposely to shatter the tower and erase all memory of it.

"I didn't want to believe your warning," said Guerin, huffing a little at the climb. "Seravain has been my home since I was seven. The thought that such evil had taken root there . . . My head just wouldn't accept it. Yet since the day your sister died, I'd noticed odd things. My room out of order. Notes disturbed. Eyes looking away too quickly. I told myself it was just students. Rumors spread like maggots in a collegia."

We sat on a slab at the head of the steep rockfall and propped our backs on the foundation stones. On a finer morning the prospect—the sprawling city falling away to the broad river and its crescent harbor—would enrich the soul. But on this gray day the river had swollen into a sea of cloud. At the base of the rocky jumble below us the treeless waste we had just traversed sloped gently down to the sheep pens and the postern road.

Guerin offered me a biscuit, pulled from a shabby rucksack. I shook my head. The last bells had rung half past the hour.

He talked between ravenous bites. "I looked into the things you wrote me about Ophelie de Marangel: her years of failure, the abrupt change, her sudden isolation, her illness and disappearance. It was all there in the archives, as you said. Blessed light . . . blood transference, torture, murder happening right under everyone's noses. I was only a student at the time, self-absorbed as we all were. But how many ignored the signs of her trouble? If you're even half attentive to your students, you'd notice something like that. And now Lianelle . . . I've tried to think what she might have been about that last morning."

"In her letter, the one you gave me, she said she had set events in motion."

He nodded. "The enchantment that killed her was her own; I told you that before. But there was no evidence she'd worked the spell in the *ravine*. So where had she done it? She frequently practiced spellwork outside supervision. I never reported it, because the mages did seem to be holding her back unfairly, and she swore to me the work was merely uncanonical magic—spells that fail to adhere to the *Encyclopaedia of Workable Formulae*— not illicit in the way of blood transference or such. Being a self-righteous ass, I never let her tell me where she did it. She'd never have worked on something dangerous in the dormitory or any of the student laboratoriums, where she might have harmed someone else."

He rummaged in his rucksack, setting aside books and papers, a shirt, a scarf. His words flowed on, as if he'd held in his thoughts for much too long. "After a day wasted searching every laboratorium where she might have had some privacy, I remembered something she had told me about the day Savin-Duplais, the librarian, questioned her about Ophelie. She'd said her nerves had near fractured when he'd hauled her off to one of her favorite places for his interview—an overgrown pergola in the outer gardens. Sure enough, tucked away under a bench in that old pergola, I found nitre powder, oil of vitriol, and sulfur—which would certainly fuel an explosion—and I found this."

He pulled out a grimy canvas bag and dumped its contents into my lap. Flint and steel, bound together with wire. A lock of hair, the sun-scalded brown curls unmistakably Lianelle's. Five silver finger rings of various sizes. Three keys dangling from a loop of leather. The skull of a small rodent—a mouse or a vole. A jumble of nonsense, it appeared.

He picked out a tightly rolled bit of paper, tied with a ribbon, and gave it to me. Unrolling the scuffed little scrap revealed a neatly written message.

> *Unable to walk out with you this evening. It is wholly improper, no matter my "heart's bidding," as you so cheekily put it. No matter that we could talk solely of schoolwork. Pass your adept's examination, milady, and you may spy a familiar face among the hordes of moonstruck swains at your feet. Until then, I must be your teacher only, and must—and shall—heed my duty to that office.*

Grief aged Guerin's face twenty years as he watched me read the message, leaving me no need to compare the handwriting to the note in my pocket, or to ask why my unsentimental little sister had cherished it. Plenty of other questions remained, however.

"Why would she keep something she treasured . . . or any of these oddments . . . alongside the makings for an explosion?" *Heed both mind and heart to understand*, she'd told me in her letter.

"I believe them to be particles," he said, clearing a roughness in his throat, "objects we use to supply the appropriate proportions of the five divine elements needed for spellwork—air, water, spark, base metal, and wood. As to why this paper, I believe—you have to understand this is a heretical suggestion, and I've no idea how one might accomplish such a thing—influencing a person's mind without using the senses. But I believe she wanted me to find her." His fingers toyed with the paper, then rerolled it so tightly, it appeared no more than a straw. "Somehow, she wove *me* into her enchantment. Enough to draw me to her. She knew I would consent; a participant's consent makes spellwork stronger. All that day, I knew she was in trouble. I just couldn't leave my younger students unsupervised to hare off after her. Why didn't she tell me what she was afraid of? Why didn't she just ask me to help?"

He waved off his pain, contorting his face with the effort. "It makes no difference. I found her, as she wanted. Walked straight down to the ravine as if she'd left me a signpost. Only too late."

But now he'd set me on the path, I caught a glimmer of my sister's purpose. "She'd no intention of risking *your* life. She understood how honor and duty would shape your reaction to this . . . disturbance . . . she caused you. Your note says it all: You'd heed your responsibilities first. As certain as I can be of anything in this world, Guerin, she was deliberate about the events of that morning."

The nireal's vision had taught me that. Magic was not whimsy to my sister. Not a childish fancy to be outgrown. "So, what do these other things tell us?"

"The skull implies she was working a spell of mortal consequence. The particular mix of air and wood that makes up bone is said to bend a spell toward death, though I think it's included as much to be a warning for the practitioner."

"Or a telltale for an observer," I murmured. "A *mortuis memore*."

"Yes." He touched the five little rings. "Silver contains all five of the divine elements—the wood, air, and spark needed for combustion, as well as base metal and water that might be needed to balance the spell's formula to make it work. Though, truly, these particles don't match any I know. Duplais could tell you more; no one knows the formulas for spell-work as he does. The flint and steel would supply additional base metal. The hair would bring water and wood to the balance—"

"No." Once I had studied even a smattering of alchemistry, the business of particles and divine elements and formulaic magic had never made sense to me. Wood and air were *not* component parts of silver. One look at a hair through an opticum lens revealed no water or wood. These bits and pieces shaped my sister's magic into a story, just as the encrypted characters on the Mondragon book had shaped themselves into its title.

"If your note designated the person she intended to find her," I said, steeling myself against incipient dread, "then perhaps the lock of hair designated her intended victim."

He looked up sharply. "But it's *her* hair!"

"You told me there were no boot prints, no signs of anyone else around her. She made sure you would come and find her once she was dead." I had thought that nothing about Lianelle's passing could slash deeper than her loss, but this truth was laid out as stark as a grave stele. "You said it: Consent is everything. She worked this explosion apurpose."

"But *why?*" His stricken cry gave voice to my own distress.

I'd been blind not to have seen it before now. Lianelle, who would squirm and wriggle and cheat to win a silly game. Lianelle, who adored living beyond reason. Lianelle, who would never, ever give up.

"She must have been dead already. Whether poisoned or wounded or trapped with no possible escape. Believe me, *nothing* else would have driven her to such a thing. She must have learned something so dangerous, her enemy could not allow her to live, not even long enough to whisk her away and leech her blood. But she made it happen on her own terms."

She had needed to pass on what she'd learned from the *Book of Greater Rites* to people who could do something about it. Elsewise, she would have destroyed the book rather than sending it on to me. As to the hurry . . . She could not allow her enemy to discover what she'd deduced, or what she'd made, or who she'd told about it. Instead, she had left me this ciphered mess and trusted me to figure it out.

"Angels' mercy, Lianelle." Whether Guerin or I or both of us said this, I could not have told.

"Who *is* this enemy? Who was she so afraid of?" The young man spoke through gritted teeth, pressing clenched fists to his forehead. "If it's the last thing I do in this life . . ."

"You'll help us expose and defeat him," I said, clutching at my own murderous desires. "Tell me, was Dante, the queen's mage, at Seravain on that day?"

"He arrived a day later. Chancellor Kajetan believed someone from outside the school should investigate her death; elsewise we might be accused of hiding illicit practices again, reviving the scandal. We—my friends among the faculty members—were surprised when this Dante came. We expected a prefect."

"And did Dante investigate her death?" I needed to understand loyalties. Were Kajetan and Dante allies or rivals?

"If you mean did he look at her and the place where she died . . . yes, certainly. If you mean did he question people, check the logbooks, and so forth, the answer is no. Chancellor Kajetan had gathered up your sister's things, as I told you, and Vice Chancellor Charlot confiscated whatever papers, reports, or magical artifacts her tutors held. This Dante scarce spoke a word to anyone save the two of them and, I suppose, Master Kajetan's friend who was staying over in his house. The chancellor—"

"Is the vice chancellor a big man? Tall? Broad?"

Guerin, frowning, studied me as if my reasoning might be written on my skin. "He's broad abeam, but scarce taller than you."

Not the Aspirant, then. "And the chancellor's friend?"

"He was a good-sized fellow, near Kajetan's height and sturdily built. Not that I saw him for more than an eyeblink for all the days he was there, as the chancellor bundled him off to the residence like a long-lost brother. I'm not sure when he left."

A fierce excitement brimmed. "So who was he? A mage?"

Guerin stuffed his belongings back into his rucksack as he scoured his memory. "I've no idea. He wore no collar; I'm sure of that. But I never saw his hand. I judged him a scholar right off, or maybe a nobleman down at heels, but I'm trying to think why. It wasn't just because he was close with the chancellor. His dress was fine enough, but plain. And his horse—a fine beast—was caparisoned in huntsman's green and black, as if the man were a nobleman or his emissary come on a formal visit. But his regalia bore no device, and he'd no retainers or servants with him. I guess the green and black made me think he was from Delourre, as those are the colors of the Delourre demesne, and they're forever short of coin up there. I just assumed the three of them were huddled up together. But as I think of it . . . I've no good reason for that. I'm not so good at logic or puzzles. Not with this, at least."

The bells rang another quarter. The mist had swallowed the city. Now its tendrils were claiming the downslope, reaching almost to the base of the rockfall.

"You've done well, Adept." Duplais might know of his mentor's friends who wore the colors of Delourre. "Did they question you?"

"Charlot asked me what Lianelle studied in my tutorial, but neither he nor Master Dante nor anyone else asked me what else she might be working on or why she might have been in the ravine that morning. As if they already knew." His skin blazed. "For certain my own inquiries have left a trail a kilometre wide. I feel like a fool and a coward."

"No, you're right to go. One hint from a student that you were fond of Lianelle, one suspicion that she confided in you or asked your help to decipher some encryption, and they'd have you on a rack or worse. You'll do my sister no honor dead."

I fiddled with the oddments in my lap, begging them to tell me more as I dropped them one by one into the canvas bag. Eventually I was left with the one we had not fit into the deadly enchantment. "What could the keys signify?"

"Base metal—"

"Not as part of a formula, but as if she had chosen them particularly to weave something into the spellmaking, as you felt she did with your note."

A sun glint shot from the hills behind us, only to die a quick death in the encroaching gloom. Guerin removed his broad-brimmed hat and scraped fingers through damp, matted hair. "Unlocking, I suppose. Something to do with spellwork itself, perhaps, as any spell that's not made active at the time of binding requires a verbal key. Honestly, damoselle, in a spell meant for self-murder, I can't even guess. I'm sorry. I should have tried the keys around the collegia."

Faint thunder shivered the ground. In any other year, I'd have called it odd to hear northern thunder on a foggy morning in Merona, where storms customarily arrived in the afternoon from south and west. As it was, the sensation merely added to the anxious urgency of the day.

"You're not the only one who feels a fool," I said, "trying to unravel this mystery while knowing so little of magic. All these years I could have been learning."

Guerin stretched his legs out in front of him. A fist-sized knob of granite tumbled down the rockfall apron toward the mist-veiled wasteland below. "She told me you—"

The adept sprang to his feet, as if the question inspired him. He clapped his hat on his head and grabbed his rucksack. "Mayhap I was follow—"

A thudding impact slammed the adept backward to the foundation wall. He slid downward, crumpling sidewise. His dislodged hat skittered down the rocks. Only my arms grabbing under his shoulders prevented him toppling after it.

"Guerin!" Father Creator, was he dead? Slithering down beside the adept, I flinched as another bolt embedded itself—impossibly—in the stone just above my head. A length of thin black cord trailed from its shank.

The adept grunted a breath and clutched the fletched base of the quarrel embedded in his shoulder. Black cord trailed from this one as well. His feet scrabbled weakly. I held him tight until he could wedge his boot in a crack.

The air whined.

"Stay down," I cried, and threw myself across his slouched form as another bolt slammed into a rock to one side of us. Sparks flew, snapping and crackling. Invisible worms wriggled in my gut.

Two horsemen barreled out of the mist from the north, joining the two crossbowmen who moved slowly upslope from the west. One of them whooped gleefully as a mechanical clatter signaled another rope-tailed bolt. The black cords, at least five of them now, each a few metres in length, had fallen slack across us. When I tried to throw them off, they coiled about my hand and arm—spidersilk the color of midnight and the thickness of my littlest finger, stiffening, tightening like live things. I kicked one aside as it curled about my ankle. But another quarrel struck the ancient foundation, showering us with sparks and shards of stone and laying a cord across Guerin's neck. It writhed, snakelike, and I yanked it away before it could choke him. It twined up my left arm instead, tethering me to the bolt embedded in the stone.

"Hold still, fair lady," shouted one of the riders from below, "and you, young sorcerer, else you'll find yourself *choking* uncomfortable." He knew exactly who we were. While the archers cranked their bows, he and his fellow dropped easily from their saddles and started climbing the rockfall. So they didn't know about the stair.

"Can you walk?" I said, wrenching unsuccessfully at the cord binding Guerin's ankles, even as another twined itself about my leg. "Let me see your feet."

He didn't answer, but clamped his teeth hard and squirmed to sitting, pulling his knees up.

"Get back down the stair," I said, slipping my zahkri blade under the cord hobbling his ankles. "Get away from the palace and out of Merona as soon as you can. I'll hold them here."

"Give me the knife," he croaked. Blue eyes filled with pain and dismay took in the black cords snaking about my arm. "I can't let you—"

"I'll be all right. I think they've plans for me. But you"—growling, grunting, I sawed at the stubborn cords binding him—"you they're going to kill."

Angels' mercy, what was this material? The zahkri might have been dull as a twig. The two riders were already up the steepest part of the rockfall. The archers had dropped their bows and begun the climb as well.

I hacked at the devilish rope, loathing and fury giving me strength. These people had hounded my mother to madness, my brother to despair, my sister to her death. They would not claim another victim, if I had to chew the cursed rope apart with my teeth. Anger surged from the smoldering fire in my gut into my veins, blinding, ferocious, devouring. The strand parted with a taut crack and white sparks. I attacked the next. And the next . . .

"Just like hers," Guerin whispered, awestruck.

I'd no idea what he meant. But there was no time for talk. As the adept's last bond snapped, I heard rocks shifting beneath the feet of the climbers. "You're going to get out of here. Hurry!"

Wrenching at the black cords that ensnared my arm, shoulder, and leg, I struggled to my feet, then helped Guerin up. He clutched his deadly limp arm, now bathed in sodden scarlet. The bone was surely shattered. His face was ashen, and the slightest jarring squeezed a choking noise from behind his clenched jaw. But I kept him moving.

We stumbled over the rim of the foundation wall and halfway across the clearing. My tethers allowed no more. My left hand was already numb.

"Saints guard you, and grace be with you forever," I said, draping my gray shawl about his shoulders. "For your life, speak to no one until you're well away. Now run."

"I'll not forget," he said. He vanished behind the massive boulder that hid the head of the stair.

"Gah!" spat one of the climbers, whose dark hair bobbed just beyond the arc of foundation stone. "He said the rope was impervious to blades! But mayhap we've still got one carp on the line." A tug on one cord jerked my ankle as if I were a puppet at a children's feste.

I backed into a shoulder-width niche formed by two tilted slabs—well away from the stair—just as the two riders clambered over the rim.

"A nasty climb you pick for a morning outing, Damoselle de Vernase." The dark-haired man wore a mask, not the Aspirant's finely sculpted leather, but cruder, like those of the riders at Vradeu's Crossing. The man that followed him into the clearing had tied a green-and-black-striped scarf over nose and mouth. It failed to hide a wispy beard or thin eyebrows the color of dried blood.

"If you know my name, then you know the penalties for assaulting a woman of the royal household." Behind my back I settled my grip on the zahkri as my Cazar uncles had taught me. The rocks felt comfortably close on either side of me. My body pulsed with heat.

The red-bearded man now held the ends of the cords, twitching them as if they were reins and I his steed. "Assault? It might be we've spotted your fugitive brother up here with you. And you've blood on your skirt. Mayhap we're *rescuing* you from assault."

"Rescuers don't wear masks. Release these devilish cords and perhaps I won't see you hanged." But I would. I'd see them dead for what they'd done.

"The lady's not stupid, brother," said the man in the leather mask, empty hands extended to either side as if he intended no harm. "We've been told that often enough. Step aside, damoselle, and we'll undo the snaketether with no harm to ye. We just wish to speak to your friend there behind you. Ask a few questions. Hear news from the south."

"What kind of man allows a girl to stand for him?" said the red-bearded rider. He strolled toward me, shaking the cords as if it might make me run or scream. "We should whip 'em both."

Closer . . . closer . . . I allowed their nattering to recede. Only actions mattered. Only distance and movement. His left hand held the tether cords. His right, stained with soot, extended slightly out from his body, the fingers open and ready.

Closer. Only a few fine hairs grew between the dried-blood wisps of beard and his ear tufts.

His right hand shot up and grabbed at me.

I struck.

Blood blossomed from the deep gash on his arm. Howling, he bulled forward.

Before he could grab hold of me, I struck again. The bloody rags of his mask sagged from the gaping crease in his jaw. He was no one I recognized.

He fell back, body arched about his pain. "Witchfire! Devil spawn!"

I waved the zahkri side to side slowly, silently. The dripping knife and my victim's blood-sprayed curses could speak my warning.

The two bowmen had climbed over the rim and were gaping at their bleeding comrade. The man in the leather mask snapped a finger at them. A stumpy fellow with a flat nose picked up the black tethers the wounded man had dropped. The ends were wound with white thread.

"Your father's daughter," said the masked leader, peering into the dark behind me. "What is your magical friend hiding? We *shall* have him."

I willed Guerin strength, wiles, and speeding feet. It wouldn't take long for these villains to realize that I defended naught but more rock. Wedging my shoulder behind one of the flanking slabs, I sawed furiously at the stretched tether cords, never taking my eyes from the leader. How dare these people murder at will? Maiming scholars. Leeching children. Rage surged through my arm like molten steel. The tether binding my shoulder snapped, spitting sparks.

He snarled. "Drag her out of there. If she loses a limb, so be it."

Though the constricting cords felt as if they might sever my ankle or slice my arm into segments, they could not budge me. The man's yanks merely ground my shoulder into the flanking slab. I didn't care.

While the leader taunted and threatened, the flat-nosed bowman circled, disappearing behind the slab of slate that protected my right flank. Sadly for him, he had to step around the rock and into the niche to get a straight pull at my leg. Well within my reach.

The zahkri split flesh, grinding against the bones of his hand. A stalwart fellow, he bellowed and hauled with his other hand. I cut that one, too. Hard and deep.

He staggered forward. And I whipped the blade across his throat.

His convulsion dislodged my foot, which flew out from under me. I fell backward, wedged in the notch, my back grating on the stone. Another man rushed forward and grabbed for my wrist. I slashed at his arms, but my off-balance strike scarce grazed his sleeve.

The zahkri went flying. As the attacker pinned my flailing arms, I kneed him in the groin. His face twisted. He groaned and curled forward.

But his bruising grip on my arms grew tighter. The leather-masked leader shoved the two of us aside and stared into the niche. At nothing.

Choking in the man's stinking embrace, my arm on the verge of breaking, spite burst from me. "You're a clever bully. Have I magicked a wall behind him? Or are you blind?"

The leader backed away, yelling, "Do *not* let go of her! Find that belly-crawling little sorcerer!"

"Stairs over here!" shouted the red-bearded man, blood and spittle flying from his mutilated face. Blood-soaked rags bound his shredded wrist. He'd never pull a bow again.

"I've vanished him," I said.

My angry guard slammed me backward. My skull whacked stone, blurring my vision with pain and frustration. I'd not held long enough. Guerin couldn't move fast with his shoulder in ruins.

Surprised shouts broke out much sooner and much closer than I expected. And my whacked head played tricks. I was sure I heard the steely clamor of swordplay. Guerin had carried no such weapon.

"You'll die if you touch him!" I screamed. My head drummed. Blood welled from the lacerating cords about my arm.

"What the devil?" My guard's bleeding hand clamped my throat as he nearly twisted his own head off trying to see what was happening in the clearing.

"Souleater's servant!" He leapt up when a black blur closed off the gap. The dark shape retreated almost immediately, dragging my yelling captor by his hair.

A brief clash of steel, a few grunts, and silence fell. And then a figure swathed in midnight was kneeling at my side.

"Are you harmed, lady?" he said, voice muffled by the black silk wrapped about his face. "I promise you don't need this." His hand gripped my wrist, forcing me to drop the sharp rock I held aimed at his face.

"Or this." He pinned my damaged arm to the ground with one knee, lest I continue using it as a bludgeon to his neck. "They're all dead. None's going to hurt you anymore. Honestly. I'm letting you loose now."

His voice quenched my fury as a squall damps fire. Entirely unlikely laughter welled up unbidden in its wake. Rescuers *did* sometimes wear masks.

He sat back on his heels and offered a gloved hand. "Can you sit up?"

I was shaking in such violent fashion that all I could do was extend my aching, bleeding arm in his direction. The black cord continued to constrict.

"Perhaps unwinding it would work better," I cried, gasping as he attempted to slip his knife blade under the cord without removing the swollen flesh.

By the time we had removed the dreadful bindings and thrown them across the clearing, where they wouldn't entangle either of us, a damp curl of flaxen hair had escaped his raked hat.

"Lord chevalier," I croaked, laughing and weeping all at once. "I believe I owe you at least one life."

CHAPTER 28

23 OCET, MORNING

My rescuer—the swordsman—spluttered a bit. Attempted to deny his identity and withdraw. But I refused to budge from my awkward seat in the notch until he pulled down his mask. I was desperate for a chance to speak with him.

"You're too much the gentleman to leave me here wounded in the company of four corpses," I said, struggling to recapture some semblance of equanimity. "And if you go, you'll never know what gave you away."

"Damn and blast," he grumbled. He removed his hat and unwound the scarf. But he refused to engage in conversation until he'd seen me settled more comfortably on his folded cloak, stuffed the four dead men in the notch, and bathed my lacerated arm and ankle in some vile-smelling liquid from a silver flask. He would have poured it down my throat as well, but I vigorously refused. My fit of explosive sneezing finally convinced him I couldn't tolerate it.

He propped his backside on a rock and folded his arms across his chest. Damp locks of pale hair had fallen into his face, and his soulful gaze made me feel like patting him on his head. "Damoselle, I must beg you . . ."

"Your secret is safe, Lord Ilario. On my honor and by the life you saved." One more sneeze. "And, truly, you just need to tie your hair up better."

"You are the damndest . . ." He mopped blood and sweat from his face with a kerchief so plain and rough the public Ilario de Sylvae would not use it to wipe his shoes. "Here I thought Portier was the world's most surprising person, a scrap of a librarian with the constitution of a dragon. And then a maiden who scarce reaches my elbow comes along and leaves one man dead, one bloodied, one frighted out of his boots, and another about to explode like a badly stuffed musket. A sweeping boy could have cleaned up the lot. I knew you'd be good for Geni . . . watch after her . . . but this is extraordinary."

His boot poked at the zahkri's scarlet tithe splattered across the rocks. "You're not going to tell me who got away, are you?" He forestalled my apology with a raised hand. "It's all right. Portier doesn't tell me half what he knows. Says it's for my own protection. I'm delighted the both of you consider that a worthwhile cause."

"It was not my brother," I said. "I've no idea where he is, and I'm terrified at what might be happening to him. And I would happily tell you many things, but I've got to get back, or Lady Eleanor will set the Guard Royale after me."

"Oh, your brother from the Spindle. Never occurred to me." He carefully brushed dust from his hat. "And you must never cross the ducessa. She could dredge up stories so scandalous about the Pantokrator he'd not allow his divine self into Heaven."

Such silliness took on an entirely different cast when spoken by a swordsman who could dispatch three ruffians in three minutes without disarranging his black tunic—a serious man of gentle manners, dry wit, and expert sword, not a self-indulgent fool. Hardly innocent, as his own half sister believed, yet noble in the finest sense of the word. No playwright had ever benefitted from so skilled an actor.

His humor prodded me to smile. "First, thank you. And thank Duplais for sending you."

"For sending—?" He rolled his eyes. "All right, I see I'm pinched between two of a kind. So have you ferreted out all *his* deepest secrets in your short time at court? Have you begun to assess his inerrant perception of righteousness? Now, *that's* a study."

Inerrant perception of right— That was Cult lore. Did Duplais subscribe to the Cult of the Reborn, too? I'd never have thought it. "We've talked a little. Can you pass him a message?"

"If you say it's important. He does try to save me back for his most critical needs." The chevalier's grin blossomed like sunrise, disarming the grandiose words—which I had no doubt were true. No informant could be so valuable as the queen's own brother. And no lady's champion could be better placed. Yet the least hint that Ilario de Sylvae had a gram of intellect, and he was a dead man. Lady Antonia could never allow a man of sense so near Eugenie.

"The Aspirant is here at Castelle Escalon."

"God of all." The chevalier's pleasant face took on a stillness and sobriety that banished the last remnants of Castelle Escalon's court fool. "Who is he?"

"I don't know. I spied him last night, masked, of course, speaking with Mage Dante. He's indeed a big man like my father. But his voice is not Papa's, even purposefully disguised. And Dante doesn't know his identity, either. They're the unfriendliest of allies."

Ilario kicked at a boulder. "I'll tell him."

"And ask Duplais who might have been guesting with his mentor at Seravain at the time of my sister's death. A big man, too. Maybe a sorcerer, but not a collared mage. Not wealthy, but with the taste for it. Impoverished nobility or an academician, perhaps. One who rides in the colors of Delourre."

"That fits no one *I* know."

"The next piece is for both of you. Lord, your foster mother intends to rule Sabria again, as she did when Soren was a boy."

"Not surprising. There are many good reasons I live as I do. Even Geni, who sees ill in no one, has become uneasy with Antonia of late. I did appreciate your warning about her, when you knew so little of me. Be aware, Antonia has many, many friends and allies. Far more than my sister."

"If the queen births a healthy son, Antonia will see both king and queen dead within the hour."

Ilario waved a dismissive hand. "She'd never dirty her own hands. We keep watch—"

"She murdered Cecile de Blasencourt. I heard her admit to it. And she was shocked when I turned up alive after Roussel and the kitchen girl ate the poisoned couchine. Perhaps in the past some personal principle stayed her hand. But no more. Not now she's so close."

His fair skin grayed. "Saints defend! Why would they want you dead?"

"I don't think the *conspirators* do. They could have killed me in the Bastionne . . . and ten times since. Lady Antonia strikes out on her own, and I don't think her partners like it. They see her as a necessary irritation."

To see his fair brow so smudged with dirt and blood was odd enough, but not half so much as seeing the sincere worry.

"And one more thing." I inhaled a great breath, not believing what I was to speak. "Do you know that Mage Dante raises King Soren from the dead?"

"Pssh, tush." Lord Ilario waved a hand and grimaced indulgently. Only the expression quickly faded and his hand fell to his side. "You believe this. You've seen."

"I've seen him three times, lord, or someone amazingly like him, even to his sword and mode of dress. I spoke with him last night in the Rotunda gardens. Your sister receives him in her game rooms." *And in her bedchamber.* "He is not a living human person."

Ilario paced three steps beyond me, then whirled back again, his hand stilled in midmovement as he raked his hair. "I've assumed the deadraising was but foolery, a screen to hide the traitors' real magic. I've never even— You've *spoken* to Soren de Maslin? You're sure?"

"We exchanged words, yes."

"Soren. Saints' glory, Geni . . ." His whispered invocation of his sister's name expressed a deep and private anguish that I had no time to probe. Passing along my information must take priority.

"Lord, you must tell Duplais: Dante's deadraising is no feint. He's perfecting it so it can be part of the rite. Tell him that exactly: part of the rite. He's making a device that contains"—I felt a fool to say it—"the essence of a soul."

Ilario did not laugh. "I'll tell him. Soren, of all the god-blasted, cowardly sons of the Souleater. My sister worshiped the arrogant shitheel."

I COULD NOT AFFORD THESE fits of the shakes. For the tenth time since arriving at the queen's bedchamber, I pressed my back to the wall of the wardrobe room and relived the sensations of the morning: the zahkri splitting skin, penetrating rubbery flesh, and grinding on bone, warm blood spilling over my hands, the raging tide of molten anger that had flowed through my veins and sinews. Creator's mercy, I'd killed a man.

My uncles had hung raw meat on spikes and ropes to give me practice with the knife, but nothing had prepared me for savaging living flesh. Rage . . . fear . . . had changed me into another person entirely.

I must remain alert. When the four attackers failed to return, someone would be thrown off balance. They'd want to know what I'd learned, who had helped me. They'd try something else.

I cradled my left arm, its hasty bandaging concealed under long sleeves, over my roiling gut. Saints sustain Guerin through his injury and speed him to safety.

Fortunately, the queen slept until almost midday. I could scarce rouse her for her first appointment, an excursion to a lace merchant's warehouse with Lord Ilario and a few of her ladies. Even then, her manner was like a spring sky, hazy and changeable, all fragile layers of unfocused light and ephemeral cloud. Her brow creased as she stepped around the sorcerer's circle, now bare of spellmaking objects, and picked up the stuffed doll that had fallen beside her screen. She set it on a high shelf, displaying only a passing sorrow, not the despair of the Rotunda. As if yet dream wrapped, she glided across the bedchamber, pausing in the middle of the floor for a long while to stare at her hand. With a fleeting smile and a long sigh, she touched her breast.

My own fingers clenched. Did she feel the brush of a soft beard and a ghostly kiss?

"Are you well this morning, my lady?" I said, a harsh and barren intrusion, as she curled up on the blue divan and closed her eyes.

"I've a plaguey headache," she said, her drowsy smile tamping down any concern. "But elsewise quite well. I'm so hungry."

Her odd behavior was likely a reaction to the sleeping draughts she'd been given. I needed to consult Roussel about the effects of such potions on a pregnancy. The smile's origin, however . . . My cheeks heated. Were such activities possible with a revenant? Imagination took me where life never had.

I blinked myself back to the present and set out the tonics she took each morning. "Perhaps tea will rid you of the annoyance. Shall I add the red tincture? Or would you prefer the peppermint elixir first?"

Though I had ensured their innocence, my ring could not tell me whether continuing or stopping them better served Eugenie's health. At the least, Antonia's interests required delivery of a healthy child. We had many months ahead to worry about murder.

"Nothing but the shellblade tisane."

Roussel's tisane. That seemed a good thing. Perhaps she was more certain about her friends and enemies than she seemed. The living ones, at the least.

I brought the tea and began brushing her hair. My wounded arm ached and stung.

Caution and mercy forbade questioning her too abruptly about the events of the previous night, so I began obliquely. "The salon is abuzz with the news of the king's homecoming."

"This is *not* Philippe's home." Her languor vanished as if I had slapped her. "His heart is in his mountains. Air so thin one cannot breathe. Sun so brilliant it blinds the eye to softer lights. Winter so deep that only the strongest can survive. Summers so perfect, so incomparably rare and glorious, the heart shatters when they end so soon. Few can thrive in such rarified climes."

I offered no rebuttal. No matter my linguistic fluency, the heart's dialect remained a mystery to me. "Shall you accompany him on his progress? The stay in Journia should not be very long."

The simplest circuit touching all ten demesnes major should take two to three months. To sit with the demesne lords, review defenses, and hear reports and complaints must stretch the time near double. Surely the king would not leave his wife alone so long.

"He'll wish to visit the northern demesnes before winter closes the roads, and be on campaign by spring, so he'll have no time to drag women along. And, of course, if I am—" Hope and regret warred in her, all ghost dreams left behind. "It's easier for him to travel with his men. A small party. Fast. He loves riding out in autumn." But what and whom did *she* love?

"Autumn is a glorious time to travel," I offered. "You might find it refreshing to get away from Merona, no matter your condition. Clean air and new sights. Adventure. Though no one appreciated home more than my mother, she claimed that travel enriched her blood, providing delights to dream on for years to come. And she rode horseback . . . scandalously astride . . . every day she carried my brother and sister. Some said Ambrose rode as if he'd been born on a horse—"

A flashing vision of split flesh, welling blood, and broken teeth, bared in pain, brought on another fit of the shakes and a shooting pain through my wounded arm. Eugenie, mistaking my silence for grief, drew my trembling hand over her shoulder and laid her silken cheek on it. "Shhh. We are a dismal pair, are we not, Anne? We could both use some distraction to give us happier dreams."

"True, lady." Our conversation fell into more mundane channels as I helped her dress. She painted chevrons of indigo beside her eyes. I had scarce pinned her sky blue mantle at her shoulders when a trumpeting tenor from the doorway brought a smile to her face.

"Morning, morning, morning! Dearest Geni, much as I treasure your company on a visit to Dame de Froid's banquet of lace—" Chevalier Ilario breezed into the room in a flash of yellow satin. "Ah, Damoselle de Vernase! My wish of divine grace must surely set your mind to visit to Dame de Froid's with us. Your natural charms could only be enhanced by a discreetly pinned fall of silk filet or perhaps a ruffle of reticella. But honestly, Geni, the hour!"

Kissing Eugenie's cheeks and sweeping a bow to me, he never missed a syllable.

"Why ever, beloved sister, must we depart so early in the day? I've enough baggage beneath my eyes from this early rising to supply a full expedition to Syanar. And no, Damoselle Anne, I have not forgotten your most generous offer to speak with me of the perils of travel and the likelihood of finding crocodiles and other beasts in the Caurean Isles. But for now all I can think of is a nap, as we await the bold flowers of the household who will venture this journey. Saints Awaiting, ladies, my eyes will not stay open."

Tossing his fashionable tall hat to the floor, he flopped on the blue couch, a perfect simulacrum of a man who came no nearer flowing blood than a meal of rare beef. I watched in vain for a glance, a wink, a raised eyebrow, or some sign that he had passed on my message to Duplais. Ilario de Sylvae was no actor, but two wholly different people.

As Eugenie relaxed on her cushions, consumed in laughter, and remonstrated that the hour was not at all early, but already midday, I began putting her medicine bottles away. My hand slowed . . . This was a rare opportunity. Only the three of us present. Anything discovered might move on to Duplais through Chevalier Ilario.

I quickly pulled out the rest of the bottles and lifted the bottom tray of the medicine box. Snatching up what I wanted, I rejoined the queen. "My lady, excuse my curiosity, but I was dusting the lower compartment of your medicine box and found something I think might belong in your jewelry case instead. Yet it could be some kind of magical remedy."

Lord Ilario sighed and began to snore.

I knelt and emptied the little copper circlet onto Eugenie's lap. Her smile warmed, despite a touch of sadness.

"I'm so happy you found this. It's unseemly, maudlin, for me to keep it when it rightly belongs in your family. And Philippe would never countenance— Well, you must have it and do with it as seems best. But

I'd recommend you keep it to yourself until all the furor dies away." She pressed the trinket into my hand.

"Me?" This was the last thing I expected. "But why, Majesty? I don't even know what it is."

"It's an infant's shield bracelet. A northern custom my dear maman held to. You place it on a male child's arm or ankle, to be worn throughout his first year. You see how the metal is soft, so you can make it larger or smaller with your fingers as you need, and light, so the little one is not troubled by it. Noble families shaped them to include the family's heraldic device. Commonfolk made them plain, or engraved kin names or god symbols or just a favored image. It ensures your son will lose neither life nor honor in battle. Desmond wore it last."

So it was no proof against sickness or murder.

"Surely your own family should keep custody of it." The device was certainly not the king's interlaced *S* and *V*.

"But it's not a Sylvae bracelet," she said, affecting a tone of conspiracy. "Neither the beast nor bird on the bracelet is a *crane*. You can envision our family crest sprawled over there on my divan: long shanks, fine plumage, a trumpeting call, and forever a wild dance when he is *awake*." Eugenie smiled at Ilario and raised her eyebrows at me. So she knew of his mode of retiring from a conversation.

Ilario gave a snorting cough, then settled into his rhythmic snoring again. Dare I imagine I saw a smile dart across his features? A heraldic crane also symbolized fidelity and eternal vigilance.

But the mystery remained. I dusted lint from the tarnished copper. "Then whose device is it?"

"Well, of course it is your father's, Anne. Did he never show you? He gave it to us when Desmond was born. He said he intended to stand protection for our son in every way."

The world, the knight, the queen, and every concern plaguing me vanished, as I stepped through yet another door into impossibility. I hurried to the window. Holding the worn circlet in the best light, I tried to discern the details. The long-snouted beast could only be a crocodile—

amusing in any other circumstance. The bird could be anything. My tremulous hands prickled as if new wakened from numbness.

"But my father never knew his true family. And Gavril de Menil—the man who raised him—wore a crest of five feathers." In all the stories of his childhood, my father had never mentioned the copper circlet. Had he ever tried to learn the symbol's meaning?

Eugenie had joined me at the window. "Your father didn't lie about this, Anne," she said, gently chiding. "He *wept* when Desmond died. More than Philippe, I think." Her hands closed my fingers about the little brace-let. "He said he'd worn this in his foundling basket, and for the required year thereafter, and had emerged from every battle with life and honor intact. What does that say about the shield magic? And what does that say about your father?"

Eugenie's jeweled finger raised my chin so I could not avoid meeting her gaze. "Michel and I were never friends. Our opinions diverged on almost everything. He pitied Philippe for finding it politically expedient to wed a girl of twelve. He considered me spoilt and ignorant, which I am, and un-worthy of an incomparable king, which is likely true, as well. But I saw him look on his own daughters, Anne—on you, especially, his firstborn, his soul's child—and he could never in this life have hurt that poor Ophelie."

Her warmth drew out my own declaration. "I doubted my father for a long while, lady. But now I believe, as firmly as I believe in anything, he is a victim of these evildoers, not one of them."

Lady Antonia's clarion tones echoed in the passage, along with other women's voices.

The dark eyes that met my own displayed no frailty, no doubt, no fear. "Then I'll believe it, too." Eugenie's conspiratorial smile transformed her into a lady of mischief. "Now, we'd best be ready."

In a rustle of satin, she returned to Lord Ilario's divan and shoved his feet aside to take a seat beside him. "I hate when duty takes us out these days," she said, loud enough the approaching company could hear her. "The city is so strange. People tell me it is some ordinary shifting of the ground that settles abandoned tunnels and drives birds and beasts from their usual lairs. I don't believe it. My driver never explains why he chooses one route over another anymore. Someday we're going to roll straight into one of these pits of Dimios."

"Not while I am with you, Geni fair," said the chevalier, sitting straight up as if someone had stuck him with a pin. He yawned prodigiously. "I shall spread my cloak across every pit and pothole, and you shall not topple. I had Jacard charm it just a few days since." He slapped one gloved hand to his mouth. "You don't suppose the charm will fail or reverse itself now he's been sacked?"

I left them to a discussion of what charms and wards they should take with them, and returned quickly to the medicine chest. As I reassembled it, I bumped the case and the lid fell, landing on my left arm. The pain nearly shot the top of my head off. I had the case only half reassembled when the ladies entered the bedchamber.

Lady Patrice accompanied Antonia, as did tall, bony Marie-Claire de Tallement, the exceedingly aloof maid of honor I'd seen at cards with Eugenie and Lord Ilario. Was she Eugenie's choice or Antonia's or Ilario's? The chevalier held her chair and gallantly offered her wine, sweets, and unstoppable conversation, while Antonia and Patrice fussed over Eugenie. Though almost as tall as Eugenie the girl never looked at his face, but she bit her lip as if a smile might be struggling to get through. Perhaps she was only reserved, not proud.

I was most pleased to note that the gouty Lady Eleanor was not in the party.

After much fussing and kissing and talk of shoes, charms, smelling salts, pastilles for nausea, and the possibility of rain, the lord and ladies departed. Hard on their heels, I abandoned my post. Cradling my throbbing arm, clutching the copper circlet and a growing excitement that gave my feet wings, I hurried off to find Lady Eleanor. She had bored me to distraction with endless exposition on Sabria's family heritage, but if anyone in Sabria might recognize this device, she would.

THE DUCESSA ELEANOR SAT IN the Rose Room, writing out the queen's schedule for the following day. Her heavy jowls and wattled chin sagged as she wiped her pen and sat back to rest her full glare on me. "What kind of question, damoselle?"

"As you know, Lady Antonia has taken upon herself the difficult duty of soliciting offers for my hand, a service for which, naturally, I am most grateful. As it happened, a gentleman approached me yesterday and asked if he might present his credentials to my goodfather's representative. He was a well-spoken gentleman and immaculately turned out, which—please excuse my frankness, my lady—the Barone Gurmeddion is not."

Eleanor's eyebrows twitched and nostrils flared in just such fashion that I could see she agreed with my assessment of the Honorable Derwin.

The copper bracelet remained in my pocket, lest she ask how I had come by it. I called upon every maidenly matchmaking discussion I had heard from my fellow maids of honor. "As I am anxious to satisfy my goodfather, the king, with the best match possible, I must not fail to present this other gentleman. Only with my sudden summoning after Her Majesty's fainting spell that night, I never got his name. I do recall the outline of the crest he wore on his tabard. Cloth of gold it was, my lady!"

Though her impressive bosom heaved an equally impressive sigh, Lady Eleanor did not hesitate to reach for the book I had never seen more than twelve centimetres from her hand. At the same time, she nodded at the stack of paper and the pen she had just abandoned. "Sketch what you recall of the device. We shall see if he has the quality of a good match or merely a good tailor."

She removed the dark leather volume of *The Grande Historie of the Sabrian Peerage and Families of Lesser Note* from its blue velvet wrappings as reverently as if it were Philippe's own crown, while I drew a reasonable approximation of the beast and bird from the bracelet. I blotted the page and turned it around to show her.

The ducessa pulled it close, squinting. She slammed her book shut, her complexion taking on the color of the age-mottled leather. "What insolence is this, girl?"

"My artwork is crude, I know. Perhaps it is not very like—"

"None wore that crest in this house," she snapped. "None wears it in any house, nor does it appear in my book. Even to draw it is to cross the law."

The room grew cold as a daemon's heart. But I had to hear it. "What did I draw, lady? I'll search out the man and discover the correct device, as I'd never wish to slander such a gentleman. But tell me, please."

She snatched up the pen and dipped it again, and with the magic of an artist born she lengthened the stretched-out bird, rounded the crocodile's snout and the bird's beak into similar heads . . . added two crescent arms and the suggestion of legs until each had the same number . . . and spun the paper to face me. "No other mark bears this exact configuration. Nose to nose. Bird and beast. Crocodile and crocodile bird. This reconstruction is all that's been seen for more than a century, and that's rare enough, bless the Pantokrator's mercy."

I *had* seen her "reconstruction"—two eight-legged beasts entwining deadly pincers in an unending battle. Dueling scorpions. The mark of Mondragon.

CHAPTER 29

23 OCET, MIDDAY

Throughout history artists had reused canvases, slathering paint over older works they disdained as out of style. But now restorers at the great schools of art spent years delicately cleaning away the newer, mundane work to uncloak the glories of Sabria's ancient cultures. What if one didn't like the work uncovered? What if you realized the portrait you had just washed away was the image you loved?

"Divine grace, damoselle. Are you well?" The man stepped from a side passage.

As fate had mandated since our first encounter, my path had crossed with Physician Roussel's yet again in the morning flow of householders.

"Yes. Certainly. Very well." I shaped a smile and folded my arms gingerly, hoping to disguise any telltale bloodstains on my sleeve. The blow from the queen's medicine box must have started it bleeding again.

A door slammed from the direction I had just come.

"Your color seems high." Brow wrinkled, he glanced up and down the corridor. From around the corner came the unmistakable thump of Lady Eleanor's cane. "If I could offer assistance . . ."

"Honestly, it is nothing. Please excuse me. I've duties." My tumultuous emotions left me nothing to offer.

"Forgive my presumption." He backed away and bowed briskly.

"Divine grace, sonjeur."

Numb feet sped me to my hidden balcony, where I huddled amid the rubble of plaster, stone, and every belief about my family's place—my place—in the world.

Long fingers of mist twined through the east gardens, teasing the eye with glimpses of color—here green leaves limned with autumn gold, there a red tile roof or a gold-tipped spire. Glimpses of truth. But not the whole of it. The trees might grow within a courtyard garden or a cultivated orchard or a lingering grove of the wildwood. The roof might cover snug rooms or open colonnades.

In the same way, these glimpses of conspiracy and murder and family and ancient evils might tell a thousand different stories. Seven-and-forty years ago, a newborn male child wearing the device of an extinct Sabrian blood family had been abandoned on a knight's doorstep. What did that mean? My left arm pained me worse by the moment, a reminder of the cost of probing deeper.

Sir Gavril's kitchen girl might have *found* the shield bracelet and put it on her child for the same simple reason she chose to leave the babe with the good-hearted knight—to protect him from harm. Yet how likely was such an artifact to be lying about? The garnet eyes were intact and valuable. And shield bracelets were passed down in families, *northern* families. As in Delourre, where my father had been born and abandoned. In Delourre, where the Gautieri had built their collegia and their library, part of the Grande Demesne Gautier. And Kajetan's guest had worn the colors of Delourre.

Papa's mother must surely have been ignorant of the symbol's meaning and the consequences of discovery. In the decades after the Blood Wars, a hint of Mondragon blood to a magistrate had you dead at the end of a spear. Unless the Camarilla got wind of it first. That death was worse.

Papa could not have known the meaning of the device, either, else he'd never have given the bracelet to Philippe and Eugenie for their child. Yet Cecile de Blasencourt had been asking questions about my father's birth. She'd a hint from somewhere. She had surely seen the bracelet, kept in a silk bag identical to that holding the scrap from her armoire.

And what of Duplais? He didn't know the older mark, either. What had he said to me about Mage Kajetan's handmark? It was *not to be confused with either the scorpions of Mondragon or the three keys of Gautier.*

Three keys! And so did another question resolve itself, while spawning ten more. On the morning she realized that death was inescapable, Lianelle had included a loop of three keys with her spellmaking particles. If the lock of hair aimed the death spell at herself, and Guerin's note designated the person she wished to find her body, then what role did the symbol of Gautier play?

Revelations came tumbling. I had seen three keys in another place, too. In the Bastionne Camarilla, in the ruined chamber Dante insisted was my father's laboratorium, the mage had shown me a topaz set in a triangle formed of three bronze keys. If a Mondragon survived two centuries after the Blood Wars, then it was possible that a Gautier had also survived. Was that what Lianelle was telling me? That the Aspirant was not a Mondragon, but a Gautier? Heaven's creatures!

A tickling at the back of my neck and along my arms signaled another onslaught of tremors and nausea. I buried my face in my arms, trying to empty my head and scour away confusion and dread.

My friend! Gods and daemons, are you well? All morning I've felt these earthquakes in the aether. But when you close your mind, I cannot— I've not been able to reach you.

I'm well. I nearly dissolved in laughter at the thought that my uneasy conscience had somehow opened the door between us and rousted him from his work. *Perfectly well.*

You're not, though. And if you believe so, then you've greater problems than you know.

What a priggish assessment!

You've no idea what my problems are. My hands trembled as they felt the zahkri grind on bone. As I imagined Guerin and his shattered shoulder trying to survive in the streets of Merona. As molten iron stirred in my belly yet again. Foul and wicked. Poison.

I've intruded where I should not, he said. *Forgive me.*

His silent withdrawal struck me like an ice bath.

Wait . . . I'm sorry. Please . . . He deserved better of me. How could I explain my state of mind without blurting out that my father's blood—my own blood—might be so dangerous as to be unworthy of life, or that it might be the very seed sparking a revival of savagery? Or that my sister had murdered herself rather than allow someone else to do it, perhaps because of this very discovery? Or that I had spoken with a dead man, who was somehow seducing my queen and part of a plot to thrust the world into upheaval?

. . . please don't go . . .

My friend's solid presence, his concern, gave me an anchor in the chaos of my thoughts. I could not bear to be left alone with all this yet again.

I'm in no immediate danger. It's just been an awful day. I walked out on an errand this morning, and a brute assaulted me. No one I knew. But I . . . struck him. Cut him. His flesh ripped and his lifeblood spilled out on my hands . . .

The words spilled as if they were my own lifeblood. I had to let them flow, lest skull and heart burst.

. . . and I know it was justified and I'm not sorry for what I did, but I feel filthy and wretched, and I keep seeing it over and over. I think I might possibly have used . . . I curled into the corner of the balcony and buried my head in my arms, holding off a redoubled onslaught of sensory memory. As some great opticum whose lenses reveal those things hidden to the naked eye, the vile insinuation of the copper bracelet magnified the morning's events. And with the closer scrutiny arrived the truth I had never wanted.

From childhood my Cazar relatives had told me I lacked the factor of the blood that sparked magic. No talent. It was a certainty as firm as Montclaire's foundation. I had rejoiced that I would never need to experience the strangeness, the uncertainties, the sickness that accompanied any proximity to spellworking. As I grew older and scholarship—and pride—led me to worship at the altar of reason, the lack made it altogether simple to deny the truth of magic.

Yet as I had slashed at Guerin's magical bindings, anger and hatred had raised this fiery torrent in my limbs. In a gnat's heartbeat, the impervious cords had split. As if by magic. As if by foul, wicked Mondragon magic.

Great gods . . . Well, of course you used your talent to defend yourself. Magic is a gift you bring to any encounter. I, too, came late to magic, so I understand the confusions power can stir. But to deny it makes no more sense than the astronomer de Vouger choosing to be ignorant because his intellect might lead him to contradict the Book of Creation. *Must a woman stop reading books or blind herself because some poor ignorant devil in Riverside cannot read? Must a tall man hunch his shoulders and never reach too high?*

Certainly not. His logic tamed my terror, but did not quench it. *It just felt— Some talent for sorcery is wicked, yes? The very nature of it . . . violence, hate, anger, a bent to evil.* My stomach spasmed again as the bowman's warm blood dribbled through my fingers.

Magic is not wicked. No more than oceans are wicked or learning or sight or weather. Certainly raw power, uncontrolled by the structure of a spell, can be dangerous, just as lightning is dangerous. And some people—some with talent; some without—have a warped, devilish spirit bent to violence. That's why a practitioner must learn control from the first inkling of talent. Emotions that touch the innermost self can cause— A spasm of outrage cut off his thought, rumbling in my soul as distant thunder rattles windows. *Did the brute injure you in such a— Is that the problem? Did* he *use magic to . . . gods . . . to violate* you?

No, no, I've only a few cuts and bruises, some from a magical weapon, some not. I found myself hastening to reassure him. *They ache and sting a bit. That's all. The man didn't get what he wanted. It's the reliving sickens me.*

The stretched moment eased. *Have the injuries seen to,* he said. *By someone who's familiar with magical injuries. Many wounds seem simple but are not. A friend taught me that, and I recall it every time I sharpen a pen. Don't cripple yourself. Promise me.*

More and more I felt certain as to my friend's identity. Indeed, Duplais bore the scars of magical wounding—burns from the ship fire that almost killed him and the king—and he had certainly come late to magic. *All right*, I said. *I'll find someone to look at it.*

And never feel guilty for defending yourself with whatever is at hand. If the incident has opened you to your own gifts, all the better.

Closing my eyes, I could almost see him, a shadowed form against a brilliant light. Thick walls surrounding him. Uncomfortable but safe. Solitary. Focused on this strange conversation as I was. Concerned about me.

I scrubbed my scalp as terror receded. I was still Anne. Plain, awkward Anne. I had been angry before without changing into a monster. *You're very good at calming hysterical women*, I said, leaning my head against the damp balusters, letting the mist bathe my heated skin. *Tell me, friend—*

I hated the thought of returning to the empty world. I yet had some time.

—do your studies progress? I know nothing of night-blooming plants. They're rare, I know. Do you find them more beautiful than day bloomers? Or perhaps you just like working in the dark?

His hesitation was as clear as my hand in front of me. Perhaps I'd made some new faux pas. *If you've other business waiting or would rather not . . .*

No, no. It's just . . . in fact, I detest the dark. Light—seeing—that's the finest pleasure the world offers. But, of course, some work has to be done in the dark . . . like studying night bloomers. Actually, there are a goodly number of them. Thornapple, of course, and daylilies and evening campion. There's a rare type of vervain that bears white flowers that open in the dark. I can't see they're more attractive than other plants. It's their response to the night that is their truly unique quality, though any aspect of their complex nature can be useful. Vervain is included in love potions and witch wards, while at the same time it serves as a wash for festering wounds, a remedy for gout and flux, and a hundred other medicinal tasks. The Cinnear used vervain to cleanse their temples of evil spirits. Any physical property can be useful in spellwork—a tree's hardness or resistance to disease or an herb's hairy stem or thick leaves—but you can also draw on the beliefs surrounding them. All these things make up the plant's intrinsic nature, the power that it brings to magic. If you choose to pursue your talent, which you ought, you must study these things—see them for yourself. Magic is all about seeing. . . .

It was as if I had opened a door in a thick gray wall and stepped through into a feast of brilliant colors, of the smells of spices, wine, and ripe pears, of whirling dancers and sparkling conversation, of jewels, candles, rippling silks, and rustling taffetas. Not even Lianelle had spoken this way of nature and magic. I drank it in.

As he moved onto other unusual plants, those that root in air or die every summer or flower only when their leaves have withered, it struck me that my sister had described a scholar who had touched a kindred part of her soul with his talk of magic. Kajetan. No, no, no, he could not be. . . .

I could not but think of Guerin and his befuddlement at the objects Lianelle had brought to her spellwork. Uncanonical magic. Heresy. And I'd just revealed I'd worked magic unsanctioned. Foolish, incautious girl! This *friendship* could be a trap. How was I to know?

Gods, I've rattled on too long, he said. *You needed to go.*

You astonish me. I never understood that to work spells you would have to know so much about customs and culture, history and language, as well as the divine elements—five of them. Is that right?

My friend slammed the door between us with such finality, I was astounded, moments later, when he spoke again. *The Camarilla Magica teaches that all matter comprises five elements granted by the Creator.* Grave and quiet, all exuberance quenched. Precise. Clear. *Be warned. For a novice practitioner of magic to contradict or question Camarilla tenets is most unwise. Those who know little of the art must listen and learn. And weigh beliefs carefully and in private . . . as I do.*

All true. The words were stripped of every accessory feeling save wariness and a trace of anxiety—for me? Perhaps he did not realize he felt such a thing.

I pushed. *What we say here is private between us. Yes?*

Yes. I could interpret nothing from this but truth.

It would mark me a lunatic to share any idea on a topic so unfamiliar, derived from a source I cannot explain, I said. *Especially when the source might very well be a product of my own deranged mind or a Camarilla practitioner who might reside in Syanar or the Caurean Isles.*

He didn't respond to my attempt at humor. *I should get back to my studies instead of prattling about them,* he said. *You'll see to your wounds? You mustn't let them fester.*

I will. And thank you for all this. You've given me a great deal to think about besides potential husbands or despicable ruffians. Or terror of my own blood.

Scholarly conversation pleases me.

And me, I said. *No one in my guardian's house cares for plants or stars or books.*

He was not Kajetan. The chancellor of Seravain and prefect of the Camarilla, a man so certain of his own worth, so admired and valued even by those wary of him, would never ask his students to weigh his view of the world for themselves—even if he could convey the request without audible speech. And filled with purpose and righteousness as he was, Kajetan would never feel lonely.

EQUANIMITY SOMEWHAT RESTORED, I RETURNED to my bedchamber. The day, still young, was already replete with revelation, including the terrifying, stomach-heaving possibility that I myself had used magic. This friendship outside the boundaries of physical presence was perhaps the least significant of everything that had happened, and yet its mystery roused the deepest wonder and the deepest confusions. I longed to know more of him. Yet he could be anywhere. Anyone. Had I truly glimpsed him for that moment behind my closed eyes? Almost anything seemed possible.

Ambrose would call me a lunatic for believing. As ever, the thought of my brother wrenched my heart, and I prayed Duplais would bring me news that he had escaped. I'd prefer him a murderer than captive as Papa was.

Clanging bells warned me that Eugenie and Antonia would be returning from the lace market at any time. Setting speculation aside, I quickly wrote a note to Lady Eleanor, apologizing again for shocking her with my incapable drawing. I promised to observe more carefully should I spy the "gentleman suitor" again and pass along his name so that she might advise me as to his suitability.

Then, with hot water and clean linen, I cleaned the wounds on my arm. Swollen, mottled purple and black with cross stripes of dark blood, the limb looked as if I'd been lashed. Worse, the spiraled cuts had grown tender and hot. The lightest touch made me wince.

Out of time, I bound it again with strips torn from a chemise, and donned a fresh bodice and sleeves the color of claret. As soon as I had opportunity, I'd ask Physician Roussel to look at it.

No sooner had I bade divine grace to Doorward Viggio than a bustle of gowns, footsteps, and muted voices announced the return of the shopping party. Yet the noise came from the wrong direction, and the excited babble was of a sober tenor, not at all the usual exuberant aftermath of an excursion.

I hurried into Eugenie's bedchamber to see the dark blue wall panel that opened onto the servant's stair standing open. Antonia, swathed in diamonds and purple ruffles, snapped direction into the dim passage behind her. "Get her onto the bed and get out. Speak a word of this and I'll have your tongues out of your heads! Out of their way, Ilario. I told you to—"

"Roussel is on his way, dama," said the lord, bursting from the doorway, his hands in the air. "Saints Awaiting, guard and protect . . ." His yellow satin doublet bore scarlet stains, and no foolery could mask his body's tense lines as three footmen carried a litter through the open panel.

"I told you to fetch the *mage*, you insufferable, milk-livered blot," spat Antonia. "Where is that Anne?"

"Here, my lady!" I stepped into view, yet my eyes did not linger on the dowager queen or the frantic chevalier, but rather on Eugenie's mantle, sodden with dark-edged scarlet. Other blood-soaked wads of fabric—her apricot-hued gown, Antonia's purple cape, the pearl gray silk cloak Marie-Claire had been wearing—fell to the carpet as the footmen gently lifted the unconscious Eugenie onto her bed.

"Attention, girl!" The lines of Antonia's face had hardened into crags. "Fetch Master Dante immediately. Her Majesty is suffering a woman's hemorrhage. Do you understand me?"

"Yes. Yes, certainly." Not a wound, then, but from inside her. Sweet angels, let it not be a miscarried child.

I didn't question the need to summon whatever aid was at hand. Yet to fetch *Dante*, who twisted Eugenie's life into a macabre travesty of maternity, revolted me. Physician Roussel should be able to catch any medical irregularities the mage might notice. But who might detect perverse magic?

As I left the bedchamber, I grabbed Marie-Claire by the wrist and dragged her alongside. The tall girl was so astonished, she failed to resist, and actually looked at me. Men could write sonnets about her cheekbones and compose airs to praise her sapphire eyes, but she had a most dreadful squint. "Someone should fetch Sonjeur de Duplais, as well," I said. "He can arrange for anything that might be wanted to serve Her Majesty and Lady Antonia in this need, don't you think?"

"Yes," she said, thoughtfully. "I'll go. I'd like to be useful."

"Good."

Thanking her, I flew down the stairs and into the corridor referred to as the mages' passage and hammered on the last door. "Mage Dante, you are summoned!"

Three times elicited no response. Yet a noise very like the insistent drumming of winter rainfall emanated from inside. Steeling myself, I opened the door. . . .

My hair rose, crackling as with the *virtu elektric*. Stomach, heart, head spun out of control with the terror of a chasm's brink . . . vertigo . . . nausea.

The mage sat on his heels inside a ring of raging flames. Sweat poured from his darkened complexion and dripped from the black hair, straggling loose from a knot at his nape. His eyes were clamped shut. One gloved hand gripped his staff, his shoulder and arm quivering with effort as if he worked to plunge the white stick through the floor.

From the upper end of the staff plumed a circle of intense blackness the exact diameter of his ring of fire—a void, a tunnel, a passage into night. A *not*.

My flailing hand gripped the unseen frame of the doorway. Surely one false step would send me plummeting into that void. Yet I could not look away. The world beyond his circle dimmed to gray.

Then cracks appeared in the hole of midnight. Silver-white streaks quickly etched a pyramid shape, shimmering like glass in lamplight against the blackness. More silver streaks bent and twisted themselves into a knotted netting that mantled the pyramid, tinkling faintly like fine silver on crystal. Thick blue spirals tangled themselves in the netting, and a broad crimson band slashed across it all, as if a disgruntled artist had chosen to ruin his work with one broad brushstroke. More colors splotched and streaked the dark canvas—livid green and stormy purple, the colors of bruises and sickness, and a vomitous brown—the strange artwork swelling into something huge and horrid and wicked, though it mimed no pattern or image that made sense to me.

Dante's right hand jerked and swept in a circular motion, as if to scoop a handful of the heated air. As if in reflection of his movement, a black void appeared in the leprous image. At the same time, a searing spike shot from my eyes to my toes, straight down through the center of me, dissipating as quickly as it had begun.

I stepped back, slapping the back of my hand to my mouth to choke off a cry. The mage did not react. He'd shown no evidence of recognizing my presence thus far, and as the vile, horrid pattern in the air continued to shift and change, his posture remained entirely focused. Saints' mercy, what was he doing?

The mage's cupped hand twisted. Three strands of the silvery net slipped free of the rest and dissolved in a burst of sparks. Another quick movement and a bilious green swirl shifted to a dull mustard hue. Shifting, tweaking, he might have been some ancient priest painting on a cave wall. Each movement plucked my nerves and sent twinges into my extremities.

I wanted to run away. Excuses flashed to mind. *The mage was out. He refused to come. The door would not open. He frightened me.* But Eugenie lay bleeding, and whatever interest this mage had in our queen might draw his skills to support her healing. I could not return without him.

"Mage!" I yelled over the roar of the flames.

His mouth, nose, and brow flinched, but otherwise he did not change his posture. Another gesture of his gloved hand split the scarlet band into three parts. My fingers stung, as if pricked by hot needles.

The scarred floor of the laboratorium was littered with glass, earth, splattered water, and coils of thin black cord that announced the source of my arm's persistent hurt. I stepped gingerly through the litter and around the ring of flame, placing me within his line of sight, and shouted again. "Mage Dante!"

His eyes flicked open. Vague, confused, they scanned me and the laboratorium behind as if we were indistinguishable. But the amber firelight that licked his cheekbones and shadowed the deep hollows of his eyes soon set the green irises aflame. His mouth hardened. Yet without altering his posture, he squeezed his eyes shut again and gripped his quivering staff. The swollen blight slowly faded. The flames quieted, dulled, and died.

As the last flame vanished with a soft pop, the laboratorium took on the ordinary colors and shapes of cloudy daylight. The amber ring dulled. The mage sagged backward onto his heels, his broad back bent, his head drooping.

Jacard had been right about Dante's works depleting the dark mage. Wrong, though, when he minimized the power of those works. Whatever wickedness this was, it had left the world changed in some unguessable way. The air felt brittle. Fragile. The temperature uncertain. The boundaries of objects and spaces slightly askew. I massaged my fingers as the hot wires threading my nerves cooled.

"You are summoned, mage. Her Majesty suffers a hemorrhage that threatens her life." My voice grated on the quiet like boots on crushed glass.

For an exasperatingly lengthy interlude, the mage stretched his neck and broad shoulders as if to relieve the stiffness of long effort, and ran a finger under the silver collar—a seamless, five-centimetre-wide band wrapped snugly about his sinewed neck. He never looked up. My Cazar uncles would have reminded me I could whip out my knife and slice the veins in his neck, ridding the world of his evils. But I doubted Dante needed to look at me to assess such a threat.

When he raised his eyes at last, the green holocaust had been controlled to a moderate blaze, his temper to a quiet menace. "Are you an entire fool to break through a mage's door and interrupt him at his work? Or has someone put you up to it?"

Perhaps his evident weariness emboldened me. Perhaps his deliberate restraint. The explosive violence that had bruised Jacard seethed just below his haggard visage, yet remained firmly in his grip. My ambiguous beliefs about the Creation stories had never been challenged with so vivid an image of Dimios the Souleater, the dark angel whose beauty had been consumed by lust for the forbidden.

"I am perhaps not such an entire fool as one who pursues such work as you do," I said.

His brows lifted in irony. "Surely the daughter of Michel de Vernase, a man who disdains human authority and mocks the divine, does not fear for my soul."

I had no time for a war of semantics; my knees already jellied under his glare. "You're correct. Not a whit do I care for your soul, assuming you possess one. But your skills are pledged to my lady's service, and she lies in mortal peril at this hour. Attend her if you have aught to offer in her need."

I made a hasty exit. I did not wish to travel even so short a distance in Dante's company.

Feeling as though I'd fought the morning's second battle, I sagged against the passage wall beside Jacard's deserted desk. The scuffed table remained a jumble of papers and what I supposed were spellworking particles—the bits of metal, fabric, bone, and biological materials that seemed to litter a sorcerer's worktable. Among them lay a short length of the black cord. As a moth drawn to flame, I touched it. It snaked up my finger.

Shuddering, I flung it off and hurried off toward the queen's chambers. It would take a month of bathing to make me feel clean again.

CHAPTER 30

For three hours Physician Roussel bathed the queen's wrists and forehead in spirits and administered repeated doses of herbal tinctures he swore would quell the hemorrhage and restore her blood. Though I trusted Roussel, I faithfully touched each vial, beaker, and spoon he used. My ring's wardstone did not change color.

To my chagrin, billowing smoke and the stink of boiling herbs forced me from Eugenie's bedside into the ladies' retiring room, where I watched and listened through the doorway. Watering eyes and incessant sneezing left me anything but useful.

Antonia alternately derided the physician's incompetence and begged his assessments, while snapping instructions at two serving women who provided steady replacements for stained linen and fouled water basins. Ladies Eleanor and Patrice tucked blankets, plumped pillows that Roussel promptly removed again, wrung their hands, and murmured soothing clucks and copious prayers. Standing as far as possible from the bed, the king's portly First Counselor, Lord Baldwin, and his own owlish secretary maintained an awkward presence, representing the king and his privy council.

Mage Dante propped his backside on the window seat, arms folded across his staff. Though he offered no assessments, no advice, and no medicaments, I doubted he was idle. The air about him quivered like summer heat shimmers. The lingering image of his disturbing magic had me expecting a crimson slash to split the steams and smokes. Everyone in the room did their best to pretend he was not there.

Duplais never arrived. I didn't know whether to curse Marie-Claire or fret about Duplais' safety. I dared not leave to seek him out myself. And so I paced and fretted and clutched my throbbing arm.

"Get out, you ninny!" Lady Antonia's annoyance at Lord Ilario, rising throughout the afternoon, shattered the quiet.

Ilario had come near wearing grooves in the floor circling the chamber's perimeters. The chevalier threw himself onto a divan in my little alcove, his sister's blood still darkening his canary garments. "Her heart races like a songbird's." His voice came soft and filled with anguish. "If this be another miscarried child, however will she bear it? If she dies . . ."

No one in the bedchamber had dared voice that wretched likelihood as yet.

Though the wide doorway left us open to view from the bedchamber, no one was likely to overhear our conversation. Nonetheless, I wandered over to the window as he spoke. The sun peered through veils of fog, naught but a solid gray disk that offered little illumination to the day.

He waved his slender hands helplessly. "As we went out this morning, she announced her intent to ride out with Philippe on his progress. To enjoy the autumn weather and the jolly company, she said, and to unburden him of the petty piffelry that complicates such a journey—the pig petting and child dandling and greetings of merchants and marriageable daughters and magistrate's wives. My lady mother near collapsed at the thought of it. The more dama pressed, the more adamant Geni was. What was she thinking?"

His report made this grievous turn of events even more wretched. Not only had Eugenie understood the meaning of my suggestion, she had added her own generous portion to it.

"I've known my lady only these few short days, lord, but she impresses me as far stronger than anyone imagines." It was not some casual soothing I offered, but a conclusion that had solidified over these terrible hours.

"She must stop this," he said, twisting one of the cushions into a knot. "No matter what the council says, no matter what she believes, Philippe will not displace her."

I busied myself plumping cushions that did not need it, straightening paintings, charms, and draperies that were perfectly arranged. "Have you witnessed what she does with Dante?" I said softly. "With the children?"

He stretched out on his back and flung his arm over his face as if to sleep. "She's told me she sees them," he murmured. "The babes. I won't participate."

"I spied on them last night after the mage worked the sorcery," I said as I rearranged the cups and pitcher on the table nearest the divan, "and it was both terrible and wonderful to behold. Your sister smiled and played with four children. Whether or not they were what Dante claims, whether or not it was a perversion of the Creator's will, her actions were as brave and painful as any I've witnessed. Who could put themselves through such grief for whimsy or stubbornness or fear? When she expresses her desire to ensure her children are not afraid in their journey through Ixtador, that is *exactly* what she intends. She does it for *them*. And so, I think that when she puts herself through this ordeal of conceiving"—I stared at the crowded bedside—"it is not for her position or duty to Sabria, but for simple love."

Though whether it was love for her present husband or her lost one, I was not sure.

"Thank you." It was the swordsman who had saved my life so many hours before who spoke gratitude. When Ilario jumped up and returned to the bedchamber, wringing his lace-wreathed hands as effusively as the ladies, that man vanished.

I sent for warmed ginger clarrey. Few refreshments were so restorative as the peppery honeyed wine. When it arrived, I ventured Roussel's smoking herbs long enough to share it out . . . and catch a glimpse of Eugenie.

The queen might have been laid out for her funeral; she was profoundly still, dark hair fanned out across the white pillows, the green spirals painted on her temples and neck reminiscent of deadhouse sigils meant to keep daemons away. Yet her eyes fluttered behind closed lids, and her cheeks and lips displayed a rosy flush. From time to time she stirred, licking her lips or pressing her hand to her belly or her breasts. The physician hovered at her bedside with his tincture vials.

I raised pitcher and cup. "Clarrey, sonjeur?"

Roussel's gaze met mine, and his grave expression softened. "That would be a m-mercy, damoselle. Let me clean up a b-bit."

Before stepping away, he suggested the ladies take the opportunity to release his patient from her restrictive garments and cleanse her in the ways a male physician could not. I followed him to the washing bowl, well away from the bedside and the hovering women. As he scrubbed his hands, I ventured a quiet question. "How fares my dear lady? She looks perfectly healthy, not even pale. And yet this blood . . ."

"It's almost stopped," he said. "And her heart has slowed. Good news all." After toweling his hands dry, he accepted the wine cup and took a long, grateful pull. "B-but she has developed a fever, causing this flush, and she does not wake. It may be a natural weakness from the ordeal. . . ."

"Or?"

He glanced sidewise at the renewed bustle of ladies and serving women at the bedside. "It may be a d-determined will to avoid hearing what I m-must tell her."

Aching sympathy filled my already stinging eyes. "Sweet spirits."

Roussel downed the rest of his clarrey and rubbed his forehead with the back of his hand. "T-truthfully, damoselle, I've seen no evidence that she was with child. Certainly she is not carrying one now."

A rapid assault of five sneezes seemed particularly abrasive in the face of such sorrow. As I pulled out a kerchief and blotted my eyes, he cocked his head in concern. "Have you a d-dose of red eyebright for that problem? I could formulate—"

"My former housekeeper makes me a helpful tonic," I said. "But later, when you're available, I *would* like to consult you on another matter." Every jar of my wounded arm now caused shooting agony, illustrating my friend's warning.

"Certainly," said Roussel, with just enough eager sympathy to warm my heart. "Anything you need. Now I'd best get back, else *he'll* step up. The man can crumble b-bones with a look."

Dante had occupied the window seat nearest his sorcerer's ring. He observed the quiet bustle, seemingly without interest. Yet a thread of white vapor drifted from his staff. I kept my voice low.

"What can he do, really?" I proffered my pitcher again. "He does not watch idly."

"I've never worked with magicians before. D-don't believe in it any more than you do. Yet I've seen him soothe the queen's headaches and nightmares by sitting at her bedside, never touching her. Somehow, using that cursed staff, he can birth flames or set the night whirling." Roussel stroked his thick brush of a mustache and stared boldly back at the mage, scowling. "Such manipulations seem wondrous. Yet I don't trust him."

"Nor do I!"

Roussel's own gaze roamed the bedchamber. Uneasy. "This day feels wholly askew, as if the p-planets have slipped out of alignment. I know that sounds foolish."

"Not at all," I said. "These past few hours I've sensed the same. As if de Vouger's principles, the forces that bind the universe, have been violated." As if I walked that sloping floor in the ruined Bastionne Camarilla.

Roussel whipped his head back to me, quickly smothering a trace of a smile. But naught could dim the spark in his gray eyes. "Exactly that."

The dowager queen's red-haired harridan, Morgansa, arrived just then, dragging a wide-eyed boy who clutched an Aubini bell-pipe. Antonia bustled the lanky youth into a corner, tied a kerchief about his eyes, and gave him a quick muttering of instruction.

Morgansa raised the lid of the incense burner above the queen's bed. Smoke billowed across the room. My ensuing barrage of coughs and sneezes drew Antonia's glare.

With a sympathetic waggle of his eyebrows, Roussel passed me his cup and returned to the bedside. I retreated.

As the deep flutelike tones of the bell-pipe rose in sleepy melody, Antonia and Morgansa arranged goblets of grapes and bundled willow withes about and under Eugenie's sickbed. Aubini women placed such talismans in their bedchambers to ensure fertility.

Though Antonia desired Eugenie to bear a male child, she did not welcome the proposal of the king and queen reconciled. The queen's collapse—a reminder of miscarriage, even if it was not that at all—would ensure Eugenie remained home when her husband rode out in nine days' time. And the ghostly Soren wandered these halls.

Suspicion flowered like a night-blooming lily. Had Antonia caused this incident to keep Eugenie here? Surely only the pressure of time could prompt her to such an appalling risk.

Time . . . fertility . . . I touched my hand where I'd felt the brush of Soren's beard, the soft breath of a kiss, so near life. Surely it was madness to wonder whose child was at risk on that great bed.

Roussel's rumbling voice spoke a few undecipherable phrases, raising a hushed babble from the others in the bedchamber. Curiosity consumed me until Ilario was banished yet again.

The chevalier dropped into a chair, elbows propped on his knees, head resting in his hands. "The bleeding is stopped. The good physician believes she will live if he can suppress this fever."

Impatience allowed me no time for kindness. "Tell me, lord, how did this sickness befall Her Majesty? She seemed well when you set out."

"As she climbed into the carriage, she stumbled," he said. "Said she was dizzy. Wouldn't hear of returning, though. Not half an hour into our tour of the lace warehouse, she asked to sit down. . . ."

"The queen stumbled *after* mentioning she planned to ride out with the king? *After* the argument with Lady Antonia?"

His head lifted. "Yes."

"Think carefully, lord. Did she have anything to eat or drink on the way to the coach?"

"I'd swear not. We sat in the salon courtyard awhile, as Antonia desired tea before setting off. The others had pastry. I tried to get Geni to eat, but she said her stomach was unsettled, the same as every day of late."

Recollection of the conversation as the party prepared to depart stilled my pulse. "Was she perhaps offered a pastille to suck on for her nausea?"

He leapt to his feet. "Sante Ianne!"

Never had I seen such a battle as ensued. The chevalier's complexion darkened to the color of clay tiles. His chest heaved and fine mouth twisted in fury. But in the space of two eyeblinks, his long fingers uncurled, and a sighing exhale cooled his fair complexion. He snatched a willow wreath from beside the doorway and spun like a whirligig. Did I not know his secret, I'd have been assured he was the world's greatest dolt.

"A hex! That's it! The holy saints can only provide when we give them opportunity to do so, and the same for the Souleater's servants."

His exuberant vocalization drew horrified looks from the bed-chamber.

"Beloved dama! The saints have answered!" He darted through the doorway, lifted a shocked Antonia into the air, and spun her around. An awkward landing crushed the sputtering woman in his arms. Undaunted, he tugged and patted her gown and petticoats into some semblance of order, then dragged her back to the retiring room with him.

"Blighted idiot!" Antonia was livid. No playacting was required for me to display mystification.

"I am inspired!" Ilario bellowed, towering over the woman once he had her seated. "In part, certainly, because the gentle Damoselle Anne was here, and I could not but think of her despicable—please, please forgive me, dear young lady—her despicable sire, who has shown such vile intents toward my beloved sister. As I begged the Hero Saint Reborn to come to Geni's aid, it struck me that we have not done our part to defend her from this desperado in the king's absence. For surely the villain de Vernase has hexed Castelle Escalon! Which means our answer is simple. Once the king arrives, he must take Geni away."

"A hex, lackwit?"

"Clearly," said Ilario. "Once they are gone, the palace can be purged of this infection. Surely a battalion of mages will be required to aid Master Dante in the work."

Dante's scorn produced a derisive snort from all the way across the bedchamber. Staff in hand, he left the room.

No matter Antonia's insults, Lord Baldwin and his secretary soon stood in the doorway alongside Lady Eleanor and a breathless, intensely interested Portier de Savin-Duplais. The ensuing discussion reviewed the dangers that impinged on Eugenie's safety, from Roussel's poisoning to the haunting of the Rotunda to the destruction of the Bastionne Camarilla, scarce two kilometres distant.

Lord Baldwin, appalled by the tales, was inclined to agree with Ilario. He commanded Duplais to install the most secure precautions to ensure my father's influence with daemonic hordes could not harm his sovereign's queen. Two loyal attendants must sit with Her Majesty every moment of her recovery, he said, as well as a willing servant to taste every portion of her foods and medicines.

"His Majesty will question your presence in this chamber, Damoselle de Vernase." The well-spoken Baldwin raked me with his incisive gaze.

"She must stay." To my amazement, it was Antonia who jumped to my defense. "Eugenie gave specific instruction that Damoselle de Vernase attend her in this bedchamber. Many have heard this. Duplais? Ilario?"

Both men acknowledged her accuracy. I was speechless. But then, she had already demonstrated her intentions of keeping me under her control, dead or otherwise.

"Until she wakes to contradict them, my daughter will expect her wishes to be heeded. She has come to love and trust Anne, despite her initial uncertainties. And Anne's husband has granted his permission for her to continue in her duties."

"Husband?" Baldwin and Ilario chimed together. Their gawking made me wish to crawl under a table.

"Lacking certain minor formalities, yes. Damoselle Anne is betrothed to my son-in-law's Commander of the Northern Passes."

"My goodfather's consent is hardly a minor formality," I said, but I didn't think anyone heard.

Baldwin recognized when argument was impossible. "Your will, of course, Your Grace," he said, inclining his back, "as long as there are *two* in attendance at all times."

"If I may, my lords and ladies," said Duplais, hands behind his back as if wholly unfazed at the discussion of poisonings and hauntings and incipient husbands. "Upon hearing of this dire event, I took the liberty of dispatching a palace messenger bird to His Majesty's current sojourn at Castelle Dureme. I've been awaiting the king's response." He offered Philippe's First Counselor a curling slip of paper.

Antonia snatched it from Lord Baldwin's hand. Her stretched forehead burnt so deep a scarlet, I thought the skin must char and split. She crumpled the slip, threw it on the floor, and returned to the bedchamber.

Ilario retrieved it, read it, and passed it on to me.

On my way. P. SV

Castelle Dureme. For a determined rider, three days.

CHAPTER 31

Throughout that night and the next day, Eugenie's condition changed little. Though she remained fevered and insensible, she seemed ever on the verge of waking. We kept her comfortable, stroking her throat until she swallowed so we could feed her bread soaked in milk and Roussel's medicines. At times she grew restless, trying to throw off the sheets and her bedgown, arching her back, and rubbing her breasts and nether regions. We bathed her face and limbs with cool water.

An elderly serving woman—Prince Desmond's old milk nurse, Mailine—came willingly out of her retirement to taste everything brought in for the queen. Mailine, a stick figure of a woman, dry as dust, spent her waking hours tatting lace with quick, capable hands. She sat in the doorward's chamber and slept in the alcove.

Duplais had made out a schedule for Antonia, Ilario, Eleanor, Patrice, himself, and me—two of us to be with the queen at all times. He had assigned either Ilario, himself, or me as one of each pairing, as we three were by far the youngest. Unfortunately it meant I was never alone with one of my allies. Likely that was his intent, which annoyed me to no end.

On the first morning of our new arrangements, Duplais and I reviewed a small change in the schedule. "Are you well?" he murmured without lifting his eyes from the page. "A swordsman friend believed you might have suffered an injury yesterday."

"Well enough." Which was wholly untrue. My arm felt like a smith was trying to heat and hammer it into a sword. But I wasn't going to waste this time. "I've so much to tell you."

"Later. I promise." Lady Patrice was bearing down on us. Duplais snatched up his paper. "I'll have a new copy made for you and each of those named."

Though Physician Roussel was not named on Duplais' schedule, he had not left Eugenie's side throughout the long night and day. He displayed a gentle hand but grew increasingly exasperated with his own inability to cool the queen's fever. None could have missed his sidewise glances at Dante, who drifted in and out at random times, offering naught that anyone could see.

"She'll wake when she's ready," said the mage on one of his visits, a pale white glow from his staff illuminating the sleeping lady. "Perhaps she's fed up with all this aristo nattering and enjoys her fevered dreaming. I'd estimate she'll sleep until . . . the Souleater's Return." Somehow in his mouth the common phrasing of world's end took on a dread reality.

By nightfall Lady Patrice insisted Roussel retire for a few hours, lest he exact more harm than good on his charge. Though I myself had caught only a few hours of sleep in a chair, I added my voice to hers. "Physician Roussel could stretch out on a couch in the salon, could he not, my lady? There he would be instantly accessible."

With only a slight disapproving sniff, the marquesa agreed. After extracting our sworn oaths that we would summon him if we detected the slightest change for better or worse, the physician latched his satchel, looped its strap over his shoulder, and withdrew.

Hours later, deep in the night watch, Patrice and I relinquished our oaths, our linen cloths, and our bedside stools to Ilario and Lady Antonia. Pinched lips painted a startling red, garments stiff and regal, Antonia would have better suited a throne room than a sickroom. She kissed me on each cheek. "So devoted you are, *caeri*. My daughter will be so grateful when she wakes."

I'd scarce left the bedchamber when Ilario came pelting after me. "Damoselle, your kerchief!"

He passed me a square of lacework that would cost Bernard's wages for a year. "It's not—"

I was halfway through my denial when I realized that a tightly folded scrap of paper had been deposited into my hand along with the linen.

"This is Her Majesty's," I said, returning the kerchief while slipping the pellet-sized wad into my pocket. He bowed and returned to the bedchamber.

I lagged behind Lady Patrice, long enough to step into a lamp-lit closet and unfold the scrap of paper. A dry, dusty pellet fell into my hand. The strong, unelaborated script on the paper was the same as on the bedchamber schedule. Duplais'.

A mild dosage of common hypericum can cause dizziness and confusion. Not bleeding or fever.

Recalling Ilario's exuberant dance with Antonia and its untidy ending, I supposed the chevalier had palmed one of the medicaments. So much for my assumptions. Perhaps the hemorrhage was nature's work after all. Or perhaps only one pastille had been laced with some devilish compound.

Confused and uncertain I hurried tiredly down the passage in Patrice's wake, supporting my painful left arm in my right. I hoped I was so spry as the brisk marquesa when I was in my eighth decade, if not so mean-spirited.

Never had I been so unsure of what future awaited me. Did I carry Mondragon magic in my veins? Was it true that the rocky slopes of Gurmeddion damped the talents of the blood? To someone like Lianelle or my friend of the mind such a fate would surely feel like suffocation. My own suffocation would be of another kind.

My head a muddle of faces, fears, and the day's bloody images, my stomach churning, I rounded the corner into the long passage.

"Damoselle."

Cold sweat rippled across my skin as fingers plucked at my sleeve. A man's figure stepped from the shadows. I jerked away, slamming my back to the passage wall and fumbling for my knife.

"Physician!" The pooled lamplight revealed Roussel's intelligent gray eyes and his black curls threaded with white. Ghostly kings, the Aspirant, Dante, assassins . . . there were a number of men I'd no wish to encounter in the night watches.

"Shhh." He drew me into the Rose Room and closed the door behind us. A single lamp burned on the writing desk. "Wouldn't want anyone to catch a m-maid of the royal b-bedchamber having a middle-night assignation with the stammering physician."

"You've no idea how close you were to having my dinner on your shoes, sonjeur. You should be sleeping. And so should I. I can scarce summon a thought." My eyes stung. The lamp's flame seemed to heighten the stink of herbs and incense that clung to our clothing.

"But you said you needed to c-consult me. Friends are rare in this place just now."

I cradled my arm, its incessant throbbing but one misery amid overwhelming exhaustion. "This can likely wait." Though my friend had advised not. Pleasure at the remembrance of his concern heated my cheeks.

"The arm, yes? I've noticed you favoring it all day. And you seem fevered. How did you injure it?"

"It got tangled in a rope this morning," I said. "Yesterday morning. Accidentally."

The physician settled me in the padded chair, turning it around where I could rest my arm on the writing table. He drew up a stool for himself, pulled on a pair of spectacles, and unlaced my sleeve. Rusty blood streaked the linen winding. As he unpinned and unwrapped the bandage, his every touch made me wince.

"Tangled in a rope? Accidentally?" He stared down at my battered limb—swollen, purple flesh scored by at least ten angular lacerations—thin black lines bordered by angry red. "My d-dear young lady, do you think I am an imbecile?"

His skeptical expression as he glanced over the top of his spectacles sparked an unlikely inclination to laugh. My head spun. The lamplight swelled and receded. "Perhaps it was not accidental. Have you experience with magical injuries?"

"I've seen very few injuries that could not be explained by simple science or stupidity," he said. "B-but, then, I took up medical studies only in the past few years, so I can't claim d-decades of experience." The physician produced a magnifying lens from his satchel and examined my chevronlike injuries. Brow knotted, he probed gently with a thin bronze implement. "And truthfully, I've never seen anything qu-quite like this. There appear to be . . . fibers . . . embedded in the lacerations, yet they—"

He pulled out several more implements, some squares of clean linen, and a mounting mechanism for the magnifying lens. With both hands free, he peered through his lens and used tweezers and a small blade to probe one particularly angry wound.

"Hold very still, damoselle. This may sting."

Tired as I was, every prick felt like a sword cut. But I held still. Before very long, Roussel picked a sheet of writing paper from the stack and deposited something on it. He shifted the focus of his magnifier to the paper and invited me to look through the lens.

A black fiber, a few millimetres in length, was clearly visible on the cream-colored paper. Roussel passed me one of his probes. "Use that to touch it."

I did so, and the hairlike thread curled like a live thing. And then it uncurled and lay still, no matter how I poked it. But when I touched the fiber with my finger, it writhed and stung and adhered to my flesh until Roussel picked it off with his tweezers and scraped it back onto the page. I shuddered and scrubbed at my fingertip.

"*Rope*, you said?" The physician dabbed at the bead of blood that marked the site of his probing. "How in the name of all d-daemons did *that* get into your arm in Castelle Escalon?"

"From a crossbow bolt," I said, mesmerized by the black thread, even after he shifted the lens mount back into place and began to probe another wound. "The bedeviled rope was attached. I'd gone out to meet a friend."

His hands stilled. "A friend who brought attackers with crossbows?"

His kind efforts deserved an answer. "The attackers were after him, not me."

"Stars' glory, why? Was he—? Oh." He swallowed his question in such a hurry, he almost choked. He bent his head to the work. "P-pardon. Not polite to pry into family secrets at such an hour of the morning," he said softly, extracting a third and fourth remnant of the black cords in quick succession.

"He was *not* my brother."

"Of course." I could see only his thick curls as he bobbed his head in acceptance.

But the ensuing silence pricked at me. "A young man came to tell me that my sister had killed herself apurpose. He didn't think it something to write in a letter."

"Ah, damoselle, I'd heard of your tragic loss." Roussel's sympathy threatened to sap my anger. I couldn't afford to wallow in guilt and grief.

"Unfortunately he could not tell me why. Or who pursued him with such weapons as this. Perhaps he has family enemies." Perhaps . . . though I knew it was no such thing.

"Did your friend survive?"

"I don't know. We took different paths to get away." Trusting Roussel with my life was one thing; trusting him with Guerin's was another. He seemed to understand that.

"Whoever he was, I'll say he has w-wicked enemies. You're going to tell me this is sorcery, aren't you, and not some alchemical marvel ignited by the temperature of your skin?" Another black fiber dropped onto the paper.

"I've lost sight of the line between science and magic," I confessed. "But the cord is Mage Dante's work. I saw a coil of it in his laboratorium today."

This time shock popped his head up. "Stars above us, what were you doing *there*?"

"Lady Antonia sent me to fetch him to the queen's chamber. Believe me, I'd never venture there otherwise."

The physician shook his head and went back to his work. "I wouldn't have p-picked you for Dante's friend, though Duplais claims the mage is an intelligent man. I hear that about you, too: languages . . . exotic cultures . . . mathematics. Physics and astronomy, too, no doubt, if you know of the celebrated de Vouger and his theories."

"My family valued education," I said, drowsiness loosening my tongue. "My father corresponded with de Vouger. Called him the most brilliant man of science of our day."

"I've heard that as well."

I was almost asleep by the time he finished removing all the remnants of the black cord from my arm. He opened a narrow-necked brown bottle and sponged an oily, foul-smelling liquid over the wounds, now pocked with his tiny incisions. By the time he was done, my arm felt as if I'd been stung by a giant bee. Other than that and an overall weariness, I felt better than I had since the coils first constricted my arm.

"No need to bind it, I think," he said as I started to reinstall the linen bandage. "The bleeding's stopped, and air will be good for healing."

I relaced my sleeve. Roussel wiped his instruments with turpentine and packed them away.

"Thank you, sonjeur," I said, rising to leave. His calm demeanor was surely as healing as his capable hands. "I cannot tell you how grateful I am."

"It was my pleasure." He glanced up from his medicine case. "I suppose I must now offer my felicitations on your coming nuptials. Though surely the gentleman must be congratulated more thoroughly."

For Roussel, I would not pretend. "No felicity is possible in this match."

"The name being bandied about the household leads me to agree. Damoselle, you must use whatever means you have to stop it. I've heard tales of this man. . . ."

"I, too," I said. "I've appealed to my goodfather. He can stop it."

"And yet with your family connections, an appeal to the king cannot be a certain reprieve."

"I've resources. Information that should convince him."

"Ah, that's g-good, then." He dropped his eyes. His cheeks colored. "Please c-count me among those resources."

"You are very kind, sonjeur."

"You see no shame in my profession or my b-birth—or this c-cursed b-blight of my tongue. That's refreshing. And you've p-prodded my thinking, which is a delight I've missed since leaving the academie. And so I must share this idea you've p-prompted." He snapped the latch on his case. "Here, gentle damoselle, is what I see as the distinction between science and magic. Once a scientific principle is formulated, anyone can follow the steps and repeat the discovery. But in the case of magic, the connection between the formulated principle and the one who truly grasps it, who can make it come alive, is so intimate and so complex that perhaps only a few others in the universe can repeat the act successfully. Perhaps no one at all."

Which struck me as a profound explanation from someone who proclaimed himself a magical skeptic. I had no time to respond, even if I'd had the wit, for he raised his eyes to mine. He must have approved what he saw, for he smiled, crinkling the sun lines at his temples. Then he lifted my hand and kissed it. Firm. Warm. Fully of flesh and living breath. "Sleep well, lady."

A short time later, as I curled my arm under my pillow with scarce a twinge of discomfort, it occurred to me that perhaps Ganet de Roussel had more experience with magical injuries than he admitted to. And that, perhaps, he had already known I had an injury that needed tending, and a prospective husband I needed help with, and that he had purposely brought up Germond de Vouger's name. Duplais was not the only quiet, well-spoken person in this palace who might be lonely in his chosen work. Next time I encountered the physician, I might ask him if he had finished his work with night-blooming plants and come again into the light.

I drifted off to sleep, smiling, grateful that a human man's kiss had supplanted the whispered breath of King Soren's ghost.

CHAPTER 32

"Damoselle Anne!"

Moonshine glared in my eyes. I threw my arm up to block the light, only to bump into a warm, solid barrier. The jarring collision set the moon wavering.

"Forgive this intrusion. I need you to wake, damoselle." The whisper came from somewhere beyond the unsettled moon, beyond the hand tapping my shoulder.

Waking quenched a flooding pleasure. The hand was not Roussel's. A forest of dark curling hair backed the physician's hand. This one—thin fingers, nails stained with ink—displayed fine, light brown hair and a gray-blue mark that shimmered in the moonshine.

I blinked. Not moonshine, but candlelight. And an interlaced *S* and *V.* The Savin family mark.

"Duplais?"

His clothing brushed softly as he set his candle on the bedside table and crouched low enough to put his face on a level with mine. The sidewise light sculpted his narrow face and fine bones. He smelled of damp skin and soap. "I need your help. Are you awake?"

"Yes." I sat up, drawing the sheet close, as if the Royal Accuser might read my immodest dreams. Movement set my mind functioning. "Great Heaven. Eugenie . . ."

"The queen remains in her unnatural sleep. No worse. But I must leave the palace for a few hours, half a day at most, and need my absence disguised. I can't divert Ilario while he stands watch with Antonia, so I've come to you."

"You're *leaving*?" I sat up straighter, appalled. "This plot is ripe enough to burst. I don't care if the pastille only made her dizzy. They've done this to Eugenie to keep her apart from the king, to keep her *here*, where they raise a revenant king who visits her in a bedchamber bedecked with fertility charms."

"Fertility, yes. But you think . . . with *Soren*? Not possible . . ." Yet his pause reeked of doubt.

"The storm is almost on us," I said. "Surely you sense it. And there's so much more. Did you not get my message? The Aspirant is *here*. Even in the dark, when he believes no one is listening, he gloats that the universe will never be the same." Somehow in middle-night, without distractions, the weight of the Aspirant's threat near crushed the breath from me. "We should be questioning every man in this house!"

"Two thousand people move about this house in a day, three-quarters of them men." His urgency to be gone set the air aquiver. "Questioning would serve nothing."

"What if the Aspirant is a Gautier?"

"It wouldn't help us identify him. I've theorized about Gautier or Mondragon survivors, made inquiries, followed leads that were little more than spidersilk, but all for naught. No portraits remain for comparison. I've uncovered no identifying characteristics. And to have lived so deeply hidden for so many years, no simple questioning is going to expose him. Why do you ask?"

I told him about the pendant Dante had shown me in the Bastionne and the three keys Lianelle had kept with her spellworking particles. "I think she learned who he was. That's why she had to die."

"Merciful saints! It would certainly explain a plot to upend the Sabrian kings—who issued orders to exterminate the remnants of his family, and tear apart the Camarilla—who agreed to terms with that king. The index to the Mondragon codices could have been passed down through the remnants of his family." His words slowed. "If the Aspirant is the man we know as Michel de Vernase, that would explain how your sister could unravel their encryption so easily. And you . . ."

He caught his breath. "Damoselle, you must not breathe a word of this possibility to anyone. No matter the differences in the world's opinions of Gautieri works versus those of the Mondragons, the law makes no distinction. Any Gautier or Mondragon connection must be reported. This will take some untangling."

"My father is not Gautier." Suspecting the far worse truth, my assertion rang hollow. "And he is not the Aspirant. . . ." I recounted everything I'd heard between Dante and the Aspirant in the Rotunda. "Dante so much as told me in the Bastionne that he aimed to trade places with the Aspirant—and also that he didn't know his master's identity. They're rivals, just as you told me at the beginning. The bearded 'prophet' who can't learn Dante's spells is surely Kajetan. But who was Kajetan's guest at Seravain, this down-on-his-luck nobleman?"

"I've not a guess as to his identity, but, it's curious; I think I've seen him."

Perhaps it was only the flicker of weak candlelight, but Duplais' gaze seemed to have lost itself in the shadows, as if a revenant had manifested itself.

"In the year I was two-and-twenty, I was stabbed, a severe wound that damaged me in many ways, far more than I understood at the time. Over many months Kajetan brought me back to some semblance of health. Someone else visited us frequently in those days. But as often as I've revisited those events, until Ilario passed on your message yesterday, I had *wholly forgotten* this visitor. Even now, the more I try to recall the man's face or voice or anything about him, the more elusive the memory. Odd, yes? Hearing your tale, it makes more sense. Is he the Gautier, living in obscurity, using such magic to hide the existence of his family line? My illness occurred thirteen years ago. It *could* have been your father, but I've never believed him involved in conspiracy for so long a time. So, I've just sent off an inquiry to a cook who worked at Seravain in those days. It's possible that you and the friend you so bravely defended have provided exactly the clue we need."

"So, what do we do now?"

"We wait. And I go. Believe me, I'd not leave for anything but this. I'll return by midday and we'll find a way to talk."

But I'd have none of it. "Yesterday as the queen lay bleeding, Dante was creating something dreadful in his chamber—as if he'd ripped a hole in the world and painted a curse over it, written in a hieroglyph I could not translate. Just looking on it left me feeling sick . . . violated. . . ."

His agitation stilled. "A hieroglyph? An abstraction, you mean. Lines and colors, shapes without obvious meaning? He showed *you* such a thing?"

"He didn't know I was there. But yes. He knelt in that abominable circle and the thing hung above him, as if woven into the fabric of the air. When I interrupted him, it vanished. What was he doing? You know, don't you?"

Like a sculptor's chisel, pain recrafted Duplais' face, leaving the creases and tightness of a far older man. He pressed stained fingers to his forehead. "Spellwork, of course, though I've no idea what spell in particular. In the days we worked together, he showed me something like. His insights . . . Glory, he is so gifted, though he wears no mark and swore to me he carries no blood-family inheritance. I don't know what it means that you could see one of these patterns without him explicitly showing you."

Perhaps my cursed blood enabled me to see Mondragon spellwork.

"I can get the book of rites, Duplais. I'll bleed all over it if I have to, and you can read it and tell me what it means. We must know what they're planning."

"Do you imagine Dante will allow you to walk in and take a book they've killed for?" Pain sharpened his words. "And what would he do when he finds it missing?"

"I promise he'll never see me."

"Even if that was possible . . . think. The Aspirant plans to work this rite. But what if the book fails to reveal what form their chaotic vision will take? Do they plan to create weapons that drive bottomless holes in the earth to swallow their enemies, or that incite plagues of rampaging beasts? Do they plan to recruit the dead to go to war with them? If the book doesn't tell us and our precipitate actions push them deeper into hiding, we'll not know when or where or in what form they'll strike."

"We could return it before he's sure what's happened."

"You couldn't possibly—"

"I can and will." My patience was long ended. "I've a way. Certainly I'd rather just cut the Aspirant's throat and be done with it. But we're still meeting in my bedchamber in the middle of the night, as we don't know who he is. I'm not stupid enough to imagine we could force Dante to reveal anything, but we ought to stop him now."

A rueful laugh bore a sincere humor. "I've got to say, I'm seeing you in an entirely new light of late. Our swordsman friend was . . . effusive . . . in his description of your ferocity."

"My mother's kin were bandits for about five centuries. Some still are, I think, and they always hoped one of us would take up the family profession. Though Lianelle and Ambrose were far more likely . . ." My despicable voice wavered.

Duplais' slim hand found mine and squeezed hard. "The evidence yet points to your father as the Aspirant. Could it be Kajetan, instead, or could Kajetan be your father's rival for supremacy in the aftermath of their plot? Yes. He is driven by the belief that the glories of sorcery must not be displaced by the science of reason, which puts him at odds with the king. Could it be this visitor in Delourre colors? Yes. No matter who he is and what he plans, we'll take him down—"

"But for now we wait and gather crumbs while the Souleater's servant tortures my brother." I could not restrain my bitterness.

"Listen to me." Duplais' fervor—solid, substantial, healthy—passed through his hand to mine. "For four years I've gathered crumbs. I've investigated odd physical disturbances . . . every whisper of illicit sorcery, blood transference, strong magic, strange magic. I've studied all that's known of Ixtador and the Veil, and traced every inquiry made about them at temples throughout the kingdom. A few times I felt I was close enough to feel the Aspirant's breath whispering his plan in my ear. But every trail withered into nothing . . . until your extraordinary sister's death. Lianelle did not die in vain, damoselle. She breached the Aspirant's fortress of secrets, and you've become her worthy successor. We are so close to the end. Yes, I do sense it. I've this conviction—I wish I could convey how strongly I believe it—that we must not abort their scheme too early. It's not just a matter of identifying the traitor at the center of an assassination plot. This work—this magic—touches on the very boundary between human and divine, between Creator and creation, on the mystery of our nature, of our future beyond this life. We *must* understand it all. Thus we must hold patience and keep our own secrets and follow this trail to its hard end. Let them grow more confident. Then we pounce."

I hated his logic. I hated his faith. That his conclusions made sense left them no more acceptable.

"Antonia thinks to marry me off or kill me. But I must be at this culminating rite. To see . . ." To save my father.

"Antonia's wishes are of no moment in the Aspirant's scheme. Think, lady: You can open the *Book of Greater Rites* for Dante. Your brother and your father cannot. Dante would never have tested you in the Bastionne otherwise. Yet he could not have taken enough blood from you that night to translate the entire book. These vile magics ravage him, body and soul, and with Jacard banished, he has no one to take any share of the work. Yet Dante's truer weakness is his inexperience with human beings. I see him watching you, and he cannot decide what you are. But for certain, he plans for you to be there."

He laid my hands in my lap and retrieved his candle. "Don't allow the Gurmedd wretch to touch you. But move carefully. Right now they believe nothing can stop them. How arrogant they are—walking Philippe's palace while planning to rape his queen. It will be their undoing."

"You're a hard man, Duplais."

"I wish it could be otherwise. But now I *must* go. I've other oaths to uphold besides the one I swore to the king at the beginning of all this, and I cannot fail. So cover my absence. Watch your back always. And let events unfold, leaving the damnable book where it is for now. I'll be back by midday, and we'll decide what to do about it. The Creator's grace shield you, lady."

Even fully awake, I scarce heard him go. I'd no chance to reciprocate his blessing or urge him to watch his own back.

Further sleep was impossible, especially as I considered all the things I should have told or asked Duplais. About Lady Cecile's diagrams. About the shield bracelet. He ought to know about the possibility that my family was Mondragon, though it would likely harden his beliefs about my father. Midday, he'd said. The hours would crawl until he showed his face again.

Ixtador. If Dante could transport souls across the Veil and shape bodies for them, and if a revenant king could converse of favorite houses and hunting grounds, then what was to prevent Soren telling us the truth about the Realm of Trial and Journey or even what might lie beyond the Ten Gates to Heaven? The seduction of such knowledge was indisputable.

History recounted the games of kings and queens and those who challenged them. The prizes were never simple knowledge, even knowledge of the divine. The prize was always power—of land, of wealth, of sea routes or harbors, of subjugation, of numbers. I knew what power Antonia wanted, but Duplais seemed to share my notion of her as a pawn who would be sacrificed when the Aspirant made his play. What power did *he* seek? What would nobles pay to learn the secrets of the dead? A merging of the Temple and the Camarilla might serve as a balance to my goodfather's temporal might. But at the trial Duplais had said they wanted chaos, not balance.

As ever my thoughts ran in circles far from my starting point. With a sigh I dragged my coverlet over to the window seat and settled there to await the sunrise. The hours before dawn were always the loneliest of the night.

I leaned my head on the window mullions, closed my eyes, and let the voices of the aether flow over and through me, battered but no longer terrified by the onslaught. *Are you there?*

A faint sense of him—the pool of quiet solidity—held amid chaos. But he didn't answer. Perhaps he was bent upon a mysterious errand or coaxing his queen back to health. More likely he was asleep, as any sensible person would be.

Far outside the maelstrom, the relentless tower bells warned me of approaching day. I'd need to be at Eugenie's side by sixth hour to take Duplais' place.

Someone's seen to my injuries, I said. *He had kind hands and knew exactly what to do. I feel ever so much better. So I wanted to thank you for your advice. And for caring.*

I left it at that, hoping my friend would hear and feel my gratitude as he woke to greet the light.

25 OCET, SIXTH HOUR OF THE EVENING WATCH

"I'M SORRY, MY LADY. I'VE no idea where Duplais might be. I presumed he had discussed the schedule changes with you." I threw open my hands in helpless surrender.

"Inexcusable." Antonia dabbed her lips with a kerchief. An unsightly blister had erupted at the corner of her mouth, and no cosmetic had sufficed to hide it.

It had been difficult enough to pacify the dowager queen when I arrived instead of Duplais to relieve her and Ilario at sixth hour of the morning watch, but when I arrived again in the evening watch, she was ready to call up the palace bailiffs. *I* was ready to call in my goodfather's legions.

"I'd wager he went shopping for flowers in the dawn market," offered Ilario from the divan in the retiring room, where we had adjourned to discuss the matter. "He knows how Geni loves them, and this late in the season all the best ones are gone by seventh hour, though I've never seen how anyone could select flowers properly so early." Ilario had taken my lead from the morning, offering excuses plentiful enough and ridiculous enough to confuse a sphinx.

"Idiot! Do you believe it's taken him twelve hours to select a few flowers?"

I returned to the window and peered into the gloom. The gardens and maze beyond the windows were naught but a blurred tangle of green, gold, and autumn red obscured by a mournful drizzle. Despite my willing, the path from the stables and the carriage road remained deserted. "Wherever he's gone, it's likely the rain has delayed him."

"That's it!" chirped Ilario. "He's trapped. Riverside markets turn into a bog with the slightest drizzle. When he extracts himself, I do wish he'd bring ale from the Baithook. It is the finest in the city—such a rich, earthy subtlety to it. Though merely stepping into the Baithook is enough to soil the roots of one's hair, it is such a den of low and villainous scum. I scarce escaped with my life! I never could fathom why Gilles de Froux chose to meet me there last Cinq and then failed to come. I had kissed his sister's hand and paid her a few compliments, and he said we should meet at the Baithook and discuss it over a tankard—"

"Still your tongue, fool, or I'll have someone put a bit in your mouth." Antonia stormed out, dispatching the chevalier to fetch one of Eugenie's two night chamber attendants to take the watch with me. The damp had forced the gout-ridden Lady Eleanor to her bed.

I lit a few candles and dampened a sponge with wine. More than in any hour since she had fallen ill, Eugenie's heated beauty seemed poised on the verge of waking. "What are we to do, lady?" I said as I moistened her lips. "If this long sleep is your choice, I beg you wake. Together we might make a plan and confound these villains."

Sitting on the edge of her bed as the gray evening deepened toward night, I smoothed her hands with rose-scented cream. To pass the time and break the heavy quiet, I told her stories of my sister and brother and the grand occasions when Papa took us adventuring in the wild.

"What must I do, lord?" Eugenie's sighing words were almost obscured by the whisper of rain on the window.

"My lady, can you hear me?" I snatched up the purple-stained sponge and squeezed a few droplets onto her lips. Her tongue ran over her lips as if savoring the pungent flavor.

"A plan," she murmured. "A plan, beloved, else she wins and I lose you forever." She shifted. Tossed her head. Shoved away pillows and picked at the silken sheets as if they were binding her. "Come back to me, gracious lord. Touch me. I'm lost here . . . alone . . . desiring you. Only you, beloved."

I patted her flushed cheek. "Your Grace, you're safe in your own bed. 'Tis only Anne, here to help you. Can you open your eyes?"

She moaned and kicked at the tangled sheets. Opening her eyes, she sat bolt upright, throwing off my hands with such ferocity, it staggered me halfway to the window. "How dare you keep me from him!"

She swung her legs from the tall bed, slid down onto her feet, and took off across the room. But after only a few steps, she halted, swaying like a wind-whipped cedar.

"My lady!" I caught her before she crashed her head into a tabletop, but hadn't strength enough to prevent her slumping weight from pressing us both to the floor.

"Sorry. Sorry," she whispered as I scrambled out from under her and ensured neither of us had broken anything. "The world's spinning."

"If we can just get you up."

"He touched me with such sweetness, then vanished." Her words flowed thick as cold honey. Lips parted, eyes vague and uncertain, awash with tears as from unremembered dreams.

I pushed my shoulder under her arm, my right arm around her slim waist, and heaved upward. "Help me, sweet lady," I murmured.

We staggered forward two steps, until she swayed again. I lowered her to her knees before we toppled.

A draft from the passage signaled someone's arrival. "In here!" I called, trying to untangle my skirts and her shift and our feet.

Firm footsteps halted at the doorway, which was, unfortunately, behind me. "The queen's dizzy," I said. "Help me get her back to bed."

The newcomer stepped around us and hauled Eugenie to her feet as if she were a child. Unfortunately she was standing on my foreskirt, which meant all I saw of my rescuer was sober gray breeches and worn black boots that had been tramping in the mud.

That was enough to flood my eyes with relief. "Duplais! Saints' mercy, where have you been?"

"Has our clerk of hairpins deserted his post? How wretched for all of us." A sleek black glove slipped around Eugenie's waist. "He'll learn better than to take on matters he's ill prepared to handle. As will you."

"Mage!" Dante's hold on Eugenie reminded me of my night in the Bastionne, when his gloved hand snaked around me from behind and pierced my finger. Of the day he touched my mother's hand and broke her mind.

The instant my skirt pulled free, I scrambled up and took Eugenie's left side. "I can support her now."

But I couldn't. It was an awkward business getting her to the bed, as I was so much shorter than the lady, and the mage seemed reluctant to touch her. Even wearing gloves, he kept his fingers curled. Once we lifted Eugenie onto the high bed, the mage stepped away almost as quickly as he had bolted my cell at the Bastionne. Back to the window, he watched as I drew up the sheets to shield the queen from his scrutiny.

"Ever your stubborn father's stubborn daughter. A consummate liar, who can convince even the holy librarian of your innocence."

"Where do you keep my father?" I said, snapping my head up to meet his black gaze. "Have you drained his blood entirely? Have you left his mind a wasteland as you did my brother's, or broken it as you did my mother's? What has my family ever done to you that you take such pleasure in our torment?"

He cocked his head, while pulses of heat and cold scraped my skin as on that day at Seravain. But the pooled fire in my gut made me strong, and I did not flinch.

Abruptly he turned away to face the night through the window, and left me to breathe again.

"The man who taught me of sorcery was a healer," he said, the words arcing over his wide shoulders like spits of ice in a winter rain. "Uncollared. Unsanctified by the Camarilla, because he claimed no blood-family alliance and because he could not read, thus was unable to study their books of formulas. He provided only a few small remedies to his customers—a balm for burns, a physic for a man's failed rising, a charm for colic. Large in importance to those in need of them, of course, for unlike most spelled remedies, they worked.

"Word spread in the town. Laborers and householders flocked to his door. Over the years, merchants and noblemen joined them, only unlike the laborers and householders who saw a competent man who ran a fair business, they saw a fat, illiterate commoner with brown teeth and grease stains on his tunic. They took his remedies, but chose not to pay. His debts grew and when he applied to the nobles for payment, their bailiffs beat him. And when he applied for payment yet again, for he was a stubborn man, too, they diddled him to the Camarilla as an illicit practitioner.

"The righteous prefects lashed him as a lesson to all—and a favor to their noble friends—and branded him on the face, and hung him in a cage in the square. A delicate lady could likely not imagine what vermin and diseases a flayed fat man in a cage attracts over the space of three months, especially in Sabrian summer. Autumn was no relief, as he was blind and gibbering by then. Dead before the season's turn."

My stomach recoiled at the imagining. Did Dante's comrades know this story? And why had he told me?

As suddenly as he'd faced it, he abandoned the window and snatched up his staff left propped beside the door. A green storm had risen under his black brows. "Do not imagine I would trade a rat's tail for a noble-man's life, whether he was born to his name or raised from dirt. Nor will I weep for his woman or his whelps, not even if he be this Divine Aspirant whose altered world might better suit my taste."

Nor would he weep for pawners or moneylenders, I guessed, nor, most especially, for the Camarilla. The room rumbled with his hate. The city suffered for it.

"When your student friend Portier returns from his crumb sweeping, tell him the time for games and secrets is ended. I will see him in Ixtador. Together we shall await the Souleater and the last day of the world." He crossed the room in ten strides and vanished through the doorway.

Though the candlelight seemed brighter after Dante's leaving, a bitter taint lingered on my tongue and in my soul. My head hammered unmercifully, and surely every muscle detailed in Vendanni's *Catalogue Anatomie Humanae* ached. But it was my spirit fared worst, pulsing with burgeoning dread. Dante and his masters believed their altered world would come to pass.

I checked on Eugenie again. Smoothed her tangled hair, apologizing for my feeble efforts that necessitated Dante's touch. I eased the edge of the sheet from her clenched hands, only to be startled out of mind when her fingers curled about my wrist and her eyes blinked wide open.

"Don't let me sleep, Anne," she whispered, her dark eyes pooled with terror. Her skin pulsed as if the thready veins were covered with naught but thin-stretched silk. "Please, no more."

"Indeed, let's keep you awake for a while," I said, hopes rising. "But we'll not go walking just yet."

I stuffed extra pillows under her back and head. Laved her hands and patted her cheeks, yet her chin still drooped. Looking around for some other means of keeping her awake, my eye fell on the smelling salts the other ladies relied on so heavily. I snatched up the etched-glass vial half filled with brown crystals, uncorked it, and waved it under her nose.

"No!" She jerked her head aside and wailed softly. "Please, no! He'll come here again. . . ."

"Who, lady? Is it King Soren who comes?"

Her huge dark eyes filled with terror. "So beautiful, so commanding, so desirable. But he leads me to that awful place. I *saw* him once without the mask . . . hungry . . ."

Her heavy lids sagged. Her shoulders slumped.

"Lady! Eugenie! Stay awake! Who did you see? Where did he take you?" I held the vial under her nose yet again. "Who?"

Her response came in a thick-tongued whisper: "The Fallen. The Souleater. In my dreams he lies with me, rousing me until I burn. He says we'll rule Heaven together. Anne, help me. . . ."

Then she was asleep again, as if she had never stirred.

Confused, I corked the vial of smelling salts and set it on the bedside table. The candlelight set the wardstone on my finger gleaming—no longer benign silver, but the color of lapis. Not the color of poison, but of dangerous enchantment.

CHAPTER 33

"Only for an hour or two until Patrice arrives, Arabella, *caeri*," said Antonia, sweeping into the room with a stout woman of fifty-odd summers, whose outlandish wig resembled the rag-mop hair of Syan idols. "You've naught to do but supervise Anne; she is so new at this."

Heart galloping, I drifted away from the medicine box, as Antonia established the ample Contessa Arabella on a settee.

Antonia's patter flowed like cream. "Just make sure the nursemaid tastes anything brought, whether food, drink, or medicine. And if Eugenie stirs, keep her abed and use her salts, lest she faint and start the dreadful bleeding again. Anne, *caeri*, where are Her Majesty's smelling salts? The vial should be right here." Her jeweled fingers tapped the bedside table.

"I'm sure I saw it earlier," I said, spinning, my fingers wrapped tight around the very vial she wanted. "Ah, over here, my lady!"

I darted toward Eugenie's dressing table, and with an obscuring sweep of my shawl and a twist of my hand, sent the crystal bottle flying. "Oh no!"

"You stupid, clumsy wretch!" Antonia's screech must surely have waked half the palace.

"I'm so sorry, Your Grace! Where can I find more of the compound? From the physician? From the mage?"

"Cursed was the day you came here!" she said. "Cursed be your family, your ancestors." Her venom scalded the sickroom air.

Lady Arabella, shocked speechless at such blasphemy, waved her embroidery needles at me in some message to do with sweeping. Comprehending, I offered to fetch a servant to clean up the splintered glass and salts.

"Yes, yes." Antonia's strangled agreement spoke more of fear than anger. Her trembling hands rattled through the medicine box.

I would have worried more about the sweeping girl or Arabella, who had set her embroidery frame and a large basket of spooled silks in the vicinity, save that the original contents of the vial were wrapped tightly and stowed in my pocket. The scattered crystals were some more benign formula I'd retrieved from the medicine box.

Clever villains, to use smelling salts as a vehicle for their enchantments. Who would think to have a taster take a whiff each time such a thing was used, more common among court ladies than swatting flies? And with so many vials at hand, they could be switched easily. Was there some aromatic compound that could cause a hemorrhage, as this one bound Eugenie in unnatural sleep? Perhaps Roussel could tell me.

Not long after Antonia and the sweeping girl had departed, Lord Ilario tiptoed through the door. After proper greetings, he flung himself on the settee beside Arabella, wrapping his long arm around her shoulder and his confidences about her ear. "Dearest Lady Arabella, a most distressing matter. Your son, the Baronet Montmorency, such a charming boy, so delicate in his choices of fabrics. Honestly, I adore his rose stripes. Not to put too fine a point on it, but he loves his wine and his delicate health causes it to affect him so dreadfully. I've just had a report of a youth . . . rose stripes and ostrich plumes . . . uh, let us say . . . discharging . . . his dinner in the Faun Fountains or perhaps it was the Troll Regarde Fountain. Thought you should know."

Mumbled commiseration soon popped Ilario to his feet. He hauled the distressed Arabella up and into his arms. "Certainly I can escort you, dear lady! We'll borrow a footman or two. Dreadful frights in the courtyards . . ."

With handiwork as neat and quick as the contessa's own, Ilario whisked Arabella and her embroidery frame away. Only a few spools of rose silk remained behind. I presumed he had a reason for removing her, and remained alert.

Sure enough, shortly after ninth hour, a soft click signaled a visitor. Yet the noise didn't come from the outer passage, but from the wall to the left of Eugenie's bed. A rectangular wall panel opened a few centimetres. Either the door to the servants' stair had shifted its position or there was a second concealed access to her bedchamber.

My hand slipped into the fitchet in my skirt. I didn't draw my knife, but neither was I inclined to step up and shift the stool that blocked the door from opening further. Would a revenant need a doorway?

When a long arm clad in scarlet and trailing a year's output of a lace maker's art at the wrist reached through and dragged the stool aside, I relaxed my guard. Not ghostly Soren, but Ilario poked his fair head cautiously around the blue panel.

"None's here but me," I said.

"Good. Thank the saints for Arabella's easily seduced brat. I needed to speak with you alone." He joined me at the bedside, his eyes all for his sister. "How is she, truly?"

"Restless and dreadfully weak. But she doesn't seem to be in pain. I might have found the cause for all this . . ." I told him of Eugenie's brief waking, Dante's visit, and the smelling salts.

"Sante Ianne," he said, anguished, "I've offered her the vial myself. When she was so dizzy in the carriage, I may have given her the very dose that felled her. If there was a child . . ." He did not hammer his fists on the wall, but I would not wish to be the first of these conspirators who ventured within reach of Ilario de Sylvae's sword.

"For what comfort it might give, Roussel does not believe there was a child." The good knight's pain but hardened my resolve. "Chevalier, where has Duplais gone? He told me he had important business outside the palace, but he should have returned hours ago."

Ilario wrenched his attention from poison and murder. "I knew nothing but what you told us, until his man brought me this a short time ago. Portier charged Heurot to deliver it if he'd not returned by the middlenight. The lad was too anxious to wait longer." He passed me a smudged scrap of paper—a handbill for a play given years ago in the town of Archenase. A message had been scribed in a neat, even script.

To the kindest man in the world from the world's most pitiful gull: Though I forbade you oath swearing, hope tells me that your promise of aid remains sealed in your heart. I am desperate. Judgment for my folly looms like a headsman's ax. I'll wait at the crossroads at Voilline until sunset tomorrow.

Two additional lines, written in Duplais' bolder hand, appeared below.

Matters must have gotten more complicated. Forgive me for not confiding in you.
Keep to your path, friend. Trust the girl.

"The idiot!" I said. "*This* is what took him away? Look at this last; he suspected it was a trap!"

"The writer is surely Maura ney Billard," said Ilario, as he perched on the edge of Eugenie's bed, absently stroking her temple. "Portier claims he knew her too short a time to truly love her, but I observed otherwise. The lady reflected the sentiment, even before he risked his life and Geni's to get her out of the Spindle." He glanced over his shoulder. "I presume *you're* the girl to trust."

"Stupid, stupid," I murmured, holding the paper close to the lamp, as if I might see additional information squeezed amid the spare prose. Was Maura dupe, victim, or traitor? And Voilline . . . something nagged about it.

"I never thought the woman fool enough—or so careless of *his* safety—to return to Sabria," said Ilario. "She's dead if Philippe finds her.

And our librarian friend will be, as well, if he's found with her. If Portier's damnable holy righteousness fails again . . ."

I snorted. Ilario must truly be an innocent as his sister believed, an idealist at the least. "I've always considered Duplais' righteousness more daemonish than holy."

"You're not a Cultist." The quiet comment drew my attention from the page.

"You subscribe to the Cult of the Reborn?" I'd forgotten he wore the phoenix ring.

"Four years ago, I was sure I witnessed the two Invariant Signs made manifest. Certainly the refusal to die without meaningful purpose."

His earnest sobriety . . . reverence . . . from a person who personified irreverence banished all inclination to amusement. "You believed *Duplais* to be a Saint Reborn?"

"I saw him step out of a holocaust as the *Swan* burned and men died around him. And none but a Saint Reborn could have survived the battering he took at Eltevire. Then, but a few months ago, Portier told me about the night his father tried to murder him because he'd failed at his study of magic—because he could not elevate their family to their 'rightful rank' as royal kin. Portier believes he actually died that night and was returned from Ixtador. Kajetan was there and coddled him back to health, but conveniently forgot ever to mention the dying part."

Threads of connection knotted themselves into a lacework. "You don't suppose *Kajetan* believes this about him?"

Ilario shrugged. "The second Invariant Sign is an inerrant perception of righteousness, and anyone who knows Portier for more than an hour can see that honor and compassion are rooted in his bones. So I always assumed he saw something in Maura worth saving, the same as he did with Captain de Santo. I feared he had the same conviction about Dante, but he didn't defend the mad mage for smashing me to smithereens. I appreciated that."

"He doesn't defend Kajetan, either," I said, "though he wants to very badly. But that doesn't make him a reborn soul."

"Certainly not. Portier himself certainly doesn't believe it. It was the matter of his dreams had me convinced. He recounted a few of them on the road to Eltevire. Vivid dreams of extraordinary deeds . . . every one of which I could pull straight out of Cult texts."

"Great Heaven, *Voilline!*" Understanding set my blood racing. Not belief that Duplais was some altruistic soul repeatedly returned to life throughout history, but the meaning of the place he'd gone to meet his fugitive friend. "This came from a history text Dante was reading, about the Gautieri and the Mondragons and the last great battle of the Blood Wars."

The text poured from my lips: " 'Abandoning the broken Ring Wall, the Gautieri retreated into the Voilline Rift. . . . Backed deep against the foot of the crags where Ianne, the first Saint of the Reborn, had brought humankind the gift of fire, the valiant Gautieri mage line unleashed the fires of Creation.' "

Did Kajetan believe this cult idiocy or was it merely that his master, the Aspirant—the down-on-his-luck nobleman, the Gautier survivor—wanted to revisit the place where his ancestors had been slaughtered by the hated Mondragons?

I shook the treacherous paper. "This was a trap, and the fool Duplais suspected it before he went. This morning, he insisted I let events unfold, as that was the only way we could comprehend this grand scheme. That's exactly what he's done . . . full knowing. I don't know what they're going to do with him, but as sure as sunrise, they've take him to the Voilline Rift. That's where they're going to work their cataclysm."

"Not the rift," said Ilario, softly. "Portier told me about places on the earth where magic works better than others. People name them holy sites, like the field where the Creator planted the first grapevines, or cursed ones, like that damnable village of Eltevire, where stories say one human first shed the blood of another. He also told me that in one of his dreams, he was chained to a rock in punishment for a crime he could not remember."

Ilario extended his hand into the candlelight and twitched one long finger, setting the gold phoenix ring flashing. When he raised his gaze from the ring to meet my question, his blue eyes burned as if a thousand candles had been lit within.

"He didn't know me then—*this* me—so I didn't mention the Cult story. And I didn't know about the battle in the rift, but your text tells you. When Ianne the Blessed brought fire to humankind on Mont Voilline, he tore a rip in the Veil to fetch the flame from Heaven. Some say the Creator punished him for the damage by chaining him to the mountainside until he died, and that's why he chose to return to the world again and again instead of moving on to Heaven. Some say the Souleater chained him to the rock in vengeance for giving fire to humans, so they were less frightened of him and his Fallen, and that Ianne remained there forty years until his human friends could learn how to break the devilish chains. They've taken Portier to the mount, Anne. God's mercy, they're going to kill him—"

"Thinking he won't die," I said. If persons and objects carried intrinsic power, as my friend of the mind had told me, what power for magic might be bound up in a being who could refuse death?

"Or perhaps that this time, he will," said Ilario. "Killing one of the Reborn before his work is done must surely alter the universe forever."

"Lord, we must get the Mondragon *Book of Greater Rites* from Dante. Tonight. That way, when the king arrives tomorrow night we can tell him what they plan."

"I can arrange a meeting with Philippe. He's the only other person that knows . . . this." He pointed to himself and rolled his eyes. "But the damnable book . . . I'm willing, but last time I ventured into Dante's laboratorium, I ended up most of dead, and I am no Saint Reborn."

"I'm no saint, either," I said, "but I know a way to get the book and decrypt it. The mage will never know it's gone. As soon as you and Antonia return for the night watch, I'll steal it. But then . . . you wouldn't happen to know enough about magic to help me *interpret* the cursed thing?"

"Glory, woman, I've managed to fill my head with a few useful things through the years, but a scholar I am not. I still maintain Philippe's clocks are daemon work and that mathematics beyond calculating the cost of new breeches is a language meant for the Pantokrator and his angels."

"I've another friend who might be able to help me," I said, teetering on the unlikely verge of laughter. Or hysteria. "I'll get word to you when I can."

He kissed Eugenie on the forehead and let his temple rest against hers for a few moments. "Stay with me, sweet Geni," he said softly. "We'll fight through this and find your happiness."

Moving quickly, Ilario tweaked a piece of a gilded pilaster. The wall panel swung open. "Saints guard you, damoselle."

"And you," I said as the panel closed. "And all of us." I wished I had more faith in saints and angels. The daemons I already knew.

I COULD NOT PROCEED AS Duplais had asked me. I hadn't his faith that unfolding events would reveal the Aspirant and his plan in time for us to do anything about it. Believing that Eugenie's poisoning and Duplais' disappearance signaled the opening salvo in the final battle, I could wait no longer to take action. I hoped I was not too late already.

Thus at second hour of the night watch, I stood outside Dante's apartments, body and spirit a riot of nerves. *Fetch the book. Learn what they plan.* Words were so simple. *If he's awake, retreat and try again later.*

Lianelle's potion, as always, had opened me to the mindstorm—tonight in full frenzy. As always I listened for my friend, not intending to delay my mission, but only to feel his steady quiet, a solid anchor in the chaotic aether. But I could not sense him. All logical reasons for dismissing Duplais as my friend of the mind crumbled. What had they done to him?

The wind had come up in the middle-night hours, sweeping away the rain and mist. The waxing moon dodged scudding clouds and gleamed through the tall windows at the end of the sorcerers' passage. I would have preferred a darker night, no matter that Lianelle's magic had rendered me invisible. Human instincts are difficult to overcome with logic, especially when one walks the most illogical realms of sorcery.

I pressed my ear to Dante's door. Hearing no hint of activity within, I summoned every discipline of mind and pressed the latch.

Heat bit at my fingertips and riffled up my left arm. Bearable. The mage did not fear determined visitors. The heavy door swung inward. Catching it before it struck the wall, I crossed the threshold and closed the door softly behind me.

The unsteady moonlight bathed the sitting area before the great windows and the sorcerer's ring in the center of the room, but did not reach so far as his worktables. It was enough to tell me he wasn't there, asleep or awake. I released my pent breath.

I'd spent my last hours in the sickroom recalling every detail of Dante's chamber, trying to guess where he'd keep such a precious book. Well hidden, I feared, with his door so easily breached.

I would dismiss the easy places first. Barefoot, slippers stuffed into my belt, I padded over to the whitewashed bookshelves. Only a moment to survey the contents. Another to scan the volumes scattered on couch and tables.

I set aside a cold lamp and opened the lid of the schoolmaster's stool, a better hiding place. But its cavity sat empty save for the decades' tally of spilled ink and dropped penknives. No dust, though. Ours at Montclaire had an extra compartment.

With a frisson of anticipation, I felt around the thin molding that framed the bottom of the cavity. A gap marred its continuity, and I fiddled and pushed until a piece of the molding slid sideways. There was a similar gap on the opposite side of the cavity. I shifted the corresponding piece and with trembling fingers lifted the false bottom.

No Mondragon book. Only a motley stack of journals and unbound pages, written in an oddly skewed script. Some yellowed; some faded. Most of them hard used. They might provide fascinating reading, but the book must remain my focus.

Bitterly disappointed, I restored all and moved to the worktables. Gloomed in shadows, the laboratorium took more care. I dared not disarrange anything. Fortunately the mage seemed to keep his books separate from the clutter of his work—the sharp edges and implements that might tear fragile pages; the liquids, plants, and dirt that might soil them. I removed the lids of baskets and crates on the floor, peered under benches. A wooden case with a small latch opened to reveal five palm-sized silver spheres. So Dante wasn't out raising the dead this night.

Such a small volume could be tucked anywhere. Fate could not be so cruel as to dictate he'd taken it with him wherever he'd gone so late.

I riffled through stacks of papers in his cupboards, shifted polished wood cases, unstacked the piled herb boxes, hating the thought of abandoning the search. But my gut was tightening. He could return at any time. Foolish to imagine I would walk straight to the book, as if the stain of Lianelle's death might leave it incandescent.

Frustrated, I returned to the center of the room and circled slowly, hunting for some corner I had missed. The odd blue light that limned the world while I was under the influence of the potion sketched out a faint rectangular shape in the end wall opposite the windows. Another doorway. How had I failed to notice it on my earlier visits?

Amid a fusillade of nerves, I halted just inside, astonished. What would I expect to find in a mage's bedchamber? Corpses? Spiders? Vats of blood or boiling oil? Certainly not a bare closet, an ascetic's cell. Narrow bed. Battered clothes chest. A writing table holding ink bottles, stacked papers, a pen case. An old leather satchel resting on the floor beside it. The only oddity a bare knife blade protruding horizontally from the desktop—a wickedly dangerous position.

I was stooping to examine litter on the floor below the blade when a booming crash from the other room stood me up straight, nearly causing me to impale myself.

Get out. Get out. Every sensible bone in my body screamed at me in warning. I crept to the doorway, hugged the wall, and peered into the great chamber.

The cloaked and hooded mage propped his staff just inside the doorway. Its support relinquished, he paused to readjust a large bundle laid across his shoulders. Hooking the wide-open door with his foot, he nudged it closed behind him. For a moment, he sagged backward, resting the shapeless burden against the oak panels. His breath grated hard enough that I could hear it from these six or eight metres distant.

The bundle's burdensome weight was confirmed when he rolled it off his back and dropped it inside the amber ring. The muffled clank of metal shivered the wood floor. Not a corpse, then.

He dropped to his knees, yanked open the mouth of the large canvas bag, and extracted a length of heavy chain, tangled and gleaming dully in the darting moonlight. And then another length. And another. Five or six in all.

Bag emptied, the mage climbed wearily to his feet, picked a few items from his shelves, and set them around the heaped chains within the circle. I could identify only a few: a knife, a copper bowl, a small skull . . .

Needles pricked my spine.

From his cloak he pulled a flask that he emptied into the bowl, a flat tin containing chips of stone that he mounded across the circle from the bowl of water, and a flat rectangular object—a bound book of some kind, both too large and too thin to be the *Book of Greater Rites*. He laid the book atop the chains. When all was arranged, he abandoned the circle and headed straight for me.

Blood-pulse galloping, I drew back from the opening and pressed my back to the wall. He passed so close I could smell the outdoors on him—sweat-damped wool, horse, the smoke of autumn fires.

After only a few steps, he halted and swung around to peer into the dark behind him. My heart near stopped. I dared not even blink.

"Gods and daemons," he muttered, ripping off his cloak and throwing it atop the clothes chest. "Lunatic." A leather jerkin scudded across the floor, and the man sat heavily on the bed, not five steps from me.

Even as I dreaded it, my nose began to itch. No matter my bare feet or the thin wool gown I'd worn apurpose to be quiet, if I so much as twitched, he would hear it. And I was well within his reach.

His forearms rested on his knees. His head sagged. Whatever his thoughts as he contemplated his boots, they did nothing for his temper. He rose abruptly and left the little bedchamber, kicking a toppled basket out of his way so hard its contents—thin branches, it appeared—scattered all the way to the embedded circle.

It required my every discipline to remain still. And indeed Dante returned almost immediately with a lit taper that he jammed into a holder on the writing desk. Its light scarce spread beyond the few papers on the desk, but it showed me something unexpected. His hands, still clad in his ever-present black leather gloves, were trembling.

Did his tremors rise from fatigue, anger, or something worse? If Dante was afraid of what he was about to do, I wanted to be well away. *Let him choose sleep now. Saints, please.*

He bent over the clothes chest and fumbled with his cloak. When he turned around, his hand clutched a small book. Unmistakably the one I sought.

Patience. Patience. I could almost reach out and touch it.

He tossed the little codex on the writing table and peeled off his gloves. The sight shocked me cold. I had never seen Dante without gloves and now I knew why. His left hand was wide, with long, strong fingers. But the right was a purple-scarred ruin, constricted into a rigid claw.

Memories bombarded me. Of those few hours ago when he supported Eugenie without using his curled fingers. Of him grabbing me so oddly in the Bastionne Camarilla, his back to my face so that his powerful upper arm clamped my right arm still, while his capable left hand pierced my finger. Of the way he so often crossed his arms across his chest, his staff tucked into the crook of his right arm. He never ate with the household and I'd always assumed it was merely his distaste for noble company.

Was it shame that caused him to hide its ugliness? Or a fear of appearing weak? Some would denounce such deformity as a mark of the Fallen—the Souleater and his kin who refused to bow to the Pantokrator at the Creation. A month ago I would have scoffed at such tales.

His unscarred hand thumbed the pages of the little book, then slammed it shut and dropped it into the satchel on the floor. He strode into the great chamber and retrieved his staff. This time he did not return to the bedroom, but to the sorcerer's ring. A wave of the staff and a mumble of words and the broad ring began to pulse with light, birthing low flames that snapped and hissed.

Blessing the kindly fates, I reached into the satchel to retrieve their gift. A razor knife scoured my hand. I yanked it back, biting my lips to keep from screaming. No blood. No wounding. But the mindstorm surged against the barriers in my head and wriggling worms curled in my abdomen.

All right, then. I plunged my hand in again. Fire surged up the bone from hand to elbow. I could not bear it long enough to grab the book. But I gritted my teeth and went straight back to it. This third time, when I pulled the little book from the satchel, I almost dropped it for the agony in my fingers. The smallest one and the one next it felt broken, and the healing wounds from the black cords stung as if packed with brine.

Dante remained outside the fiery ring, his forehead resting on the white wood of his staff. The air felt tremulous, unstable, a withering quiet. . . .

Jaw clenched, book clutched to my breast, I edged through the doorway. I had witnessed the intensity of the mage's concentration as he worked. That should obscure any telltale of my presence. I picked my way through the scattered branches. Past the worktables and cupboards. As I crept behind the mage and angled toward the door, the flames gave me a good look at the object Dante had placed atop the chains. A well-worn brown folio, cloth bound. No one who knew Duplais would fail to recognize his journal, which made the story of this enchantment— Holy gods!

The firelight shivered. Ruthless, I reined in fear and anger. The book was all. Take an extra step or two past the opening and I could crack the door only slightly, slip through, and be away with my prize.

But as I reached for the latch, a boiling fury erupted all around me.

Dante hurled his staff across the room. The stick struck one of his worktables, setting off a noisy cascade of toppling boxes and shattering glass. Roaring, he crumpled the emptied bag and lobbed it at the hearth. White flames exploded around and through it, illuminating the dirty canvas and consuming it almost as one.

His rage made his display at the Arothi reception seem but a mime. Though the violence was not directed at me, its pressure drove me backward until my back slammed against the bookshelves and my head jostled the little painting on the wall. The lighthouse. So small. So lovely. The artifact that did not fit in this daemon's den.

The mage scooped up the scattered branches and launched them at the hearth, followed by stones from a broken urn that clattered like hailstones against the marble mantelpiece. Stray missiles flew into the flames, causing them to blaze high in bloody scarlet.

The moon's light dimmed as my head filled with black fire. Molten iron flowed in my veins, scorched my heart, seared the raw edges of mind and feeling with words and images of grief and loss: *Blighted days . . . harsh duty . . . blistering fate . . . plans wholly awry . . . too far . . . too deep . . . Something incomparably rare . . . the fragile roots ripped out . . . every blessed thing in this life twisted to murder and blood, darkness and death . . . Oh, gods, too cruel a death . . . for the past, for a fancy, for a whim . . . This selfish hunger for something of order, of beauty, of light and worth to fill these caverns and pits of midnight . . . tainting the gift . . . squandering the glory . . . for what?*

The burden of anguish, of terror, anger, despair, and regret swelled huge in my skull, and I did not understand why, because fear had wiped my thoughts clear of anything but escape. Only I dared not move lest the madman discover my presence and turn on me.

He flung up his arms, and I tried to melt into the wall because surely his rage would bring the plastered ceiling down on our heads, and the roaring came louder as he wrapped his arms over his head and bent near double.

Pain tore through my gut. Paralyzed my chest. . . . *Must* not *feel this . . . Necessity will leave me a husk . . .* feeling *it will leave me dead . . .* Nonsensical thoughts.

Why didn't the entirety of Merona wake to his bellowing?

The flames on the circle hissed softly and went out. The mountain of ash in the hearth slumped with a soft plop. My ears registered the sounds clearly. The chamber was quiet, the mage huddled—soundless—around his gut. Yet the grief and anger raged on, and blocking my ears did no good . . .

. . . because all of it was inside me. None of these thoughts or feelings was mine. They echoed from the lonely chaos of the mindstorm. That voice . . .

As a flight of arrows strikes close targets one upon the next upon the next, so images and phrases raised from memory slammed my reason in rapid succession:

A mutilated hand . . . *the perils of untended wounds . . . don't cripple yourself . . . a lesson recalled when sharpening pens . . .* and a knife blade protruding from a desk with shavings on the floor beneath.

Night-blooming plants and uncanonical magic . . . *All Dante cares about is magic . . . his extraordinary gift.*

My work does not go well of late. Answers elude me. And in a different voice, a different venue: *the nireal working eludes me.*

He has no understanding of people. . . . I've no experience of exemplary marriage. . . . Nor any understanding of family, of jests, or of whimsy.

The blast of malevolent fury that had driven me to huddle in a corner that first night in the throes of magic and scream into the mindstorm . . . the same night a quiet, passionate voice had spoken to me, *Gods, there has been no one ever. . . . Trust me.*

Light . . . seeing . . . that's the finest pleasure . . . these uncovered windows . . . *I detest the dark . . .* and a hunger for *something of order, of beauty, of light and worth to fill these caverns and pits of midnight.* And the single item in these daemons' chambers that spoke of something beyond magic—the delicate watercolor of a lighthouse . . .

Dante. I screamed the name into the aether. His head snapped up.

Magic was all about seeing. And at last I saw my friend of the mind.

CHAPTER 34

26 OCET, BEFORE DAWN

I wrenched open the door and fled Dante's chamber, revulsion and denial boiling out of me unchecked, unguarded. To think of him inside me . . . the monster who had broken my mother, who had raped my brother's mind . . . the madman who challenged the boundaries of Heaven, toying with dead souls and feeding on grief. I felt filthy. Violated. I had told him things I'd shared with no one else in the world.

I pelted through the corridors of the east wing, careening through the ragged arch onto my hidden balcony just in time to vomit over the rail. Then I backed into the corner and gripped my rattled head with shaking hands. *Be calm, girl*, I said. *Think. Get the mindstorm under control.*

Shock and terror had smashed my barriers to dust. Nothing could have been hidden from him in that moment.

Not since that first night of chaos had I struggled so to build the barriers that kept me from madness. One by one I tried shoving the clamoring voices, the fretting ones, the laughing, the fearful, aside. But it was like herding snakes or building a wall of leaves in a gale. Creator's fire, of all things in the world, I had a strong mind. Knowing him now, knowing the danger, I could not allow him to destroy it.

I tried again. This time I didn't search for that quiet island I had clung to these past days. As on the first night of this madness, I carved out my own.

Think, Anne. I couldn't hide on the balcony. I needed to separate myself from the *Book of Greater Rites* and tell someone where to find it. Ilario's man had left the piled rubble in appropriate disarray when he'd removed the ugly dream charm. Had that been Dante's idea, too—to evoke dreams of a woman's burning parents? Despicable.

My shaking hands slid the book under the stones and shoved the chunks of plaster, splintered wood, and rotted molding around to disguise it. Now . . . a message to Ilario. He must find someone trustworthy to translate the book or destroy the wretched thing. If I could spark fire as Dante could, I'd burn it here and now. Yet Lianelle had given her life to preserve what it could tell us.

I abandoned the balcony as quickly as I'd come. Ilario would be with the queen for hours yet. The good physician would certainly pass a message for me, but Ilario had been sent to fetch him, and Roussel, ever diligent in his care, would stay with Eugenie through the morning. That left Heurot, which meant I needed Ella.

Brushing off my gown, I took out for my bedchamber, nodding to a sleepy chambermaid carrying tea, and a slouching footman posted at the clock. The girl dipped her head. The footman stiffened his back. So the potion had worn off. Good.

Duplais' stool at the corner of the passage remained ominously vacant. "Angels guard you," I murmured, trailing my hand along the planed curve of the seat. "And if you are what your chevalier friend believes, this would be a fine time to show us."

I rang for Ella, but it would take her a little time. As I waited, I splashed my face and dusty hands with the cooled water from the pitcher. Then I transferred a few items from my hidden drawer into a large kerchief: the copper shield bracelet, Lianelle's nireals, Lady Cecile's book, and the scrap of paper from her drawer that I did not yet understand. They needed to go to Ilario with my message.

I set out paper and ink and began sharpening a pen. Steadying my shaking hands, I shaved the curve into the tine. Inevitably I recalled the blade embedded in Dante's writing table. He had devised a serviceable method for a man with only one usable hand to do this simple task, but a dangerous one, requiring one to be ever vigilant. He could not do just anything with his magic.

We must speak. I'll not harm you. His words struck like javelins sent straight to the mark. Staggering in their strength, but devoid of emotion.

Words before actions. That surprised me. Perhaps he'd not yet discovered his book missing. Perhaps he thought I was stupid.

To prolong this contact was the last thing I wanted, yet I needed time. *Why would I believe anything you say? You told me you were a teacher. I felt no warning of untruth.*

You told me you were plain, dull, poor, and had no family connection likely to lure a desirable suitor. I felt no warning of untruth. Obviously, from your frame of reference, you did not lie, yet many would dispute your statements.

It's not the same— No, I would not be drawn into argument. Already my hands betrayed me, warming at the mere sensation of his speaking. As if he'd touched them.

I was revolted. What could he possibly have to say to me?

Safety was no longer an issue. If he wished me dead, he'd not hesitate to strike. Once I had passed on my bundle of evidence and the book, I would have done what I could to satisfy Lianelle's purpose. Perhaps I could buy time for Ilario to get it away from Merona. And, indeed, curiosity would not be denied.

Face-to-face only, I said. I needed to see him, hear his true voice. *In one hour. In a public room.* Whatever his plan, I should have a witness, be it a sweeping girl or a kitchen boy.

There followed a moment's withdrawal, one of those intervals we used to reshape our words to keep them true. To hide what we would not tell. To protect secrets. Father Creator, such secrets he had been hiding!

Yet why bother with reshaping if he could manipulate my perceptions? The things I had learned of my friend could not be truth. Not when that person was Dante.

Face-to-face, then, he said. *In one hour. But I cannot allow my allies to see us together, any more than you can allow your queen or her courtiers to see you treating with me. Choose a place we'll be private, and swear you'll not reveal our meeting to anyone. I say again, I will not harm you.*

Could he detect my own lies? He might just have made a lucky guess that night we quizzed each other. But he hadn't hesitated even for a moment. I'd best keep to the truth.

One more mistake would not make this greatest of follies worse, yet I would not yield all of his conditions. *The summerhouse in the heart of the maze*, I said. *And I promise to tell no one of our meeting before it occurs. You'll have to convince me not to do so afterward. As to harm, I don't believe you.*

One hour from now. If you have second thoughts, you know how to tell me.

And he was gone. No threats. No attempt to deny who he was or the things he had done. That surprised me. He was no quiet eddy in the mindstorm, either. That did *not* surprise me.

He was right that a public conversation would do my reputation no good. One hint of my connivance with Dante, a man despised and feared by everyone in both households, and suspicions would be raised about my loyalties. Lady Eleanor would recall my query. Mention of the device I'd shown her would recall the copper bracelet to Eugenie. And even if the queen never woke, my interest in a forbidden symbol could link my father's murky origins to the Mondragons. The remnants of my family would be exterminated.

"Damoselle? Are you ill? Damoselle Anne?" Ella's round face poked into the room, even while her fingers tapped a roundelay on my door. Her cheek wore the red crinkles of her pillow and her hair was bed-tousled under her cap.

"Dear Ella." Emerging from my own mindstorm, I threw my ring in the kerchief with the other things and tied the corners into a knot. "Sorry to drag you out so deep in the night. Can you pass a message to Heurot? Right now?"

"Now? Well, I doubt—" She blinked. "Aye. He planned to sleep in Sonjeur de Duplais' room, as he was so worried about him not coming back when he was expected. But you'll not tell anyone, damoselle, will you? It's presumptuous, and he could be accused—"

"I'll not breathe a word. And Ella, I'll ask your same discretion about what I'm doing. This is for Sonjeur de Duplais' safety and the queen's."

"You know I'll do anything for you, damoselle."

"You're a good girl, Ella," I said as I set about writing a message to Ilario. "You were my first friend here. I'll never forget that."

Her expression crumpled in worry, bereft of its ever-present caution. "Oh, damoselle, are you leaving us?"

I smiled and shook my head. "Not until I set some things to rights."

"About your family? It must be so awful, the things I've heard." She whose father made bricks sixteen hours of every day, and whose drunken mother had been trampled by a carriage horse.

"My father didn't do the things they say. My sister, not much older than you, died because of it, but she was as strong as you and immensely brave, as much as any Sabrian knight ever was. So I must be strong and brave as well."

I scribbled the note to Ilario, outlining the meaning of the items in the bundle and telling him that the object of my search was in the same place he'd found "the devilish bracelet." I told him that the person who had held the object was sure I'd taken it and was forcing me to meet with him. Ilario was not, under any circumstance, to trade the book for my life.

If worse came to worst, I hoped he would ignore that last and come riding to my rescue. My feeble courage did not extend to self-murder.

"Heurot must deliver this letter and this packet into Chevalier de Sylvae's own hand at seventh hour of this morning's watch, unless I inform him otherwise. He is to use every precaution to keep it from the attention of anyone else. Duplais' very life may depend on it. Is that clear?"

"Aye. I can get them to him in a clean slops jar. None will ever look in that. We'll figure a way to get them to . . . Did you say Chevalier de Sylvae? Are you sure?"

"You needn't worry. Lord Ilario will pass them on to someone with more wit and forget about it before he has his breakfast."

Her smile was tight. "I suppose that makes sense."

Ella fetched the promised slops jar, and we stuffed the bundle and the note inside. One more thing to tidy up. "If at any time I should vanish without telling you . . . if no one in the palace has seen me . . . I want you to take the jewelry and money from the hidden drawer in the armoire and run away, as far from this palace, as far from Merona, as you can get. Take Heurot, if he'll go." I dropped the key beside my grandmother's tessila.

"Oh, damoselle!"

The bells rang a quarter past fourth hour. The palace would soon be waking. A quarter of an hour and Dante would be waiting.

I dispatched Ella with a hard embrace. One drop of Lianelle's potion and I was off. I wasn't an entire fool.

CHAPTER 35

The *escalon*, or maze, that gave my goodfather's palace its name was a whimsical garden, mingling colorful wildland flowers like gorse and broom with cultivated blooms like hibiscus and cascading bougainvillea. Poppies, wallflowers, and myriad colorful denizens of the maquis popped up in unexpected places, making the winding paths wholly different and wholly beautiful in every season. One needed Lord Ilario's height to see over the tangled walls.

In the heart of the maze stood a rustic summerhouse. Even in the summer doldrums, a breeze could find its way through the latticed walls and bentwood arches to those who played or read or conversed beneath the vine-clad roof beams.

The airs were not so benevolent in these tarry hours before dawn. The moon hung huge and low in the west, almost obscured by racing clouds. Humid gusts thrashed the slender branches and whipped them into my face. But I gripped my shawl and welcomed the wild weather, the better to disguise my presence at the verge of the clearing.

No light shone through the latticework. The sorcerer had arrived minutes before, dark head bowed into the wind. Alone.

A cold raindrop struck my cheek as I circled the grassy clearing before venturing inside, assuring myself that no one else lurked in the shrubbery. Silly for me to take some solace from that. He might be able to summon the Aspirant with a call of the tangle curse.

The wooden step creaked under my slipper. I cursed silently, but his startled jerk allowed me to pick him out of the dark. He perched cross-legged atop a table pushed into a corner. His staff, gleaming white in stray moonlight, was propped against the wall at the opposite end of the elliptical structure. Was that to lull my fears?

It didn't.

Deeming it best to let the invisibility potion wear off in the deepest shadows, I slipped around the periphery toward a stretch of solid wall. The floor might be less likely to creak along the edge.

Dante jumped up, halting my steps. But he merely moved to one of the arched openings and rested a fist on each facing. Raindrops spattered on the steps and whispered across the grass beyond him. Uncloaked, his gaunt frame stood outlined against the night. He wore no gloves.

As the potion lost potency, the mindstorm faded into a muted chaos. Somehow all the incisive opening volleys I had planned along the way faded as well. In the dark, scarce able to pick out his shape, all I could remember were snips of past conversations . . .

No, not dead. Just buried in a place I'd rather not be.

It is so . . . fine . . . to hear another . . . to know I am not the only one.

The aether is the medium of souls.

Yet the most memorable part of our exchanges had not been the words themselves but the richness . . . the completeness . . . of their speaking: all the shyness, longing, wry humor, sympathy, emptiness, the shared wonder at the sky and its principled behavior, our awe at magnificent ideas, yet another form of seeing.

How could a daemon who had *little understanding of people* falsify such perceptions? How could one who demonstrated such . . . exaltation . . . at the marvels of the natural world scheme to upend it? He had expressed a reverence for magic and a prickly sensitivity to injustice. He had bought me a reprieve. *To prison you with an unworthy partner would be abomination.*

"Where is Duplais?" I said, reclaiming anger with memories of Ambrose's terror and Eugenie's blood and children with empty eyes—true abominations.

He spun, startled, picking me out of the shadows. "Is there no end to the lady's surprises?"

The cold, flat baritone, so different from that other voice, banished my febrile imaginings.

"You wished to speak," I said. "So begin. Tell me how you came by Duplais' journal. He would not part from it willing."

"We've a great deal to discuss before we get to that. Such as how you were present in my chamber without me seeing you. And you must return—"

"Why did you break my mother's mind?"

He turned his back on me then, returning to his position in the doorway. "You are blind, muleheaded, and naive. I saved your mother's life."

I almost choked. "A life of chewing her nails until her fingers bleed? Of setting her home afire to purge it of daemons? Of forgetting her children's names?"

"She was going to be silenced one way or another. She is not dead. Someday you may be grateful for that."

"*Grateful?* Then I'm sure to be delighted at what you've done to my brother. Where is he?"

"I've no idea."

"I don't believe you."

"Then there is little point in asking questions." The air between us crackled. "I said we needed to talk, not interrogate one another."

"I say nothing more until you tell me one true thing. Anything." And then my tongue made a liar of me, continuing without my consent to the question threatening to fracture my skull, as if my eyes were trying to see two distinct bodies occupying the same space. "What *are* you?"

A complete and utter lunatic.

His answer struck me with such astonishing clarity, and such abject, reluctant, bitter *horror*, as if he had been forced to strip naked and reach into the maw of a lion, that for one moment I did not realize he'd spoken in that other voice and not the one directed at my ears. And if deep and abiding belief made an assertion true, then no one had ever spoken more honestly. I was speechless.

"I could give you a thousand reasons for that assessment," he snapped, his manner redolent of his night's fury. "Wanting what I want. Living as I do. Imagining that the one honest man in the world gave me a purpose that only I could fill."

He reversed positions but remained in the doorway. The night trapped in the summerhouse left his visage a cruel imagining.

"But let me begin with my lunacy with regard to *you*. Born in a *tent*? Delivering *foals*? Gadding about the wilderness with a collection of schoolmasters, reciting legends of *star patterns*? And naive—gods save me from abject idiocy—trusting a person you've never seen and traipsing off to meet Raissina Nialle, who makes dockside thief lords tremble. The moment Raissina reported she had no information about you to sell me— and I did *not* ask her for it, by the by—I should have known you had managed a deception I believed impossible in the medium of souls."

His vehemence drove me backward.

"This astounding person, so oddly simple, so incredibly complex, so . . . jubilant . . . unlike anyone I've ever encountered—gods, you asked me if I was *dead* as innocently as if that might be possible without corruption. Made me want to inquire if you were one of these angels the damnable peacock lord babbles about. Who could guess that this clever maid in the aether, sharing a curse I'd come to believe was mine alone, could be the aristo knife-tongue, the daughter of Michel de Vernase, a woman who in less than a month confounded Warder Pognole, the most calculating brute in five kingdoms, wormed her way into the queen's bedchamber confidences, and rousted the sneaking vermin Jacard to a panicked mistake the size of all Sabria . . . the same woman who *reeked* of power and illicit secrets from the day she walked into Castelle Escalon, yet hid it all behind the most formidable mental barriers this side of the Aspirant himself? Even yet I've not disentangled that enchanted powder from your bedchamber."

He paced like a chained beast, never coming so much as a step closer to me. A good thing, that. Light-headed, my nerves pricking as if spiders traveled along them, I was near bolting.

"Once only did the notion pass through my mind that the two might be the same person, but I dismissed it, assuming it was a result of this work I do. Overreaching . . . undoing in the night all I do during the day . . . creeping corruption . . . this incessant, flaying, devouring need to strike . . ."

I gasped . . . confounded . . . remembering: *light . . . that's life's finest pleasure . . . but, of course, some work has to be done in the dark.* "Stars of Heaven, you're still Duplais' man!"

He blew a rude disparagement. "The cursed librarian knows naught of what I do. Or, rather, he put me here and goaded me to do it, but he has no understanding. He would not approve my course, and I don't care a whit what he would approve. But he is naive, like you. He wanted the scheme unraveled with clean hands; then he arranged for inquisitors to haul me to the Bastionne, where I learned that such was impossible. A price must be paid for knowledge. I've done so many— But those things don't matter. Do not expect me to apologize. Yet if any value is to come from all this, if you want the truth, if you want this stopped . . ."

His hand flew to his hair, yanking on his queue as if to wake himself, yet succeeding only in pulling more wild strands loose. "Gods, I've not actually talked with anyone in four years, so I'm prattling nonsense like the popinjay, and you're sure I am the Souleater's minion . . . or a murderous lunatic . . . which I surely am. But the world teeters at the brink of a chasm from which it will not recover, and I don't give a horse's ass about the world, but they're going to make me kill the self-righteous little prick to accomplish this rite, and I'm already mad, as I've told you, so I've this notion that you're the only person in the world who can help me stop it . . . and save his annoying, godforsaken, priggish balls."

The summerhouse trembled as he stomped down the steps and into the spattering rain. He didn't go far. As my knees had turned to wet cotton with this vehement outpouring of arrogance and grief, that was just as well. It meant I didn't have to chase after him to confirm that Duplais was the *self-righteous little prick* he wanted to save. He stopped a few paces from the steps, letting the rain hammer on his head and sluice over his shoulders and back, while the silks of this malevolent tapestry, animated like his black snaketethers, wove their murderous story.

A man with no family, no connections, no friends. Even Duplais, who had brought Dante here, who had formed some sort of bond with the prickly sorcerer, had come to believe him corrupt and vicious. Yet Dante had taken exactly the path Duplais propounded. *Keep your secrets. Let events unfold. Do the hard things that are necessary.* Duplais had said the sorcery the mage pursued drove him deeper into the dark, ravaging him body and soul. And then came this night, when his masters told him he must murder the man he believed the one honest man in the world.

Anguish at what his course demanded—and fear at the price he would pay for it—had sparked his tirade this hour past. Chains, knife, Duplais' journal . . . *so cruel a death* . . . uncanonical spellwork. *Necessity will leave me a husk* . . . feeling *it will leave me dead.* . . .

The rain should be stirring the scents of the dying garden: lingering flowers, drying leaves, hardy green grass. Instead it reeked of sulfur. A world teetering at the brink of a chasm.

I crossed to the door. The gray raindrops spattered in unnatural patterns, some leaping high like balls of hard rubber, some looping, some not rebounding at all, but chasing other droplets across the step. Chaos.

"What do you mean by undoing what you do in the day? The queen lies ill and despairing. My mother remains confined. Father Creator, did you send my sister to her death?"

He faced neither toward me nor away, but exactly at right angles. His arms were folded across his chest, empty without the staff. Different. Less formidable, his frantic energies spent.

"I did not kill the girl, nor did I advise it, drive her to it, or ignore its prospect," he said in his more customary even measure. "It happened very suddenly. But certainly I bear responsibility. I have consorted with those involved. I made sure it was not investigated. As with all this, you must believe as you please."

I could not answer. What use a list of crimes, when he had already conceded guilt?

"As to the undoing . . . The Aspirant's objective—this magic I help them work—is no less than the permanent overturn of natural law. Portier saw a hint of it at Eltevire, but he had no idea of the scale. The Aspirant believes that if we penetrate the Veil sufficiently, create a big enough hole and seal it open, we will invert the order of nature entire—the laws of physics and alchemistry, the behavior of weather, of oceans, the instincts of animals. It will be madness. With the natural world no longer predictable, a terrified populace will turn back to mysticism. To sorcery. But, in truth, I don't think the Aspirant cares about the result so much as the doing."

Hand of Heaven . . . to hear it stated so bluntly . . . Reason called his claim absurd, and yet the things I had seen in the city . . . in the Rotunda . . . in Dante's own chamber . . . whispered that reason no longer held sway.

"The efficacy of this rite, the mystery, is founded in the nature of the realm beyond the Veil."

"Ixtador," I offered.

"Aye. The Aspirant withholds what he knows of Ixtador's history, teasing as he does. But I've gleaned it is neither a divine state—else why am I not seven times god-struck for breaching its boundaries?—nor is it some common aspect of the universe that we've only discovered in these hundred years since the Wars. I've never believed in gods or angels or Heaven, not since the day I first told someone I could hear voices in my head, but whenever I reach beyond life with this work I do"—his neck twisted and his shoulders hunched, as if to fend off a blow—"what I perceive is perverse, aberrant, a festering wound hidden deep inside the body of the natural world. Even if we halt this rite and defeat the Aspirant and his minions, we cannot simply close the *Book of Greater Rites* and walk away. Which means—"

"We have to let events unfold. Learn more. Know what we are dealing with."

He jerked his head in assent. "Exactly so. Do you know much about the Mondragon codices?"

"Duplais told me their history."

"The Aspirant keeps the index volume. I decipher what I can from the other three, practice and perfect what I learn, then formulate the spells in a more traditional way and teach them to the Aspirant. The magic is"—he closed his eyes for that moment, not to summon a word, but as if to recapture something treasured—"magnificent. Also complex and difficult. But alongside this work—unshared with my colleagues— I've developed a skill at visualizing spellwork, the patterns and shapes of it, as you might see the hidden structure of a leaf beneath an opticum lens. I can then translate my understanding into simple forms that can be manipulated."

The hieroglyphs, certainly. Dared I tell him I had seen?

"My patterning allows me to detect when someone uses these spells I've taught them. If I'm alert and if I've the strength of mind, I can go in and—"

"You alter the spells!" Enlightenment flashed as clear as Dante's fire. "You corrupt their work and then taunt them for their failures. It makes you necessary to their plan." That's what I had seen him doing two nights previous, altering a spell in subtle ways.

His head snapped around to stare. "How could you know that?"

"Logic."

He strangled a retort and averted his face again. "If I can ensure that *I* work this culminating rite on the day the Aspirant chooses, I can ensure the worst does not happen. That'll not be as simple as it sounds. The As- pirant is magically capable"—distaste heated his telling—"as long as he uses leeched blood to enhance his innate gifts. And he is highly intelli- gent. He keeps a close watch on what I teach him, matching it with what *Diel Voile Aeterna*—the index—leads him to expect. If he gets an inkling that I've been thwarting him, and decides he's learned enough of what the books can teach to work the rite, he'll dispense with me and attempt it on his own. I must take him down first."

But my blood could open the books to the Aspirant. Did the Aspirant know that? "You still don't know who he is."

"No." Dante returned so far as the lower steps and sat. Hard drops pelted his already sodden garments. He rubbed the back of his neck, tugging at the silver collar as if it chafed. "This is where matters get nastier, of course."

"The Aspirant is not my father."

"That conflicts, just a spit, with your testimony against him." He glanced over his shoulder. I was close enough to make out the prominences and hollows of his face, the dark brows and unshaven chin against the paler skin, but no finer detail.

"On the same night I heard you for the first time, I heard my father's voice in the aether. There was no mistake."

"Does he share the tangle curse? Did he hear you speak back to him?" Never had I felt a mind snap up my words so quickly.

"I don't think he heard me. And I've not heard him again. He's your friends' prisoner."

"They've hiding places all over. Laboratoriums, dungeons. I've visited at least three besides Eltevire. But I'm not allowed to see their prisoners. I am their hireling—useful, but ultimately not of the same rank. Not to be trusted." He leaned back on his elbows and turned his face up into the rain. "I need the book back, else everything is wasted. Your keeping it will get me dead, which will not grieve you, but it'll not save anyone— not your father, not your king, not Duplais."

Of course it would come back to the book. But I was not ready to join hands with my mother's destroyer. "What do they plan for Duplais?"

"His death is to be a part of the rite, but as I've translated only pieces of it as yet, I don't know which part. The index guides the whole working. Unfortunately it references a missing page of the *Book of Greater Rites*. The Aspirant gave *Diel Schemata Magna* into Orviene's custody once, years ago, before I joined their little cadre. Orviene claimed *he* could translate it. When forced to give it back—because, of course, the banty rooster could not do what he said—a page was missing. We've spent a great deal of time trying to reconstruct the missing information from the other parts we know. That's tricky. Dangerous. Knowing the power involved, I'd not like to think we'll get it wrong . . . which may be only slightly better than getting it right."

"What was on the page?" Surely he must detect my rising excitement.

I'd never imagined Cecile's fragment to be a part of Lianelle's book . . . not merely complex, but *encrypted*.

"Diagrams. Maps, you might say. They would describe the arrangement of participants—the principal practitioner, which I intend to be me, and the assistants who will work supporting spells. Also the arrangement of the objects whose energies will shape the magic—persons, plants, animals, stones, or the like. Unlike the nonsense the Camarilla spews, the power for true enchantment does not come solely from the practitioner's blood, but from the complex energies of nature, bound in physical reality and shaped by use and history and belief . . ."

For that one moment, I heard the voice of my friend of the mind . . . the teacher . . . the man who relished the properties of planets and night-blooming flowers, who reverenced magic. Dante. They were truly the same man.

". . . and there might be other markings, describing the sequence of the work or aligning the layered spells to the particular location or . . . activities. This is a rite intended to rend the Veil between life and death. I've some ideas about what must be involved. Fundamental things. Powerful evocations of life and death."

Like the death of a man who could not die. And necromancy . . .

I was torn between rushing off to incinerate the page and confessing I had it. "It's never been found?"

"No. Whatever she did, whatever she said, your sister shook the Aspirant. He feels pressed for time, as if he's seen a flaw in his scheme, and he's pushed me to be ready much earlier than planned, whether or not we ever find the diagrams. He made the mistake of prodding Antonia about the missing page. She was convinced someone had got hold of it, as Orviene was always trying to impress people with his great magic. The crone took it upon herself to manage the situation, but she didn't come up with it."

Dante spoke of Cecile's murder as little more than a lady's pique. "Naturally you helped Antonia manage this *situation*."

My disgust must have struck him square on. He shifted around on the step. The graying light revealed his face hard as hewn granite, instantly banishing any idea I might have of casual murder.

"And *you* are unsurprised to hear your mistress's mother is a murderess. You associate with the woman every day, yet allow her to walk free unaccused, poisoning and manipulating your aristo lady. You are indeed an *agente confide* worthy of Portier's mentoring." His flint-hard eyes were the color of jade. "I did not do this murder. I'm kept back to deal with the larger magics. The Aspirant threatened to bleed the witch if she did something so stupid again. He insinuated he'd use her viscera in the very rite she thinks will give her Sabria to rule. He may do so yet. I'd not weep."

Though I had no love for Antonia, I wouldn't wish the Aspirant's vengeance on anyone, even a traitorous, conniving murderess. "She conspired with a sorcerer to do the murder. If not you, then who? Jacard?"

"Jacard would piss himself if he smelled blood. Kajetan has more followers than just the mewling nephew. His mindless sheep from Seravain will do anything to further his holy mission."

My head spun yet again. "Jacard is Kajetan's nephew?"

"That's why I couldn't get shed of the incompetent little vermin until he threw his panic fit. Evidently you told him that I'd tortured your brother. He decided you knew everything and were ready to expose us. I thought Kajetan would strangle him for having you hauled to the Bastionne."

He glanced around, as if he sensed the blaze in my gut. "I visited your brother one time only and left him useless to the Aspirant. I could not help the rest."

"You're despicable! He was innocent . . . a boy!"

"Pognole paid in kind for his crimes, which involved many prisoners besides your noble kinsman." Disdain frosted the air. "Most such crimes involve other than aristo families. Yet after all, it was the *noble* king of Sabria who put his own goodson in the Spindle with no care for who watched out for him. Do not believe that because I've come to treat with you, because I have . . . opened . . . myself to you in ways I never— Do not imagine I believe the wrongs done your family somehow worse than those afflicting others in this world."

I had heard Dante's tragic story of his teacher. But I had also heard this argument before. Too often it served as an excuse for further cruelty. "Injustice to *any* person should breed a deeper determination to justice, not indifference."

"Pssh."

I'd heard that before, too. My father had called it the inarguable riposte, the tool of an empty-handed debater.

Water sluiced from the roof in a steady fall, reminiscent more of winter than autumn. The morning would not lighten much from this. The last bells had called out the change to the morning watch—sixth hour. I had only one hour to decide whether to reclaim my packet from Heurot.

It had been so easy to fall into this conversation, seduced by answers, craving hints of what I wanted to believe—that the person I had opened my soul to was no fiend, but an intelligent, brave, and immensely talented man caught up in a diabolical plot, a generous soul who could demonstrate that I was mistaken about the worst things he had done.

Dante was not that paragon. Nor was he misunderstood. My mother, my father, my brother, and likely others were bound in torment this hour because he would not risk his purpose by breaking his silence. Nor had he apologized, save in offering these grudging hints of the reasoning behind his deeds. That his work wore on him, savaged him, scarred him, was no absolution. He was what I saw, not what girlish imagining might invent.

But he had claimed, albeit reluctantly, that I might help him undo the Aspirant's plan and save Duplais . . . and by implication Eugenie and Philippe and the myriad souls this chaos might consume. It was time we came to some resolution.

"Is Kajetan the Aspirant? Even Duplais suspects him."

"No. Kajetan is worse." Dante near spat the prefect's name. "The Aspirant freely admits he wishes to do this because it amuses him. He says he finds the exercise *stimulating*. Kajetan pretends he is on a divine mission to protect the glories of magic. He spews fatherly affection for both gifted and ungifted, while *using* Portier . . . his student . . . his charge . . . his worshiper. When Portier took him on as his mentor, he gave Kajetan implicit consent for whatever he did, and then Kajetan gave him over to the Aspirant to do *experiments* on him. Gods, he came near getting Portier killed, revived him from the brink, then let him believe for nine years that he had slain his own father, whom he rightly despised, but nonetheless . . . That sort of thing bothers Portier. Then the holy prefect installs this mind block that destroys Portier's ability to work magic. I tried to break it. Thought I had, but evidently not."

He shrugged as if his failure were no matter, but his vehemence had already put the lie to that. It was not my place to reveal Duplais' secret. And we had many important things yet to discuss.

"I don't think the Aspirant's motives are entirely whimsical," I said. "A visitor was staying with Kajetan at Seravain when my sister died. . . ." I told him then about the man wearing Delourre colors and Duplais' belief that the man had visited him frequently during his recovery.

By the time I had done, Dante was outside the summerhouse yet again, his unscarred thumb and forefingers squeezing his temples. Moments ticked away. Only with difficulty did I hold patience. Seventh hour was approaching.

"Gah!" He returned to the steps, shoving the dripping hair from his face with the back of his scarred hand. "Had you asked me straight out who was sharing Kajetan's house when I arrived, I'd have said no one. Charlot, the vice chancellor, popped in and out; the toady does what Kajetan says with as little thought as possible. But when Kajetan sent for me to clean up their blunder, I was already halfway along the road, as I needed to do some reading in their vault, so I arrived a day earlier than expected. Until this moment, I'd forgotten that. And someone else *was* there. Damnation, why can I not remember?"

He ripped a broken lath from the latticework and launched it into the soggy garden. "I saw the devil without his mask, and he's gone and cut it out of me."

"Duplais sent an inquiry to a servant who worked at Seravain," I said. "We might yet hear something of worth. And someone here at court must have Delourre connections. I could inquire. . . ." The prospect of something to do besides letting doom fall around me was exhilarating.

"Gods, no!" Dante's refocused attention knocked me backward a step or two. "Do nothing that puts you at risk! Don't you understand even yet? Your gift— You've truly no idea. The tangle curse is a predictor of talent for magic. I am *very* good at what I do—but the strength of your voice tells me you could be even better. Tonight when I realized it was *you* with all this raw talent, and I knew we had this connection that we could use, that no one could suspect—" He swung around abruptly. "Damn and blast, you've not told Portier about it—our conversations?"

Portier, who was destined to die in this wretched game. Who had not wanted to know my secrets, lest they be forced from him. My chest constricted. "I've not told anyone."

He expelled a tight breath. "Good. If this plays out to the end, and I attempt to subvert their devilish rites and fail, I will have lost the biggest gamble this world has ever known. But together—if you allow me to draw on your power—we can snarl them in their own horrors and cast them all into the Souleater's pit."

Draw on my power? My gorge rose. "You think to *bleed* me?"

"No, no. As long as you're close by, I believe it can be done through the aether . . . as if we were speaking. I'll make up some reason I need you there—to bring the conspiracy full circle, to punish you for daring interfere, for exciting Jacard's panic and disgrace and thus causing me more trouble and more work. I'll throw a tantrum and sizzle their hair—"

"But the Aspirant knows my blood *will* unlock the book."

"As it happens, he doesn't. The sample I passed them—your blood taken in the Bastionne, so they believe—would *not* unlock the Mondragon ciphers." His hand gripped the arched wood as if to tear the supports from under the summerhouse, yet he held his voice steady. "Maybe it needn't come to this, but the time is ripe. The Aspirant is edgy. The king's movements unsettle him. And, after everything, I—" He had to force it out. "I judge I am not enough to do this alone. So I must know. Will you work with me?"

Bathed in the searing green of his gaze, rational thought was impossible. I crossed the summerhouse to the eastern arch and let the damp morning cool my heated skin. Dante had immersed himself in lies. He had cooperated in loathsome acts. He admitted his own corruption, his fascination with wicked magic, his lack of moral scruple. All this could be a ploy to make naive Anne yield the Mondragon book, to induce me to walk calmly up the gallows steps so he could drop the noose about my neck.

But the tapestry of events had woven itself into a pattern, and not a single strand belied the story it told. I had felt the fire in my veins on Merona's ridge. I lived in the mindstorm, and I knew the truth of my father's blood. Dante said he wanted to stop what was to come and ensure it could not happen again, and had confessed he needed my help—the last ploy a proud, ruthless man would choose for deception. Beyond logic, reason, and caution, I believed him.

I retraced my steps across the summerhouse. Papa had once said that no matter the weather, he could never get warm on the night after a battle. Body, mind, and soul had been stretched to their limits, leaving nothing for the ordinary functions of life. I knew exactly what he meant. No matter how tightly I wrapped my shawl, I could not stop shivering.

Dante, drenched to the skin, awaited me on the steps.

"One more thing I should tell you about Duplais," I said. "It's possible Kajetan, at the least, believes him a Saint Reborn—unable to die until he consents to it. Legends of such strength often have roots in truth. You and I may even have touched on that topic in one of our . . . exchanges. That's one reason they've chosen Mont Voilline for the rite. That *is* the place, yes?"

"Night's daughters . . ." Dante said this almost prayerfully. A quiet, desperate prayer. "Yes. Voilline."

"As for the book . . . I've some others need returning to the royal library," I said. "You'll recognize them. By ninth hour, I'll have the *Book of Greater Rites* shelved beside *Divine Harmonies and Discords of the Air.*"

"You'll—? Well, good. That's good." It came out something less than his usual bluster. "It would be most excellent not to end up dead the next time the Aspirant summons me. I never know when that might be from one time to the next, and he always wants to see the book."

"Then it's as well I'm not planning to give you the missing page until—"

"You have it?" He sagged against the arch, weariness and astonishment escaping his control. *"You?"*

"Yes. But I'll not give it until we meet again. Then I'll prick my finger and we'll read what the cursed book says. Together." He was truly crazed if he thought I would go into this without knowing what I was getting into.

"No!" His relief vanished as quickly as it had come. "This is just as well. I mustn't know the complete rite—the exact binding words, the keys, the focus—before the day. That's how I hold him back. While our Aspirant is not the world's most talented sorcerer, we cannot underestimate him, especially not now, hearing how he's played games with Portier's mind and mine. The Aspirant must not know; therefore I must not know. All the more reason to have you there."

"All right. We keep you ignorant." I was pleased we were speaking with voices, where intent could not flavor my agreement with untruth. My determination to read the cursed book was unchanged. Perhaps it was only my imagination that his head lifted in suspicion.

"Duplais believes you Fallen," I said. "I heard it, clear as sunrise, whenever he spoke of you."

"Good." The clipped answer came very quickly. "That's what I wanted."

"Were you ever going to tell him otherwise?"

This answer came slowly. "I was tempted fairly often at first. Whenever I learned something new. But as time went on and I went deeper . . . It doesn't matter. He'll never trust me."

I wasn't so sure of that. "So answer me one more thing. Why did you trust *me* with all this? I could cheerfully see you dead for what you've done to my family. You could have forced me to the rite without me knowing anything more. And yet you chose to do it this way. To ask. To tell me all and trust me to keep your secrets."

"Great gods of the universe, I've told you. We *cannot* lie in the aether." He threw his hands up. It was all I could do not to look up to ensure that the roof was ready to crash down on us.

But he reimposed discipline as quickly as he'd lost it, and the words flowed onward with the quiet intensity of my friend. "Everything that went on between us was truth. To use you, to take your power without consent . . . I *know* you, Anne de Vernase. The world would fall to ruin before you would permit it."

CHAPTER 36

I left the maze first, his pronunciation of my name graven in my bones. Never had I heard it pronounced with such . . . fervor . . . such intimacy . . . such understanding. I wasn't even sure he knew how he said it or that I'd heard. I would have liked to linger, to spend the next hours hidden from the frantic business of the day, reconsidering the most extraordinary conversation I'd ever had in my life. To decide if *I* had become the lunatic by agreeing to ally with the man I despised and feared most in the world.

But the three-quarter hour bells had rung, forcing me to hurry straight across the sodden grass and onto the carriage road instead of taking the circuitous gravel path through the rose gardens. Which was why I emerged from behind the stable and walked straight into some twenty of the Guard Royale, massed before the east doors of the palace.

Instinct pulled me back, but not before an alert young guardsman challenged me: "Identify yourself."

"Damoselle Anne de Vernase, Her Majesty's maid of the bedchamber."

I wouldn't have believed me, either—a woman haggard from lack of sleep, dressed in common woad-dyed wool soggy to the knees, and whose hair had long responded to the wind and damp by escaping any semblance of restraint. There was no use yelling or asserting my authority. They'd been sent to guard the palace doors. They must—"Please forgive our commander's requirement, honorable damoselle"—verify the identity of any who lacked a badge of office.

And so seventh hour came and went before Lady Patrice appeared on the east steps, rolled her eyes, and confessed in high dudgeon that, yes, I was exactly who I claimed to be. With only a raised eyebrow for the young guardsman, she plucked my sleeve and swept under the portico and into the east atrium.

"Dragons' teeth, girl, have you no sense of responsibility?" snapped the spry little marquesa. "Bad enough you show so little respect for your office that you tattle about in rags the chambermaids would discard, and so obnoxiously hold yourself above the rest of the household, as if a sad history and gifts of the mind are somehow superior to gifts of simple grace or an earnest determination to make the best of one's family expectations. I had at least conceded your feeling for the woman we serve. You seem genuinely to care about her. Yet as Eugenie weeps for her empty womb, you've been haring about in the muck like a tavern girl."

Though it was impossible to explain that my activities might benefit Eugenie more than any bedchamber service, my calculated excuses evaporated. I, the *knife-tongued aristo*. The *fierce little scrag-dog*. Where had I lost *Anne*?

"Lady, I sincerely love and admire our mistress. She's shown me favor far beyond expectation. I'll strive to do better."

Patrice pursed her thin lips. "I believe you. Now see that you do. I'd rather not be fetched to the steps like a steward."

"But why are these guardsmen posted here?"

"You must *attend*, Anne. You live in the royal city now, not your rustic countryside. The king has returned to Merona."

The earth shifted again. My goodfather. The sole arbiter of my future, assuming any of us had a future. I could be confined to the Spindle in the next hour. "I didn't think he could be here before night."

"He's not in residence as yet," she said. "Prefect Kajetan and Tetrarch Grabian must greet him at the city gates and welcome him home on behalf of the Camarilla and the Temple. I doubt he'll brook any other delay. We'll all be called to account then. Keep your wits about you and your tongue still."

As we passed through the gilded doors into the household, I could scarce sort through the day's possibilities. "Is Her Majesty awake now?"

"Fitfully. The fool brother has had a sensible idea for once, suggesting she be moved to the country, where fresh air and happier associations might revive her. The physician approves it. Who knows what the king will say? Many things could change today."

"Indeed. But it sounds an excellent plan." Especially if Antonia and her schemes and the revenants of dead kings could be left behind.

I hadn't asked Dante about the possibilities of procreation with a revenant. *Asked Dante* . . . The idea shivered me to the marrow . . . along with the thought that I *could* ask him when I had a moment, out there in our meeting place in the aether. Somehow the prospect of our next such conversation left me breathless. *Dante. Impossible . . .*

As we climbed the stair into the inner household, Patrice dismissed me to my bedchamber, saying she would roust Eleanor or Arabella to join her in relief of Antonia and Lord Ilario. "Sleep for a few hours, Anne. You've given good service these past days. And for the love of Sabria, take the time to dress appropriately."

"Thank you, my lady," I said. "I do feel a bit frantic. There are more dangers around this palace than illness. I'd not have our mistress harmed in any way."

"Nor I. You're not the only one who watches. I've heard you were a bit clumsy earlier. Very clever. Walk carefully."

"Yes, indeed I will." I was near stammering with astonishment. I suppose seven decades of palace intrigues could make a sharp-eyed woman used to almost anything. "Divine grace, Marquesa Patrice."

As the bells rang eighth hour of the morning watch, I watched her go, brisk and precise in her movements. Perhaps the natural order of the universe was already reversed.

———

THE BOOK WAS GONE FROM the balcony rubble, and with it my hopes of an hour's sleep. I could not allow Ilario to do anything drastic—assuming, of course, that Ilario was the one who had taken it. My confidence in my plan seemed suddenly flimsy, with Dante's life in danger every moment of delay.

I'd taken two drops of the potion, hoping to avoid entanglements along the way. Now my state of invisibility did naught but make my search for Ilario more difficult. He was not in the bedchamber, where Patrice and Arabella were bathing the sleeping queen in preparation for her husband's arrival, nor in the private dining room. I slipped into his apartments in the wake of his wizened, impatient little manservant, John Deune, as unlikely a pairing of servant and master as any I'd seen, but the chevalier was not at home. Neither was he in the queen's salon.

The household ladies and maids of honor were all atwitter about what the king might do when he arrived. Cautious whispers agreed that "executing certain terrifying sorcerers" would be wise, but extremely dangerous, if not impossible. One craggy contessa was convinced the king would set Eugenie aside within the month. The king's privy council had prepared the order of *cerrate vide* months ago, she said. This collapse would be the last straw.

My name was whispered, too. Most of the women assumed that I would be shipped to the Spindle the moment Philippe found me serving in Eugenie's bedchamber.

"That would be a shame." Chins dropped when Marie-Claire spoke up. "Anne saved our lady's life yesterday, and watches out for her carefully. She is very wise."

Rumor spread faster in Castelle Escalon than late-summer fires in the maquis. Marveling at my two unlikely new defenders, I abandoned Marie-Claire at the center of a murmuring group, repeating all she knew, which was very little and mostly wrong.

The experience was incredibly strange, the voices of the aether roaring through my head as I flitted unseen among my companions of the court. Hearing myself discussed. Was this what it was like to be dead?

Having gleaned nothing of Lord Ilario's whereabouts, I sped down to the viewing gallery that marked the division between the queen's household and the public rooms. Increasingly I feared he'd taken my treasures and ridden off to his country house with them. Yet I couldn't imagine him deserting Eugenie.

Debating whether to head for the stables or the kitchens, both known for Lord Ilario's frequent visits, I hurried down the gallery, past the entrance to the mages' passage. How differently I saw it after these past hours. Despite his violent temper and unrepentant wickedness, I could summon no fear of Dante.

Which was idiocy. He had not changed. Not four hours previous, I'd written Ilario, my faithful chevalier, not to approach him—

Father Creator, he wouldn't!

Reversing course, I sped down the passage toward Dante's door.

Ilario stepped briskly from behind a cupboard, hand appallingly near his sword hilt. "Who's there?"

"Lord, hold," I said, skidding to a stop. "I'm all right. Wholly intact."

He spun in place, every fiber of him on the alert. "Damoselle?"

"Right here." When I touched his arm, he jerked away and backed toward the windows, color draining from his fair complexion. A knife had appeared in his hand as if by the finest magic.

"Who's there? Where are you? Ianne's breath, are you—?"

"Don't be afraid. I'm right here. He didn't hurt me."

He took a deep, shaking breath. "Are you sure?"

My admiration for Ilario reached new heights. A laugh bubbled up from somewhere. "It's only a seeing charm diverts your eye. My sister's work, not his at all. Here"—I took his hand and laid it atop my head—"if I were a ghost I'm sure I would be taller and have lovely silken hair."

"And yet you sound something different." He removed his hand—not without a press firm enough to ensure I was substantial. "Did you not meet up with the devil after all?"

"I'm just relieved," I said. "He yelled at me a great deal. Tried to frighten me into giving back the book. But he couldn't explain how I could've taken it without his seeing me. Eventually he let me go. He's nervous about what's coming. You'd not want to cross him just now. What were you planning on doing here?"

"Ending it in the only way I know how," he said. "This has gone on far too long." All smiles withered. The hair on my neck prickled.

"Lord, you can't. Not yet." I kept my voice low and backed into the corner, lest anyone happen by and see me reappear. "Duplais was most insistent that we let things proceed so that we're not held hostage to the Aspirant's threat from now on. You surely know his mind better than I do. Do we trust his judgment or not?"

He struggled with that. Yet after a few moments, even in the dim light, I could see his body transform from the private man to the public. He bent over the place I had been standing when he touched my hair. "Could we . . . mmm . . . go somewhere else? I'm talking to walls."

"First fetch the book," I said, my moment's exhilaration drowned in the passing hour. My search had gone on much too long. "We've got to take a look before I give it back. Then meet me . . . where?"

"Follow me." Ilario took a lamp from a wall sconce and turned it brighter. "You can't . . . uh . . . walk through walls, can you?"

"No better than you."

Which was ironic, as the next quarter hour took me on an entirely unexpected journey through the walls of Castelle Escalon. We began in an abandoned stool closet, which had a movable wall panel in its dusty recesses, and then proceeded through a series of passages, wardrobes, and odd-shaped rooms occupied solely by spiders and mice.

Every few steps Ilario looked over his shoulder and whispered, "Are you still there?"

"I'll stay close," I said. "We need to hurry."

By the time we'd climbed a few steps through another closet, the subtle alteration in the light and the mindstorm told me I was visible again. Ilario almost dropped his lamp the next time he checked on me.

We emerged in a small, comfortable suite of rooms that overlooked the east gardens. The windows and the game table laid with green baize and set with painted cards hinted that this was Eugenie's game room, the suite where she entertained her private guests . . . including her dead husband. The quiet rooms felt deserted, despite vases filled with fresh flowers and a carefully banked fire, just waiting the stir of a poker to spring to life.

Ilario yanked open a blanket chest and lifted out the bottom. "Geni's forbidden anyone to come here uninvited, save old Mathilde, who's cared for the place since we were children and would cut off her arm before snooping. Even Antonia obeys the rule. Geni gave me an exemption, but I honor her wishes . . . for the most part. She doesn't exactly know about this chest. Our father kept his mistresses' gifts and portraits in here."

As he drew out my knotted kerchief and a bundle of linen tied with string, I espied a pile of black silk, a plain-hilted sword in a black scabbard, and the other accoutrements of my masked rescuer.

"Here they are," he said, passing me the bundles and reconstructing the chest. "I've got to say, I'd rather kill the damnable mage. Should have done it that night after the trial, when I saw what he'd done to your mother."

I couldn't bear thinking of my mother as I prepared to partner with the fiend who'd hurt her so dreadfully. How would I ever reconcile it? "Why didn't you?"

"I intended it. Barged into the mage's room and confronted him. Portier told me that Dante had sunk so deeply into this role of collaborator that he had a difficult time crawling back out. The mage had admitted to him how the sorcery he worked ate away at his mind. Of all men I understand the difficulties of a double life. Sometimes I think I'd better just bash my head against a stone wall so I can forget, and I've been at it a lot longer than Dante.

"But on that night the mage just stood there, stone-faced, and let me yell at him. I cursed him, called him the Souleater's servant for what he had done, told him I'd come to defend Madeleine's honor. I kept thinking he'd explain. But he just stood there. To draw my sword meant exposure. After twenty years. In the end, I couldn't do it. Stupid. I didn't even see the first blow coming. He bound me in some wretched enchantment that left me looking a proper helpless fool. Portier arrived just in time to see him tire of the game. Just in time to watch him break my sword arm and five ribs. Just in time to haul away the scraps. I've tried to get him to start exercising so he can arrive a bit earlier next time."

"So that's what convinced Duplais that Dante was past saving," I said. "The crowning blow, delivered *after* he arrived."

"That, and what was done to your mother. He'd seen her, too. I don't think anything else would have made him give up his faith in the god-blasted sorcerer."

An inerrant perception of righteousness. I carried the book to the game table, burying wonder deep inside me. If I only believed in saints and angels, Ilario might have converted me to the Cult of the Reborn right then.

The bells were ringing another quarter hour gone. I'd no time left to read the whole book, but I could not yield these treasures without a look. "I need a clean, sharp knife and your steady hand," I said, unwrapping the kerchief bundle.

"*Cut* you?" he said, when I stuck out my finger and told him what to do. "Have *you* gone mad now, alongside the rest of us?"

"This is a page from a spellbook. I've got to read it, and this is the only way." The thought of cutting my own flesh revolted me.

"But I can't—"

"Please, lord, just do as I ask."

"Santa Claire, protect all queens, fools, lunatics, and madwomen."

I heartily concurred with his prayer as I touched my bleeding finger not to the *Book of Greater Rites*, which I had no time to read, but to its missing page—Lady Cecile's fragment. The key to unravel it had been with me all this time. Mage Orviene's loose tongue had let slip the essential question: *M vitet or G vitet?* Mondragon blood or Gautier blood to unlock the encryption? I already knew it was Mondragon. As I knew the key. *"Andragossa."*

The mindstorm surged, this time in raucous energies that battered my tired skull. But as Ilario hissed over my shoulder, the letters and symbols labeling the three diagrams shifted and rearranged themselves into a puzzle worthy of Montclaire. I could not deny my excitement.

Atop all sat a compass rose, indicating the top of the diagrams as east.

Each circled triangle bore a prominent title that seemed to signify sequence as well as purpose. The leftmost, *Opening*; the center, *Passage*; the rightmost, *Inversion*. Dante had described this as a map designating positions of the practitioners, objects, and activities involved in the spellwork. He said he intended to act as *principal*, so it was easy to interpret the labels *principal*, *mediator*, and *guide* that appeared at the vertices of each triangle. These would be the sorcerers.

Each side of each triangle displayed one or more symbols. The first diagram showed a plumed bird, a set of three waved lines, and three interlinked ovals; the second, a skull, a cluster of three tight spirals next to an empty vessel, and two concentric rings. Positioned on the third were a tree, a similar vessel but with a knot inside it, and what appeared to be an oval mirror reflecting a three-lobed knot.

"I've learned these are patterns for spellwork," I said. "They describe a magical rite to rend the Veil, linking all these preparations the conspirators have made to the chaos Duplais fears. If we can interpret this, perhaps we'll know what we face and how to counter it. I know these three—the alchemical symbols for water, air, and earth." I pointed to the waved lines, the three spirals, and the vessel. "And I was told that in spellwork, the skull represents mortality."

"If we're to interpret these as parallel ideas, then not simply mortality," said Ilario, touching the two symbols that corresponded to the skull, "but *death*. Because the bird is a phoenix, as we use in cult texts to represent the *undeath* of the Reborn, and the tree is the Temple representation of the Creator's gift. *Life*."

"The others, though . . ." I stared at the links, the concentric circles, and the reflecting mirror, willing them to reveal their meaning. "The things my sister brought to spellwork told a story. And I think Dante's magic works that way, as well. So what story do these tell? *Opening*, as in opening the rent in the Veil, must be created by *water* and *undeath*, and these links . . ."

Symbols appeared in the center of each triangle. Inside the first appeared the same symbol of two concentric rings that appeared beside the second diagram. A dotted line connected the two symbols, as if the first fed the second. I considered the phoenix and the Cult of the Reborn, and recalled the earth and water set in the sorcerer's ring and scattered across the Rotunda during Dante's deadraising. In the night just past, Dante had arranged water and stone in his circle of magic, along with Duplais' journal. And chains—links. *They're going to make me kill the self-righteous little prick.*

"This first diagram must be about Duplais. If they believe he is a Saint Reborn, it's about killing him, chaining him to the mountain, as in his dream. The water? I don't know. But Duplais' death—or the undeath of a Saint Reborn—must rend the Veil, allowing the *passage* shown in the second diagram. Perhaps the symbol in the center of each triangle is the result, because each diagram is linked to the next." In the center of the second diagram, two curved arrows were drawn head to tail. *Passage* in both directions. And centering the third, what I first thought to be an inkblot might actually represent a hole . . . a void . . . an emptiness. . . .

"I'm thinking the concentric circles could be the lens," said Ilario, crouching beside me. "Think of a spyglass collapsed. Portier told me that at the Exposition, Dante made the Rotunda into a lens, a larger version of Gaetana's spyglass, through which one could see past the Veil. He said that those dreadful lights one sees floating inside the dome leak through the lens, like sun glints through an imperfect window."

Eager, I took up his chain of reasoning. "Assuming they've opened the way, then in this second diagram the principal practitioner would use the lens to facilitate a passage between the realms, an *exchange* symbolized by the opposing arrows. We know they plan to use necromancy, and so we raise the revenant . . ."

"But someone would have to die to make it happen." He tapped the skull. "And then what?"

The second dotted line led from the symbol for air into the third diagram, where it looped about the vessel, the alchemical symbol of earth.

All the bits and pieces I'd seen and heard fell into place. In the third diagram appeared the mirror—the nireal, the soul mirror that I believed brought vivid life to a revenant. I tapped the three spirals. "Air, the revenant spirit, given passage from beyond the Veil and provided a body made of earth"—I touched the empty vessel—"and instilled with a soul." I touched the mirror. "And here is the tree of life." They would be using *fundamental things*, Dante had said. *Powerful evocations of life and death.* "Soren, the ghost king, the revenant, would be brought here, where the second vessel waits beside the tree of life."

"Eugenie." We spoke together.

I was more and more appalled as I recalled Eugenie's dreams, her flushed cheeks, her *need*. "They've been preparing her for what's going to happen there at Voilline. Eugenie and Soren are to make a child . . ."

. . . and the result was the blot, the emptiness, a gaping hole in the cosmos. *Inversion.* Chaos.

Ilario upended the little table, sending the book to the floor and the page flying. "Burn the daemon book, and I'll kill the cursed mage. Let's be done with this madness."

My own impulses clamored the same. How was I to reconcile Duplais' beliefs and Dante's with the drives of Ilario's good heart and the promptings of my own god? The Lord Reason insisted we stop this today and worry about the future later. To do otherwise required proceeding on faith, which I had so long disdained.

And yet, Reason had—and still—proclaimed my father's guilt. Intellect and logic gave me no other answer to the handwriting of the treacherous letters . . . the phrasing that so clearly echoed his own . . . the spare sentences, direct and clear and unambiguous. Lacking faith, I had betrayed him. But I had learned a different truth in the aether. My father's voice proclaimed his innocence and I believed.

"Yes, burn the page. But we can destroy neither book nor mage," I said, "not yet. For one, the conspirators have Portier. My father and brother, too, I believe. They're all dead—or worse—if we move now. And I've concluded that the Aspirant himself is a sorcerer. Even if we remove Dante, it's possible he can proceed on his own. Secrecy . . . deception . . . is our only advantage, the only way we can be sure we destroy their threat."

"Then what, in the name of all saints, do we tell Philippe?" he snapped, kicking at the overturned table. "He's not going to stand by and allow them to do this to Eugenie on Portier's word or mine, and certainly not on yours."

"We'll think of something. But first I have to return the book before Dante discovers it on me. It's already far later than I'd planned. Please, I need to go now." I hated lying to him, but if I told him our hope lay in a half-mad sorcerer who spoke in my head, he'd likely chain me up, too.

We poked the banked fire to life, watched it consume the blood-marked page in flames of purple and green, and without further conversation, hurried through the wall panel and into the web of passages. Only when Ilario deposited me in a closet nearest my own room did he speak. "I'll fetch you as soon as I've arranged an audience with Philippe," he said. "You'll take care as you return the book, damoselle? The mage will surely be watching."

"He'll not see me. I promise."

As I turned to reinforce my lies eye to eye, the lamp illumined Ilario's handsome face, perfectly composed and slightly foolish. Neither worry line nor whitened knuckle betrayed the man inside the fool.

Deception lingered in my mouth like sour milk. I felt dirty and weak. Corrupt.

I had just pulled open my bedchamber door when the blast of trumpets overwhelmed the soft gurgle of rain from the gargoyle spouts outside my window. A ripple shook the mindstorm, or perhaps it was my own shudder. It was difficult to tell the difference anymore. The King of Sabria had come home.

CHAPTER 37

"So you vouchsafed a return to duty, did you, damoselle?" An annoyed Lady Patrice snagged me as I hurried into the royal apartments. "When I encouraged you to spend a few hours making yourself decent and ensuring your alertness, I had no intention of your using half a day."

"My apologies, my lady. I'm ready to sit with Queen Eugenie as long as needed."

The *Book of Greater Rites* was safely shelved in the royal library. My face and gown were clean. Negotiating the crowds flocking to the entry hall to witness Philippe's arrival had taken more time than either task.

"As matters stand"—the marquesa glanced over her shoulder toward the bedchamber, where two footmen blocked the passage—"you must turn right around and return to your own room. His Majesty is on his way here, and Ducessa Antonia has instructed that you are not to be present. Indeed, she insists that you are not to intrude yourself on the king at all in this mournful time. She deems it best you remain in your chambers."

Shock devised my retort. "How does the lady intend to enforce this rule? The king is my goodfather. He's surely aware of my presence and is quite likely to summon me, don't you think?" Especially as I'd asked Ilario to arrange a meeting.

Not that I was looking forward to telling my goodfather that his wife was to be mated to a dead man in a rite to throw his kingdom into madness. Convincing him to allow events to move forward without interference might get me hanged.

"An audience is highly unlikely. The king does not allow your father's name to be spoken in his presence. And it has been learned that it was *not* His Majesty's order to summon you to Castelle Escalon. As Sonjeur de Duplais is conveniently not present to explain his reasons for acting on a false premise, it could be surmised that you falsified the summons yourself or in concert with him."

Or that I had arranged Duplais' disappearance. I'd announced before witnesses that I was the last to see him. My arms prickled.

"Come, let's ensure you've left no personal item here." Patrice propelled me into a cloakroom. "Anne, do not dispute this instruction. Antonia's antipathy for you has reached a dangerous pass." The lady had shed her imperious manner. "No one has challenged her authority so successfully in decades. Truly, I've never seen her so angry and . . . frantic. I fear for her reason."

"I'll not hide from her." But fear already nibbled at bravado.

The marquesa's voice came a whisper. "Antonia claims she mentioned to you that the queen's smelling salts seemed to have no efficacy, and that she proposed suspending their use until Mage Dante could examine them. She whispers that you seemed nervous at this prospect, and only then caused the accident that broke the vial. The mage has analyzed the residue the servants collected, and Antonia reports that they were not aromatics at all, but something unknown."

Hot blood pounded in my hands, feet, and head. "I didn't. I would never—"

"I know that," she said crisply. "Many of us know that and will speak to it when asked. Certainly Antonia herself cannot bear too close an investigation. But the truth might come too late for you." She heaved a deep sigh. "Obey her directive and naught will come of this. Now go. The queen will not be harmed while I draw breath. I've enlisted Roussel to push this scheme to get Eugenie away from Castelle Escalon. Though he's common, he has a respectful manner and intelligent approach. The king will listen to a man of science. The very air here is poison."

"Thank you. Honestly, lady, thank you. Did everyone on the queen's watch hear this? Eleanor, Arabella . . . Lord Ilario?" Ilario had to know the danger before prompting the king to summon me.

"She announced it to all the inner circle. In *confidence*, naturally." Patrice's sarcasm reflected my own feeling. Confidentiality did not exist at court. But at least Ilario had wind of Antonia's intent.

Though a seething morass inside, I left the royal apartments without further argument. If anyone breathed the words *poison* and *Anne de Vernase* in the king's hearing, I would be dead before the day was out. The poisoned salts I'd saved from the broken vial were tucked away in my locked drawer, but they could more easily be deemed evidence against me than in my favor. I could prove nothing.

IN MY BRIEF ABSENCE, A folded letter, sealed with an unfamiliar device, had been left on my bedchamber table. I ripped it open, sinking to the bed as I read.

> *The Honorable Derwin de Scero-Gurmeddion will depart Castelle Escalon for Palazzo Gurmedd at seventh hour of the morning watch on 27 Ocet. He asserts his betrothal rights and commands his affianced bride, Anne de Vernase ney Cazar, prepare herself to accompany him. From this hour, she is to have no physical or verbal communication with any male unless in the presence of, and with the permission of, her betrothed husband. Appropriate garments for the barone's maiden bride will be delivered beforetime.*

I flung open my window and gulped the sultry air, rejecting one panicked solution after another. Eventually, hands shaking like a palsied elder,

I mixed an additional supply of Lianelle's potion. I would become a ghost myself before submitting to the Honorable Derwin.

With time and forceful discipline I gathered my wits. The timing of Derwin's assertion of rights could be no accident. Antonia's doing, certainly. *Think, Anne.* Duplais believed the conspirators needed me at Voilline. Dante had sworn to ensure my presence. Derwin was Antonia's tool, and the ducessa would never jeopardize her triumph for spite. Rather, I should read this development as a good sign. Antonia was nervous. More chances for mistakes. My purpose here was to throw them off balance, and surely that was her own purpose—distraction, so I'd not suspect their true plan for me. Or, even more likely, Derwin had agreed to transport me to Voilline in return for Antonia's connivance in my betrothal.

The more I thought of it, the more it made sense. *Keep the girl away from the king. Ship her through Castelle Escalon's gates with her contracted husband.* No one would question.

My efforts did not reduce my dread at the events to come, or my revulsion at yielding to Derwin of Gurmeddion even for a few hours' ride to Mont Voilline, but at least I could think again.

I sat by my window, quieted my unruly thoughts, and opened myself to the aether. *Friend?*

No response. No island of quiet. No solid anchor.

I needed to tell Dante that Derwin was charged with transporting me. I needed to ask where he imagined we would find the breaking point in the Mondragon ritual. Even if we upended the Aspirant's plan, might it not be too late for Duplais or Papa, Ambrose or Eugenie? Was Dante's power enough to protect the innocent as well as thwart the wicked . . . and would he care? His method of protecting the innocent was to ravage minds. Indeed, I needed to hear my friend of the aether and be reassured I had not been a naive fool all those hours ago.

I tried again. Searched. Listened. After a while, desperate and worried, I opened all barriers as I had never done. Swept up by the mindstorm, I hurtled through the anarchy of grief and anxiety, excitement and fear, one autumn leaf amid millions in the heart of a hurricane. *Friend, are you here?*

A touch. Distant, faint. *Not now* . . .

Both relieved and disappointed, exhausted from lack of sleep, I struggled to retreat from chaos and reassemble my defenses. One step to suppress desire, another for each sense . . . A brick at a time, I must rebuild the wall. Only on that afternoon, I could not. I buried my head in my pillows and let chaos drive me into storm-racked dreams.

"DAMOSELLE. WAKE UP, DAMOSELLE. GRACIOUS, you're all askew." Ella's insistent politeness dragged me out of a black stupor. I fought off sleep, blinking, focusing on the girl's face swimming in the candlelight.

"What's the time?" I said, gripping her arm, overcome with a horrified certainty that it was seventh hour of the morning watch and Derwin of Gurmeddion had come to claim me.

"It's gone eleventh hour of the evening watch. I've brought a message from Heurot."

That meant Ilario! "Yes, yes, all right. Where is it?"

"It's not writ this time. Heurot says you're to meet the gentleman in the portrait gallery at middle-night exactly. You'll know which gallery, he says. And whatever you do, you mustn't be seen. Though I'm not sure at all how you might do that. There's the most awful two fellows out in the passage. None passes them that they don't question and . . . ogle . . . in the crudest way. It's enough to make me want a wash right there and then."

Derwin's men. No mistaking.

"Thank you, Ella. I'll manage. The men in the passage . . . they didn't know you were coming to me?"

"I told them that *all* my ladies charge me to empty the slops jars before middle-night so they wouldn't have nasty dreams in the late dark. Didn't think they'd know the habits of a fine house."

"You are exceptional, Ella," I said, hugging her with a fierce pride. "We could all do with fewer nasty dreams. And don't worry. I'll be all right with this."

With a sidewise grin, she dipped her knee and scurried away with my night jar.

Refreshed by the sleep, veins coursing with excitement, I dressed carefully, donning the elegant brocade jacket Melusina had made for my last visit to Merona. The wardstone ring gleamed on my finger, and Lianelle's nireal hung from my neck. Vials of the potion were tucked inside my bodice, in my skirt waist, and in the spall pouch tied to my belt. The zahkri sheath on my thigh was snug; my rambunctious hair tidied. Lady Patrice, Lianelle, and my Cazar uncles would all approve my turnout.

As the bells struck half past eleventh hour, I took exactly two drops of the potion. Thus the two ruffians in the passage had no one to ogle as I slipped past and began the long trek to the west wing. I kept to the public rooms of the palace. A quiet drizzle yet owned the skies, and I needed to present myself to my goodfather fairly, not a draggled mess. On this occasion, *portrait gallery* could only mean the Kings' Gallery.

Ilario was talking to the air when I arrived. Every few moments he would duck his head and whisper, "Damoselle? Damoselle?"

I had mercy and called out softly. "Here, lord."

To his credit, he blew a long, slow exhale and scanned the gallery, only a bit wild in the eye. "Saints . . . come along, then."

"Thought I'd never get the chance," he said as soon as we'd entered his warren of closets and passages. "Philippe spent two hours with Geni and another interrogating the physician. Poor Roussel was a stammering wreck, but I think he came off well. Told Philippe this was not another miscarried child, but more likely a reaction to the strain of her position and the herbs she'd been taking to help with . . . you know . . . these things. Conceiving. Philippe approved the idea of sending her to the country. The rest of the night he's spent with the Privy Council and then Lord Baldwin alone, and only just now run them off. He's expecting us." He—the King of Sabria.

We ducked out of a niche behind a statue, darted across a wide passage, and into a storage room that contained one of his ubiquitous wall panels. "Believe me—he was not at all happy to hear about you being here. When

I told him all you'd done for Geni, he didn't quite boot me out. I didn't say anything about the rest. Thought I'd leave that to you."

My sudden reappearance just then caused only an abrupt, "Hah. Well, then . . ."

A narrow passage sloped gently downhill for a few metres, a draft carrying the scent of old leather. I pressed my handkerchief to my nose, hoping to prevent yet another bout of sneezing.

The sound of a metal catch and the solid movement of a wall panel, and we crowded into a dim room crammed with bags, boxes, and trunks. The walls were lined with shelves of folded linen and wooden racks hung with old-fashioned robes of scarlet, purple, and green. Illumination was supplied by two slivers of light, the exact size to frame another panel doorway.

Ilario opened a tiny slot in the panel. The lights beyond the door were muted, and two quiet voices could be heard, though I couldn't make out the words. Moments ticked away. I brushed cobwebs from my shoulders and tried not to fidget.

The voices quieted. A solid *snick* sounded like a door closing. Moments later, Ilario tapped lightly on the door in a short, rhythmic pattern.

"Come," said a voice that I remembered.

Only firelight and a single small lamp illuminated the room, which was not at all what one might expect for a king's bedchamber. No gilt, brocades, or velvets. Simple furnishings polished to a dull glow. Brass lamps free of tarnish. A shelf of well-thumbed books. A carpet of solid maroon, figured in black. The windows were open, drawing in the scent of the rain . . . pleasant tonight. My goodfather sat in a padded leather chair next the fire, a glass of wine sparkling like a giant ruby in his hand, his stockinged feet propped on a stool.

For a moment I felt very small. Though he had dandled me on his knee and listened with serious good humor to my first forays into adult conversation, Philippe de Savin-Journia had forever been a dashing young god to me. He was a man who led armies, ruled cities, and dispensed justice to the most powerful kingdom in the world. And here was I, a woman of little experience and no sophistication, setting out to tell him of a monumental event that aimed to bring him to his knees. I was grateful for the dim light to hide my flush of embarrassment.

Ilario perched on the arm of a chair away from the fire. I dipped a knee, bowed my head, and waited.

"Ani Sophia Madeleine." A brisk movement of his hand brought me to standing. "The years are cruel to pass so quickly. You were but a wide-eyed child full of literary enchantments last time we had a visit. I recall you were ready to embark on a voyage of exploration to Atlas's Pillars, and wished to know if your king would provide you a ship."

After all the misery of the past five years, why was it at such a moment that my tears began to flow? Was it that he sounded so like my father, or that his words brought back those happy times so vividly? I was furious at myself—it was such a "girlish" thing to do, just when I needed to be serious and convincing. The last time Philippe had *seen* me was at my father's trial, when he thrust the damning letters in my face and demanded I say again whose hand had written them. Tonight *I* was on trial.

"I would still like to take that voyage, sire, but the Creator's servants have plotted a different course."

"Indeed. I heard you were here and fully intended to find the time for a chat. I never considered inviting you at middle-night, and me not even in boots. But our friend here seems to believe you have a tale that must be told before I've picked the dirt of the road from my beard. So tell what you will. We've hours yet until daylight."

"I'd wait if I could, sire, but the matters are of utmost urgency, and I'm to be taken from Castelle Escalon at seventh hour of the morning watch, betrothed to a man your wife's foster mother has selected for me."

His chin popped up. "Betrothed? To *Antonia's* choice? I thought I had some say in that particular matter. Who is it?"

Tempting though it was, I would not begin with Derwin. So much had changed since I'd left my appeal in Simon's hands.

"That's only one piece of a very long story. I ask your indulgence to hear it entire. I understand you'll receive everything I say with skepticism, but I beg you to believe that I wish only your good."

"So you give me the most difficult part to swallow right at the beginning." He tilted his head and propped it on a curled fist. But there was nothing casual in his manner. "I hear reports that young Ambrose has slipped his bonds and murdered his lawful jailer. I hear reports that my cousin Duplais has mysteriously vanished from the palace after open hostilities with you, and that you were the last to see him. I hear reports that you serve in my wife's bedchamber—powers of night, in her *bedchamber*— and she lies in this stupor that no one seems to understand. I hear tales of poisoning and murder in this house—the widow of my noble friend Blasencourt, my wife's physician, a kitchen girl—all since your arrival. I know you, Anne Sophia Madeleine de Vernase ney Cazar, and I know the bond you shared with the man I entrusted with everything precious to me, the friend who betrayed his every oath. Why in the name of Heaven should I imagine you wish my *good*? Why should I not have you thrown into the Spindle or into the sea this night?"

He never raised his voice, never spoke anything I'd not considered already, but his quiet outrage trembled my bones. Yet it took me only a moment to summon my own from the heated iron in my belly. "Perhaps for my mother, your friend, who weeps in madness. Perhaps for my brother, your goodson, who rotted four years in your prison, beaten, starved, and abused in the most obscene ways because you did not heed your responsibility to him. Perhaps for my murdered sister, whose tale I've come to tell you. And if nothing else, then for the debt you owe my father. By saving your life, he gave you this kingdom."

The king leapt from his chair. "He *betrayed* this kingdom! He stole its future and my wife's peace! With pleasure and malice, Michel de Vernase murdered my *son*. You didn't know that, did you? He slaughtered the noblest young lord Sabria had ever birthed as if he were a crawling beast, then dumped him naked on the floor of my house."

His wrath fell on my head like a mighty river from a cliff top. It was all I could do to remain standing. Yet the words confused me as much as the power of their speaking. *Noblest young lord?* Desmond was but a year old when he died. That was years before the conspiracy, the assassination attempt, the investigation. *Threw him naked . . . ?*

The image in the Rotunda reshaped itself in my mind, limned with pain beyond bearing . . . and enlightenment. No wonder the king could not live in this house anymore. "Edmond de Roble was your son."

"And that's my difficulty with anything you might say. Only four people in the world knew that truth. Myself. Ilario de Sylvae. Edmond's mother, who is not my wife. And your father. Neither his mother nor Ilario wrote the letter pinned to my son's dead flesh. No one knew the words to put in such a message that would identify the writer, and the handwriting was as familiar to me as it was to you. You risk your life walking in here and asking my indulgence, Anne de Vernase."

He returned to his chair, propped up his feet, and drank his wine, staring at me.

The ramparts in front of me were much more formidable than I'd guessed. But the very reason I could grasp the magnitude of my goodfather's grief and anger was because they mirrored my own. Edmond and my parents, Ophelie de Marangel, and Lianelle had been the Aspirant's first targets. Duplais and Ambrose and Eugenie were the next. And after them the rest of us . . .

So I stood my ground. "Four years ago you rendered judgment that my father had committed treason against you, conspiring with corrupted sorcerers to do murder—this despicable, unholy outrage to your son and other innocents—in order to tear you from your throne. When I bore witness against my father, I believed fully in his corruption. Just as you did, I felt betrayed by a man I had believed worthy of all my love and honor, and if he had showed his face at Montclaire, I would have turned him over to your justice. But four-and-thirty days ago, everything changed. That was the morning my sister, Lianelle, your other gooddaughter, knew she was going to die and arranged to leave us a message. In an act of extraordinary magic and extraordinary courage, she pointed us to the truth. . . ."

I told him the story of Lianelle and her books of magic. I recited her letter from memory. As I told him of Lady Cecile and the page she had stolen from Orviene, of the down-at-the-heels nobleman, and of Warder Pognole and Ambrose's middle-night visitors at the Spindle, Philippe de Savin-Journia pulled his feet from the stool and leaned forward, forearms on his thighs, knuckles taut. But he said nothing and let me continue.

When I came to Eugenie, Ilario's words blended with mine, explaining his conviction that I might provide his sister some shelter from Antonia's smothering wickedness. And he told how Duplais had set him to watch and protect me, while giving the household to believe we were at odds. "He used her, sire, to force them show themselves, and so they did, beyond his expectations. And he was convinced of her innocence."

I told him of the Bastionne, of Soren and the children, of the aether and the mindstorm, of hearing Papa and knowing in my bones and heart that he was innocent. Of all, I omitted only the tale of my quiet friend who happened to be Dante. Neither of them was going to believe that until they saw it for themselves. And no matter the honor of these two, there were doors and peepholes everywhere. I dared not risk news of Dante's duplicity reaching the Aspirant. He would believe.

I even told the king of the copper shield bracelet. By this time, I dared pause long enough to venture a question. "How did he explain its origin, sire?"

"He said it was found on him when he was born. The Delourre demesne records recorded no such device, so he assumed it was the kitchen girl's god token."

And then I risked all, because if the king chose to ignore my warnings, my family's safety wasn't going to matter. I told him my family's name.

"That's why they've kept Papa," I said. "To bleed for their magic. And if the Aspirant knows his name, then he's kept him for vengeance."

"Mondragon. Michel a sorcerer. Impossible . . ." The king's soft utterance gave lie to his denial.

"It explains the manacle." Ilario now sat cross-legged on a stool between the king's chair and me, absorbing the details of the story he'd not yet heard. "Ophelie's manacle," he answered to the king's puzzled stare and mine. "Ophelie de Marangel was held prisoner in the royal crypt. A burst of magic from a fellow prisoner set her free—raw power; that's how Dante described it to Portier. Portier assumed Michel was Ophelie's warder, because someone scratched the Ruggiere device on the wall. But we never found out who the prisoner was and we decided it couldn't be Michel, because she was freed by magic."

"Michel would have gone mad at watching them bleeding a young girl," said the king.

"That's exactly what happened to me on the ridge," I said, blinking back tears at the imagining and at the burgeoning grief coloring my good-father's voice. "It enabled me to cut the snaketethers. I used magic, though I've no idea how or whether I can ever use it again."

And then came the difficult piece . . . our plan. "We must have faith in Duplais, sire. He believes we can stop this evil, bring the Aspirant to justice, and repair the damage he's done only by letting events move forward without overt interference. We've . . . sensed . . . powerful forces that work to our benefit, that confuse the conspirators' cause and spoil their magics and that must be allowed to play out. Only when the time is right will Duplais and I and our allies, known and unknown, find the resources to undermine these mysteries. I've come to believe he's right, lord, as deeply as I've ever believed anything. But I would feel much better about it all if the King of Sabria and my noble bodyguard were watching, as well, prepared to come drag us out."

The fire snapped, its last burst of energy before fading out. Having poured out so many words, I felt as if I were fading, too.

The king's cold anger was more fearsome than his earlier outburst. "So you would have me send Eugenie into this obscenity? I will not."

"No. They couldn't have based their plan solely on the queen." The conclusion had come to me as I outlined the plot. "Antonia's aims are irrelevant to their larger purpose, and your actions could never have been entirely predictable. They must have an alternative . . . vessel . . . in mind—another woman who will be there and prepared. Likely another captive. So we rattle them again by sending our lady somewhere safe with people you trust. Neither of you can go with her, else they'll be suspicious right away. And by all means, don't tell *me* where she's taken! It's a risk, but a safe one, I think. I'll go with Derwin in the morning; that must be the plan to get me there. And then Duplais can do . . . whatever it is he believes will stop this. And you, sire, can bring down your full might on their heads when you get our signal—well, you'll have to think of a signal, as I'm entirely out of ideas. But I don't see that we have any choice in any of this. . . ."

Eventually I persuaded them to see it my way. Both were convinced I was mad. Likely I was. But they didn't know Dante would be working with me. Dante was everything.

CHAPTER 38

At half past fourth hour of the night watch, a small cadre of the Guard Royale rode out of the postern on their way to a new posting in Arabasca. Half an hour later, a carriage marked with the gold feathers of Enderia clattered out of the stableyard and through one of Castelle Escalon's minor gates. The gate guards took no note of passengers other than the hysterical Marquesa Patrice, who was called to her ailing sister in Challyat, and the physician trying in vain to comfort her . . . though they might have observed a tall serving girl asleep in the corner. I didn't witness these occurrences, but I had helped plan them.

"Have we disrupted the divine order by sending Geni away?" said Ilario as we watched the wheeling stars from his balcony. "What if we've thwarted Portier's mission here in the world, and he dies truly . . . forever . . . forbidden to come back? Cult teachings are ambiguous when it comes to failure."

"I'm the last one to ask about divine order," I said, fingering the king's little signal packet. "But it seems to me that the very definition of saints, according to your beliefs, implies they are a random influence in the world, directed by their own innate sense of what is right. So, Portier chose his risk. If your sister had been more than halfway lucid, I would have said let her choose her own role in this, as well. But she's too much under the influence of poisons and fertility charms, incense and ghosts. Physician Roussel will see to her health, and Lady Patrice to her well-being. I hope they've taken her somewhere winters are mild."

The cadre of the Guard Royale—Philippe's handpicked ten—would meet Patrice's carriage outside Merona's gates and escort it neither to Arabasca nor Challyat, but to a place far from Voilline. The king told Roussel and Patrice only that he had received threats on Eugenie's life and chose to keep her journey and her refuge secret. They surely suspected more.

How odd it was to find so many friends at Castelle Escalon, against all expectation. None better than the extraordinary man standing next to me.

"I'd best go now, lord chevalier," I said. "Derwin's sent me a gown the color of a frog's belly, a *modesty veil* that's the size and quality of a fishnet, and a flask of his favored perfume, which smells like rotted seaweed. My toilet will take some time and a strong stomach." Two hours remaining. I needed some time to breathe.

"Saints mercy, damoselle." Ilario's face crumpled. "I think I'd rather face my foster mother when she discovers Geni gone than that disgusting wretch. Portier will have a deal to answer for when this is over, convincing you to proceed with whatever these devils plan."

"Voilline is but three hours' ride. You'll have to deal with Antonia for much longer. Lord, you must watch your back when they come for the queen." Antonia couldn't abduct the Queen of Sabria on her own. "I'll be anxiously awaiting my noble rescuer." I waggled the small packet of crystals that would make any fire burn green.

"I've a lifetime's practice watching my back." He walked me to the wall. The panel remained open from our arrival half an hour since. "Can you find your way? I'm thinking to catch some sleep while I can. Dama Antonia is an early riser."

"First right turn. Down three steps and right again. Second left turn. Fifteen metres and look for the latch. Divine grace, good lord."

"Exactly so." He bowed and kissed my hand, merry blue eyes peeking up through his flaxen hair. "But truly, Damoselle Anne, any lovely lady I entertain in my chambers in the predawn hours must call me Ilario."

And before I could laugh at him, he raised my hand to his forehead. "May you find the grace of the divine, the courage of all saints, and all angels' blessings this day."

ILARIO'S MOMENT OF GRACE WAS but a single treasure in a chest of worries. My accounting of Raissina Nialle's evidence had been more than enough to induce my goodfather to halt my marriage. But he refused to issue his denial of consent until I returned to his custody. If I agreed to ride out with Derwin without being legally betrothed, I would be labeled harlot and ineligible for any decent marriage. Though I preferred the title *harlot* to *betrothed wife of Barone Gurmeddion*, my goodfather was adamant, and I had tested his patience enough. Titles would not change what was to come—for better or worse.

While traversing the quiet route from Ilario's rooms, I tried again to speak with Dante, but could not touch him even so slightly as before. Was he already gone to Voilline? To inquire of his whereabouts among the householders would be as subtle as setting geese loose in the east wing. Anyone in the palace could be Antonia's spy. The more I considered my *friend's* identity, the more stupid I felt. How could I possibly trust him?

"Damoselle de Vernase!" As I angled into the main passage, a youth from the steward's office hailed me softly from the stair. "I've letters."

"Post messengers must travel on the night wind," I said, curious at the sizeable stack.

"Nay, damoselle. These were actually held for Sonjeur de Duplais, but he instructed Secretary de Sain that if he was out of the palace for more than a day to forward his post to you. The secretary heard you were to be leaving this morning, so he says I should bring them early."

I sent him off with my thanks and a spark of anticipation. Only one reason Duplais would have his letters sent to me—hope of an answer to his inquiries about Kajetan's noble guest. I riffled through the stack as I hurried past the two gawking Gurmedd men yet loitering in the passage.

Two letters were from a tailor, one from a wine merchant, and three from libraries around Sabria. Four or five had no identifying marks. I separated those from the rest.

Pushing open my bedchamber door, I'd only a heartbeat to wonder why Ella had left a candle burning. Before me, grinning and fingering his tongue, stood Dagobert de Gurmedd.

"Come to fetch you, wench. We've chose to leave early, as we've been told you might have friends thinking to snatch you away." The two Gurmedd ruffians blocked the doorway behind me.

Despite the bile stinging my throat, I lifted my chin. "Doubting the bride's honor is a poor way to begin a marriage. I keep my agreements."

Dagobert flared his nostrils. "You've had talk with men. Conspired. I can smell it on you."

My face heated before I could even ask how he could possibly know.

The youth grinned in triumph. "He said you'd blush at that. My sire will teach you obedience, he will. Now ready yourself." He thrust the atrocious garments into my hand. Squirming, he cast a sidewise glance at his companions. "And yer not to wear drawers nor lady linens 'neath the gown, neither. We'll have no uppity ways in Gurmedd."

Sheerest will kept me from drawing my knife. "Get out, Dagobert. If I'm not to converse with men, then I'm certain my betrothed husband would not wish men to observe me dressing or even to *think* about it. *You'll* be the one disciplined when I tease your father's ear with sweetnesses and at the same time tell him how you tried to sneak a look at his naked bride!"

Dagobert's jaw dropped, seemingly astonished that anyone could figure out his nasty scheme. Red-faced, he shoved the two snickering guards from the room and was halfway out the door before he could think of anything to say. "Make it fast or we'll drag you out by the hair. Da'll skin us if we're late."

I slammed the door, hoping it broke his nose. Only a few hours to the Voilline Rift. I could bear that.

Retaining my "lady linens" and gray petticoat, I donned the spangled gown and ankle-length, fishnet veil. Commanding my shaking hands to cooperate, I used the zahkri to cut a ragged slit in the gown's seam, and made sure it allowed me access to the precious knife. The perfume, I tossed out my window. The veil stank badly enough.

My stomach churned with doubts. Sheathing my knife, I clenched my hands to my forehead. *Friend?* I called, reaching . . . searching. *I could use a reassuring word just now. Please.*

. . . *father lives* . . . The response was so faint, I could scarce believe I'd heard correctly.

My father lives?

Portier, too, for now. The words brimmed with fervid satisfaction. And truth.

My eyes welled with tears. *My brother?*

Not yet. Already the mindstorm was submerging his voice. *No other answers yet.*

Disappointed, yes, but hopeful. *I'm on my way. No tantrums needed.*

For a moment, I feared he'd not heard. But then more words took shape, stronger, more solid, wrapped in his own relief and glinting with amusement. *You'll be welcome . . . fierce ally . . . sunset tonight . . .* It was not the mindstorm that carried these, but a cold, dark current that filled my head, my chest, my spirit—a river, deep and black, not a morbid darkness as commonly thought, but as richly textured as ermine, as substantial as liquid ebony, as mysterious as midnight with all its exotic scents and eerie cries, its unexpected wonders, secrets, hidden passions, dangers, violence, and risky pleasure. Infusing all was a fierce and abiding joy that blazed with the pungent heat of good wine. It felt as if my friend had ripped himself open to send these fragments to reassure me, exposing this singular flood, this pungent darkness. It was his lifeblood . . . his magic.

In that moment every other person I had known—father, sister, mother, brother, those friends I had just come to appreciate—faded into insubstantiality. I *knew* Dante. I *understood* him as I understood no one in the world. He had trusted me, exposing his essence in all its dark and terrible beauty. So much to explore and learn. Angels' mercy, I did not want ever to look away.

"Get out here!" Muffled grumbling outside my door demanded my attention. I stuffed linen, soap, clothes, and towels into the tapestry traveling case pulled from under my bed, and Duplais' letters and the packet of signal crystals into my bodice. Still glazed with wonder, I pulled open the door and walked out of my life.

OUR UNSETTLING DESCENT OF THE servants' stair to the east doors recalled my transport to the Bastionne Camarilla. But instead of being thrown into a wagon, I was lifted to the back of a bay mare. Torches flared and smoked in the yard.

"Took you time enough." Derwin's snarl banished the lingering magic of the mindstorm. Though the netting veil obscured my vision, I spotted my betrothed lord not far away.

"What are you doing?" I said. The two guards had set the stirrups for me, but didn't stop there. They looped an extra leather strap through the irons and about each ankle. I had poked my hands through the proper holes in the veil to have the use of them, but the men bound my wrists together so I couldn't pull them back again, and hooked the spangles on the hem of the veil to metal loops on the hem of my skirt. I was locked inside the horrid garment as if it were a cage.

"Can't have our prize jumping off, now, can we?" Dagobert sniggered and flung himself onto his own mount.

As Derwin's party, some twenty strong, formed up around the lord and me, a small, stiff figure in a scarlet cloak and hood descended the palace steps. "You know your orders, Gurmedd lord?"

"Homeward bound with my prize, good lady. And never a look back—lest my gold and new horses be not waiting."

"All is arranged." The wind lifted the hood from Antonia's piled curls. "Gold at Sessaline, remounts at the Crenci Waystation, the Challyat border, Navella, and the rest, and the last payment waiting at the Gurmedd Pass. Ride hard and by midmorn you'll have her out of reach. Then you can enjoy the interfering little vixen at the roadside for all I care. She is insolent and proud and needs a strong master."

Cold dread seeped upward from my toes. *North? Crenci? Out of reach?*

Voilline was southeast of Merona, nowhere near Crenci. Dante had confirmed the location of the rite.

"Lady Antonia, what are—?"

"Surprised, are you?" she said. "These men—this Aspirant—thought
to use and discard me. He kept me playing games he never meant for me
to win. But I listen beyond the words and hear his scorn and recognize the
poison's taste in my tisane in time to wreak havoc before I die. And when
a friendly bird whispers of new arrangements made, I pounce. If I cannot
have my prize, they shan't have theirs. Analyze it in the days ahead, Anne
de Vernase. Calculate where your vaunted intelligence guessed wrong as
you lick your lord's boots in the deeps of mountain winter. I hope he
keeps you in chains."

Her cloak whipped about her ankles as she ascended the steps.

"Move out!"

"No! Wait!" Stung with dismay, sick with fear, I started yelling. "Betrayed! Help me!"

Surely someone—a stable boy, a kitchen girl, Ilario from his balcony—
would see what was happening. Someone might think the screaming lady
was worth mentioning.

Guards halted us at the palace gate, and though the Gurmedd riders
kept me surrounded and well apart as Derwin showed them our betrothal
contract, I shouted to get their attention. "I'm the king's gooddaughter,"
I yelled. "I'm abducted! Tell the king we ride north."

"These fine ladies never understand the business of dowries." Derwin
chuckled and slapped the gate guard on the shoulder. "They prance and
preen to attract a man's favor, then get their tits in a twist 'cause we men-
folk must look square at the cost of upkeep—dresses and follies and tasty
bits to eat. No matter it's legal, they're scared to lose their maidswatch, so's
they raise a fuss. Ah, now you've stamped the paper, we'll be on our way.
My bride'll cheer up once we're cozy in my keep. She'll tame just fine."

"We've been betrayed!" I yelled. "Tell the king!"

The square-face guard grimaced at the Gurmedd lord. "Such a
message'll do no good today, sonjeura. His Majesty rode out not half an
hour since, like the Souleater was on his tail."

No! The king had moved too early. It didn't make sense. Eugenie was safe with his own bodyguards. And Antonia poisoned? *Dying*? Everything was wrong!

Derwin laughed and bellowed. "On to the Iron Hills!"

Derwin led us at a fast walk through the deserted city and the first few kilometres on the road. No one could see well. The coarse mesh of the veil obscured just enough to leave me blind in the late dark. But as soon as the sky began to gray, the Gurmedd barreled northward as hard as he dared push. They had taken the reins from my mount and attached a lead rope to Dagobert's saddle. I'd no choice but to ride.

Dante, hear me! They're taking me north. Was panic blinding me to his voice or muting my own? Was he spellworking? Sleeping? Or was this his doing, a grand deception by the master? Lure the naive girl with images of truth. Gain her trust. Set her on a course . . . and crush it.

Impossible. His horror at the requirement to kill Duplais had been genuine and displayed before he knew I was watching. Did daemons grieve for their victims? He had shared his essence. He had sent me to Raissina to save me from this. I could not . . . could not . . . be wrong about him. I clung to belief as I clung to the horse, because to relinquish either was unthinkable.

Our mounts' hooves thundered on the good road. The horses would be blown by Crenci. But with fresh mounts we'd be into Challyat before midday, too far ahead for anyone to catch us, even if someone discovered where we'd gone. Even if there was anyone left at Castelle Escalon to come looking.

On any other day, the surge of muscle underneath would have thrilled me. But as I curled forward, clinging desperately to mane and pommel, every step took me farther from the place I needed to be. Great gods, my *father* was at Voilline. A sword in the gut could be no more painful than the knowledge that I was helpless while he suffered. Any imagining that my father would survive the Aspirant's triumph was flimsier than the mist draping the vineyards to either side of us.

"Don't slow, Dag," said Derwin, goading his son's horse with a snap of his crop. "Wouldn't want the girlie to have time for magicking."

Would that I *could* control that molten fire I'd felt on Merona's ridge. But I'd no idea even how to begin.

Sunset, Dante had said. Easy to imagine sorcery most effective at the time of day when the mysteries of the world felt strongest, when the change from light to dark fed our most profound anticipation and most abject fear. Sunset would come at Voilline, and Dante would have to dredge up the book's spells for himself . . . sapping his strength for the difficult work of the rite and the even more difficult work of unraveling what his partners did. No one would drop a packet of crystals into a fire, signaling the king to take down the conspirators. Duplais would die in his chains.

Speed and pain wrenched a sob from me. The world streamed past, a blur of green and gold through the flapping veil.

We'd ridden perhaps five kilometres when our pace abruptly slowed. Those at the front of the party shouted at one another and those behind. Even without knowing their language I recognized fear and uncertainty.

"*Griv yagnat!*" Derwin, pushing to the front. Dagobert followed, dragging me along behind. As well as I could see, the road plunged down-ward into a bank of yellow-brown fog. Autumn fog in Louvel's hollows was not so unusual, especially near the river. Not so usual were the crisp lightning bursts inside the cloud wall, and the immediate, ear-splitting cracks of thunder, as if an entire storm had been trapped between two swales with blue sky above us.

"Forward," snapped Derwin. "No detours. My gold waits at Sessa-line."

Sessaline. I'd heard that name. But where?

The fog slowed us to a walk, elsewise we risked the horses stumbling into a ditch or a wall. Derwin quickly ordered Dagobert to dismount and lead us through so we could keep to the road. The men fell silent, save for mumbled curses. The horses snorted and jinked, tossing their heads in protest. Every lightning strike set them off.

The fog enveloped us like wool, smothering sound and making every breath difficult. Sweat dripped and trickled under my thick clothes. It took all my skill and concentration to keep the mare steady. With my ankles bound to the stirrups, she'd crush me in a fall.

"Houses ahead!" Dagobert shouted. "Alloo! It's the Gurmedd lord come. Step out and speak. What place is this?"

No one stepped out. Even his assertion of houses seemed doubtful. The ill-defined shapes could as easily be rocks as dwellings.

Derwin ordered a halt and dispatched his son and another man to inquire if this was Sessaline. Dagobert detached my lead rope, and Derwin shouted at the others to form up around me.

The men vanished. Everyone else stayed close. You could lose a legion in such a fog.

"Dimios's balls!" A nearby warrior threw down his water skin and spat repeatedly. The skin's contents splattered on the rutted roadway, droplets the size of eggs bouncing into the air, stretching and shifting like bubbles. Some dissolved into the fog that twined around the horses' legs. Some settled on the man's stained trousers, then rolled off slowly, shattering like glass when they struck dirt again. "What devil's work is this?"

Devil's work! Duplais had mentioned Sessaline when he was talking about the anomalies in the city—the exemplars of our new world under the Aspirant.

The warrior couldn't stop swiping the back of his hand across his face. A few of the men laughed uncertainly, as if they thought someone had played a prank. Others backed away from him, their fingers twitching witch signs. Derwin, positioned at the front, stared into the fog ahead as if to will his men back with his booty.

Free of the lead rope, I nudged the mare gently.

Soon the barone sent two more men after the first. One returned immediately, stopping dead in his tracks when he confronted his lord.

Derwin slashed the man's face with his crop. "I said get thee after, Vigger."

"But, lord, I was walking straight ahead. Fog's thick as mustard."

I nudged the mare again toward the edge of the party. Bring her around and I would bolt, fog or no. Blind or no.

Some of the Gurmedd warriors began mumbling of withdrawal. Some simply shouted louder.

Just as I forced the mare a little farther beyond the group, I felt a firm tug on her bridle. A soft cluck was accompanied by, "Sshh."

My stomach hollowed and I strained to see, but raised no alarm, allowing the unseen hand to lead me deeper into the fog. In moments the Gurmedd warriors were out of sight, and their calls to their comrades were muffled as with down pillows. Hands fumbled with my ankles, tugging fruitlessly at the straps. Then a sawing pressure released my right ankle.

Hurry . . . hurry . . . I willed the indefinable bulk to get quickly to the other side of me, and the shouts of Derwin's warriors not to change into warnings.

As the strap on my left ankle fell free, I whispered, "Hands," and held them as far down as I could reach.

A man's sturdy, capable fingers found mine. A knife obligingly cut through the binding cord. As he held the mare's head, I wrestled out of the damnable veil, threw it to the ground, and pulled out the zahkri.

"Now show me your face," I said softly. If it was a Gurmedd, I'd shove the blade in his eye.

He moved closer, running his hand along the horse's neck. Indeed I recognized the hand first—wide, well tended, a forest of curling hair—before his head of gray-streaked curls came into view. "Saint's mercy," I breathed. "Roussel."

CHAPTER 39

The physician laid a hushing finger across his wide grin, then used it to shift my shaking knife blade away from his face. I swallowed my thanks and questions.

He tugged on the bridle again. Slowly, quietly, we moved away. Saints please, we would not turn back on our tracks as the Gurmedd warrior had! But the physician seemed sure of his course, and before I knew it we came on his own horse tied to a metre post.

He motioned me to bend down. "Can you ride a b-bit more?"

"To Syanar, if need be."

He squeezed my hand and mounted. We moved out at a painfully slow walk.

About the time we broke out of the fog into the watery sunlight, a bellow burst from behind us. "Witch woman! You'll wear chains at your wedding, girl! Find her!"

"Shall we go, lady?"

Never had I experienced such a glorious gallop. Free of the fog, the veil, the bindings, and the vile Gurmedds, I could indeed have ridden to Syanar. We retraced the morning's route, and almost before I knew it Sante Paolo's Pillar rose in the distance. But my horse was laboring.

I shouted at Roussel to slow. "The mare's blown," I said, breathless myself. Though a glance over my shoulder evidenced no pursuit, my blood drummed with Gurmedd hoofbeats. The sprawling vineyards and fields left the road exposed.

He coaxed his own beast closer and peered at mine. "We'll walk her. It's not so far. You'll soon be safe behind Merona's walls."

"I can't stop at Merona."

"But these Gurmedd—" He pursed his lips, frowning. "I can see there's no arguing. A freeholder I know k-keeps a few horses not far from here. We'll exchange and take the circuit road around the city, while you c-convince me not to turn you over to your g-goodfather's safekeeping."

"How in the name of Heaven are you here?" I said, taking advantage of the slower pace. "The queen—"

"She is quite safe. I've been watching the vile G-Gurmedd since learning of your prospects." He ducked his head and lifted his shoulders in resignation. "There are advantages to b-being an invisible person. Last night I heard him bragging of his bargain with the Lady Antonia. I didn't quite understand all of it, but . . . sometimes a man is forced to take action. Our mistress agreed."

"Eugenie's awake?" The morning took a yet brighter turn.

"She'd not been away from the p-palace a quarter hour before she shook off her stupor entirely. When I expressed my misgivings at your fate, she almost b-booted me out of the carriage to be on my way to your aid. I left her in the capable hands of the m-marquesa."

"Bless you, sonjeur. I shall be forever grateful." More than he could know.

He pointed to a stack of flat stones a few metres ahead. "Turn eastward at the cairn."

A track led through a stripped vineyard, the golden leaves half fallen. On any other day, the poignant reminder of Montclaire and the season's completion would have tempted me to dismount and wander for a while. But my father was waiting.

I urged the panting mare to yield a little more, as my thoughts raced ahead to Voilline. How could I surrender myself without raising the Aspirant's suspicions?

"Be at ease, lady," said Roussel, coming up from behind. "They'll not catch us now."

"It's not entirely Derwin. There are other matters pressing . . . even more dangerous."

"Heaven's gates, is the king *c-complicit* in this marriage? I c-can't believe he'd hold so hellish a grudge."

"Not that at all. It's—" Though relief and gratitude urged me to spew every detail, my friends had too many secrets I dared not reveal, even to my latest savior. Yet getting myself into play on my own was going to be difficult. A plan began to take shape. . . .

"Would you be willing to help me more, sonjeur? The circumstances would be far more dangerous than those you've just ventured."

"I am at your service, of course. Our mistress c-commanded." He bowed from his saddle. "Yet to accompany you into danger . . . I'll confess, I've no d-defensive skills of any worth. Better I see you safe with friends or family who can help you."

"I don't want a warrior, and I cannot afford delay. I need to reach Mont Voilline by sunset. Though it sounds awful, I need you to *deliver* me to the people there, as if you overheard Antonia bragging of her betrayal and saw an easy way to improve a physician's poor pay."

Shock struck him rigid. "Great heavens, lady, we've just g-got you out of slavery!"

"This is very different. A good friend is in mortal danger. The story would take me days to explain, but I swear to you, I am acting in the interests and with the consent of the King of Sabria."

"The king's consent?" He seemed to relax a bit. "Clearly I've missed some fascinating twist to your presence at Castelle Escalon. Your c-confidence honors me. Tell me what to do."

With the expenditure of half an hour and a debt to a grizzled, taciturn hostler named Favreu, we were racing southward.

Autumn sunlight mantled the fields behind us in gold, as Roussel and I hiked up Mont Voilline's northern shoulder, otherwise known as Ianne's Hand. Warblers and woodchats twittered from atop rocks and shrubs, or startled as we approached, then settled back to harvesting the year's crop of berries. Though the sun had gone from the east-facing hillside, the lingering heat still carried the resinous fragrances of the maquis: juniper and tree heath, leathery smilax and madder. Spiny leaves scratched our arms, and midges swarmed our ears and noses as we trod the narrow pilgrim path. Horses had come this way in the past hours. We'd hobbled our own mounts a few hundred metres down the slope so they'd not give us away.

The mendicant brother at the cult shrine in the village of Voilline had told us that Ianne's Hand provided the best view of both the holy mount and the daemon-touched rift, as well as the easiest path to the site of the warrior saint's imprisonment. He'd also cautioned that wise pilgrims would do well to keep away, for the sky had burned red the previous night, as if the Saint were at last cleansing the blood from his land.

My stomach fluttered in anticipation.

"The battle in the Voilline Rift effectively ended the Blood Wars," I told Roussel as we approached the summit of the low ridge. "Two blood families almost exterminated each other that day. In the ensuing months the people of Sabria finished the job."

"I've read a bit of history," he said. "A dreadful day that was, here on holy ground. Some call the slaughter the greatest sacrilege ever committed."

"Are you a Cultist?" I said, startled by the suddenly serious turn in his mood. He'd shown no particular reverence at the shrine. And throughout our long ride from Sessaline, our short stops to buy bread and cheese and rest the horses, and this sweltering climb, he had seemed singularly dedicated to bolstering my spirits. Laughing off incipient saddle sores, blistered feet, and uncomfortably unsuitable dress, he had professed simple delight at being outdoors in Sabria's most glorious season.

"My father was a Cultist. I don't subscribe to most of their trip-trap, but I do believe truths can be found in their legends. It doesn't make sense that our essence would be lost when the heart stops. It's one reason I chose to study medicine after years of other studies. I do find it fascinating that your mysterious mission brings us to the holiest site in cult lore and the holiest site in the history of magic."

"Not the holiest," I said as the delicious breeze of the heights welcomed us to the crest of Ianne's Hand. "The most depraved . . ." And then the expansive landscape stole the rest of my argument, my questions, and my words.

On our left Mont Voilline bared its craggy white face to the westering sun, afire in gold light near blinding in its brilliance. Easy to see how stories might arise here of a courageous young man who breached Heaven to bring fire to humankind.

To our right and looping back to the west to form a U shape stood a palisade of jagged pinnacles, vertical bands of white stone and seamed vales thick with joint pines and prickly juniper. To the south—the open end of the U—Mont Voilline's south shoulder fell away in long rills of white rock, like pale fingers plunging into the dusty green forest of Ardienne. Blue shadows had settled into the narrow vale between these bastions of stone—the rift.

A gentle slope led from our position on Voilline's shoulder down to a sun-drenched tableland that jutted from the mountain's sheer face before plummeting into the depths of the rift. This was the holy place, where pilgrims came to honor Sante Ianne. A black scar marked the scene of countless bonfires. Rags and ribbons fluttered from wooden poles jammed into cracks in the rock. Legend said that when the wind snatched the rotted fabric away, it was truly the Saint of Wisdom's hand, answering the prayers of the one who tied it there.

Yet it was not the common exhibits of reverence that transfixed me, but the image of Lady Cecile's stolen diagrams reflected upon the broad shelf. Thirty-six stone pillars, as ancient as Ianne's story, stood in three giant rings set side by side.

"Undeath, death, and life," I murmured.

"Sante Ianne's holy mystery," said Roussel at my shoulder.

The leftmost circle was centered by a deep rectangular basin. A system of stone troughs seemed designed to divert the myriad seeps from their natural channels off the mountainside to feed it. Both channels and basin were dry. Beside the basin sat a slab exactly the size of the opening.

A raised stone platform stood in the middle ring. Centered on the platform, a metal plaque or plate gleamed in the sunlight.

In the rightmost circle, a single, small azinheira grew right out of the rock. The breeze swayed its pendulous lower branches, the dark leaves trailing on the stone tableland. Ever green, the azinheira was the tree that blazoned Sabria's ensign, the sign and seal of my goodfather's kingdom. On the otherwise barren rock it spoke everything of tenacious life.

Though nothing moved on the tableland save windblown rags and azinheira branches, we had come to the right place. My skin itched; wind teased my hair, tickling my ears with ghostly fingers. Every sense cried out that something lived here beyond sun and wind and tree, and that if I would just look a little deeper, listen a little more carefully, touch a little more reverently, I would plumb the world's mysteries.

Friend, can you hear me? I've come to Voilline. For the tenth time since leaving Sessaline, I opened myself to the aether. On the road, the farther we were from Merona, the more the mindstorm had settled into a quiet murmur, like twittering birds on a summer morning or the brush of falling leaves when walking an autumn wood. But here, in this vast and mystic wilderness, I felt as if I stood in the Plas Royale on Feste Morde, two hundred thousand drunken Sabrians wailing for loved ones dead and the coming of winter. But none of them was Dante.

I needed his voice. Doubts lingered on my palate like the taste of bad fish.

Somewhere the Aspirant waited for sunset. One of the pennons flying from the prayer poles was striped green and black—the colors of Demesne Delourre, once known as the Grande Demesne Gautier.

"This is a fascinating place," said Roussel, offering me first pick of two rocks to sit on. Even in such vastness, we needed to stay low. "The columns are marble. Some say the Cinnear floated them down the river from the quarries in Coverge, then hauled them here with teams of mules. The basin is called Eilianna's Sink. It's named for the woman the Creator charged to wash Ianne and soothe his thirst in the years he was chained to the mountain. She lived in one of the caves, it's said. Several of them are quite deep."

"You've been here before?" He'd not mentioned it at the shrine.

"My father, as I said, was a believer, and brought me here as a boy. No matter one's own doubts about the holy cosmos, it raises your neck hairs to stand around the bonfires in the center circle on Ianne's Rock and hear the Cultists chanting. Or to see the echoing bonfires lit on the Ring."

"The Ring Wall, Germond de Gautier's magical defense . . ."

"Aye." He pointed to the pinnacles beyond the rift. "Every few hundred metres along the ridgeline—wherever they could find a saddle or a flat spot large enough to hold wood for a b-bonfire and a few spelled artifacts, they built a small defense work. They hoped to make it a c-continuous boundary to provide safe shelter from their attackers, but it was destroyed before it was completed. With a spyglass you can pick out their ruins from the rest of the rock. Now, are you ever going to tell me what we're doing here? Why would anyone need rescuing from the Saint's holy place?"

I didn't want to tell him. This place . . . the eerie quiet . . . the sense of things unseen . . . had my nerves jangled and my skin buzzing. Yet I needed a way into the game, and I'd come up with no alternative. The physician's enveloping admiration, his half-hidden smiles, his warm and eager solicitation promised he'd do whatever I asked. But justice demanded I tell him what he risked.

"An unholy rite of sorcery will take place down there in the circles tonight. I know this sounds preposterous, but its purpose is to engulf Sabria in chaos. I aim to stop it."

"Stars' g-glory! Sorcery? I didn't think you even believed . . ."

"I'm not sure what I believe anymore. But these people are murderers who plot the world's ruin. I've some skills . . . language skills . . . that might help defeat their plan, so I must be there. Unfortunately I can't appear to be there of my own will, else I'd never ask you."

"P-please don't apologize." He cupped my hands in his larger ones and gazed down at me, his well-proportioned face sober. "I am honored, lady. You truly would put yourself in my p-poor hands?"

"Your hands are most capable, physician. There are few I'd trust so well."

He leaned down, his gray eyes sparkling, not at all shy today. "In t-truth, damoselle, I've not seen such adventure since I was fifteen, when my life turned in upon itself and left me this self-absorbed island of study and work. I've needed a challenge. And I c-cannot think of a person I'd rather share it with."

A month previous, or a tenday, Ganet de Roussel would have been everything I could ask for in a man—kind, good-humored, modest, intelligent, a big, well-favored man whose imperfection of speech only made his charm more human. I should grasp what he offered, relish it and hold it precious as we embarked on the dangers to come. That my thoughts kept drifting to an arrogant, half-mad, unrepentant villain of a sorcerer was lunacy. Yet Roussel seemed like the reflected image in a mirror glass, neither so marvelously vivid nor so painfully flawed nor so filled with passionate life as the quiet scholar who spoke in my mind. So I pretended I didn't understand him.

My companion's earnest kindness unknotted one thread of anxiety, at least. "All right, then. As soon as we see someone preparing"—or as soon as I could exchange a word with Dante—"we'll do as I proposed at the beginning. You'll bind my hands and take me down there. While I struggle and protest, you'll barter with them, telling the story we've agreed on. Keep your distance, though. If they refuse to pay or give you any reason to believe they don't trust you, you must leave. Without question. Without argument. Without *me*. These are not gentlemen, but ruthless rogues and murderers. Promise me, Ganet de Roussel."

"Obviously there's no point in arguing that *you* have no place among ruthless rogues and murderers, either. But I do wish you'd tell me what in the name of perdition an intelligent young woman with no training in magic thinks to do about such dire events. I am a man of science, and I very much dislike risking your life—or mine—by going in blind."

His rueful expression dredged a smile from my worries. "If all goes well, I'll tell you everything," I said. "If it goes badly, then nothing I could say will matter."

He sighed in resignation. "Does anyone ever win arguments with you? We'd best discuss something more pleasant than venal sorcerers. That day in the royal bedchamber you mentioned de Vouger's theories. . . ."

As we awaited some sign of life in the pillared circles, we kept our heads down on the breezy ridgetop, drinking from his water flask, eating the remainder of our bread and cheese, speaking no more of magic or the ruin of the world. Instead we talked of physics, and how strange it was that an anvil, the filled water flask, and a tiny pebble would land in the rift at exactly the same moment if we dropped them from the edge of Ianne's Bench at the same time.

"The wind would make a difference, of course," he said. "The lighter objects could be slowed by the wind. One has to consider the ideal. . . ."

It rankled when he doubted I really understood how this applied to planetary movements, but I exposed the fundamental principles as Dante and I had explored them.

"Well-done, damoselle! As clearly as the astronomer himself could explain it."

"I've a teacher who explained it *better* than de Vouger did in his own writing." My mind drifted in that dangerous direction again. "Weren't you going to check on the horses half an hour ago? The daylight wanes."

"Ah, you send me on errands instead of letting me refute your premise. But I've come to serve. Perhaps your nefarious sorcerers chose not to work their scheme today." The creases in his brow belied his light tone. He kissed my hand and vanished back the way we'd come.

Indeed the sun was getting perilously close to the spiny tops of the ridge across the chasm. The wind was cooling rapidly. If all went according to plan, my goodfather and his men would find their way up here to Ianne's Hand as soon as it was dark, and on my signal would swoop down and take the Aspirant and his henchmen prisoner. By that time we would know the Aspirant's identity. The Queen of Sabria and—if I was lucky, her maid of the bedchamber—would remain inviolate. De Vouger's principles of objects in motion would remain stalwart.

Head resting on my drawn-up knees, I again lowered the walls in my mind to reach for Dante. The mindstorm had swelled to a raging hurricane, battering, stretching, lacerating thought. *Friend, I'm here. Roussel rescued me from Derwin and will play the mercenary to bring me in. Where are you?*

After only a few moments, I was ready to give up.

Gods, you're here! His voice sliced through the tumult. *We had a report that Antonia was dead and you were taken north with that . . . abomination.* His blunt horror and outrage and relief warmed my blood, more even than Roussel's mannered gallantry. *They've kept me buried in trivial work all day, so I've just now got to work at the book, and it's damnably obscure. No fear the Aspirant will have scrounged it from me beforetime, even if he deigns to show his face this moment. You say the physician is here with you? Never imagined he'd discomfort himself for anyone. How——?*

I couldn't wait. One question trumped all others. *Please, my father?*

This time he withdrew, in our way, shaping his words carefully. *He will hurry this to its end. They've bled him . . . four years.*

Thank you for your honesty. I held my grief to feed anger. If that was the only way I could rouse Mondragon magic, then so be it. *What of Ambrose and Portier?*

Portier's here. A shiver of outrage reminded me this was Dante. *No hint of your brother. But these caves are bottomless, and I've the notion that there are more prisoners than I've seen. Can you see the circles of pillars?*

Yes. And I read the missing page and believe I've an understanding of it. Portier is supposed to die—or not—in the leftmost circle.

Aye. Urgency bound his every word. *I'll place you close to him. You must convince him to hold on. I'll keep him breathing, if he can just not yield to what they do . . . what we do. When he followed the false trail, knowing well it could be their trap, he consented to be used. But he must not consent to die. Tell him a student must trust and obey his master. That exactly.*

I will. What else? I hungered to get on with this. At the same time, I felt a pleasing ripple of ferocity that was not my own. His melded with mine, strengthening it as braided rope becomes stronger than the sum of each strand.

Stay open to the mindstorm, no matter what. It wears, but you've reserves you've never tapped. Believe that. When I tell you, think of that page you read. Draw it on the canvas of your mind—every detail you can remember. I'll see it, and it will be much faster than trying to explain it in words. I must stay ahead of them. Anything you can do to that end is good. And be prepared for anything. Despite the news of the witch's betrayal, Kajetan wears an unhealthy smirk. Gods . . . must leave off—

He broke off abruptly, before I could tell him that Eugenie would not arrive. He would likely be furious at my changing the plan, but I still believed it the right choice. As for the king . . .

The wind seemed to urge the encroaching shadows more swiftly now. Why had my goodfather left the palace early? Had he changed his mind about letting this move forward?

I scanned the hillside behind me. Where was Roussel? Maybe he had found better grazing for the horses. Exposed grass was sparse in the maquis, only a few little patches between the rocks.

I tried to assuage my guilt at drawing Roussel into this. The Aspirant wouldn't care about him. He had no blood mark on his hand. But if the physician insisted on staying close to help once I was in the Aspirant's hands, he needed to know about the king and our signal. Perhaps I should give him my knife, still strapped to my thigh beneath the vile Gurmedd gown. Perhaps I should give him some of Lianelle's potion and tell him how to use it.

I reached under my jacket to make sure the vials remained secure and undetectable to anyone searching me. One was bound with my breasts, one in the rolled waist of my underskirt. In my fumbling, my fingers came across a thin packet of folded papers, limp with old sweat.

Stars of night, Duplais' letters. The abrupt departure with Dagobert had completely erased them from my mind. I stuffed the notes from tailors and merchants under a thornbush and devoured the others. Nothing. Nothing. Nothing. Until I opened one addressed to *Libarean Duplais* and smoothed it on my knee to read . . .

The Soul Mirror

Sonjeur de Duplais,

*It is fine to heer from you. You were soorely missed at Se-
ravain these last years. Students and tuters alike made comment
on it. And shure the master lammented the loss of your company
dinning. Though he is large in frends, he cares for none so much
as you.*

*As to yoor queriess. I bide well, living with my dawter Ja-
nille and her children, bakeing for the shop here in Tigano. As
for Master Kajetan's guest, Nieba last, I had already left the
collegia behind, so cannot be shure. But there is only one likely.
He came oft when you were so ill—bless the santes that brought
you back to yourselff—and some since you've gone. I oft won-
dred why he stopped when you were well. And yes, he forewer
wares that green and black that made him look so sallow com-
plexcted, and always arguing sience, magic, magic, sience with the
master. De Voojay was his name. The master nammed him
Jermond.*

*Yoor frend and hummbel servent,
Patinne de Gano*

Germond de Vouger the amoral Aspirant? A Gautieri *sorcerer*?

Bursting to my feet, I stared at the awkward script as if it created some daemonic cipher my mind was incapable of decoding. The man who had brought reason and good order to the ever-mystical heavens was the man who conspired, murdered, tortured, ruined all, in order to destroy the very order he championed? Impossible. Wholly, entirely impossible.

I crushed the page into a ball and threw it to the ground. My chain of reasoning must be faulty. Kajetan and de Vouger, two men so powerful and passionate in their chosen disciplines, could certainly find intellectual challenge in an acquaintance. Each would relish a friend worthy of debating. It didn't mean they conspired to alter nature—the very platform of their conflict.

Yet the man in Delourre colors had been at Kajetan's house when Lianelle died. He had been closeted with Kajetan, so Guerin had told me. He had visited Duplais often when he was ill, but not before or after, when Duplais might note his face. And neither Duplais nor Dante could recall so much as his existence without prompting—a mental lapse of such coincidence, it must defy credulity. And the Aspirant's ruined chamber in the Bastionne Camarilla had contained star charts and a planetary . . . but not my father's . . .

Once the door to belief was cracked open, the deluge came. My father's letters—the nagging evidence I had not been able to reconcile with innocence. Who better than Germond de Vouger—my father's correspondent for more than twenty years—to create a perfect facsimile of both Papa's prose and his script? Every phrase in those damning letters could have appeared in Papa's correspondence at one time or another, available to be copied, practiced, perfected. Which explained perfectly why the thieves at Montclaire had stolen de Vouger's own letters from my father's desk.

But what could explain why a man who could predict, and devise experiments to prove, the very phenomena that Roussel and I had just marveled at would conspire to unravel those phenomena? Though he might be a Gautier, brought up in common circumstances and nourished on the bitter stories of his family's fall, he had reached the pinnacle of respect in a world that embraced his talents more every day. Scholars revered him; kings sent him laurel wreaths; brokers bought and sold his papers and his signature. Surely petty vengeance rang hollow when you had already regained what your family had lost.

But then I recalled what Dante had told me about the Aspirant: *Because it amuses him . . . he finds the exercise stimulating.* Where would a man of science who believed he had unraveled the fundamental mysteries of the physical universe find a greater challenge? De Vouger could demonstrate that he was not only the unraveler of scientific mysteries, but their master, and then he could move on to challenge the mysteries of the divine. Kajetan, believing Duplais a reborn soul, had given his student over to the Aspirant *to do experiments on him.* Opening a new adventure.

Adventure . . .

The sun settled toward the pinnacles, distorted, flaring silver as if to outshine the stars and moon that would follow . . . as night ever follows day . . . as insight both follows revelation and spawns it anew . . .

I needed a challenge . . . not had such an adventure since I was fifteen. I stared at the back of my hand and felt ghostly kisses . . . heard charming laughter . . . shy questions . . . and felt the sun slipping away.

Where else had Germond de Vouger's name surfaced in this mystery? At the Collegia Medica when he recommended a cobbler's son who had come late to medicine because he needed a new challenge. At Castelle Escalon when he recommended a man of science for the queen's household . . . a man of science who had access to Eugenie de Sylvae's smelling salts, who brewed her tisanes, who lurked in the background, listening . . . always listening and watching . . . who might whisper tidbits of information in Antonia's ear like a little bird . . . who could poison Antonia's tea when she was of no more use, and poison a couchine to fake his own illness and persuade a naive woman to trust him. A subservient man who might confess minor magical skills that could assist the dowager queen with untidy ventures like murder. A big man who would be recognized did he appear in the Rotunda unmasked, but who could vanish into the household in a moment because no one paid attention to a cobbler's son who stammered and dealt with the unwholesome business of sick bodies. Father Creator, everything explained . . .

Footsteps crunched on the pilgrim path, and I took off running, down toward Ianne's Bench, because there was nowhere else to run. But his legs were longer and the chains were in his hand. He had changed into his gown of green and black stripes and wore the topaz pendant made from three keys, and he led me to the first circle, shoved me to my knees, and linked my chained wrists to an iron ring seated in the rim of the empty pool. To his credit, he did not gloat or smirk or threaten. I felt transformed from a person into an instrument.

"Anne de Mondragon ney Cazar, you have consented to put yourself in the hands of Germond de Gautier ney Roussel," he said, without a trace of a stammer. "Now we can begin."

CHAPTER 40

I had no leisure to contemplate the magnitude of my errors. Moments after Roussel . . . de Vouger . . . Gautier vanished beyond some hidden entry in the cliff face, Mage Kajetan and several men and women in adept's gray emerged from it. While the adepts wheeled barrows of wood to the middle circle and stacked glazed urns and clay bricks outside the first, Kajetan came to me. He was barefoot.

"I wish I could comfort you," he said. "The moon will rise on a new world, glorious in possibility."

Hands close tethered to the dressed stone rim of the basin, I had to twist my neck to see his face, towering two metres above me. "A world birthed in my sister's blood? In Ophelie de Marangel's blood? In my father's torment, my mother's mad tears, and my brother's degradation? I want no part of it. Tell me, Prefect, will you kill Portier yourself? Or will you have someone else do it and continue to pretend your hands unsoiled?"

The words flew, though I knew better than to engage him. Whatever advantage remained to Dante, Duplais, and me could only be jeopardized by careless flailing.

He tilted his head as if I were a curiosity. "The Aspirant suspects you've read the missing page. Describe what you saw there, and the night will go easier for all."

His patronizing grated worse than Derwin's obscenities. "Shall any of us be less dead? Will the world be less broken? You and Gautier and your daemon mage may leap headfirst into the rift."

"Do not demean yourself with childishness. This was not an easy choice. . . ."

I refused to listen. Bending forward, I touched my forehead to the sun-warmed stone, wishing I could cover my ears as well.

All I could do was keep my promises. Dante had said I needed to hold myself open to the mindstorm. Thus I lowered the walls inside and delved into the maelstrom to warn him of my ruinous error.

He didn't respond.

He'd know what I had done soon enough. How I had allowed Roussel to manipulate me. How I had delivered Eugenie into Roussel's hands with her nearest blood relative's consent. As for the king himself, he wasn't going to be here. Only the news of Eugenie's abduction would have caused my goodfather to ride out early. An easy misdirection. Even Ilario, our most secret reserve, would have been lured away by such a report. They could be on their way west to Arabasca or north to Delourre itself for all I knew. Roussel likely even knew I was a Mondragon. He had been waiting outside the Rose Room on the day Lady Eleanor had shown me the truth. How blind I'd been. How naive.

"I need the book." Dante's voice, cold as my spirit, lashed the twilight outside my skull. "As you've gone to this ridiculous trouble to get her here, the Vernase girl can read my transcript and release the rest of you to the work itself. But if something goes awry, I'll have to refer to the book as we go."

"In time. Our expectations for the night have shifted slightly," said Roussel. Though he was more truly Gautier, for the Aspirant had sloughed off the gentlemanly, good-humored physician as a snake sheds its skin.

"As you will," said Dante. "I presumed you wished this to succeed. So, am I to continue designating you as the Aspirant, or do you prefer one of this sudden excess of names?"

"Names are but masks upon the intellect. Perhaps we shall outlaw names in the future we build, and designate persons by their defining urge. What would yours be, mage?"

"Impatience. The sunset power is wasting." Dante walked away. "Here, adept, empty that bag just there. . . ."

Had Roussel planned to tell the others his identity tonight? It committed him to finish what he started. There could be no going back to either of his lives—not if any one of us survived. Yet he had donned the Aspirant's leather mask. Perhaps he preferred that none could read his expressions.

A clanking crash yanked my attention to the opposite side of the basin. From a gray canvas bag, an adept had emptied the chains I'd seen in Dante's chamber. For Portier.

Dante, Portier, and I were committed to this night as well. The only way to free Sabria from this threat—and to rescue those held captive here—was to turn Gautier's great rite against him, making sure he could not try this again.

Now. The page. Dante's silent instruction came so quickly, I almost missed it. But it was accompanied by a determination and reassurance that spurred me to action.

I visualized the opening circle on Cecile's page—the labels, the symbols of plumed bird, water, and chain links, the concentric circles, and the dotted line that connected them to the second circle. Dante touched the image I gave him, binding us together as securely as the chain on my wrists attached me to Mont Voilline.

"As your partners failed to locate the missing chart, I must assume we set up the usual triangular configuration," said Dante. "The principal practitioner easterly; the mediator north; the guide south."

Incomparably strange to hear him speak with tongue and voice at the same time we were linked in the mindstorm. My head felt like to split with it, in the same way it had when I spoke to Ambrose of birds while writing him the story of treachery.

"The reader can remain beside the subject as long as she speaks loud enough for all to hear," Dante continued. "Does your index indicate otherwise?"

"Nothing in the index contradicts your configuration, Master. Proceed. Ceynaud"—Roussel's call drew one of the adepts—"bring the librarian. Set Master Dante's other materials as he prescribes."

Dante marshaled the adepts. "Place water bowl beside our master, branches beside Master Kajetan, chains next the subject . . ." Exactly as the diagram showed. He was proceeding with this abomination.

A glance revealed only his back, the indigo gown, the half-unraveled braid, the head of the white staff taller than his own. Doubts swept in with the onrushing night. *Dante . . .*

Hear this and tell me which is truth. The intrusion blazed through my skull. *My right hand was burnt in my father's forge. I have revealed this fact to another person now living.*

Both statements stung. The first like fire—a hated, painful truth; the other like frost—a nerve-scraping, ephemeral lie. Together an avowal of trust from one who rarely trusted.

Remember it through all. Tell Portier what I said. I will sustain him through this.

"All is in place, Master," said a breathless assistant.

No position was going to provide me any degree of comfort, but I scooted closer to the dressed blocks that rimmed the dry pool. That way I could sit up a little and see.

Two adepts guided a dark-haired man into the circle of pillars. He hobbled—or, rather, hopped slowly on one leg, the other scarce touching the ground.

"Creator's mercy, Portier."

He lifted his narrow chin as I murmured his name. A deep laceration creased one of his slender cheekbones. Split, swollen lips clamped tight to smother a choking agony at every jarring hop. One eye was scabbed shut; the other glazed with pain. I could not tell if he recognized me.

Of his myriad wounds, it was certainly the leg that wrecked him. The shreds of his hose revealed a limb that was just . . . wrong, knee and ankle twisted wholly out of alignment with his hip. A bloody shard, bone perhaps, protruded from his ankle.

At Roussel's direction, the adepts carried him down the steps at one end of the dry pool and dumped him on his back. Portier lay gasping through clenched teeth, arm flung across his eyes.

The deep basin looked very like a wide coffin. It was only a slight comfort to note the carved openings in the lid that lay only a few steps away. Should they replace it, he wouldn't suffocate.

"Take your position as principal, Dante," snapped the Aspirant. "Prefect, you are guide."

Kajetan burst out, indignant, "But I should be—"

"You will *obey*, Prefect."

Huffing in offense, Kajetan moved to a pillar on my left. Dante, flames flicking from the head of his staff, took the position at the apex of the circle's eastern arc. Roussel, cloaked and masked as I had seen him in the Rotunda, joined me beside the basin, bending onto one knee as if in genuflection. He reached down and gently removed Duplais' arm from his face. "Open your eyes, librarian. I wish you to look on me."

Duplais' breath came in tight, shallow bursts. But he opened his eye to the beautiful and terrible leather mask.

"Nicely obedient," said the Aspirant—Roussel. "Now, did I not tell you we had all the time in the world to learn your secrets? I know what you are."

"You're wrong." Duplais' hoarse words were scarce audible, each forced out with a growl. "Cannot . . . see . . . righteous—"

"Dante says failure and self-loathing leave you blind." Roussel leaned forward and spoke softly. "Ironic, that."

Water dribbled in the diversion troughs. A stone lip shaped like an angel barred it from spilling into the basin. Roussel scooped a handful of water. "Whatever you imagine your great destiny, Portier de Savin-Duplais, tonight changes it. Your service now belongs to me. Your life, your death, your sustenance rest in *my* hand."

He dribbled the water on Duplais' cracked and bleeding lips like a mother teasing her child to eat. Duplais clamped his mouth shut.

Roussel threw the water in his face. His Aspirant's mask, naturally, remained serene. On the rim of the basin, he laid two hand-scribed pages. The oddly angled script mirrored that on the pages in Dante's schoolmaster's stool.

"Mage Dante has found a use for you, damoselle," he said. "On his signal you will begin reading from beginning to end. You will speak loud enough that all can hear, pausing after each instruction, so that we three can do as the text requires or repeat words that must be woven into the spellwork. You've no need to distinguish between the instructions and the words of power. Beyond the skill of reading, your mind is irrelevant to this task." His cloak snapped in my face as he rose.

"Are you mad?" I called after him. "Why would I do anything you tell me?"

"Prefect," said Dante, before Roussel could answer, "demonstrate what happens if the woman fails to read correctly."

Hissing in annoyance, Kajetan descended the steps into the basin and pressed his boot on Duplais' left ankle.

Duplais screamed, a hoarse agony that was quickly dissipated in the settling night, as if he had screamed a great deal already that day. He wrapped his arms over his head, one hand clawing at his hair, the other forearm clamped over his mouth to smother his cries. His upper body rocked from side to side as if in some frantic attempt to distract himself.

I near broke my wrists in my desire to reach for him, to comfort, to apologize.

Glaring at me as if I had done it, Kajetan returned to his place.

"We've no reason to stop, you see," said Dante, as if discussing the grape harvest. "Do as you're told." The basest and most basic of threats . . .

Or a reminder of my promise. What was changed, save my bound hands? These devils did not know of the tangle curse. Dante and I could still do what was needed.

The yellow flames hissing from Dante's staff—our only light—took that moment to wink out, abandoning Ianne's Bench in tarry darkness. He cursed and bellowed that some adept had cast a spell in error. He would have to rework it. A girl piped up with excuses, and Roussel snapped at them both to get it done, as the night was deepening.

This could not be coincidence. As Dante's accusations roared, I lunged forward as far as I could over my bound hands and the rim of the basin, whispering, "You must not consent to die, Portier. *He* will keep you breathing. He says to tell you a *student* must trust and obey his master."

The words made no sense. The last person Duplais should trust was Kajetan. But when Dante's staff blazed high again, this time in a shower of purple and red, Duplais lay still, save for a quiet trembling. His hands were clenched together and pressed to his forehead as one did to acknowledge a divine gift. Evidently the words made sense to him.

"Read," snapped Dante.

I began. "'As the light of nature fails, seal the circle with phoenix hue.'"

I paused. Dante waved his staff around the first circle and purple-red flames tipped with gold burst into life atop each column, illuminating the circle with a wavering glow. A low thrum shivered my bones.

My mind fully open to the churning aether, I had to concentrate on each word to get it right, leaving it impossible to make sense of the whole. "'Particulae settled in triune power . . . drawing forth what lives to join and bind . . .'"

At each pause I felt a new shiver, as if a different string were plucked on a monstrous violone. The tones did not fade, but blended and swelled and transformed one another, growing the magic.

"'. . . to break and rend . . . subject, spelled weapon, primal element . . . as sigils marked upon the eternal Veil . . .'"

My father had described the hour before battle thus: The world, a trebuchet straining at its tether. The mind, a spear hand reared back. The gut, a crossbow cranked taut. So it was in the first circle at Voilline.

"'Each of three grope for the crossing, the frayed and glissome warp and weft . . . as glass encircled to see beyond . . . infuse power into the three tethers. . . .'"

The water in the narrow trough began to burble, slopping over the angel's wings that blocked its passage. The Aspirant touched a glazed bowl at his feet. When the water flared emerald green, he brought it to the dry pool and poured it over Portier's chest. Kajetan laid living willow branches across a blood-smeared knife.

" 'Draw in the chosen element, touched in power, and enact the marriage of death and life.' "

The stars quivered through the veil of smoke. Roussel returned to his pillar, while Kajetan descended into the basin and wrapped Duplais' wrists in a length of chain.

"Master," rasped Duplais, "I am not what you think."

Kajetan leaned down and laid his clean, long-fingered hand on Portier's bruised forehead.

"You are everything I hoped you would be, my son: noble, generous, a mind for the ages. Never will I love another as I have loved you." Then he pulled a length of chain from the tangled pile and laid it across Duplais' chest. Another went across his thighs, and two more diagonally from each shoulder to the opposite hip.

I didn't understand it. Duplais was too broken to move. They'd no need to put him through the agony of binding him. But then the prefect shifted the stone angel, allowing the rising water in the trough to spill into the basin. These chains were not bindings, but weights. God's mercy, they were going to drown him.

"Savage!" I said, appalled, outraged. "Love does not murder!"

Kajetan grabbed my hair and yanked my head back, forcing me to look into his heated gray eyes. "Silence," he whispered. "You do not wish to know the forces you disturb. Read."

Without releasing my hair or my gaze, he yanked another length of chain from the pile and dropped it across Duplais' ankles. What small struggles Duplais had managed stopped abruptly. His head lolled. My punishment for disobedience.

Kajetan returned to his pillar. The water splashed cheerfully. Trembling with hate, I read all the way to the end of Dante's transcription.

" '. . . by will and intent and consent are subject and universe joined. And so will the rent remain forever unhealed.' " And that was the end.

Duplais' hair was floating. He remained insensible as the rising water swirled away dirt and blood. The surface of the water would be forty centimetres above his face before the basin began to overflow.

When the cool water licked at his cheeks, Portier's undamaged eye flicked open, widening as he tried to move. Even to inflate his chest against the weight of the chains must be a supreme effort. The movement sloshed water over his face. Panic overcame pain, and he writhed and struggled against the cold iron. "Master," he croaked. "Please . . ."

The three sorcerers remained in their positions. The flames atop the ring of pillars thundered.

Molten fire in my veins, I strained forward again, whispering so none but Portier might hear. "Do *not* consent to their villainy. Your friend will sustain you as long as he has strength to give. A student must obey and trust. . . ."

The words stilled his terror. He fixed his gaze on me as if searching for some answer in my face. "Tell him—" But the water lapped the corners of his mouth. He nodded deliberately and closed his eye.

Five times more I repeated the message, the last through five centimetres of water. Bubbles floated idly to the surface. The flames atop the pillars died, and the dark water hid his face.

CHAPTER 41

The wind gusted fitfully across the tableland, damp and heavy, its skirling music eerie in the dark. Elsewise all was hushed movement and whispers, joined with the quiet dribble of water as it seeped out of the filled basin. The night smelled of cedar and juniper, dry grass and old leaves, touched with moisture and laced with a faint tinge of rot. The mindstorm had quieted as well, as if its riotous participants had been notified that the world was changing, and they were holding their lives in check to see what came of it.

It was only inside me that anger and hatred boiled like liquid fire. I wanted to slash something, to hit something, to fight, not sit here waiting for doom to fall. I needed to know how to wield it to some purpose.

Grinding my jaw, I yanked on my wrist chain, pulling this way and that as if I might worry the ring from the stone. When it failed to budge yet again, I wanted to scream. But I would not. Not here beside Duplais.

I rested my head on my hands, dreading the moment they would make me abandon him in his watery coffin. If he was dead, it would be sacrilege. If he lived, it would surely be torment for him, to be abandoned in the dark with only a relayed promise. Once they settled the basin lid in place, no pilgrim would ever know a man lay under the water.

Something brushed my cheek. A windblown hair, a leaf torn from the maquis? A world away, it seemed, that afternoon hour in the steamy, fragrant heat with Roussel.

Another brush, tickling. I rubbed my cheek on my forearm, but the sensation didn't stop. The soft touches were cold, tainted.

I lifted my head. Purple and green threads floated in the air above the pool, their numbers in the hundreds, multiplied by their reflection in the dark water. A lens, Ilario had said. Just as Dante had created in the Rotunda, they had created the lens here, the symbol of concentric circles on the diagram. Were the floating lights a result of imperfection, Dante's subtle work to keep the villains dependent on his magic? I should have insisted Dante teach me how to use my own magic.

Now. The second and third circles. Dante's unvoiced command was hardedged against the quiet, like stars in a winter sky.

Relieved to be of use, I did not waste words, but sketched out the diagrams of passage and inversion—the skull, the three spirals, the concentric rings, the passing arrows, the dotted line that carried the alchemical symbol for air forward to the vessel and the tree of life. Already he was allocating places and positioning urns of earth and water within the shelter of the tree.

What's our plan? I said. *We must end this.* I wanted to spend this seething fury that threatened to split my skin.

Leash your rage. Focus it. It was a warning, yet surely his matched my own.

Kajetan arrived to unfasten my wrists and deliver me to the second circle. I spat on him. It was not at all as satisfying as it should have been. He ignored me.

The platform I had seen from the mountain's shoulder was raised above the level ground by four or five wide steps. A hinged trapdoor of thick bronze stood open in the center of the slab, a small circle of bronze gridwork set in the middle of it. The Aspirant emerged from the hole in the slab as Dante waited on the steps.

As Kajetan led me around the platform, someone behind me sighed wearily. I glanced backward and Dante's warning became clear.

A man sat resting his head against the pillar. Or perhaps he was no man, but a scarecrow stolen from a barley field in Challyat. His garments were rags, his long limbs fleshless sticks, his unhealthy hair and beard tangled and filthy. A strap of leather circled his rooster's neck and tethered him like a dog to the pillar.

I wrenched my hands from Kajetan's grip and ran to him, my knees skidding on the hard stone. Though nothing on this person resembled the man who five years ago had twirled me in his powerful arms, thrown himself on his favored stallion, and galloped away from Montclaire, I would know my father anywhere.

Crosshatched cuts marked every centimetre of chest, belly, arms, legs, back—fresh wounds layered across older scars. Scarificators, the blockish instruments that popped ten blades at a time into the skin, were much more efficient than a single lancet for milking a mule's blood.

"Papa," I whispered, dashing aside murderous tears before touching his hair with my bound hands. "Papa, look at me. I know you're innocent."

He twisted his neck, as if his head was too heavy to lift. His mane of hair fell aside. Saints, they had scored his brow, cheeks, and neck, too. But his sunken eyes flared, and his colorless lips stretched in the ghost of his ebullient smile. "Ani, love," he whispered. "You've come."

"Am I not your mind's child?" I pressed his bony hand to my forehead and my heart.

His other hand, palsied like that of a man fifty years his senior, caressed my hair. "Never dreamt you so real as this before."

"I'm no dream. I'll save—"

Kajetan yanked me away from him. "You've work to do, damoselle."

Papa turned away without protest as they fixed me to Kajetan's pillar. Perhaps it was better he thought me a dream. I memorized his skeletal form and leashed my swelling rage.

"You *what*?" Dante's scornful question rang out, an offense against the pregnant night. "You've never once worked a successful summoning. Would you infuse the entirety of his blood directly into your hand, this wretch's *carcass* would summon a revenant sooner than you."

"Nonetheless, I shall serve as principal practitioner for the second rite," said Roussel. "You've taught me well, mage. The prefect shall serve as mediator. That should give you adequate time to translate the book. Your transcriptions of the second and third rites seem quite lean."

Dante had assumed he'd introduced enough flaws in the other mages' spellwork that he would always serve as principal practitioner. Something was wrong. "So where is the book?"

"I've deposited the personal attractors for our revenant in the vault as you specified. The index requires that the nireals be positioned with them for the second rite and removed to the third circle *after* the summoning. The adepts are busily preparing the royal lady, so you must see to the nireals yourself. It's just as well, as you're so meticulous about such things. When you've done, take your place as guide, and I'll give you the book."

"I did not become traitor and apostate to do adepts' chores," Dante spat. "You've not ever worked—"

"If you note the summoning slipping out of my control, Master, halt the work and we'll shift positions."

The aether link between us rumbled.

I peered into the night beyond the ring of pillars. The first circle, where Portier lay, remained dark and silent, save for the floating threads and trickling water. Ivory lights flickered from the third circle. It appeared at first as if sylphs danced around the azinheira. But the dark shapes were just the tree's trailing lower branches shifting in the wind. I'd often played or read in the cool green bower formed by an azinheira's branches. That's where the adepts were *preparing* Eugenie to create a child with Soren—not for Antonia, but to bridge the gap between life and death. A supremely unnatural being whose conception would upend the laws of nature.

Dante retrieved the five silver spheres from a box outside the pillar circle. He fumbled with them, dropped several, as the clawed fingers of his right hand could not grasp more than one. Growling, he propped his staff on the pillar and gathered the silver spheres in his arms.

Wait! Dread and warning burst from me. But he had already swept across the circle, mounted the steps in two strides, and descended into the space below the trapdoor. A flash of brilliant yellow seared the night from the opening in the platform, accompanied by a short, sharp bark of surprise. Only when the dark form emerged from the vault did I breathe again.

The bronze door crashed shut. A bolt clattered. "There you are, you arrogant devil," he shouted through the grate. "Never saw sweeter than you locked in a pit. In the *dark*."

The knot in my gut exploded fire into chest and limbs, turning bone to porridge. The dark-robed figure was not Dante, but Jacard.

"Did you not think we'd wonder why the spellwork you granted us never worked as your own did? Did you not think we'd notice that the prisoner in the Spindle was useless after your visit? And did you think to lure a Mondragon witch to your hermit's bed by lying about her blood?"

"Enough, adept!" said the Aspirant. "Fetch the shield plate for this grate. And make sure your master's staff is well outside the circle."

Vermillion lightning burst through the grate, accompanied by a shattering resonance that shivered stone and sky. A concussion of rage . . . of pain . . . of profound dismay . . . ripped through the aether and into my skull.

I blinked and squinted, the painful red glare subsiding only slowly. *Dante!*

"He's not my master. Not anymore."

Roussel mounted the steps and crouched over the grate in the trap. "Hear me, Master Dante, and be very clear," he said. "I've no desire to kill you. One does not destroy a resource of your considerable value. But I cannot brook intentionally flawed spellwork today, and I've a more efficient linguist at hand to translate my book. Alas, we've no sorcerer's hole at Voilline, so I've left you a Gautier family heirloom called a contrabalance, intended to occupy the talents of a captive mage when no other containment is at hand. With an application of your power you can shield yourself from its effects. But ignore its eruptions at your peril; I allowed

Jacard to select the particular torment it will apply. You are a dreadful lash-tongue with your inferiors, and he is a vengeful creature. Now, excuse me. I've business."

As the Aspirant descended the steps, the lightning flashed again.

"Ah, Portier," said a soft voice behind me, "I believed you had exacted the world's most astonishing deceit, convincing me you had embraced your humble calling. But Dante a *king's* man? Nothing shall ever surprise me again."

I had forgotten Kajetan, who stood behind me, shielding his eyes as he watched the scene play out.

Friend, tell me you're all right. What do I do? Another scalding flash. I looked away, but still the red glare obscured my sight.

Jacard hurried up the steps, carrying a flat square of steel. He propped the metal sheet on its edge. "Magic is all about seeing, you told me. *Uncover the windows, weevil. Get out of my light, weevil. Can you not make the simplest fire spell? You are blind, groveler . . . insect . . . weevil.* Well, who is the weevil now? Enjoy the light I've made for you."

He let the sheet fall. Yet another flash of searing orange-red was shut off with its dull clank.

All I could think was of one friend drowning in the dark, the other in that flaying fire. I called Dante again.

We continue, he said. *Just give me time. I've lost Portier. . . .* Confused, desperate, riven with pain.

The Aspirant joined Kajetan and me. "You really must leash your kinsman, Prefect. Teach him respect, at least until his talents measure up to those of his foes. If he fails us tonight, you and he will both join Dante in the oubliette."

"My nephew alerted you to the mage, Aspirant. He deserves the chance to prove himself."

"That, and Antonia's vicious little end play that required this morning's northward chase, give him this opportunity. With Dante's loyalties compromised, I needed the girl more than I needed a better guide. And so . . ."

Roussel dropped the *Book of Greater Rites* in my lap. He crouched beside me, and without ceremony produced a knife, stabbed it into my right index finger, and touched my stinging, bloody finger to the open page. "Now speak the key. The consequences of your misbehavior will be applied to your father. Do not imagine he is beyond pain."

"Andragossa." The letters shifted and twisted into readable text.

Grunting in satisfaction, he pointed at the middle of the page. "When I signal, read from this point through the mark of the skull."

He did not wait for a response. "Jacard, prepare."

The night settled around us as Roussel and Jacard took their positions.

You're to translate the book?

"Of cou—" For a moment I'd thought it was Kajetan. *Yes. This is my fault. Stupid . . .*

I had offered the kindly physician my arm, allowing him to pull out the fibers, giving him free taking of my blood. Naive. Thick-headed. My blood had proved Dante false.

We're all fools. But now you must tell me what they do, every gesture, every pause. I'm holding Portier, for the moment, but to accomplish any other work, I have to see. The words first. And quickly.

Dante's impatient prodding taught me right away that I didn't have to comprehend in order to show him the page. I skimmed through the words to the mark of the skull. *Now everyone's positions . . .*

I described Jacard beside my father and Kajetan looming over me. Roussel had returned to the principal's pillar, where Dante's fading staff yet cast a faint light. The physician pulled out a small brass tube, a syringe like those used to suck putrefaction from wounds. Yanking up his sleeve, he plunged the sharp end into his arm. But instead of drawing out the ivory plunger, he depressed it.

My curiosity must have intruded on my description.

Your father's blood. The Aspirant told me he'd perfected the infuser, allowing him to deliver the blood, cleansed of imperfections that might sicken him, directly into his veins. I didn't believe him. Dante's colossal self-reproach was a reflection of my own.

The syringe clattered to the stone. Roussel raised a hand. "Begin!"

I read. "'Within the hour of rending, tighten the lens, sealing with the hues of royal might, dual circles, one and then the other.'"

My reading paused, but my narrative continued, describing how Roussel waved his hand twice in a circle, and gold-tipped flames of purple and indigo blazed from the tops of the pillars.

But he's not satisfied, I said. *He's halted my reading and tries the gesture again.*

He's done it wrong. A fierce approval. *It should be purple on the pillar circle. Indigo on the—*

Mountaintops, I said. Flames of indigo and gold blazed on the Ring Wall. All the world beyond that dual ring faded into insignificance.

I read on. "'Particulae settled in triune power . . . the embodiment of undeath holding the way. . . .'"

I could not say what Dante did as I read. Unlike the rite of the First Circle, the three sorcerers faltered frequently. Never did any of them speak beyond the instruction of the book, but Roussel's hand extended my pauses, giving me ample time to describe what Dante could not see or feel. Yet always we moved forward again.

"'. . . mediator conjoins the physical attractors for the one to be summoned with bulk matter to shape the physical manifestation.'"

Another halt while Kajetan repeated some working with incense, earth, and water.

Dante's disruptions did not come without a price, for we'd not even finished the first page when he began to tire. *Repeat,* he would say, or *Again. Eastward or toward the center? Which sorcerer?* Or, *Gods, I'm losing him . . .* And his frantic grief told me he had slipped control of the spell that maintained Portier's life. *Slower . . . read slower.* He had to split his attention and his power between the rite, sustaining Portier, and defending himself against the Gautier device.

The assaults of the contrabalance came with the regularity of a cannonade. He would withdraw momentarily, then growl, *Go on.* The pain and visceral fear borne on the words shook me. The very fact that I could perceive it told me how harried he was. But he refused to acknowledge my concern, and we continued.

Eventually, as the rite moved on to the second page, Dante stopped speaking at all. I sensed when he could not listen and would dawdle until Kajetan kicked me. The magic surged unimpeded. The night felt swollen. Huge.

Of a sudden a great wind howled across the tableland, as if the windows of the world had been opened, sucking the air through the constricted enclosure of the two great rings. Colored lightnings split the sky above, and the earth below us shook.

"'. . . and with the dissolution of the sacrifice, so is the exchange accomplished and the passage readied.'"

The final words remained meaningless until I looked up to describe the subsequent occurrences for Dante. That's when I noticed Jacard watching, waiting for me to look at him. And then he smiled and slammed a knife blade into my father's chest.

"Papa!" My scream should have ripped out Jacard's heart, flattened Mont Voilline, toppled the pillar beside me, or at least torn out the bolt that bound me to it. Anger and hatred erupted from the molten pool waiting in my gut. Fire seared my lungs, scorched my limbs, and shriveled my heart. I wrenched at the chain and beat my bleeding fists on the pillar, ready to break the one and splinter the other.

But a quiet, calm, desperate voice interrupted my fit: *Gods, I thought you would never take hold of it! Yield me this power, Anne Sophia Madeleine. Grant me the fruit of your anger. We can only do this together . . . as I told you . . . I've an answer half wrought, but we've a way to go as yet, and I've nothing left.*

Take it! Kill them all! Shatter this mountain and end it.

Tell me I can, he said, steady, though racked with pain and exhaustion and the storm at the end of the world. *Invite me. Yield everything without condition. Think, and only then consent.*

His words gave me pause, as he meant they should. I summoned the ragged remnants of mental discipline. He did not lure me with the possibilities of vengeance or victory or salvation of those I loved. He merely asked for my trust. Anger had enabled the question, but anger could not—must not—give the answer. Yet my rage left no room for doubts. *Have you other names?* I asked.

I felt the spasm of disbelief . . . and a despairing humor as only a man utterly without recourse might summon. *No, just the one.*

Then hear this, Dante, my friend of the aether: Come into my house and take what you need of me. I place my magic, my soul's life, and my hope of right in your hands.

And in the moment I yielded, the molten chaos of my blood was re-shaped into an artwork of reason and color, light and strength, I'd not known existed this side of the tales of angels.

CHAPTER 42

"To the third circle," yelled Roussel, as the wind of the universe whipped the fires of the second to a thundering blaze. The flames of the Ring Wall raked the starless sky in frenzy.

The Aspirant left Kajetan and Jacard to bring me along. My head drooped; my arms were wrapped about my middle. But eyes and ears were ready. Listening. Searching. Black fire simmered just beneath my skin.

"Where is the revenant?" whispered Jacard, as they detached my wrists from the pillar. The younger man's gaze darted into the wavering lights and shadows. "We opened the way. Sent the dead man. Shouldn't it be here now? You said Dante's raised one ten times over."

All this Dante saw and heard through my senses. No longer did I need to relay what I perceived or recalled. My will released the impression or memory, and he knew.

"In the past he's forced the rising, yes," said Kajetan, jerking on my bloody wrists to get me up. "With bulk matter and refined memory, he enticed spectres to shape bodies and become revenant. He even instilled a semblance of wholeness, but only for a few hours. No true life was renewed. He didn't have Portier to seal the rent in the Veil. He didn't provide the exchange. No, it is the lure of the woman in heat will incite this revenant to become complete."

And the nireals would infuse the revenant with a living soul, making him *engasi*—a true person with memories and history and emotions, a living being who could mate and create a child. I understood these things as if it were I who had studied and practiced for so many years. Dante and I had been bound together by will and intent and consent—the fundamental triad of spellmaking. I understood that, too.

Kajetan and Jacard left my father lying in the dark, ragged and exposed, as they had abandoned Portier in his watery tomb. But I felt the thready beat of Papa's life pulse held in one of Dante's spells, just as I felt the slow filtering of gaseous air into Duplais' lungs maintained by another. Because of our bond of power, I could actually envision the spellwork as Dante did—intricate, ethereal structures of color and light, arcs and spirals, blocks and ramps and spires, each spell a virtual cityscape of magic. The hieroglyphs were only an abstraction, Dante's way to comprehend and communicate the complex structure as he analyzed it, in the same way the Syan used a few brushstrokes to communicate complex ideas like *love* or *thought* or *illness*. Dante could manipulate the spells by manipulating the hieroglyph—altering colors or shifting or removing shapes. The whole was staggering.

Kajetan bound my wrists to a pillar of the third circle. I did not resist and did not raise my head. Let him think me defeated.

"Check the placement of the nireals, Prefect, and that the vessel is properly prepared." The Aspirant threw aside another syringe and shoved down his sleeve. "If Dante has carried the true nireals into the oubliette, your nephew will fetch them."

Jacard huffed, the image of wounded pride.

Kajetan darted through the leafy veils, returning almost immediately. "The nireals are positioned as you and the mage agreed—one at each corner of the bed, and one embedded in heaped earth and pooled water at the base of the tree. The vessel is secured and writhes in lust."

The vessel. Holy angels, sweet Eugenie. I'd hardly given her a thought. They spoke of her as if she were a dog. Darkness choked my soul.

Attend! Her hope is in our deeds. The words you read must convince the Aspirant to hold the fifth nireal in his hand, no matter what his index has taught him. Everything hinges on that. And be ready . . . He hesitated. *Even together, we'll have only one chance to finish this.*

I'll do what's needed. Though his pause had been slight, I wondered what he was withholding.

"Begin, reader," said the Aspirant, the physician who had prepared kind, loving Eugenie for abomination. "Pausing, as before, and all the way to the last sentence."

And so I began. " 'Within the hour of summoning, raise the Circle of Inversion, sealing with the hues of life's bounty . . .' "

With a sweeping gesture, Roussel lit the third circle with emerald fire. It was only just possible to glimpse Roussel and Jacard. The azinheira branches obscured the lines of sight.

As before, I read and paused, read and paused. From behind the rustling branches came small, swallowed cries of hunger . . . of heat . . . of need. Outrage torched my heart.

" '. . . draws the revenant with the craving for breath . . . subject to the hunger for human touch . . . lust of long deprivation . . . to ravish the vessel and deposit his seed . . .' " Between every word I watched for Soren.

Close your eyes.

The largest of Dante's spell structures gleamed in my mind's darkness, a new spire geysering upward as we observed. As if drawing me alongside him by the hand, Dante explored its lines and curves. The shimmering edges sliced my spirit like well-honed steel or the brittle beauty of thinnest glass. *Here,* he said, directing my attention to a grand arc of rose and silver that supported the entire structure. *This is where we destroy them.*

In moments he'd sketched the hieroglyph . . . blocks of color, chevrons, spirals. *These blue and brown chevrons represent that supporting arc,* he said, *the earth and water we provide the chosen spirit to shape a body. The silver circles are the nireals, the promise of a soul, memories, thought, and choice.* Each description was accompanied by a surge of effort, as he linked the true spellwork to its abstraction.

"Reader!" Kajetan kicked me.

"'. . . setting the four soul mirrors opposing to reflect the new life to come, one for Heaven, one for the netherworld, one for the living world, one for Ixtador, each to be home for the Holy One, the child who shall bridge all realms. And the fifth nireal, positioned at the root of life to be . . .'"

I paused. The Aspirant's hand waved me onward. Here. This was the place. "'And the fifth nireal to be brought to the hand of the principal to match soul and spirit with intent and will,'" I said, crafting words that might have been written in the cursed book.

For a single moment, Roussel hesitated.

My chin drooped to my breast. I sobbed softly—not difficult when body and mind felt as if they were disintegrating.

Then he gestured to Jacard, who scurried underneath the azinheira branches. In moments, the adept placed the silver sphere in the Aspirant's hand.

In a surge of power that seemed to draw my entrails out through my head, Dante erased the two chevrons from the hieroglyph and shoved a red spiral into its place beside the silver circle, altering the underlying spell structure. The red spiral, I knew, represented Roussel.

Dante's furious will left no time to assess what that meant.

I read, "'Principal, mediator, guide, together summon the revenant to true life, to plant the seed in the vessel prepared creating the Holy One—'"

I flipped the page forward and back again, squeezed my pierced finger, and pressed one more drop of blood to the thin paper. But the text ended in midsentence.

"'—who straddles life and death.'" The Aspirant took up where I had left off, reciting words cached in his index or his family's memory. "'And so shall the rent in the *voile aeterna* be made permanent, and Ixtador Beyond the Veil nevermore be dissolved nor shaken nor altered in its composition.'"

The three chanted, "*Revienne, vitae, aeterna.*" Return, live, eternally.

And now, friend, said Dante, as gently as his driving urgency would allow, *someone must die. We must provide the exchange to enable passage through this rent in the Veil. You have to let your father go.*

Let Papa go? No! I could feel his blood-pulse. *I promised him here in the aether that I'd save him.* As Dante had promised Portier to keep air in his lungs. *He will not die here.*

To make my scheme work, to end it, we must go on. We hold Portier and your father in our hands and have no other weapons. I know Portier would agree if we asked. But your father will welcome it. How else do we choose?

You know nothing about my father! Logic, reason, love, friendship . . . It was not fair, not after all they had endured. How dare he make me choose! I would not.

The droning chant continued, higher pitched, more insistent than ever. The Gautier device struck Dante again—flaying fire he could no longer shield from me.

Choose, he said, pain stretching his beleaguered patience. *It must be now. I cannot—*

I won't! Desire, consent, will . . . The molten darkness inside me reived the barrier of my flesh, a geyser of flame the color of night.

The chains about my wrists shattered and fell to the ground.

For my father's fragile life, for faithful Portier, for Eugenie and Lianelle and my mad mother and my vanished, tormented brother, for Dante, balancing the world's fate in his incomparable mind, I reached through the ripped seam of my filthy gown and drew out the Cazar dagger, lunged upward, and slammed the blade beneath Kajetan's ribs. My hatred held him up and crushed him into the pillar, and I watched his scornful disbelief bloom and curl and fade all in one moment. In that same instant Dante claimed our joined magic and spoke the word that bound the Mondragon spell.

Fire and storm and winter raged through flesh and bone as one, scouring, dizzying, as if I'd drunk an entire harvest's wine, as if the howling wind of the universe blew straight through me. My bones felt hollowed like a bird's, my flesh dried and crumbled, as if the next wind gust might tumble me across the tableland and into the chasm. In the dark behind my eyes, fountains of scarlet and indigo burst from one massive structure of light, collapsing its arc and spires.

It was done. The night within the rings of fire yawned. The wind blustered across the mountain's face, its throaty howl creasing the silence.

Kajetan's weight slumped sideways. Unable to hold, I let him fall.

"Uncle!" squawked Jacard, abandoning his pillar. It needed no finger to throat or mirror to mouth to know Kajetan was dead.

"You've killed him, you cursed witch! I'll have your heart out of you."

But the bloody knife in my shaking hand held him away. With a glare of searing hate, he snatched up the *Book of Greater Rites* and ran.

Gautier/de Vouger/Roussel could not attend. As fog creeping down from the highlands in winter, so cloudy fingers embraced the masked Aspirant as he held the nireal high. A faint outline of a man appeared within the fog, not Soren, but a man even larger than Roussel. His ankle-length tunic and sleeveless surcoat, garments of centuries past, were emblazoned with three gold keys.

"What's this?" Roussel tried to brush away the solidifying presence. "Prefect, examine the text. Did the reader err? Water and earth await at the root of the tree. Not *here!*"

He tried to step away, but the wind whined and fog swirled and pressed him to the pillar at his back, splaying his arms above his head. "Lord Grandsire . . . Master . . . the vessel awaits your *rightful* flesh, not mine. *This* body is not yours. No! No!"

Roussel's cries became increasingly strident as the manifesting spectre enfolded him, licking at his face, at his neck, fondling his groin, his mouth . . . craving flesh, craving life.

"Earth and water be your shaping. This flesh is mine!" Only there was no earth or water at hand. The nireal, woven into the summoning, the promise of a living soul, lay in Roussel's hand.

The Gautier revenant peeled Roussel's mask and clothes away and began to reshape the bulk matter of his great-grandson's body into a body of his own. That's when Roussel/de Vouger/Gautier began to scream.

I sank to the ground, hands over my ears.

So we stop it, said Dante, and he drained the molten murder from my veins into the nireal, melting the silver sphere with its work only half done.

When the screaming stopped, the Aspirant lay still—the shape of his body entirely wrong. I averted my eyes.

Hurry. Dante's voice was faint, or perhaps my inner hearing had been deafened by the screaming or perhaps it was the swelling mindstorm . . . fury . . . hunger . . . lust . . . hatred . . . anger. . . . *We must destroy the lens. But Portier first. I cannot maintain— Hurry!*

I needed no spur. I rolled Kajetan out of his cloak. Holding tight to the zahkri, I sped to the second circle, where my father lay slumped like a discarded rug. His heart was beating, faint and uneven, the wound in his breast seeping slowly. I wadded his ragged tunic over the wound and used the leather leash to tie it in place. Then I tucked Kajetan's cloak around him, and with a kiss and a promise moved on to Portier. Angels' grace that they had not laid the stone lid over him.

I splashed into the frigid water, ducked under, and wrenched away the chains that held him down. Once he was free of the chains, the water supported his upper body as I reached under his shoulders and lifted his face above the surface. Spirits, he was cold. The water might have flowed straight off a glacier. I searched in vain for breath or heartbeat.

"You are n-not dead," I said through chattering teeth, tugging him toward the steps. "N-not dead. Not dead." I sat on the steps, hauling him up one step, then backing up to the next, and hauling him up again. Eventually he was out of the water far enough that his sodden frame became too heavy to drag farther. Just as well. Another step and the exposed bone of his leg would scrape on the lowest step. Even if he was dead, I couldn't do that to him.

The wind howled. One by one the flames atop the pillars winked out. Night had swallowed the floating lights. *I've got him*, I said through the raging mindstorm, *but I've no idea if he's alive.*

Needs warmth. Make a fire. Use my staff.

I started laughing. Drenched, freezing, clinging to a corpse, for all I knew, and Dante was asking me to work magic again. I could scarcely pump breath in and out. *I'll need you for that. Let me get you out of there.*

No time to play with locks. Just do as I say. Hurry . . . The last was pleading . . . strained . . . as if he were holding up the roof of the sky.

Perhaps he was. Above my head an inky blackness rippled, shivered, and bulged as if someone pushed on it from the other side.

Babbling apologies, I left Portier and retraced my steps through the wind-blasted dark. Dante's staff had been left near the principal's pillar in the second circle. I felt my way, one pillar and then another and another. I tripped on a discarded urn and barely missed crashing my head on the pillar. But wood clattered on the stone just in front of my nose. I hesitated . . .

Don't be afraid. Patient. Controlled. *A handspan—a bit more than your handspan—from the top, you'll find a carved triangle with a smooth depression in its center. Touch it . . .*

A cool, soft wave rippled through my center and through my finger into the stick. White flame popped from the staff. Only a touch was required to ignite the wood piled in the bonfire scar. And then it was a matter of hauling Duplais and my father close to it. With weeping apology, I used Kajetan's cloak to drag them near and covered them both with its ragged remnants.

Now for you, my friend. And then poor Eugenie. Wearily I climbed the steps to the bronze trapdoor and shoved the metal plate aside, exposing the grate. I should have done that first thing. At least now he could get the reflected light from the bonfire. *Take heart; it's almost dawn.*

Not a nice dawn. A livid glow now illuminated the pillar circles. Not enough to push back the inky void of the rift. Not enough to show me Dante through the bronze grate.

I doubt it's dawn you see. We've work yet to do before dealing with locks. They're coming.

Eyes bleared with weariness and wind tears, head bulging with voices and cries I could not begin to hold back, I glanced up. My mouth dropped open. Though I believed myself incapable of another emotion, pity and horror filled my heart.

A gaping hollow in the night was jammed with colorless shapes . . . men, women, children surging forward, crowding against an unseen barrier. Emaciated, eye sockets of solid gray, yearning, starving . . .

They don't belong here, said Dante. *They're but spectres . . . phantasms . . . not souls. I need you to help me close the way.*

How did he know? Was she there . . . my sister? I couldn't just slam the door on her without a word. *Wait!*

My frozen fingers clasped her pendant still hung about my neck. *We won, Nel. We followed your clues and found the shitheels who hounded you to death. I've found Papa.*

The little nireal flared a brilliant silver, an echo of the fiery sunset over the pinnacles, and stung my enveloping palm with the winter frost. The scent of dead leaves flooded my nostrils. Cold dry air . . . desolation . . . threaded my skin and bone. *Help us, Ani! Don't leave us here. It's all wrong. . . . Can you see? Trapped . . . souls leached away . . . Your friend can tell you.*

"Nel?" I stared up at the surging mass of hunger. She was not one of them, but somewhere else . . . behind them . . . hidden.

Gods, hurry . . . can't hold . . . Dante's plea was a knife in my temple.

I had no choice. We had nothing left to help my sister, even if I knew how. This night had to end. I let go of the nireal, thinking of Roussel and his whims that had caused so much death and misery . . . and his ancestors and mine whose lust for knowledge had conspired to create this horror. Smoldering fury and hatred caught fire again, and I closed my eyes.

The shimmering structures of the Mondragon spells lay in ruins, the great spires and arcs collapsed or vanished altogether, the colors dulled. Only a great wheel remained, glittering like faceted glass, spinning. The lens, the opening to Ixtador.

Take it, I said. *All I have . . .*

And in a surge of destruction worthy of the world's end, Dante harnessed the remnants of his cold, dark river and my fiery flood, and shattered the wheel, destroying the hole in the sky.

I sank to the stone, sobbing, as if we'd murdered Lianelle and all the others yet again.

Thunder rumbled in the distance. I needed to find the key to unlock Dante's cell, and see to Eugenie and Portier and Papa . . .

———

"Ani. Are you wounded? So much blood on you. Come, Ani. Wake up and tell me."

The slap on my cheeks was going to get the soft-voiced man's head removed. Half of me was freezing and half burning. All I wanted was to sleep, and he was shining blazing fire in my eyes and dribbling wine into my arid mouth.

"Ani, please. They need to ask you some questions."

"We've settled with the villains in the caves," said a different voice, filled with gravel. "Saved the king the trouble. Once he sees what was done to his men and that woman down there, he would have bricked up the lot of them and let them eat one another. If he ever gets a hint of what we found under that tree, he might do for us all. It's good the chevalier got us here first."

The king . . . the chevalier . . . I needed to wake up. I had important things to do. "I'm not injured," I croaked.

I sat bolt upright, bumping heads with the man bent over me, the one who'd called me Ani. But when I glimpsed his grim face, every other thought left my muddled head. My hand flew to my mouth as my gaze encompassed the rangy young man, clean and unwounded, dressed in fine leathers, with a sword sheathed at his waist. I burst into tears.

"Spirits, Ani, what's happened here?" His thin hand, marked with a zahkri and myriad scars, jerked away when I reached for it. "Don't—"

But my arms flew around my brother. "I thought you were dead . . . that they'd bled you."

He suffered my embrace, rigid as the stone column behind him until my arms dropped away.

"That was the intent. But your friends kept a watch on the Spindle. When I was dragged out, the chevalier came after us. Killed the lot of them. Convinced me he was your friend. He hid me at his house. Gave me a weapon and promised I'd get to use it. Swore not to tell anyone where I was until this was over. Or ever, if I wanted."

The chevalier . . . my friends . . .

Anxious, I peered over his shoulder. A scarecrow huddled under a clean blanket beside the raging bonfire. As he slept, a mustached man, my brother's gravel-voiced confidant, was dressing a wound on his arm. Beyond the two, a slender man with short, dark hair was propped up by one of Ianne's pillars, looking very ill. At the sick man's side knelt another swordsman, dressed all in black, tall and thin, hair like flax—the chevalier.

Never had I felt so depleted. Names rattled in my empty skull like dried peas. Anxiety tried to match them with bodies. Ambrose. Papa. Duplais. Captain de Santo. Ilario. Eugenie . . . Sweet angels! "The queen?"

"Naught but frightened and groggy, so says the chevalier. Here, lean back. The king wants to speak with you, Ani, to find out where the villains have got off to."

I could scarce comprehend the question, much less an answer. "I need to be up. I'm not hurt." An unnamed urgency drove me to the sick man. He ought to be dead. And others . . .

"Says she's not hurt, lord," said Ambrose, keeping me from tripping over my own feet. "But she won't stay down."

"Anne!" The flaxen-haired man beamed. "Saints' grace to see you awake and whole, and basking in the embrace of this sturdy young *cousin*. That *unidentified man* there"—his widened eyes flicked to my sleeping father—"insists *he* will be perfectly well if he can but see the angel who holds him in her wings."

Even in my empty state, his warnings were clear.

I touched Papa in passing, but sank to my knees beside the other sick man. I needed him to tell me what was missing.

He was coughing and shivering. No wonder that, as he was soaking wet. Pain had ground terrible lines in his thin face. Some deeper hurt had left its mark as well. His eyes were closed.

"We could use a physician's skills just now," whispered the swordsman in black . . . Ilario. "Alas, you surely know we found poor Roussel, what was left of him. And we know who did for him. Found this." He picked up a leather mask and tossed it back to the ground.

Memories of the night trickled back . . . the blood on my hands and gown . . . Kajetan . . . the leather-faced Aspirant . . . "No! Roussel *was* the Aspirant."

"Roussel!" I could not answer Ilario's sputtering disbelief.

"Yes." Why was it I wanted so much to weep? "We won. We stopped it."

Though his chin rested heavy on his chest, the sick man's hand—Duplais' hand—reached for me.

I enfolded his thin, cold fingers. "You live," I said softly.

He lifted his eyes, such an unfathomable gaze as to shiver my blood. "It would seem so." A wan smile eased my disturbance. "Thanks to you and—"

Memory concussed head and heart. "Dante!"

"Where is the cursed villain?" called Ilario and de Santo, instantly alert.

But I was racing into the dark second circle and up the platform steps. I hammered on the trapdoor and wrenched at the recessed locking bolt.

"I'm here!" I called through the grate. "I passed out and they've come for us, and I've only just come out of it with a head like an empty wine vat. Portier lives. And my—the other victim lives . . . and, holy saints, why can I not get this open? Somebody help me! Tell me you're all right." I couldn't hear him. Couldn't feel him in the surging current of the aether.

It was Captain de Santo who located some kind of lever and snapped the bolt. I raced down the steep steps into the dank pit, Ambrose and Ilario on my heels, weapons drawn and calling for a light.

"Put those away," I said, unable to see where to put my foot next. "It's a friend down here."

De Santo clattered down the steps behind us with a torch.

Dante was huddled in a corner of the cramped, filthy hole, shaking uncontrollably, his haggard face the color of ash. "I'm fine," he said in a throaty whisper. "Just need my staff. Would appreciate them not puncturing me."

He was not at all fine. Despite de Santo's torchlight flooding the oubliette, Dante couldn't name Ilario or Ambrose. Neither did he blink or squint or look directly at any of us, nor did he acknowledge my proffered hand as he struggled to his feet, his good hand groping the wall. A small, blackened pyramid sat in the center of the mud-grimed floor, spitting orange-red sparks. Veins of the same fiery hue floated in his dull, aimless eyes.

Magic was all about seeing, and Dante, whose lifeblood was magic, who believed light the finest of the Creator's gifts, was blind.

CHAPTER 43

AFTERWARD

"He's not one of them! He saved us all! He'll give his parole until we can explain!"

Ignoring my repeated protests, soldiers dragged Dante out of the filthy pit and shoved him to his knees. They bound his hands, eyes, and mouth, and tied separate ropes to his waist. In a gnat's breath they had him stumbling up the path to Ianne's Hand surrounded by nervous soldiers bristling with weapons.

"You fools, he can't see!" I yelled. "He can scarce walk. Lord Ilario, please. He protected her!"

Ilario, Ambrose, and de Santo had withdrawn as my goodfather's men took charge. But a lift of Ilario's chin sent Calvino de Santo charging up the hill. The former guard captain bulled his way through the ring of soldiers and grabbed Dante's arm, ensuring, none too gently, that the mage stayed on his feet.

Dante had spoken not a word as they bound him. Perhaps he was incapable of speech. The mindstorm dribbled through my skull unchecked as if I were a gutter spout on the palace roof, my silent calls washed away like stray leaves.

The king rode out soon after. He commanded his men to treat Portier, his gooddaughter, and "the abused stranger" with utmost care, but he did not stop to speak with me. He had emerged from the azinheira bower carrying Eugenie, wrapped in blankets. He relinquished her only long enough to swing into the saddle and take her back.

"Lord chevalier, they must not harm—"

"Oh, my dearest Damoselle Anne!" Ilario rode up, transformed into his other self. "His Majesty asked me to assure you that he will consider all pleas as soon as we are sheltered at Barone Crief's house. Saints' glory, everyone so damaged and no one knowing who did what or making sense of anything. They tell me the barone's house—not the most comfortable of houses, but more suitable than inns or village houses—has a sorcerer's hole, as most do in this region. They'll stow Mage Dante there until the events of this night are sorted out. My aide and I"—he nodded toward Ambrose, also mounted—"will ride ahead and ensure that all proceeds fairly. You three will be brought along more gently."

The assurances built into his foolery calmed me only slightly. "He must not harm Dante, lord," I said softly, gripping his boot. "You *must* believe me. Because of him, Portier lives and the lady is inviolate."

Yet how could anyone possibly understand? Only two days had passed since my own eyes were opened, and Dante and I had been through events no one could imagine.

Ilario bent down from the saddle. "There's been death enough this night," he said softly. "Tomorrow we'll see."

He and Ambrose galloped off after the king's party. They didn't believe me.

With tender care, the remaining guardsmen bore Portier and my father on litters over the mountain's shoulder and down to the road. They treated me as if I were made of spun glass. They likely thought I was mad.

THREE DAYS WE SPENT AT Barone Crief's fortress near Voilline. That first morning I slept like the gray stones of the barone's walls. I woke unrested, frantic, ready to strangle anyone who stood between me and the king. Fortunately they'd posted Ambrose at my door. He showed me Papa, who had been washed and fed the kitchen's best broth, and now slept safely in a clean bed for the first time in five years. Philippe's own field surgeons were attending Portier. The sorcerer remained confined in the sorcerer's hole. Explaining the events of the night to our goodfather would fall to me, my brother told me, but only when I was ready. Awake and sensible.

Ambrose returned me to my room, the apartments of some favored daughter. Dolls of porcelain, straw, and cloth sat on every shelf and surface of the room, peeped out of trunks, and lay in heaps on the floor, where they'd been swept from the bed when I was laid there. The pervasive dust suggested the girl was long married off, far from home. Silly that the sight made me weep.

The baroness kindly did not press me with her society, but sent clothes, breakfast, and a quiet chambermaid who supplied a welcome bath. I ate and took care with my toilette. Though hating the thought of Dante confined, I did not rush. By the time I sent word that I would speak to the king, I had gathered my thoughts and as much dignified calm as I possessed.

A full day it took to persuade the king not to execute Dante. Three times I repeated the story of how I'd come to learn of the mage's long, terrible service as Philippe's *agente confide*, unable to tell anyone of his purpose without ruining all chance of its success. Unwilling to reveal the secret of the tangle curse without Dante's consent, I attributed all to Dante's unique magic and my Mondragon blood. Yet even after I'd convinced my goodfather that Dante and I had worked together to stop the rite before it touched Eugenie or caused catastrophe, it enraged Philippe to think of the terrible things Dante had done.

And so he dragged me into the bowels of the barone's palace. A guard unbolted a slotlike opening in a thick door, then left us. The reek of camphor from the darkness beyond the slot revived dread memories of the Bastionne Camarilla.

"You are on trial, mage," said my goodfather. "I am Philippe de Savin-Journia, and I am your only judge this side of Heaven."

"As I am not allowed to step out of this hole and stand my defense, this seems a waste of our time." The voice from the dark was cold and dry as the iron band on the door.

I hated that I could not see him, and I hated common speech that could tell me so little of his state. He did not respond to my overtures in the aether.

"My gooddaughter has made your defense."

"I need no maudlin aristo female to speak for me," Dante snapped.

"Speak gently, mage. By her word only are you yet breathing." Anger rumbled under Philippe's judicious manner. "Yet despite Anne's testimony as to your deeds at Voilline, I've a mind that you're too dangerous to live. You have terrorized my wife and my household. You have tormented my goodson and destroyed the mind of his mother. You've caused havoc in my house and in my city, and have abetted, if not accomplished, the torture and murder of my friends and subjects, innocent as well as guilty. For all I know your treacherous talents have planted these stories in Anne's head, and you but bide your time to impose your own perverted vision of nature on this kingdom. Tell me why I should not kill you."

"Do it if you want. I'd as soon be dead just now anyway. But do not accuse me of crimes and at the same time of failing to live up to our agreement in a proper manner. I swore an oath to Portier that I'd discover the person who shot a spelled arrow at you, and why, and what might be done about it. And so I have. No one bothered to tell me you didn't care anymore, or that you only wanted these things done if I stayed in the kitchen with the other servants and dogs, or avoided breaking the crockery."

And that was all. Dante refused to say more, no matter that the king commanded it or that I pleaded for it. My furious goodfather slammed the shutter and shot the bolt that sealed the sorcerer's hole. "You have a damnably perverse ally, Anne."

In the end it was Portier who tipped the balance. As soon as the surgeons finished setting his leg, Ilario had told him of our impasse. Though in terrible pain, Portier insisted on testifying. And so on the second morning at Barone Crief's, the king and I sat at his bedside. Again my goodfather asked why he should not avoid future risks and slay Dante before he recovered full use of his power.

"Because it would be unworthy of you, sire," said Portier, hoarse and panting with fever. "He protected your wife, her very sanity, I think, many times over. He saved your kingdom. Saved your cousin's life."

"*Anne* dragged you out of that pool. Gods' balls, she is a Mondragon sorceress. She might have done it all."

Duplais managed a weak smile. "Determined, talented, intelligent as she is, she could not possibly have saved me, lord, or done any save perhaps a few of the more . . . explosive . . . feats on her own. I was drowned more than three hours, and your gooddaughter is untrained, incapable of true spellwork. Believe me, no one in the world has been watched more closely than she these few years."

But the king would not be satisfied. "How do you know it was Dante and not Jacard or some other of the sorcerers who performed this monumental sorcery that I don't yet understand?"

Portier laughed at that—though the movement robbed his face of what little color it displayed. "The message Anne relayed called me *student*. Back when we were partner *agentes*, Dante always called me *student* when he was trying to teach me, to make me listen. As I look back, I'm thinking that for all these years, he's tried to point me in the directions I needed to go. He dropped hints that I pounced on as his own lapses. My queries turned up one anonymous lead after another, and I never questioned how they were so effective in putting me on the Aspirant's trail. Yes, he did terrible things along the way. But his courage and skill, and Anne's, have saved us from chaos that would make the heyday of the Blood Wars seem like a household spat. He has given— You cannot imagine what he has given, lord. You should grant him whatever boon he chooses."

With misgiving and ill grace, the king relented.

Portier asked that Dante be allowed to stay with him, if the mage was willing. He faced sepsis or amputation, crippling at best, and offered that understanding the details of the magic we had worked might take his mind off his grim prospects. *And Dante's off his*, I thought. In return, Portier would stand for Dante's parole.

To my astonishment, Dante agreed.

And so on that second afternoon, Dante was released from the sorcerer's hole. Haggard, unshaven, filthy, he was escorted out of the barone's house and given temporary accommodation in a remote guesthouse, until such time as the king's party left for Merona. Though I stood on the barone's steps and spoke Dante's name as he stumbled past, he did not speak or turn his head my way. He didn't look at anything.

Heartsick, I ran inside and consulted Portier, then persuaded Ilario to return to Voilline. Portier said Dante's staff was like a third arm. By evening, he had it.

SO MUCH LESS WOUNDED THAN my friends, I believed myself well recovered from the ordeal at Mont Voilline. To sit at my father's bedside and feed him, to hear that Portier had survived another day, to read the king's proclamation that Michel de Vernase and his son were cleared of all charges, enabled me to put aside the harsh truths of that dreadful night.

Such was clearly not the case. Five days after the Mondragon Rite, my father, brother, and I returned to Merona. From my first step into the city, the mindstorm raged through me unchecked. I was wholly incapable of rebuilding the mental barriers that had kept me sane since Lianelle's magic had waked my tangle curse.

By nightfall I could not stop weeping, babbling about voices screaming in my head. Lost in the mindstorm without an anchor, I repeatedly relived that night of blood, murder, drowning, and starving spectres. Terrified the murder lurking in my veins might burst out to harm those near me, I barricaded myself in my room and screamed into my pillows. When I collapsed into sleep, I dreamt of being chained in Derwin's cellar as a savage revenant tried to reshape my body.

The king's physicians could not explain my frenzy and gave me sleeping draughts until I could not tell night from day or friend from spectre.

In the end Ambrose visited Portier, imploring him to say what might be wrong with me. Portier consulted Dante. Portier wrote me later that Dante had near set him afire for not informing him of my state sooner, heedless of the fact that Portier himself did not know. "Get her out of the city," Dante had told him. My mind had suffered from the events at Voilline like that of a soldier who had stood too close to a cannonade. I needed quiet, away from people. He didn't mention it was because we had together expended such magic that left the world thin and gray, or because I truly experienced the passions of tens of thousands of Merona's residents in my head and was unable to subdue them.

And so Papa and I were taken to Ilario's country house together, because I would not hear of being separated from him when his health was yet so fragile. It was a blessed place, comfortable and quiet. Very few servants, and those accustomed to discretion. Within hours, the world took on its more usual color. I felt whole again, even if I was not.

Eugenie herself was recovering there, enjoying the devoted attentions of her brother and frequent private visits from her husband. She remembered very little of Voilline, she told me one afternoon as we strolled Ilario's dying gardens. A yellow-brown fog had engulfed her party on the road not far from Merona. Philippe's guards, unable to see, had been quickly killed or taken prisoner. We grieved together for Marquesa Patrice, who had pulled a knife from her bodice and died defending her queen. Her masked captors had forced Eugenie to drink a potion that gave her scandalous dreams she blushed to recall. I didn't tell her they likely weren't dreams.

We spoke a little of Antonia, who had died the same night as the Mondragon Rite. Eugenie mourned her foster mother's true affection, while confessing Antonia's imperious ways had made life difficult in her household. "How could I condemn her, Anne, when I understood so perfectly her feeling of helplessness? For half a year she ruled Sabria and did many fine things, and then was told that a council of ill-educated men and a thirteen-year-old boy could do better. I thought that if I allowed her to rule me, it might make up for that a little. I never imagined her conspiring against Philippe, or, saints' mercy, murdering Cecile."

No purpose would be served by sharing my suspicion that Antonia had murdered Eugenie's children. When I made a sidewise reference to Soren, Eugenie blushed. "I tried to tell Dama Antonia that I had only admired him, as a girl child admires any man so handsome and powerful. He was her child, as Desmond and the others were mine. Perhaps she worried about his Veil journey. I didn't know the meaning of love—or the bitter price of loving a king—until I married Philippe. Did Soren's visits please me? I knew he was not real, and yet . . ." She shook her head. "Life is complicated."

Eugenie adored Philippe and feared him, terrified to lose him and terrified to love too unreservedly, thereby, inevitably, losing herself.

I was beginning to understand that.

AND SO THE DAYS OF autumn passed. I slept and reveled in the quiet. Once Papa was strong enough to feed himself, I read him the nonsensical stories and essays I found in Ilario's library. He slept prodigiously, slowly regaining strength, though physicians warned that he would never be aught but frail. His mind began to wake from its starved torpor, but he had not yet convinced himself that the bed, the food, Ambrose, and I were not dreams. We didn't argue. Too much pain awaited him in the real world.

My brother dealt with his own pain. He could not bear walls or any sedentary occupation. Nor could he abide being touched. For hours on end he practiced his swordwork in Ilario's fencing yard, but without poetry or joy. I could not help him, save by understanding. Though we walked in the gardens, we rarely spoke beyond triviality. He was not ready to speak of his ordeal, any more than I could explain what troubled me.

I didn't know who I was anymore—reserved, scholarly Anne de Vernase, dutiful daughter and sometime mistress of Montclaire, or Anne de Mondragon, a dangerous, untrained sorceress who found power for magic in hate and vengeful murder. Who relished it.

I believed violence and murder barbaric, yet my blood would not cool.

Every thought of Jacard, Kajetan, Gautier, or the Camarilla brought my knife to hand. And why could I not stop thinking about a sorcerer who baldly confessed his violent nature and his disdain of so much I valued? I felt as if I'd left my soul on Mont Voilline, drowned in a dark river of murderous magic.

CHAPTER 44

A month or so after coming to the country, I received a packet from Merona. It contained a small tin of five pastilles and a terse message.

Give her one of these each day for five days. The keyword is sallebruja. You'll thank me.

"What do you suppose they are?" asked Eugenie.

"I've no idea," I said. "The keyword means *southern witch* or something like."

"Burn them," said Ambrose. "It's that Jacard, hunting vengeance."

It was true that neither the king's men nor the Camarilla had been able to locate Jacard, who had disappeared at some time in the last frenzy of the rite on Voilline, along with the *Book of Greater Rites*. And the script was uneven and angled oddly, little better than a child's ragged scrawl, as if meant to disguise the writer. Yet the packet was addressed to me, thus the *her* must be someone other. Not Eugenie. Blooming with health and happiness, the queen had abjured all medicine, tisanes, and inhalants.

You'll thank me. . . . My companions likely thought me having a relapse into madness when I leapt from my chair.

Warmth, wonder, and lunatic hope rose as one. Dante had spoken those very words in the escalon on that morning of revelation. Certainly his hand would be awkward now he couldn't see. And I knew only one *southern witch*. "Ambrose, these are for Mama. Do exactly as it specifies. Yes, I'm sure. I swear I am not mad. Ride!"

A MONTH LATER I FIRST told my father about my mother's madness, and at the same time read him Ambrose's letter about her astonishing awakening, as from a long fever. She would be ready to come home early in the new year. I also told him about Lianelle that day. Papa was still quite fragile. I kissed him, left him my brother's blessedly descriptive letter, and shut the door so he could weep without shame.

At about this same time Portier came for a visit. To our cheers and applause, he demonstrated his facility with his cane, which looked to be his lifetime companion. After dinner, the two of us left Ilario and Eugenie to a game of cards and walked out in the garden.

We shared our stories, shaking our heads at our blindness. I was sorry to hear that he'd seen no sign of Maura ney Billard. The Aspirant had not bothered to tell him if the note was forged. Both of us, it seemed, had been left with unsettled questions.

"As soon as I'm able to sit a horse, I'm off to Abidaijar," he said as we sat in the weak sunshine. "Ilario told me of a man expert in the teachings of the Cult of the Reborn, but more in the scholarly line than the priestly, if you know what I mean. If he'll have me, I'll spend the winter with him. To say truth, I'm ready for a little desert clarity." He stared into some distance beyond the fingers that gripped the head of his cane.

"Go on." Too much remained unspoken since the night on Voilline.

"I am no reborn saint," he said. "I don't believe in them. Never have. Holy mercy, if I'd come back from Heaven for something important, you'd think it would be what we just went through, wouldn't you? Instead I'm lured into a trap, and spend one night being twisted into jackstraws, and another sunk to the bottom of a puddle. Yet I must confess. . . ." He would not look at me. "I drowned three times that night. Three times I felt Dante lose hold of me. Three times he fetched me back."

"Creator's Hand!" Horror at the imagining stole my breath.

"Maybe I died," he said, "or maybe I didn't. I was half crazed. But the sensations were very like thirteen years ago. That pervasive smell of dead leaves, dry grass, and rot, and the feel of it—the dry air, the emptiness of time and purpose. Not the best evidence. I still couldn't force myself to open my eyes. But this time, perhaps because it happened at Voilline or because of the magic Dante worked that night, I felt . . . others there. Not spirits, not wandering souls as I expected, but beings very like a spectre that plagued de Santo when he was trapped at Castelle Escalon. Savage things, angry, hungry . . ."

"Ravenous. Trapped. As if they were what was left when the soul is leached away from a dead spirit." Exactly what Lianelle had shown me as I held her nireal. "And blind, I think."

"Yes," said Portier, glancing up sharply. "Dante told me that a spectre was not a soul but a lingering image of something that once lived. That's what they were . . . what they *are*, for I've no reason to think they aren't still just beyond the Veil. It's not merely that they prefer being alive to being dead. They're not *where* they're supposed to be and they're not *what* they're supposed to be. And it wasn't just that I didn't belong there. *No one* belongs there."

A chill shivered me despite the amber sunlight. *Your friend can tell you.* Lianelle had truly spoken to me. She had known my friend Portier was in that place.

"You were there," I said. "It was all true. Roussel and Kajetan believed you couldn't die. They intended to seal you in that pool forever, to keep the rent in the Veil open by your continual passage between . . ." I told him of my sister's nireal then, and what I'd heard as it scalded my hand before we closed down the rent in the Veil.

Portier blew a pent breath and shook off a visible horror grown throughout my tale. "I've told Dante some of this," he said. "He believes the Mondragons created Ixtador by mistake. When the Gautieri learned what their rivals had done, they would not rest until they controlled it— and the knowledge and use of it—for themselves. And so we got Germond and his diabolical scheme. Certainly the place where I was, whether Ixtador or something else, is not divine, but an aberration, a disorder."

"Our beloved dead *pay the price of Gautieri greed.*"

"What's that?"

"It's from a history—Reviell de Mondragon's warning, as he was being executed at the end of the Blood Wars. And the Mondragon rite confirms it." Eager, appalled, I dredged up the words. "Creating a child who straddles the realms of death and life would not only cause the inversion of the natural order the Aspirant wanted, but see *Ixtador Beyond the Veil nevermore dissolved nor shaken nor altered in its composition.* Ixtador, this unnatural place, would become permanent. We stopped that—for the moment—but Ixtador remains."

He rubbed the back of his neck. "It all fits. And it does not comfort me that we've recovered neither the Mondragon codices nor Dante's four remaining nireals."

No one had told me that. "Jacard took them?"

"We presume so. Dante says it's not a concern, as Jacard hasn't power enough to work vermin wards, much less translate the books or use them."

Portier's rueful head shake reflected my own misgivings.

"I've had this thought," he said, "and this is where Dante vehemently disagrees with me, that Ixtador's existence disrupts that part of natural law that encompasses what we know as magic. Perhaps that's why even our most reliable spells don't work so well since the Blood Wars. Perhaps that's why Dante's work, the purest, most natural magic I've ever experienced, devours his body and drives him to this brink of control. I doubt he was ever mild mannered, and, yes, he worked hard to convince me of his wickedness, but the explosive rage was never playacting. And now this injury threatens everything he is . . . everything he values. I fear the consequences of leaving Ixtador as it is, and we need our best magical practitioner to turn his mind to the problem. But even more, I fear for my friend."

All my unspoken anxieties came into focus. "He's found no remedy, then?"

"He can find no residual enchantment to counter, and has no faith that the damage will reverse itself on its own. Worse, he is convinced that this sensory deprivation will inevitably destroy his magic. He's at a loss."

Duplais massaged his leg with a grimace, then propped his chin on his cane, glancing at me in a most peculiar fashion. "How you worked with the man is beyond me. Any mention of you sets him chewing the walls worse than he does already. He damns you with profane names, then in the next breath brags how you kept him from sacrificing me, for which I thank you, or your father, for which I'm sure *he* thanks you. He expounds at obscene length on what you were able to contribute to the work that night, while scorning any suggestion that 'an aristo child-woman' might actually *develop* such immense potential."

He stopped. Twiddled his cane. Glanced sidewise at me again. I sensed he was not finished.

"Such a compliment from Dante, even awkwardly given"—Portier shook his head like a sage of ninety summers—"you know how rare that is, yes?"

Why did my skin feel like summer noonday? "I've a glimmer."

And still Portier fiddled. He heaved a deep breath. "He's forbidden to return to Castelle Escalon. But the king has offered him a small house called Pradoverde. It sits on a few hectares of meadows and woods near the village of Laurentine in northern Louvel. Isolated, which he likes. A royal gift, which he doesn't, but might be persuaded to accept. Secret, which is necessary, as we've heard a thousand calls for his execution. I've loaned him Heurot to do for him until he is more accustomed to his condition. Dante hates it, but Heurot is staunch, patient, and not easily discouraged. All necessary, as you might imagine. And I pay the lad well. The mage threatens to disembowel anyone who offers him help. It would take a ferocious will."

"You want me—?" Unnecessary even to complete my question. As ever, the master logician had laid out his case precisely, and in so doing had resolved my own turmoil into a clear—and scarce conceivable—course of action.

Portier hauled himself to his feet, pulled a brass ring from his pocket, and pressed it into my hand. The hairs on my arms rose with the telltales of enchantment. "Give him this. Tell him his *student* says he must consider taking up teaching."

"I'll visit as soon as I believe it safe," I said, "and stay as long as you need me. But I don't belong at Montclaire anymore. I've other responsibilities."

I felt guilty telling Ambrose that I could not go home, especially when our parents faced months, perhaps years, of recovery, and I was leaving the burden solely on him. It had been even more difficult to tell him that I planned to live, unmarried, with a man who had contributed to his torment. But I was not yet ready to reveal the gift—or curse—I shared with Dante, or my conviction that any future away from him would condemn me to only half a life. How could I explain what set my own hands trembling? So I couched my decision solely in terms of magic.

"This Mondragon blood festers inside me," I said to him as we took a last walk through Ilario's gardens. "I feel like a volcano, ready to spew murder. I stabbed a man in cold blood and relished it. I mutilated a man's face and another man's hands and hungered to hurt them more. And I killed one of them. No matter justification, I hate it. As of now, I've no desire ever to use magic again. But before I can live among people, and especially people I love, I must learn how to control it. I'm not willing to go to the Camarilla, who looked aside while Lianelle and Ophelie died. They're busy rousting out Kajetan's followers anyway. Duplais is traveling. That leaves Dante. Trust me, brother. You'll see."

"I won't come there, Ani," said Ambrose, scarce suppressing his own anger. "I won't come rescue you. I won't speak to him or welcome him to Montclaire. I would kill him gladly and without guilt. I've done as you asked thus far and refrained, but I won't pretend he's somehow nobler than the others who ruined us, just because his personal interests at the end *happened* to coincide with ours."

My brother walked away without word or touch. I couldn't blame him, though it twisted my heart. But this was the best I could do.

Ilario was equally horrified, swearing me to summon him at the slightest difficulty.

Only Eugenie understood. "Like clear glass," she said to me, smiling, "blown into the simplest, thinnest shape. May it ring with perfect clarity and catch only the truest colors of the light."

It only remained to convince Dante.

AND SO IT WAS THAT I found myself at the lovely little country house called Pradoverde in the middle of Estar's month, on a morning when frost limned every twig, leaf, needle, and blade. I strolled up the path, leaving Ilario and the horses heading for the shelter of a likely looking shed. The muted light on the frost crystals reminded me of the structures of magic. My heart slammed against my breastbone as if trying to escape its fate.

Heurot knew I was coming, though his new master did not. The young man opened the door to my knock, grinned, and ushered me into a study, frigid despite a blazing hearth fire. It appeared the drapes had been torn down from the wide windows. The sight wrenched my heart.

"A lady visitor, Master Dante. She is most insistent."

"I told you to turn them all away." Seated at a table jumbled with the paraphernalia from his palace laboratorium, he was ripping pages from a stack of journals—those I'd seen in the schoolmaster's stool. "Tell her I'll hex her unborn children—her grandchildren if she's crone."

"I'm not a crone," I said. "My name is Anne Sophia Madeleine de Mondragon, aged two-and-twenty, and I've discovered an unexpected talent for magic. I need someone to teach me how not to kill people with it."

He did not face me, but his knuckles turned as white as the staff propped idly in the corner. "Go away. I've no further business with you."

I joined him at the hearthside, making sure my steps were noisy. "A former student gave me this and recommended you as a mentor." I pressed Portier's ring into his hand.

He threw it across the room. "Get out of here. Him, too, if he's skulking about."

"Portier left for Abidaijar this morning," I said. "To study, he says.

He'll be back. He hasn't fulfilled his purpose in the world as yet. Frightening to think that."

Dante snorted. "He and the peacock have infected you with this cult nonsense. Now leave."

Friend . . .

"Stop," he snapped. "That is over and done."

"Over and done? Are you mad?"

"Clearly so. I torture, murder, and cripple innocent minds when I believe it necessary. I also find it most annoying that people use my madness to excuse such crimes. Yet if they did not excuse me, they could rightly hang me for them. What could be more lunatic than that?"

"You spent four years without speaking truth with another human being."

"You see my point? You are a sentimental aristo woman and make excuses I don't want." By this time he was on his feet. He reached for his staff but misjudged and came up with nothing. His cheeks flamed. "Do you think I don't know what you're trying to do?"

"You know a great many things, mage, but you've no idea what I'm trying to do."

He fumbled for the stool and sat down again, taking up one of the torn pages and crumpling it into a knot. It might have been Jacard's face. "I told you I cared nothing for aristos, nothing for their wives or whelps. I don't want you here."

"Is it the blindness in particular that shames you?" I said as if discussing his decorating preferences. "You've lived with crippling injury since your hand was burnt. I've heard you managed your life in your forest hermitage quite well. And I doubt if three people at Castelle Escalon guessed about your hand."

"It is *not* the blindness," he snapped, shoving the stack of journals to the floor. "I will deal with that in my own way if I can just be left to it. I am not shamed, and I do not want your pity . . . Portier's pity . . . anyone's pity. I will certainly not indulge my own. Do you comprehend? I just want to be left alone."

But I had known better since the first time I'd heard his other voice.

There has been no one . . . ever. No, this battle within him was more than blindness, just as my malaise was more than reaction to horror. I was determined to force him to confront it as I had. I had prepared my approach carefully. "Why did you ask Portier every day if he'd heard how I was getting on with my screaming fits?"

"Because—because I needed to know that my actions did not damage you."

"Why?"

"A sorcerer is a moron if he does not understand the consequences of his work."

"That morning in the maze, why did you tell me of your friendship with Portier, the first honest man you'd ever met?"

Surprise crossed his face but did not slow the answer. "I had to convince you to work with me."

"In Eugenie's bedchamber, why did you tell me the story of your teacher? At that point, you didn't know I was the one you shared the tangle curse with. Why would the aristo enigma, Anne de Vernase, reeking of magic and secrets, care about the origins of your hate?"

"I needed . . . I've no idea. I was trying to warn Portier that the day of the rite was at hand. That *he* was in mortal danger, and that the conspiracy was all to do with this idiocy of reborn saints and Ixtador. He wasn't there, so I had to tell you. And then you looked at me with such bald disgust, as if I were a monster, inhuman—which I had spent those years trying to be, so I couldn't care. But I saw my reflection in you and couldn't—" His complexion flamed. "This is ridiculous. I want you to go. The king granted me this house to be private."

But I was not ready to give in. "At Voilline, why did you tell me how your hand was burnt, when you've kept that piece of information private from every other person living?"

"How is that relevant?"

"Why did you *tell* me?" One thing I'd learned: I could be as stubborn as he.

"To remind you that we could only speak truth in the aether. So you would do what was necessary."

And why will you not speak to me in the aether now? I said. *I'll tell you. Because you know that when you insist you've no wish to be near me, I'll hear your lie. You've no way to shape it into a truth, because there is another part of you that is just as real as this arrogant, unrepentant daemon before me. You knew those revelations would speak to me because we were already irrevocably linked. Don't you see? Our outward seeming is nothing like what lurks inside our souls. We are the reflection of each other, not joined through a common looking glass, easily parted, but as if a nireal has bound us together into a whole—a fractious whole, for we have as many contradictions between us as we have within ourselves. I don't despise you. I don't pity you. I know you. I see you, and—saints have mercy on all lunatics— everything I see I value.*

"Gods . . . Anne . . ." For that one moment, wonder and astonishment glinted like fireflies against a midnight of pain. It was enough to banish my lingering doubts, if not my fear.

I pulled out the nireal Lianelle had made for me, the one etched with an olive tree. I had bound it as her letter had instructed, considering everything in the world I treasured. Now I dropped it around his neck. *My sister and I made this. When you are ready, the key is* luminesque. *I will not leave you, Dante, my friend of the aether. I cannot. Not now. Not ever.*

His unscarred fingers grasped the silver pendant, and his head twisted slightly, as if he were listening.

But he did not speak the key, and his face hardened into its customary cool mask. "I've no patience for teaching. I tried once. Wasted my time."

A smile he could not see teased at my lips. His eyes, so dull when I arrived, now sparked with curiosity. I retrieved Portier's ring from the dusty corner and folded his fingers around it. "Your *student* says differently." Even a brief touch of the brass circle prickled my skin.

Still and intent, Dante turned the ring over and over in his capable fingers. His mouth twitched. "Well, then. Perhaps my efforts weren't wasted. But I've no—"

I interrupted his excuses. "As I'm sure you would disdain either Collegia Seravain or any other Camarilla tutor for a promising talent, I must study here. You've no need to fear I'll intrude on your privacy. I understand you've a reasonable guesthouse. I'll bring my chambermaid. She can take care of both houses and, together with Heurot, chaperone our arrangement. If you require it, my family will pay a yearly stipend, as they would at Seravain, though I'll say my brother's none too pleased with the idea."

His color high, Dante stewed, fidgeting, crumpling more papers. I let him, happy he couldn't see my own fingers twisting as I awaited the outcome of his battle.

When he heaved a deep, tight breath, I knew I'd won. "I won't go easy because you're a woman. No days off. No coddling. No argument about arrangements."

"Understood."

He reached for his staff again and this time found it. "I don't want your father's money. And I'll take the guesthouse. You take whatever's up the stairs here. Ground floor is for work. Books. Materials. You'll have to get dirty."

"I've worked a vineyard, patched roofs, and a thousand other things you wouldn't guess. I can do what's needed."

"We'll see, won't we?" Had my heart not been soaring, his grim tone might have set me shivering.

Without another word he marched stiffly from the room, only occasionally hesitating to touch the surroundings with his staff. I watched him set out for the modest cottage set behind the main house. Halfway across the yard, he paused, fiddling with something pulled from his pocket.

Music floated on the air—the merriest, most annoying piping one might imagine. Dante snatched the ring from his finger and launched it into the brown grass that rustled with the frost of beauteous winter.

For that moment of grace, I laughed, blessing the saints . . . or at least the one I knew. Then, with a deep, shaking breath, I climbed the stairs to survey my new home.

ABOUT THE AUTHOR

Carol Berg is a former software engineer with degrees in mathematics from Rice University and computer science from the University of Colorado. Since her 2000 debut, her epic fantasy novels have won multiple Colorado Book Awards, the Geffen Award, the Prism Award, and the Mythopoeic Fantasy Award for Adult Literature. Carol lives in the foothills of the Colorado Rockies with her Exceptional Spouse, and on the Web at www.carolberg.com.